# THE
# COLOR
# LINE

*Walker Smith*

SONATA BOOKS

2004

*The Color Line*
Copyright © 2004 by Walker Smith
Published by Sonata Books, LLC

For further information, you can contact the author at:

Sonata Books
403 Barataria Boulevard
Marrero, LA 70072

or by email:

*walkersmith@sonatabooks.com*

*Book design by The Floating Gallery*
*www.thefloatinggallery.com*

*Cover concept by Walker Smith*
*Photography and cover design by David Williams and Joshua Slack*

Printed in the United States of America

*The Color Line*
Copyright © 2004 by Walker Smith

Library of Congress Control Number 2004109137
ISBN 0-975932-0-5

# Acknowledgments

My eternal thanks to the following individuals: David Williams, Theresa Walker, Michele Silas, Eddie Pugh, Jack "The Rapper" Gibson, Dr. Makungu Akinyela, Walter Jenkins, Carmela Emanuele, Cheryll Greene, Carol Smith, Sharon Tisdale, Sandy McPherson, Carolyn Butts, Layding Lumumba Kaliba, Clairesa Clay, Debo Kotun, Yemi Toure, Elizabeth Quinn, Steve Gutman, Donna Douglas, and Dennis Williams. Their encouragement, criticism, and technical assistance were invaluable in bringing the truths of this story to light.                                                                W.S.

*Sing, Antoninus, sing.*

— DALTON TRUMBO

This book is dedicated to the World War I unit
of the 369th U.S. Infantry

—*The Harlem Hellfighters*—

for their spiritual guidance in the telling of this story.
The characters are a blend of fiction and history.
The depiction of the African-American experience
in the war is anchored in truth.

*The problem of the Twentieth Century
is the problem of the color-line.*

—W.E.B. DUBOIS

# Harlem—August 1925

The Imperial Lodge of Elks buzzed with whispers and baritone murmuring as a tall, distinguished looking man stepped up to the podium. His complexion was only a shade lighter than the neatly pressed sienna brown suit he wore, and his expression was all business. The room quieted as he arranged his papers, then his booming voice swept through the air like wind before an electrical storm.

"Good evening, gentlemen. You all know why we're here, so let's get right to business. For those of you who don't already know me, my name is Asa Philip Randolph, and I'm here to help you organize this battle you're about to mount. Now, we've been studying your problems and have come up with a list of conditions we propose to present to Pullman management. Condition number one . . . a fair raise in wages." A loud cheer went up, prompting Randolph to raise his hands for quiet. "Number two . . . on the question of hours . . ."

Jack Hawkins stood watching from the back of the room, fanning himself with his straw Borsalino. As he listened, random remembrances of the war jumbled together with Mr. Randolph's words. All the horror of No Man's Land came rushing back—the fear of death and the trading of innocence for a pair of skillful, murderous hands. He remembered hunger—the food kind and the learning kind. And he remembered Serval.

*Why ya think folks start wars, Serval?*

*Hell, that's simple. War's easier than peace. For peace you need nations led by decent men—men of good will. And they seem to be extinct—like dinosaurs. For peace you need equality and justice for everybody. Unheard of. At least in our lifetime. But war . . . War requires only two things— oppression and hate. And there seems to be enough of both to keep the war industry thriving for generations to come, wouldn't you say?*

". . . unity equals power, and you can't have unity unless you organize!" Randolph shouted from the podium. "Number five . . ."

Jack fanned furiously at the heat under his collar as he listened, then impulsively stepped into the center aisle and strode up to the small table in front of the podium. Pulling a fountain pen from his vest pocket, he signed his name in a slow, deliberate scrawl on the top line of the membership sheet. As he turned to leave, the other men began filling the aisle and swarming around the sign-up table.

By the time Jack made his way to the exit door, the murmuring had grown into an excited chant: *Union, union, union!*

He stepped outside, smiling and moving in the long, purposeful strides of a conquering soldier. But halfway down the steps, he froze. Without moving his head, he searched up, down, and across the street to identify the out-of-place element that had stopped him. To his extreme right he made out the rigid forms of two men in dark blue. Police officers. Suspicious police officers waiting for the mysterious lodge meeting to conclude. But to his left lay a street where even his most joyful memories melted into sorrow. Fifth Avenue.

Fishing a cigarette out of his pocket, he leaned against the rail and reflected on the events of the tense days leading up to the revolution that had just begun inside the lodge.

*A war with no blood,* he mused. *'Least so far . . .*

A great shout rumbled the lodge walls, and Jack cut his eyes at the officers. Alarm registered on their faces, then they stepped up onto the sidewalk and posted themselves under a street lamp. Jack took a long pull on the cigarette, as he watched one of the police officers tip his hat in the direction of a polished black limousine prowling past. Jack exhaled hard, sending a rush of smoke skyward. *White folks. Cotton Club white folks . . .*

He dropped his half-smoked cigarette, crushed it under the toe of his shoe, and continued down the stairs to the street. Turning his back on the police officers, he confronted Fifth Avenue.

The sun was long gone, but its heat lingered. Jack stopped at the corner to slip off his jacket and roll up his shirtsleeves, then pushed back the brim of his hat so that it rested cool on the crown of his head. Fifth Avenue might not be so painful on such a good night. But with each step forward, his mind traveled back. Five years ago, he and Serval would have spent a night like this roaming the streets of Harlem in search of the rowdiest speakeasy. Serval would have entertained him with one of his truth-stretching tales until it was time to head back home to Opal. No matter how late the hour, Opal always laughed when their noise woke her, then complained about the chaos of too many cooks in her kitchen. Jack laughed out loud. *Jus' like a Mack*

*Sennett comedy . . . All we needed was the organ player from down to the Bijou . . . Those was sho' some good times . . .*

The abrupt blast of an automobile horn and the sound of screeching tires interrupted Jack's musing. The passenger door of a black Lincoln opened, and an attractive light-skinned woman emerged wearing a silver-beaded fringe dress. She paused for a moment, then smiled and hurried toward him, stopping short of stepping up onto the curb.

"Jack!" she said, peering up at him. "I knew that couldn't be nobody but you, with them long, skyscraper legs a'yours. What'cha doin' walkin' around all by yourself on Fifth Avenue?"

"Creola." Jack removed his hat and forced a smile to cover his discomfort at saying her name. "Uh, didn't 'spect to run into you. Who you with?" he asked, leaning down to peer into the automobile window.

She shrugged one shoulder and sighed. "Oh, just a date is all."

Jack nodded in understanding. It was nobody special.

An awkward silence made it impossible for him to avoid her eyes. They were as sad and empty as the last time he had seen them.

"So, how's—uh, everybody?" she asked.

"Oh . . . good, I guess."

"Good. That's real good, Jack."

"And how 'bout you? You' sho' lookin' prosperous," he said, eyeing the extravagant dress. "You mus' be doin' awright."

"Mm-hmm. Good, I guess."

Another long silence. Jack fidgeted with his hat and Creola smiled crookedly as she backed away. "Well, I guess I better go now, Jack. I just saw you, ya know, and thought I ought'a stop and say hello."

"Well, it was good seein' you again, girl. You take care'a ya'self, hear?"

As she opened the automobile door, Creola turned to look at him over her shoulder. "Aw, you know me, Jack, I'm always gonna do that. 'Cause ain't nobody gonna take care'a Creola but Creola." Their eyes locked in another long gaze, then she disappeared into the Lincoln.

As he watched the tail lights speeding away, Jack put on his hat and was suddenly struck by something Opal always said: *Those blues'll get'cha, Jack, if you're not careful. You can catch somebody else's blues just like you can catch a cold.*

Jack pushed his hat back the way he liked it and began walking rapidly to shake off Creola's blues. The next street sign told him he was crossing 59th Street. *Eighteen mo' blocks.*

Vivid images began to appear in his mind, followed by the sounds and the emotional goosebumps. He could almost feel the February chill in the air on the day the 369th marched home from the Great War. The cheers and singing of the crowd reverberated in his ears, and his feet picked up the rhythm: *Over there, over there, send the word, send the word over there . . .*

Crossing 42nd Street to the New York Public Library, he caught sight of the first of two stone lions gracing its steps, and it began. A flood of conflicting emotions, running the gamut from joy to pain, rushed through him unchecked. He swallowed back the taste of tears and removed his hat as he stared out at the street. It was there, as always, waiting for him. The most indelible image of all inhabited this particular stretch of Fifth Avenue: neat formations of Negro soldiers on an eternal march past the grand library, under the lion sentries' prideful watch. First, the uniforms, then the ghosts of faces emerged in Jack's memory, and once again he recognized the collective flicker of hope in their eyes. It was a silent exchange. The soldiers bared their souls to him about death and injustice, honor and struggle, as he stood by to pay his respects.

After a long stretch of time, he turned to climb the library steps. His fingers wrapped around a careworn piece of notepaper in his trouser pocket. Stopping to touch the lion's stone paw, he smiled up into the knowing eyes. "Bet'chu seen a lot in yo' time, Mistah Lion."

Jack retrieved the notepaper from his pocket, unfolded it, and turned again to face the street. He checked to his right and then to his left. No one in sight. Only the Hellfighters of the 369th, standing at attention in his memory's vision. "I ain't the one wrote it," he said softly, "but this is for y'all." He cleared his throat and began to read: "Dawn . . . priz—prismatic mornin' colors re—refractin' lies . . ." He stopped, annoyed at his halting recitation, and continued reading in silence. By the end of the second line, it was Serval's voice he heard:

> *Dawn—prismatic morning colors*
> *refracting lies called "white" and*
> *a war called "Great" leaving*
> *Dark Paradise eclipsed by light*
> *Uncle Sam wants you too!*
> *Fight for the country your father built and*
> *your mother suckled and nurtured and*

*tried to make clean*
*A renaissance dream laid bare*
*as New Negroes line up for "nigger" weapons*
*at the armory of shovels, mops and*
*shoe-shine rags*
*To serve at dream-stealers' feet*
*"over there, over there . . ."*

Jack closed his eyes, unable to finish and unable to shut out the sound of the crowd's singing: . . . *Send the word, send the word over there . . . that the Yanks are coming, the Yanks are coming . . .*

Sinking heavily onto the cool step, Jack leaned against the pedestal and stared toward the street. The imaginary parade was in full swing now, and Serval was waving at him from his place in line—fourth row, second man from the left.

As the day progressed in his memory, Jack realized that he had seen Creola on the library steps long before being introduced to her. He smiled at the recollection of Creola's sour expression as she was pulled along by a fast-moving young woman, whose coat kept sliding off one shoulder. Opal. She'd been a stranger then, but he remembered laughing with delight at a colored girl bold enough to push past all those rows of white folks so that she and her friend could stand in front. Creola's pale skin and prim expression blended in with the crowd, but Opal was as conspicuous as a dancing rainbow. Jack still remembered it all; her dress was olive green, and her coat reminded him of wheat— gold and ready for harvest. She turned his way, and he saw that smile— on a face as smooth and brown as a pecan. Even after she disappeared into the front row of annoyed onlookers, Opal was easy to spot; perched on her head was a bright hat the color of spring grass.

Jack sighed. Thoughts of Opal filled his mind until the tapping of a nightstick against the pedestal startled him back to the present.

"And just what're you up to, boy?"

"Boy" echoed in Jack's ears. He looked up into the pale gray eyes of a uniformed beat cop, Irish, by the sound of his accent.

Jack took care in composing his answer, and kept his eyes on the nightstick the officer swung in his right hand. "Jus' takin' a walk is all, suh."

"A walk?" the officer said, studying him. "Well, ya don't seem to be walkin', now do ya? Up with ya. It's late and you're a long way from home, I'll wager."

"Jus' takin' a res' was all, suh." Jack rose slowly and watched the gray eyes widen as they took in the sight of his six-foot, seven-inch frame.

The officer took a step back, and his tone became more cordial. "Faith! But you're a tall one! I don't believe I've ever seen a fella tall as yerself."

"Yes, suh. Guess I'm a pretty big fella, awright. That's the truth."

"Well. You'd best be movin' along now. You're in the wrong neighborhood, ya know."

Jack gazed once again at the parade, which had all but evaporated with the intrusion, and shrugged. "Oh, I don't know. It was feelin' kind'a like home right on these here steps. But you' right, I guess. It's time for me to be movin' on . . . suh."

# 1899

---

*Duke Ellington is born.*

*Eighty-five reported lynchings of Negroes in the U.S.*

# Creola

# Chapter 1

Creola's name, just as most people suspected, was not the name she received at birth. She was born Addie Dunbar, the third daughter of Pete and Effie Dunbar, and a great disappointment to her father who had prayed for a son's physical strength to help out in the family blacksmith business. Pete and his brother were the only colored men in the Baltimore area with their own thriving operation, and Pete wanted it to remain family owned and operated. He viewed daughters as worthless for his needs. To add to his disappointment, Addie was the palest Negro baby he had ever seen, several shades lighter than his other children. After a few nasty remarks from neighbors and relatives, Pete attempted to beat the truth out of Effie.

"Effie, it ain't no way on earth a man dark as me could'a fathered that yalla child!"

Effie endured the beatings in terrified silence, wondering how nature could have played such a cruel trick on her. Addie was indeed Pete Dunbar's child; her light complexion was merely the result of some old renegade gene left over from a plantation owner's clandestine visit to slave row scores of years before.

When Addie was four years old, her father died. The silent, bitter giant of a man who had frightened her with his unsmiling face was gone, and Addie wasted no time missing him. Besides, her mother's new gentleman callers were more fun, bringing gifts of saltwater taffy and bouncing Addie on their laps.

She was eight before she began to understand that the gentleman callers were the reason for the disapproving whispers among the neighbors. But she also understood that more frequent visits from the gentleman callers meant more food on the table and prettier dresses to wear.

*No wonder Mama don't take in washin' no more . . .*

But Addie welcomed the gentleman callers for another reason.

They gave her the first realization that her light complexion was a trait to be prized. No one ever commented on her older sisters, but more than a few fussed over Addie like surrogate fathers, calling her "the pretty little red baby."

Addie basked in their attention until she turned eleven and one of her mother's visitors attempted to express his admiration for her delicate coloring on an up-close-and-personal basis. She escaped late that night to the soft maternal haven of her favorite aunt's arms. Aunt May embraced Addie without question, as if she had been expecting her. Addie knew that Aunt May had always disapproved of Effie's "messin'" and assumed that her aunt would take her in. A secure feeling pushed the man-fear from her mind.

But three days later, Addie was told about "short finances" and "family problems" that she couldn't understand. Aunt May's solution was to put Addie on a train bound for New York, where she would stay with a cousin-by-marriage, who had moved there and was working as a lady's maid. The woman was a devout churchgoer and Addie was told to call her Aunt Ella, despite the fact that she was not an actual blood relative.

It was in New York, while staying with Aunt Ella, that Addie had her first glimpse of a real Creole lady from New Orleans who had moved into their boarding house. The lady ate evening meals with the rest of the boarders just like a regular person, but Addie believed that she retired straight back to heaven afterwards. Addie knew her only as Miss LaRue and learned that she was a singer of that new music everybody was talking about—ragtime. From her honey-colored hair to her delicate ankles, Miss LaRue was a breathtaking vision to an impressionable eleven-year-old girl. Addie made up her mind to walk like Miss LaRue, talk like Miss LaRue, and laugh like Miss LaRue. But she found one feature impossible to imitate. Miss LaRue possessed a pair of green eyes that made Addie's heart race. If she could have yanked her own eyeballs out of her head and traded them in for green-marble substitutes, Addie would have gladly endured the pain. But for now, imitation of Miss LaRue's every mannerism, down to the tiniest detail, would have to do.

Addie continued to resent her dark brown eyes long after Miss LaRue moved on. Judging by the gossip and table-talk of the boarders in her building, Addie was sure that being white was the best a person could hope for, and she knew that she was closer to it than any of them. Miss

LaRue was the only exception. A new word danced into Addie's ears and sent shivers through her body as she eavesdropped on grown folks' conversations about Miss LaRue: *exotic*.

When Addie was thirteen, she began helping Aunt Ella with her housemaid work. Although the work was tedious, she loved the sound of the change jingling in her pocket as she walked to L.L. Bailey's Sheet Music Emporium on payday. Mr. Bailey had begun to stock a small selection of phonograph records, a few of which were the latest ragtime and blues recordings. Ever loyal to the memory of Miss LaRue, Addie cranked up Aunt Ella's Victrola and played the phonograph records until the black shine wore off. Despite her thin, colorless singing voice, Addie was satisfied with the reflection of her dancing skills in Aunt Ella's armoire mirror. She was sure she had what it took to be an entertainer just like Miss LaRue—someday.

As she grew closer to womanhood, her practice sessions began to evolve into hours of fantasy. When she was sure Aunt Ella was out for the whole day, Addie would strip down to her chemise and perform like the cooch dancer she'd seen once after sneaking into a Burlesque theater. Her improvised movements were instinctively erotic, and always led to the same heavenly climax: she would change her name and marry a French painter, who would buy her a cabaret that would feature her as the main attraction: Addie LaRue, Creole chanteuse and cooch dancer extraordinaire from New Orleans. Her nude portrait, painted by her handsome husband, would hang over the bar taunting man after man until each one would blow his brains out in a desperate need to possess her. But being the classy lady of her own imagination, she would attend each funeral in respectful benevolence, and sing a mournful blues number, after the preacher finished his turn at the pulpit, of course.

Unbeknownst to Addie, Aunt Ella had begun to pray fervently for a halt in the child's physical development. But Mother Nature had been more than kind to Addie, and no amount of praying seemed to prevent her body from blooming with an abundance of womanly endowments. So over the years, Aunt Ella was forced to shift the focus of her praying from the child's uncontrollable body to her soul.

By the age of seventeen, Addie was fully aware of male eyes scrutinizing her every move. She was as mouth-watering as a summer peach, and she had no intention of being left on the tree. Addie Dunbar had plans of her own. They were unclear plans until she spotted an announcement hanging on the wall of Mademoiselle Tess's House of Beauty. The House of Beauty was the only beauty parlor in Addie's neighborhood that stocked a full line of Madame C.J. Walker's beauty preparations, including Walker's exclusive "Skin Brightener," for which Addie gladly plunked down thirty-five cents once each month. She stared up at the words on the posted notice, and smiled.

*Singers and dancers wanted for the Grand Opening of*
*THE DOUGLAS CLUB in six weeks! Chorine auditions*
*this Saturday at 1:00 p.m. High-tone beauties only!*

Snatching the paper from the wall, Addie dashed out the door. A new marcel could wait, at least until Saturday morning.

\* \* \*

By Saturday afternoon, Addie was reborn. Still breathing rapidly from her audition, she stared out at the man who held her fate in his manicured hands. When he spoke to her, she jumped nervously.

"Step forward, please."

Addie licked her lips and took a deep breath as she stepped forward.

"You're a good dancer, young lady."

"Thank you."

"Name?"

Her moment had finally arrived and Addie was ready, having lain awake half the night trying on names. Feeling a certain disloyalty at stealing "LaRue," she had tossed and turned until the perfect name came to her. And now, feeling pleased with her audition, Addie stood on the stage basking in the admiring scrutiny of the choreographer and the musicians who had remained to watch after their own rehearsal. Her nerves were suddenly calm as she lifted her chin to speak her new name publicly for the first time: "My name is Creola. Creola Dorshay."

\* \* \*

When she discovered that she was the lightest girl on the line, Creola's confidence quickly escalated into arrogance. She flaunted her butterscotch skin-tone like a golden dressing gown, and captured the attention of the men with whom she worked, from the choreographer and musicians to her dance partners, and even the carpenters who were there to put on finishing touches before the grand opening.

Animosity came as no surprise to Creola. It was apparent that the other girls on the line hated her by their loud comments and laughter.

"Creola? Huh! What kind'a joke-name is that? That Negro child 'bout as Creole as my dog, girl!"

"You know that's right! Miss Uppity wanna be white, that's what her problem is!"

"Mm-hmm. Ought'a go ahead and call herself Mam'zelle Lily Whitefolks and be done with it!"

"No, girl! I know, I know! All she gotta do is bleach that nappy hair a'hers and make sure she keeps that trusty hotcomb on a high flame . . . then 'bout another inch'a that flour-barrel face powder she uses . . . and wah-lah, honey! We got ourselves a new headliner—Her Majesty Snow-White Dorshay!"

But Creola ignored it all, and instead cultivated the attentions of the choreographer and the club manager. Within a month, she was rewarded with a private dressing room. Painted on the door was a large white star and the name "Miss Creola Dorshay" written in gold script letters. By opening night, all the laughter had stopped.

# 1906

—————

*Morehouse College welcomes John Hope
as its first Negro President.*

*Sixty-two reported lynchings of Negroes in the U.S.*

*Opal*

# Chapter 2

Leon Jackson eased the Mercedes Benz touring car around the curved driveway leading to the Saunders mansion and glided to a stop. Glancing over at his little girl, he laughed. "You sho' lookin' elegant in this fancy car, Miss Opal. Even if ya feet barely reach the edge'a the seat."

Opal grinned and bumped the toes of her new high-button shoes together. "I do?"

"Mm-hmm," Leon said as he shut off the motor. "I bet'chu gonna have fun helpin' Daddy drive the white folks around today after you meet Miz Saunders."

"Yes, sir!" Opal bounced in her seat until her father walked around the automobile to open her door. As he lifted her into his arms, she squirmed. "No, Daddy! The runnin' board, 'member?"

Leon laughed. "Oh, that's right. I forgot." Setting her feet on the running board of the car, he stepped back and began counting. "One, two, three!"

Opal giggled, then hopped into his arms. "Now swing me around, Daddy!"

"Later, baby," he said, putting her down. "Now le'me fix them braids. . . . There ya go. Now, come on in the house and meet Miz Saunders."

Clinging tightly to her father's hand, Opal climbed up the back stairs to the biggest house she had ever seen. It was her fifth birthday, and so far it had been the best day of her life. She had been taken for her first ride in the grand automobile owned by her father's employers, and now she was about to step into their fancy home.

Opal was taking in the sight of the kitchen, with its chrome appliances and sparkling copper pots and pans hanging from the high ceiling, when she heard her father suddenly speak to a tall dark woman standing at the stove.

"Hey, Aida. Well, here she is! This' Opal—my little girl!"

Aida stopped stirring, then wiped her hands on her apron as she turned around. Opal caught her breath. Aida's angular face glowed with the same burnished highlights as the pottery hanging just above her head. And when she smiled, her teeth were like a row of perfect white pearls.

"You' so pretty, ma'am," Opal murmured.

"Well, well!" Aida laughed. "You' pretty too, Sista!" Placing her fists on her hips, she cut her eyes at Leon. "Now Leon, how'd you make such a beautiful baby wit'cho ugly self?"

Leon tilted his chauffeur's cap over one eye and smiled. "Ugly?! Aww, Aida! Don't try to act like I ain't the handsome man of yo' dreams. You know you' always been in love with me!"

Aida rolled her eyes and laughed as she leaned down to extend her hands to Opal. "Well, Sista? Ain'tcha gonna give Aida some sugar wit'cha sweet little self?"

Leon pushed Opal gently and said, "Go on, child. This here is Miz Aida Johnson. If I was you, I'd make real good friends with her 'cause she makes the best oatmeal cookies in the whole world."

Opal stepped closer and kissed Aida's cheek before reciting her rehearsed line. "My name is Opal, and I's . . . uh . . . *I'm* very pleased to meet you, Miz Johnson, ma'am."

Aida grabbed Opal's hands and covered them with quick, tickling kisses until the kitchen was filled with giggles. "Ooh, you' a sweet child! Just look at those big eyes and that pretty little face, and so smart, too! She's talkin' like a grownup, Leon! You ain't got a thing to worry 'bout. Your landlord troubles are over, friend. Once Miz Saunders sees this baby, she's bound to let you be a live-in."

Leon held up one hand to show Aida his crossed fingers. "Well, let's all hope so. 'Cause if not . . ."

Aida laughed. "Aww, stop worryin'! You' as good as in!"

Leon leaned down to smooth Opal's hair. "Okay, let's go on in and meet Miz Saunders, baby."

Opal was amazed when they went through another door into a larger room. Feeling the cushion of carpet beneath her feet, she wanted to fall down on all fours to feel the softness with her hands, but one look at her father's solemn expression told her that she shouldn't. A soft rattling noise caught her attention as Mrs. Saunders glided into the room. Opal's eyes widened at the vision of the elegant white lady.

Rose Saunders was a tall woman, almost five feet, nine inches, and carried her height proudly. Her smokey-blond hair was pulled up in a loose chignon, which softened the harsh angles of her face. She wore a long, high-necked dress of dove gray, and a long double string of pearls, which was the source of the rattling sound Opal had heard. Smiling stiffly, she extended her hand. "You must be Opal. What an enchanting name, my dear."

Opal reached for Mrs. Saunders' hand and forced her shaking knees into a curtsy. "Muh—uh . . ." Glancing at her father, she gulped and continued, "My name is Opal and I—I'm very please—pleased to meet you Miz Saunders—ma'am."

Mrs. Saunders laughed musically and patted Opal's head. "She's a delight, Jackson!" She gazed distractedly at Opal's tilted brown eyes for a moment. ". . . And so pretty!" The word "pretty" came haltingly from her lips, and in her voice was a note of surprise. "Well. I don't see why she would cause a problem. I'll speak to Edward about your taking up residence in the basement servants' quarters. I'm sure this little angel won't be a problem at all."

As suddenly as she had appeared, Rose Saunders was gone, leaving Leon and Opal standing in the study alone. Leon sighed and Opal tugged at his sleeve. "What, baby?" he said, patting her head.

"Didn't I say it right, Daddy?"

"Yes, baby. You was perfect!"

Opal frowned. "Then why that white lady laugh at me, huh?"

Lifting Opal high in the air, Leon laughed. "She wasn't laughin' at you, child! That was delight! See? You was jus' delightful, baby! Matter'a fact, you was so doggone delightful, we got us a new home!"

"Where, Daddy?"

"Here! My little fairy princess gonna live right here! Smack in the middle of her own enchanted castle!"

*    *    *

The first morning Opal woke up in her new room, she forgot where she was for a moment. But when her eyes focused on her favorite storybook next to her pillow, she remembered. "Oh! We' in the castle now! Like the fairy princess!" Scrambling out of bed, Opal ran out of the room and was halfway up the stairs when her father's stern voice stopped her.

"Opal! Get back down here now, you hear me? Ya can't jus' go rippin' 'round here like you own the place! What'sa matter wit'chu, child?"

Reaching up for the rail, Opal slowly descended the stairs and stopped at the door to her room. "Ya mean we have to stay down here all the time, Daddy? Can't I go in the kitchen wif Miss Aida? She told me I could help her make some cookies . . ."

Leon lifted Opal in his arms and smiled at her. "Well, sho, baby. You can do that. It's just that—see, you gotta ask Daddy 'fo you go up-stairs, okay? Mr. and Miz Saunders might have some company or sump'm. Now, you look at'cha picture book while I takes me a bath, and then we'll get you dressed and both of us'll go see if Aida' gon' make good on her promise about them cookies, okay?"

"Yes, sir."

\* \* \*

When Leon and Opal arrived in the kitchen, the heavenly smell of oatmeal raisin cookies was already hanging in the air. "Mmm-mmm! Aida, you is one talented cook, girl! I know some of them cookies is . . ." Leon stopped abruptly when he spotted the blond head of the Saunders' little girl Edna beside Aida's hip.

"Oh! Morning, Jackson," Edna chirped as she glanced back at him. When she saw Opal, she turned completely around and pointed at her. "*Who* are you?"

"Look, Daddy," Opal whispered, "A *little* white lady. Do I 'posta curtsy to the little ones too?"

"Mm-hmm."

Opal curtsied neatly and said, "My name is Opal Jackson and I'm pleased to meet'cha."

Edna smiled and reached for a cookie. "Want one, Opal? I helped Aida make 'em and you can have one. Then we can go play. You wanna play outside with me?"

Opal gave her father a pleading look. "Please, Daddy?"

"Okay. But you be good and don't go wanderin' off."

"Yes, sir!"

Edna shoved two cookies into Opal's hand and then pulled her toward the back door. Within seconds, the sounds of little-girl giggles and squeals floated in through the open window.

Aida crossed her arms and gazed out at them. "Well, well. Leon,

looks like your little girl's gettin' along just fine. Now sit ya'self down
and have some of these cookies."

*   *   *

Opal waited patiently in bed for her father to return from his last run
of the evening. He had promised to get home before she fell asleep so
that he could read to her. When Opal turned the last page, she sighed
before turning the book over to start again. It was the third time she had
looked through all the pictures in the book and picked out the words
her father had taught her to read. "The Tale of the Enchanted Fairy
Princess," Opal said loudly, trying to imitate her father's voice. She was
determined to learn all the words and read the whole book by herself,
but she knew she would never grow tired of watching her father act out
all the parts as he read.

As she gazed at the picture of the blond fairy princess in her blue
gown, Opal was suddenly struck with a way to overcome her boredom.
Scrambling to the floor, she reached under the bed for her box of
crayons. The box of broken crayons had been a gift from Edna, when
she had received a new box. Opal searched through the colors until
she found the one she wanted. Taking the brown crayon, she slowly began to color the fairy princess's face, careful not to scribble outside the
lines. When she finished the face, she started on the arms, then the
hands and the ears. Peering at her handiwork, she decided the blue
eyes didn't look right on the brown face, so she colored the eyes with
the black crayon. She was just finishing when Leon walked in.

"You still awake, honey?"

"Yes, sir," Opal said, holding up her storybook. "Look!"

Leon stared at the colored version of the picture and laughed. "Well,
now, you know what? I think that's jus' what that little fairy princess
needed—some color! She was lookin' a little pale to me too, come to
think of it."

Opal smiled proudly. "Now she looks like me—and Mama, huh?"

Leon sat next to Opal and gathered her up in his arms. "I know you
miss yo' Mama, honey. Hey, who knows? Maybe she'll come back
someday."

"How come she didn't take us wif' her, Daddy?"

Leon gave her a squeeze and sighed. "Baby, ya Mama had places
to go and folks to see. She knew I'd take good care of her baby. And
ain't I?"

"Yes, sir." Opal eased her thumb into her mouth, and Leon pulled it back out.

"No, baby," he said firmly. "We don't want'cha teeth to grow in all stickin' out, now do we?"

"No, sir."

"Okay, now. I think it's 'bout time for the story, right?"

Opal nodded her head and snuggled into the space between her father's chest and arm—the space she seemed to fit into so well.

"Well, now that you done painted Miss Fairy Princess like a chocolate drop, I think we gonna have to call her sump'm else, what'cha say? Now, I'm thinkin' she looks a lot like a pretty little gal I know, so I think I'ma call her majesty 'Princess Opal.' That okay wit'chu?"

Opal grinned. "Yes, sir. Uh, Daddy?"

"What, baby?"

"Tomorrow I'ma color all the pages, okay?"

"Okay. I think that's a real good idea."

*　　*　　*

Opal stayed in her room all the next day laboriously coloring each picture of the fairy princess. Late that afternoon she tiptoed to the top of the stairs and peeked around the corner to make sure that Mr. and Mrs. Saunders were not in the front room with company. With one daring dash, she burst into the kitchen and presented her book to Aida.

Aida wiped off her hands and opened the book. "My, my, Sista! Look what you done here. Did your Daddy say you could color all over your picture book like this?"

"Yes, ma'am," Opal said, nodding her head.

"Well, then, I think you did a real good job. A pretty colored princess! My, my! You have got one hard-workin' imagination, child!"

As Aida settled herself at the kitchen table to look through the book, Edna walked in. "Aida, please could I have some milk?"

"Well, of course, Miss Edna. I'll get it for you, honey."

Edna gave Opal a frosty look as she approached the table. "Oh. So this is what you were doing all day. I was waiting for you to come up and play."

"I—I'm sorry, Miss Edna. I didn't know . . ."

Edna peered intently at the book and began to laugh. "A colored princess? Oh, Opal, you're so funny! There are no colored princesses!"

Aida stopped pouring the milk and looked up.

Opal's eyes narrowed and her lips tightened together in a straight line. "It is too a colored princess. And it's—it's me!"

Edna collapsed onto the floor laughing. "You? Oh, Opal, you're just a little girl! You're just Jackson's little girl!"

Opal's eyes filled with tears. "My Daddy's name ain't Jackson," she snapped. "It's *Mister* Jackson. Mister Leon Jackson! And he' a—a king! King Leon!"

Edna continued laughing until Opal turned to leave the room. "Oh! Wait, Opal. I'm sorry, okay? You can be a princess if you want to. We'll go in my room and play, okay? I'll ask Mother. Now come on. And stop crying! I was only teasing you, silly!"

As the two girls headed out of the kitchen hand-in-hand, Opal turned back to smile at Aida, who was still standing with the milk bottle poised in mid-air. "Is it okay, Miss Aida?" Opal asked.

Aida put the milk bottle down on the table and settled onto one of the kitchen chairs. "Po' child got so much to learn about white folks," she murmured, staring absently at the milk.

"Ma'am?" Opal asked.

Aida smiled. "Nothin', Sista. Go on and have fun."

* * *

When Rose Saunders enrolled Edna into the first grade class at St. Sebastian's Elementary School in Manhattan, Leon Jackson's leisurely afternoons became a thing of the past. His weekdays were now broken up into three long trips downtown from the Saunders' home at Irvington-on-the-Hudson. Leaving the mansion at 7:30 a.m., he first dropped Edna at school, then continued downtown to Mr. Saunders' Wall Street bank office. But before picking up Mr. Saunders at 7:00 p.m., which was usually his last run of the evening, Leon now had an additional afternoon trip to collect Edna at St. Sebastian's.

Opal spent the days with Aida, and soon grew accustomed to her father's routine by creating one for herself. About an hour after Leon left to pick up Edna from school each day, Opal would climb up onto a chair near the big kitchen window where she knelt to watch for his return.

"When do I get to go to school, Miss Aida?" Opal asked.

"Next year, Sista. When you turn six."

Opal sighed. "Daddy been gone a long time, Miss Aida. Ain't it three-thirty o'clock yet?"

Aida glanced up at the kitchen clock and removed her apron. "It's nearly four, honey. And you ain't got to say 'o'clock' when it's on the half-hour."

Opal turned from the window with a puzzled expression. "Ma'am?"

"Never mind," Aida laughed. "You can say it that way if you want to. Anyway, Miss Edna's late 'cause her Mama took her shoppin' up at that fancy department store downtown for a fancy new party frock. So your Daddy won't be home for awhile either. He' got to wait out in the car 'til they get through shoppin' and then bring 'em on home."

Opal climbed down from the chair and leaned her head against Aida's hip. "How long does fancy shoppin' take, Miss Aida?"

"Well, you' about to find out, Sista."

Opal twisted one of her braids and smiled. "Me?"

"Mm-hmm. I get off at four, and I'm fixin' to take you shoppin' for a pretty little frock of your very own."

Opal gasped. "You are? Did Daddy say we could?"

"He did. He's the one gave me the money. And you know what else he said?"

"What?"

"He said if I had enough left after we buy the frock, that we could buy you a fancy Sunday hat for church."

Opal jumped up and down in a circle. "Thank you, Miss Aida! Oh! Maybe we'll see Miss Edna at the fancy store!"

Aida shook her head and reached for her sweater. "No, sweetheart. I'm takin' you to a different store."

"But it's fancy, right?" Opal said, grabbing Aida's hand.

Aida leaned down and pressed her index finger against the tip of Opal's nose. "It's just like the palace in your fairy princess book, Sista."

"Can we go right now, Miss Aida? Please?"

"Run downstairs and wash your hands, and we'll be off."

Opal got as far as the kitchen door, and stopped. "Do we get to ride the bus too?"

"The fanciest bus you ever saw," Aida said with a wink. "Now scoot!"

\* \* \*

When Opal stepped off the bus, she clung tightly to Aida's hand. Horse-drawn buggies and chugging automobiles crowded the street, and important-looking people hurried along the sidewalk. She turned her head slowly, taking it all in, until she felt Aida jiggle her hand.

"This is it, Sista—Harlem. And there's your fancy store right across the street."

Opal gaped at the large shop window sparkling with a reflection of the late afternoon sun. Behind the glass she saw an elaborate collection of ladies' hats trimmed with ribbons and flowers of every imaginable color. A portly Caucasian man with long sideburns and a neatly-trimmed silver beard stood at the entrance door waving goodbye to a young woman with hair almost as red as the dress she wore. A round black hatbox dangled lightly from her arm, and perched atop her head was a hat piled high with black taffeta and swirls of red ribbon.

"Ooh, Miss Aida!" Opal shouted. "Could I get a hat like that white lady got on?"

Aida laughed and rolled her eyes. "Lawd, Sista! If you walked into church wearin' that hat, so many knees would hit the floor to pray for your Daddy, it'd sound like thunder!"

"Huh?"

"Never mind, Sista. You' gonna love the hats they got for little girls. You jus' wait an' see."

As they approached the entrance, Opal studied the gold printed letters etched in the window glass. "Mill—milli . . . Miss Aida? That don't say 'hats.'"

Aida laughed. "It's millinery. It means a hat store."

Opal shrugged her shoulders and smiled. "Sounds funny, but awright."

"Come on, Sista," Aida said. "The dress shop is up the street a ways, so we'll get the hat first."

"Yes, ma'am. But Miss Aida? You sure we got enough money?"

"I got paid yesterday, so if we run short on your Daddy's money, I'll make it up. But you ain't got to tell him that. That'll be our little secret, okay?"

Opal grinned. "Yes, ma'am. Our hat secret."

Aida nodded politely to the proprietor, who was still standing at the entrance. "Good afternoon, sir," she said.

"Good afternoon. Is Madame interested in a hat for herself, or are we shopping for the little one today?" he asked, smiling down at Opal.

"For the child, sir. I believe I saw a lovely little girl's Sunday bonnet the last time I was here—the one with lilacs and white lace . . ."

"Ah! I know the one," he said. "Follow me."

A tiny bell rang above her head when Opal stepped inside, and she stayed close to Aida's skirt as she gawked at the rainbows of color. A large floral arrangement in an azure blue vase stood on a towering pedestal in the center aisle like a great perfumed mother to a nursery of flowered hats. At the front of the shop, an elderly lady posed before an ornate full-length mirror as she tried on a gray velvet creation with yards of black netting. Opal stopped to watch her until she heard Aida's voice from behind the vase of flowers. "Oh, yes, sir! That's the one. Come here, Opal. Just look at this sweet little hat!"

Opal hurried over and stared at the object the proprietor held in his hands—a white lace crescent, covered with lilacs and long pink ribbons trailing nearly to the floor. Her mouth fell open. "That ain't no hat, is it, Miss Aida?" she whispered.

The proprietor laughed. "All the fashionable ladies will be wearing ribbons down their backs this spring. You want to be fashionable, don't you, young lady?"

Opal nodded and reached for the hat, but the proprietor suddenly snatched it from her grasp. His smile was gone.

"I'm sorry, sir," Aida apologized softly. "She don't know."

"Will you be purchasing the hat, Madame?" he asked stiffly.

Aida jiggled Opal's hand. "Is that the one you want, Sista? I'm sure we can find a nice white frock, and then I'll embroider you a pink sash to match the bonnet."

Opal was still staring at the proprietor. "I wasn't gon' steal it, Mister—'cause thou shalt not steal, right, Miss Aida? See, I learned my ten commandments awready an' everything. I was jus' . . ." She turned and pointed at the woman near the mirror.

"No, no, Sista," Aida said quickly. "You can't try it on. Just look at it. Now ain't it pretty?"

"Yes, ma'am, but . . ."

"We'll take it," Aida said. "Uh . . . how much, sir?"

"A dollar twenty five."

Aida reached into her pocketbook and counted out the money as the proprietor placed the hat in a round, green-striped box. "Thank you, sir," she said, pulling Opal by the hand.

Once they were outside, Aida gathered up her skirt and crouched down so that she was face to face with Opal. She smiled, but her eyes were serious. "Listen, honey. Harlem is a real nice neighborhood. White folks don't be openin' their doors to colored folks all over, you know. Some high-tone colored folks even got houses up here. So we gotta mind our manners. We don't wanna give 'em no excuses to throw those good colored folks out they' nice homes, do we?"

"No, ma'am, but . . . I jus' wanted to look in that big mirra like the white lady was doin'—to see my new hat."

"I got a big mirror in my room, Opal. Tell you what we gonna do— I'll stand you up on a chair, and then you can look at your new hat and your new dress—all together. Won't that be nice?"

"Yes, ma'am, but . . ."

Aida smoothed Opal's braids and kissed her forehead. "It's jus' the way things are, Sista."

\* \* \*

The next morning Opal woke up suddenly when she felt her father shaking her foot. "Wake up, baby!" he said. "And hurry! I gotta drive Miz Saunders to the city, but she say she wanna have a little talk wit'chu first, child! Now, here's ya dress."

Opal scrambled up and slipped on her dress, then climbed up on a chair to fetch the buttonhook and stockings from the dresser. "Daddy?" she asked as he fastened the buttons on her left shoe.

"Mm-hmm?"

"Could I wear my new hat today?"

"Not today, baby. Sunday. Now gimme ya comb so I can drag it 'round on that big head a'yours."

Opal giggled. "My head ain't big!"

Leon winked at her. "See can I make them fancy braids the way you like 'em."

"Yes, sir. But not too tight. And don't forget the pomade. You forgot yesterday."

"Yes, ya highness."

Twenty minutes later, Opal marched up the stairs and into the front room, hand-in-hand with her father.

Mrs. Saunders was adjusting Edna's collar as they approached. "Oh, there she is! Well, hello, Opal. How are you this morning?"

Opal curtsied. "Jus' fine, ma'am."

"Well, we've got to fly now, so I'll make this quick. Edna and I are go- ing into the city to have breakfast with a ballet instructress from Russia. She danced with the Bolshoi, Opal! But of course, you don't know what that is, do you? Neither did Edna. Well, let me tell you. The Bolshoi is the finest group of ballet dancers in the entire world. And Opal,

Edna has asked me if you would be permitted to take the classes with her, so she won't be so lonely. We want her lessons to be private, without a class full of giggling girls to distract her. But I'm sure Madame could handle the two of you. So how do you feel about it?"

Opal blinked nervously at the three faces studying her. "Ya mean dancin'?" she asked. "Like school, ma'am?"

"Yes! That's it. Dancing school. But you and Edna will be the only students. Won't that be fun?"

"Yes, ma'am. But I ain't six yet."

Edna giggled. "Oh, Opal! You don't have to be six for dancing school!"

"Oh." Opal was quiet for a moment as she thought about the fun she'd had the previous summer when her aunt taught her "the cakewalk." Leaning her head back to give her father a pleading look, she waited for some sign of approval. When he answered her with a quick wink, Opal broke into a smile. "Yes, ma'am. I likes to dance."

"Splendid! Come, now, Edna. We're off to meet Madame Romanov."

*   *   *

On the morning of their first lesson, Edna and Opal were a single bundle of giggling nerves. Squirming into the leotards and tights was a fun sort of challenge that sent them into squeals of laughter. Their curiosity about the new dance class was heightened as they waited in the specially prepared dance room for Madame's arrival. The upstairs sitting room of the Saunders' mansion had been cleared of furniture, and a railing called a "barre" had been installed along one wall. The rest of the room was equipped with floor-to-ceiling mirrors "for studying progress of form," as Edna's mother had explained. But on the morning of their first lesson, Opal and Edna gave no thought to progress of form as they hopped and spun around before the wall of mirrors. Opal finally got things organized by teaching Edna to do the cakewalk, but everything came to a halt at the sound of a woman's deep voice from the doorway: "Good morning."

Madame Romanov swept into the room like a multi-colored butterfly, a vision of blue, purple, and magenta. Lithe of body and each move ethereal, she wore a lavender leotard, over which many layers of chiffon floated in the form of a skirt. Her face was a narrow ivory-colored oval, out of which peered two of the strangest eyes Opal had ever seen. They were the palest of blue, against the startling contrast of ink-black lashes and eyebrows. Her black hair was parted in the middle and captured in a tight bun at the nape of her neck. Without turning around to look at Edna and Opal, she barked in an almost baritone voice, "We begin!"

Edna and Opal stared at each other and giggled, not knowing what to make of this colorful whirlwind with the funny voice.

"Ici, s'il vous plait! Ici!" Gazing at the bewildered girls, she tapped a black cane three times on the floor. "Ici!"

Mrs. Saunders suddenly appeared in the doorway and said softly, "Madame, my daughter does not understand French and, of course, neither does Opal."

Madame Romanov arched one eyebrow menacingly and glowered at Mrs. Saunders. "To donce za ballet, Madame, zey will learn za Francais!"

Mrs. Saunders nodded. "Well, yes. Edna, French would be fun to learn, don't you think? Now, honey, 'ici' means 'here.' She wants you and Opal to step closer."

Timidly, Edna and Opal edged closer.

As Madame Romanov circled them, Opal felt the blue eyes crawling over her, and shivered. When the cold white hand touched her chin, she stiffened and aimed her gaze in the opposite direction. She knew she would have nightmares about Madame Romanov's see-through eyes in the nights to come.

Opal heard her murmur *beaux yeux*, but had no idea what it meant. Madame Romanov clapped her hands sharply and shouted, "Vite, vite, vite! Please to lie down on tummies? Oui. Tres bien. Now. Push little knees out—like little froggies."

Opal and Edna squealed with laughter as they wiggled into the desired position.

Opal twisted her head around to see the blue eyes staring at her again. Then she felt Madame Romanov gently press down on her buttocks until her legs lay flat on the floor.

"This does not hurt little legs?"

"No, ma'am," Opal said. "Only a lidda bit."

Madame straightened up and gasped, "Ma foi! Such potential! Za perfect turnout!"

Mrs. Saunders voice was sharp as she said, "Madame? May I speak to you a moment, s'il vous plait?"

"Certainment." Madame stepped closer to Rose Saunders, and the girls sat up to watch the exchange.

Rose Saunders gave Madame a long, silent stare before she spoke. "Madame . . . I believe you are here to teach Edna the finer points of the ballet, is that not so?"

"Oui, Madame."

"The amount we agreed to pay you is satisfactory, is it not?"

"Oui, Madame."

". . . For which I expect nothing short of your all, Madame. I expect you to mold my child into nothing less than a prima ballerina. That is why we are starting her out with someone of your background, instead of sending her to some local dance academy. I want her background to be the same as yours—the Bolshoi. The talk is that soon the United States will have a ballet company of its own, and if that's true, I want Edna to be a part of it. Being trained by someone from the Bolshoi will get her instant attention when the time comes. I'm serious about this, Madame. Now. As for the little colored girl, she is nothing more than a play-thing for my child—a life-sized doll. She is the daughter of our chauffeur, for heaven's sake. Edna just wanted Opal to keep her company during her ballet lessons. That is *all*. Now, Madame. Do we understand each other?"

Madame Romanov smiled and bowed her head. "Oui, Madame."

\* \* \*

For the first two weeks, each ballet lesson began the same way—three taps of Madame Romanov's cane on the hard wood floor, followed by the words: "And now we begin. Please to pay attention, young ladies. Today we study again za positions and za plié. First position, s'il vous plait. Aaand begin . . . Plié! Un, deux, trois . . . No, no, Mademoiselle Edna! Please to keep za back straight. Regardez . . ."

After Edna struggled through two more pliés, Madame Romanov smiled warmly at her and patted her back. "Magnifique, mon petite! Such za pretty little doncer!" Glancing quickly at Opal, Madame Romanov nodded her head and said in a clipped voice, "Keep za plié exactement za way you are doing it, Shoo-Shoo. Exactement. And did Madame say to stop? I think not! Please to plié. Twenty-five times!"

In the months that followed, Opal experienced anger, frustration, and pain, both physical and emotional, as she struggled to understand why Edna received constant praise while her own efforts seemed to go unnoticed. But Opal persevered. There was something in the words Madame spoke at the beginning of each class that ran a tingle down her spine. *We begin.* A chance to try again.

*   *   *

For eight years Opal studied ballet alongside Edna, training dexterity into each muscle and developing the brutal discipline it took to create elegant pirouettes, chainés, jetés, glissades, and arabesques. In addition to Madame's lessons, which were conducted on Monday, Wednesday, and Friday evenings, with a longer, more intensive lesson on Saturday mornings, Opal rushed home from school on Tuesdays and Thursdays to practice alone in the dance room. While Edna became absorbed in outside activities with her friends, Opal preferred solitude, happiest when slipping her feet into her perfectly broken-in blocked-toe pointe shoes. Madame had taught her to soak the ends in alcohol, rub and pound them against the floor, then knead them with her hands until the hardened burlap toe encasement softened just enough for a perfect roll-up from flat feet to the pointe position. It had been eight years of sore joints and muscles, bleeding blisters, and raw, aching toes. But when she gazed at her reflection dancing on pointe in the mirror, Opal smiled. She was a ballerina.

*   *   *

At the end of the eighth year Madame Romanov announced to Rose Saunders that the girls were ready to pick up the pace.

"Edna is like za little shining candle," she said. "Za flame needs to be turned brighter! Every day now, Madame. For Mademoiselle to be ready to donce as za prima ballerina, it is za time to begin za serious study!"

Visibly thrilled, Rose agreed and immediately wrote Madame Romanov a check. As she wrote, she murmured, "By the way, Madame, how is Opal doing? She certainly has thrown herself into the ballet, hasn't she?"

Madame Romanov measured her answer carefully. "Ah, Madame Saunders, Opal is competent doncer, is true. But she will never be real doncer. She tries to donce like Edna, but she is nothing more than companion for Edna."

"Well then, perhaps Edna should continue her lessons by herself, Madame. I mean . . ."

Madame Romanov's eyes widened. "Oh, no! I—I mean, you see, Madame Saunders, is good thing for Opal to continue. Edna needs za—how you say it? Za measure—za competition, so she can be better, Madame."

Rose smiled and handed Madame Romanov the check. "Whatever you think is best, Madame."

Madame Romanov bowed from the waist as if for a curtain-call.

\* \* \*

It happened when Opal was fifteen—the monumental turning point hidden in such a fleeting moment, that she felt it for only a heartbeat—its sole witness, Madame Romanov's discerning gaze.

All week, grande jetés had been Madame's paramount concern. As she observed the height of Opal's leaps, she was filled with anticipation. It was a rare occurrence—the breaking of the boundary between simple dancing and actual flight. By Friday evening, she found it difficult to wait for the girls' regular lesson to end so that her private lesson with Opal could begin. Finally, the large clock hanging near the door displayed the time she had been waiting for: 7:00. The routine tap on the door, Aida's announcement that dinner was served, and Edna's instant drop from high fifth position to flat feet were routine indicators that the lesson was over. Edna grabbed a towel and hurried to the door.

"'Night, Madame! See you tomorrow!"

"Good-night, my prima ballerina! Tomorrow we work again on grande jetés."

Edna sighed. "Yes, Madame. Coming, Opal?"

"Oh, I think I'll be stayin' a little longer, Miss Edna. Daddy won't be back 'til eight or so, and I always wait for him."

"Okay."

The door closed, and Madame began humming as she cranked the Victrola. "That was lie, Shoo-Shoo. Your Papa is one who must all za time wait for you."

Opal smiled and executed several pirouettes. "You don't really mind, do you, Madame? I guess I do keep you late a lot, huh?"

"And Papa eats dinner alone a lot too, no?" Madame said, laughing. "Now. What questions will my Shoo-Shoo have for me tonight?"

A worry line creased Opal's forehead. "Well, Madame, I need you to show me what I'm doin' wrong on my preparation."

"Your preparation is perfect, Shoo-Shoo."

"But Madame, it just kind'a seems like I'm not gettin' up high enough."

"And why do you think this?"

Opal laughed. "Prob'ly 'cause I keep on hearin' this lady with a funny accent hollerin' 'Higher! Higher!'"

Madame chuckled as she guided Opal to the center of the room. "Is wise thing to mock za teacher, Shoo-Shoo? I think not. So please to listen instead to lady with funny accent. You must aim higher. To fly beyond za air with lightness of tiny bird. Not to donce, Shoo-Shoo. To fly. Now is za time for you to fly."

Opal's wide brown eyes met calmness in Madame's blue eyes. "You mean I don't need to worry 'bout my form or anything?"

"Hah! Your form is like to breathe za air now, Shoo-Shoo. To fly is to begin something new. And you are now ready for something new. Tonight. I have decided." She closed one eye and tapped her temple with her index finger. "I know these things because I am teacher." She stepped back and leaned against the barre. "Just—fly now. Begin, please."

Opal wiped the perspiration from her neck and grinned. "Fly, huh? Just like that, Madame? Fly?"

Madame nodded. "Please."

Opal's smile faded, and her face took on the diligent expression Madame loved. She watched Opal's first three grande jetés, and nodded her approval. "Again, please. Begin." Opal paused before the fourth attempt, and covered her face with her hands for a moment.

"You are all right, Shoo-Shoo?" Madame asked.

Opal extended her arms in middle fifth. "Mm-hmm. I was just thinkin' 'bout what wings feel like. Le'me try it again."

Madame clutched the towel she held in her hand. This time, there was something different in Opal's preparation. The spring of her launch appeared more powerful than before. As she watched the upward sweep of Opal's right leg, Madame held her breath. The right foot arched in perfect aim for the ceiling corner, like a spear about to pierce the heavens. Opal rose, and Madame's eyes calculated the height: *Five feet. No. Higher . . .*

The aerial split threatened to break the aesthetics of a 180 degree angle, and the back leg soared behind, arcing until the pointe of Opal's battered black toe-shoe met the back of her head in a gentle kiss. At the pinnacle, Madame could only stare in awe at the impossible vision hanging before her, seemingly in suspended animation. Opal was perfection of form—a bronze Firebird in full flight.

Time spun backward in Madame's mind until the music in the room was no longer the scratchy emission of a gramophone, but the colorful performance of a living, breathing Russian orchestra. Once again, her white satin toe-shoes lifted her above the shouts and applause of a devoted Bolshoi audience. She was Anna Arkadyevitch, the Firebird, held aloft on new wings—Opal's wings. *I know, Shoo-Shoo. To fly over za gates of heaven is fine, fine moment.*

Opal finished as she had begun, pure and flawless, landing with the silent grace of a cat on soft grass. Only then did she exhibit a shocked realization of her journey. She wobbled and took a half-step back, as if struggling to reacquaint herself with gravity, before sinking to the floor in an emotional heap. "I—I did it, Madame," she whispered. "Didn't I? That was—flying."

"Yes, Shoo-Shoo," Madame whispered. "Pardon, please." She slipped out of the room to collect herself, and nearly bumped into Aida, who was standing just outside the door. Her mouth was frozen in the shape of an "O" and her eyes were moist. Madame patted her arm and eased her into the hallway, closing the door behind them.

Aida placed the tray she was holding on the narrow hallway table. "Madame," she whispered, "Did that child jus' do what I think she did? I—I didn't mean to peek in like that, but . . . well, when I heard you tell her to *fly*, I was . . . well, beg your pardon, ma'am, but I was about to come in there and give you a piece'a my mind . . ."

Madame covered her mouth to muffle a laugh, and pulled Aida away from the door. "Is all right, Aida."

"But Madame, she did it! You told the child to fly, and doggone if she didn't do it! Is—is Opal good as all that? I mean, I see 'em jumpin' 'round in there every time I come up to announce dinner, and I ain't *never* seen Miss Edna do *nothin'* like that!"

"Aida, za child is not good. I tell you this: What you saw in that room tonight was greatness. Please to remember, because never may you see such greatness again."

Aida gasped and blinked back tears to no avail. "You mean she'— she' really all that much better than Miss Edna?"

"Ma foi!" Madame laughed. "Better? Aida, our little Shoo-Shoo is . . . queen of za firebirds, and Edna is—is . . . toad."

"Toad?" Aida whispered, swallowing back a laugh. "Miss Edna's a—a toad?"

"A toad," Madame repeated with a jerk of her chin. "But Aida, please . . . One thing you must promise . . ."

"What's that, Madame?"

"Madame Rose Saunders must never, never know she is Mama to such za toad. And Opal must not know she is queen."

Aida smiled. "Well, I'd drink muddy water 'fore I'd be the one tellin' Miz Saunders her child's a toad. But why can't Opal know how good she is? All that greatness you talkin' 'bout? Seem' like that'd make the child happy."

Madame shook her head and frowned. "Shoo-Shoo is on long, hard journey, Aida, to reach za dream. Praise will wait. Now she must work. Do you understand?"

Aida nodded her head and picked up the tray. "I think so. It'll be our little secret, Madame. Now, you think it's awright if I take this sandwich and milk in to the queen?"

"Certainment! After flying for first time, za queen must have her feast!"

*    *    *

For the next year, Madame worked diligently with the two girls. While encouraging Edna's efforts, she quietly cultivated Opal's blooming talent. From time to time, a nagging concern surfaced in her mind: Both Edna and her mother were convinced that Edna was a future star. Madame Romanov knew that if Edna's talent were ever put to the test, her deception would be revealed. But each time the thought surfaced, she pushed it to the back of her mind and concentrated on Opal.

Inevitably, the dreaded day came. In the middle of a Saturday lesson, Rose Saunders bolted into the dance room, grabbed Edna's hands, and spun her around. "Edna! Madame! They're coming!"

Madame Romanov and Opal exchanged an amused glance, and Madame stepped over to peer out the window. "Who is coming? I see no one."

Rose Saunders' eyes widened. "Madame! You haven't heard?"

"No . . ."

"The Ballet Russes! The Ballets Russes de Sergei Diaghilev is coming to the Metropolitan Opera House for a big gala, Madame!"

"Oh, Mother!" Edna cried. "We're going, of course, aren't we?"

Rose Saunders clasped her hands together under her chin and
beamed. "Not only are we going, Edna, but here's the best part. Part of
the two-day program will be a recital spotlighting local talent from the
United States. Don't you see, darling? Your big opportunity has arrived!"
Turning to Madame, she said, "Tell her, Madame."

Madame opened her mouth, but her private terror prevented words
from forming.

"You're always telling me how good she is, Madame. This is her big
chance. With your influence, you can see that she is part of the program. The biggest names in international ballet will be at this recital
and I want Edna center stage! Do you understand me?"

"Oui, Madame. Of course."

\* \* \*

For the next two weeks, Opal felt abandoned as Madame Romanov
pushed Edna to exhaustion in preparation for the big night. They
had selected a solo from *Giselle* with only minimal pointe work, due
to Edna's weak ankles. Opal watched quietly from the barre, and
mentally danced each step until she had memorized the entire performance.

On the evening before the gala, they were just finishing up when
Rose Saunders opened the door and smiled. "Lesson over?" she asked.

Madame sighed. "Oui, Madame." Handing a towel to Edna, she
shook her finger at her. "Rest tonight, my dear."

Edna shrugged. "I hope I remember everything, Madame."

Madame nodded. "You will do . . . fine."

Edna left the room, but her mother remained at the door watching
Opal, who was performing stretches on the floor. "Opal? May I have a
word with you, dear?"

Opal scrambled to her feet. "Yes, ma'am?"

"I have some good news for you, Opal, but I'm afraid I also have
some bad news. Which would you like to hear first?"

"Well, I guess the good news, ma'am."

"All right. Edward and I talked it over and we've decided that Aida
just can't handle everything around this big house any more. We were

discussing the possibility of hiring a maid when it occurred to us that you're sixteen now and could probably use a little pocket money. You could help Aida after school and on weekends, and by the time you graduate, you'll be ready to take it on full time, leaving Aida more time to concentrate on the cooking." Rose Saunders paused expectantly, but Opal only stared at her. "Well, Opal, what do you think? When I mentioned it to your father, he said it was fine with him, if you wanted to, of course. I mean, you've both been with us for so long, you're like family. Wouldn't it be better than having to go off every morning to some stranger's house to clean?"

Opal felt her breath coming rapidly as she stared at Mrs. Saunders. *But I'm not a maid . . . I'm a dancer.* But as she looked into the cold, expectant eyes, Opal heard her own voice go flat with resignation. "Thank you, ma'am," she murmured.

"Of course, we'll pay you, Opal. Now. I guess that brings me to the bad news."

Opal was already on the verge of tears. *Bad news. Oh, no . . . I forgot this mess is gonna get worse.*

"I know how much you enjoy your little lessons with Madame, Opal, but I'm afraid they'll cut into the time we'll be needing you around the house. If we're going to pay you for your work, you'll have to take the responsibility seriously."

Opal shot a quick look at Madame Romanov. In her eyes, Opal saw something she had never seen before. Madame's eyes were a mirror reflection of her own fear and disappointment. Opal broke the stare by looking at her feet and mumbling, "Yes, ma'am. Guess it's time for me to get to work and help Daddy and Miss Aida."

Rose smiled and patted Opal's head. "Good girl."

*　*　*

At eight o'clock the following night Madame Romanov sat in the orchestra section next to Mrs. Saunders, waiting for the program to begin. Closing her eyes, she wondered what would have happened if her covert attempt to present Opal in the gala along with Edna would have been revealed to the Saunders. Although the visiting Russian organizers had been amenable to the suggestion, once the American Ladies of the Arts Committee learned that Opal was a Negro, the answer was a contemptuous "out of the question!" Madame Romanov squirmed uncomfortably in her seat, remembering the horrified expressions of the pompous old crones.

She stared glumly at members of the orchestra as they began warming up in a soft cacophony of scales and musical segments from the program. Suddenly aware that Rose Saunders was staring quizzically at her, she pulled her compact from her pocketbook and nervously dabbed at her perspiring forehead with a powder puff. As she pondered the ramifications of her years of deceit, she realized that the end was near. In the hours to follow, not only would Edna's dismal lack of talent be revealed, but her own position as instructress would end, severing her connection to Opal. *Opal should be dancing here tonight. Ahh, how my little Shoo-Shoo would dazzle them!*

The conductor strode out, and the orchestra fell silent as he bowed to a thunderous ovation. Madame sighed and stared at the curtain. Edna Saunders' debut was at hand.

*   *   *

Backstage, Opal assisted Edna in her costume preparations. Kneeling on the floor to adjust the ribbons on Edna's toe-shoes, she whispered, "Aren't you nervous, Miss Edna?"

"Yes! I hope I can remember it all the way through, Opal. You know that part I always mess up on . . ."

"Miss Edna! Madame wouldn't call you her prima ballerina all the time, if you weren't good!"

Edna sighed. "I guess that's so, Opal. Well, wish me luck."

"Oh, yes! Break your leg, Miss Edna! And don't worry. It's gonna go real good, I just know it. I just wish . . . I mean . . ."

"What, Opal?"

"Oh, nothin', I guess."

"No. Tell me. We've never had secrets. You wish what?"

"Well, I just wish I was dancin' tonight, too, that's all," she murmured as she watched Edna begin her warm-up stretches.

"You're colored, Opal," Edna said simply. "You were only allowed backstage 'cause you're our maid."

Opal gulped back a pained gasp. "I know. I just wish, that's all."

Edna hoisted one leg up onto the back of a chair and grinned as she stretched her chin over to her knee. "Like your fairy princess wishes, Opal?"

"Oh, I was just little when that happened. I didn't know any better."

"Gosh, Opal. It must be hard being colored. There are so many things you can't do. Too bad, too, because you're a pretty good dancer. Not a prima ballerina or anything, but pretty good."

Opal froze for a moment as she fought back the stinging in her eyes. She turned around and busied herself picking up Edna's clothes off the floor. "Well, you better go ahead on, now, Miss Edna. The orchestra's playin' the overture."

The minute Edna left, the tears came anyway. Opal regarded her reflection in the mirror for a moment, then rose on tiptoes and extended her right arm as if dancing. She closed her eyes and imagined the sound of Madame's guiding voice: *Exactement, Shoo-Shoo . . . Now. We begin . . .*

Opal opened her eyes and laughed at the irony of her reflection. The creature in the mirror was half-dancer/half-servant, clutching Edna's skirt and slip tightly in her left hand while standing poised for her big solo on the stage of the Metropolitan Opera House. "Begin?" she shouted, throwing the clothing to the floor. "But what do you do when they won't let you begin?" A gentle hand on her shoulder startled her and she looked up to see another reflection in the mirror. "Madame! I—uh . . . I . . ."

Madame Romanov was standing behind Opal, dressed in the same shade of blue as her eyes. Opal covered her face as a sob escaped her throat.

"Shoo-Shoo," Madame whispered, "Don't cry. Tonight is not Edna's night. You do not know it, but tonight is your night, mon petite Shoo-Shoo."

"My night? Madame, how's it gonna be my night when they won't let me . . . I'm colored, Madame. I can't dance the ballet. They won't—they won't let me." Opal's voice broke, and Madame Romanov gathered her tightly into her arms.

"Shoo-Shoo, this is very sad night for you, I know this. If Madame tells you something, you will believe me?"

"Yes, ma'am. I guess so."

"Then look at me, Shoo-Shoo." Opal felt Madame's cool palms on her face, and looked up into the familiar blue eyes. "It is time for you to know something," she whispered. "You are . . . Shoo-Shoo, you are za greatest doncer ever I have seen. *Ever.*"

Opal gasped and shook her head, but Madame held on. "Sh-sh-sh!

Listen to me, Shoo-Shoo. Is true! With little more work, you could be greatest doncer of all time—in—in whole world! Do you hear me, Opal? Za greatest! I tell you this: In Russia, you would hear za bravo and make them to stand with za—za tears to stream down their faces! Madame would never lie to you about this. Madame's only lie was Edna. Don't you understand? Tonight is very sad night for me too, Shoo-Shoo. They will present Edna as my protege. Many people know me, and my reputation will be ruined when they see how—how—oh, what is right word? How *ordinary* she is. Edna is no prima ballerina! I say that only so I can stay near you. You are one with real talent! I wanted to teach you everything I know! And you learned, Shoo-Shoo! How you learned! Edna is finished after tonight, but you? You must continue to donce. Madame Saunders will dismiss me after tonight, I am sure of this, so I have decided. You must come to me on your own."

For a moment Opal couldn't speak, and only stared at her teacher, reeling from the revelation. "But Madame, I—I don't have any money and . . ."

Madame Romanov threw back her head and laughed. "Ma foi! Cherie, have you not listened to anything I have told you? It is now za time for you, Shoo-Shoo, to learn something new—always we must learn something new."

"What, Madame?"

"You now must learn za difference between za queen and za toad."

Opal blinked. "Huh?"

"Za toad will cry tonight, Shoo-Shoo. But za queen I now crown za new prima ballerina. You, Shoo-Shoo. *You* are queen. You are prima ballerina, no matter what za toads and toad mothers say. And I will be honored to teach you." Clasping Opal's hands in her own, Madame leaned her forehead against Opal's and whispered, "*Now,* Shoo-Shoo . . ."

Opal giggled. "We begin?"

"Yes. We begin."

# 1908

---

*Thurgood Marshall is born.*

*Jack Johnson defeats Tommy Burns to become the first Negro Heavyweight Champion of the World.*

*Eighty-nine reported lynchings of Negroes in the U.S.*

# Jack

# Chapter 3

Portia Hawkins squinted at her gangly eleven-year-old son without straightening her back or breaking the rhythm of her picking. "Jack! Pull ya hat down over ya face, son."

"Yes'm." Sighing, he pushed the old straw hat back for a second to wipe the perspiration from his forehead before pulling the brim down firmly over his eyebrows.

"And keep up, boy! You fallin' behind!"

"Yes, Mama."

Portia pushed all of her children to the limit during the harvest, knowing that the more cotton the family brought in, the better her chances would be to get to bed without a beating at the hands of her husband Andrew. The work was backbreaking, and it broke Portia's heart to watch her children endure the punishment.

Eleven years earlier, when Portia first held Jack in her arms, she prayed that her most beautiful child's skin would not have to be spoiled by the beating sun, and she vowed to make a better life for him. But in addition to his copper complexion, Jack had the misfortune of growing taller than his older brother by the time he was nine. When Andrew told her it was time for Jack to work, Portia talked back to her husband for the first time in years, in defense of her youngest child.

"No, Andrew. He' jes' a baby . . ."

After slapping her hard for her insolence, Andrew glared at his wife in disbelief. "I's so damn tired, Portia! I gotta bring in double what you bring in, else Mistah Davis be thinkin' I ain't pullin' my weight 'round here. Now, that boy big as a man and he can take some'a the load off'a me. He' goin'. Next crop come in, he' goin'! Heah me?"

\* \* \*

During his first day of picking, Jack truly thought he would die in the blazing heat. He didn't understand his mother's obsession with keeping his skin covered with a heavy, long-sleeved shirt and a large straw hat. When the sun was at its highest point, he grew so dizzy that he lost consciousness and pitched forward into the cotton. Andrew cursed loudly as he hoisted his rangy son over his shoulder and carried him back to the house.

But after a few weeks, Jack managed to go through the motions without so much as a sway, and by the end of harvest time he was picking nearly as much as his older sister Elsie, while longing for school to begin again.

Jack attended the Beacon School for Colored Children with Elsie and their brother Andrew, Jr. Too shy to reveal his enjoyment of the songs and learning games Miss Wells taught him, Jack was the quietest student in her class. Miss Lucy Wells was a young lady in her mid-twenties with a round build and a smooth, honey-brown face that always smiled at him, even when he made mistakes in his reading. During his first session of school, Jack developed a secret crush on Miss Wells and it showed no signs of diminishing. Her singing voice was sweet and clear, and whenever she walked past him, the scent of lavender soap lingered in the air. Each time she brought a picture book for the class to pass around, she always let Jack hold the book the longest. At least it seemed that way to him.

Jack had only been to two sessions of school and struggled with reading and writing, but found arithmetic easier. It made sense to him because he could relate it to counting sacks of cotton, and being paid the correct amount. Although he was bashful in his halting attempts to read in front of Miss Wells, he didn't mind trying when he was at home with his mother. She listened patiently as he sounded out the words, and praised his efforts even when he made mistakes.

Miss Wells' attention and his mother's love were the only gentle things in Jack's life that softened the horrors of the cotton fields. Even during the harvest, which was the most punishing time of year, Portia gave her youngest son one small gift to make things more bearable. Each night after the rest of the family was asleep, Portia whispered to Jack that it was time to pray. Together, they knelt at the foot of her bed and gazed up at the only picture hanging in the tiny shack. The white face of Jesus was surrounded by a glowing halo, and his blue eyes stared heavenward. To Jack, the picture was the living, breathing essence of Almighty God, Himself. At times, while listening to his mother's whispered prayers, Jack felt a twinge of guilt that his brother and sister were not included, and suspected that if he had been born dark and they had been born lighter, they would have been the ones in that white God's favor. Something about it seemed unfair, but he never complained. At these times, he attempted to redirect his thinking and prayed, *Please Lawd, let it be cooler tomorrow,* or *Make me understand spellin' for Miss Wells, Lawd,* depending upon what time of year it was.

As hard as he tried not to dwell on it, the closing of each session of school brought all of Jack's horrors to the forefront of his mind: the heat, feeling dirty all the time, the dried cotton-ball stems ripping his fingers to shreds, and, worst of all, his mother's fretting about keeping his skin covered with the hated long-sleeved shirts.

By the end of his second year of picking, Jack had grown another two inches. He now looked his father in the eyes when he stood next to him, which pleased Andrew. "Boy, you jes' fill out some and you gon' be a sho' 'nuff man! Next year, I'ma keep you next to me when you pick. See can you keep up wit'cho Daddy!"

But the following year, Jack failed to live up to his father's expectations due to a lack of manly muscle power and the agility and speed that only come with years of experience. Andrew, Sr. snatched his son by the collar and roughly pushed him in Portia's direction. "G'on, boy! You' big, but you ain't no man yet. Get on behind ya Mama and pick. See can you keep up wid'a woman."

His father's mocking words were like a slap, and Jack's reaction was to withdraw into himself. Day after day in the cotton fields, he drifted in and out of a heat-inflicted delirium, wondering if the sun would kill him as it had killed so many before him. Sometimes he imagined himself a prisoner and the sun his cruel omnipotent captor. His only escape was thought. He spent hours recalling details about school: his classmates, the storybooks, and always Miss Wells.

One sizzling afternoon a memory of a picture of the snow-capped Swiss Alps assisted him in his struggle to fill his sack with cotton. Closing his eyes, he could see the image clearly, remembering how Miss Wells had passed the book around for all the students to see. He squinted at the field of cotton and imagined it a field of snow. *Shoot. Wish it was cold like snow. Wonder what snow really feel like? Sho' wish it could snow right now. Then . . .*

In an instant, his mother's sharp tone melted the snow. "Jack! I done told you to roll them sleeves down, boy! How many times I gotta tell ya?"

"Aww, Mama. It's too hot. Please, can't I take my shirt off like . . ."

She stopped picking and glared back at him. "Boy! What I tell you? Don'tchu sass me if you know what's . . ."

Jack cut her off with a resigned "Yes'm." He knew the rest.

\* \* \*

That night Jack sat aching from head to toe, as the family ate their supper in silence. *Only one mo' week a'pickin'. School starts end'a next month.* He smiled at the thought.

"What'chu grinnin' about, boy?" Andrew asked suddenly.

Jack squirmed. He preferred invisibility to being caught in conversation with his father. "Nothin', Daddy," he mumbled.

"Speak up, boy! I axed ya what'cha grinnin' at. And don't tell me it ain't about nothin'!"

"Yessuh. I mean, uh, I's thinkin'—'bout school, that's all."

Without looking up, Andrew growled, "Ain't gon' be no school dis year. I need mo' help 'round here. Elsie—she' goin'. One mo' year. But you and Andrew—y'all gon' stay here and work. Y'all men now."

\* \* \*

Portia Hawkins died of old age in the spring of 1917. She was thirty-six.

The family, being an efficient piece of harvesting machinery, seemed outwardly not to miss her. Andrew permitted no talking in the fields, so the pain of Portia's three children was only shared by an occasional exchanged gaze. But Jack was deeply affected, and swallowing his pain for the sake of work created a cold bitterness inside. The devastation of his mother's death haunted him in the only privacy he possessed, the quiet corners of his mind. Over the years, his hatred for his father had grown into a dangerous beast, and Jack's fear of unleashing it compelled him to work feverishly in the cotton fields—his only outlet for frustration. He picked his own share and more than his mother's share of cotton that summer, and spoke to no one. Driven by his grief, Jack outlasted even his father day after day.

But his cycle of pain and backbreaking work was brought to a halt by global events. On a trip to town for supplies, he heard two white men outside the feed store excitedly discussing their plans to join the army. Inside the store, the clerk was reading aloud from the front page of a newspaper as several wide-eyed townspeople listened: "After wavering for nearly two years, President Wilson has finally decided to commit

American troops to the global fight for freedom. All able-bodied American males should consider it their duty to drop everything and join the war effort . . ."

As Jack listened to the voices raised in reaction to the news, he began to formulate the plan for his escape. *War.* The idea shot a perverse thrill through him. He was sure that fighting for his life on a field of battle would be better than suffering a passive death on a field of cotton.

*   *   *

The journey home was quiet. But the minute the wagon rolled up to the Hawkins house, Jack hopped out, inciting an angry outburst from his father.

"Boy, where the hell you goin'? Git'cho behind back here and unload dis wagon!"

Ignoring his father, Jack strode inside and grabbed the box containing the family's clean clothing. He fished out two pairs of underwear, overalls, and his only other shirt, then tied them in a bundle before grabbing a loaf of bread from the kitchen. By the time he stepped back outside, he knew that his life had already changed. He coldly stared down into the eyes of his father for what he hoped would be the last time.

"Dis big ol' mule jes' quit, Daddy."

*   *   *

President Woodrow Wilson sorted through his usual neat stack of documents on the right-hand side of his desk, having been briefed about the contents of each one. After hastily scrawling his signature at the designated space, he blotted the ink and placed each one at the top of the "Executed" stack to his left. Any document that appeared to be inconsistent with his understanding, or for which he had a question, he set aside in his "For-Further-Consideration" stack. Things were moving along at a swift pace until the President stopped to stare at a document entitled "Anti-Lynching Bill." He had seen it before, and was fully aware of who was responsible for its sponsorship. Pressing his pen firmly on the paper, he scrawled one word: Rejected.

# 1916

---

The NAACP leads nationwide protests against
D.W. Griffith's film "Birth of a Nation" for
its negative depiction of Negroes and for its
blatant glorification of the Ku Klux Klan.

Woodrow Wilson re-elected for second term
as President of the United States.

Fifty reported lynchings of Negroes in the U.S.

# Serval

# Chapter 4

Serval Rivard stood smiling at his reflection in the mirror as he dried off after his morning bath. It was a day he wanted to imprint on his memory for the rest of his life. Not only was it his eighteenth birthday, but two weeks earlier he had graduated high school at the top of his class. After acceptance by both his top college choices—Howard and Morehouse—Serval Rivard had a man's decision to make.

His smile faded for a minute as guilt invaded his reverie. Although his father dismissed his concerns as ridiculous, Serval knew that his life was not representative of most Negro boys his age. A constant nagging thought had disturbed him since the age of seven; his father's position as Chairman of the Sons of the Freedmen's Economic League had opened doors for the Rivard family that remained shut to many of Serval's less fortunate friends. Serval's father, Charles Rivard, also held the distinction of being part of what W.E.B. DuBois called The Talented Tenth. By their own ascent, members of The Talented Tenth were somehow supposed to lift the entire race. Serval tried to believe in this theory, but there was something about it that he found fundamentally unworkable. The name had bothered Serval when he first read it in Dr. DuBois's newspaper *The Crisis*, and it bothered him today.

Although he knew that his father would have something to say about his lateness at the breakfast table, Serval continued to stand in the bathroom, giving his thoughts free reign. He was reminded of something said by the man who was rapidly becoming his hero. Ever since the morning he stopped at the corner of 135th and Lenox Avenue to listen to the man with the booming West Indian accent, Serval couldn't seem to stay away. By questioning a couple standing next to him, he learned that the man spoke there regularly, and a strong, instinctive stirring compelled Serval to return again and again.

Although Serval had never experienced shame about his dark coloring, he knew that others of his own race considered it a flaw, while white people simply considered it subhuman. But the man who held court at 135th and Lenox talked about things Serval had never heard before. He spoke about the rich beauty of dark-skinned people and their nobility as descendants of kings and queens in Africa. Always a child of instinct, Serval loved his black skin, so these words were like a song to him.

Serval studied his dark reflection. He was an even six feet in height, and the muscles had finally thickened over his formerly rail-thin frame. *Strong,* he decided. *I look strong and quick, like the cat I'm named for.* After enduring all the childhood teasing about his name, he was finally beginning to appreciate it. Turning his hands over, he first examined his palms, then stretched out his fingers before tightening them into fists. He leaned closer and peered at his even features in the mirror: prominent cheekbones, high and proud, a nose which resembled neither his mother's nor his father's; it was a nose inherited from some African ancestor. The fullness of his lips conveyed the serious side of his nature until the left corner turned up, revealing a wicked grin. He smiled broadly for a moment, just enjoying how he felt, until he found himself staring deeply into his own eyes, searching. Ever since reading that the eyes were the mirrors of the soul, Serval had cultivated an aptitude for finding a person's true nature in the depths of their eyes. He had tried it on himself many times, but had failed until now. *Who are you, Serval Rivard? Where are you going and where did you come from?* The deeper he looked, the blacker his eyes appeared until he heard the words echo once again in his mind. *Kings and queens.*

This moment of self-discovery seemed to answer the question that he knew most people asked about him. "How can Serval be so confident? Almost arrogant, just so sure." He knew that when girls first met him, they weren't impressed with his looks; his complexion was too dark to entice the modern society girls of Striver's Row. Good looks to them meant wavy hair and pointed, non-African features on a light to moderately brown face. But somehow, even with his unfashionable African features, the kinky tightness of his close-cropped hair, and skin the color of darkest sable, girls fell under his spell. Serval was well-liked and now he knew why. The people who met him recognized something in him that was much older than their Americanized notions of handsomeness, whether they were conscious of it or not. In his eyes and in the way he carried himself, they saw Serval as the ideal reflection of their true selves—descendants of African royalty.

Satisfied with this revelation, Serval closed his eyes, and slowly, lovingly ran his hands over his body; down from his chest, over the neat row of muscles in his stomach, pausing at his genitals to enjoy the tingling sensation generated by his own touch; then down the front of his thighs, flexing to feel their power, and barely grazed his knees with the tips of his fingers, before beginning the journey back up. When he reached his face, he opened his eyes and smiled at himself. With his right fist, he pounded the center of his chest once and shouted his favorite slogan: "Up! You mighty race! You can accomplish what you will!"

Pulling on his bathrobe, he hurried into his room and sat down at his desk. He opened the right-hand drawer and pulled out a thick, black leather volume. He turned the pages, crowded with his own handwriting, until he found a blank one, and made his first entry of the day:

*June 15, 1916—*

*I am a man today. Not because I am eighteen, and not because I will soon leave my father's house to attend college. One cannot truly call himself a man until he finds his purpose for the life he is given. In finding the answers to my most disturbing questions, I have now found my purpose. I know why I spent so many sleepless nights troubled by "The Talented Tenth" and my father's pride in being part of such a group. Why should the injustices inflicted on a people be carried on the shoulders of a tenth of the victims themselves, instead of borne by the whole of their oppressors? And why do we continue to hold such low expectations of ourselves? A tenth? We should strive for excellence at one hundred percent! Somewhere in this discovery lies the purpose for my life's work. I will begin by learning everything I can about every subject. I will stand in the light of teachers like Marcus Garvey, and I will reject the history books of my childhood. I have no doubt that with this beginning I have placed my feet on the difficult path to leadership. It is time for my days as court jester to end, and all toys of childhood to be put away. I was born to lead, of that I am sure. Serval Rivard is a man today.*

\*   \*   \*

Kathryn Rivard smiled as Serval walked into the dining room. He returned the smile and kissed her before taking his seat at the table.

"Good morning, Serval," she said. "Many happy returns of the day, son."

"Thank you, Mama." The left corner of his mouth twitched in a rebellious half-smile as he shot a quick look at his father to see if he had noticed the word "Mama." Since Charles Rivard insisted that Serval call Kathryn "Mother," Serval persisted in calling her "Mama," and reveled in his father's resulting outbursts.

This time Charles appeared not to hear, and folded his newspaper before looking up. "Oh, good morning, son. You're looking pleased with yourself today. Has it something to do with the fact that it's your birthday?"

"It's a good birthday and a good day, Daddy," Serval said as he scooped scrambled eggs onto his plate.

"Well, you certainly look older than eighteen years. Kathryn, our son is a man, no longer a little boy. And many happy returns of the day, son."

"Thank you, Daddy."

"And of course, I know you've been up all night pondering your decision. Well, Serval, don't keep us in suspense any more. What's it to be? Morehouse or Howard?"

"Morehouse. Definitely Morehouse."

"Good school. It's farther away, but college years instill independence in a young man, so distance shouldn't be a factor. Good decision, son."

"So no more talk about me enlisting in this war that's brewing, I hope. 'Cause I won't be able to go. I'm a college boy now, Daddy."

Charles sighed loudly. "Serval, I hope that isn't your motivation for going to Morehouse, because if it is . . ."

"No, Daddy. You know how much I want education. And you're always drilling it into me—'A good education is the only path to gainful employment.'" He put down his fork and directed an impish smile at his father. "But to be honest, Daddy, aside from gainful employment, I want education because I want to be better at their game than they are, themselves."

Charles put down his fork and leaned back in his chair. "And to *whom* are you referring, Serval, when you say 'they'?"

"You know damn well to *whom* I am referring," Serval said.

Kathryn's brow wrinkled into a frown as she rose from the table. "Cursing again! At the breakfast table, too, Serval. And you, Charles, provoking him on his birthday. I—I thought you two could at least be civilized today of all days. I won't sit and be witness to this again. I just won't! I'll be upstairs."

"Kathryn!" Charles called.

"No, Charles," she said stiffly. "I'll be upstairs."

Charles glared at Serval. "Why do you always have to stir up trouble, Serval? You've upset your mother again with all this."

"But Daddy," Serval said, grinning, "like Mama said, I was provoked."

Charles slammed his palm against the table. "You will not use your mother's words against me! I don't care if it is your birthday." As he rearranged his napkin on his lap, Charles muttered angrily. "I've spoiled you. That's what this is. I've spoiled you rotten."

Serval sighed and reached for a slice of toast. "Okay, okay, Daddy. I apologize. Let's be civilized like Mama said."

"Yes. There's no reason we can't have a discussion like two civilized men. Now, son, I suggest that you think twice about world events because when you get to Morehouse, you're going to find a lot of fellows who are thinking along the lines of Dr. DuBois on this subject and . . ."

Serval chewed his toast and half-listened to his father's speech until a devilish idea occurred to him: talking with his mouth full—about his father's latest nemesis. "Daddy, ya know what Maacus Gahvey said va uvah day, hmm?"

"Swallow your food, Serval! What in the world are you trying to say?"

Serval swallowed. "I said, do you know what Marcus Garvey said the other day? I heard him speaking on . . ."

"Stop right there, Serval. No one in his right mind takes that charlatan seriously, and I will not discuss any of his nonsense at my breakfast table."

"But Daddy, everybody's talkin' about the war. If you could only hear what Mr. Garvey has to say about it . . ."

"Drop it, Serval. I will not have that madman's name spoken in my house."

*   *   *

During his first year and a half at Morehouse, Serval was so busy with his studies and debate team matches that he only returned home once to visit during the Christmas holidays. On that occasion, it became evident to him that being away at college had greatly improved his relationship with his father.

But several months later, preparations for his second visit home were made with considerable trepidation. Since the last time he had seen his parents, the nightmare in Europe had become a full-blown global conflict that newspaper columnists referred to as "The Great War." Up until that time, Serval had lived with his father's measured but constant pressure about enlisting, but with the new developments, he had no doubt that all subtlety would be abandoned.

As Serval packed, he decided that the best approach would be to avoid the subject altogether. He could not imagine leaving More-house, with its fascinating professors and its wealth of books, for a grim battlefield in Europe to fight for white America. He prayed for a peace-ful visit, but he knew his father's temperament as well as he knew his own. As he buckled his suitcase, he began compiling a mental list of conversational topics other than the Great War and Marcus Garvey. Reaching into his pocket, he pulled out his father's most recent letter:

> . . . *and your sterling academic performance during the past year at Morehouse has far exceeded my expectations. I am pleased, son. Fondly, Your Father*

Serval folded the letter. "No arguments this time," he said firmly.

*   *   *

Once home, his vow lasted for one hour. After listening to his father's veiled insults at the recent attention-grabbing actions of Mr. Garvey, Serval, in his usual style, broke the house rule by not only speaking the name of Marcus Garvey, but also challenging his father to a debate about him.

"Why are you so closed-minded about Mr. Garvey, Daddy? Can't you even . . ."

Charles Rivard folded his copy of *The Crisis* and sighed. "All right, Serval. Since you seem to have been so influenced by this man, I'll dis-cuss him with you, but just this once. It is my job to guide you, after all."

Serval resisted the urge to roll his eyes. "Okay, Daddy, I'm listening. Guide me."

"I'm not saying the man's intentions are not good, but only as far as the racial pride angle goes, Serval. Can't you see how all this pie-in-the-sky talk about going back to resettle Africa is damaging to our people?

I guarantee you, son, he'll raise their hopes the same way he's raising yours, and his dream will never materialize."

"Wait a minute, Daddy. No disrespect intended, but I think I've got you on two points. One, the end of slavery was viewed as a pie-in-the-sky notion not that long ago. And two . . ."

"Serval . . ."

"Let me finish, Daddy. On the debate team, we're not allowed to speak until a man finishes."

Charles removed his glasses and rubbed his eyes. "The debate team. Oh, all right, Serval. Finish."

"And two, what's the difference between what Mr. Garvey's trying to do and what Dr. DuBois is doing? DuBois is telling us that if Wilson commits troops to the war that Negroes will finally get their chance to be viewed as equals by the white man. Come on, Daddy. That's worse."

"And just how is it worse, Serval? Fighting for our country is a noble ideal. It wouldn't hurt you to think about enlisting. Morehouse will still be there when you come back. With the benefits of a veteran added to your education, you'd have so many offers of gainful employment, why, you'd have your pick of . . ."

"Daddy, stop! Gainful employment and enlisting! Are those the only two things we can talk about?"

"They're important issues, Serval."

"Yes, but I have my own opinions, Daddy. You might as well know that I'm as dead-set against Negroes fighting in this war as Mr. Garvey is, so you can drop the subject of my enlisting. It's just not going to happen. You want me to go and fight for a country that holds me back and calls me derogatory names—from the president on down! Daddy, I don't even know how you can call it *our* country. Are we talkin' about the same plutocratic, capitalistic America that only thrives because of slavery?"

Charles sighed. "The past is the past, Serval, and best forgotten . . ."

"Forget slavery?! And what about all the Indians who were killed because they were in the way? We forget them too, I suppose. And the Mexicans whose land was stolen . . ."

"What do you propose the government should do about it now, Serval? Every organized, functional nation is guilty of oppression against some other group. It's an ugly fact of history, but we're stuck with it. We must survive in the here-and-now, son. Capitalism works. If we learn to function within it instead of fighting it, it will work for us too. To achieve economic betterment for our people, we'll simply have to deal with the white man, and it's time you faced that fact. If we tried to go back to Africa, we'd find worse conditions. And besides, Africa is not our home."

Serval narrowed his eyes and drummed his fingers on the tabletop, searching for a rebuttal. "Hey, Daddy. Home is where the heart is."

Charles took a deep breath. "Serval, all I ask is that you think twice about the things Garvey is saying. Wait and look for concrete results before you go believing his rantings."

"And all I ask, Daddy, is that you *don't* look for concrete results of what DuBois is trying to do. Because the only results of us joining the white man's army will be to get Negroes killed in vain. Don't you think that's more damaging than just not making it to Africa?"

"It's called sacrifice, Serval. I'm talking about long-term results here."

"Well, I still say you're wrong, but I guess only time will tell."

"I just don't want you to be disappointed when your hero fails. He's all talk. Everybody knows that. So now that I've conceded to your wish for this discussion, I'd appreciate it if I never have to hear the man's name in my house again, Serval."

But Serval couldn't resist having the last word. "Just one more thing, Daddy. See, you said that Mr. Garvey's all talk. But I heard that he's organizing a Negro shipping line. Wouldn't it be funny if he could help us all become millionaires and get us all back to Africa at the same time? Then you and I could finally agree on something. We'd be rich Africans. Whadaya think, Daddy?"

Charles glared at him. "You are not an African, Serval. You are an American!"

Serval sighed and shook his head. Keeping his voice at a reasonable level, he tried to find the playful mood he had just been in. "You know, Daddy, I can't help but wonder why you named me after an African wildcat, when anything African seems to get on your nerves."

"I told you, son, it started out as a sort of joke about what a restless baby you were, but the more I said it—Serval—well, I liked the sound of it. It sounded like, well, it sounded like 'civil' and . . ."

Serval rolled his eyes and groaned.

"That's right, son, I said 'civil.' Ironic, isn't it? Since that's the one thing you can't seem to be these days."

"Aww, come on, Daddy. Can't we just agree to disagree? I mean,

I don't really have anything against Dr. DuBois. I've even been known to sneak and read your copies of *The Crisis* when you ain't lookin' . . ."

Charles's face registered extreme pain. "Don't say 'ain't', Serval. Please!"

Serval pressed on. ". . . but I still say he's wrong about Garvey, and he's wrong about the war, too. Things won't change for our people if we go fight. You mark my words."

Charles stood up, signaling an end to the conversation. "When you talk like that, I'm more sure than ever, son. No. We cannot agree to disagree as long as you're spouting the ravings of that West Indian madman!"

As Charles strode angrily out of the room, Serval shouted after him, "He's not a madman! And there's nothin' you can do to stop me from . . . Daddy? Damn!"

*In the villages the negroes were the office holders, men who knew none of the uses of authority, except its insolences . . . to put the white South under the heel of the black South. The Ku Klux Klan—a veritable empire of the South, to protect the Southern country. . . . It's history written with lightning. And my only regret is that it is all terribly true.*

—PRESIDENT WOODROW WILSON
on the film *Birth of a Nation*

# Chapter 5

By 1917, the violence of war loomed in the global consciousness like a great Pandora's box, opened to release humankind's most self-destructive maladies at home and abroad.

Following a series of race riots, most notably the bloodbath in St. Louis that summer, the subject of race relations rivaled even the Great War as the dominant topic of conversation among Americans. Negroes searched for answers to the continued violence rained upon them, and concerned Caucasians were shocked at the news of black retaliation. But slavery's wounds had never been tended in America, and the result was pain compounded with anger—old wrongs demanding retroactive redress.

A generation of young Negroes rejected the use of their parents' chosen term of identity, "colored," opting for a more progressive description of themselves: "New Negroes." New Negroes were unwilling to passively endure the terrorism of marauding nightriders, and rare incidents of black reprisal began to occur. The events in St. Louis incited a barrage of heated commentary from American newspapers as diverse as the men who published them—from William Randolph Hearst's *San Francisco Examiner* to Dr. DuBois's *Crisis*. The prevailing point of agreement was that America was embroiled in not one, but two Great Wars.

Edward Saunders, who normally enjoyed a rousing political discussion, dismissed the topic of Negroes. But he was unable to escape the subject when Eastern National Bank made it a major point at a heated meeting of the board of directors. It was decided that financial assistance to local Negroes would set an example of good will for hot-headed white residents, and insure against the possible occurrence of a St. Louis-style episode in New York. The next step was the selection of a spokesman. After a vote was taken, Edward Saunders found himself Eastern National Bank's liaison to the Sons of the Freedmen's Economic League. The boardmembers finished their business by scheduling the first meeting with the League's representative, Charles Rivard, at Edward

Saunders' home to maintain the appearance of societal equality. Edward Saunders nodded a curt acceptance and strode from the boardroom.

*   *   *

By the designated Saturday of the meeting, Edward Saunders had worked himself into a nervous frenzy. "For God's sake, Rose—help me with this tie! My fingers seem to have stopped working properly."

Rose stepped between her husband and the dressing mirror, and smiled patiently as she reworked the knot on his gray tie.

"Black devils!" Edward hissed. "A pack of these savages revert to form and start rioting in St. Louis and the whole of civilized society panics!"

"Well, then, Edward," Rose said softly, "why didn't you turn the board down? Perhaps they could've selected someone else to meet with this man."

Edward grimaced. "You don't understand, Rose! Cooperation and leadership are the only paths for advancement in matters of business."

"All right, all right, then, Edward. This Rivard person won't be here that long, will he? It'll be over before you know it."

"I suppose so. But my God, Rose, he'll be lounging around on our furniture like a regular guest!"

"Edward, be reasonable. After all, Opal and Jackson have been with us for years and they don't bother you. I'm sure this man is no different from them."

He shook his head emphatically. "It *is* different, Rose. Jackson and Opal are servants. This Rivard fellow is coming here expecting to be treated . . . Oh, God! Was that the bell? Don't tell me he's here already!"

*   *   *

Downstairs another tie was being straightened as another heated discussion took place.

"Now, Serval, none of your childish antics, do you understand?"

Serval rolled his eyes, but answered with a dutiful "Yes, sir."

"This man has the ears of the board of directors, and he can make the difference between economic progress and failure for our people. Now, pay attention to what's said here today, son. I want you to learn; that's why I brought you along. Do me this one favor before you go back to school. Please be on your best behavior."

"I'll be good for the white folks, Daddy."

"Serval!"

The opening of the door froze Charles's reprimand on his lips, and he flashed a toothy smile. But as Serval took in the vision of the girl who opened the door, he felt the corners of his own mouth turning upward. The Saunders' maid was a brown-skinned girl of about eighteen, who possessed a pair of the longest, curliest eyelashes Serval had ever seen. On her face was an expression of discomfort, and her dark features were a bit uneven. But when she spoke, her lips parted in a luscious, shy smile, and Serval felt an overwhelming urge to kiss her right there in the doorway.

"Afternoon, gentlemen," she said. "You must be Mr. Rivard. Mr. Saunders is expecting you. Come right in."

Serval couldn't keep his eyes off the maid, and his tone was overtly flirtatious when he spoke to her. "Good afternoon, lovely lady!" This earned him the expected "Serval!" from his father, but Serval was beyond caring. He fleetingly realized the meaning of the term "floating on air" when he suddenly found himself in the study; he couldn't for the life of him remember how he had gotten there. As he watched the maid exit through the large double doors, he got his first glimpse of Edward Saunders. Stony, tight-lipped, and detached—just as Serval had pictured him. Saunders strode past the maid as if she were furniture, and finally met the gaze of Charles Rivard. A serpentine smile crawled across his flushed features as he extended his hand.

"Mr. Rivard, is it?"

Charles smiled as he shook the proffered hand. "Yes, sir. Good to make your acquaintance, Mr. Saunders. I brought my son Serval along. I hope that was all right . . ."

"Certainly, certainly!" Edward turned to Serval. "Hello, uh, Serval, is it? Well, well. Unusual name."

Serval drilled a hard flat look into the watery blue eyes of Edward Saunders. "Yes," he said.

"And . . . well, how is a name like that spelled?"

"Oh, it's not the word you're thinking of, sir. It's not S-E-R-V-I-L-E, which we all know describes the personality of a slave. My name is spelled S-E-R-V-A-L." He smiled sweetly and basked for a moment in Saunder's crooked expression before continuing. "In case you've never been on one of those African safaris that are all the rage with your set, you've probably never heard of one. It's a wildcat indigenous to Africa."

"What is? Oh, of course. A serval. Well, well . . . uh, such a clever name."

"I think so," Serval said. "Ironic, isn't it? Two words sounding exactly alike but with two completely different meanings. African wildcat. And it fits, too." Out of the corner of his eye, Serval saw his father close his eyes and shake his head slightly, and coughed to cover a laugh. *Let's see . . . What're you tryin' to tell me with that look, Daddy? . . . Stop this display of impudence at once!* A litany of sarcastic remarks came to mind, which Several kept inside, but he couldn't shrink his impish grin. He had the feeling that he had grown ten or twelve new teeth since meeting Edward Saunders.

Saunders broke the silence. "Well. To be sure. So I suppose a big strapping lad such as yourself will be joining up soon to go fight for your country . . . Or have you already signed up?"

Serval sensed his father's tension at the question, and gritted his teeth. He met Edward Saunders' gaze and kept his tone cordial. "No, Mr. Saunders. Actually, I'm busy with collegiate pursuits."

"Well, well! A path well taken, my boy!"

Charles smiled broadly.

Mr. Saunders gestured in the direction of a deep green leather sofa. "Well, gentlemen. What's say we get down to business?"

As Serval and his father seated themselves on the sofa, Mr. Saunders settled into a large chair and leaned forward to shuffle through some papers on an expensive-looking mahogany coffee table. He suddenly looked up. "I apologize. Would you care for something to drink?" Before Charles could answer, Mr. Saunders bellowed, "Opal!"

The maid appeared at the door and curtsied. "Yes, sir?"

Serval smiled. *Opal. So that's her name.*

Without acknowledging Opal, Mr. Saunders asked, "What'll it be, gentlemen? Coffee? Tea?"

Charles answered quickly. "Tea would be just fine, thank you. My son will have tea as well."

Opal curtsied again and was gone.

Serval fought to maintain a respectful silence as his father spoke to Mr. Saunders in the perfect clipped sentences he had rehearsed so fervently the night before. But the day wasn't a total loss; after all, he had met, or at least seen, the loveliest girl he could ever remember seeing. *Opal. What a pretty name.*

When Opal returned with the tea, she curtsied and said, "Telephone call, Mr. Saunders. Mr. Huggins from down to the bank, sir."

"Oh, will you excuse me, gentlemen? I've really got to take this. It may take me a few minutes, so please enjoy the tea and I'll be back just as soon as I can."

Charles rose. "Certainly. Not a problem at all."

Serval rolled his eyes, but followed his father's lead and stood up.

As Serval followed Opal with his eyes, his father spoke to him in angry hisses. "Serval! What's wrong with you, boy? You were not raised to comport yourself in such a manner. Such a display!"

Charles's lecture bounced off Serval, who was intently studying Opal. As she glided about the room setting out the accoutrements for the serving of tea, he became fascinated by her every movement. She walked with a fluid elegance that seemed natural and devoid of affectation. Even her hands were graceful as she lifted the teapot to pour. When she leaned toward him, Serval was again overwhelmed by an urge to let his lips meet hers, before continuing with an examination of her long velvety neck. But he settled for a darting glance at her slight cleavage. When she took a sudden step back, he realized that he had been caught. He offered a smile, which she did not acknowledge, but he still couldn't take his eyes off of her. There was something athletic about her, something lithe and vibrant, but at the same time delicate. Her small maid's cap was a stark white crescent of lace resting neatly on the crown of her head, surrounded by a profusion of tight black curls cut in a stylish bob. Serval smiled. Her hair appeared never to have been touched by a straightening comb. He was so lost in his exploration of her charms, Serval suddenly realized that she was asking him something for the second time.

"Oh, I'm sorry. What did you say, Miss—uh, by the way, what is your last name?" he whispered while looking deeply into her eyes.

After a couple of bewildered eyeblinks, Opal whispered back, "Jackson. And I was askin' you if you wanted cream or lemon . . . uh, sir."

"Opal Jackson," Serval murmured, smiling adoringly at her.

Charles, who had been lecturing nonstop during the exchange, suddenly stopped in mid-sentence. "Serval! Are you listening to me, boy?!"

Without acknowledging his father, Serval extended his hand to Opal and whispered, "Please call me Serval. Please. Or just call me." He tried his most beguiling grin, which earned him an impatient glare from Opal. It was apparent that she did not appreciate being caught in the middle of the father/son battle heating up.

"Cream or lemon, sir?" she repeated. She jumped at the sound of another sharp "Serval!" from the elder Mr. Rivard. "Okay, *buster*," she hissed at Serval, "since you can't choose, you're gettin' both!" She splashed a sloppy dollop of cream into his cup with one hand, then plunked a lemon slice onto his saucer with the other.

By the time Opal turned her back to tend to his father's tea, Serval had stopped laughing. He fought to keep his hands from reaching out to encircle her waist. When she was a safer distance from him, he became aware that his father was treating her like a servant just as Mr. Saunders had done. He flashed his father an irritated look when he heard ". . . and these people are descended from the pioneers who came to this country on the Mayflower."

Serval leaned back in his chair and took a sip of his tea. "Daddy, you're in luck! We've been studying the history of those folks on the Mayflower in school. You know, our people were enslaved by other countries long before it became the rage in America. When I get back, I'm gonna do some research and, hey, who knows? Maybe it'll turn out that the white folks on the Mayflower brought along their slaves on the voyage. And even though it's a stretch, well, maybe one of them was named Rivard, which would make their slaves' names Rivard and . . ."

"Serval!"

". . . and then you could say you were a direct descendant of the Mayflower . . ."

"Serval! You will stop this display at once!"

Opal shot a wide-eyed glance at Serval, and muffled a giggle.

Basking in the warmth of her smile, Serval took aim at his father one last time: "Hey, Daddy, hope springs eternal."

\* \* \*

If Opal had known Serval Rivard, she would not have been surprised when he rang the Saunders' front door bell the next morning. She opened the door and blinked several times before speaking. "Uh, Mr. Rivard? Mr. Saunders isn't up yet, sir."

Serval smiled. "I'm not here to see Mr. Saunders. I'm here to see you, Miss Jackson. It is 'Miss'? I mean, I hope it's 'Miss Jackson' and not 'Mrs. Jackson.'"

Before Opal could answer, the door was roughly pulled open from behind, and Mr. Saunders' voice boomed, "Who is it at this hour, Opal?"

Serval appeared cool as he stepped forward to extend his hand. "Serval Rivard, Mr. Saunders. Beautiful morning, isn't it?"

Edward Saunders glared at Serval, but kept his tone civil. "Uh, well, yes. I, uh . . . I don't recall another appointment . . ."

Serval looked squarely at Mr. Saunders. "No, sir. Sorry to have disturbed you. I'm here to ask Miss Jackson to dinner this evening."

Silence.

Serval looked from Mr. Saunders to Opal, then back again. "Is that a problem?" he asked.

Edward Saunders muttered something unintelligible and walked away. Opal gave Serval a blank stare.

Serval waved his hand in front of her face and snapped his fingers. "Well, Opal? What time do you get off? Do you think you'd like to have dinner with me or not?"

Opal nodded her head slowly and began to push the door shut.

Serval laughed and wedged his foot in the doorway. "Wait a minute! What time should I pick you up?"

"Huh? Oh, seven, I guess. . . . Lord, you are one strange fella, Mr. Rivard."

*    *    *

By seven-fifteen that evening, Serval was sitting comfortably in the Saunders' study, waiting for Opal to finish dressing for their date. When he saw Edward Saunders passing the doorway, Serval couldn't resist drawing attention to himself. He cleared his throat loudly, and Saunders looked up with wide eyes. Serval's teeth smiled, and he waved. "Hi."

Saunders muttered something Serval couldn't hear, then stomped up the stairs.

A few seconds later, Serval heard the quick, light steps of a woman coming down the stairs, then heard the voice of Rose Saunders. "Opal!" she called. "I'll have a word with you before you leave."

Serval rose from the settee silently, and crept into the hallway where he saw Mrs. Saunders waiting at the top of the basement stairs. When he heard Opal running up, he ducked into the shadows.

"Yes, ma'am?" Opal said.

Rose Saunders pulled Opal by the arm and hissed, "You have put us in a very uncomfortable position, young lady."

Opal looked down at her shoes. "Yes, ma'am."

"Mr. Saunders is quite upset at this Rivard boy stopping by any time he pleases to—to sniff around after you and . . ."

Serval stepped up behind Rose Saunders and tapped her shoulder lightly. Her body jerked in surprise, and she spun around to face him.

"Excuse me, Mrs. Saunders," Serval said. He directed a polite smile at Rose while protectively linking arms with Opal to draw her to his side. "I didn't mean to startle you," he said, "but I did not come here to *sniff* anyone. And especially not this lovely young lady. I'm not a bloodhound, after all. What I am, Mrs. Saunders, is a young man. I'm just a young man who wants nothing more than to enjoy Miss Jackson's company over a nice dinner. In fact, I believe we do it in much the same manner as you Caucasians do." Leaning closer to Rose, he whispered, "This may shock you, but I even know which fork is used for the entree and which one is used for the salad."

Rose Saunders' face reddened as she glared at Opal. "I will speak to your father about this!" Avoiding Serval's unyielding stare, she hurried out of the room.

Serval smiled into Opal's wide eyes, as if nothing out of the ordinary had occurred, and rubbed his palms together. "Ready?"

*   *   *

As Opal's eyes took in the plush surroundings of *La Belle Etoile*, Serval's eyes remained fixed on her. When they were seated, Opal leaned across the table and whispered, "Mr. Rivard, I never knew colored folks could go to a place like this. I mean . . ."

"The owner of this restaurant is a Negro, Opal. He and his family are friends of ours from New Orleans. I guess that's why they gave it a French name. *La Belle Etoile* means . . ."

"The beautiful star," Opal said softly as she stroked the blue linen napkin next to her plate.

"You speak French?" Serval couldn't help being surprised.

"Oui, monsieur. Tres peu."

Serval laughed with pleasure at her shy smile. "Well, I'm sure I speak 'tres peu' less than you. I only know a word or two, probably 'cause my Daddy wanted me to learn it so bad. I'm—I'm kind'a stubborn that way."

"I know."

"Oh, you do? And just how do you know how stubborn I am, Miss Jackson?"

Opal narrowed her eyes and jerked her chin. "I was there when you went to settlin' your Daddy's hash the other day, remember?"

Serval threw back his head and laughed. "Is that what I did? Settled his hash, huh? Well, well. You know what I think, Miss Jackson?"

"What do you think, Mr. Rivard?"

"I think tonight is gonna be a lot'a fun, that's what I think. Know why?"

Opal smiled, revealing a dimple that made Serval catch his breath. "Why, Mr. Rivard?"

"'Cause you are the most charming, refreshing young lady I've met in a long, long time. Now, tell me something."

"What?"

"Where did you pick up French?"

Her smile faded. "I—oh, I don't really know much, just a few words and phrases."

Serval was mystified as to why his question seemed to change her mood, but decided to change the subject rather than ask. "Well, would you do me a favor, Miss Jackson?"

The smile returned. "Maybe . . ."

"Call me Serval."

"If you call me Opal."

"Okay, Opal. And since you're being so agreeable, then maybe you wouldn't mind calling me by my real name."

"And what's that?"

"Honey."

Opal rolled her eyes and laughed. "You're one silly child . . . honey." But when she opened her menu, she was suddenly all business. "Now. Let's get down to what's really important. What'cha gonna buy me for supper?"

*　　*　　*

Opal's wry sense of humor delighted Serval, who was more accustomed to stuffy college girls from Striver's Row. Several times through the meal, he found himself reaching for his water glass, to keep from choking on his food as he laughed at her stories. He couldn't help wondering about her mysterious reaction to his question about speaking French, but figured she would eventually explain.

All too quickly, a waiter approached the table and broke the news to the couple that *La Belle Etoile* was closing. Serval looked around for the first time, and realized that he and Opal were the last two patrons left. After paying the bill, he reached for her hand and led her outside. Suddenly at a loss for words, they slowly walked the quiet streets in no particular direction. For the first time, Serval felt comfortable sharing silence with a girl.

\* \* \*

Late that night Serval lay in his bed staring at the ceiling. He'd always told himself that when he really fell in love he'd know it, but the anticipated fireworks had failed to appear until Opal Jackson walked into his life. Only two hours earlier, he had said goodnight to her, and already he couldn't wait until their next date, which he'd impulsively set for the following morning. Serval was accustomed to girls seeking him out, but in Opal, he had met his match. Only one disturbing thought nagged at his mind. Serval was as keenly aware of his shortcomings as he was of his strong points, and one of his most childish tendencies was to do exactly the opposite of what his father wished him to do, no matter what the consequences. Having been pushed into numerous dates with girls from "good families," Serval knew only too well what kind of girl Charles Rivard had in mind for him. When Serval married, his father would be expecting a lot more than a love match for his son; Charles Rivard wanted a family alliance. And Serval was sure that a maid, a chauffeur, and a runaway mother were not his father's idea of a good family. He wondered if his all-consuming attraction to Opal could be linked to his father's expected disapproval of her. But as Serval drifted toward sleep, he conjured up an image of Opal's soft hypnotic eyes, and smiled. His father was suddenly the furthest thing from his mind.

\* \* \*

The next morning, as he waited for Opal, Serval was surprised at his own nervousness. He paced beside a park bench, rehearsing a few clever lines until he caught sight of her. He grinned broadly, yanked off his hat, and then affected a scowl of disapproval as he checked his wristwatch. "You, Miss Jackson, are late!"

"Oh, no I'm not," she snapped. "You, Mr. Rivard, must be early! You said eleven in the mornin' and . . . well, if I had a watch I'd show you just *how* early!"

Serval moved his arm closer to point out the time: eleven-ten.

Opal cut her eyes at him, but smiled. "Okay, I'm late. But I guess you must think I'm worth waitin' for since you're still here!"

Serval impulsively placed his hands around her waist, but she pulled away. Using his most ingratiating smile, he said softly, "One kiss."

Opal hesitated, but only for a moment. "Okay, Mr. Rivard, but just one. A little one."

Placing both hands behind his back, he leaned down to give her a chaste peck, but found himself kissing her more seriously than he had intended. "Good morning, Miss Jackson."

Opal's eyes fluttered open and she cleared her throat nervously. "Uh, good morning. Now, where are you takin' me today?"

"It's a surprise."

"Give me a hint."

"Well, let's say it's something . . . educational."

Opal scowled. "Not enough. Give me a better hint."

"Okay. Let's see . . . It'll inspire you—I hope. Come on."

Hand-in-hand, Serval and Opal sprinted up an alley, taking a short-cut to Lenox Avenue. A large group had gathered near one corner, and broke into sudden applause when a man stepped up onto a makeshift platform. Serval pulled Opal along behind him as he threaded through the crowd in an effort to get closer to the speaker. Finding a satisfactory spot, he stood behind Opal and leaned close to her ear. "Listen to him, Opal," he whispered. "Some of it might surprise you but I think you'll find it fascinating."

"But who is he, Serval?"

"Shh," he whispered. "His name is Marcus . . . Mosiah . . . Garvey."

Opal gazed up at the words written in bold black letters on a banner hanging high over the podium: "Universal Negro Improvement Association," she read aloud. A commanding, heavily-accented voice rang out, and Opal's gaze settled on the speaker.

Marcus Garvey was a dark, portly gentleman, possessing eyes that peered at his audience with intense blackness. He punctuated each statement with animated hand gestures, and wore a military-looking uniform, topped off by an ornate headpiece bedecked with plumes. He was all magnificence, like an admiral. His demeanor was one of confident leadership that came from a clear knowledge of his history. He spoke of his descendancy from the Maroons, whose name still struck terror in the hearts of white men in the mountain regions of Jamaica. His voice danced with the musical lilt of the Islands, but his use of language was formal with perfect enunciation, a reflection of an extensive education.

Serval could tell that Opal was mesmerized as Garvey spoke about the dignity of Negro people, backing it up with a condensed global history lesson. She glanced back at Serval and whispered, "Is that really true, Serval? Where did he learn that?"

"Perhaps it's more a case of unlearning than learning," Serval whispered back. "We stand here being surprised when a scholarly man takes us back into our own history, further than slavery, to days when we stood as kings and queens. He wants us to unlearn the negative history we've been taught for generations by the ones who enslaved us."

"Mm-mm-mm," Opal murmured. "There don't seem to be anything this Mr. Garvey doesn't know. Even about the war, Serval! I mean, I don't follow all that politics stuff myself, but I've heard Daddy fussin' with his friends about this war. They all been reading Dr. DuBois's newspaper, talkin' 'bout we ought'a go fight on account'a it bein' a good way for colored folks to get respect, but Daddy says Negroes got no place in a white man's war. Miss Aida—she's like a second Mama to me—she's got a newphew who joined up, and she don't care who's right or wrong. She's just worried about Eugene. Wonder if Daddy ever came out here to listen to Mr. Garvey, Serval? I bet he'd really like him!"

Serval smiled and squeezed her hand. Garvey was wrapping up his speech with his shouted slogans, which the crowd repeated in call and response fashion. "Back to Africa! Africa for the Africans! Up! You mighty race! You can accomplish what you will!"

After the crowd broke up, Opal and Serval collected a few brochures and walked through the park as they talked. "Sorry I was chattering so much, Serval," Opal said. "But that man sure stirred up my brain! A colored man with his own ships?" she said. "That'd really be sump'm, wouldn't it!"

Serval laughed. "Hey, why not? Negroes can achieve anything if they just stick together, Opal. That's what Mr. Garvey says. You watch. I happen to know he's got this shipping line in the works already. I wonder what it would be like to live in Africa? Of course, in certain sections, it's as bad as America, even worse, if that's possible."

Opal gave him a curious look. "You don't have it so bad, Serval. Seems to me, if you and your Daddy got invited to the Saunders' for tea, y'all must be kind'a high-tone colored folks."

Serval answered in a patient voice. "Opal. My family is . . . my family is the exception. I know I ought'a feel lucky but I'm still angry. I'm angry for all my friends who live in poverty just because they're skin is like mine — black. And as for us being high-tone, hey, there's no such thing, whether my Daddy wants to believe it or not. For all his accomplishments and polish, white folks would call my Daddy nigger just as fast as some poor bum livin' in the gutter. Our achievements don't matter to them. We're black. That's all they see."

Opal gazed absently at Serval's chest and touched it. "Know what, Serval? I think you're right. Mr. Saunders wasn't treatin' you and your Daddy the same way he treats white folks. I mean, me and Daddy work for him but you were guests, and he was still acting different somehow."

Serval shrugged. "We were only there because of some appointment by his bank. It was good politics. If Edward Saunders threw a party for fun, believe me, my father would not be on the invitation list, and, well, we know how he feels about me. Oh, by the way, you didn't get in trouble because of what I said to Mrs. Saunders last night, did you?"

Opal laughed. "Oh, no! She told Daddy, and he told her he'd wear me out, but then we just had a big laugh about it. If he really beat me the way he tells Mrs. Saunders he does, I'd be ridin' around in a wheelchair! And Daddy hollered when I told him what you said to her! He said he already likes you, and he hasn't even met you yet."

"Well, from the sound of him, I like him, too. So when are you gonna introduce me, now that we're hopelessly in love?"

"Oh, Lord, Serval, you're a crazy one. I've known you for two days. I do *not* fall in love in two days, and I *never* get hopeless. . . . Oh, wait a minute! Serval, let me look at your watch . . . Aw, I knew it! I'm late!"

"Wait a minute, Opal. Where are you off to in such a hurry?"

But with the agility of a deer, Opal was already halfway to the street, and only turned back to smile at Serval as she threw him a kiss.

*　*　*

Kathryn watched with concerned eyes as Serval picked at his food that night at supper. "Son, are you feeling all right?"

"Huh? Oh, sure, Mama. I've just got sump'm on my mind, that's all."

"Leave the boy alone, Kathryn," Charles laughed. "He's probably just mooning over some pretty girl."

Serval chuckled. "So you thought she was pretty, too?"

Charles looked up. "Who? I was speaking generally, son. Don't tell me you've gone and really fallen in love?"

"Well . . . it feels like it, Daddy."

"Well, I hope it's the Williams girl. Good family. I remember now. You took her out a couple of times the last time you were home. Is she the one?"

"No, Daddy. Didn't you see how hard I was workin' to catch that cute little maid's eye at the Saunders' last weekend?"

Charles put down his fork and leveled his eyes at Serval, then threw his napkin onto his plate. "That cute little *maid*? Serval Rivard, you will not be consorting with some common uneducated girl who—who scrubs toilets for a living when your mother and I have struggled to introduce you to some of the finest young ladies in Harlem!" He paused and took a deep breath.

Serval rose slowly from his chair, his eyes glittering and his teeth clenched. "Goddamn . . ." he muttered.

Kathryn's attempt to intervene came out as a weak croak heard by no one: "Oh, Serval . . ."

Serval planted his fists on the table and leaned dangerously close to his father. "You social-climbing son-of-a . . ."

Charles interrupted him by pounding the table with his palm. "Stop that gutter language at once, young man!"

Serval leaned closer, undaunted. "I'm gonna tell you something and I'm only gonna say it once. I don't care if you are my father . . . don't you ever call Opal Jackson common in or out of my presence! You just . . ."

Charles shot out of his chair and drew back his hand, but stopped short of backhanding Serval. His arm froze in mid-air as he glared at him.

Serval narrowed his eyes and leaned even closer. "I wouldn't recommend it, Daddy. Because you know it's about that time . . ."

"Oh, Serval!" Kathryn gasped.

Charles smirked, lowered his hand and sat back down in a pretense of calm. "Time for what, Serval? The old fable of the son challenging his father to a fistfight? That won't be happening in the Rivard house. We will remain a civilized family, I assure you." He gave Kathryn a patronizing smile and patted her hand.

Serval sat down and mimicked his father by fussing with the arrangement of the napkin on his lap. "No, Daddy. I would never challenge you to a fistfight. But if you had gone ahead and smacked me the way you wanted to so badly just then . . ."

"Then what, Serval?"

"Look, Daddy. It's just that Opal makes all those girls you keep throwin' at me look like . . . I can't even find a word derogatory enough to describe those empty-headed snobs, Daddy! Opal's a warm, beautiful girl and I'll see her whenever I goddamn well please!"

"That's enough! You will not curse around your mother, boy. That's those ruffians you insist on running around with. That's their influence on you, Serval. Such filthy language! Kathryn, perhaps you should go upstairs while Serval and I talk this over."

Kathryn stood up and glared at them. "This sort of thing cannot go on."

"But, my dear . . ." Charles began.

Kathryn held up one hand, silencing him, then left the room.

After her departure, Charles softened his tone, but only managed to sound patronizing, which frayed Serval's nerves. "Son, be reasonable. I didn't mean you couldn't see the girl at all. I mean, we're both men. We can discuss this sort of thing."

Serval shot his father a warning look. "What sort of thing, Daddy?"

"She was a pretty little thing for, well, we've never had a discussion about sowing your wild oats. I'm a man, too, son. I can see how the girl might have turned your head after a couple of romps with her and . . ."

"Romps?" he shouted. "Oh, you mean sexual romps? Who the hell said anything about sex, Daddy? Why do you assume that just because she's a maid, she's the type that would lay up with a fella after only knowing him for a couple of days? Goddamn . . ."

"Serval! Stop it at once!"

Serval fought to lower his voice. "All right. I'll restrain my gutter language, Daddy. You're right. I'm a Rivard and I've probably got a nastier mouth than a lot of those common uneducated servants out there, huh? But it's important that you know this, Daddy. Not only have I not had sex with her, but I've barely kissed the girl! No. I mean, the lady! Believe it or not, Daddy, a maid can be a lady, too."

"You are impossible when you're like this, Serval. This conversation is over."

As Charles strode angrily out of the room, Serval called loudly after him, "Oh, yeah, Daddy, one more thing . . . That girl you said would be such a prize fiance? Lon Williams' sweet little flower? Aw, shit, what the hell's her name? Oh, yeah! Daphne! Well, Daddy, you might be interested to know that sweet little Daphne spread her legs for half the fellas in my senior class in high school! Still want me to marry her?"

*   *   *

Two days later, Serval was faced with the indignity of calling for Opal at the rear servants' entrance of the Saunders mansion. She had been warned about her personal visitors calling for her at the front door, and she told Serval that if it happened again, she and her father would be dismissed. The temptation to enrage Edward Saunders by knocking at the front door was strong, but Serval suppressed it. He pulled his Pierce-Arrow around to the back of the house, and was still trying to convince himself that pride could indeed be swallowed when he spotted a dark-skinned man, who looked to be about fifty years of age, polishing the Saunders' touring car.

*Leon Jackson! You've just got to be Leon!* Serval parked his car and stepped out, meeting Leon's gaze with a smile. "Mr. Jackson?"

Leon Jackson's greeting warmed Serval. "You jus' got to be the famous Serval Rivard that done stole my baby's heart!" Wiping his hands on a towel, Leon let out a long whistle as he approached Serval's Pierce-Arrow. "That's a real grand automobile ya got there, Son!"

Serval shrugged self-consciously. "Well, thank you, sir. It's—my Daddy thought I should—well, thanks." He grabbed Leon's hand and took an instant liking to him. "I've heard a lot about you, Mr. Jackson! I hear you've got these white folks 'round here wrapped around your little finger!"

Leon hooted. "Naw, naw, son. I wouldn't go and say that! It's true, but I wouldn't say it, not out loud anyhow!"

"Well, I've been lookin' forward to meetin' the man that brought such a beautiful child into the world." Serval bowed deferentially from the waist, sending Leon into a fit of laughter.

"I can't take all the credit, now, but she is a sweet child. My baby's the apple of my eye, don'tcha know!"

"Well, then it looks like we've got that in common, sir."

"Look' like it. Well, now, Serval, I know you and Opal got places to go, so le'me go inside and see can I rush that child up a little."

"Wait, uh, Mr. Jackson?"

"Yes, son?"

"I must be crazy to ask," Serval laughed. "But aren't you gonna give me the usual lecture about takin' good care of your baby and I better act like a gentleman and all that?"

"Listen, son," Leon said. "Opal never was one to mess with fools. And from what she done told me about you, I know my baby's in good hands."

Serval grinned, feeling a blend of pleasure and curiosity. "Uh, and what was that? I mean, what did she say about me?"

Just as Leon opened his mouth to answer, Opal stepped from the side door off the kitchen, which was several yards away. The sun was setting in the distance behind her, setting the sky ablaze with every imaginable shade of red and gold. A gentle breeze stirred, and her long skirt billowed in a rose-colored cloud around her legs. She was such a breathtaking vision, Serval almost wished she wouldn't move and spoil the picture. Their eyes met, and he heard Leon's voice behind him: "What she told me was that she done finally met herself a real gentleman. And if I do say so myself, my child is a good judge of character. So, son, I ain't worried."

* * *

As soon as Serval escorted Opal inside the Clef Club, he regretted bringing her there. The Club's popularity had soared when James Reese Europe's band made it their home, drawing record numbers of patrons. Even after the popular bandleader's enlistment into the army, the Clef Club remained the favorite nightspot of the college set during holidays. It was a loud outrageous place that Serval usually loved, but it didn't seem to fit with his feelings for Opal. The minute they sat down, Serval glanced at his watch. "We'll just stay a few minutes," he said.

The expression on her face told him that she hadn't heard him. A couple dancing a drunken foxtrot suddenly bumped her chair, and the girl stumbled.

*That bum Raymond Hill and gin-swilling Sally Eldridge,* Serval thought miserably. He gave Opal a weak smile and sank lower in his chair when Raymond swept Sally into his arms to carry her back to their table. Opal gazed at Sally who was sprawled on Raymond's lap, giggling and tugging at his necktie. Serval considered dancing Opal to the far end of the room, but he wasn't sure whether or not she liked to dance. He searched her face for signs of disapproval, but she only smiled.

Still, Serval began thinking of an alternate plan for the evening. He suddenly noticed Opal mouthing something from across the table.

"You're gonna have to really shout, Opal. I can't hear you over this music and the noise these fools are makin'!"

"I said, don't they ever play soft music in this place, Serval?"

"Huh?"

"I SAID . . . Oh!"

Just as her voice reached its maximum volume, the band's loud rendition of "Maple Leaf Rag" abruptly ended, and Opal clapped her hand over her mouth.

"I don't know why I brought you here anyway," Serval laughed. "I mean, come to think of it, they never do play soft music and that means I won't get an excuse to put my arms around you. Let's go."

As Serval stood up, he felt a hand on his shoulder and heard a familiar voice. "Not so fast, buddy."

Serval spun around and threw his arms around the neck of a slender, dark-skinned young man wearing wire-rimmed eyeglasses. "Joseph! When did you get home?" Serval shouted. "Opal, I'd like you to meet one of my best friends in the whole world, Joseph Winfield. He beat me up in the first grade, and we've been like brothers ever since. We went all through school together—all the way to graduation. Joseph, this is Miss Opal Jackson."

Opal smiled and stretched out her hand. "Nice to meet you, Joseph."

Joseph shook her hand. "A pleasure. And since your date brought up the subject of our education, has he told you anything about that second-rate college of his?"

Serval laughed. "We fought like crazy over college choices. He was hellbent on Howard, but I knew that Morehouse was the better choice."

"Hah!" Joseph shouted. "We'll see who was right. But wait, I'm being rude." Joseph put his arm around a plump young woman with tilted, feline eyes and a bright smile shining from a glowing copper-colored face. "I'd like you both to meet my fiance, Millie Henderson."

Serval stepped back. "Fiance? Joseph—you're getting married?"

Millie stuck out her left hand and jiggled her fingers to show off her small engagement ring. "He asked me so many times, I finally had to say yes."

"Aww, congratulations, man!" Serval said, hugging Joseph again. "But Millie! Are you sure you know what you're doing?"

"Oh, I'll take my chances," Millie laughed. "It's nice to meet you, Opal, Serval."

"Hi, Millie," Opal said. "You're gonna make a lovely bride. All the best."

"Thank you."

As the band broke into another loud rag, Serval pointed toward the exit and led the way. Once they were outside, he asked Joseph, "So you're home on break?"

"For two more weeks. You?"

"Uhh, I'm keeping my options open," Serval said, grinning at Opal.

Joseph rolled his eyes. "Same ol' Serval. Cutting classes, inciting riots, and chasing pretty girls. I'll bet the professors keep you after class to clean the chalkboards. He was always in trouble, Opal. I'd ditch him if I were you. He'll come to no good, this one."

Serval doubled up his fists and took a playful jab at Joseph. "Oh . . . tryin' to come between me and my girl, huh? Why I ought'a . . ."

Joseph laughed. "Listen, Serval, we were just leaving. Dinner at my future in-laws, you know, so we don't want to be late."

"I understand. I'll call you, Joseph. Tomorrow. We'll compare notes and see whose professor has planted the more potent seeds of brilliance."

Joseph shook his head as he walked away. "It's the soil, Brother," he called over his shoulder. "Potent seeds are wasted unless planted in fertile soil. And I believe your whole field has gone to the worms. But call me. It's my duty to share the superior academic bounty of Howard University with my less fortunate Morehouse Brother."

"Superior, my ass!" Serval called, then clapped his hand over his mouth. "God, Opal," he whispered, "I'm sorry."

"It's okay this once," she sniffed. "Just remember, I'm not the bathtub gin type." She smiled and waved at Joseph and Millie. "Bye! Hope to see you again!"

Serval took her hand. "Okay. So we know it's too noisy for any intimate, soul-searching conversation inside the Clef Club. So . . ."

Opal nodded. "So where to, Mr. Rivard?"

He smiled and took her hand. "Someplace quieter, Miss Jackson."

*    *    *

At the north end of 118th Street was an expanse of grass that served as the neighborhood children's baseball diamond. "Ooh!" Opal squealed, stepping off the curb into the street. "Let's go walk in the grass, Serval!"

Serval gave her a puzzled look, then smiled. "Okay. Why not?"

When they reached the edge of the worn path between first and second base, Opal kicked off her shoes and leaned down to peel off her stockings. Serval laughed as he grabbed her arm to steady her.

"What're you laughin' at, Mr. Rivard?" she snapped. "I'm not about to get my good shoes and my only pair of stockings all messed up walkin' in this grass. Besides, grass feels best on bare feet. Try it. Come on! Take off your shoes."

"Okay, Miss Jackson," he said, sitting down to remove his shoes and socks. "But I had no idea you were such a wild child."

"Oh, hush. I know when you're makin' fun of me, Serval."

He scrambled to his feet and stuffed his socks into his shoes. "I'm not making fun of you. I'm really not. Okay, my shoes are off. Now, if you mess around and walk me into a bunch of brambles, I'ma have to—to settle your hash, young lady."

Opal smiled. "Huh! Like to see you try that!"

As they walked along the perimeter of the field, Serval began to enjoy the simplicity and quiet. He smiled and wrapped his arm around Opal's waist. "Hey, you know what? This grass *does* feel good on my bare feet. Real cool."

"Told'ya."

"Listen—you didn't think I was really makin' fun of you before, did you, Opal?"

"Well, I know you're not used to girls like me, Serval. I mean, you're probably used to those high-tone girls."

"High-tone? That's not a description I'd ever apply to Miss Sally Eldridge."

"Who?"

"The, uh, dancer who was stumblin' around the Clef Club lookin' for a lap to roost in."

"Oh," Opal sniffed. "Her. You know her pretty good?"

"Well, I've danced with her a few times. But that's all. She never ended up in my lap, the way she did with Raymond. But see, that's the reason I like you as much as I do. You're not like her. Believe me, Opal, you're a hundred times more interesting to me than Sally or any of those spoiled Striver's Row girls."

"Oh, I know I'm interestin' and all that, but . . ."

"But what?"

"Well, those girls seem like they know how to show a fella a real good time. Sittin' all in their laps and drinkin' and all that nonsense. If you like that sort'a thing."

Serval grinned. "I'm here with you. What does that tell you?"

Opal cut her eyes at him and gave him a sly smile. "Tells me you're smarter than I thought you were, Mr. Rivard."

*   *   *

Opal Jackson began consuming almost all of Serval's thoughts. Only two things bothered him. One was the fact that his break from school was almost over, which would end his time with Opal. The other problem wasn't actually a problem at all; it was more of a mystery. On four occasions since he'd met her, Opal had suddenly rushed away or even refused to make a date with him at all, on Thursday and Saturday afternoons. This time, he was determined to find out where she went. Although she told him she had something important to do on Saturday, he convinced her to meet him at a cafe for lunch.

After finishing lunch, Serval watched Opal closely as she sipped her coffee. "Why are you so jumpy, Opal?" he asked.

"Are you sure it's not two yet, Serval? Le'me see that watch."

"Opal. You're gonna make me think you're secretly married or something if you don't tell me where you always go on Thursdays and Saturdays."

"It's—it's not—just don't worry about it, Serval. Now I gotta go."

"Opal . . ."

"I said I gotta go." Turning on her heel, Opal left quickly without looking at him.

Realizing that he had angered her for the first time, Serval watched her walk away, and wondered what to do. Curiosity got the better of him. He tossed the money on the table for the check and dashed after her, keeping a safe distance between them. *To apologize, if nothing else*, he told himself, knowing it was a lie.

Peering around the corner of a building, he saw that she was standing at the bus stop with her back to him. His car was parked several yards in the other direction, so he sprinted up the block and climbed in to wait. After a few minutes he spotted the bus in his rear-view mirror and started his engine. When the bus slowed to a stop, Opal climbed aboard, and Serval followed the bus along its route. He fell back a good distance behind it at each stop, and, shortly after passing 102nd Street, he saw Opal step off. Pulling over, he parked his car, and took up the chase on foot. She walked two blocks up to West End Avenue and turned right. Ducking behind an ice wagon, Serval watched her cross the street and run up the steps to a brownstone—number 870. Once she had disappeared inside, he considered turning back, but quickly found himself at the top of the steps with his hand on the foyer doorknob. The sound of classical music that he recognized as a Tchaikovsky piece floated out the open front window to his left. He froze when he heard Opal's voice.

"I'm on time for a change, Madame! What'cha think about that?"

She was answered by the sound of another woman's throaty laughter followed by a foreign accent: "Ah, Shoo-Shoo! He's cooling! Your young man is letting you get away easier these days!"

"Oh, Madame, I guess I ought'a tell him but . . ."

"But what, Shoo-Shoo? This prince of romance you have told me about—surely he will understand, no?"

"He might just think I'm, well, chasin' rainbows, Madame. Sometimes that's what I think, too. I know you're tryin', but sometimes I think they'll never let me . . ."

"Shh. No more of that, Shoo-Shoo. Now. We begin."

The mysterious exchange left Serval bewildered as to what was going on with this "Madame" person. He leaned over the railing, and through the fluttering curtains caught sight of Opal and her surroundings reflected in a large mirror hanging on the wall. As he watched, his eyes widened and his mouth fell open in shock. The skirt and blouse she had worn at the cafe were hanging on a coat rack, leaving Opal dressed in form-fitting black tights and a leotard. She stretched her right leg up over her head and leaned it against the wall. Then she stretched the left leg in the same manner and executed several barre maneuvers before positioning herself in the center of the room.

The sound of "Madame's" voice seemed different, more commanding, when she said, "Elevé, mon petite Shoo-Shoo. High fifth, s'il vous plait."

"Oui, Madame."

Serval leaned against the rail and closed his eyes. *French. That's how she knows French.* He heard the scratching sound of a phonograph needle being abruptly lifted from a record. The silence made him curious, and he took another peek. A slender white woman with graying hair vigorously cranked the Victrola handle a few times, and then carefully placed the needle back at the beginning of the record. She backed away slowly toward the far wall, providing Serval with an unobstructed view of Opal. She was dancing.

The music seemed to transform the sweet girl he thought he knew into a complete stranger. She was too many new things at once, and he couldn't comprehend her for a moment. This ethereal creature was surely an angel or a wood sprite from some children's fairy tale — certainly not the same girl who had walked barefoot with him through the neighborhood baseball diamond. He shook his head and blinked. One second she was as delicate as a wren in flight, but in a sweeping shift of movement, she was the wind at hurricane velocity. He had never seen her legs before, and he stared at their shape and limber strength; they were the legs of a finely tuned athlete.

The music rose in a crescendo of fire, licking her body until she became one with it, responding to its every leap and descent in perfect synchronization. Suddenly, she was all surging power, like a wild horse running at immeasurable speeds, but tempered by the grace and fluidity of a woman's form. Through it all, her face was a blend of concentration and passion for the supernal world she was in, as if leaving it would be the death of her.

After watching for several minutes, Serval felt an unfamiliar sting somewhere deep inside, and came to the realization that it was loss. Opal Jackson was not the free-spirited chauffeur's daughter he had fallen in love with. She was the possession of Tchaikovsky's music and a foreign ballet teacher she called "Madame." He descended the steps slowly, confused but still mesmerized by her dancing image in his head.

# Chapter 6

Three days passed with no calls or surprise visits from Serval, and Opal was unprepared for her emotional reaction. What began as listlessness ended in confusion and depression. After finally drifting into a fitful sleep on the third night, she felt Aida shaking her shoulder.

"Sista! Wake up!"

"Huh? Miss Aida? What's wrong?"

"That young man is outside and wants to speak to you, child! He tossed a few pebbles at my window—guess he thought it was yours—and I jus' hope Mr. Saunders don't wake up! He'll raise the roof, I know it! Now get ya'self together, Sista, and get on out there!"

But Opal was already up and pulling on a dress. "Miss Aida, if Daddy wakes up, tell him I'm with Serval and not to worry, would you, please?" She grabbed her shoes and kissed Aida quickly before running quietly up the stairs and out the side door.

She paused at the top of the outside steps when she saw Serval's unsmiling face. They stared at each other for a long silent moment before the sudden spatter of several drops of rain sent Opal running down to him. Pulling her by the hand, Serval sprinted down the driveway to his car and opened the passenger door for her.

Opal stared at the glowing numbers on the dashboard and listened to the tires spin as Serval pressed the accelerator. He twisted a knob and the windshield wipers began a rhythmic slap across the glass. After riding for several minutes, Opal broke the silence. "I know how mad you are, Serval."

"What makes you think I'm mad?"

"The way I keep runnin' off and not tellin' you where I'm goin'. I know men don't like that sort'a thing. Y'all just want us to be there waitin' when you're ready to see us."

"Opal . . ." He stopped talking and pulled the car over to the side of the road. Leaning his head back, he said softly, "I'm not mad at you. I'm—I'm confused. So many things are going on, and I don't know what I feel. Did you know I'm supposed to go back to school in ten days?"

"How could I know that?" she said. "You didn't tell me."

"I know. I was thinking about extending my visit . . . Opal, I don't know if I can stand to leave you. I know that doesn't sound . . . What I mean is . . ."

"I know, Serval. You're the independent type, huh? You've never been tied to anybody so it scares you. But don't worry. I don't have you tied up."

He sighed. "How come things are so—so uncomplicated for you, Opal?"

"Things only get complicated when you let 'em. See, I'll miss you when you go back to school, but I'll just write you letters, and wait 'til you come back, I guess. I'll keep busy and . . ."

"How will you keep busy?"

"Huh? Oh, I've got my work to do, you know, and I have—interests, Serval."

"Interests?" he asked in an edgy tone. "What kind of *interests*?"

"Oh," Opal said, crossing her arms. "Look's like you just danced us back to the front door, huh? You want to know where I've been going. . . . Oh, I guess I should've just told you from the beginning . . ."

Serval touched her arm. "Wait."

"What?"

"You don't owe me any explanation, Opal. In fact, I've got a confession to make to you. I *know* where you go."

"Huh?"

"I followed you last Saturday to your dance class. I watched you through the window. It was wrong, I know, but I just had to know."

After a long silence, Opal murmured, "I knew you'd be upset."

"I'm not . . . I'm just, see . . . I mean, you were good, Opal. You dance the ballet beautifully, but . . ."

"But it's white folks' stuff, huh? That's what's got you so upset."

He stared at her with wide eyes. "How did you—I mean what makes you think that?"

"Well, I know how proud you are, Serval. That's the thing I like best about you. I mean, you might be a little full of yourself sometimes, but mostly, it's nice to be around a man who's not scared of white folks. And you make me feel brave too, just bein' around you. So I was worried that if you saw me dancin' the ballet, you'd think I was just . . . I don't know." She paused for a moment. "Serval, the white folks won't even let me dance, but Madame keeps tellin' me I've *got* to dance. She—she thinks I'm, uh . . ."

"What? Don't be bashful. Tell me."

Opal squirmed and looked away. "She told me she thinks I'm— great. You know, what'cha call a 'prima ballerina.' But it seems she's the only white person on earth who thinks so, Serval. Sometimes, I just feel like I'm wastin' my time."

"Then why do you keep going back?" he asked gently.

A faraway look crept into Opal's eyes and she smiled. "I feel like . . . It makes me feel happy, I guess. Sometimes I feel just like a—a bird. For those three or four hours when I'm at Madame's flat . . . Oh. That's what those foreigners call an apartment, Serval—a flat."

Serval smiled.

"Anyway, when I'm there, I feel like I'm not colored or white or a girl or a boy . . . I—I wish I could explain it to you. I just feel free and powerful—like nature. Like mountains or a bird . . ." She turned and stared at him with tears standing in her eyes. "Serval . . . do you know . . . I can—fly?"

Serval suddenly grabbed her tightly. "Yes," he whispered. "I saw you. I—maybe that's part of what scared me. But I think I understand now. You just love to dance, don't you? Just like Mr. Garvey wants to sail us all back to Africa. I guess it sounds far-fetched to some folks, but dreams always sound far-fetched—until they come true. So, Opal, you know what you should do? You should keep dancing—and flying."

She squirmed away from him and searched his eyes. "Are you sure you understand?"

"No. I've never known a girl who could fly before," he said, grinning. "But I'll get used to it. Be patient. Please?"

✻ ✻ ✻

Listening to Opal's uncomplicated take on their situation cleared Serval's mind like rain clears the air. As confused as he had been for the previous three days, the hours they spent talking in his car left Serval with a feeling of peace. Returning to school no longer loomed like the end of the world with Opal's promise of a steady stream of letters and plans for several visits over the year to come.

They were sleepy but contented by the time the first streaks of morning lit a partly overcast sky. The colors on the horizon became their shared focal point, quieting all conversation for a long stretch of time. It was a majestic sunrise filled with abstract portent—like liquid gold reconciling two purple clouds in a dispute over whether or not to rain.

Serval yawned. "It's like being in an art gallery, huh?"

"Mm-hmm. Looks like God used up all his paints on the sky this mornin'."

"Well said. Hey, Miss Jackson. You hungry?"

"Mm-hmm. I could eat."

"Okay. Pop Duval's place might be open."

"No, wait. I've got an idea, Serval. We're not too far from Madame Romanov's flat. How 'bout if we go there? She cooks me breakfast all the time on early class days. She won't mind fixin' another plate."

Serval looked at his watch and laughed. "It's only a little after seven, Opal. You really think she's up?"

"I know she's up. She's goin' to visit her sister in California, and her train leaves at noon. And besides, she's been dyin' to meet you, Serval. Don't let it go to your head, but I talk about you all the time, you know."

"You do?"

"Mm-hmm. Come on. And let's walk, Serval. I feel like walking. I promise you'll like Madame—even if she is white folks."

*   *   *

When Madame Romanov opened her front door, her surprised expression immediately melted into a warm smile. "Good morning, young lovers! Please to come in!"

"Mornin', Madame!" Opal chirped, proudly clinging to Serval's arm.

Madame nodded her head and raised one eyebrow as she studied him. "And this is of course za magnificent Monsieur Rivard! You were right, Shoo-Shoo. He is most beautiful." Turning to gesture toward the sofa, she smiled at Serval. "You are being good to my little Shoo-Shoo?"

Serval smiled and cleared his throat. "Yes, ma'am. Uh, Shoo-Shoo?"

"She means it like 'teacher's pet' or sump'm," Opal whispered.

"Please to sit down and make yourself at home," Madame said. "You wish coffee, Monsieur Rivard?"

"Yes. Thank you. But please call me Serval."

"Such za elegant name. Serval. Like za graceful cat, no? Oh, ma foi, Shoo-Shoo! That reminds me! Please to remember about feeding my little Meow. Every day. You will not forget?"

"No, Madame. I won't forget."

"Here is key and za food is in kitchen. Now, Madame will fix you both grand breakfast. Sit and talk. I will be back in only little time." Turning back to face Serval, she smiled. "Please to call me Anna."

Opal looked surprised. "I—I never knew . . . Madame, why . . .?"

Madame laughed and shook her index finger at Opal. "You, Shoo-Shoo, are student. Monsieur Rivard is guest."

During the visit Serval marveled at the warm relationship between Opal and Madame Romanov. Never had he felt so at home in the presence of a white person. He found himself laughing at her stories about Russia, told in her broken English, until he almost forgot the racial difference.

The time passed quickly, and Serval was surprised when Opal pointed out the time on his watch. "Guess it's time for us to go, Madame," she said. "I know you've gotta finish your packing."

"Yes. Is true I should be packing. But when I return, you must bring your charming young man again to visit. I would be most happy."

Serval smiled and reached for her hand. "Thank you—Anna."

As they descended the steps of Madame's brownstone, Opal grinned up at Serval. "Well, what do you think of Madame?"

"She's different, I'll tell you that. But I think I know why."

"Why, Serval?"

"She wasn't raised in America. No residual effects of slavery. No Jim Crow. Too bad white folks here aren't like her. Things could be so different. Hey, girl! Ain'tchu sleepy yet? We've been up all night."

"No. Not a bit. Serval, let's walk to the park."

Serval grimaced and pointed over his shoulder with his thumb. "Haven't you had enough walking for one morning? How 'bout we go up the road and get my car, then I'll *drive* you to the park."

"Aww, Serval," Opal pleaded. "Come on. Let's have a nice, romantic stroll."

Serval squinted up at the gray sky. "All right. But I bet'cha it's gonna rain."

"No it won't. Not today. It wouldn't dare."

\* \* \*

Three hours later, caught in a torrential downpour, Serval and Opal dashed back to Madame Romanov's flat. Noticing the drawn blinds, Opal murmured, "She must've left already."

"I knew we shouldn't have walked this morning," Serval moaned. "My car's a mile down the road."

Opal began digging around in her handbag for the key. "Don't worry. Madame won't mind. Oh, but just be sure to watch out for Meow. Mind you don't step on his tail or sump'm, hear?"

Once inside, Opal hurried into the bathroom and returned with a stack of blue bath towels. Stopping abruptly in the doorway, she stared at Serval as he peeled off his wet shirt.

He grinned at her, then wrapped his arms around his body and pretended to shiver violently. "Uh, any of those for me?"

"Huh?" Opal redirected her gaze toward the floor, then hurried over to him. "Oh, uh, yeah. Here you are."

"It really is cold in here, isn't it?" Serval said as he began drying off. "Maybe you ought'a go into the bedroom and get out'a that wet dress. I'm sure your teacher's got a robe or something in there you can put on." He tapped her chin playfully and smiled at her. "And don't worry. I'm not planning to take advantage of the situation or anything. Now go change."

Opal disappeared into the bedroom for a few minutes. When she returned she was wearing a long, blue chenille wrapper and a patchwork quilt around her shoulders. Serval broke into a grin, and Opal giggled.

"Lord, I must look a sight!"

Serval rubbed his chin and studied her through squinted eyes. "Hmmm . . . Well, let's see . . . Hah! I've got it! You look like a little brown half-drowned mouse . . . with kinky hair. And you never looked more beautiful."

Opal rolled her eyes and laughed. "Come on. A nappy half-drowned mouse does *not* sound beautiful to me."

Serval's smile faded as he stepped closer and touched her chin. "And your eyelashes are all wet and stuck together in little points," he whispered. "Makes your eyes look like stars. So you're not just beautiful. I think that maybe you're something from the heavens."

Opal gulped, then hurried over and tapped the radiator. "You know what? It's cold in here, Serval. Isn't this radiator workin'?"

Serval chuckled. "Mm-hmm. But we're soaked to the skin. It's gonna take a minute, but we'll warm up."

She eyed his soaked trousers still clinging to his legs. "Not you. Not unless you take off those trousers. Uh, I mean . . . Here, you take this quilt and wrap up in it. I think I saw an extra blanket in the bedroom. I'll go get it."

When Opal returned with the blanket, Serval was bundled in the quilt and hanging his clothes on the backs of the kitchen chairs. "I've got an idea, Opal. Let's turn on the oven in here and sit on the floor in front of it. I can't remember ever being this cold before."

By the time they were huddled comfortably together on the floor of the tiny kitchen, Serval noticed that Opal hadn't said a word for several minutes. "Hey. You all right? You're suddenly so quiet, Miss Jackson."

Opal snuggled against his chest and shrugged. "I guess—I just guess I'm embarrassed, that's all."

"Why? There's nothin' to be embarrassed about. You haven't done anything wrong."

"No. It's not that, Serval. I'm embarrassed 'cause of the way I was lookin' at you before. I—I guess I was starin' at you."

Serval laughed and tugged at one of her curls. "Hey, I didn't mind."

Silence.

"Opal, don't be scared of me. I'm the same person, in clothes or out of clothes."

"I'm not scared of you, Serval. I guess I was scared of—me. I mean, you didn't know it, but I almost . . ."

"You almost what?"

"I almost put my hand out and touched you on your chest, Serval, because you just looked so—so pretty."

Serval stared at her for a moment, marveling at her combination of innocence and earthy sensibility. Her simple honesty about a sexual stirring threw him into a sudden uncharacteristic state of nervousness.

"Opal, listen to me for a minute. I know we haven't known each other for very long, but I have strong feelings for you. I—I mean, uh, feelings I never had before." He cleared his throat and continued. "I guess I—I'm falling in love with you—and . . ."

"Me too." She blinked at him once before returning her head to his shoulder.

Momentarily stunned, Serval finally found his voice again. "You . . . love me?"

"Mm-hmm."

"Opal. You must be the most direct, honest girl I've ever met. Maybe that's why I feel the way I do. At least one of the reasons."

"You're honest, Serval."

"Well, I try to be, and sometimes I even succeed. But you just—I mean, I have to think about what I'm gonna say, and then while I'm still trying to find the right words, you just say it. Short, simple and very much to the point." He scratched his head and grinned. "Come to think of it, you would've been great on my debate team."

Opal scowled and nudged him with her shoulder. "You know what? It's hot, Serval. This oven got hot quick, huh?"

Laughing, Serval gathered the quilt around his body and pulled Opal to her feet. "Let's go back into the front room."

After they settled themselves on the sofa, Serval grabbed another towel from the stack and began to rub Opal's hair in gentle circles. "Your hair's almost dry, Miss Jackson," he whispered.

"Mmmm . . . Too bad, 'cause that sure feels good."

"Opal?"

"Yes?"

"Tell me what you were thinking, when you—when you wanted to touch me before."

"Well . . ." she began slowly, "I wasn't thinkin' really. I was just havin' a feeling is all."

"What kind of feeling?"

After a pause, she smoothed her hair and gave him an earnest look. "Can't remember. Show me your stomach again, Serval, and I'll try to figure it out this time."

Suppressing a laugh, Serval eased the quilt down around his waist and waited.

"You won't think I'm bad if I—if I touch you, Serval?"

"Miss Jackson, nothing you could do would be bad."

Watching her expression, Serval caught his breath when she rested her palm on the left side of his chest. The softness of her fingertips held the instinctive caress of a woman experienced in pleasures of the flesh, but in her eyes was the naive curiosity of a child. Feeling a bead of perspiration roll down his forehead, he was beginning to think it impossible to endure another second of her feather-light exploration of his chest and arms, when she suddenly squeezed his shoulder lightly and smiled.

"You're strong, huh?"

He cleared his throat. "Uh, not at the moment, no."

After continuing her finger-tracing of each curve and indentation of his upper body for a moment more, Opal folded her hands in her lap and looked into his eyes. "Okay, Serval. I'm ready to tell you what I'm feelin' now."

He exhaled. "All right. What?"

"You are . . . well, remember the way the sky looked this morning?"

Serval grinned. "I'm cloudy? Colorful?"

"Be serious. You said it yourself. It was beautiful. And you're beautiful like that sunrise to me, Serval. I know men are supposed to be handsome, but you're not handsome. You're just beautiful. And when I touch you . . ." She stopped and lowered her head.

"What? Don't look down, Opal. Tell me. I really want to know."

"I'm not a child, Serval. I know about what goes on between men and women. It's just that—I guess I never felt it before. Not like this. But now I understand. Nature just makes you crave each other, huh?"

Serval leaned close and kissed her before answering. "Crave. Yes. So, is that what you're telling me? That you crave me?"

She touched his mouth lightly with her fingertips and nodded. "It's not like—I mean, I've been kissed before, you know. And fought fellas off too."

"I bet."

"But I never felt like this. This is different. You won't think . . .?"

"No. I won't think." Keeping his eyes locked on hers, he eased the blanket off her shoulders and ran his fingers down the side of her neck.

"Mmmm." A sudden look of panic crossed her face.

"That's okay. It's okay to show what you feel. I'm the only one here, and I promise you, Opal, you can trust me."

As slowly as he could, he slid his hand inside the robe and around her waist. When the robe fell open, he pulled her close and felt the warmth of her bare breasts against his chest. Hearing an almost imperceptible gasp, he pulled away slightly. "You want me to stop?"

"No. I . . ."

"What, baby?"

"I want to begin. I—I just don't know how."

He wrapped his arms tightly around her and brought his lips to her ear. "Nobody knows how," he whispered. "All you have to know is what you feel. So if you're sure about what you feel . . ." He stopped and peered into her eyes. "You have to be sure that I'm the one you want, Opal, because I'm serious about you. For the first time in my life, I'm really serious. So be sure, because this is where we begin."

Opal closed her eyes and leaned her forehead against his chin. "I'm sure."

"Good. Then just hold onto me, and we'll begin."

\* \* \*

Serval Rivard was in love for the first time in his life, he was sure. After taking Opal home that night, he felt a strong compulsion to have a talk with his father. Inspired by a long day of soul-stirring passion, Serval's mood was buoyant when he blasted through the front door of his parents' house. "Daddy!" he shouted. "Are you up?"

Charles yanked open his bedroom door and glared over the bannister at his son before quietly closing the door behind himself. "Serval!" he hissed. "Your mother is asleep! Now what in the world would possess you to come into the house screaming like a wild man? Serval?" He hurried down the stairs and found Serval standing in the formal dining room.

Serval pulled out a chair from the table and nodded at his father. "Have a seat, Daddy. I've got something to tell you and you'll take it better sitting down."

Charles sat down and rubbed his temples. "Oh, Serval, stop being so dramatic and get to the point." Suddenly, his annoyed expression changed to one of eager anticipation. "It's not that . . . Son, don't tell me you're going to enlist after all?" Charles's hopeful eyes met confusion in Serval's.

"What? No, Daddy. That's not what . . ."

"I know you don't want to talk about it, son, but it really is the right thing to do. Not only for moral reasons, but for the benefit of our people, and then there's your own future to consider. There are innumerable benefits in being a war veteran, son. Besides, with all this talk of conscription, President Wilson's bound to call for a draft any day now, and then you'll have no choice. It's not as if you'd really be at any risk—well, any real risk. Now that we Yanks are involved, the whole thing'll be over in no time."

"*We* Yanks, Daddy?" As soon as he heard his own voice say the words, Serval threw back his head and laughed wildly. He had come home to announce his plan to marry Opal, and instead was on the verge of another shouting match with his father over politics, as usual. "Please, Daddy, can we just . . . Look, this is not what I came home to discuss with you."

His father sat quietly, glaring at him. "What could be more important than the war, Serval? Haven't you even considered . . ."

"I—wait. No, Daddy. Forgive me, but I haven't suddenly been inspired to join President Custer's cavalry. What I wanted to tell you was—I'm going to marry Opal Jackson." Leaning back in his chair, Serval was the picture of contentment as he waited for the explosion.

But Charles remained calm. "I expected this, Serval. You always do exactly the opposite of my wishes. Answer a question for me, Serval. Do you think I'm a stupid man?"

Serval rolled his eyes. "No, but . . ."

"That's right, I'm not. Son, it's time you tried to grow up. Hasn't it occurred to you that the reason you're drawn to this—this girl—is that you knew I'd . . ."

Serval shot out of his chair so violently, he not only knocked it over, but broke one of the legs. "Shut up, goddammit!"

"Stop the vulgar language at once and listen to me, son . . ."

"*You* stop! Stop trying to spit on my feelings for Opal!"

"This is important, son. You've got to listen to me . . ."

"No. This time you're gonna listen to me. Yes, it occurred to me, in the beginning, that I might have an ulterior motive for wanting to be with her, but I'm not a boy any more, Daddy. I thought it over carefully and . . . Aw, shit! Why do you have to make everything so wrong? Why can't it be that I just happened to fall in love with a girl who's not from Striver's Row? Why can't you accept the fact that everything I do isn't somehow connected with the almighty Charles Rivard?" Suddenly feeling drained, Serval pulled up another chair and dropped into it. "Daddy, I love her. It's just that simple. I really do. Why can't you just be happy for me?"

"You're not seeing this thing clearly, Serval. Love isn't enough."

"But . . ."

"Don't interrupt me, son. Listen. You go around quoting your precious Mr. Garvey about the progress of Negroes, but when it comes to sacrificing your own selfish interests, you behave like a spoiled child. You're a hypocrite, Serval."

Serval clutched his head in his hands and gave his father a wild-eyed look. "What in holy *hell* are you talkin' about *now*, Daddy?"

"Love is not enough. We Negroes have very little power in these United States, as you know. You're looking at things on a very small scale, son. You think you love a girl so . . ."

"I *know* I love her."

Charles sighed impatiently. "All right. You love her. To you, it's as simple as one, two, three. You fall in love with some girl, you marry the girl. You don't want to go to war, you don't go. But what would happen, Serval, if Dr. DuBois is right? What if young Negroes going to this war could lift the race? What if it does win us the respect we deserve? White people aren't perfect, Serval . . ."

"That's the first *accurate* thing you've said all night, Daddy," Serval mumbled, resting his head on the table.

Charles continued. "If they see that we're *with* them, shoulder to shoulder to protect America, how can they possibly continue these practices? It takes thinking on a larger scale, Serval. You've got to start thinking big."

"Okay, Daddy," Serval said, gritting his teeth. "Just for argument's sake, let's say I go to war and save the white folks, win every medal for valor and all that. Then in, oh, say twenty years or so, in their abundant *gratitude*, they elect me President of the United States. Swell. But what in the *hell* has all this got to do with Opal?! *How* is my marrying Opal Jackson gonna be the ruination of the Negro race? Answer me that if you can." When he finished, he plunked his head back on the table, harder this time.

Charles stiffened and narrowed his eyes. "If you'll lift your head off that table and act like a man, I'll tell you."

Serval sat up, puffed out his chest theatrically, and crossed his arms. "Okay, Daddy, how's this? Manly enough?"

Charles refused the bait and continued his lecture. "What if you could be instrumental in joining two *influential* Negro families, Serval? Don't you understand that when power joins power, then a stronger, more invincible power is created?"

"So you're sayin' I shouldn't marry for love, I should marry for economic development? Is that it? Well, hell! Why didn't you just pick out a wife for me when I was a baby the way they did in medieval times? Or, shit! What am I sayin'? You probably did! When do I meet her?"

"Serval, if you don't stop that cursing . . . Look, I'm not talking about an arranged marriage. It's just that there are so many young ladies to choose from, and you've only known this Jackson girl for a few weeks, son. And Serval, you can laugh all you want about economic development, but that is the way our race will rise in this country. And by God, if you say anything about going back to Africa, I swear, Serval, I'll take a strap to you!"

Serval's eyes widened, but he remained silent. Charles softened his tone.

"Son, didn't you understand what that meeting at Mr. Saunders' home was all about? *That* was about economic development."

"No it wasn't, Daddy." Not caring that he was rounding a forbidden corner, Serval spoke his piece anyway. "Mr. Garvey's plans for a shipping line—now *that's* economic development—*independent* economic development. What *you* were doin' was goin' to the white man beggin', Daddy. You know, like the white folks say, call a spade a spade."

Charles rose slowly, staring at Serval with empty eyes. The tense silence bore witness to the wreckage between them, of the bridge that had just been burned.

"You go ahead and marry the girl, Serval. Not that you'll receive my blessing, because you won't. But marry her. If she has any feeling for you whatsoever, she won't want to see the division she's caused between you and your family. Don't ask me to do something I can't." Turning his back, he headed toward the door.

"And don't *you* ask me to do something I can't, Daddy," Serval shouted. "Because there's no way in hell I'll marry anybody other than Opal Jackson."

Charles stopped and turned around. "Oh, Serval. One more thing. Since you don't believe in economic development, then you'll understand when I don't send your regular check to Morehouse for next semester. If you're not man enough to fight for your country, then you have no right to the benefits of an American education. See how long your little maid stays with a penniless, unemployed coward. Good night."

# Chapter 7

Joseph Winfield was scheduled to return to Howard University that Friday morning, but when Serval showed up at the Winfield family home late Thursday night, his plans changed.

"I'll leave Sunday, Serval. It's all right. Now come upstairs and tell me what's wrong. But be quiet. My mother's asleep."

Serval followed Joseph up the stairs and into his room, then flopped down on the twin bed near the window.

Joseph laughed. "Make yourself at home."

"Don't laugh! Do you realize that this bed feels more homey than my own bed in my parents' house?"

"Uh-huh, I thought so. Another verbal prize-fight with Charles Rivard, am I right? And from the tragic look on your face, I'd say it was bare-knuckles."

"Bullseye." Serval sat up and gave Joseph a hard look. "I told him I was gonna marry Opal, and he hit the roof. I told you her father's a chauffeur, didn't I?"

"You did. And I'm getting a pretty clear picture of how the discussion went."

"Discussion? Try Little Big Horn. Gettysburg. The American Revolution. Or even that mess goin' on in Europe right now. Anyway, it was a war."

Joseph sat on the other twin bed and rubbed his eyes under his glasses. "And it was all Daddy's fault, right?"

Serval cut his eyes at him. "One hundred percent, buddy."

"Who won?"

"Well . . . not me, that's for damn sure. I never win my Daddy's wars. Anyway, it was a two-part war. He doesn't want me to marry Opal, and then there was the same old lecture about enlisting in the army. But I'm marrying Opal just the same. And I'll be damned if I enlist. I don't care what he says."

"Then it sounds like you *did* win."

"Oh, no. He pulled out his big gun at the last minute and blasted me six feet under the goddamn lilies."

"Which big gun?"

"The big tuition gun."

Joseph fell back across the bed and groaned. "Ouuch! Withholding funds. So the senior Mr. Rivard prevailed after all."

"No. I guess you'd have to call it a draw."

"Wait a minute, Serval. You can't quit school. Please tell me that's not what you're doing."

"I can't beg him, Joseph."

"Nobody said you have to beg. Just apologize."

"No! You don't get it! He doesn't want an apology. He wants to control me!"

"Well, compromise then."

"Joseph, my Daddy's idea of a compromise would be for me to dump Opal, the woman I love, marry some spoiled rotten Striver's Row socialite, who I don't love, and then offer up my ass as a sacrifice for the glory of the U.S. Army! How can I make him see how wrong he is? What do you think about all this? I mean, I have to admit I'm not in the best financial position, but damn! What the hell should I do?"

"You're asking for my opinion?"

"Well, hell! You see the mess I'm in, Joseph! Don't you think I need guidance?"

After a long silence, Joseph said, "You won't like it, Serval."

"Joseph! Don't tell me you're sidin' with my Daddy on this!"

"Oh, not about your girl, Serval. He's wrong about that. But this war . . ."

"What?! Come on, buddy. You get just as excited as I do when we listen to Mr. Garvey. I know you're not lining up with DuBois and my father on all this."

"Calm down, Serval. That's one of your worst shortcomings, you know. Always has been. You need to listen more, instead of blowing up before you've had a chance to really turn things over in your mind."

Serval rolled his eyes, but said nothing, so Joseph continued.

"I still believe Mr. Garvey's right, about Africa being home and about the shipping line to build our own financial reserves to get there. I believe in all of that."

Serval glared at him. "But not the war."

Joseph shot Serval an impatient look. "Man, would you listen? For once?"

"All right," Serval sighed. "I'm listening."

"Mr. Garvey encourages independent thinking, Serval. How do you think he came up with all the revolutionary ideas he has? So I've been giving this whole global situation some thinking on my own. Independent thinking, meaning, I guess, that I'm just trying to keep an open mind. I mean, no pun intended, but the question of this war is not a black or white issue. There's a lot of gray."

"I'm still listening, Joseph. But get to the point, would you?"

"Okay. I believe in Mr. Garvey just like you do. It's just that I think, realistically, it might take quite some time for the whole back-to-Africa plan to work, that's all."

Serval's eyes narrowed. "Nobody ever said it would be next week, Joseph. Certainly not Mr. Garvey."

"I know. My point is, what's going to happen to our people in the meantime? I mean, while we're sitting around waiting for our turn to sail back to Mother Africa, how many more lynchings will there be? How many more Negro children will starve because so many of our people live in such God-forsaken poverty? Don't you see what I'm driving at, Serval?"

"Frankly, no. But you definitely have my attention."

Joseph took a deep breath. "I'm enlisting."

Serval blinked. "You *just* lost me."

"Well, I won't enlist until I finish next semester. But if all this is still going on then, I'll be enlisting. I've given it a lot of thought, and I'm playing the odds, Serval."

Serval held up his hands and shook his head.

"Okay, okay, man. I'll try to explain. I'm with you on doubting DuBois and his pie-in-the-sky notion that things'll suddenly be jake for Negroes if we go fight. Like Mr. Garvey says, they'll never treat us as equals. Not a hundred percent. *But*, even if it gains us a modicum of respect—ten percent—no, even five percent . . ."

Serval groaned. "Fractions again. Talented tenths and now respect at five percent."

"Damn, Serval! Stop interrupting me so I can make my point!"

"I apologize. What's your point, Joseph?"

"Even five percent is better than nothing."

"Bullshit, my friend," Serval said coolly.

Joseph leaned forward in his chair and stared hard at Serval. "*Not* bullshit, my friend. Not if you measure the totality of Negro lives in percentages. Five percent would equate to more than a few lives, Serval. All I'm saying is this: If a couple of racist crackers change their minds about lynching one Negro in the south because he's a war veteran— *one*, Serval—then DuBois is right. I don't know about you, but if we're going to sit around and grieve for one soul lost to a lynching, then we ought to be willing to stick our necks out to save one other soul. Just one. And the odds are that it'll be more than one."

Serval rubbed his eyes. "Pure speculation. And besides, while you're talking about changing two crackers' minds to save one of our brothers, how many Negro soldiers lose their lives in Europe? Your theory's cockeyed, pal."

"I thought of that. And that's where it comes down to the real confrontation everybody has to face sooner or later, Serval."

"Which is?"

Joseph stared intently at his hands. "Death. If I want to go fight on the outside chance that I might help my people, even in that small five-percent way, then that's my personal decision. Don't you understand yet? I know that white men are enlisting for a completely different reason than I am. And I'm fully aware that I'll probably have to fight twice as hard, take twice as much shit, and get five percent of the recognition that white soldiers get, but I'll know my reasons. I haven't changed, Serval. I sure didn't turn into goddamn Johnny Appleseed overnight. I know it's a weird, roundabout way of helping to lift up the race, but it makes sense to me. And if I find myself lying in some French battlefield breathing my last, at least I'll know my death wasn't in vain. Don't you think rolling the dice for some dignity for our people is a good idea? As long as we're stuck here anyway organizing for this big exodus back to Africa, we might as well fight to make things as bearable as possible in the meantime."

"But Joseph . . ."

"Don't, Serval. This is between me and my own soul. We all have to die sometime, and when I do, I want to be able to rest."

\*   \*   \*

After Joseph fell asleep, Serval lay awake in the twin bed across from him, wrestling with his thoughts. In addition to the anger at his father, he now had the specter of Joseph's words to contend with.

Each time he convinced himself that everything was his own fault, his father's words surfaced in his mind, setting his temper ablaze. *I can't be like him! I just can't. . . . But what about Opal? I won't be able to support her . . . And how's this gonna make her feel?* Knowing that Opal would blame herself for the rift between him and his father, Serval repeatedly turned the situation over in his mind, searching for a solution. After hours of scattering his mental energy, to Serval's surprise, it was Joseph's five-percent speech that finally clarified things. He made a difficult but definite decision and at last, slept.

*　*　*

It had been three days since the blow-up with his father when Serval returned to the Rivard house and let himself in the back door. Walking quietly to his room, he pulled out his suitcases and began to pack as quickly as he could. In the stillness of the early hour, he was suddenly aware of another presence in the room, and spun around. Charles Rivard stood in the doorway staring at him as if he were a stranger.

"Your mother has been worried," Charles said.

"I'll speak to her."

"She's asleep. Speak to her later."

"I won't be here later. I—listen, Daddy, sit down for a minute. I have a proposal for you."

"Too late, Serval. It simply isn't in me to ever forget the things you said to me."

"Give me five minutes, Daddy—two minutes."

Charles pulled out the desk chair and sat down stiffly, his face an unreadable mask. "Well?"

"In school, I don't know if you knew, but the thing I excelled in was the debate team. And I don't just mean the arguing part. The professors told me I have a flare for the art of practical negotiation, believe it or not. You know, negotiating on certain points of dissension, quietly, reasonably. I'd like to propose a compromise with you, Daddy."

Charles stood up.

"I'm enlisting," Serval said quickly.

Charles froze, then turned to stare at him.

Serval nodded. *That got his attention.* "I'm packing a few things and gettin' out since you and I can't seem to be under the same roof without fighting, but as soon as they call me to ship out, I'll go. I've fought you long enough on this and I'm ready to concede . . . as part of my negotiation." He leveled his eyes at Charles, and waited for him to counter.

Charles cleared his throat. "And exactly what is it you want in return, son?"

Serval flinched. *I tell him I'll go fight for the white man and suddenly I'm "son" again.* He shook off the feeling and pressed on. "I'm going to marry Opal Jackson, Daddy. Her father's given his permission, and I want you to welcome her into this family with open arms. I never want her to feel that you're looking down on her—that she's not good enough for me."

Charles stared at the floor as the grandfather clock in the great room chimed seven times in slow succession. "All right," he said finally. "She'll be—a Rivard. But, son, you didn't even mention continuing your education. You know you'll have to complete your studies in order to secure a position when you get back. It's never too soon to think about gainful employment."

"Daddy, all I care about is Opal. And if I get my ass shot off in this damn war, believe me, I'll die laughing at myself, but I'm willing to take the risk. So, yes, it's that important to me. Opal is *that* important to me." He closed his eyes and sighed. "My God, Daddy! My life is— God, the whole *world* is suddenly changing, and college just seems a million miles away. So, is it a deal?"

Charles rose and extended his hand. "It's a deal. And we'll discuss college when you get back. You'll see, son. The benefits of being a veteran will make it all worthwhile. In the meantime, you can consider your army experience as your first real job."

As Serval grasped his father's hand, he could feel the palpable joy in the grip and wondered how one single decision could have such opposite effects on two men. His decision to enlist had evidently thrilled his father, but Serval had a nagging feeling that he was living out the story of Faust. He did his best to focus on Joseph's five-percent theory, but rapidly sank into depression as he gazed into his father's smiling eyes. It occurred to him that for years they had been speaking two different languages, and that somehow, somewhere along the way, something vital had been lost in the translation.

\* \* \*

Two days later Opal sat beside her father in the Saunders' touring car as he drove down Seventh Avenue to the Rivard family home for brunch. "It was nice of Mr. Saunders to let us use the car today, huh, Daddy?"

"Mm-hmm," he said. "But don't let me forget them errands I gotta run on the way back."

"The package at the bank and the meat market for Mrs. Saunders' dinner party tomorrow night. I won't let you forget." Opal glanced over at her father's grim expression. "You must've told him it was a special occasion for him to let you keep the car all day."

Leon jerked up his chin. "I wasn't 'bout to show up at them fancy folks' house in my ol' truck, I'll tell ya that." He fell silent, and neither of them spoke for several minutes.

"What is it, Daddy?" Opal finally asked. "What'cha got buzzin' around in that head of yours?"

"Aww, now, child, ain't nothin' for you to be worryin' about. I'm just feelin' a little nervous, that's all."

"Daddy, don't you let Mr. Rivard worry you. Just because he's kind'a well-to-do doesn't make him better than us."

"Yeah, I know, but I ought'a be the one payin' for this weddin', ya know. Makes me feel kind'a . . . I don't know."

Opal rolled her eyes and laughed. "Men! Y'all got more than your share of pride, I'll tell you that! Daddy, I don't care about a dress or a wedding. Me and Serval have been talkin' about just goin' off to the Justice of the Peace. His parents are the ones who want the fancy ceremony. But I'm hoping Serval can talk 'em out of it."

Leon grinned over at Opal. "You sure, baby?"

"I'm sure, Daddy. This is all for them, not me. And there's no sense in you worrying about payin' for their big party when it's nothin' but showin' off for all their society friends. Only reason I'm goin' along with it, if I have to, that is, is so I don't start off on the wrong foot with 'em."

Just as she finished, the upscale houses on Striver's Row came into view, and Leon's smile faded.

"Here's the turn, Daddy. 138th Street," Opal said, pointing. "It's the third house."

Leon pulled the touring car over to the curb and stared at the ornate double-mahogany doors of the three-story brownstone. "Good Lawd," he moaned. "These folks much be rich as the Vanderbilts."

"No, they're not, Daddy. Now come on. We'll get it over with quick and run those errands, and then get back home. Me and Miss Aida's gonna fix you a big supper tonight, remember?"

Opal pulled Leon by the hand as they started up the front steps, and felt her teeth grinding together, a habit that always accompanied her occasional sparks of anger. By the time they reached the vestibule, she was planning her attack, in case Charles Rivard said or did anything to hurt her father's feelings. Although Leon was nearly six inches taller than she was, Opal tried to drape her arm around his shoulder. She stuck out her chin in a show of ferocity—a dangerous lioness protecting her overgrown cub. Ready for battle, she rang the bell.

Kathryn Rivard opened the door quietly and smiled the same way. Everything about Kathryn Rivard was quiet, making Opal feel that she should whisper. It was only the second time she had met Kathryn, and Opal still found it difficult to believe that this woman and Serval actually shared the same blood. Kathryn was a petite, caramel-colored woman with wavy salt-and-pepper hair which she always wore in a loose chignon. Her pointed features and constantly-blinking eyes reminded Opal of a mouse with a nervous condition. "Good morning, my dear," Kathryn said.

But before Opal could respond, she caught a glimpse of Charles Rivard's reflection in the entry hall mirror, and his sour expression sent all thoughts of whispering out of her head. "Good morning, Mrs. Rivard. Is that your husband *hiding* around that corner?" she snapped. Opal was surprised at the volume and nasty tone of her own voice, but she offered no apology.

Charles suddenly appeared at his wife's side and smiled as he extended his hand to Leon. "Mr. Jackson, I believe? Come right in. We've been expecting you and your lovely daughter. Lots of planning to do for these young folks' wedding, you know!"

Opal rolled her eyes, then followed her father inside. *Good thing you didn't stick out your hand at me. I'm in a bitin' mood today!*

Serval was sprinting down the stairs, buttoning his shirt on his way. He wasn't smiling, but Opal saw the amusement dancing in his eyes. When he reached the landing, he spun her around before whispering in her ear, "You keep on handlin' Daddy the way you just did, and you and me are gonna get along just fine, baby."

Opal's giggle captured the attention of Charles, who cleared his throat and glared at Serval. "Son, it might be nice if you'd finish dressing before coming downstairs to greet guests, don't you think?"

"I'll try that next time, Daddy," Serval said, winking at his mother.

Kathryn laughed softly. "I'll go and see about brunch."

Grabbing Opal's hand, Serval said, "Mr. Jackson, Daddy, please excuse us, but I've got to speak privately with Opal for just a minute. We'll be right back."

Serval pulled Opal into a small sitting room and closed the door. "I thought you were staying at Joseph's!" Opal whispered.

Serval shrugged. "Mama asked me to come back until the wedding, and with all this talk about me goin' off to war, well, she started crying. So I figured it'd cheer her up if I stayed here until the wedding."

"So you didn't tell 'em?"

"About the wedding being off? I was just fixin' to do that."

Opal gasped. "Right at the table? At your Mama's nice breakfast?"

"Brunch."

"Oh, all right—brunch. But your Daddy won't like it."

Serval grinned. "No, he won't. But don't worry, baby. I think Daddy's about to give up on me ever developing good table manners."

*   *   *

The conversation over brunch was strained; everything but the marriage was discussed. Charles and Serval were like two racehorses at a starting gate as their debate over politics heated up. Kathryn interjected with polite table-talk about the weather and her new great room portieres. Leon nodded and smiled, shooting puzzled glances at Opal, who busied herself by eating everything on her plate.

"Eat, Daddy," she said, nudging his arm. "Try the, uh, omelette. Maybe we ought to see if Miss Aida knows how to make this sauce . . ."

"Mr. Jackson!" Charles said. "What's your opinion on conscription? I've been trying to make my son understand . . ."

Suddenly, Kathryn surprised everyone by standing up and loudly tapping her water glass with a teaspoon. She smiled at the resulting silence.

"That's better. Now, perhaps we can proceed on a more appropriate note. Opal, my dear, after brunch, how would you like to try on a few wedding gowns?"

Opal coughed, apparently having trouble swallowing her toast. "Uh, well, ma'am . . ."

"Don't be nervous, my dear. With all these rushed wedding arrangements, there's no time like the present. We've scheduled the church for, oh, what was that date, Charles? Well, it's three weeks from today, anyway."

Opal shot Serval a "help me" look, and he nodded his head.

"Mama," he said, "things have changed. About the wedding, I mean."

"What is it, son? Don't tell me . . ."

"Wait, just let me explain. I went to the induction center yesterday for my physical, and once they passed me, they said I've got to report for training camp in three weeks. Now, I appreciate all you're trying to do, both of you, but we'd like a little honeymoon before I have to leave, so . . ." Taking a deep breath, he reached for Opal's hand and continued. "Opal and I are going down to get our marriage license and we've decided on a plain civil ceremony. I know, I know, it won't be the social event of the season, but there's a war on, Daddy, as you well know. Lots of my buddies are doing the same thing. We'd appreciate it if, instead of spending all this time and money on a wedding, you'd help us find a little place where we can set up house. And just let us have these next three weeks to ourselves."

Kathryn slowly sank into her chair. "A—a civil ceremony?"

"Yes, ma'am. A civil ceremony." When Serval's eyes met his father's, the unspoken message was clear. Nothing was mentioned in their deal about a lavish wedding.

Charles cleared his throat. "Well, there *is* a war on, after all, so I suppose this is understandable. I'll call a realtor today, son."

"And Daddy," Serval said, "nothing fancy. Just a simple apartment— something I can afford by myself when I get back. I'll probably go back to school, but that won't stop me from finding some kind of work."

Charles beamed. "Gainful employment."

"Yes, sir. We wouldn't even be asking for your help except for the shortage of time and money. So if you can help us find something fast, we'd like to get married this week."

"I'm sure it can be arranged, son."

*   *   *

On the morning he was to be married, Serval rolled over in bed and squinted at the thin blazing ribbons of light framing his window shade, then turned off his alarm clock without looking at the time. He sat up and focused on his surroundings. The room was clean, but when he had left for Morehouse, his mother had taken care to leave the symbols of his boyhood undisturbed. The dresser was still home to his athletic treasures—the game-winning baseball signed by his high school team; the football he'd caught at the cost of a broken ankle in his junior year;

and his battered canvas track-and-field shoes. Above his desk, which was still covered with books and stacks of paper, hung a bulletin board filled with blue ribbons won at spelling bees and debate team matches. Among the myriad of pictures and clippings tacked up over the headboard of his bed was a team picture of the 1913 New York Lincoln Giants, autographed by Smokey Joe Williams and Louis Santop. Beside that hung a framed newspaper clipping, dateline July 4, 1910, Reno Nevada, featuring the yellowing image of heavyweight champion Jack Johnson. Serval's gaze drifted over to the four large bookcases lining the opposite wall, and a title caught his eye: *Call of the Wild* by Jack London. He laughed softly as he stood up. "Seems like a million years ago . . ."

Crossing over to the window, he lifted the shade and blinked at a glittering sun in a cobalt blue sky. A cool breeze carrying the scent of his mother's roses gently rustled the branches of the tree he had climbed as a boy, and, for a fleeting moment, the sweetness of a perfect morning blurred the years between adolescence and manhood. He thought of Opal and smiled. "It's a good day for a wedding."

*   *   *

Two hours later, Opal, Leon, and Serval stood nervously waiting in a dimly-lit hallway outside Room 103 of City Hall for the civil marriage ceremony to begin. At Serval's suggestion, Opal had broken tradition by wearing the rose-colored frock that he loved so much. When his parents arrived, they eyed the dress in a long, chilly silence before finally greeting the bride and her father.

"Good morning, my dear," Kathryn said, nudging her husband with an elbow.

"Oh, yes," Charles mumbled. "Good morning, Opal. How are you, Mr. Jackson?"

Leon smiled broadly and reached for Charles's hand. "Mornin', folks! You two is dressed to the nines, ain'tcha? Miz Rivard, you look like a bride ya'self this mornin'."

"Thank you, Mr. Jackson." Kathryn smiled at Opal and touched the sleeve of her frock. "Opal, my dear? What happened to the white party dress you told me about? Were you planning to—to change, dear?"

"No, Mama," Serval said. "This *is* her wedding dress. It's my favorite one, so she wore it for me."

"But . . ."

Leon grabbed Kathryn's white-gloved hand and patted it. "Ain't no rule a weddin' dress gotta be white, Miz Rivard. My baby always did like puttin' color on things that needed it. Ain't that right, baby?"

Opal snuck a look at her future in-laws. "Yes, Daddy. Whatever you say, Daddy," she snapped, keeping a tight grip on her bouquet of crimson and white roses.

Serval grinned and kissed her cheek. "Nervous, baby?"

She glared at him. "No!"

"Liar," he whispered.

At that moment, the door to Room 103 opened and a middle-aged woman stepped out. "Excuse me, folks. Justice Lang is ready for you now."

Leon hurried inside, followed by Serval's parents, and they took seats in the row of folding chairs at the front of the room. Opal clutched Serval's arm. "Well, here we go, Mr. Rivard."

As they stepped inside, a tall white man in flowing black robes motioned to them. "Right up here, please." He peered at them over the top of his glasses, but offered no smile. "I'm Justice Palmer Lang, and I'll be presiding over the ceremony. My secretary's already checked over all your paperwork, so let's get started. Repeat after me . . . I, Ser—uh, *Ser-val*, is it?"

Serval sighed and rolled his eyes. "Serval. Yes."

After the initial stumble over Serval's name, the vows tumbled out of Justice Lang's mouth in a rush, and Serval repeated them slowly as he gazed into Opal's eyes. After firmly reciting his "I do," he nudged Opal. "Your turn."

Justice Lang looked up with an annoyed expression, then continued. "Opal Jackson, do you take this man to be your lawfully wedded husband, for richer, for poorer, in sickness and in health 'til death do you part?"

Opal gulped and blinked back a flood of tears. "I do. Oh, Lord, I'm married."

"I now pronounce you man and wife," Justice Lang snapped. "*Now* you're married. Thank you, folks, and good afternoon," he said before striding out.

Serval glared at Justice Lang's back, then held up his hands. "Wait a minute. Everybody sit back down. We don't need the judge for this part. I have not yet kissed my bride, and I will not be cheated out'a that. Come here, Mrs. Rivard."

The kiss was long and intimate, leaving the parents of the bride and groom in a long, awkward silence. Charles cleared his throat and Kathryn's face began to redden, but Leon smiled broadly at the couple as he slipped his camera out of its case.

"Now jus' le'me get a few pictures with my Brownie here, and then y'all children better go on home and get to it! Only got two and a half mo' weeks, ya know!"

Charles closed his eyes and counted to ten.

*     *     *

Serval slowed the car to a stop in front of a well-kept brownstone apartment building on 130th Street. "Well," he said, "here we are."

"Home, huh?" Opal said, smiling up at the brownstone.

Serval hopped out to open the passenger door. "I'm sorry we had to sign the lease without you seeing it, but the guy was leaving and we ran out of time. I wanted you to have this front apartment with the big windows. I know how you like those window gardens. But if you don't like it, just remember that leases can be broken. I mean it, Opal, if you don't like it, we'll move."

Stepping out onto the sidewalk, she gave Serval's cheek a quick kiss. "I love it."

"But you haven't even seen the inside!"

Opal swept past him and ran up the steps. "Well, I'm about to . . ."

"Wait a minute, Miss Jackson!" Serval shouted. "Uh, I mean Mrs. Rivard . . . You just hold on a minute. Stop right there!"

Opal blinked at him. "Why? Oh. Guess I'd need the key, wouldn't I?"

"I've got 'em," Serval said, dangling a set of house keys from his finger. "But that's not why I told you to stop." Sprinting up the steps, he sighed and rolled his eyes. "You really don't know what I'm talking about, do you?"

Opal shook her head, but followed him through the foyer to the first door on the left. Still clutching her bouquet in her hands, she stared at the number on the door as Serval unlocked it. "One-A. Our home, huh?"

As the door swung open, Serval raised his hand, stopping Opal, then swept her into his arms and carried her inside. "The threshold business, remember?" he said, closing the door with his foot.

"Forgive me," Opal said, laughing. "I've never been a bride before. I forgot some of the rules."

Serval kissed her, then set her on her feet. "It's pretty empty, but look around all you want."

Opal shook her head and wrapped her arms around his neck. "All of a sudden, I don't need to see it. I just need to be with my new husband."

Serval grinned. "Husband. Wow. I like the way you say that, Mrs. Rivard."

"And I like the way you say *that*."

"Then follow me. There's a wedding gift from your father in here."

"From Daddy? Where, Serval?"

"Close your eyes."

"Okay. They're closed."

Guiding Opal to the end of the hallway, Serval opened the bedroom door, then pulled her by the hand until she stood at the foot of a large double bed fitted out with crisp white linens and a sky-blue bedspread turned down on one side. Standing on a small table next to the bed was a vase containing two dozen long-stemmed red roses. Serval kissed the back of her neck, then whispered, "You can open your eyes."

Opal's eyes fluttered open and she gasped. "Ooh, Serval! Daddy bought us a bed!"

"He sure did. He said we couldn't be married without a marriage bed. And I don't mind telling you that it's my personal favorite of all the wedding gifts we got. Hmm . . . Ya know, baby? Sump'm tells me Leon's anxious for some grandchildren."

Walking around to the left side, Opal sat on the edge of the bed and leaned her face into the roses. "And these?"

Serval sat next to her and raised one of the buds to his nose. "Oh, these are from me."

"But you already gave me . . ."

Shaking his head, Serval took her hand and ran his lips across her fingertips. "I could sure use a kiss, Mrs. Rivard."

"I love you," she whispered.

"Good. Then let's get this honeymoon started." He began a slow succession of kisses starting at her shoulder, moving up her neck, and settling at her ear. "I've got everything planned," he whispered, then laughed softly. "Stop squirming."

Opal giggled. "It tickles!"

"It's supposed to tickle. Now, as I was saying, there's a stove in the kitchen, and a pantry and a cooler, both stocked with food. So you see,

baby . . . with the exception of the ice-man, the world will not be seeing Mr. and Mrs. Serval Rivard for two weeks."

* * *

On the morning of his departure, Serval woke suddenly after only an
hour of sleep. Opal was still in his arms, her head resting just under his
chin. Feeling her breath steady against his bare chest, he sighed with
arousal and buried his face in her hair. He tried to memorize the smell
of it, but the depression he had been fighting all night descended upon
him, too heavy to ignore any longer. Opal stirred and looked at him.

"Didn't you sleep at all, Serval?"

"A little. I'll sleep on the train. What time's your Daddy picking
us up?"

"Nine. Think we ought'a get up now?"

"Not yet. I'm all packed. Just stay close to me awhile longer. I need it."

Feeling a sudden warm wetness on his chest, Serval stared at the
ceiling and stroked Opal's short curls. He knew that within weeks, he
would look into man's incarnation of hell at the front, and marveled
at how the woman beside him eased even that fear. In their brief time
together, he realized that she knew things that could not be taught
with words. Serval had always recoiled in confusion at the sight of a
woman crying, but found solace in the tears he now felt trailing down
his shoulder. *It's just another learned thing . . . knowing how and when
to let a woman cry.*

* * *

Grand Central Station was its usual hub of bustling activity when Leon
dropped off his daughter and new son-in-law later that morning. The
cavernous main concourse echoed with the familiar sounds of arrival
and departure announcements, but the war had changed the typical
costumes of male travelers from suits and skimmers to crisp new military uniforms. Departing recruits were at every gate, hastily kissing
tearful girls, before scrambling to catch trains headed for points unknown.

Opal clung tightly to Serval's arm as their legs picked up the quick
rhythm that seemed to pulsate up from the floor and into the shoes of
anyone setting foot in Grand Central. As they passed a familiar "I want
you!" poster of Uncle Sam, Serval chuckled. "Look at that! He's pointing right at me!"

Opal scowled at the poster. "But I want him too, you ugly ol' white man," she mumbled, tightening her grip on her new husband's arm.

Serval laughed and patted her hand. "Hey. You *got* me, Mrs. Rivard. And you're stuck with me now that we're married. You remember that while I'm away, okay? Now where'd Leon say he'd meet us?"

"The clock, Serval. He said to wait for him under the clock."

"Okay. I can see if my train's on time while we wait. Maybe we'll get lucky and it'll be late." His attempt at a smile faded when he saw the frantic look in Opal's eyes. "You okay, baby?"

"Mm-hmm. It's just harder than I thought it'd be, Serval. I'm sorry. I said I wouldn't cry."

As they made their way to the center of the terminal, Serval once again felt the strange sting of loss. He grabbed Opal suddenly, and wrapped his arms tightly around her, afraid to move. Staring up at the time, he imagined that the hands on the large brass clock would stop, and that there would be no train to catch, no war to fight. But Leon's breathless arrival broke the spell.

"Lawd!" Leon gasped. "Thought I'd never find a place to leave that big ol' automobile! Now, what track you on, son?"

"Fourteen," Serval said. "I guess we'd better head over there now."

When they arrived at the platform for Track Fourteen, the train stood waiting like a menacing metal beast, and Opal threw herself against Serval's chest. "Don't go!" she sobbed. "Please, Serval! Don't go, *please?*"

Any doubts Serval had harbored about his hasty marriage to Opal dissolved as he gently pushed her into her father's arms. The emotional pain of releasing her hand was sharper than anything he had ever felt, and the fear in her eyes sent a ripping shudder through him. *She thinks I'm never coming back. She's seeing me dead.* He barely felt the Pullman porter tugging at his sleeve.

"Come on, son! Train's runnin' on a schedule, ya know!"

Serval grabbed the porter's outstretched hand and hopped onto the train's steps just as it began to move. His brain registered a series of urgent messages: *Wave. Smile at her.* But he was paralyzed by the pain, and could only stare at the ominous terror in Opal's eyes. *She's seeing me dead.*

*The real purpose of these savage demonstrations is to teach the Negro that in the South he has no rights that the law will enforce.*

—IDA B. WELLS

# Chapter 8

Despite Serval's fond memories of his alma mater, his first day at Camp Wadsworth made it clear that Morehouse College was only a small oasis of Negro dignity located smack in the middle of a racist wasteland. As he listened to the nauseating drawl of the red-faced drill sergeant pacing in front of the Negro unit, Serval gritted his teeth.

*So this is the real South*, he thought. *Shit.*

The sergeant bellowed his name: "Sergeant Fairgate, Sir," then stopped in front of a recruit down the line to Serval's left.

"What the hell you grinnin' at, boy?" the sergeant snarled.

The recruit hesitated. "Uh . . . nothin', Sergeant Fairgate, Sir."

"Y'all niggers like to grin, don'tcha?"

Silence.

Serval closed his eyes. *Daddy, what the hell have we done to me?*

Sergeant Fairgate continued his verbal assault on the unfortunate man. "Where the hell ya git that red hair, boy? And you better answer me this time, if ya know what's good for ya, *boy!*"

"I guess I got it from my grandmama, Sergeant Fairgate, Sir!"

Laughing derisively, the white man circled the recruit and stared at his hair. "A nigger with red hair! Ah'll be damned! What's your name, boy?"

"William Watts, Sir."

"No it ain't. Your name's Dogshit. Ya got that? You answer to Dogshit Watts from now on, you hear me, boy?"

After a pause, Serval heard the answer, and anticipated Fairgate's response.

"Yes, sir, Sergeant Fairgate, Sir."

"I can't hear, ya, Dogshit!"

"Yes, sir, Sergeant Fairgate, Sir!" Watts shouted.

Serval managed to avoid being singled out by Sergeant Fairgate on his first day, which was a relief, but at the same time a disappointment. He was sure that his temper would have erupted, sending him to the brig and, with any luck, back home.

With the worst of their grueling day behind them, the faces of the new recruits all wore expressions of shock as they filed into the stark Wadsworth barracks. Following Sergeant Fairgate's orders, they hurried to their assigned bunks, unrolled the mattresses, and stood at attention as sheets and blankets were distributed. In quick order, they learned to make precise folds and tuck tight hospital corners until the narrow bunks were two long rows of identical army-green rectangles. After unpacking duffel bags and arranging the contents of their footlockers, they suffered through inspection, and, at last, Sergeant Fairgate was gone. When it finally seemed safe to talk to each other, Serval walked over to William Watts' bunk and introduced himself.

"Damn, buddy, you had it rough out there," he said, extending his hand. "I don't know if I could've stood up to that abuse like you did. Name's Serval Rivard."

Watts smiled broadly and grasped Serval's hand. "My friends call me Red. And man, you ain't never lyin' when you called it abuse. That Fairgate is some far cry from Colonel Hayward, ain't he?"

"Yeah. Where's Hayward when we need him? But I hear this is standard treatment. In training camp, even the white boys get treated like . . ."

"Dogshit?" Red said, grinning.

Serval laughed. "Right! And from one dogshit private to another, it's good to meet you! So where are you from?"

"Brooklyn. You?"

"Harlem. So Red, tell me . . ."

An unexpected interruption came in the form of a deep basso voice from the bunk next to Red's. "Man, you two make me sick."

Serval looked up and tried not to show his annoyance. "What's the problem?"

The voice belonged to a thickly-muscled, dark-skinned man sitting cross-legged on his bunk playing solitaire. He stopped playing, and met Serval's stare with a loaded silence.

Serval studied him from a safe distance, noticing a tense stillness in the man's eyes that reminded him of a tightly-coiled snake ready to strike at the slightest provocation. Sensing that a handshake was not in order, Serval stood at the foot of the bunk and shrugged his shoulders.

"Look, buddy, we're just tryin' to make the best of a bad situation. You want to be left alone, hey, we won't bother you."

The reply was monotone, almost mechanical—a perfect match for the eyes. "First of all, I ain'tcho buddy. And second of all, we was *born* in a bad situation and there ain't no good can be made of it. But I ain't here to start no mess wit'chu fellas. I jus' ain't got no patience for folks foolin' theyselves." He stood up and scanned the faces of the other men. All eyes were on him, as if waiting for some earthshaking announcement. He turned in a slow circle, meeting each gaze before he spoke. "'Cause this ain't about makin' friends. This is about learnin' how to kill."

*   *   *

Serval soon learned that the man's name was Jimmy Coles. After discreetly watching him for several days, Serval decided that he was a loner who should be avoided. He did his best to forget Coles, until the day the company was informed of their duties as "soldiers" of the United States Army.

Sergeant Fairgate's voice colored each assigned duty with malicious sarcasm. "Some'a y'all git kitchen detail, but y'all'a be spendin' most'a yer time cleanin' latrines. Then ya gotcher laundry detail, and last but not least, you will shine the boots of any military personnel, no matter what rank, as long as he's white. And ya better make them gotdamn boots shine, boys."

*You hear that, Daddy?* Serval thought. *Your educated son has found gainful employment with the U.S. Army as a rising young shoe-shine boy.* He couldn't keep from stealing a quick look at Jimmy Coles. His face twitched, and the eyes radiated some unthinkable evil. In that split second, Serval revised his original impression of Coles. This man was not just a loner. Jimmy Coles was dangerous.

*   *   *

Serval's inevitable confrontation with Sergeant Fairgate rolled around early the next morning. As the white man stood before him screaming maniacally about a scuff on his left boot, Serval's anger was suddenly replaced by physical revulsion. *Damn! How can anybody have such foul breath?* he thought. *This sonofabitch must eat shit for breakfast!*

"Did you hear me, black boy?!" Fairgate's red face was so close to

Serval's, he could now feel, as well as smell, the hot breath assaulting his nostrils.

*Goddamn! And I thought latrine duty was bad!* Gritting his teeth, Serval shouted back evenly, "I hear you quite well, sir!"

"Quite *well*? You hear me *quite well*? What're you? One 'a them northern college niggers?"

"No, sir! Men."

"*What*? What did you say, boy?"

"I'm not a boy, sir. I'm one of those college educated *men*, sir." Serval's eyes exposed no emotion as they stared straight ahead, cutting through Fairgate as if he were a bit of monotonous scenery.

Fairgate's face turned purple and contorted with rage, and Serval knew that a racial insult was on the way.

"Y'all s'posed to be experts at shinin' shoes, ain'tcha? It's about the only thing y'all go-rillas can do without messin' it up. So, what'cha gonna do about it, boy?"

Serval suppressed a laugh. *Is that the best you can do, you ignorant 'Bama cracker? Go-rilla?*

"Answer me, boy!" Fairgate screamed. "I said what'cha gonna do about it?"

"Get it right next time, sir!"

"You'll get it right! Right now, boy! Git'cher ass back inside and don't come out 'til them gotdamn boots shine!"

"Yes, sir!" Serval answered without moving.

"Well? What the hell ya waitin' for, boy?!"

"Waiting to be dismissed, sir!"

The mounting tension released itself in a burst of muffled laughter from the rest of the company. Fairgate shot Serval an evil look and hissed, "When you finish those boots, yer gonna run ten miles with a full pack!"

Unfortunately for Red, he was unable to contain one last snorting laugh, and Fairgate descended on him. "You ugly gotdamn nigger! You think he's so gotdamn funny, you can run with him! Full pack!"

The corners of Red's mouth twitched upwards as he answered. "Yes, ss . . ."

Before he could finish the word "sir," Fairgate slammed his fist into Red's ribs, doubling him over. Serval lunged to his defense, but Jimmy Coles was already at Red's side, catching him as he collapsed in a heap.

Without so much as a look at Sergeant Fairgate, Jimmy Coles helped Red back to the barracks.

"Gotdammit!" Fairgate screamed. "That's it! Whole company! Fifteen miles! Full pack! Rivard! . . . Your dismissed! And git'cher ass in there and shine them gotdamn boots! The company's leavin' now and you gotdamn well better catch up with 'em!"

"Yes, sir!"

Serval sprinted to his bunk, then yanked a shoe-shine rag from his footlocker as he mocked Fairgate under his breath. "Ya better make them gotdamn boots shine, boys! Cain't have no gotdamn scuffs when yer runnin' through all that nice, clean mud, now can ya? . . . Aw, Daddy, I knew this army shit wasn't for me." He looked up when he heard Jimmy Coles instructing Red to lie on his side for a minute. "Hey, Coles."

Jimmy Coles turned to look at him. "What?"

Keeping his eye on the door to watch for Fairgate, Serval ventured a sly grin. "Thought you weren't here to make friends. Stickin' your neck out for Red was a pretty friendly thing to do, don'tcha think?"

Jimmy Coles shook his head and sighed. "You still don't get it. This is about war." Serval tried to respond, but Coles held up his hand. "No, Rivard. I'm not talkin' about *their* war. I'm talkin' about *the* war."

Serval hoisted his knapsack over his shoulder and stared hard at Coles. "You're wrong as you can be about me. I know exactly what war you're talkin' about. You don't want to be friends, okay. But believe me, Coles, you and me are fightin' on the same side."

*   *   *

For the next few days, Sergeant Fairgate did his best to make life as hellish as possible for Rivard, Coles, and Watts. But as he devised new tortures each day, a larger force was working to dramatically alter the course of events for the trio. The battle of Verdun had been a costly turning point for the Allies, and an urgent communication dictated the need for every suitable man at the front for combat duty. While many U.S. Army officials considered Negro enlisted men suitable only for menial labor, and refused to humiliate their white soldiers by forcing them to fight side-by-side with Negroes, the French questioned American racial attitudes, especially in the face of a global war. The French Government, more concerned with the massive losses suffered in the bloody battles fought in their country, at last convinced U.S. Army officials to send the Negroes to them, to fight under French command. Once the decision was made, France waited for the 15th from New York with open arms.

When Sergeant Fairgate received the orders to prepare his unit for combat duty, he delayed making the announcement. He was aware of the company's desire to fight, and did not relish delivering news that would undoubtedly thrill them. But orders were orders. The most recent directive had been an order for the names of his best leadership material for the remote possibility of officer training. After lying awake all night battling between his personal feelings and military orders, Fairgate got out of bed and began the task of making a list.

With great difficulty, he wrote the name "Coles." Coles. *Sump'm 'bout that guy just ain't right.* With a sigh, he put down his pencil and forced his mind to think objectively. With the exception of his defense of Watts during their first week, Coles had excelled in every aspect of military training and was the finest overall soldier in the unit. Fairgate wrote the name "Watts" next, then scratched it out, and wrote it again. Watts was quick to grasp complicated assignments and displayed unwavering obedience to orders. *Rivard. Best written test scores and best tactical man. A real smart smartass.* It occurred to Fairgate that if Rivard were a Caucasian, he would quickly ascend in rank, possessing all the leadership qualities of a fine officer. No matter how he scrambled the list, his three biggest annoyances always came in on top. Yanking a fresh piece of paper from his desk drawer, he composed his final list: 1. Coles, 2. Rivard, and 3. Watts.

*   *   *

Two days later, Serval found himself on a Mac Bulldog transport truck with Red and Jimmy Coles, among others, on his way to a remote location where they would be put through intensive combat training to prepare them for what awaited in France. The feeling he experienced was not new, easily identifiable as excitement in the face of adventure, but another disturbing sensation filled his mind as the truck bumped along. Gazing over at the vacant eyes on the face across from him, Serval knew that the chill in his bones had something to do with Jimmy Coles.

# OFFICIAL ORDER

DATE: *August 7, 1918*
TO: *French Military Mission Stationed
with the American Army*
FROM: *General Pershing's Headquarters*
SUBJECT: *Secret Information Concerning the
Black American Troops*

*. . . 1. We must prevent the rise of any pronounced degree
of intimacy between French officers and black officers. We
may be courteous and amiable with the last, but we cannot
deal with them on the same plane as with the white American officers without deeply wounding the latter. We must
not eat with them, must not shake hands or seek to talk or
meet with them outside of the requirements of military service. 2. We must not commend too highly the black American troops, particularly in the presence of white Americans
. . . 3. Make a point of keeping the native cantonment population from "spoiling" the Negroes. Americans become
greatly incensed at any public expression of intimacy between white women and black men.*

# Chapter 9

After days of punishing training for trench warfare, which included gas mask drills, weapons instruction, and maneuvers through muddy obstacle courses, Serval's unit was given liberty.

"Damn!" Red said, shaking his head. "In three days, we'll be on the boat! You ready, Rivard?"

Serval finished buttoning his shirt and grinned over at Red. "Le'me see . . . We get off the boat, follow the signs to Armentières and turn left. Or was it right? Then we crawl on our bellies lookin' for the nearest trench, but avoid the barbed-wire. Or was it look for the barbed-wire and avoid the trench? Shit, yeah! I'm ready. And can't speak a lick'a French. But we ain't got much choice now, boys!"

Red's laughter ended in a fit of coughing. "Damn, Rivard. First you gimme a cigarette and then you make me choke on it! Anyway, I know I ain't ready. But like you say, ready or not, we' goin'."

Jimmy Coles stood up and stretched, a languid smile creeping across his face. "Well, *I'm* ready. I been ready to kill white boys all my life."

Red laughed. "Jus' make sure you don't make a mistake and shoot one of ours."

"Ours? Hell, Red. Ain't none of 'em *ours.*"

Serval gazed up at Jimmy Coles and forced a laugh. "Just try to stick to the Germans, Coles. Ain't they white enough for you?"

"Shit, what's the difference?"

"Big difference. You kill white Germans, you get medals. You kill white Americans, you get a tag on your toe."

Jimmy Coles let go with a roaring, free-sounding laugh, which shocked Serval. It was the first time he had ever heard such a sound come from him.

"I'm in a real good mood tonight," Coles announced. "Why don't we go into town and get drunk? Then we can sleep on the ship tomorrow. Come on, fellas. Let's celebrate gettin' the hell out'a the United Jim Crow States of Ameri-K-K-K."

*Jimmy Coles drunk. This I gotta see*, Serval thought as he grabbed his cap.

*   *   *

On the outskirts of Spartanburg they found a small roadside tavern called "Raleigh's Roar." Serval stood across the dirt road with Red and Jimmy Coles, listening to their debate as he watched the faces of the white men who went inside.

"Look," Coles was saying. "We been walkin' for over an hour and this is the only place we found so far. I say we walk in like any white man and order some gotdamn drinks."

"I don't know, Coles," Red said. "This is the south—Jim Crow and all that. They'll probably throw us out."

Coles cut his eyes at Red. "Damn, Watts! Walk three blocks out'a Harlem in any direction and tell me a white man wouldn't throw your black ass out'a his joint too. Jim Crow might live in the south, but he got lots'a Northern cousins, man."

Red shook his head. "I don't know, Coles . . . Rivard? What'chu think?"

"I don't know . . . Look, Coles, if we *do* get thrown out, do you think you can control your temper?"

"Aw, hell," Coles groaned. "I ain't killed Fairgate yet, and they can't be no worse than him."

Serval murmured a skeptical "uh-huh," and rubbed his chin. "Well, who knows? They *might* let us in . . . give us a nice cozy table—right in the middle, so we can be thoroughly *surrounded* by our kindly white brethren."

"Hey," Coles barked. "I ain't scared'a these simple-minded country ofays, Rivard. Besides," he said, breaking into a grin, "with some luck and plenty'a fast gulpin', I'll be drunk in fifteen gotdamn minutes. Then everybody'll be the same color—plaid."

Serval laughed. "Okay, okay. I mean, we *are* in uniform, and we *are* gentlemen. Well, at least one of us is a gentleman. So I'll tell you what . . . I'll just waltz in and have a snifter of Napoleon brandy while you oxen slurp at the trough."

"Kiss my ass, Rivard," Red laughed. "Okay, let's ask politely and see what kind'a mood the crackers are in tonight."

The trio crossed the road and removed their uniform caps as they approached the door. A short, stocky white man who was wiping off the bar looked up when they stepped inside. "Uh . . . Wait right there." Glancing around at the patrons, he hurried over to the door. "Now, fellas, I can bring y'all out a beer, but . . ."

"Sir?" Serval interrupted softly. "We're not troublemakers. We're shipping out tomorrow for Europe, and we just wanted to have a drink in a nice place like this before we left, that's all."

The proprietor sighed. "Europe, huh? Well . . . tell y'all what. You go on around back and I'll let'cha sit in that corner off by the kitchen. That's the best I can do, boys. It's that or nothin'."

Serval glanced back at Red, who shrugged and nodded, then at Coles, who managed only an expression of disgusted resignation. Serval turned back to the proprietor. "Thank you, Mister."

After letting them in the back door, the proprietor hustled them to a tiny table which was almost completely obscured from the other patrons' view. Within a minute, he reappeared and dropped a large washtub on the floor beside them. It was filled with ice and dark unlabeled bottles with cork stoppers. "Drink up, boys," he said. "This is the best I can do. I couldn't do it if y'all wasn't soldiers. Well, drink up."

Red reached into the tub and held up a bottle. "Think I ought'a try it?"

"Sure," Serval said. "*You* be the first to die."

Red uncorked the bottle, wiped off the top, and took a drink. After swishing the liquid around in his mouth and contorting his face into a series of unreadable expressions, he nodded and swallowed it. "Not bad."

After passing bottles to Serval and Coles, Red leaned forward in his chair. "Hey," he whispered, "Why you think all these white boys keep goin' in the kitchen?"

Serval shrugged, and two more men filed past their table, assailed them with their eyes, then disappeared into the kitchen. A few seconds later, a man came out carrying a plate and returned to his table. Serval, Red, and Jimmy Coles sat for a long time in alert silence, like three pieces of finely-tuned surveillance equipment; eyes, ears, and every nerve ending at keen attention. After a half-hour with no incident, they allowed themselves to relax.

"Mmm-mmm!" Red said. "I smell fried egg sandwiches. So that's what everybody's been carryin' back from the kitchen. I wonder if . . ."

Serval shook his head. "Not for us. We're lucky to get our tub'a swill. We'll eat tomorrow."

When the washtub was half-empty, Jimmy Coles drifted into a long talking jag, which amused Serval until the stories took a turn for the morose.

"Did I ever tell you fellas . . . how my Daddy died?"

The change was so abrupt, Serval was unsure of how to shift from raucous laughter to the subject of death. "Uh, no. Guess you never told us that, Coles."

"White men. White men killed him." He slammed his bottle onto the table and leaned back in his chair, as if finished. But his eyes suddenly held that flat expression that haunted Serval. There was more.

"Shot him down in the street right in front'a me and Mama. Here was about ten white men—armed white men—right in his front yard, and my Daddy was standin' there wavin' his arms around makin' a speech to the colored men on the block, even though none of 'em stepped off they' gotdamn front porch. Damn fool heads out to the street like he fixin' to lead a gotdamn Garvey parade, talkin' 'bout, 'We gotta stand up to 'em! Show 'em we' men!' Shit! You think one'a them sissy bastards stepped off they porch to help him? Hell, naw."

Serval was chilled by Coles' voice—a low monotone, and he couldn't stop staring at the flat black eyes. The words began to run together until he no longer heard them; he was preoccupied with a need to understand the disturbing chill of those eyes. A faint shiver went through him when he sensed the answer dangling just beyond his mental reach. He peered over into the depths of Jimmy Coles' eyes, afraid of what he might see, but unable to stop probing, like a child picking at a scab until it bleeds.

Abruptly, the eyes that had been fixed on space drilled into Serval's, as if to say *Here. You want to see? Go ahead and look.*

Serval stopped breathing. *Death.* The impossible anomaly. Death was alive in Jimmy Coles' eyes. The instant he perceived the fact of it, Serval at once knew the why of it. Hatred was eating Jimmy Coles alive, from the inside out.

"Jimmy."

Coles' expression changed to one of surprise. No one in the outfit ever called him Jimmy.

"What, Rivard?"

"Don't. . . . Don't let 'em do it to you," Serval said quietly.

"Gotdamn right! I ain't lettin' 'em shoot *my* ass down in the street like a dog!"

"That ain't what I meant."

Coles rolled his eyes. "Shit, Rivard. You' drunk."

"I certainly am. But not so drunk that I can't see . . ." He stopped when a red-faced man, standing about six feet tall and weighing well over two hundred fifty pounds, lumbered up behind Red and roughly knocked his cap off his head. Serval blinked. His focus did not remain on the white man as it should have, but shifted to Coles. The look was back.

"What the hell you gotdamn niggers want here?" came the intruder's syrupy drawl.

Serval stood up and raised one hand in a conciliatory gesture. "Just havin' a drink, Mister. We're not lookin' for any trouble."

The red face smiled, revealing a missing front tooth. "Well, too gotdamn bad! 'Cuz ya shore found some!"

The proprietor approached wearing a worried expression. Patting the much larger white man on the back, he spoke in a voice that exposed none of the tension in his face.

"Wade, now these boys ain't causin' no trouble."

"Well, what the hell they doin' in here in the first place?"

"They're U.S. Army soldiers, Wade, not no nigger field hands. They're shippin' out tomorrow, and I jus' figured I'd let 'em set over here in the corner a few minutes. Now jus' come on over here and have a drink on the house, buddy." The proprietor gave Serval a pointed look, and jerked his head in the direction of the back door. "These boys was jus' leavin'."

"Naw!" Wade shouted, pointing at Jimmy Coles. "I don't like the way that black one's lookin' at me. Gotdamn!" he chortled. "I didn't know they made niggers black as you, boy!"

When Jimmy Coles stood up, Serval went cold. "Wait, Coles . . ." Too late.

From Coles' first lunge at the white man, everything seemed to move in slow motion. Whether it was the liquor or the fear gripping him, Serval didn't know. He and Red did their best to pull their friend off the white man, but Coles shook them off roughly. Within seconds, tables and chairs went flying, and a full-blown brawl ensued. Before Serval could think another disjointed thought, everything went black.

\* \* \*

When he woke up, it took several minutes for Serval to figure out where he was or how he had gotten there. Sitting up slowly, the thumping in his head quickly forced him back down. *My bunk. How the hell did I get back to my bunk?*

In answer to his question, his stomach churned wildly before erupting with a surge of vomit. "Awww, shiiiit!" He rolled over onto the floor, landing on his hands and knees near a pair of shiny dress shoes—the kind worn by officers. He tried to vomit in the other direction, and heard an angry voice from above.

"Rivard!"

"Yes . . . uh, uh, AWWW, jusaminute sir!"

When he finished, he attempted to catch his breath and felt a towel drop on his head. He quickly made use of it, first on his face, then on the floor.

"Get a mop and disinfectant from supplies, Rivard! Clean up this mess and then clean yourself up. Then report to my office! And don't keep me waitin'!"

"Yes, sir," Serval moaned, unable to stand. He offered a limp salute, figuring that with the trouble he was in, a salute on his knees was better than no salute at all.

\* \* \*

Serval did a passable imitation of standing at attention in Captain Hancock's office until he swayed forward and grabbed the edge of the captain's desk. He steadied himself and silently vowed never to drink again.

Captain Hancock rolled his eyes. "At ease, Rivard. In fact, sit down before you fall down."

Serval sat.

"I'll make this short," Hancock began in a bored-sounding monotone. "Your train is leaving in three hours. If you miss it, you'll also miss your boat. So, it's up to me whether you make it overseas this trip, or at all, for that matter. I was tempted to throw you and Watts in the brig, but the proprietor of the tavern told me you two did your best to stop Coles and defuse the situation. I'm not a stupid man, Rivard. I know y'all niggers hate whites. That's why I want you to know that it was because of a white man that you're still alive. If those folks at the tavern would'a had their way . . . well, you get my meanin'."

Something about the way Captain Hancock paused disturbed Serval, but he knew it was no time for questions.

"The French need reinforcements so desperately, they're even beggin' for niggers, so I guess I got no choice but to let you and Watts go. You two might not have started that business last night, but you shouldn't have been forcin' yourselves down those folks' throats, either. Next time, just stick to one'a those colored juke joints." He paused to sigh. "God only knows what's gonna happen in France. Those people got no sense of decorum when it comes to dealin' with colored. Anyway, your punishment, yours and Watts', is to run fifteen miles with a full pack out on that road through the woods behind the barracks. You stay on that road, you hear me? Don't take any shortcuts. And you better report back here in time to catch your train, you hear me, Rivard?"

*Run?!* Alarm bells went off in Serval's head and his intestines fluttered. *Awwww, damn! . . . Couldn't you just execute me instead?*

"Rivard! I asked you a question, soldier, and I damn well expect an answer!"

"Yes, sir. Fifteen miles, no shortcuts, and don't miss my train. Understood, sir."

"One more thing, Rivard."

"Yes, sir?"

"You remember it was a *white* man that saved your ass. You remember that, you hear me? You owe your life to a *white* man."

"Yes, sir."

"Dismissed."

Serval managed a crisp salute and turned on his heel. *Goddamn cracker! I don't owe my life to anybody but my Mama and my Daddy.*

*   *   *

By the time Serval dragged himself to the designated starting point for his punishment run, Red was waiting for him. Their eyes met, but neither man spoke. Serval winced with the first footfall, and groaned continuously for several yards.

"Red."

"What?"

"Running and hangovers do *not* mix."

"No shit."

"Hold up. Wait a minute."

"Damn, Rivard! We gotta hurry!"

"I gotta throw up again . . ."

"Aww, man . . . Remind me never to go drinkin' with you again!"

"Okay, wait . . . all right . . . okay, it passed. I guess I'm all right. Come on."

"You seen Coles?"

"Naw. But I know where he is—the brig. Where you and me almost ended up. And the way Hancock told it, he ain't goin' to Europe."

Serval's remark sank in, and the two men ran in silence for a few minutes.

"Damn," Serval finally said. "I don't know what's gonna happen to Coles if he can't get that killin' out'a his system."

"That's what I was thinkin'," Red said. "He wanted to kill Germans so bad."

"Mmmm."

"Rivard?"

"What?"

"I don't think . . . I guess I ain't like Coles."

"What'chu mean, Red?"

"I mean, well, when Coles talked about killin' Krauts . . . I don't know. He acted like he was goin' to Coney Island or sump'm. I ain't lookin' forward to killin' *nobody*. I mean, I don't exactly love white folks neither, 'specially Krauts, but I ain't just *itchin'* to kill 'em. You think that's bein' a coward?"

"Naw, Red. I ain't lookin' forward to killin' anybody either."

Serval came to an abrupt stop, and Red turned around, sighing impatiently. "Aww, shit, Rivard! Don't tell me you gotta throw up again?"

Serval dropped to his knees as if the bones in his legs had suddenly gone soft. His right arm extended forward as if reaching for something, and he stared in disbelief in the direction of a large tree set back a few feet from the road. Twice he opened his mouth to speak, but no words came.

"What's wrong with you, Rivard? What the hell you . . ." Red's complaint faded to silence, followed by a sharp intake of breath.

Hanging from the tree was a body, rigid in death. Although the face was swollen and beaten almost beyond recognition, the identity was certain. It was the body of Jimmy Coles. Neither Red nor Serval spoke or moved.

Serval's first coherent thought was that he was suffocating; somehow the mid-day air was suddenly too thick and hot to breathe. He finally managed a gulp, and found the strength to stand up. He slowly approached the tree, and Red followed.

"We gotta—do sump'm," Red whispered.

"Too goddamn late, Red," Serval hissed.

"But, we can't just *leave* him here . . . We gotta . . . we'll go back and tell somebody, and then . . ."

"Goddamn, Red! Don't you think they already know?"

Red gaped at Serval in horror. "You mean you think the *Army* did this?"

"Shit, Red, the Army ain't nothin' but the Klan in a different uniform."

"Damn! Damn! But we gotta do sump'm, don't we, Rivard?"

Serval only shook his head.

"We gotta bury him or sump'm," Red whispered.

"Shit! With what?"

"I—I don't know, but . . ."

Serval pulled out a small pocketknife and handed it to Red. "Here. We gotta cut him down. But you do it, Red. If I try to climb that tree, I'll throw my guts up."

Red was shaking, but moved quickly up the trunk of the tree and out onto the limb holding the body. Serval took a deep breath and stepped closer to the dangling feet as he waited for Red to cut the rope. When Jimmy Coles fell, Serval caught him and fought a strong surge of nausea. His own physical senses screamed witness to the violation inflicted on the man he held in his arms. The sights, smells, and disorientation of mind and spirit would never leave him, he was sure. An unimaginable stench that was bile and urine mixed with blood and scorched flesh. An indelible close-up view of rigor mortis in the macabre contortion of a snapped neck. The eyes that Serval had studied so intently the night before were no longer eyes, but dried, unseeing bulges on a grisly death-mask. Serval gritted his teeth and swallowed hard when he felt the clammy sensation of Jimmy's face brushing against his own. *So this is death.* He eased the body to the ground and tugged at the tight noose until he was able to slip it off. "There," he whispered.

He stared down at Jimmy's exposed throat, and a lifetime flew by in the seconds it took. The open wound was a flaming rainbow of colors, but most prominent was a raw, outraged red. Serval's fingers hovered over the ripped flesh in a state of suspended animation as his thoughts raced from curiosity to a wish that touching the horror could somehow heal them both. The second his fingertips brushed the skin, he drew back his hand, stunned that the intense heat of violence could leave such cold in its wake.

Red hopped down from the tree and slowly approached the prone body. "Aww, shit!" he sobbed. "Look at him! Oh, God. We can't just leave him here."

Serval stood up in a series of small, uncontrolled jerks, and placed his hand on Red's shoulder. "Red . . ."

Red recoiled from the comforting gesture. "No!" he shouted. "Aww, damn! We gotta *do* sump'm, Rivard!"

"Red. Calm down and listen to me. Even if the Army didn't do this, they knew about it. Hancock told me to stick to this road because he *wanted* us to see Coles."

"Then we gotta do sump'm!"

"What, Red? We can't prove shit! It's our word against the Army's. And you know how close we came to endin' up like Coles? Right now, the best thing we can do is survive. We can't do a *goddamn* thing if we don't survive. We're gonna have our day, Red. This kind'a shit can't go on forever."

But the words sounded hollow, even to his own ears. Serval slowly knelt again, and began scraping together a mound of wet fallen leaves. He paused for a moment, trying to stop the shaking in his hands, and then began covering Jimmy's body with the leaves. Red watched for a minute before pitching in. Once the body was covered, Red stood up and brushed his hands against his shirt.

"Damn! This ain't no kind'a burial," he moaned. "We ought'a say some words—a prayer or sump'm."

Serval rose unsteadily and shook his head. "You do it, Red. 'Cause I can't think of a damn thing that quite fits the occasion."

Red mumbled some words Serval was too numb to hear, and then nudged him. "What now, Rivard?"

After a long silence, Serval cleared the lump in his throat, but his voice was still a whisper. "Now . . . I think we ought'a get on that god-damn boat, and go kill some Krauts for Jimmy Coles."

*If we must die—oh, let us nobly die,*
*So that our precious blood may not be shed*
*In vain; then even the monsters we defy*
*Shall be constrained to honor us though dead!*

—CLAUDE MCKAY

# Chapter 10

Opal dashed up the steps to Madame's flat, muttering to herself: "I can't believe I'm late again! Oh, please let her be in a better mood today . . ." Having only received one letter from Serval since his departure, Opal found it difficult to sleep nights, and had fallen into the bad habit of oversleeping in the mornings.

In addition to lectures about tardiness, Madame seemed to find fault with everything Opal did, and told her so in an uncharacteristically sarcastic tone. Opal wondered if her last failed audition had been the final straw for Madame. On that occasion, Mrs. Alexander and the sponsors of the newly budding New England Ballet Company had been among the few that actually allowed Opal to dance for them before rejecting her. But when she finished the audition and looked out at their disapproving expressions, she knew that the answer would be the same. Perhaps because her hopes had been raised so high, the New England Ballet Company's "no" had been a crushing blow to Madame, sending her into a state of irritable depression.

Opal sighed. "And now I'm late again! Shoot! I know she's gonna have sump'm to say about that!" Fixing a smile on her face, she tapped on the door.

"Come in, Opal."

*Uh-oh. She only calls me Opal when she's mad. Oh, well. Like Daddy says, catch the fly with honey, not vinegar. She can't stay mad forever.* Stepping into the front room, Opal tried to make her voice as cheery as possible. "Mornin', Madame! What're we workin' on today?"

"Wait. I have something I am doing. I am busy in kitchen," she said with an impatient edge. "Just warm up at za barre and I will be there in only little time. After all these years, *surely* you can warm up by yourself."

Opal angrily yanked off her pumps and jammed her feet into her toe-shoes, as she mimicked Madame's accent under her breath. "*Surely you can warm up by yourself!* Huh! Sure can! Who needs you, you old bat!" *Oh . . . I'm terrible. She's just gettin' old and grouchy is all.*

Peeling off her sweater, she tossed it onto the sofa and plunked her left leg onto the barre to begin a series of stretches she could do in her sleep. *But old or not, she's gonna have to stop takin' it out on me!* She stopped grumbling when Madame walked into the room stirring a cup of tea.

With a tired sigh, Madame sank onto the sofa and suddenly rolled her eyes, muttering. Rising to her feet, she made a big show of pulling Opal's sweater out from under herself and said, "This is how you keep your own house, Opal?"

Opal again.

Releasing a loud sigh, Opal broke Madame's cardinal rule of maintaining perfect balletic poise between exercises, and slouched into the most easily identifiable position of body language. Arms folded, one hip jutting out with the opposite foot tapping impatiently on the floor. Anger.

"Madame!" she snapped. "I'm sorry about the sweater, but I've just gotta tell you sump'm. Whatever your troubles are, I'm gettin' real tired of you takin' 'em out on me. The last month or so, you've just been, well, you've been a real—witch!"

Madame stared at Opal for a moment, then slowly folded the sweater and placed it in her lap. She gazed down at it for nearly a minute before speaking. "I—I was planning a wonderful surprise for you, Shoo-Shoo," she said softly. "My own company, so no one can say no to you again. You would be za star, Shoo-Shoo. I almost had a benefactor interested and everything, but something stopped me. I am so sorry, Shoo-Shoo. My own disappointment I turned on you. You are right, of course, about Madame being a witch to you. Za only excuse is zat, you see, Shoo-Shoo, za old witch is sick. Very sick, I'm afraid, and za trouble is, I am not so good at being sick."

Opal stood rooted to the spot, gaping at Madame. "No! What—what is it?"

Madame reached for Opal's hand. "Cancer, Shoo-Shoo. Za doctor tells me it is too much in my body and . . . I am—dying."

Opal stared for a moment, then collapsed on the floor at Madame's feet, sobbing uncontrollably. "No! *No*, Madame! There must be some kind of treatment, isn't there? You *can't* leave me too! Mama left me, and then Serval. What if he doesn't come back, Madame? I'll need you! . . . Why does everybody leave me?"

Grabbing Opal's wrists, Madame shook her and spoke in her

teacher's voice. "Shoo-Shoo! You will stop at once! Do you hear me? Your young man will be back! Listen to yourself! Madame has never seen you act like such za child! Blaming your mother and your beautiful husband for—for things they could not help? No more than I can help dying, Shoo-Shoo?" Stroking Opal's hair, she whispered, "We all do our best, Shoo-Shoo. Sometimes it is not fair, I know. We all wish to live long time, but to grow old and feeble is not fair either."

"Oh, Madame!"

"Ach, Shoo-Shoo! To die is not so bad. For za greatest doncer not to donce . . . This is much worse. For Madame's eyes never to see my prima ballerina on Metropolitan Opera House stage is not fair. But it will happen for you, Shoo-Shoo. And if there is God in heaven, and He is good to me, I will see it yet. I will watch over you, Shoo-Shoo, for za rest of your life—each time you donce." Her voice trailed off, and she rested her cheek against Opal's head. "Shhh . . . shhh."

*High noon—blinding eyes to truths of*
*a lynching en masse—over there*
*Shovels gladly traded for colored pride*
*Hut, two, three, four—move out!*
*Sharecroppers, chauffeurs and*
*ragtime-side-men*
*French heroes overnight*
*over there*
*in burning blasts of light and*
*rocket's red glare*
*blind and lost to white man's truths*
*Talented tenths—*
*percentages caught*
*in a barbed-wire noose . . .*

# Chapter 11

After several months in France, the horror of war had saturated every fiber of Serval's being until he thought of his own body as nothing more than a walking vessel of hell. His external reality was bone-chilling cold, stinging eyes, and crawling lice. But when he tried to escape in sleep, his inner vision was tinged red with blood. Dead and dying men—half-faces attached to half-bodies—found eternal life in Serval's mind, along with Jimmy Coles. Some days it took great effort for him to conjure up his one tenuous connection to peace, a memory of Opal's smiling eyes. But the image grew dimmer with each day that passed without word from her. She hardly seemed real any more.

At the halfway point between Paris and Verdun, Serval's unit pitched camp in a remote wooded area of the French countryside. The tall trees and overgrown shrubbery created a deceptively peaceful sanctuary, with only the distant muffled sounds of war to remind them of the imminence of death. After a day of hiking and burying the dead, Serval stretched out on his thin bedroll near a small open fire and lit a cigarette. He stared up at the ghostly clouds floating rapidly across the dark sky and pondered their course. *Northwest.* Sitting up suddenly, he opened his backpack and dug around for paper and a pen. After writing the words "My Wife, My Heart, My Soul," he held the pen still for a moment, then began to write his thoughts rapidly.

*Today was bad, baby. It was the kind of day that grinds a soldier down. Don't worry—I wasn't on the front line. We lost another man to the wire, and the only thing that allowed me to keep my sanity was a little poem I've been writing for you—in my head. I hope it helps you through a bad day, the way it did for me. This was my first chance to commit it to paper, so here goes:*

> *It is always darkest before the dawn—*
> *Thank God for the darkness!*
> *Because without it*

*the moon and the stars would remain hidden*
*in the light*
*and we would miss the birth*
*of the new morning . . .*

*Trying to remain "upbeat"—as the fellows in Lt. Europe's band*
*say. You know how I like dabbling in poetry-writing. I'm sure I'm*
*not very good at it, certainly no James Weldon Johnson, but it has*
*a soothing effect on my spirit. I've been struggling to put my feelings*
*into a poem about this war, but I keep getting stuck. Maybe I'll*
*need to get home to you first, to find some perspective.*

*Speaking of getting home, I've been feeling the need to get*
*something off my chest. It isn't my intention to upset you, Opal,*
*but there are a few things I want to say now—in case I don't get a*
*chance to say them in person. . .*

Several minutes later as he was finishing the letter, he heard Red's
familiar sigh, followed by the rattle of buckles being unfastened, and
the sound of a heavy backpack hitting the ground beside him.

"Hey, Rivard. Where you been? I ain't seen you all day."

"Drew put me on burial duty," Serval said as he folded the letter
and slipped it into an envelope. "Four graves. How 'bout you?"

Red yanked off his helmet and wiped the grime from his forehead
with the back of his hand. "Diggin' latrines for the unit comin' behind
us. We're movin' out tomorrow."

As Red laid out his bedroll, Serval wrote Opal's name and address
on the envelope and sealed it. Then he stretched out on his back again
and turned his attention back to cloud-watching. "The Argonne Forest
at last, huh?"

Red groaned as he lowered himself onto his blankets. "Yep. This is
it, brother—the big show. Hey, gimme a cigarette."

Serval tossed a cigarette to Red, and lit a fresh one for himself. "See
those clouds?"

"Mm-hmm. Movin' fast, huh?"

"Northwest—the direction of the front—where we'll be in a few
days. Guess those clouds are leading the charge."

Red snorted. "Too bad they ain't armed."

"Red?"

"Mm-hmm?"

"Listen . . . I've been thinking about sump'm . . . What do you think you'd do if—if I got hit real bad? You know—if I died? What would you do?"

No answer.

The distant rumble of bombs seemed louder in Serval's ears. "Red?"

"What the hell would make you think I want to talk about *that*, man?"

"Goddamn, Red. We can't just bury our heads in the sand. We're in the middle of a war, on our way to the front. We've gotta talk about it. Like families talk about it. You're my only family out here, man."

"So what do you want from me, Rivard? What was the question? What'll I do if I have to watch you die? Like Coles? Shit, I'll probably cry like a goddamn woman. Is that what you want to hear?"

Serval turned his head to look at Red. "You still think about Coles?"

"Shit. Every night. Just before I fall asleep. And even after that sometimes."

"Nightmares?"

"Hell, yeah! Don't you have nightmares?"

Serval sighed. "Aw, hell, maybe I started off wrong. Here's what I want you to do if . . . Look, Red, I only have two requests. One, if anything happens to me, I'd appreciate it if you could get this letter to my wife." He handed Red the envelope he'd just sealed. "But only if—if I don't make it. I wrote some things in it that . . .that she won't need to read if I ever make it out'a this hell."

Red stared at the envelope. "It's like a goodbye letter, huh? Maybe I ought'a write one to my parents . . . just in case. And you could give it to 'em. Okay, Rivard. I can do that, I guess. But what was the second thing?"

"Well, the second thing's a little harder. If I get hit, and you're there, just . . . well, just stay with me until—until I'm dead. I don't want to be like Jimmy. I don't want to die alone."

Red sat up and crushed the end of the cigarette in the mud. "Shit. Jimmy wasn't alone. He had plenty of crackers around. It was a goddamn party and he was the guest of honor."

"That's the worst kind of alone, Red, and you know it."

"Yeah, I know. No allies." Red shot Serval an annoyed look. "This the kind'a morbid stuff you write about in that book you carry around?"

"Sometimes," Serval snapped.

"Sorry," Red said, holding up one hand. "I didn't mean to crack wise about it. I know it's important to you."

"It's okay. Look, Red, all I'm asking is that you—be my ally," Serval said softly. "That's all."

Red tilted his head back and stared at the sky. "Those clouds sure are movin' fast, huh?"

". . . Only if you *can*, Red. I ain't askin' you to die with me."

"I know what you're askin' me, Rivard. Damn! It's just that . . . damn! I'm twenty-one years old and I'm sittin' here talkin' to you about dying." He let out a long sigh and closed his eyes. "Damn, Rivard. You know my answer. I'll be your ally. 'Cause I know you'd do the same for me."

"Thanks, Red. That means a lot to me."

*    *    *

By dawn the next morning, Serval and Red were standing at parade rest, equipped with full packs and clean, loaded weapons. The rumble of an approaching truck interrupted roll-call, and Colonel Hayward stepped out and strode toward the unit. Top Sergeant Drew sprinted past the unit to take his position at their left flank, and cupped his hand around his mouth: "Ten-hut!"

The men came to attention, and Hayward nodded at them. "Good morning, boys," he said.

Serval sucked in his breath. *This is it.*

Colonel Hayward paced back and forth in front of the unit, nodding his head as if pleased with what he saw. "At ease. We're on a tight strategic schedule, so I'll make this short. There's not much time for praise during wartime, but I wanted to let you boys know before we advance to this next offensive that I'm damn proud of you. I'm sure I don't have to tell you that there were many who expected you to fail, but I was never one of them. I expected a lot from you, and you never failed me or your country. I understand that many of you are angry about the order that came down stripping the Negro officers of their rank, and I can't say that I blame you. It is my personal belief that a soldier should be ranked according to his ability and record, not his race. I'm not sure what good it will do, but my views on this situation are a matter of public record, and I intend to do everything in my power to see that history treats you right. They told me that Negro recruits were only good for manual labor, and now you're headed to the front—a band of the best fighting men I've had the privilege of knowing."

He stopped pacing suddenly, and Serval heard him murmur, "Yes, sir, the best."

"Now," Hayward continued in his booming voice. "I'm sure you've all heard about the Argonne Forest's geographic import to the outcome of this war. I'm proud to tell you that the upcoming offensive that will take place there is being personally orchestrated by our own General Pershing, and I am privy to enough information to assure you that our endeavors there will be victorious. General Pershing will accept nothing less. We'll still be in the trenches alongside our French allies, but you will answer to me and Sergeant Drew, as usual. Now. We have a long, dangerous hike ahead of us, and a mission for only the strongest of wills once we get to the front. So let's get there." He saluted the unit, then headed in the direction of the truck and barked over his shoulder, "Sergeant Drew, give the order!"

Sergeant Drew reappeared at the lead spot and raised his right arm. "Move out!"

\* \* \*

The messy business of trench warfare, together with the controversial employment of a weapon introduced by the Germans, noxious chlorine gas, were major strategic devices of the war. But more disturbing to the troops was the treacherous use of an invention originally intended to confine cattle on U.S. ranches—barbed-wire. All along the labyrinth of trenches snaking across the European countryside, barbed-wire had been quickly adapted by both sides as a barricade, but also functioned as a ground-level deathtrap. It was simply and respectfully referred to as "the wire." Necessity dictated that raids and troop movements be conducted under cover of darkness, therefore putting soldiers at risk of stumbling into the dreaded metal spikes of the wire and becoming entangled like flies in a spider web. In the struggle to free himself, a soldier's movement could be detected by enemy units monitoring the traps from a safe distance, tipping them off to his presence. Inevitably, gunfire followed within minutes. For this reason, the wire was feared more than any other single weapon of the Great War. It was almost always a terrifying prelude to certain death.

To Serval, the wire's psychological effect was as bad as its bloody reality. During his first weeks in France, he waited out the nights in the trenches, longing for the reassurance of each sunrise as a milestone of survival. But as the fighting intensified, even that small joy was taken from him. He began to dread morning as nothing more than a revelation of night's horror—countless bullet-riddled bodies hanging askew in the thorny wire mazes. To Serval, the image was a thumbnail sketch of two Great Wars, the one raging around him, and his own internal war. Even in the blessed silence of a temporary ceasefire, he often felt as trapped as the dead men consumed by the wire, who were sometimes extricated for burial, and sometimes left behind, depending upon the risk to the living.

*   *   *

The night before their final push into the depths of the Argonne Forest, Serval and Red were both assigned to the late watch. The day had been one of the worst they had seen, with a staggering number of casualties, and watch duty gave them their only opportunity to talk since the previous day. They found each other in matching somber moods.

"Foggy tonight, huh?" Red said in a tired voice.

"Yeah."

"Think it's foggy enough to sneak a smoke?"

"Shit, Red! You holdin' out on me. You got cigarettes?"

"Well, jus' one, I think." Red fished out a badly battered cigarette from his pocket and lit it. "You see Reynolds today?" he asked quietly, passing the cigarette to Serval.

"I saw him. He was . . . pretty mangled. Tucker, too."

"Oh. I didn't see Tucker. Guess he didn't get buried either, then."

"That was their third raid together."

"Yeah," Red said. "They were a good team. Wonder what went wrong?"

The question was left hanging in a long silence, until Serval changed the subject. "Did I ever tell you about the time I took a joy-ride on that policeman's horse in Manhattan when I was a kid?"

Red grinned and shook his head. "Naw. You never told me that one. Was that the same time you wandered around lost 'til your daddy found you in that tavern with the winos?"

Serval had to dig deep for a smile, but finally found one. "Naw, man. That was when I was six. I didn't work my way up to stealin' police horses 'til I was eleven."

*   *   *

As Serval's unit prepared to move out the next morning, they were joined by several other units to form a massive battalion of reinforcements headed for the Western front. Serval watched row after row of men fall in, one behind the other, until he couldn't see where they ended. For the first time since his arrival in Europe, he sensed a strong stirring of hope, because arriving with the new divisions was a new rumor: the war was ending. If this last push proved successful, the Allies would be in a position to demand German surrender.

Serval checked his ammunition and secured the straps on his knapsack as he scrambled to join his unit. A tap on his left shoulder stopped him, and he turned to face an unfamiliar American officer wearing captain's bars on his sleeve. Serval saluted. "Yes, sir?"

The captain's weather-burned face creased into a network of smile lines. "At ease, soldier. They tell me your name's Rivard. That right?"

"Yes, sir."

"I'm Captain Welch of the 77th. I've got something here that might interest you, Rivard." Welch swung his knapsack off his shoulder and reached inside, producing a bundle of fat envelopes. "Looks like ladies' lip rouge on the back of some of these. Thought you might be glad to get 'em."

Serval grinned at the sight of his own name in Opal's handwriting, and he quickly thumbed through the envelopes, counting them: twelve. "Thank you, sir!"

"It's tough getting the mail through to the front, so when we were assigned to give you boys a hand, we caught double-duty—as mailmen. Got another delivery to make to your unit as a matter of fact . . . You know a fella name of, uh . . . Connor? Edward Connor?"

Serval shook his head slowly as he stared at the second bundle the captain had retrieved from his knapsack. "We lost Eddie Connor three weeks ago, sir. I think it was three . . . Yeah. Three."

Captain Welch gazed into the distance over Serval's head for a few seconds, then stuffed Connor's bundle back into his knapsack. "You sure, soldier? You saw him?"

"Yes, sir."

"But was he—pronounced? Mistakes happen during wartime. Why, just last month we had a hell of a time trying to apologize to a family in Kentucky who was told their boy was killed. All that grieving—a funeral and everything—and it turned out he was just laid up in a field hospital. And I don't have to tell you how often the dead can't be identified." He paused, and his voice softened. "How does a mother say goodbye to a dead son who's only listed as missing? I'll tell you . . . she doesn't. She keeps hoping—and wondering where her boy is. It's just plain cruel, and that's why I need you to be sure about this Connor boy . . ."

"Captain Welch, I . . . I buried him, sir."

The captain's gray eyes suddenly locked on Serval's, and they stared at each other for a long silent moment. Finally, Welch took a deep breath and extended his hand. "I'll get the word to H.Q. so they can notify his family."

Serval made no move to shake hands, and Captain Welch took a step closer. "I know, I know. Goddamn stupid order if you ask me. It's war, and men are dying. White men *and* colored men. Even women and children . . . But if you and I can't shake hands, then none of this shit makes sense, does it?"

Serval shifted the bundle of letters to his left hand, then gripped Welch's hand with his right. "No, sir. But with all due respect, sir, handshake or no handshake, this shit still doesn't make sense. None of it."

Captain Welch nodded. "Carry on, Rivard."

"Yes, sir. And thanks again for the letters."

Serval watched him stride away, and then broke the string on his bundle of mail. But before he had time to pull the first letter from its envelope, dated five months earlier, he heard the command to move out. Cursing the timing, he tucked the letters safely inside his shirt. His eyes instinctively searched for Red, and found him.

*   *   *

An ominous silence hung over the front as Serval scrambled over the last rise of lumpy terrain into a deep trench with his unit. The sounds of shelling that had disturbed his sleep the night before were hushed, and neither the departing wounded nor the reinforcements spoke. Colonel Hayward exchanged quiet words with Sergeant Drew as he pointed out positions on the large map they held up. After rolling the map and tucking it under his arm, Colonel Hayward saluted the men and disappeared into his temporary quarters—a small dugout at the far end of the trench. Without a word, Sergeant Drew pressed his back against the muddy, sloping wall, then slid down to a sitting position. The other soldiers followed suit. Night had fallen, but a nearly full moon bathed the trench in its pale light, casting eerie shadows on the faces across from Serval. They were two neat walls of men, waiting in an eternity as quiet and still as death.

Serval closed his eyes. Only an hour earlier, when the unit had stopped for its last rest before reaching its destination, he had watched the gray winter afternoon sink into the distant silhouettes of charred trees in a serene, purple sunset. *If only I could freeze that moment and then multiply it,* he mused, . . . *that would be peace. That's all it is—stringing a million quiet minutes together with no blood or screaming. No hate. I gotta tell Red. He'll tell me I'm crazy, but he'll think about it, and it's a nice thought.*

One of the men coughed, and a night bird cried out, as if in answer. Serval opened his eyes to find Red, and saw him staring up at something.

"You hear that?" Red whispered.

A soft whistling sound suddenly became a piercing scream, then a thunderous blast that shook the trench, knocking great clumps of dirt out of the walls and sending the men sprawling.

"Gunners! Commence firing!" Sergeant Drew shouted, as he began grabbing men by the arms. "Take your positions, boys! This is it!"

Within minutes of the first bomb blast, the night sky was illuminated by a hellish frenzy of fire. A new law was being passed in No Man's Land—unspoken but written in blood: Each foot of land was to be defended to the death by any man standing on it.

Serval felt the sergeant pushing him. "Rivard! Up and over the next rise—about thirty feet in front of us before the wire. There's a foxhole at two o'clock—you'll see the mound of sandbags. Get in there and do as much damage as you can to their front line. You and Hardy! Go!"

Red wedged himself between Serval and Hardy. "Sir . . .?"

Drew nodded. "Yeah, you too, Watts. Now move!"

Serval scrambled out of the trench and crouched low as he ran, counting twenty steps and angling to his right. Suddenly, his right foot hit a sandbag, and he dove over it into a narrow chasm. "Red!" he shouted.

"Rivard?"

"Down here!"

Serval felt Red brush his shoulder as he fell in beside him, then heard Hardy grunt as he thumped against the trench wall. "Goddamn! I didn't even see it!"

"This ain't no trench," Red moaned. "It's too shallow!"

Hardy stood up, then quickly crouched back down when a bullet whizzed past his ear. "Damn, Rivard! We're gonna get our heads shot off in this goddamn gopher hole!"

Another shell landed nearby, sending a spray of dirt and rocks rattling down onto their helmets. "Quit griping and get up here!" Serval shouted. "We gotta get them before they get us!"

The three men stood shoulder-to-shoulder for several minutes firing their weapons in the direction of a short line of continuous red blasts about twenty yards away. Occasional screams and groans rose over the roar of gunfire, and Serval wondered how many of his shots had hit their marks. As he watched the deadly, purposeful skill of his own hands reloading his rifle, something broke in his heart. "You can be proud of me, Daddy," he muttered. "I'm a good killer. Gainful employment with the U.S. Army." He choked back the feeling and scrambled up alongside Red to fire at a trio of advancing Germans. But before he could squeeze the trigger, another bomb blast shook the ground and Serval was thrown back, completely disoriented. If not for the familiarity of his position in the trench, he would have had no conception of north, south, east, or west. He reached for Red's outstretched hand and regained his footing.

Hardy pulled his helmet down low on his forehead and shouted, "This is goddamn suicide! I'm goin' back!"

"Back where?" Serval shouted.

"Back to the *real* trench where Top and the gunners are! Out'a this goddamn shallow grave!"

"Wait, Hardy! At least . . ."

Before Serval or Red could stop him, Hardy was out of the trench. "Cover him!" Red screamed. They fired several rounds in rapid succession, and Red turned around.

"Did he make it?" Serval asked as he reloaded.

"I think so," Red murmured. "I hope so. You think we should go back too?"

Serval glanced over at Red. "Man, I'm so goddamn scared right now, I don't think I could run."

Red nodded. "Me too. So I guess it's just you and me—allies."

Serval took a deep breath and held it to steady his aim, then squinted at the target area as he squeezed off a round. "Yeah. Allies."

Over the next few minutes, the fighting escalated, and Serval suddenly slid down and jerked his left hand off the barrel of his rifle.

"What the hell you doin', man?" Red shouted.

Serval shook his head. "Louder! I can't hear you!"

"I said what the hell you doin'? What's wrong with your hand?"

"It went to sleep! Look out, Red!"

Red dropped to the dirt, and a projectile whistled over his head. Before he could get to his feet, two French soldiers rolled into the trench, knocking him on his back. "Damn!" Red shouted.

"Pardon!"

After scrambling to his feet, one of the French soldiers sighed impatiently as he blinked at Serval and Red. He was evidently dismayed that they were Americans, but managed to convey the urgency of his message in broken English. Motioning upward and to his left, he spoke haltingly: "Colonel Hayward—he say za order! Ah . . . we—we move out. We go! Now!"

Serval and Red exchanged a glance, then nodded at him. As he climbed out of the slippery trench behind Red and the two French soldiers, Serval winced at the familiar aching feeling of adrenaline pumping into the muscles of his legs. He stumbled over something soft and motionless, and knew from experience that it was a body, probably dead. In the bright light of a succession of blasts, he couldn't suppress the urge to look down. He gritted his teeth at the sight of a man with his head and the left half of his torso completely blown away. The remaining right arm was still jerking in a death spasm, and Serval went cold, remembering Captain Welch's words: *How does a mother say goodbye to a dead son who's only listed as missing?*

Serval was screaming even before he dropped to his knees. "Aww, damn! Who were you, goddammit?! What was your name? Where—where's your goddamn dogtags?!"

Red's repeated shouts finally snapped him out of it. "Rivard! Rivard! Hurry up!"

Serval scrambled blindly over a rise of dirt into the open, which was a vortex of pyrotechnic chaos. He blinked in disbelief at flames streaking through the air like horizontal lightning and bombs erupting with volcanic force. Something hot and wet spattered his face and sleeves, and he stopped in his tracks. *Oh, God . . . God! It's raining blood . . . Somebody's blood . . . Please make it stop . . .*

The whistle of crossfire startled his legs back into action and he hurried to keep up with Red and the others. The French soldier in the lead gestured and began to move to his left, but his companion shouted something in French and headed to his right. Red hesitated, and Serval wondered which one he would follow. But an abrupt rattle of a rapid-fire machine gun sent Red straight up the middle into an alley of darkness—the only area that was not blazing with live ammunition. Serval did his best to follow, but stumbled. He struggled to his feet and ran a few steps to catch up, but Red was suddenly gone.

"Red! Red!" he screamed. His next intake of breath brought with it a sudden acrid odor, and his eyes, nose, and throat began to burn. He began to cough as he turned in a circle, blinking and rubbing his eyes to clear his vision. He finally spotted what looked like Red's silhouette a few feet ahead, and shouted again, "*Red!* Wait!"

The bombing had ravaged the terrain with deep crevices, causing him to stumble several more times as he ran in Red's direction. He made one desperate lunge, but was abruptly clotheslined by two strong arms grabbing him around the neck from behind. When Serval's back hit the ground, his feet flew out in front of him, and he felt the sharp sting of the wire cutting into his ankles and calves. At that moment another blast lit up the night, and he saw a man directly in front of him, hanging like a macabre marionette puppet in a massive tangle of barbed-wire. Serval froze, taking it all in at once: the gore of a gaping chest wound and a familiar pair of eyes staring death. It was Red.

Serval offered no resistance when he was yanked roughly out of the wire's spikes, even as they tore several gashes into his legs. He felt himself being dragged for some distance, and then falling with a thump into the darkness of a muddy foxhole. Hearing the sound of a match scratching against a rough surface, he rubbed his eyes and blinked. In the glow of the matchlight, he peered warily at the giant Negro looming over him.

"You awright?"

Serval nodded, unable to speak.

"I tried to stop that fella you was yellin' at, but he jes' jumped at the wire 'fo I could snatch him up."

Serval fell into a fit of ragged coughing, and rubbed his throat.

"Must'a took ya'self a swallah a'that gas," the stranger said. "But don't worry. It be downwind from us now."

The match burned out and both men were suddenly aware of an eerie silence. An occasional gunshot rang out, but, for the most part, the fighting had ceased.

Serval sat quietly in the dark as the stranger cleaned his cuts with water from his canteen. He felt the heat of tears streaking down his face, but made no attempt to wipe them away. Reaching inside his shirt, he clutched at Opal's letters, still unread, but even they held no power to comfort him. Red had been lost to the wire, and he had died alone.

* * *

The fighting resumed a few hours later, and continued in sporadic bursts for the next two days. The tall stranger occasionally ventured out of the foxhole, returning with supplies he managed to find. He wordlessly urged Serval to eat and drink, and then bandaged his cuts. Three days passed before Serval finally read one of Opal's letters.

*My Husband, My Heart, My Soul:*

*I was so happy to get your letter I smiled all day. Mr. and Mrs. Saunders probably thought I was crazy. This apartment sure is lonesome without you, Serval. Miss Aida's helping me fix it up though. Your mother keeps on buying things and bringing them over. She's being nice to me but she keeps on telling me to quit my job over to the Saunders' house. But Serval, Daddy's there all day and so is Miss Aida, and if I didn't have them to talk to I'd miss you too much. So my job keeps me busy and passes the time till this silly war gets over and President Wilson lets my new husband come home. Your mother doesn't understand that I guess. She like to died one evening when she came over and caught me in my maid uniform. But I don't care. All I care about is you. Are you taking care of yourself? Not as good as I could, I bet. When you get back I'm fixing you the best supper you ever had, but that's for the second night. The first night I'll be too busy kissing you!*

*I think about our honeymoon all the time. Especially at work. Did you know Mr. and Mrs. Saunders don't sleep in the same bed? Not even in the same room, Serval! Mr. Saunders has his room on one end of the hall and Mrs. Saunders is down at the other end. White folks sure are strange. Wonder how they ever have babies? I can't imagine sleeping in a room by myself if you were somewhere in the same house where I could get to you. (Smile)*

*My legs are sure sore today. Madame is getting me ready to audition for a dance company they are forming here. I don't have much hope but I'm working hard on my leaps, especially grande jetes (the one where I kick one leg clear to the back of my head). Sounds crazy but it looks very pretty when I see it in the mirror. I practiced that one at least a hundred times yesterday! That's why my legs are sore I guess. I'll show it to you when you get back.*

*Mr. Garvey had a big UNIA rally last week and I took Daddy. I'm sending you some of the leaflets they passed out. Daddy really likes Mr. Garvey, Serval. He heard of him before but this was the first time he saw him up close. That man can sure stir up a crowd! Folks were hollering and carrying on! You know how Mr. Garvey feels about the war but he said he doesn't blame you soldiers. He said you are just trying your best and we should pray for all the Negro soldiers to come home soon so they can be soldiers in the army for freedom! I know you'll like that army better than the one you are in now.*

*I went shopping with Miss Aida yesterday and she helped me pick out a new hat—special for when you come home. It's green silk, Serval, very bright, so you can see me in the crowd. I'll be waiting for you in my snappy new hat! And Miss Aida says hi.*

*I try not to worry like you told me, but I can't help it. I have dreams about you getting hurt and I wake up crying sometimes. You better remember your promise and come back to me. I miss you too much. Sometimes I think I even love you too much. I don't know what I'd do if anything happened to you. So be careful and be sure to wear your helmet. I hope it's not as bad as my dreams. Be sure and pray a lot Serval and I'll pray too that you come back to your wife safe.*

*I love you too much to measure. Your loving wife,*

*Mrs. Opal Rivard*

*P.S. Don't be messing with any of those French girls. I never told you but I'm the jealous type!*

When he finished reading, Serval was surprised to feel himself smiling. Death had accompanied him like a shadow since the murder of Jimmy Coles, but when it claimed Red it clung to him like a second skin. Opal's first letter was like a soothing anesthetic to the pain. He tore open the second envelope.

By the time he finished reading the letters, her face was clearly imprinted on his mind, and some of his emotional strength had been restored. He stood up and walked around unsteadily in the limited space before approaching the tall man with whom he had passed two days in silence.

"Guess I never thanked you, did I?"

The stranger looked at Serval, but offered no smile. "Ain't got to."

"I know. But thanks anyway. I'd be dead if it wasn't for you. My name's Serval. Serval Rivard. What's yours?"

"Jack."

". . . Jack what?"

"Hawkins."

"Well, hello, Jack Hawkins. Hey, you are one big fella! How tall are you anyway? About six-five?"

Jack closed his eyes and let out a long sigh. "Six-seven."

"Wow. Uh . . . So Jack, what unit are you with? You can't be with the 369th—I know I would've noticed you towering over everybody."

"371st."

"The 371st? Wait a minute. When did the 371st get here?"

"They didn't. Only me."

"Only you?"

"Mm-hmm. Got separated from my unit and covered a lot'a ground by myself 'fo I found y'all. They prob'ly thinkin' I deserted, but'cho commandin' officer done tol' me he'll fix it up once we get out'a here."

"Yeah. He'll take care of it. Say, you ever run across a soldier named Winfield in all this roaming you've been doing? Joseph Winfield? He's a friend from back home, and he should've made it out here by now."

Jack shook his head. "Nope."

Serval sighed. "I keep looking for him, but now with all these new units scattered all over, I'm beginning to think I'll never run into him."

Serval fell silent, waiting for Jack to say something, but Jack remained quiet.

"So . . . you're with the 371st, huh?" Serval pressed. "I think I heard about you fellas. You're the first ones who had all that trouble over the Negro officers in your unit. They replaced 'em all with white officers. Had too many, huh?"

Jack answered with a silent shrug of his shoulders.

"Yeah," Serval continued, "all that rank-strippin' shit got around to us, too, French command or no French command. Damn. It's at least ten times harder for a Negro to become a commissioned officer, and then when they do, they find out it has no meaning. White folks don't want to let us get too much starch in our collars, huh?"

"Mmm."

"Like that Negro flyer Red was just telling me about . . ." Serval stopped and swallowed hard. "See, Red was my buddy. He was the one back there who . . ."

Jack nodded.

"And he was—he was just telling me the other day about this flyer . . . They called him the Black Swallow of Death. If anybody deserved a commission, it was him. You must'a heard of him—some fella from Georgia. Aww, what's his name? Anyway, he joined the French Foreign Legion, probably to get the hell out'a the South, and after the Battle of Verdun, he started flyin' and got himself quite a reputation as an ace. I know you must've heard of him, didn't you?"

Jack stared silently with no expression, so Serval continued.

"Anyway, the way Red told it, when America joined the war, they called back all the Americans who were flying for the French to serve under U.S. command. They all got commissions for their time served, but not our man from Georgia. Little too dark complected for a commission, no matter how much of a hero he was, so they grounded him. Guess that was a close call for the white folks, but now their fair-haired golden boy Rickenbacker's gettin' all the glory without any competition from the Negro upstart. Shit! White folks're back on top, God's in his heaven, and all's right with the world."

"Bullard," Jack said suddenly.

"Huh? Oh, yeah! Bullard! So you did hear of him! That was his name, all right. Eugene Bullard, The Black Swallow of Death! I wish you could've heard Red talk about that guy. He was a real hero, and nobody even talks about him any more. Damn, Jack! Even when the Red Baron got shot down—a Kraut—the stupid Allies started makin' toasts to him and still talk about him like he's some kind'a god . . ."

"Yeah," Jack growled. "And he was a *enemy*."

"Yeah. But he was *white*."

Jack smiled at last.

"Yeah, Jack," Serval continued. "When the enemy's white, he gets a burial with honors, even behind enemy lines, like Richthofen. Wonder what kind'a burial Bullard would'a gotten if he was shot down?"

Jack shrugged.

The unit was enjoying a temporary break in the fighting, and Serval was surprised at the soothing effect of simple conversation.

"So, Jack—where are you from?"

"Montgomery."

"Alabama?"

"Mm-hmm."

". . . You don't talk much, do you?"

Jack shot Serval an irritated glance. "Naw. I don't."

Serval scratched his head, then smiled. *Hell, somebody's gotta do the talking.* He launched into a long stretch of storytelling—about his boyhood, Harlem, Red—anything that came to mind. But after an hour of listening to nothing but the sound of his own voice, he again tried to engage his quiet companion in conversation. He asked him a few polite questions, which Jack answered in monosyllables. Serval rested his voice for awhile, thoroughly stumped. *Maybe he just thinks I talk too damn much.*

After a stretch of silence, Jack began scratching a small design in the dirt with his fingertip. "Uh, listen . . ."

"What is it, Jack?"

Jack shrugged his shoulders. "Uh, mind if I ax ya sump'm?"

Serval smiled. "Anything, buddy."

"Well . . . What kind'a name is 'Serval'? I mean, well . . ."

Usually touchy about comments concerning his name, Serval found a wealth of patience for Jack and smiled again. "It sounds too much like 'servant,' huh?"

"Well, yeah. But do it mean sump'm?"

"You know, Jack, you're the first person who ever asked me that. Most folks just think my parents were tryin' to get fancy, but actually, it does mean sump'm. A serval is a wildcat from Africa. My father said I was the wildest, blackest, sqallin'est baby he ever saw, so, after searching through names of the wildest animals he could find, he picked out what he considered to be the perfect name for me. Serval."

Jack grinned. "Is that the troof?"

"Yes, it is. Okay, now you tell me sump'm. I don't know how you knew about that wire but . . ." He paused to force the image of Red from his mind. ". . . but it's obvious you posted yourself there just to keep fools like me from gettin' caught in it. It was so dark and isolated over there, too. How'd you spot it without gettin' caught yourself?"

"Oh. . . . I jes' watched them Krauts roll it out."

Serval blinked in disbelief. "You *watched?* When?"

"I been steady followin' 'em all that day. Guess that's how I got separated from my outfit. See, two a'my buddies got caught up in the wire and shot 'fo I could do a damn thing. I was jes' sittin' there, froze like ice, starin' at 'em hangin' there—same way you was when yo' friend got it. Then I seen three Krauts come right up on 'em, stickin' 'em wit' bayonets. When they moved on, I followed 'em—real quiet."

"But—why? I mean, you were one man against three. Why didn't you just . . ."

"I was figurin' on killin' 'em—sneakin' up on 'em—one by one. But then I seen 'em get real excited—crouched down behind some brush an' got to whisperin' an' pointin' at sump'm. It was y'all makin' ya troop movement. I could see y'all skitterin' down low in a line an' droppin' into that trench, and them Krauts was watchin' y'all good. But see? I was watchin' them when they was watchin' y'all. When ya top sergeant marked down where all the wire traps was on his map, they waited 'til dark and moved 'em—then rolled out a few mo'. When the shootin' started that night, I jes' got myself over to that big one and laid down on the groun'."

"How many men you think you saved?"

"Aww, maybe 'bout sixteen, I guess. Kilt about twelve Krauts that night, too. I got them three I was followin', I know that." A familiar smile suddenly appeared on Jack's face, sending a shiver down Serval's spine. It was Jimmy Coles' smile.

Jack glanced over at Serval. "Sorry 'bout'cho buddy."

Serval extended his hand. "You couldn't save both of us. I'm just lucky you saved me. You're a hero, Jack."

"Naw, I ain't."

"Sure you are, Jack," Serval said. "You're as much a hero as Henry Johnson."

"Henry Johnson," Jack murmured, nodding. "Ain't he the one gutted that Kraut?"

"And killed about ten more after him. And he's a plain dogface private, just like us. He was on watch that night in the Montplaisar sector with his buddy. The Krauts cut through their wire barricade, and Johnson ended up running a whole regiment of 'em back to the Fatherland!"

Jack let out a low whistle. "Did he get to go home?"

"No," Serval said. "He's still laid up in some field hospital. Rumor is he refuses to go home."

Jack stared at the far corner of the foxhole. "I sho' would like to go . . ."

"Home?" Serval asked.

"Well. Somplace else but here," Jack said softly.

"Well, I still say you're as much a hero as Johnson. I'm proud to know you, Jack. Now let me ask you sump'm else."

Jack squirmed. "You sho' be axin' a lot'a questions . . ."

"But wait . . . It's obvious that you're a better tactical thinker than I am. So, I hope you don't mind me askin' this one last question. Did you ever put in for a commission yourself? I mean in the beginning—before they made it impossible. You're a quick thinker. Somebody like you would've made a good general."

"A *niggah* general?! Man!" Jack shook his head. "Anyway, a general gotta have schoolin'." The smile faded from his lips and he jerked his chin up. "I did go to school—some—when I was a kid. But I guess I ain't learned much."

Serval nodded, encouraging him to continue.

Jack leveled a wary look in Serval's direction, then shrugged. "See, we was sharecroppers. Only had one school for everybody. School was on in—I think it was November to February on account'a March was plantin' time. But I went awright, when I was little. Then when I got big enough that next November, Daddy said naw I ain't goin' back. All that pickin' I done all summer, too."

A faint smile twitched at the corners of Jack's lips. "I had me a real nice teacher. Wonder whatever happened to her? Well, anyway, Daddy figured on needin' another man around for the cho's, and I was it. I wasn't nothin' but ten, but you see how big I is . . ." He stopped and his face registered alarm. "I mean—am. How big I *am*. That's right, ain't it? . . . Aww, hell. You must think I's the biggest, dumbest niggah you done ever seent."

After a long silence, Serval said, "I don't think you're dumb, Jack. Don't ever say you're dumb. You're uneducated, not dumb. There's a big difference. The only thing I've got that you don't is my fancy education at those wise-ass schools my daddy paid for. So, I read a few books. So what? Anybody can learn to read. I've got a feeling that you know a lot'a things I need to learn. Like . . . I don't know. Stuff you can't learn from a book. But look, I can teach you the book stuff if it means that much to you, the same way I got taught. It's all a matter of habits. So, if you don't mind me correcting you now and then, I'll try to help you." He grinned at Jack and jabbed him with his elbow. "And maybe you can teach me not to hang my ass out on the wire like a damn target and get it shot off."

Jack lowered his head. "Ya think I could learn? If I could talk propah like you, shoot, I might got a lot to say." He laughed softly and added, "And man, that sho' is the troof."

"Truth, Jack," Serval said gently.

"Huh?"

"Lesson number one. You said troof, and it's truth."

Jack swallowed hard and stared at Serval. "Truth," he said, then shrugged his shoulders and smiled. "Feels funny."

"You'll get used to it, Jack. It's just a habit. You've been hearing folks say troof all your life so, of course, that's how you're gonna pronounce it." Serval laughed. "But hey, man, if the *troof* be told, we ought'a both be sittin' here with our black asses worryin' about speakin' Swahili correctly instead of English, huh?"

Jack cut his eyes at Serval and chuckled. "Yeah. And that sho' is the *truth!*"

*They are positively the most stoical and mysterious men I've ever known. Nothing surprises them. . . . called for twelve volunteers for a raid and the company fell in—to the last man. All wanted to go. Do you wonder that I love them? Every one? . . . None of my men have been captured so far and the boys wear a blue French uniform when they go on raids. I've been thinking if they capture one of my Puerto Rican men in the uniform of a Normandy French regiment, and this black man tells him—in Spanish—that he's an American soldier from a New York National Guard regiment, it's going to give the German Intelligence Department a headache trying to figure it out.*

*The first thing I knew, all there was between the German Army and Paris on a four mile stretch of front was my regiment of Negroes. But it was fair enough at that; all there was between us and Berlin was the German Army. They tried pretty hard to get by us, but they never did. No German ever got into a trench with my regiment who did not stay there—or go back with the brand of my boys on them. I feel it has been a tremendously important experiment, when one considers the host of colored men who must come after us. I wish I had a brigade, a division, or a corp of them. We'd make history and plant the hobnailed boot of the heavy, Ethiopian foot in the Kaiser's face, all right!*

—COLONEL WILLIAM HAYWARD, from his journal

# Chapter 12

After her initial reaction to Madame's revelation about her illness, Opal began spending more time at the flat, sometimes functioning as a nursemaid as well as a ballet student. But Madame would only take so much coddling, insisting instead that Opal's lessons increase in length. Opal obediently complied, and worked harder than ever at her craft.

It was during this time that Madame invited a young male dancer by the name of Rudolph Zinskaya to work with Opal on the finer points of the pas de deux. Rudolph was the protege of Madame's former teacher in Russia, and his style had been lauded as comparable to the great Nijinsky. The American newspapers had trumpeted his arrival, referring to him as the possible cornerstone of a newly-formed ballet company in Boston. But personal loyalty and strong Russian ties compelled him to continue his study with Madame Romanov before making any final decisions. From his first observation of Opal's talent, Rudolph was in agreement with Madame, and baffled by the reluctance of the cultural elite in America to embrace such a gifted dancer.

Madame was almost able to forget her illness as she watched Opal and Rudolph surpass the great dancers of her memory. As a result of her declining health over the next few months, she was forced to teach from a prone position on her sofa. Her corrections and comments came with less frequency, and her stern teacher's voice was softened by awe.

"Good, very good, Shoo-Shoo," she murmured. "Such za lovely composition! But please to not fight him at height of lift. Work *with* Rudolph, darlink."

Opal stepped out of character for a moment, shocked but smiling. "*Darling?* Shoot, Rudy, we must really be sump'm! I have *never* gotten a darling out'a Madame as long as I've known her!"

Madame clapped her hands sharply, but her reprimand came with a smile. "Ach! Shoo-Shoo! Back to work! Now. Like in za wedding vows, no? Za two shall become one. When he lifts you, your body should . . . Oh, what is word? Ah, yes. Your body should *melt* into his. Begin again, please."

After repeating the pas de deux, Opal looked over at Madame. "Well, how was that one? It felt smoother . . ."

Madame held up one hand. "Please. Please, Shoo-Shoo. I know we have agreed not to discuss my illness, but you must promise me . . ."

"What, Madame?"

"Please, even when I am gone . . . no, no, listen, Shoo-Shoo. You must donce! In a place where people will see you. Keep doing what we have been doing. Keep going to za auditions. Somebody will let you donce, Shoo-Shoo. You must train your eyes to see za admiration in their eyes. You remember za last one? Za fool was stunned! I saw his eyes, Shoo-Shoo! I know . . ."

"But Madame," Opal said, sighing softly. "He still didn't ask me to join his company."

Madame's face twisted in an expression of disgust. "Posh! His little nothing company! There was nothing that fool could have taught you, Shoo-Shoo."

Opal smiled as she plumped up Madame's pillow. "I know. That's 'cause I've been taught by the best."

\* \* \*

Over the next few weeks, Opal kept herself so busy with her job at the Saunders' home and her dance lessons that she was almost able to forget about Madame's failing health. To accommodate Rudolph's busy schedule, their joint rehearsals were held at 8:00 a.m. on Tuesdays and Thursdays.

Opal dashed up the steps to number 870 and tapped on the door. *Oh, shoot! I'm late again. I'm always late on Rudy's days! Madame's gonna skin me!* "Madame?" she called. "It's me."

No answer.

Opal's heart began to thump. *Now she was feelin' better just yesterday.* "Madame?" With a shaky hand, she tried the door and found it locked. *Oh no . . .* As she stepped back, she spotted a white envelope at her feet. She picked it up and gasped when she saw her own name written on the front.

Sinking down onto the top step, she opened the envelope carefully. As she slipped the letter out, the key to Madame's front door fell onto her lap. The sight of the key elicited the first of many tears. The letter began: *My beautiful child . . .*

> *. . . That is right, Shoo-Shoo. I call you my child because after all these many years, that is truly how I feel about you. I remember first time I saw you—little beautiful brown angel with legs of tiny dancer! Oh, Madame was so strict and ruthless to such a sweet angel. But it was only way, as you know now, Shoo-Shoo. I watched you grow into lovely young woman to fall in love with beautiful prince (who will return, remember) and I tried all my life to give you the dance—the ballet, my second love.*
>
> *Please do not be angry with Madame for leaving this way. It was only way I could care for you, my child. How could Madame die with you to watch and hurt all alone? My sister is old like me with a hard heart to stand pain. Only old age gives this protection, Shoo-Shoo. Your young heart is too tender to bear any more pain. So I go to my sister in California and she will take care of me to the end. I am too tired to pretend for you any more, Shoo-Shoo. I am now too sick to teach—to even sit up for long time. So please to do three things for me. Do not try to find me. Just remember Madame in better days and always, Shoo-Shoo, please—dance.*
>
> *I said three? Ah! Madame is old liar. It is four. Please to use key to open my door, and you will see what other favor I must ask of you. Perhaps this favor will make you smile when you see how much Madame trusts you. And my beautiful child, how much I love you. —Anna*

Opal sat hugging her knees and crying softly for several minutes before she was able to unlock the door. Blinking in the dim room, she focused on something located in the center of the floor. It was Madame's black and white cat Meow, who was perched atop a large floral hatbox. He squeaked his own name and then ran to her.

"Mornin', Meow," she sniffled. "What's that you were sittin' on?"

Cuddling Meow on her shoulder, Opal opened the hatbox and looked inside. After carefully lifting the tissue paper, she found two photographs.

"Madame was right, huh, Meow? She said I'd smile."

Gazing up from the first picture was the image of a much younger Madame at the height of her Bolshoi career, posed in a breathtaking tutu layered with white feathers. Opal turned the picture over and read: "Anna Arkadyevitch as Odette—Swan Lake performance—St. Petersburg, 1891." The second picture was of Opal at the age of eight, standing on pointe in a pair of oversized white toe-shoes. Two smiling women were standing with her like tall bookends, each holding one of her hands—Madame at her left and Aida Johnson at her right.

Opal pulled aside another layer of tissue, and discovered Madame's favorite toe-shoes at the bottom of the box. As she pressed them to her cheek, it suddenly occurred to her that they were the same shoes worn in both pictures. The only times the special shoes had come out of their box had been for Opal's auditions. *For luck, Shoo-Shoo*, Madame had always said.

Opal stared at the worn point-ends of the shoes and the frayed edges of the satin ribbons. "Only you and me, Madame . . . ," she murmured. "Only you and me could ever understand all the hard work and all the hard dreamin' that's in these old toe-shoes."

"No, Sista," a familiar voice said. "Now that jus' ain't true."

Opal spun around to see Aida Johnson standing quietly in the doorway.

"Miss Aida! What are you doin' here?"

Aida smiled patiently. "Madame called me last night before her train left, and told me everything. Now I know you' a full-grown married lady and all, Sista, but we both thought you might be needin' a shoulder today. So . . . I'm here."

Opal's bottom lip quivered. "I'm glad you're here, Miss Aida," she whispered.

Aida nodded and stepped closer. "But you know you' wrong about you and Madame bein' the only ones knowin' about all that hard dreamin' you did in them shoes, Sista. I understood too. I always did. Jus' 'cause I ain't no ballet teacher don't mean I didn't hurt inside every time they told you no. Wasn't that me at all those auditions rootin' for my ballerina-girl?"

Opal's face contorted with the beginnings of a full-blown crying spell. "Standin' in the back—giving me that good-luck wink. They always made you stand in the back of the theater. Oh, Miss Aida, I'm so sorry! All I ever thought about was . . . Oh, I did shut you out, huh? But I swear I didn't mean to." Opal fell into Aida's arms, sobbing. "I'm sorry you always had to stand in the back."

Aida stroked Opal's hair for a moment, then laughed softly. "Shoot, child! You crazy? It's a *good* thing they made me stand in the back, 'cause Lawd only knows how many kinds'a fool I would'a acted if I'da been close up enough to smack a few'a them silly high-society heifahs. You were always the best dancer, Sista. Every time. Madame knew it and so did I."

"She's dying, Miss Aida," Opal whispered. "I can't believe she's dying."

Aida pressed her handkerchief into Opal's hand. "Shh. . . . I know, Sista. It's a terrible thing when good folks go."

"I love you, Miss Aida. I'm so glad I've still got you."

"Me too, Sista. So that makes two of us. Well . . ." Aida cut her eyes at Meow and shook her head. "Better make that three, 'cause the way Mista Cat's snugglin' on you, it looks like he's pretty glad to have somebody too. Now, come on. Let's get all this stuff together and go on back to your apartment. We'll do some hard prayin' for Madame, and then I'll make us a batch of cheer-up cookies. How's that sound to you, Mista Cat? You like cookies?"

Opal finally smiled. "His name's Meow, Miss Aida. And I think he'd do better eatin' some'a that fishy kind'a food out of the can."

Aida sighed. "Oh, Lawd. I thought I was doin' good callin' the fleabag 'Mista.'"

"Mister Meow," Opal said, laughing. "Okay, just let me get his food from the kitchen, Miss Aida. I'll be right back."

"Well, hand him over—and give me some'a that stuff ya got there, Sista. We'll wait for you out on the stoop."

After handing Meow and the hatbox to Aida, Opal hurried to the kitchen to look for the cat food she knew would be waiting there. She smiled when she saw the brown grocery box on the counter. Written on the side of the box were the words "For my little Meow—tuna and sardines—for you to be fat happy cat." After taking a long look at the corner where she and Serval had cuddled under blankets over a year before, Opal gathered the box into her arms and walked back into the living room. As she took in the sight of the empty room, her gaze came to rest on the ballet barre still affixed to the far wall. The old Victrola was gone, but when Opal closed her eyes she could still hear the echoes of its music mixed with Madame's voice in an eternal marriage of sound: *Higher, Shoo-Shoo! Time for you to fly! Now, we begin . . .*

Opal reached for the doorknob. "Yes, Madame. I'll try."

# Chapter 13

A group of six schoolboys huddled near the entrance to The Douglas Club ogling a large framed photograph of the nightclub's star attraction. When a brightly polished, blue Lincoln touring car pulled up to the curb, the boys whirled around, revealing six expectant smiles. The Douglas Club's doorman hurried out and opened the rear passenger door before the driver had even shut off the engine.

"That's her car!" the tallest boy hissed, smacking one of the younger boys on the shoulder with his cap. "Take yo' hat off, stupid!"

Suddenly a pair of green satin dancing pumps appeared on the Lincoln's running board, followed by a pair of shapely, tan legs. Each boy's eyes were riveted to the beaded hemline of the green skirt as it slid up, exposing a scandalous view of the thighs beneath it.

"It's her, awright!" the tallest boy whispered.

Taking the doorman's proffered hand, Creola Dorshay alighted from the Lincoln, and smiled at the boys as she smoothed her skirt. "You boys didn't see sump'm you wasn't supposed to, now, did ya?"

A collective sigh rose from the bashful faces.

Creola glided over to them and touched the smallest boy's face with a gloved hand. "Ain't this a school day? What'chu fellas doin' out'a class, huh?"

The smallest boy stared at her with open-mouthed awe. The tallest boy cleared his throat, but couldn't hide the adolescent crack in his voice. "Uh, Miss Dorshay—uh—we cut class 'cause we found out what time you come to rehearsal, and . . . see, we ain't old enough to go inside, so, uh . . ."

"Her autograph, dummy! 'Member?" someone hissed.

"Oh, yeah. Uh, Miss Dorshay . . ."

Creola laughed. "What'cha got for me to write on, sugar?"

The smallest boy finally spoke. "Oooh, Miss Dorshay? You could write it right here!" Stepping forward, he closed his eyes and pursed his lips for a kiss.

Creola laughed. "Well, ain't you sump'm! Awright, boys, line up. Ain't got time for autographs anyway. So ya all gettin' a kiss. How's that?"

As Creola busied herself giving each boy a lingering kiss that threatened to break the boundary of decency, the club's choreographer and manager, Chappie James, poked his head out of the entrance door and rolled his eyes.

"Creola! What the hell you doin'? One of these kid's mama goes by and sees you *educatin'* her son, we gon' have the law on us, girl! Git'cha yella behind in here!"

Creola giggled and trotted away from the boys, waving at them. "Bye, babies! Y'all come back in a few years when you' grown enough for the rest!"

Chappie remained at the door and shook his finger at the boys. "Go on away from here now, and get back to school before I call the truant officer!"

All but one of the boys broke into a run. The smallest boy stood rooted to the spot, staring into space with a dazed expression.

Chappie snapped his fingers. "Hey, kid!" he shouted. "Go home!"

The boy blinked rapidly, apparently startled, then scowled at Chappie. "You tell her Willie Grover in love wid' her, man! She gon' be *my* woman!"

Chappie lunged at him, and the boy took off like a shot.

Once inside, Chappie found Creola at the bar. "What the hell you do to them *minor* children, Creola?" he asked, rolling his eyes.

Creola laughed and stirred her highball. "It's called charm, Chappie."

Chappie shook his head. "It's called tacky, Creola. But that's not what I wanted to talk to you about."

Creola shrugged. "Well, what *did* you want then?"

"Maggie quit. Maggie, of all people. She was our best draw, 'cept for you."

"Huh! I don't see why you say that. She wasn't all that pretty *or* good."

Chappie rolled his eyes. "She could sing circles around you, even if she couldn't cooch dance as hot. But she was *damn* pretty, and a lot'a our patrons liked her. And you know it."

Creola flashed a syrupy smile and fluttered her eyelashes at him. "Well, if she' gone, she' gone. Not that I care, but why'd the heifah quit anyway?"

"Pregnant."

"Huh! Stupid. She could'a . . ."

"I know. But the fool went off and married the fella! Can you beat that? Now you hear me good, Creola. If that ever happens to you, you come to me, like I told you. I know a lady who can fix you right up. We sure can't afford to lose you. Patrons'd be liable to storm the damn place if you weren't dancin'. Anyway, what I'm gettin' to is this. We've got some girls comin' in to audition for her spot, and I got to be someplace at six. I'll look at the ones who get here before that, but I need you to look at the rest of 'em. You've learned enough about dancin' to know if any of 'em got talent or not."

Creola dug out a nail file from her purse and began to work on her nails. "Oh, awright, Chappie. But what about tonight?"

"Shit! Guess we'll be one girl short is all! Oh, and Creola?"

"Mmm-hmm?"

"If I haven't picked somebody by six, I don't wanna come in here to-morrow and find out you picked some ugly, no-dancin' *dog* so you can play beauty and the beast, you hear me?"

Creola stopped filing her nails and shot him an evil look. "Shut up, Chappie!"

*   *   *

By 5:30 that afternoon, Chappie and Creola had suffered through six pathetic auditions. Chappie sighed and slumped in his chair, and Creola giggled softly. "Shit, Chappie! That one danced like a plow horse!"

"Shut up!" he hissed under his breath. "Thank you, uh, Susie, was it?"

"Yes, sir," came the nervous answer from the stage.

"Well, thank you, Susie. We'll be in touch if, uh . . . we'll be in touch." With an exasperated look at the piano player, he called, "Okay, Ray, I got time for one more. Who's next?"

"I didn't get her name, but damn, Chappie! You ought'a see this sheet music! Man, you know . . ."

"Can you play it?" Chappie asked impatiently.

"Well . . . ain't played nothin' like this since I was a kid takin' lessons, but I guess I can try." Ray put on his glasses and began picking out the notes on the piano. Chappie grimaced and approached the side of the stage.

"What the hell kind'a shit is that, Ray?"

Without stopping, Ray leaned closer to squint at the sheet music. "Classical."

A young woman suddenly appeared on the stage. She was dressed in lavender tights and leotard, and in her right hand she held a folded red fan. Chappie scrutinized her for a moment. She was too dark to meet the usual standards for his chorines, but he saw a distinct elegance in her facial features, and the lines of her body intrigued him. He opened his mouth to ask her name, but when she smiled at him he forgot his question. "Well, ain'tchu just a pretty bunch'a brown sugar!"

"Thank you, sir," she answered softly.

Straddling his chair, Chappie found it impossible not to smile at the girl. "Go on, Ray. Let's see if you still know how to play *real* music."

After another pass at the intro, Ray played it with more confidence. At a dramatic pause in the music, he nodded at the girl, who whipped open her red fan and was suddenly on her toes in high fifth position. Chappie laughed softly, delighted at such a polished departure from the standard audition fare he'd seen that day—bashful school girls stomping out their clumsy variations of the time step or the tight-skirted girl whose greatest talent was jiggling her hips while singing a breathy, off-key rendition of "Won't You Come Home, Bill Bailey." The classically trained girl who commanded his stage now was unlike any dancer Chappie had ever seen.

Creola mumbled something and then grunted in disgust. Chappie ignored her. As the number progressed in complexity, his smile faded into an expression of awe. He had been exposed to only a minimal amount of classical ballet, but his dancer's instincts still recognized greatness. It took three nudges from Creola before he responded. "Huh?"

"I said, *tell her*, Chappie!"

"Huh? Tell her what?"

"Tell her what kind'a club this is. It's a jazz club, Chappie. We ain't got no use for that high-brow kind'a dancin'! Chappie! You listenin' to me? Our patrons would laugh her off the stage! And if we played music like that, shoot! The joint would empty out in five minutes!"

"Shut up, Creola."

"What?"

"Shut *up*. I might not know a whole hell of a lot more than you about ballet, but I know some. And there's one thing I know that you don't. When somebody can dance like *that*, then they can dance anything else you throw at 'em. Shit! If I work with her for a week, she'll stand this joint on its head!"

Creola cut her eyes at him. "But ain'tcha forgettin' somethin',

Chappie? The sign out front says that Chappie's Chorines are 'high-tone beauties,' 'member? Shit! She look like one'a them African natives in National Geographic magazine!"

"Shut up!"

"Ought'a be stirrin' a big ol' pot full'a white folks up on the stage or somethin'!"

"Goddammit, Creola! Shut *up!* If she hears you and leaves, I swear I'll belt you! Why don't you go on to your dressin' room and—hell, I don't know, put on some more make-up or sump'm."

Creola glared at Chappie for a moment, then flounced off to her dressing room, muttering all the way.

Chappie didn't move, and thoroughly enjoyed himself throughout the rest of the segment. When the music stopped, the girl bowed and smiled shyly at him.

Chappie grinned at her like a helpless fan. "What—uh, what'cha call that piece you just did, young lady?"

"It's from a ballet called *Don Quixote.*"

"Oh. Well, it sure was sump'm. Anyway, down to business . . . First, let me say, our kind'a dancing isn't quite as high-tone as any *Don Quixote.* We're more jazz oriented—classy jazz, you understand. But if you want the job, it's yours. Second, where in the world did you learn to dance like that? And third, what's your name?"

Placing hands on hips, the girl revealed dimples and a generous share of the personality that had stolen Chappie's heart. "Well, Mr.—Mr., uh . . . ?"

"Chappie. You just call me Chappie."

"Okay, Chappie . . ." Holding up three fingers, she counted down. "First, yes, I want the job or I wouldn't be here. Second, I learned to dance by . . . studyin' a long time with a real good teacher. And third, my name is Opal Rivard."

Rising, Chappie approached the stage and extended his hand. "Well, Opal Rivard, welcome to The Douglas Club."

\* \* \*

Two weeks later, Creola sat seething in her dressing room. Not only had Opal learned all the chorine routines in record time, but she had effortlessly made friends with Chappie, as well as everybody else at The Douglas Club.

Creola slammed her hairbrush on the dressing table and made a face at herself. "Oh, well. You still got the star spot. Nobody's gonna take that." Momentarily insecure, she dabbed on more lip rouge. Hearing a tap on her door, she called, "Hell, it ain't ten yet, is it?"

The door opened a crack, and Opal Rivard peeked in.

Creola frowned. "I'm busy."

"I know. I just . . . Listen, could I talk to you a minute, Miss Dorshay?"

Creola turned her attention back to the mirror. "Aww, shit. Call me Creola like everybody else. Sit down, I guess. But I ain't got much time. I'm on in a minute."

Opal sat down in the extra chair and Creola stared at her reflection in the mirror. "Well?"

"I know you hate me," Opal said.

Creola groaned. "Oh, hell. You're all right, I guess. Why are you worried about what I think anyway?"

"I just don't want you to hate me, that's all. Look, I'm not out to steal your thunder or your man. I'm a happily married woman, you know."

Creola cocked her head to one side in surprise. "Well, congratulations on bein' married, but I ain't worried 'bout you stealin' *anything* from me, girl. And who the hell did you think my man was anyhow?"

"Chappie?"

Creola laughed. "Chappie? Shit. I dumped Chappie a long time ago. And you can take that as a warning, honey. Chappie tries to get in all the new girl's panties. He'll get around to you, don't you worry."

Opal's eyes widened. "I don't *want* him to get around to me. I've got my Serval."

"You got your *what?*"

"Serval. That's my husband," Opal laughed.

"What the hell kind'a name is that?"

"It means an African wildcat."

"Well, well," Creola said, lifting one eyebrow. "Sounds sexual."

"Huh?"

Creola rolled her eyes. "Oh, Lord, Mary Pickford, I *said* it sounds sexual. Is he wild in bed?"

"Wild?" Opal was quiet for a moment and then said, "No. He's not what I'd call *wild*. He's beautiful—you know, sexually."

Something about the way Opal said "beautiful" made Creola lick her lips. "Hmm. Well, looks like ol' Chappie might jus' strike out for the first time. Okay, Opal. You wanna be friends with Creola? Here's what'cha do. Just don't try to dance your way into the lead spot 'cause that's mine. And since you're so happily married, I guess I ain't got to worry 'bout you goin' after the same men as me, so yeah. I guess we can be friends."

"Good! Oh, and Creola? I think you're a real good dancer. But if you're ever interested in learning about ballet, you just let me know and I'll be happy to show you. As good as you dance, I know you'd learn real fast. Well . . . I guess I should let you finish getting ready . . . so bye."

Creola sat in stunned silence until the door shut behind Opal. "Damn little *pygmy!* Thinks she's gonna give *me* lessons! Huh!"

*It is my desire to record the fact that the 369th was under fire for 191 days, all told, and during all this time never lost a prisoner, a trench, or a foot of ground.*

—Colonel William Hayward, from his Official Report

# Chapter 14

By the close of 1918, the rumor about the war ending had worn into a threadbare joke, and Serval began to wonder if he would ever go home to Harlem. The latest hardships suffered by the Negro soldiers were an unexplained termination of their pay, followed by the Army's failure to include them in the special holiday rations enjoyed by Caucasian soldiers during Thanksgiving and Christmas.

Even talk about Colonel Hayward's attempts to rectify their situation only angered Serval. He saw them as well-intentioned words that accomplished nothing. The most recent report had confirmed German surrender, which toppled the final obstacle to peace. But New Year's Eve came and went, and still Serval's unit awaited orders to leave No Man's Land.

Serval sat in his corner of the foxhole cleaning his rifle and muttering. "Sonofabitch! Six months in the mud!"

Jack retreated to the farthest corner from Serval, and lowered himself to the ground. Pulling his collar up around his ears, he adjusted his helmet over his eyes and crossed his arms—his standard nap position.

Serval glared at him. "I *said* . . . six goddamn months, Jack! Somebody needs to tell the Krauts the war's over 'cause some'a these fools are still shootin'. And I'll be goddamned if I'm gettin' my ass shot off when it's supposed to be peacetime!"

Without opening his eyes, Jack said, "Serval."

"What?"

"It be over when it be over."

Serval scratched furiously at a raw spot just above the small of his back. "These goddamn lice are eatin' me alive! . . . Jack! Hey, Jack!"

"What?"

"If the Krauts surrendered, then what the hell else needs to happen? Why the hell ain't I home makin' love to my woman? Huh? . . . Not that she'd let me touch her. Not with my ass crawlin' with these goddamn lice! Hey, are you listenin' to me?"

Jack sighed. "Serval."

"What, goddammit?!"

"You holla if you need me. I'm goin' to sleep."

Serval opened his mouth to protest, but stopped when a pair of muddy combat boots bumped his shoulder. He looked up, but couldn't avoid being knocked off balance by a soldier who dropped into the fox-hole. Recognizing the intruder as Davis, he launched a verbal attack on him before either of them could get to their feet.

"Shit! I'm so sick of these damn trenches! Can't anybody look before they jump in and knock everybody's ass down?!"

Davis grinned. "Speakin' of asses, you can shut up and kiss mine twice, Rivard. Ya got mail! Here. And don't bother thankin' me."

Serval rubbed his chin and smiled in Jack's direction. "Uh, whadaya know? Some mail got through."

Jack chuckled and opened one eye. "Mm-hmm. And the way you' grinnin', it must be from Opal."

"Mm-hmm."

"Good. Now maybe you could shut up so I can get me some sleep."

*  *  *

Reading Opal's letter lulled Serval into a restful sleep, complete with an erotic dream. But the dream began to unravel when the taste of Opal's mouth was replaced by the gritty drizzle from a leaking sandbag. He tried to ignore the interruption, but the dream vanished completely when he felt a boot nudge his ribs.

"What the hell . . .? Aww, shit! Now what?" Spitting dry sand, he scowled up at Jack, who was grinning at him. "Oh. So you think a mouthful of sand is funny?" Serval snapped.

Jack shook his head. "Listen," he whispered. "Listen hard."

"Listen to wh . . .?" Before the words completely left his lips, Serval became aware of the sounds of running feet, the clacking of rifles against belt buckles, and the buzz of excited voices. They were sounds he had heard countless times before as the units prepared to shift positions, but the usual tension in the voices was replaced by an uncharacteristic joy. Reaching for Jack's hand, he scrambled up and joined the other men just in time to hear Sergeant Drew's impatient command:

"I said fall in!"

Verbal confirmation was not necessary. Serval smiled along with the other men, certain that he was finally going home.

"Move out!"

A baritone voice behind Serval broke into a spirited marching-cadence song, and the others joined in:

> *Oh, Mademoiselle from Armentières—parlez vous*
> *Mademoiselle from Armentières—parlez vous*
> *She'll do it for wine, she'll do it for rum*
> *And sometimes for chocolate or chewing gum*
> *Hinky-dinky, parlez vous . . .*

\* \* \*

For the duration of their tour of duty, Negro soldiers had been denied leave, but the Armistice prompted a slight relaxation of the policy. On the night before Jack's unit was scheduled to ship stateside, Serval and Jack ventured a visit to Paris.

Serval sidestepped the flying legs of a shrieking woman as a drunken doughboy swung her around in his arms. As the couple collapsed onto the sidewalk, Serval tried to help them up, but they only laughed and waved him away.

Serval grinned and saluted the red-faced doughboy. "Carry on, sir!" he said.

The doughboy planted a sloppy kiss on the woman's left eye, then waved his cap in the air. "Aww, hell, Chocolate Sholdier! You don't gotta call me shir! I los' muh shtripe, shee? An unforshunate inshident involving . . . chicken-shitedness . . . But I don't give a good goddamn! I got both muh legs and arms, don't I? Ish Armishish! Uh, Arm-mitsish . . ."

"Armistice," Serval laughed.

"Yeah! Thash the word. Anyway, we're all goin' home!"

"Yes, we are."

As Serval and Jack made the turn from Rue Saint Dominique onto a wider avenue, the crowd grew thicker and rowdier, and every reveler, whether a French citizen or an American soldier, seemed to be singing. Strains of the French national anthem, "La Marseillaise," floated on the night air, along with drunken choruses of "Pack Up Your Troubles In Your Old Kit Bag" and "Hail, Hail, The Gang's All Here."

"Whee-eww!" Serval laughed. "I don't know which is worse—them trying to sing these silly English songs, or drunk doughboys trying to sing in French."

Jack shook his head. "I don't know. All I know is folks is sho' happy in Paris."

"Got plenty of reason to be, don'tcha think? Having a war right in your back yard can't be too much fun. So, Jack, what do you wanna do on your last night in France?"

"Eat! I'ma eat all the food I can hold, and then I'ma drink me some'a that French wine the fellas been talkin' 'bout. But first thing I wanna do is ditch this crowd."

"Ditto, buddy. Okay, I see what's going on," Serval shouted, nudging Jack and pointing to his right. "There's the Eifel Tower. That's where this mob must be headed."

Jack gestured in the opposite direction with his thumb, and Serval nodded. "Just keep a lookout for M.P.'s, man. You know they'll find any excuse to cut our night short."

After ducking through several alleys and side streets, they stepped out onto a narrow cobblestone lane lined with tiny shops, a laundry, and a boulangerie.

Jack stopped to peer through the boulangerie window. "A bakery!"

"Yeah, but it's closed. But sump'm tells me we're on the right street, Jack."

"Which is?"

"I don't see a sign. Let's just follow our noses to the nearest restaurant. Hey, it won't be long before you'll be eating home-cooking, huh? You got a girl waitin' in Alabama for you?"

"Naw. Tell ya the . . . the *truth*, Alabama don't feel like home no mo'. Aw, damn . . . no *more*. But I ought'a go back and 'least let 'em know I'm alive."

"Jack, look. If you go back and find you don't want to stay, just come up to Harlem. Lots of Southerners are doing it, you know. I mean, we have problems too, but conditions are better for Negroes in Harlem than in Alabama. I told you about Mr. Garvey. Well, maybe you could work for the UNIA."

Jack smiled down at Serval. "Well, I'll think about it. You send word to the Western Union in Montgomery 'fo ya go back, and maybe I'll jump a freight train up Nawth or sump'm."

"I'll send a wire the minute I get my ship assignment." Serval stopped and grabbed Jack's arm. "Hey! Here's what we've been looking for. Grand Monde Bistro."

"What' that mean?"

"Hell, I don't know. I barely know enough French to scrape by, Jack. But man, smell that food! And look, not an M.P. for miles!"

"Ain't gotta say it twice. Let's see if they let us in."

As they stepped inside, Serval and Jack were greeted by a stout, middle-aged Frenchman with a warm smile. "Entré! Americain!"

"Oui, Monsieur," Serval answered. "Je—uh, aww, hell . . . Oui. Americain. Sorry."

"Parlez vous Francais?"

Serval held his thumb and index finger close together to indicate his limited knowledge of French. "Tres, tres peu. Let's see, uh . . . s'il vous plait, merci beaucoup, and qui va là? That's about it. Sorry."

The proprietor laughed. "Qui va là? Is all right, Monsieur," the proprietor said. "I talk za Anglais—ah . . ." He mimicked Serval's thumb-and-finger gesture and laughed. "Little Anglais. We do—how you say? We do okay. I bring wine for you? Bread?"

Rubbing his palms together, Serval grinned. "That sounds like a great start. Wine and bread. All you can bring us, uh, s'il vous plait. And merci, Monsieur uh . . .?"

With a loud belly-laugh, the man slapped Serval on the back and said, "I am called Louis Marchand. Please to call me Louis." He pronounced it "L'wee."

"Well, merci, Louie!"

Louis Marchand clapped his hands and bellowed something in rapid French as he pushed through a curtain-covered door behind the bar. The only word Serval and Jack caught was "Harlem." Within seconds, a plump, middle-aged woman appeared, swinging a bottle of rosé above her head with a flourish. "Ayyy! Bonjour, zhentlemen!"

Louis was right behind her, carrying a plate of steaming bread, fresh from the oven. "I present my wife, Nicole."

Nicole's smile was as welcoming as Louie's. Reaching up to grasp Jack's shoulders, she enthusiastically kissed him on his left cheek, then the right, before repeating the gesture on Serval. Jack sat down in stunned silence, as Nicole Marchand clasped her hands together under her chin, beaming at them as if they were her own sons. Placing one hand on her hip, she filled their glasses and chattered amiably in French with a few semi-English words like "champion Negré" and "honored patrons" thrown in. "Aide-toi! Mangier!" she commanded.

Jack blinked at Serval, who answered him with a laugh and a shrug.

Nicole tore off a hunk of the hot bread and held it to Serval's mouth. "Mangier!" she repeated.

"Oh!" Serval said. "It means eat! Well, Miz Louie, you ain't got to ask me twice. I'll be happy to mon-jay all the food you've got!" He shoved the plate of bread toward Jack. "Mon-jay, man!"

From a nearby table, a French couple raised their glasses and shouted at Serval and Jack, "Bon appétite!"

Serval and Jack returned the gesture. "Merci!"

The bread and wine served as modest precursors of what followed. After several servings of Nicole's coq au vin, followed by creme brulee for dessert, Serval and Jack pushed their plates away and begged her to stop. Just as Serval convinced her that they could hold no more, two young women, dressed in provocative, clingy dresses, walked in and sat at the adjacent table.

Jack glanced over at them and smiled. Without hesitation, the women rose and approached the table, taking seats on either side of him. Serval barely suppressed a laugh when the blonde woman began stroking Jack's face in the brazen manner of an experienced prostitute.

Jack smiled bashfully at her. "Bonjour," he mumbled.

"Bonjour, mon Capitan Chocolat!" she gushed. "Parlez vous . . .?"

"No, ma'am," Serval interrupted. "Anglais."

"Oh!" Turning to her companion, a dark-haired beauty with a quieter demeanor, she whispered, "Seulange . . .?"

Seulange smiled at Serval and blinked at him with eyes the color of melted butter. "I am called Seulange, and this is my friend René. René says, uhh, how you say? Your names. She wishes to know your names."

"Oh! Well, I'm Serval and this is Jack."

"Ooh! Jacques!" René cooed, stroking Jack's leg.

Serval coughed to conceal a laugh. "You, uh, speak English very well, Seulange."

"Thank you, Monsieur."

"Uh, Seulange . . ."

"Yes?"

"We, uh, I mean, I can't speak for Jack, but uh, I'm not really look-ing to . . ."

Seulange placed her palm on top of Serval's hand. "No, no. But you do not understand, Monsieur Serval. You are—mmmm, how you say? On za house. No francs for za Argonne soldiers—za *Negré* soldiers."

Serval grinned and kicked Jack under the table. "You mean the, uh, Negré soldiers get it for free? What about the white soldiers?"

Seulange threw back her head and laughed. "No, no, Monsieur

Serval. My Onglish, she is not so good. Za *Harlem* soldiers—in za Argonne, no?"

"Oh! Well . . ." Noticing Jack's apparent interest in René, he kicked him again under the table and gave him a pointed look. "Jack was a big hero of the Argonne conflict. You might want to give him a special deal . . ."

Seulange leaned closer and gazed deeply into Serval's eyes. "But you, Monsieur, I like," she cooed. "No francs for you too. We are, ahh, how is za word . . .?"

René suddenly piped in: "Off duty! We go?"

"Wuh-wuh-wait a minute!" Serval laughed. "No! Uh, I mean . . . I, uh, I've got to get back tonight and . . ."

Jack spoke up. "Uh, can I talk to you a minute, man?"

Smiling weakly at the two women, Serval rose. "Would you excuse us, ladies?"

"Certainment."

Nudging Serval into a small alcove near the kitchen, Jack sighed. "Look. I *likes* that René, if you take my meanin'."

"Believe me, Jack, I took your meaning the minute she sat down," Serval laughed. "You go ahead, man. Have some fun! I just . . . I just can't. I've got my mind all full'a Opal and I think it'll be nice to be with her again in a state of complete starvation, if you take *my* meaning. But wait a minute . . . I thought you said you've got no use for these pale French girls."

"Well, she is awful ghos'ly-lookin', huh? But she' sort'a pretty though. Uh, seem like they some kind'a team, huh? I mean, ya think you could just talk to Seulange for a while or sump'm? Just talk is all. I don't want 'em to leave. I ain't told ya this before, Serval, but it ain't no time for pride now."

"What?"

"I been steady listenin' to yo' stories about the girls you done been *friendly* with and all . . ."

"Jack!" Serval laughed, "You're not tryin' to tell me . . ."

Jack's angry eyes stopped him. "What'chu think, Serval? That sharecroppers throws a dance every Saturday night where young fellas can meet 'em some girls? Everybody don't live in no fancy house in no Harlem, man. Wit' rich Daddies who sends 'em to high-tone colleges and such. Hell, my life wasn't nothin' but hard work ever since I was nine. And time I was old enough to be thinkin' about girls, well, that's when Mama died and . . . Anyhow, the only girl I ever done it with was durin' trainin' camp, right 'fo we shipped out."

"I'm sorry, Jack. I didn't mean it like it sounded. Look, if you've only been with a girl once, then, by all means, go have some fun with René. You've earned it."

"Well," Jack said, smiling, ". . . what I said was—it was only one *girl*, but b'lieve me, it was mo' than one *time*. I mean *more*. Much more."

Serval laughed. "Uh-huh. As much more as you could get, I'll bet, huh? Okay, *Jacques*, I'll keep Seulange occupied for a couple'a hours. You and René go have a brief love affair with my blessing."

Jack was already headed back to the table when Serval grabbed him by the collar from behind. "Hey! Two hours," he hissed.

"Two hours. And thanks!"

René needed little coaxing. After a few minutes of heated nuzzling, she left the bistro, pulling Jack by the hand.

"Remember, Jack. I gotta be gettin' back in two hours," Serval called after them.

No answer.

Serval squirmed uncomfortably under Seulange's knowing smile.

"I think, Monsieur Serval, that you do not have to go back tonight. You are married, no?"

Serval laughed and shrugged his shoulders. "Guilty."

"Truly married."

"Oui. Truly married. And thanks for understanding."

"Ah, Monsieur Serval, I am not so understanding. I—ahh, accept, yes? But, mmmm . . . Je'regret. You are quite za beautiful man."

Serval closed his eyes. "That's what my wife told me once."

"What is Serval? What is za meaning of this name?" Seulange asked.

"Oh, uh . . . ." Serval tugged at his collar and cleared his throat. "A serval is a—a wildcat. A wildcat from Africa."

"Oohh-la-la!" Seulange laughed. "Très tentant."

"Huh?"

"A very tempting name."

"Aww, well," Serval laughed, "I've had a lot of razzing about my name, but that's the first time anyone's called it tempting. But what about your name? What does Seulange mean anyway?"

Seulange opened a gleaming silver case and offered him a cigarette. Leaning closer to him as he gave her a light, she gazed into his eyes. "What is her name?"

Serval blinked. "Who?"

"Your wife," she said softly.

"Oh. . . . Her name is Opal."

"Opal. Ah, Monsieur Serval, if I found someone to love me za way you love your Opal . . ." She shrugged one shoulder and gazed blankly into the cigarette smoke curling into the air. "La vie est moins l'amour et la beaucoup de guerre. No?"

Serval grinned and held up his hands. "You lost me."

"I say only that life . . . life is filled with so little love—and too much war." She laughed softly. "And so . . . I am a whore."

"Hey, don't be too hard on yourself, Seulange. We all do what we have to do to survive. But I can't understand these Frenchmen. You're a beautiful woman. I should think they'd be fighting each other to take care of you." Noticing the gold eyes suddenly go flat, Serval realized he had said the wrong thing. "But then, I guess I don't know your story, do I?"

Apparently unwilling to pick up such an obvious conversational cue, Seulange quietly changed the subject. "I have thought about going to America, you know. It is very wonderful, no?"

"You're definitely asking the wrong man," he laughed. "If you want to hear about *wonderful* America, you need to ask one of the white soldiers."

"No, no," she murmured sympathetically. "I hear these things. How za white ones are cruel to za Negré in America. Why is this?"

"That's the eternal question—why. They want to be superior, I guess."

After a long pause, she murmured, "But they are not, and they know it deep in za soul. That makes za anger, no?"

"Maybe." Smiling at Seulange, Serval raised his glass. "Well, vivé la France! That much French I know."

Lifting her left eyebrow in a seductive arch, she murmured, "No. Vivé la difference."

"Touché," Serval laughed. *I must really love Opal. The old Serval would've had this girl in his lap by now.* A sudden twinkle in Seulange's eyes gave him the uneasy feeling that she had read his thought. He cleared his throat nervously before speaking. "Uh, anyway, all that vivé la difference stuff is well and good here in France, but it seems to me that difference is what's causing all the trouble in America."

"How boring if everyone is za same," she sniffed. "White Americans are boring, no?"

"Well, if you're askin' me, they're boring, *yes*," he laughed. "Not that I couldn't think up some more appropriate descriptions. . . . So, Seulange . . ."

"I see it myself," she interrupted him softly. "One Negré soldier I, ahh, entertained . . . they arrested him on za street—za white American soldiers. How you say? Za M.P.'s? For only walking with me."

Serval nodded. "Under orders from the President."

"No!"

"Oui."

Over another hour of conversation, Serval sipped his wine sparingly. Seulange suddenly leaned back in her chair with a sigh, and aimed an intense stare at him.

"Seulange . . . you never told me what your name means."

Seulange smiled. "It is a long time since I spend za evening with a man talking, Monsieur Serval. It is most passionate."

"Huh? Passionate?"

"Is wrong word?"

"Uh, well, in our situation, yes."

"Ah, l'affaire quel tragiqué." Smiling, she rose from her chair. "Come. We go."

"Look, Seulange. I'll be happy to walk you home, but that's as far as I go," he said firmly.

"Bien entendu—I understand. But I know well my little friend René. If Jacques is not rescued, she will never let him go."

Serval laughed and offered her his arm. "Well, then, I guess I'd better go rescue Jacques. But I've got a sneaking suspicion he won't feel rescued—exactly."

Louis Marchand hurried over to the table. "Monsieur, you go so soon?"

"I'm afraid so, Louie. But I appreciate your hospitality. America could definitely take lessons from France in racial relations." Reaching into his pocket, Serval pulled out his wallet. "Okay, Louie, how many francs? What's the damage?"

Louis Marchand's face registered disappointment, and he muttered something in French before regaining his composure. "No, no, Monsieur Serval. Maison de Louis is honored to serve soldiers of Harlem. Fight like hell for Paris! So, Monsieur Serval, how you say? Is free!"

"Free?!" Serval shouted. "Louie! We ate everything but the walls! I can't let you . . ."

Seulange pulled him gently toward the door and whispered, "No, cherie. You offend him! Say only thank-you, and go."

Serval gave Seulange an exasperated look before smiling back at Louis and Nicole Marchand. "Monsieur, Madame . . . you are too kind. Merci and, uh . . . oh, yeah! À bientôt."

"À bientôt, Monsieur," Louis said, bowing. "But it is we who thank *you*."

* * *

Walking through a dark, crumbling corridor in Seulange's building, Serval was disturbed at the conditions endured by Parisians as a result of the war damage to their city. At one end of the hallway, an entire wall had been blasted away, and he wondered if the building was safe for the two women to occupy. Seulange stopped and tapped on a door.

"René," she called softly.

No answer.

Serval rolled his eyes. "Oh, Jacques," he called loudly in a sing-song voice.

"Shhh!" Seulange giggled. "Please do not wake Monsieur Beauchamp! He will scream and call za gendarmes!"

"Who the hell's Monsieur Beauchamp?" Serval asked, teasing her with a grin. "He in there, too?"

Seulange placed a finger to her lips. "Shh! No, Monsieur! Za neighbor!"

At that moment, René, wearing only a thin black chemise, opened the door and let them in. In the candlelight, Serval spotted Jack across the room, shirtless, splashing his face and neck with water from a porcelain wash bowl.

"Bonjour, Jacques," Serval whispered. "Sorry, but time's up, pal."

Jack shot an impatient look over his shoulder, but said nothing.

Once Jack was dressed, Serval stood at the door waiting for René to finish with his friend. As the good-bye kiss dragged on, Serval smiled nervously over at Seulange who was stretched across the bed, lying on her side with her head propped up on one fist. She stared at him sadly for a minute and sighed. "Ahh, Monsieur Serval, quel le chagrin."

Serval quickly pointed his eyes at his own feet, definitely a safer target, and mumbled, "Oh, swell . . ." Nudging Jack's arm, he said, "Jack. Let's go, man."

As René cooed sadly in French, Serval nodded and smiled, then gave Jack a hard yank. "Thank you, ladies. It really was an enjoyable evening." With one last look at Seulange, he touched his cap in a small salute. "I mean it. You gave us our only beautiful memory of France. Take care of yourselves. Good-bye."

"Bon nuit, Monsieur Serval."

Just as Serval reached the stairs, he heard Seulange call out softly, "Monsieur!"

He turned around and saw her silhouette against a jagged patch of deep blue sky, where part of the side wall had been blown away. "Yes?"

She took two steps forward, then stopped. "You asked from me for za meaning of my name."

"Yes. Seulange. What does it mean?"

"It means . . . za lonely angel—Seulange." She shrugged her shoulders and stared at him with empty eyes. "One cannot fight a name, n'est pas?"

Serval didn't try to respond; he could only gaze at her until she disappeared in the darkness. He barely felt Jack nudging his arm.

"Hey, Serval. Come on, man."

"Huh? Oh, yeah. Right behind you, buddy."

Once outside, Serval pulled up the collar of his jacket and lit a cigarette as he walked alongside Jack. A pale sliver of moon hung low in the dark sky, and the horizon glowed with the first streaks of dawn. After several minutes, Jack broke the silence. "Why ya so quiet?"

Serval chuckled. "I can be quiet sometimes, Jack. I don't run my mouth constantly, you know."

"Hmm. Since when?"

"Okay, okay," Serval laughed, "I know you're dyin' to tell me. So, how was it? I mean, how was *she*?"

A grin spread across Jack's face, and he rubbed his chin for a moment before answering. "Well, ya know how we talked about me not havin' much schoolin'?"

Serval immediately liked the direction the conversation had taken. "Yeah."

"Well, I done been to school now, Serval. I done been educated."

Serval stopped in his tracks and grabbed his head with both hands. "Damn, Jack! It just hit me! I passed up a chance to have sex with a professional! A goddamn French professional. Opal Jackson Rivard!" he moaned, "I must really love you!"

"Guess you do," Jack laughed. "'Cause that René done some stuff I ain't never even *heard* about, from the fellas or *nobody*."

Serval turned so that he could see Jack's face and began walking backward. "Okay, start at the beginning, and don't leave anything out. From the first minute . . ." He froze in mid-sentence when a bright light suddenly blinded his eyes.

"Goddamn!" he hissed under his breath. "M.P.'s."

"Who goes there?" barked a voice from behind the spot of light.

Serval and Jack stopped and saluted. "Corporal Serval Rivard, 369th Infantry, sir."

"And Corporal Jack Hawkins. 371st, suh."

"Your unit's shipping stateside in a few hours, Hawkins. Isn't that right?"

"Yes, suh."

The tone of the M.P.'s voice changed suddenly. "It's almost six. Party went a little late, wouldn't you say, boys? You haven't been consorting with any of these white Parisian women, have you? We wouldn't want to have to detain you. You might miss your boat."

Serval placed a hand on Jack's arm. "No, sir! No white women, sir. Wouldn't dream of it."

"Well, don't move, either one'a you. Stand right there for a minute."

Serval heard the M.P's murmuring among themselves, but couldn't make out what they were saying. Finally, one of them shouted, "It's your lucky night, boys. We're gonna let you go this time, but you get back to camp on the double! We catch either one of you out here roaming the streets again, and it's the brig—or worse!"

"Yes, sir!" they replied in unison.

Serval and Jack saluted, then beat a hasty retreat toward the road leading to their encampment near the Marne River. Their boisterous conversation of moments before was dead and forgotten. Now the only sound breaking the silence of the early morning hour was the weary shuffle of boots on cobblestone. Serval sank into the loneliness of his own thoughts as he reflected on what disappointments he and the other Negro soldiers would face when they returned to America.

# 1919

Pan-African Congress convenes in Paris.

Nationwide eruption of the bloodiest race riots
ever recorded in the U.S.; referred to by
newspaper columnists as "Red Summer."

Seventy-six reported lynchings of Negroes in U.S.

---

*Black men here are never truly honoured. Don't you believe like
colored Dr. DuBois that 'the race problem is at an end here,' except
you want to admit the utter insignificance of the blackman. It was
never started and it has not yet begun . . .*

—Marcus Garvey

*New Negroes are determined that they shall not travel through the
valley of death alone, but some of their oppressors shall be their
companions.*

—Asa Philip Randolph

*We return.
We return from fighting.
We return fighting.*

—W.E.B. DuBois

# Chapter 15

Jack Hawkins recognized the feverish feeling in his head. It was the cruel heat of an Alabama sun. Momentarily confused, he looked around and was horrified to find himself standing in a mile-wide field of cotton that he alone must pick. There was no time to waste. Reaching up to wipe the perspiration from his forehead, he grimaced at the sight of the starched cuff on his uniform shirt. *Damn! That's a demerit for sho' if I mess up my uniform . . .* But he sensed his father's eyes locked on him from somewhere, and reached down for an empty bag to fill. The familiar texture of the rough burlap on his fingertips sent a wave of nausea through him, and, before he could straighten up, he felt a pair of hands grabbing his shoulders. "Daddy!"

But when Jack looked into the eyes of the man shaking him, it was not his father, but a man from the 371st, Joe Walker.

"I said wake up, Jack!" Joe hissed frantically. "We gotta get off this train, man! Look what's goin' on down on that platform!"

Jack shook off the effects of the dream and reached into his pocket for a handkerchief to wipe his face. "What'chu talkin' about, Joe?" he murmured.

"If ya lift up the damn shade and look out the winda, you'll see what I'm talkin' 'bout!" The fear in Joe's voice prompted Jack to obey.

He blinked at the sight that met his eyes, wondering if it was a continuation of his dream. An angry crowd of Caucasian townspeople surrounded four Negro soldiers, pushing them and spitting at their uniforms.

"Mobile's idea of a welcomin' committee," Joe whispered.

Above the jeers of the attackers, one voice carried the message clearly: "You niggers think yer big shots now that Wilson let'cha tote guns and kill Germans, huh? But this here's Alabama, so don't be gettin' no uppity ideas!"

As if to back up the sentiment with manpower, a group of white returning soldiers pushed their way through the crowd and began pulling at the Negroes' jackets.

"What they doin' now?" Jack asked, rising from his seat.

Joe took an angry swipe at his eyes. "Look' like they tearin' off they uniforms. Aw, man, we gotta go help 'em, Jack."

But the train had begun to move and Jack heard the faint call of the conductor from a few rows up. "Next stop—Montgomery."

Joe fell heavily into the seat next to Jack. "That's us. And we the only two fellas from Montgomery. Hell! Wonder what we got waitin' for us?"

Jack thought for a moment, then reached under his seat. "You got civvies, Joe?"

"Huh? Well, yeah, in my duffel bag."

"Git 'em. And then change. 'Least change ya shirt. Pants too—if ya can."

Joe jerked his head. "Naw, man! That ain't right. We' heroes too, jus' like them white boys, and we done earned our right to wear this uniform."

"I know, but it don't mean nothin' to them, not long as we' the ones wearin' it. You can be a hero to ya family, but'cha gotta git home first. Now change."

*   *   *

"Montgomery!" The conductor's voice boomed above the train's tired shushing sounds as it approached the platform.

Jack stood up and gathered his gear before glancing down at Joe, who had not moved. "Look, Joe," he whispered. "We' gon' do what we got to, but that don't mean you ain't a hero. Ain't nothin' white folks can do to change that. Now, come on."

Joe nodded, then followed Jack to the door and down the steps to the platform. A small group of grim-faced Caucasian citizens armed with sticks, baseball bats, and rifles stood in a tight group scanning each male passenger that exited the Jim Crow car. A current of fear ran between Jack and Joe, and they reverted to their old Southern mannerisms. Heads lowered, they moved inconspicuously through the crowd in their civilian clothes. Jack risked a glance at the car to his left where mothers, wives, and children crowded around the disembarking Caucasian soldiers. As happy reunions took place, the air was filled with female voices shouting names and wailing, until the men began drifting over to join their families. Joe nudged Jack, and Jack nodded. They were safe.

After walking to the edge of town, they reached a crossroads that would lead them each in a different direction. Jack extended his hand to Joe and smiled.

"I'm proud'a you, man. I'm sorry I got separated from y'all at the end, but I know you done good."

"Thanks, Jack. Hell, we both done good!" He paused and looked at the ground. "Man, I'm happy to be gittin' home. My Mama always be makin' a pie when it's sump'm to celebrate."

Jack smiled. "Bet she be makin' 'bout nine pies tonight then, huh?"

"That's what I been countin' on since we got on the boat, man! Home and Mama's pies! Hey! Bet'chu got some pies waitin' for you too, Jack."

"Naw. My Mama passed right 'fo I enlisted."

"I'm sorry, man. I ain't meant to . . ."

"That's awright. Livin' was hell, and she never did sleep good. But she' sleepin' real good in heaven. That's how I'm thinkin' 'bout it anyhow."

"You still plannin' on headin' up nawth, Jack?"

"Yeah, prob'ly so."

"Well, maybe we' still see each other sometime 'fo ya go."

"Maybe so. Might haf'ta come out and try some'a yo' Mama's pie sometime 'fo I head nawth. Anyhow, you take care'a ya'self, soldier."

"You too, Jack . . . But naw, wait. That ain't good enough." Dropping his gear, Joe stood straight, his head held high, and executed a sharp military salute.

Jack dropped his own bag and returned the salute.

Without saying goodbye, Joe gathered his gear and headed down the dirt road that led to the place he called home.

Jack stood watching Joe until he could no longer see him through the haze of red dust. With a sigh, he hoisted his bag onto his shoulder and headed for his father's house—a place Jack Hawkins had never called home.

*        *        *

The house looked smaller, so much smaller that for a moment Jack thought he had made a mistake. But the three mason bricks, two red with a gray one in the middle, that served as a step for the porch, assured him that this was the right place after all. He stepped from the bricks up to the porch and peered through the ragged screen door. "Hello?" he called. "Anybody home?"

No answer.

Just as he was wondering whether or not he had the right to go in, he spotted a dark-skinned woman in a faded yellow dress carrying a basket of laundry from the back of the house. She walked slowly until she spotted him, then dropped the basket. "Jack?"

"Elsie?" Jack had to remind himself to smile. Elsie looked as old as his mother just before she had passed away. "Elsie?" he repeated, stepping down to greet her.

The minute she smiled, Jack was sure. Although the past two years in the cotton fields had aged her mercilessly, her smile was young and familiar. She broke into a run and squealed as she threw her arms around his neck. Wrapping his arms around her waist, he lifted her and swung her around.

"Put me down, Jack! Shoot, I'm pregnant, ya know! My stomach can't take all this nonsense! Lawd, I don't know where you done run off to, but wherever it was, it sho' seem' like it agreed wit'cha! You sho' happier than when you lef' out'a here!"

But Jack stopped listening after the word "pregnant." "Elsie. Did I hear you say you was — pregnant?"

She slapped his arm and laughed. "It's awright, Jack. I done got ma'sef married since you lef'."

Jack smiled. "Well, then, congratulations. Who the lucky fool ya trapped into that?"

"I ain't had to trap nobody, thank you very much. His name be Joshua. He' the preacher's son from down to the church."

"Church? When Daddy let y'all off work long enough to go to church?"

"Daddy passed, Jack. Last summer," she said nonchalantly.

"Daddy . . . passed? You mean . . . he' dead?"

"Mm-hmm."

Jack swallowed hard. "Well . . . how' he die?"

"Shoot, I don't know. It was in the field, though. His heart give out, I guess."

"So, uh, who tendin' to the fields and all that now?"

"Joshua and Andrew, Jr. I was helpin' fo' a while, 'til I got pregnant. Then Joshua say I gotta stay home. And you know me, Jack. Any excuse to get out'a that clawin' cotton. Shoot, I'm plannin' on havin' me a real, *real* big family!" she laughed as she opened the screen door. "Come on in, Jack and sit on down."

Jack ducked his head as he entered the tiny house and lowered himself into the same old chair that had once served as his bed. It felt considerably smaller. As he listened to Elsie chatter about family events, minor and major, he took note of her colorful personality. The misery of his own adolescence had so preoccupied him that he had never considered the possibility of the Hawkins children possessing personalities. He laughed at something Elsie was saying, although he hadn't really heard it. Her animated facial expressions were an entertaining show in and of themselves. It was apparent that she loved to talk.

"You seem real happy, Elsie," he said. "Joshua make you that happy?"

"He' a good man, Jack. And he don't be worryin' 'bout the cotton all the time like Daddy done. I mean, he work' real hard and all, but if he don't bring in much as Mr. Davis say he got to, he jus' stands right on up to him. He tell' him, 'Our loss, ain't it? We' find a way to make ends meet, wit the Lawd's help.' And you know what Mr. Davis say? 'Jus' do the best y'all can.' Can you believe that? Daddy had us thinkin' that if we was short on cotton, Mr. Davis gon' skin us alive or sump'm! But I believe he' easier on us on account'a Joshua's Daddy bein' a preacher and all. Mr. Davis be a real church goin' man, 'member? So things goin' pretty good, I guess. But what about you, Jack? Tell me where you been all this time. I was so worried!"

"Me? Aww, I jus' been off fightin' in the war."

Elsie's mouth fell open. For the first time since Jack's arrival, she was speechless.

Jack laughed. "I been off in Europe since I lef' out'a here."

"Jack," she breathed. "Was it awful and bloody as they say? Tell me . . ."

"Well, it ain't nothin' you need to be hearin' 'bout, girl. I wish I ain't seen it ma'self, tell ya the troof. I mean . . . the *truth*. But it growed me up. I wasn't nothin' but a big-talkin' boy 'til I seen all that killin'. And I know what day I finally felt like a man. I woke up one mornin' right up next to a dead man, and I ain't even felt like screamin' or nothin'. I just got up, took his rations out his knapsack, and walked on off away from him like he wasn't nothin'. I been a man since that day, Elsie."

Elsie's eyes were moist and wide open, but she said nothing.

Jack fidgeted and cleared his throat. "Aww, it wasn't all so bad. I won me a medal." Reaching into his bag, he retrieved the box and opened it. "See? French government give us that for helpin' to save Paris."

Elsie turned the heavy cross over in her hands and stroked the ribbon with her fingertips. "Ooh, Jack! You' a real hero, huh?"

Feeling the warmth creep up his face, Jack quickly returned the medal to his bag and changed the subject. "Uh, how Andrew, Jr.? He married too?"

Elsie's expression changed from one of awe to one of fear. "Naw. Andrew jus' . . . well, he . . . First off, he ain't like it when anybody call' him 'Andrew, Jr.' He jus' go by 'Andrew' now. I guess the only way to tell you . . . Jack, Andrew jus' like a walkin', talkin' *Daddy*. He' mean and ornery and don't never smile. Guess he jus' stay wid' us 'cause he ain't got noplace else to go."

Jack stared at the floor for a moment, thinking that Elsie's description of Andrew, Jr. sounded like a description of himself before joining the army. "Where they at now? Andrew and Joshua?" he asked without looking up.

"Town. They went to get supplies. And when they gets back, tell ya what. I'ma make a chocolate cake for our war hero! You stayin' a while, ain'tcha?"

Jack stood up suddenly and looked down at Elsie. "Naw. I'm sorry, Elsie. I promised a buddy I, uh . . . see, we got some plans to go into business together up nawth. I got me a train to catch."

"Naw, Jack!" she protested. "You can't leave! You just got here!"

Hugging her tightly, he murmured, "Got to, Elsie. But it sho' was good to see you again. It was good to see ya so happy."

Suddenly serious, she gazed up at Jack and rubbed his cheek. "I ain't gon' turn out like Mama," she whispered.

"Naw, you ain't, baby girl," he said, smiling. "You sho' ain't. . . . Listen, I'ma write and let'cha know where I end up, hear?"

"Okay, Jack. I sho' hate you didn't get to meet Joshua. But the nawth! That do sound excitin'!"

Jack smiled and kissed her cheek before gathering his gear and ducking through the front doorway. "Bye, Elsie. You take care'a that man and that baby, hear?"

"I'll do that. Uh, Jack?"

"Mm-hmm?"

"Uh . . . I love you, hear?"

His eyes met hers in understanding. Theirs was not a family to express such sentiments, and he knew how uncomfortable she had been saying it. "I love you too, Elsie. I really do."

As Jack strode toward the main road, he considered the possibility of meeting Andrew on his way back from town with Joshua. In the distance, he spotted a slow-moving wagon, and headed for the cover of the roadside trees. His visit with Elsie had been a pleasant one. He didn't want to destroy his one happy memory of Alabama by seeing images of unbearable days past in the coldness of his brother's eyes. He quickened his step and stayed away from the main road.

*     *     *

Things hadn't changed much in downtown Montgomery, and Jack quickly found a place to stay. After renting a room in a colored boarding house, he impatiently waited for word from Serval. Each morning before breakfast he checked in at the Western Union office, and on the fourth day a telegram finally arrived. Jack thanked the Western Union employee, then handed the telegram back to him. Leaning close to the window, Jack whispered, "Please, suh. Could ya read it to me?"

The man nodded and adjusted his reading glasses. "Le'me see . . . Says . . . J-Jock . . . Uh, Lord, son! What 'n tarnation kind'a name is this? Jock-quez? That your name?"

Jack chuckled and nodded. "Jacques. Uh, that be French for Jack. See, we was in the war and . . ."

"Oh, I get it. Little joke, huh? Well, le'me finish here 'cause I got a line formin' behind you, boy. Le'me see . . . Says here, 'Finally shipping out. Stop. Get yourself to New York City by bus, train or mule. Stop. Will meet up somewhere along parade route on Fifth Avenue on February 17. Stop. Near library. Stop. Ask anybody for directions. Stop. Serval Rivard.'"

Sunset, shadows—enigma of twists
Mama's tears and sweetheart's kiss and
Jim Crow's mocking grin
Sing it loud!
Here Comes My Daddy Now!
A sho'nuff natural man—at last . . .

# Chapter 16

On a crisp morning under a clear blue sky, New Yorkers of every race and social station lined both sides of Fifth Avenue to welcome the pride of Harlem. The buildings across from the New York Public Library were decked out with colorful welcome-home banners suspended from high flag poles, and dignitaries watched from elevated viewing platforms draped in red, white, and blue. When James Reese Europe's Ragtime Military Band began tuning up to lead the parade, the crowd buzzed with anticipation. From atop one of the stone lions gracing the library steps, two small Harlem boys shouted and waved their caps in the direction of 34th Street where their heroes stood in neat French formations.

The soldiers from Harlem had experienced several incarnations over the past year. They had departed as the 15th of New York, incorporated into the 369th U.S. Infantry. After assignment to the 161st Division of the French Army, their heroism in the Meuse-Argonne Offensive earned them the title "Harlem Hellfighters." Decorated with the Croix de Guerre, the highest award for valor bestowed by the French, the Hellfighters far exceeded the U.S. Army's expectations, making their triumphant return twice as sweet.

Suddenly the erratic squeaks and thumps of band instruments quieted; Europe's voice echoed the count; and a jazz rendition of *Over There* bounced its rhythm off the facades of skyscrapers lining Fifth Avenue. The spectators' recognition of George M. Cohan's enlistment anthem was immediate, transforming their cheers into song:

> *Over there, over there*
> *Send the word, send the word over there*
> *that the Yanks are coming, the Yanks are coming!*
> *The drums rum-tumming everywhere*
> *So prepare, say a prayer*

*Send the word, send the word over there*
*We'll be over, we're coming over*
*And we won't be back 'til it's over over there!*

But the fanfare was lost on Serval, who waited quietly for the march order. He squinted up at the sun, half-expecting to see God sitting there, ready to answer all his questions. But when he closed his eyes, the blinding orb had burned its image into his eyelids as a twisted red ball of the wire, complete with every corpse he had ever seen it consume. He responded to Sergeant Drew's command like an unfeeling automaton.

"Forward, harch!"

The big parade was underway.

As Serval marched crisply with his unit, his dismal mood began to lift. Soon he would see Opal. Touch Opal. Hold her in his arms. He blinked to sharpen his peripheral vision. *The library. She said she'd be on the library steps.*

Suddenly he spotted a familiar shape jutting out ahead to his left. He craned his neck and caught sight of a pair of large outstretched paws resting on the front edge of a raised pedestal. Two more steps brought the familiar proud chin and lion's mane into view, and Serval smiled broadly for the first time in weeks. Breaking military form, he raised his left hand to his lips and blew the stone lion a kiss.

As he scanned the crowd for Opal's face, the cheering from the library steps began to escalate. The spectators were a blur of motion, but the observance of racial ranking was evident; white faces swarmed close to the street for the best view of the parade, with dark faces visible only in the background. Serval bristled at the irony, and his mood descended. *Look at this shit. Lettin' yesterday's niggers be the big heroes for one day. What about tomorrow, Mr. White Man? Back in my place, huh?*

He blinked, and Jimmy Coles made a spectral appearance on the inside of his eyelids. Shifting his gaze to the top of the library steps, he searched intently. *Opal, Opal . . . Where are you, baby?*

A sudden bright flicker caught his attention, but was gone the next second. Something green. He surveyed the area again and spotted it. A grin spread across his face. . . . *a green silk hat, Serval, very bright— special for when you come home . . .*

\*   \*   \*

From their vantage point at the top of the library steps, Opal and Creola scrutinized each face as the soldiers passed. "Opal, this is silly," Creola grumbled. "I don't even know what he looks like."

"I showed you his photograph, Creola."

"Yeah, but all these soldiers look alike," she snapped. "Uniforms and hats pulled down, damn near coverin' up their eyes. And look how many of 'em there are! Opal, there's gotta be at least a hundred men in each one of those groups or divisions, or whatever you call 'em. And there's one, two, three, four . . . Opal, there's hundreds of 'em! How am I supposed to pick out one fella out'a all . . ."

Opal let out a sudden gasp and clutched wildly at Creola's arm. "There he is! I see him!" Grabbing Creola's hand, Opal pulled her along as she threaded her way through the crowd and down the steps toward the street. "S'cuse me, sir. . . . Thank you. Pardon us, ma'am, we need to get by. . . . Thanks. Oh, Creola! There he is!" Opal waved and shouted, "Serval! *Serval!* Oh, why isn't he lookin'?"

Creola shook Opal's shoulder. "Honey, calm down! He ain't supposed to look up, I don't think. They' at attention or sump'm." Creola pointed to her left and shouted, "We'll catch up with him at the end of the street where they' all been stoppin'. Up there, Opal, see? Up by 45th Street. It might take awhile though . . ."

Suddenly, to Creola's horror, Opal ducked under the ribbon that separated the spectators from the parade. She then stepped off the curb, and began to run up Fifth Avenue toward 45th Street. "Oh, damn!" Creola groaned. The last thing she wanted to do was run, especially with rows of pulsating manhood marching by, and after spending her last dime at the beauty parlor on a new marcel. But Opal seemed unstoppable. "This child could prob'ly win the damn Triple Crown, the way she's goin'," she muttered as she hurried after Opal. "Damn! I hope my hair don't turn back. I'll kill her if my edges nap up!"

Serval's regiment came to a sudden halt at 45th Street, inciting another explosion of cheers just as Creola caught up with Opal. She shoved her fingers into her ears and muttered, as Opal bounced up and down, pointing at Serval. "See him? There my baby is, right there! The second one in this line, see, Creola?"

Studying Serval from a three-quarter angle, Creola's face contorted in an expression of distaste. "Him? He's so, well, so *dark*, Opal. He didn't look that dark in his picture . . ."

Opal sighed. "Isn't he beautiful?"

Creola's eyes widened at the sight of the soldiers resuming their march up Fifth Avenue. As she turned to question Opal, she realized that she had been left behind. Opal was several yards ahead, skipping alongside Serval's unit.

Creola ran to catch her. "Wait a minute, Opal!" she shouted. "Wait just a damn minute!" She grabbed Opal's arm and spun her around. "How long is this damn parade anyway? How far are they goin'?"

"Harlem," Opal said. "Come on, Creola. They're gettin' away and I want to stay near Serval."

"Harlem?!" Creola stood rooted to the spot in disbelief for a few seconds. But after taking another look at the large number of potential dates in the street, she shrugged and ran to catch up with Opal. "Opal! Answer me one question . . ."

"What's that, Creola?"

"Why the hell did we come all the way out here when we could'a just waited up in Harlem?"

No answer. Opal was blowing a kiss in Serval's direction. Creola rolled her eyes and muttered as she trudged along behind her.

* * *

By the time the parade reached Harlem, Creola felt a scratchy dampness under her arms, and her stylish alligator pumps had rubbed blisters on her heels and three of her toes. Muttering under her breath, she peeled off her burgundy wool coat, and hobbled behind Opal until she caught sight of the 110th Street sign. "Thank the Lord!" she shouted.

As the soldiers rounded the corner from Fifth Avenue onto 110th Street, the band broke into a rousing rendition of *Here Comes My Daddy Now*, which sent the crowd dancing into the street to get a real down-home, Harlem-style celebration under way. The unit came to a sudden halt and the crowd roared, causing a delay in the dismissal. The officer waited nearly a full minute for quiet so that the command could be heard.

"Oh, Lord, Creola, why don't their boss let 'em go?" Opal shouted into Creola's ear. "Why they got to stand there so long like that?"

Creola slipped off her right shoe and gazed down at the bleeding blister on her little toe. "Oh, *Lord*, Opal. I sure the hell don't know."

When the command finally rang out, even Creola jumped.

"At ease!" was followed by a quick, "Dismissed!"

Serval shot out of his rigid stance toward Opal, who screamed as she catapulted herself into his arms. The street was suddenly pandemonium as similar human collisions occurred, with only Creola remaining on the sidewalk, attempting to avoid physical injury while protecting the perfectly-formed curls of her fresh marcel with her hands.

Her ulterior motive for accompanying Opal to the parade was to meet some of Serval's friends, one or two of whom she was sure would be unattached. But unable to spot even one returning veteran who wasn't being wildly hugged or kissed by someone in the over-zealous crowd, Creola had just decided to walk home barefoot when she found herself staring open-mouthed at Opal and Serval. They were locked in an intimate kiss, the only two inhabitants of a world all their own, despite the chaos surrounding them on 110th Street. Creola's first assessment of Serval as unattractive vanished, and a disturbing warm feeling between her thighs made her look closer. There was something about the way his dark hands tangled themselves in Opal's hair, as he appeared to consume her whole mouth like a starving man. She watched his hands roam from Opal's waist down to her hips, before reaching behind for the roundness they craved. Creola stopped breathing for a moment when she saw his eyes roll back in his head for a split second, as if he were momentarily losing consciousness. She watched his arms wrap around Opal to ease her lower body closer to his, and she recognized the hunger in his eyes. But there was more—a sort of reverent connection between them that she knew she had never experienced. They created an erotic, mysterious tableaux in Creola's mind, and she was unable to shake the faint twinge of jealousy she suddenly felt.

She was touched by his apparent fight for self-control as he eased away from Opal's body to give her a gentlemanly kiss on the nose. By the time the couple headed in Creola's direction, she was beyond caring about the dampness on her forehead that was crinkling up the edges of her perfect marcel.

"Creola," Opal said breathlessly, "This is Serval! My husband, girl! Serval, I want you to meet my friend Creola."

Serval stared adoringly at Opal, and appeared not to have heard the introduction. Creola seethed at his indifference toward her, until at last, he met her gaze. Stepping up onto the sidewalk, he extended his hand. "How do you do?"

Creola's knees suddenly went soft, and her voice was a weak croak. "H-hello, uh, Serval. Welcome home." His closeness was unbearable to her. Or maybe it was the two of them. The mutual desire between

Opal and Serval created a separate palpable entity more powerful than any aphrodisiac Creola could name. She felt faint.

Serval suddenly broke into an impish grin. "Wait a minute. What was that name again? Creola? *Creola*, huh? Come on, what's your *real* name?"

Creola frowned. The spell was broken. "Serval?" she snapped. "Serval, huh? Come on, what's *your* real name, buster?"

Serval raised his eyebrows and laughed. Leaning over Opal for another kiss, he suddenly looked up and shouted, "Hey! Over here! Jack!" He waved his arm over his head, then said to Opal, "Baby, this is the fella I wrote you about—Jack Hawkins. I'll be damned! He made it!"

Creola reacted to Jack like a well-oiled mantrap. Taking a deep breath to ensure that her breasts were displayed to their fullest advantage, she shifted into automatic, allowing her eyes to scale Jack Hawkins' six-foot-seven-inch frame. Stopping at his face, she gazed intently into a pair of hooded eyes with an exotic slant. "Hello, Mr. Hawkins," she purred, extending her hand, "I'm Creola Dorshay, just one of the folks you were over there fightin' for. How can I *ever* thank you?"

Jack glanced at Serval and then nodded politely at Creola. "'Mawnin', ma'am. But ya ain't got to thank me. Uh, I had lot'sa help."

Serval opened his mouth to say something, but Opal nudged him sharply and he laughed. "Okay, baby, okay. So Jack. What do you think of Harlem? Ain't she swell?"

"Uh, she?"

"Oh, yeah. Harlem is definitely a lady. All dressed up to receive her suitors."

"Well, she sho' lookin' happy today. And prosperous too."

"I told you. So did you wait up here for us? I looked for you when we passed the library, but . . ."

"Oh, I was there. Standin' right by one'a them big ol' lions. He looked right friendly, lettin' them kids ride on his back, so I jus' made friends wid'im while I was waitin' for y'all. I seen you, awright, but it ain't looked like y'all was stoppin', so I jus' followed behind." Jack smiled at Opal. "I seen yo' Missuz and her friend skippin' along. I would'a said sump'm, 'cept I didn't know she was the famous Opal I done heard so much about."

Opal grinned and snuggled against Serval's arm. "I'm so glad you're home, Mr. Rivard. You too, Jack. You're welcome at our home anytime."

"Thank you, ma'am."

Creola had taken advantage of the exchange to study Jack and consider his possibilities. He turned his back to her for a moment to point at a billboard, and she watched the muscles strain under the sleeve of his ill-fitting jacket. *Oh yeah, country-boy. You'll do just fine for Creola tonight.* When he turned back to face her, she smiled seductively at him and snaked her arm around his. "Hey, Jack. Why don't you let li'l ol' Creola show you 'round? How 'bout that, huh? Bet you and me can find ways to have a whole lot'a fun together!"

Jack took a deep breath and patted her hand. "Awright, ma'am. That's right nice'a you." He leaned closer to Serval and grinned. "Ya know sump'm, man? I think I'ma like the Nawth."

\* \* \*

Serval sighed as he stared up at the front double windows of the brownstone apartment building on 130th Street. "God, it's good to be home!"

Opal hurried up the steps, pulling him by the hand. "Well, you're not quite home yet, Serval. Wait 'til you see how I fixed things up. Come on!"

When they reached their apartment door, Serval hoisted his duffel bag up to his shoulder and put out his hand. "Key, please."

Opal giggled as she handed him the key. "Yes, you should do the honors."

After unlocking the door, he pushed it open and blinked at the darkness. "Where's the light?"

"There's a floor lamp just to your left, Serval. And the chain's right . . ."

The room was suddenly bathed in a soft light, and Serval grinned back at her. "Found it." He stepped to the center of the room, dropped his bag on the floor, and removed his cap. He said nothing as he turned in a slow circle to survey the room. The first thing he saw was a new rolltop desk with a green reading lamp in the right-hand corner. Just above the desk was a large placard that read: "Welcome Home, My Husband, My Heart, My Soul."

"Your mother had that made for you, Serval. It's bigger than regular desks—some high-tone designer made it . . . What did she call it? Oh, yeah. Custom-made. She said your old desk was always cluttered up and that now you'd be needing a man-size desk. Oh, and the welcome-home sign was custom-made too. By me."

He smiled over his shoulder at Opal, then walked slowly toward the fireplace. Facing the hearth was a slate-blue Queen Anne-style sofa with a patchwork quilt folded across the back. In front of the sofa was an oval coffee table made of a dark hardwood that matched the small end table as well as the floors. The mantlepiece was covered with an assortment of framed photographs—scenes of their wedding day, family pictures, an oval studio portrait of Opal with Aida Johnson, signed by James Van Der Zee, and the ballet pose of Madame as a young woman with the Bolshoi. The two largest pictures were of Serval and Opal as babies, carefully placed in the center in a large, silver folding frame. Against the far wall stood a long, narrow table that held a neat stack of phonograph records and a tabletop Victrola with a large black horn. A spotless dark blue rug covered the center of the floor, and crisp white curtains fluttered at the windows.

"Well," Opal said, "what do you think?"

Shaking his head slowly, Serval pulled her into his arms. "It's home. You made it a real home, baby. It was nothing but an empty room full of unpacked boxes the last time I saw it."

"Miss Aida helped me. Now come see the kitchen!"

Serval laughed. "Well, baby, I'd love to see the kitchen, but if you don't mind, after that long party at my parents' house, all I want to do is get out of this uniform and into a hot tub."

Opal sighed as she pulled off her coat. "Me too. That was some long walk, from 42nd Street all the way up to Harlem. I feel pretty gritty."

"That's right," Serval laughed. "You followed us all the way, didn't you? Well, then, ladies first. While you take your bath, I'll start a fire and poke around the old residence—figure out where everything is."

"Okay. I just hope you remember the way to the bedroom."

"Oh, the bedroom I can find with my eyes shut. So you just try to set the record for the world's fastest bath, Mrs. Rivard, because I'll be doin' my best to beat your time when I get in there. *And* I hope you have an appropriately frilly little negligee for my first night back."

Opal cut her eyes at him and gave him a sly smile. "Oh, I'm not through surprising you, Mr. Rivard. I'll see *you* later."

*   *   *

Serval scrubbed his body twice and refilled the tub for a clean rinse. Staring into the water, he searched for any trace of blood. It was clear.

He reached for a towel and pressed it to his face, then rubbed hard until the stinging made him stop. Holding the towel up to the light, he stared at its whiteness, then checked his fingernails. *No blood*, he told himself. *It's all washed off. All of it.*

A fleeting image appeared in his mind—rusty red water swirling around his feet and into the drain—his first thorough shower after leaving the front. His stomach did a small flip-flop, but he made up his mind to shake off the memory. He grabbed a fresh towel and took in its freshly laundered smell. *No more de-lousing*, he thought, then said it out loud to his reflection in the mirror to convince himself. "No more burning, stinking, goddamn de-lousing. Serval Rivard has returned to civilization, do you hear me? Towels and Ivory soap, goddammit! Clean sheets. Bed." He gazed into the mirror at a grin he hadn't seen since his wedding night. "A bed with a wife in it!" Taking a deep breath, he rubbed his hands together and opened the door. The hallway was dark.

"Hey!" he laughed. "Who turned out the lights?"

He was answered by the muffled sound of Opal giggling.

"Oh, somebody wants to play games, huh?"

"No games, Mr. Rivard," she called. "Just a welcome home. Now, you *said* you could find the bedroom with your eyes shut."

"Just keep talkin', baby," Serval said as he felt his way along the hallway wall. "With you waiting in that bed, don't you worry. I'll find it."

Suddenly something furry brushed against his leg, and he jumped. "Damn, baby! We got rats? Okay, wait, don't get nervous . . . Damn, it's a big one though! Opal! Turn on the lamp so I can see him and, uh, I'll get him . . ."

"Serval!" Opal laughed. "That's not a rat! It's just Meow! He must've hid when he heard a strange voice in the house. Remember? I told you Madame left him with me. We've got us a cat now."

"Oh, that's right. I thought it felt too soft to be a rat," he laughed. "And speaking of soft . . ." Dropping his towel on the floor, he felt his way to the bed and reached for Opal. His hand found her knee, and he fumbled and caught himself, then let out a laugh. "Why, Mrs. Rivard! I do believe you're naked!"

Another giggle. "This isn't like that fancy party at your parents' house, Serval. This is what'cha call a no-frills welcome home. No fancy dinner and no fancy dress. Just me."

"Mrs. Rivard, you know me too well. Wait, just a minute . . ." Springing out of bed, Serval felt around for the window and bumped his knee on Opal's vanity chair. "Aww, shit! Oww! *Damn!*"

Opal was convulsed with laughter. "What are you doin', crazy man?"

"I'm trying to find the string for the shade on this window, and hoping for a full moon, Mrs. Rivard! I'd like to shed some light on the subject."

"Lord, Serval, if you still want me to turn on the lamp . . ."

"Naw, uh-uh. Moonlight'll be quite effective for my purposes and . . . Here it is. I think I have it . . ."

Suddenly, the shade flew up and the brace holding it broke, bringing the entire apparatus crashing to the floor and sending Opal into a fit of breathless laughter.

"Well . . . you said you wanted moonlight, Mr. Rivard. Looks like you got a whole window full!"

Peering out the window, Serval whispered, "Hope the neighbors are asleep. Looks like their shades are down."

"Our lights are out, Serval. Nobody can see us. Now, come here and let me welcome you home proper."

He winced as he eased into bed next to Opal, but sighed at the touch of a silky thigh. Running his fingertips over the curve of her hip, he followed the path of his hand with a hungry gaze. "Mrs. Rivard," he whispered, "The way this moonlight's shining on your skin, you look . . ." Pausing, he squinted at the top of her head, which was in shadow. "Is that . . . Oh!" he laughed. "Your green silk hat! Nice touch. I especially like the way it goes with your bare skin. Quite the daring fashion statement, Mrs. Rivard. You'll have to excuse me if I fail to give your jaunty little hat the attention I should, but . . . back to your body. I was trying to figure out what it reminds me of . . . Wait! I've got it! It looks like one of those bronze statues in a museum . . . right after somebody polished it. And may I say that you're the most gorgeous sight these eyes have seen in a long, long time!"

"Aw, go on," she said with a wave of her hand. "I wouldn't be anything without my hat."

Serval laughed. "You might be right. Here. I'm taking off the hat, just to see if it ruins your ensemble . . . Ah-ha! Just as I suspected. You're still gorgeous, hat or no hat."

Opal giggled as Serval pulled her into his arms. "Wait a minute, Serval!" she said, reaching into the nightstand drawer. "I have a welcome home present for you."

Serval sat up on the edge of the bed and began rummaging through his duffel bag. "I completely forgot! I've got one for you too, but you distracted me with your wicked costume. Here it is!"

They laughed as they presented each other with almost identically-sized boxes.

"You want me to turn on the lamp?" Opal asked.

"Naw. It's bright enough in here for you to see it. Go ahead. Open it."

"Serval, when did you find time to shop for a present with a war goin' on and everything?"

"Just open it."

"Okay." Tearing off the ribbon, Opal opened the box and laughed. "A watch! Very funny. Now I guess this is supposed to make me be on time, huh?"

"No. It's to keep you from always grabbing my arm to see what time it is."

"I never had a watch before. And this one's so pretty, too! Are those diamonds?"

"Just little ones."

"Oh, thank you, Serval. Well, now I don't have any excuse for being late all the time. Okay, now open yours."

Serval eased back against his pillow and tore open the box. Nestled in the blue velvet lining was a small gold medallion on a chain, gleaming in the reflected moonlight. He stared silently at the inscribed letters: J.C.

Opal nudged him. "Turn it over."

He hesitated for a moment and looked at her before turning the medallion over to discover the initials he knew he would find: W.W.

"Jimmy Coles," he whispered. "And William Watts—Red."

"See?" Opal whispered. "Now they'll always be with you."

Serval didn't speak or move for a moment, then jerked himself up to sit on the edge of the bed. Resting his forehead in one hand, he held the medallion in the other and stared at it.

"Oh, God," Opal moaned. "I didn't mean . . . Serval?"

At last, Serval pulled the chain over his head, and swallowed hard. He squeezed his eyes shut at the metallic sound of the medallion dropping against his dogtags. "Why do people wear chains around their necks?" he murmured. He felt Opal's arms around his waist, then the warmth of her face against his back.

"Oh, God," she said. "You don't like it, do you? It was a bad idea, I guess."

"No . . . No it wasn't. It's okay."

"No, it's not. It makes you hurt all over again, doesn't it, Serval? I'm sorry. I only meant it as a kind of a . . . a remembrance."

Serval finally turned around and managed a smile. "I know."

Opal sank back against the pillows and pulled the sheet up around her shoulders. "It was a stupid, thoughtless thing to do . . ."

"No, it wasn't," he whispered, easing back into bed. "It's just that . . . Look, it's gonna take some time for me to adjust, I guess, that's all."

Opal's eyes began to fill with tears and she wrapped her arms around his neck. "Was it that bad, Serval?"

Serval opened his mouth, but made no sound for a long while. Finally: "Don't think I've gone looney on you, but you know what I almost started to believe?"

"What?"

"Well, sometimes it came to me in dreams, but sometimes when I was awake, I'd almost . . ."

"What, Serval?"

"The wire, Opal—the barbed wire. It was like this—this demon butcher all over the landscape. It snatched human life like it was *nothing*—men with souls—and swallowed 'em. It was the devil, sitting right there in the open, making us kill each other when we didn't even know why. We were like—like an army of goddamn puppets, and he just laid out there and waited for a fella to make one false step so he could swallow him down right into hell."

"Oh, God, Serval," Opal whispered. "That sounds horrible! *God*, Serval!"

Serval kissed her forehead. "Sorry. I didn't mean to scare you."

"I'm not scared. I'm sad, I guess. I just wish I could make you forget it—take it out of your head. I—I knew it was bad—'specially after your letter about Red, but . . . Oh, now I'm cryin'. Shoot! I knew I was gonna cry!"

"It's okay, Mrs. Rivard. Come closer. You can cry to me."

"Can't get any closer," she laughed, sniffling.

"Mmm-hmmm," he whispered. "Yes there is. There's one way to get closer, remember? Remember when I had to show you how to begin?"

"I remember."

"Well, now I need you to teach me—how to begin."

Opal chuckled softly. "Serval. You were always the teacher in that department, weren't you? . . . Serval?"

"Opal . . . I need you to teach me who I was—before the war. I don't . . . I don't think I know how to live anymore. Just *live*. Do you understand? Opal, I need you to help me begin life—all over again."

# Chapter 17

Waking up in his own bed completely disoriented Serval for a minute or two, especially when he discovered that Opal was not beside him. Stumbling out of bed, he suddenly remembered the window, and grabbed the sheet from the bed to wrap around his bare body. His confused arrival in the kitchen startled Opal into laughter.

She fixed a stern expression on her face and lowered her voice in imitation of Serval's father. "Perhaps it would be a good idea, son, if you got dressed before coming to the breakfast table!"

Serval bared his teeth at her and threw one end of the sheet over his shoulder, toga-style. "Please, baby. You sound just like him, and I had quite enough of Daddy yesterday. All those photographs. Yuck. And I don't appreciate my wife laughin' at me even if I'm not the most stylish fella this morning."

"Aww, what's wrong?" she laughed. "Couldn't you find your clothes, crazy man?"

"Hell, I don't know. I got lost trying to find my way to the bathroom."

"Aww, po' baby. But I see you didn't have any trouble findin' your way to this food, huh?"

"Baby, I can't tell you how heavenly those biscuits smell. Hope you made enough for about ten men 'cause that's what it's gonna take this morning." Easing up behind her, he wrapped his arms around her waist and began nuzzling her neck. "Mmmm. . . baby, I'm so hungry."

"Mmm-hmm. I know. And you were *so* hungry last night too, huh?"

"Mmmm. Still am. Did I ever tell you how extraordinarily *sexy* you look when you're cooking? Don't make me choose between you and my breakfast. Please."

"Serval! Quit foolin' with me so I can finish cookin'! Now go over there. *Way* over there, and sit down. You eat, and then we'll talk about your other hunger, okay?"

Serval grinned impishly at her as she pushed him down into the kitchen chair. "One kiss," he begged.

"Serval. I've got hotcakes to make . . ."

"Just one kiss. Then I'll be good, I promise."

Opal rolled her eyes. "You've gotta eat now. I never told you this, but I don't like skinny, little weak men and . . . Oh! Serval!"

Before she could finish, Serval swept her up in his arms and headed for the bedroom, laughing wickedly. "Who are you callin' skinny and weak?" Just as he stepped through the bedroom door, the sunlight streaming through the bare window stopped him in his tracks. He stood holding Opal with an annoyed expression on his face. "Damn! Remind me to fix that window-shade today, baby."

Opal laughed. "Okay, sheet-man, so now what'cha gonna do with me?"

"Ah, don't count me out just yet, Mrs. Rivard. Your brilliant husband always has a Plan B. There are other rooms suitable for lovemaking in this apartment, you know. Rooms with shades!"

*　*　*

After a few weeks of typical honeymoon behavior, Serval attended his first UNIA meeting at Liberty Hall, and volunteered for leaflet distribution in the community. The resulting street-corner discussions stimulated him, but upon returning home each night, concerns about unemployment fell across his mind like shadows. By the end of March, Serval had become an authority on the mission of the UNIA, but had not earned a dime.

The sun was setting on another Sunday of leaflet distribution, as he trudged up the steps to his apartment. Stepping through the front door, he shook his head when he heard the sound of Opal humming contentedly. He headed for the kitchen and sighed as he straddled a chair across from her. "Another Sunday night . . ."

Opal looked up from the bowl of peas she was shelling. "Why do you say it like that? My, my, Mr. Rivard. So grim. And where's my kiss?"

Serval leaned over and kissed her cheek twice, then shrugged. "On Sunday nights, most folks sit around complaining about Monday morning rolling around too fast. I sure wish I had a job to complain about."

"Serval. Your Daddy said you could have an apprentice position at his firm anytime you're ready."

He groaned. "There's gotta be sump'm else I can do. I couldn't stand the drudgery. You've never been to my Daddy's firm, Opal. He used to take me there sometimes when I was a kid—I guess he thought it was a thrill. All these bluenose guys in starched collars and pince-nez glasses bent over numbers all day long. And you never heard such silence! You got a chorus of shushes if you so much as sniffled. Opal, those guys at my Daddy's office make the public library look like Coney Island on the Fourth of July. No thanks. I'd get fired before lunch hour on my first day."

"Well . . . I could always go back to work for the Saunders," Opal said quietly.

Serval leaned back in his chair and exhaled sharply as if he'd been hit with a straight right. "Wait, I—I didn't mean . . . Look, I don't want you working, baby. Especially not for Edward Saunders. It was okay while I was gone, but now I want to take care of you."

"Well, we've gotta do sump'm. You said the kitty's gettin' low. I don't mind workin', Serval, and I don't want you workin' at a job you hate. If I worked, you could find sump'm you like, or maybe you could go back to school. I mean, aren't there some schools you can go to that're a little closer than Morehouse?"

Serval pulled the bowl of peas into the center of the table and helped with the shelling for awhile before answering. "Opal, you certainly have a way of putting things into perspective for me," he said softly. "Apparently, the only problem I've got is that I'm spoiled rotten. Other fellas work at jobs they hate, and I'm just gonna have to swallow my pride, that's all. Our savings are nearly gone, and I'm not about to ask Daddy for a handout. I'll get a job, even if it's only as a common laborer. Think you'd mind sittin' down to breakfast with a husband who wears overalls instead of a suit? 'Cause I'd rather dig ditches than work at my Daddy's firm."

Opal studied him for a moment and asked, "But why, Serval? I mean, at least it's a colored business and . . ."

"No, Opal. They're just a subdivision of a larger firm. Daddy tries to make it look like he's independent, but he's got to answer to the white man for every dime."

"But at least they help colored folks, don't they, Serval? I mean, all the clients he's got are colored. Doesn't that count a little?"

Serval smiled. "I guess. A little. But I get so sick of watching our people settle for just a little. Sorry, baby, but you married a proud man. I guess I'm too proud for my own good sometimes."

Opal stood up and carried the bowl to the sink. "There's no such thing as too proud in the UNIA, Serval. Descendants of kings are supposed to be proud."

* * *

Early the following morning, Opal sensed the empty spot where her husband should have been, and sprang to a sitting position. "Serval?"

Serval stepped back into the bedroom from the hallway, as he fastened the top button of his uniform shirt. "Right here, baby."

"Serval, what are you doing in your uniform?"

"Got somewhere to go this morning, that's all. I've put it off for too long as it is. And it's gotta be done in uniform."

"But you never said anything about it . . . You're not in any trouble, are you?"

"No, nothing like that. I just decided it was time to get myself organized. To face my fears and weaknesses. Let's just say that it's time for the U.S. Army to pay an official visit to some folks. And I'm the representative. Unofficially, that is. And after that, I'm getting myself a job."

Opal watched him remove his French medal from his uniform jacket and place it into its box, but didn't question him.

He leaned over her and took her face in his hands. "One kiss, baby. For luck."

* * *

Serval's first stop was 630 Miller Avenue in Brooklyn at the home of Mr. and Mrs. William Watts, Red's parents. After reminiscing about Red over breakfast, the conversation inevitably drifted to the subject of his death. Avoiding the grisly details, Serval reassured a tearful Mrs. Watts that her son had died valiantly, without the lingering pain suffered by so many others. After promising to stay in contact, he left them to pay a second, more difficult visit.

Upon arriving at 1220 Ettinger Street, Serval hesitated before climbing the steps. After standing on the sidewalk for several minutes, he took a deep breath, and stepped up to ring the bell. It took three rings before the door finally opened. Serval's rigid military training was the only thing that kept him from gasping out loud. Peering out at him were Jimmy Coles' eyes, but in the face of a middle-aged woman. She was almost as tall as Serval, with dark skin and graying hair tied back in a blue scarf. The eyes traveled slowly and suspiciously up and down his uniform and finished with a scowl.

"What'chu want?" she snapped.

"Mrs. Coles, ma'am?"

"I'm Miz Coles. And I *said* what'chu want?"

"My name is Serval Rivard. I—I was a friend of Jimmy's."

Her eyes narrowed. "You' a damn lie. Jimmy ain't had no friends. Now y'all awready done tole me he' dead, so . . . so why you still botherin' me?"

Serval hesitated, but the break in her voice prompted him to continue. "Mrs. Coles," he said softly. "I was with your son . . . well, when he died. And you're wrong. Jimmy did make two friends in our outfit— me and Red Watts. He was . . . he meant a lot to us. A lot more than you could ever know. Please. Could I come in and talk to you for just a few minutes?"

After studying him for a moment more, she stepped back and motioned for him to enter. The shades were drawn, leaving the interior of the house in shadows. One small lamp gave off an eerie glow in the far corner of the room. The absence of sound and natural light created a lifeless void—the dreary evidence of Mrs. Coles' solitary existence.

Waiting for her to sit down, Serval noticed a small table holding nothing but a silver-framed picture of Jimmy. An involuntary shudder ran through him, carrying with it the unshakable memory of that day: the tree, the bloody rope, the burial . . .

Mrs. Coles was staring at him. "Sit down, young man."

"Uh, yes, ma'am. Thank you, ma'am." Serval sat directly across from her on a faded gray settee. Gazing back at the picture of Jimmy, Serval murmured, "He was a good man, Mrs. Coles."

"Hmmph. Now I know you lyin'. That chile wasn't nothin' but a troublemaker. Never was right ever since . . ."

Her abrupt halt gave Serval the opening he had been waiting for. "Ever since his father was murdered. You see, Mrs. Coles, I did know Jimmy. He told me all about that."

She bowed her head and stared at her hands, which were clasped tightly in her lap. Serval watched her closely, and flinched when a teardrop fell from her eye to the top of her hand. She swiped at it with a handkerchief and then met his gaze. "He wouldn'ta tole you that 'less he trusted you. Seem' like he was 'shamed of the way his Daddy died. So I guess you must be tellin' the truth, Mr.—uh, I'm sorry, chile. What'cha say yo' name was again?"

"Serval Rivard. Please call me Serval, Mrs. Coles."

She smiled at him for the first time. "Serval. Well, Serval . . ." She paused and stared at the picture. "Like I done tole you, seem' like

Jimmy was mad at the whole world after his Daddy died. He was only nine, and he saw . . . the whole thing. He saw everything them white men done to my James. And he didn't jus' hate white folks after that. He hated everybody. Even took to hollerin' at me, wantin' to know how come didn't nobody help his Daddy. Gettin' into fights at school and backtalkin' his teachers 'til they jus' throwed him out the schoolhouse. Well, anyway, he finally did straighten up some when he started talkin' 'bout gettin' in that Army. That was the first thing I ever seen him get so excited about. But I guess he didn't get to be a soldier for too long, huh? Not from what that other Army gentleman done tole me. My boy died soon as he got over there."

The hairs on the back of Serval's neck bristled. "He . . . what? I'm sorry, Mrs. Coles, just what did that other Army gentleman tell you?"

"He jus' tole me that my boy . . . my Jimmy was killed the first week after his boat got to France. You said you was there . . ."

"Oh, yes, ma'am." Serval nodded with false conviction. He had expected a cover-up about the lynching, but had only guessed at what form it would take. "Was he in uniform, Mrs. Coles? The man who came to tell you the news? Was he an officer?"

"Yes." She leaned forward expectantly. "You tryin' to tell me sump'm, boy?"

Serval blinked at her. *Oh, God. I can't break her heart with the truth.*

"Please answer me, son. You tryin' to tell me sump'm. I can see it in yo' face."

"Yes, ma'am. I am." Serval smiled to cover the fact that he was improvising. *Good,* he thought. *If the lyin' bastards saw fit to relocate Jimmy's death to a French battlefield, then hell. Just change the enemy from a gang of southern crackers to the German Army, and Jimmy's an official hero . . .*

Mrs. Coles reached across the coffee table to touch Serval's arm. "What is it? Please . . . what'chu tryin' to tell me, son?"

Serval patted her hand. "I'm just angry, Mrs. Coles, because the officer who visited you obviously didn't tell you how courageously your son died."

Her eyes widened. "Jimmy? No, the gentleman didn't say nothin' 'bout that. What he said was that Jimmy was diggin' latrines when his unit got attacked by some, uh, oh, what' that man call it? Random fire. Some'a them German bombs or sump'm."

Serval swallowed hard. "Latrines? They told you he got killed—

diggin' latrines? . . . Listen, Mrs. Coles. You—you know they don't
want us to get too proud. I bet that's why they killed your husband,
wasn't it? He was probably standin' up to 'em. Am I right?"

Her bottom lip quivered when she answered. "Yes. I feels guilty to
this day for all that troublin' I gave that man. I stayed on that po' man's
back tellin' him to jus' leave it alone and don't give 'em no backtalk.
Wasn't 'til I buried him that I understood. He knowed his boy was
watchin' that day. He jus' couldn't let Jimmy see his Daddy get kicked
down by that white trash no mo'. So he jus' went ahead on and died—
like the natural man he was."

Serval closed his eyes. *Like father, like son.*

"Well, Mrs. Coles, that's why I came to see you today. To make sure
you got the right story. I wanted you to know that your son died a hero.
He fought right up to the end. . . . Oh! I almost forgot the most important thing."

Serval opened the box containing his own Croix de Guerre, and
handed it to her. "It's the French medal of honor," he said softly. "The
Croix de Guerre is the highest honor the French government bestows,
and all of us earned it, especially the ones who gave their lives for . . .
for freedom, like Jimmy."

Mrs. Coles dabbed at her eyes. "You mean—you mean this a medal
my Jimmy won? It's for him?"

"Yes, ma'am."

Lifting the medal from the box, she whispered, "Well, how come
you ain't wearin' yours?"

Serval was surprised at the smoothness of his own quick lie. "My
parents have mine on display in a china cabinet where everybody can
see it." He smiled. "Maybe you ought'a do the same thing. Put it over
here by his picture, Mrs. Coles."

"I will. I think that's a real nice idea. I—I want folks to know my
Jimmy turned out awright after all. But now, tell me sump'm, son. How
come that Army man didn't give it to me when he come to tell me
about . . . about my boy dyin'?"

"We fought under French command, Mrs. Coles. We should've
won American medals too. But we're not holding our breath about
that. And it's all right. I'll take the sincerity of the French over the . . .
well, let's just say we never expected anything from the U.S. Army. Not
after the way they treated us. We had our own reasons for fighting, Mrs.
Coles. So you just be proud of Jimmy. I know I am."

\* \* \*

Serval considered going home to change clothes after his visit with Mrs. Coles, but decided that his military uniform might be an asset at his next scheduled stop.

He climbed the steps to the office at 120 West 138th Street, and quietly stepped inside. The Liberty Hall office was small, with two desks and several file cabinets crowding an entire wall. Hanging over the door leading to a hallway was a banner: *One God; One Aim; One Destiny.* The office appeared deserted until Serval heard a heated discussion between two men speaking in clipped West Indian accents, then saw them approaching from the long hallway. When they stepped into the room and saw Serval, their conversation came to an abrupt stop. Serval knew the man nearest him as William Mathis, the author of the leaflets he'd been distributing. The other man eyed Serval suspiciously and strode over to one of the desks. "Is there something we can do for you, young man?" he asked.

"Yes, sir," Serval said, removing his hat.

William Mathis tapped his temple with his forefinger and smiled. "Ah, yes! You're one of the leaflet volunteers, aren't you? I didn't recognize you in your uniform. What was your name, son?"

"Serval Rivard, sir."

"May I present Mr. Cyril Crichlow? He's one of our organizers for the commission to Liberia."

"Oh! Yes, sir," Serval said. "I read about that on the leaflets. Very exciting!"

Cyril Crichlow nodded and gestured in a rapid circular motion with his hand. "Are you here for more leaflets?"

"No, sir. I mean, yes, I'll take more, of course. But what I really came for was . . ."

William Mathis patted Serval's shoulder. "We don't mean to rush you, my boy, but we have a million things to do today."

"I'd like a job, sir," Serval blurted out.

The two men exchanged an amused look. "And what sort of a job do you think you're suited for, Mr. Rivard?" Mathis asked.

"Anything, sir. I don't require a high wage, just enough to support my wife, and I'll do anything, sir. I'm a dues-paying member of the UNIA, and I believe in the precepts and . . ."

Mathis laughed. "Quite a dedicated lad we have here, eh, Cyril?

Now, Mr. Rivard, why don't you take a seat at the secretary's desk over there while she's at lunch, and fill out our standard employment form. Please be thorough about your skills and educational background." He handed Serval a pen and pulled out the chair for him. "Now. I have a short meeting in another room, but I'll be back in a few minutes to see what you have to offer the UNIA."

After the two men left, Serval carefully answered each question on the form. He was pacing impatiently when William Mathis returned fifteen minutes later.

"All right, Mr. Rivard," Mathis murmured as he perused the form. "I'm sure you've heard about the many UNIA undertakings. Perhaps we can find something for you . . ." He looked up at Serval and smiled. "You attended Morehouse?"

"Yes, sir."

"And I can only assume that your reason for not graduating had something to do with the war?"

"Well, yes, sir."

"But may I ask why you are not continuing your education now that the war is over?"

"Sir, as I said before, I'm starting a family . . . I may go back to school someday, but right now I need gainful employment."

Mathis nodded his head as he continued reading. "Since you understand military structure, I'll explain it this way, Mr. Rivard. No one begins with a high rank in the UNIA. Just as in the U.S. army, even a general must begin as a private."

"Of course, sir."

"We must be assured of your willingness to toil in even the lowliest of positions before delegating more responsibility to you. Now I'm sure you've heard about our efforts to branch out into the shipping industry. But in addition to that, we operate our own grocery stores, a laundry, a restaurant, a tailoring shop, and we publish our own books and newspaper . . ."

"*The Negro World,*" Serval said, smiling. "I've always liked writing . . ."

Mathis held up one hand. "Ah, ah, ah. Not so fast, young man. We begin with small steps. I'm sure you won't forget how to write in the next few months. And if things work out, that may very well be the position you'll win. But as it happens, we have a position which needs filling at the laundry. How do you feel about that?"

Serval nodded. "Anything, sir."

"Very well, then. Be here at 8:00 o'clock tomorrow morning, and we'll put you to work for the UNIA."

"Thank you, sir."

*   *   *

When Serval turned off the bedroom lamp and kissed Opal goodnight, he anticipated the worry-free sleep of a gainfully employed man. But after Opal fell asleep, the thrill of his new job with the UNIA was replaced by thoughts of his visit with Jimmy Coles' mother. Her voice elicited visions of death, and the disturbance followed him into sleep.

The image of Red hanging tangled in the wire shifted and blurred until it was Jimmy Coles swinging toward him from the tree in training camp. A crowd of featureless white faces swarmed around him. Jimmy's eyes were dead, and when he opened his mouth, he spoke in Captain Welch's voice: *How does a mother say goodbye to a dead son who's only listed as missing . . . ? It's cruel, it's cruel. Help me! . . . Don't leave me here, Rivard! Don't leave me here . . .*

Serval reached for him, but stopped when the barbed-wire began to bite and cut into his legs. He kicked at it and struggled to scream, but a tightness in his throat silenced him. *The wire!* Tighter. He gulped for air, and at last the scream came, a feeble croak. "Help me! Don't leave me here!"

He heard Opal's voice in the distance, and moved toward it. "Serval?" she called. "Serval, what—what is it?"

Serval sprang from a prone position to his hands and knees in the center of the bed. He stared at Opal with wild eyes, his chest heaving. She cringed against the headboard, watching him. The swinging medallion around his neck terrified him, and he clawed wildly at it. "Get it off me! Get me out . . ." He blinked at his surroundings, and dropped his arms to his sides in an abrupt stillness. The broken chain and medallion lay in front of him on the bed.

Opal reached for him and hesitantly touched his chest. "Oh, Serval, you're soakin' wet! Let me get you a towel to dry off with."

When she rose, he clutched at her hand. "Don't leave me here."

She sat back down. "I'm right here," she whispered. "I'm not going anywhere." Wrapping her arms around him, she kissed his neck, then drew back suddenly. "Serval! Look what you did to yourself! You're all scratched up! Le'me go get sump'm for it."

He grabbed her wrist roughly. "I said—don't! Don't leave me here!"

"But I'm only . . . All right, Serval. I'm here. Was it—was it a dream?"

He answered her with a series of confused eyeblinks followed by a nod.

"Here, Serval. Lay down next to me and tell me the dream. It helps to tell it."

He leaned against her stiffly, and a long silence passed before he spoke. "It was—a lynching. That was the dream, Opal. I dreamed . . . at first it was Red, but then it was Jimmy Coles. I could see it all so clear. But this time, I was there—watching. I couldn't help watching because . . ."

"Because why?"

"Because . . . I was in it. I was caught. I was caught in the wire. I couldn't get loose and I had to watch those crackers . . . everything they did to him. I saw the way his—his body jerked when they—when they hoisted him up. The way they . . ."

"Shh. It was just a dream, Serval."

He moaned. "No. Don't you see? It really happened. And it's still happening." After a long silence he continued. "I felt so helpless. I couldn't see their faces, but I know it was the same ones at that bar in Spartanburg. They stood around laughing and drinking like it was some kind'a goddamn party. I wanted to help him."

"Of course you did."

"I *really* wanted to help him, but I couldn't reach him. It was horrible. I kept trying to—to reach him."

Opal stroked his back and whispered, "Well, it's over now. It's all over."

"But that wasn't all of it. All of a sudden . . ." He stopped and his heart began to pound again. "All of a sudden, it was *me*. I could feel it around my neck—tighter and tighter . . . cutting me. And they all just stood there while I choked . . . It was *me*, Opal! And I was so afraid they'd tell Mama I was missing . . . 'cause I knew I was dead."

# Chapter 18

Serval reported early for his first day at the UNIA laundry facility to familiarize himself with his surroundings. Three young women were already at work, standing at a long tub that ran the length of one wall. A series of large spigots dotted the wall above the tub, with a scrub board under each one. Clouds of steam carried the combined smells of laundry soap, starch, and bleach, and two motorized washing machines jerked and shimmied in the far corner, splashing suds onto the floor. In the center of the room stood an assembly of long folding tables, rolling clothes racks, and canvas hampers. A neat row of ironing boards jutted out from the far wall, equipped with eight modern electric irons and two coal-heated flatirons. Serval was taking it all in when he felt a hard tapping on his shoulder. He turned around and took his first look at the formidable woman he would answer to in his new job.

Mrs. Lilah Abernathy was built like an old oak—solid and tall—a full two inches taller than Serval. She wore a long white apron with large, bulging pockets over a no-nonsense black muslin dress that nearly reached the ankles of her scuffed high-button shoes. Her complexion was the reddish-brown of Tennessee mud, and her graying hair was gathered into a crinkled bunch at the nape of her thick neck. She looked angry as she stood staring at him with her fists planted on her hips. "Mr. Rivard," she shouted over the roar of the electric washing machines. "I'll show you how to operate the equipment just once, so pay attention."

"Yes, ma'am," Serval replied.

Mrs. Abernathy shook her head. "Louder, Mr. Rivard! You gotta have a powerful set of lungs to work in here! Gotta holler all the time to be heard over these machines."

"Yes, ma'am!" he shouted.

She moved rapidly from the washing machines and ringers to the metal steaming cylinders, gesturing and shouting instructions over her shoulder. Serval studied her sturdy hands as she twisted knobs and turned cranks, and nodded, even though he heard only about half of what she was saying. She turned around to face him, then shouted his assignment: "And you'll be my pressing man, Mr. Rivard. These flatirons are heavy, so I've got my women splitting their shifts between washing and ironing. But you've got strong arms. You ought'a be able to handle the irons for a full shift." Her eyes did a cursory sweep of Serval from head to toe, as if inspecting a workhorse. "You ever help your Mama with the ironing?"

Serval shrugged. "No, ma'am."

Mrs. Abernathy shook her head. "Mm-mm-mm. You ain't never ironed a lick, have you boy?"

"No, ma'am. But I can learn."

Reaching into a canvas bin, Mrs. Abernathy pulled out a pair of damp, rumpled trousers and handed them to Serval. "Lay 'em out, Mr. Rivard. I find it's best to let somebody give it a try 'til they mess up, then correct 'em. That way, they remember better. Now how do you figure to press these pants?"

Serval held up the trousers and thought about how he liked his own creases set. After spreading the trousers out on the ironing board, he smoothed them into what he thought was a logical arrangement, then reached for the iron. He glanced over at Mrs. Abernathy, expecting to see a pleased expression.

She stood in the ever-present steam, fists on hips, frowning and shaking her head.

"What's wrong?" Serval asked.

Mrs. Abernathy rolled her eyes and held one hand to her ear.

"I said, what's wrong?" he yelled.

"Pockets, Mr. Rivard!"

Serval blinked at her, his hand still gripping the iron. "Pockets?"

Mrs. Abernathy yanked the trousers from the ironing board, turned the waistband portion inside out, and shoved his mistake under his nose. The left pocket was bunched into a rosette shape, and the right contained a bulge. Reaching inside the right pocket, she produced a wallet, shook it at Serval, then dropped it into her pocket. "All personal items you turn in! Now flatten out these pockets and try again! And once you set it right, you keep that iron moving! They'll scorch the fabric if you leave 'em on too long. Even with a stubborn crease—no more than five seconds, Mr. Rivard. Understand?"

"Yes, ma'am."

Serval smoothed the trousers, inside and out, and again reached for the iron. He turned to look at Mrs. Abernathy, who stood as still as a stone. He pressed the iron against the damp pants leg and slid it back and forth as billows of steam assaulted his face. When he set the iron aside to turn the pants, he felt Mrs. Abernathy jabbing his shoulder with her fingers. "Use the trivet, Mr. Rivard!" she shouted.

"Huh?"

She lifted the iron from the white cotton surface of the ironing board to reveal a light brown scorch, then rested the iron on its trivet. "We'll be lucky if you don't burn down the whole laundry, Mr. Rivard."

"Oh! Sorry, Mrs. Abernathy. I'll be more careful."

"And you got a double crease on that pants leg," she snapped. "Fix it."

Serval squinted at his crease and saw that there were two. When he looked up, Mrs. Abernathy had disappeared into the steam. "Okay," Serval mumbled. After smoothing the trousers again, he bent down as he lowered the iron to see his work up close, but the heat of the steam blasted his face and he jerked his head up. After working on the trousers for nearly twenty minutes, he placed the iron on the trivet, then inspected his creases. "Perfect! Well, almost perfect." Reaching into his pocket for his handkerchief, he wiped the perspiration from his forehead, then smoothed an ill-placed crinkle and pressed it out with the iron. "Now they're perfect," he said, smiling. He reached over for a hanger and hung the trousers on one of the rolling racks. "Excellent work, Mr. Rivard," he said, mimicking Mrs. Abernathy's voice. "Even with my cryptic training in screaming Mongolese, you're the best trouser-presser the UNIA has ever produced!"

He felt a familiar jab on his shoulder, and spun around to see Mrs. Abernathy standing behind him. "One piece?" she yelled. "Is that all you've done since I left you here, Mr. Rivard?"

"Well, I was . . ."

She shook her head as she turned to leave. "Snap it up, Mr. Rivard."

"Yes, ma'am."

\*    \*    \*

Serval worked doggedly during his first week, despite a lack of sleep. After waking in terror to variations of his nightmare on three successive nights, the idea of sleep filled him with dread. Mrs. Abernathy had informed him that Saturday and Sunday would be his days off from the laundry facility, so that Friday Serval opted to stay up all night.

Once Opal was asleep, Serval filled the void of silence by reading and scribbling observations in his journal. His last entry brought a smile to his lips, despite his growing concern: *And where the hell is Jack Hawkins? What has that panting, half-white Theda Bara vamp done with my poor, defenseless country-boy buddy?*

As morning broke, he was filling the percolator with water for his second pot of coffee. The telephone rang, and he hurried into the living room to answer it. "Hello?" he said softly.

"Why ya whisperin'?" a familiar deep voice asked.

"Jack! Oh, Opal's still asleep and I'm trying not to wake her. It's about time you called! I thought you were dead! Where the hell have you been?"

"Well . . . I know you saw that Creola. Opal's friend? Uh . . . well . . ."

"Say no more. I saw the way she was lookin' at you."

"Mm-hmm. Well, that's where I been. But, uh, it ain't like I can stay here much longer and . . ."

"Jack. I told you before we came back that you're more than welcome to stay with Opal and me. I *told* you that."

"Well, see, Creola' been real, uh, nice to me since I got here and, well, I thought you and yo' wife be wantin' to be alone awhile 'fo I showed up."

Serval laughed. "Well, I can't argue with that. We've been makin' up for lost time, my baby and me. But Jack . . ."

"What?"

"Do you mean to tell me that you've been stayin' there with that—Creola . . . all this time? You're not gettin' serious about her, are you?"

"Well, she ain't zackly a marryin' kind'a girl, but I don't think she' be wantin' to get married no way. I mean, she ain't like Opal. Yo' wife be the kind'a girl a man be proud to take home to meet his Mama."

"Thank you, Jack. I'm a blessed man, all right. But let's get back to you. When are you comin' to stay with us?"

"Well, if you sure it be awright . . ."

"I'm sure."

"Ya know I ain't found me no job yet . . ."

"Well, I finally found one. I get to press pants while my face melts off."

"Huh?"

"I work in a torture chamber, Jack. The Krauts must've invented laundries. Slow death by steam."

"What'chu talkin' 'bout?"

Serval laughed. "I'll explain when you get here. Come on over and bring your gear. Besides, Mr. Garvey's speaking tomorrow night and I want to take you. Oh! Guess you need a ride, huh?"

"Naw. Creola's friend got a car. She' takin' her to that nightclub she' work at, and they said they could drop me on the way. See, I was kind'a countin' on ya, brotha."

"Good. We'll be right here waiting for you. You still have the address?"

"Creola say she know where y'all live. Hey, thanks a lot, hear? 'Cause, Serval, between you and me, this woman was wearin' me out!"

\* \* \*

Opal and Serval welcomed Jack like a prodigal son come home. Despite Opal's repeated protests about too many cooks in a too-small kitchen, Jack and Serval insisted on helping her prepare a large, unconventional supper. After tasting full-course samples of each other's masterpieces, they settled down near the fireplace for coffee.

Jack rubbed his stomach and stretched. "See? I told y'all I could make cawnbread."

"Aww, I don't know," Serval said. "Your cornbread was all right, but my baby's spaghetti was the best thing on the table. Next to my catfish, that is."

Opal rolled her eyes. "Catfish, cornbread, and spaghetti. Oh, well, I guess that was what'cha call a real balanced meal, huh? See, Serval? That's what happens when you men start foolin' around in my kitchen. From now on, if you fellas want to cook supper, be my guest. But when I'm cookin', I don't want to see either of you set one big foot in there, you hear me?"

"Yes, ma'am!" Serval winked at Jack and they both saluted Opal.

Jack chuckled softly. "Shoot, I'm full. I don't know who be makin' up the rules 'bout what go' wit' what on a plate, but it sho' tasted good!"

The telephone rang and Serval groaned. "I can't get up, baby. Would you get it?"

"Oh, Lord, Serval, I sure spoiled you rotten fast." She stood up, threw a sofa pillow at him, and headed for the telephone. "Hello?"

After a long pause followed by a gasp, Opal said, "Don't worry, Daddy. We'll be right there." She returned the receiver to the cradle, and walked back toward Serval with a dazed expression on her face. "Mr. Saunders just fired Daddy!"

\* \* \*

Leon Jackson wasted no time scrambling into Serval's car when they pulled up to the Saunders' home. "Drive, boy!" he commanded.

Turning around in her seat, Opal fretted, "Just one little suitcase, Daddy? What about the rest of your stuff?"

"Don't worry, child. I'll get it later. Jus' get me on out'a here. Mr. Saunders say if I ain't off the place instantly—you know how he' say that, Opal, 'do such-and-such *instantly*. He be meanin' business when he use that word! Anyway, he done looked out that front window three times, and I jus' knew the police was comin' any minute!"

"The police?! Daddy, what kind'a trouble are you in?"

Leon shrugged and suddenly took notice of the large man sitting to his right in the back seat. Jack hadn't spoken a word, but even seated, his height was startling.

"Damn, boy! You' one big fella!"

Serval did a quick introduction. "Jack Hawkins, this is Opal's father, Leon Jackson. Leon, this is Jack Hawkins, an army buddy of mine. He was with the 371st over in France with me. He was the one . . ."

"Aww, sure! You the fella that saved my son-in-law from the Krauts! Opal read me the letter 'bout that! Well, son, it's good to meet'cha!"

Opal let out a loud sigh. "Daddy, please! *What* did you do to make Mr. Saunders call the police on you?"

Glancing first at Jack, then at the rear view mirror into Serval's expectant eyes, Leon said ruefully, "Well, baby, I—I . . . guess I been—bootleggin'."

\* \* \*

Upon their return to her apartment, Opal tossed her pocketbook onto the coffee table and squared off with her father. "So, Daddy. How long have you been a criminal?" she snapped.

"Oh, Lawd, Opal. It ain't like really bein' a crim . . ."

"Didn't you hear about the Volstead Act, Daddy? It was in all the newspapers, you know."

"Honey, I jus' needed a little mo' money and it seemed like a way. I mean, you ought'a know that little ol' pay I was gettin' from Mr. Saunders wasn't . . ."

"It used to be enough before you met that *Manché* woman, Daddy! And don't call me honey!"

Leon sighed. "Opal, ya ain't got to say her name like that. She' a real good woman. She jus' like' to have a good time, is all."

"Huh! A damn expensive good time, if you ask me!"

Serval's eyebrows shot up and he suppressed a laugh at hearing her swear for the first time. He stood between Opal and her father, amused at her nonstop attack and at Leon's feeble attempts to defend himself. The argument began to resemble a comedic tennis match, prompting Serval to give Jack a furtive "let's-get-out-of-here" look.

But Leon spotted them meandering toward the door, and seized the opportunity for a break in Opal's inquisition. "Oh, no, fellas! Y'all ain't got to leave. Hey, I know. Look, here. I got a little hooch in a flask . . . y'all fellas want some?"

"Daddy!" Opal screeched. "You get that stuff out of here right now! Oh, I never knew I could get so mad at you! I—I'm goin' to bed!" With that, she stomped down the hall and slammed the bedroom door.

Serval couldn't hide his amusement as he slowly backed out of the front room. "Uh, Jack? I showed you where the blankets are. Just show Leon, and, uh, you two just work out your sleeping arrangements, I guess."

"You ain't goin' to bed too?" Jack protested. "It ain't but nine o'clock."

"Hey, I'm a considerate husband, Jack. I don't want my wife to get lonely. Besides, I think Leon's countin' on me to soften her up a little so he won't have to go another round with her in the morning. Right, Leon?"

Leon nodded. "You' awright, son. Yeah, go soften her up. Lawd, she was mad!"

Serval grinned at a glaring Jack, then saluted and executed an about-face before heading to the bedroom.

"G'night, Mistah Hospitality!" Jack called. ". . . Hey, Leon. You play poker?"

# Chapter 19

Early the next morning, from his blanket on the floor, Jack watched with amusement as Leon gathered his belongings and tiptoed toward the front door. Raising up on one elbow, he debated over whether or not to say goodbye. Leon's attempt to silently unlock the front door failed, and Jack swallowed back a laugh when the lock mechanism clicked loudly. Leon cursed under his breath and crouched low, like an escaping convict caught in the searchlights.

"Ain't gotta worry 'bout wakin' me up, Mr. Jackson," Jack said, laughing. "I been awake since sunup."

"Shh!" Leon shot a worried glance in the direction of the hallway leading to his daughter's bedroom and then tiptoed closer to Jack. "It ain't you I'm worried 'bout wakin' up, big fella. I don't want Opal askin' me where I'm goin' is all. Lawd! That child got her Mama's temper, that's for sho'!"

Jack chuckled and sat up, yawning. "Ya mean you ain't stayin here?"

Leon grinned. "Naw," he whispered. "You young fellas ain't got the market on the ladies, ya know. I know Opal don't like Manché, but she ain't got to. I'm a man and I wants to be with my woman. That's natural, ain't it?"

"Yes, suh. Mighty natural."

"Well, see, to Opal I ain't nothin' but a Daddy. She worries about me too damn much. Shit! I knows how to take care of ma'self! I know she' gon' be mad when she figures out where I done gone, but if I'm quick, I won't haf'ta listen to it!"

"Well, take care'a ya'self, Mr. Jackson."

Leon grinned. "Ain't got to, big fella. Manché takes good care'a me. Mmm-mmm-mmm. Manché, Manché . . ."

"Uh, what kind'a name is that anyhow—Manché?"

"Oh, she' half squaw, man! Her Mama was a runaway slave and her Daddy was a full-blooded Comanche. She got some real long Indian name like, uh, Sun-Risin'-on-the-Hill-Over-Yonder or some mess, so everybody jus' called her Comanche since she was little. When she started singin', she jus' kind'a fancied it up wit' that French soundin' Man-shay. Pretty as she wanna be, too!" With a worried glance down the hall, Leon whispered, "Don't you tell Opal where I went. Jus' say I was gone when you woke up, hear?"

"Yes, suh. Uh, Mr. Jackson?"

"Mmm-hmm?"

Jack grinned and rubbed the top of his head. "Make sho' ya don't rile that woman, hear?"

*　*　*

Manché Redriver lived above her place of employment, a speakeasy called The Brass Door, in a small coldwater flat. Many of the first-time patrons of The Brass Door were surprised at the name, upon facing a regular oak door like any other. It wasn't until they were led through the foyer to the second door that the name was explained. At eye-level on the second portal, was a tiny, hinged square of gleaming brass, which opened from the inside. As a pair of eyes peered at the patrons through the brass opening, they were expected to relay a code word that was changed weekly.

Local police had begun to tighten up on the illegal serving of liquor, hoping to cash in on Prohibition, as had so many others. The day of the payoff was at hand, but Max Hightower, the owner of The Brass Door, was a holdout, refusing to fatten the bankrolls of greedy police officers in exchange for a raid reprieve.

The situation worried Manché, who loved to sing, but was unaware of the extent of her natural talent. After her third husband left her, she had frantically worried about taking care of herself with no prospects for employment. Sheer desperation gave her the courage to audition for Max Hightower, and she was shocked to be hired. But this new trouble with the police brought all her old fears back to the surface. If The Brass Door closed down, she feared the loss of her livelihood. Once again, poverty loomed.

Her singing was not the kind that caught the attention of club managers vying for the brightest vocal stylists, but Manché possessed a distinctive sound. Her unique raspy tones lured patrons back night after night for her melancholy stories told in song. And the more stingers she drank, the bluer her tones became, intensifying her powers of mesmerism over her audience until the wee hours of the morning. The first time Leon Jackson heard her, he became an ardent admirer.

Manché Redriver was not the most beautiful of women by conventional standards of the day, but her plumpness was concentrated in all the right places, at least as far as Leon was concerned. Her features seemed to defy time itself, wearing her forty-five years well. With narrow, black eyes, deeply set above prominent cheek bones and shadowed by a proud forehead, she was the color of burnished copper and epitomized the nobility and earthy beauty of the American Indian. But it was her long thick mane of black curls that Leon loved best. She was a perfect blend of African and Comanche characteristics, and she was Leon Jackson's angel.

Manché stood at the sink filling a large pot with water to heat downstairs for a bath, when she heard Leon's knock. Opening the door a crack, she peered out over the chain lock before letting him in.

"What'chu doin' here, Sugah? Wasn't expectin' you this mornin'."

Leon sat heavily on the edge of the bed. "Aww, baby. Have I got news for you. But 'fo I start the story, I need a favor. Ya think it'd be okay if I stayed here wit'chu for awhile?"

"Why, sho', honey. You can stay right here wit' Manché long as you need to. Oh, and Leon?"

"Mmm-hmm?"

Leaning over to kiss him, she whispered, "Did'ya bring Manché sump'm to drink, baby?"

*     *     *

Opal prepared breakfast for Serval and Jack in a noisy manner, slamming pots and pans around and muttering under her breath, which left the men unsure of how to react. Deciding that silence was the best approach, Serval and Jack ate their breakfast of scrambled eggs, hotcakes, and biscuits with their heads down and no conversation.

Opal suddenly turned around and glared at them.

"Serval."

"Mm-hmm?"

"You don't have to act like I'm some kind'a complete ravin' lunatic, you know."

Glancing up at Opal, Serval risked a smile. "Well, ya might not be a complete lunatic, baby, but you were definitely raving!"

"Daddy just makes me so doggone mad, Serval! I mean . . ."

"Uh, uh, uh," he said shaking his head and pulling her into his lap. "Don't get started again, Mrs. Rivard. Don't you think it might be time for you to let your little Daddy fly out of the nest?"

Opal sighed. "I guess you're right. I mean he is a man, and we all know what fools you men can be!"

Jack chuckled. "Well, this here fool gotta go find a job today. Don't know about that other fool you hangin' onto, Miz Rivard, but I gotta get movin'."

"Where to, Jack?" Serval asked.

"Well, I thought maybe haulin' or sump'm. Maybe I can pick up some day work down at them docks even if it is Sunday."

Serval shrugged. "Well, it's my day off, so maybe I ought'a go with you. We can use the extra money. Baby, we'll be back when we're back, so don't bother cookin' anything." He kissed her and grinned. "Just wait 'til we get home and me and Jack'll help you cook."

"Oh, no you won't! I am not eatin' any more catfish-and-spaghetti dinners, thank you very much! I'll cook by myself and keep sump'm warm for you. Now, you two get on out'a here before you get any more crazy ideas!"

*    *    *

When Serval and Jack returned that evening, Opal evicted them before the door was shut behind them. "Oh, Lord! You two smell like dead fish! Get out!" she shouted, pushing them back out. "You're stinkin' up the whole apartment!"

Serval stumbled backward against Jack until they were both back in the hallway, then Opal firmly shut the door. Knocking lightly, Serval leaned close to the door and called out in a pathetic voice. "But baby! We're hungry! You aren't gonna turn us away after we worked so hard all day, are you? We've got money, see? We found work on a shrimp boat."

"A shrimp boat, huh?" Opal shouted back. "What did you do, Serval? Bring a bunch'a shrimp home in your pockets? Ooh, Lord, y'all stink!"

"Baby, be reasonable. If you let us in, we promise to take baths before we sit down at the table."

"Yeah," Jack called. "I'll wash up right out on ya front—uh, hey, Serval, what'cha call a porch out here again?"

"A stoop."

"Oh, yeah. Hey, Opal! I'll wash up right out on the stoop if ya jus' throws me a cake'a soap an' a bucket a'water. But ya neighbors prob'ly won't like it much."

Holding her nose, Opal finally opened the apartment door and stepped back as the two men sprinted past her toward the bathroom.

"Leave those nasty clothes outside the bathroom door and I'll come and get 'em," she shouted. ". . . Then I'ma burn 'em."

By the time Serval and Jack had scrubbed and sat down at the kitchen table, Opal was ladling hot gravy over heaps of mashed potatoes on three plates. "Got some good news for you gentlemen, now that you *are* gentlemen again."

"Oh, baby, this food smells good. What kind'a news?"

Opal sat down and folded her hands, grinning at them like the Cheshire cat. "Well . . ."

Serval laughed. "What are you grinnin' at, baby?"

"I've got a job for Jack. A *real* job."

Jack and Serval looked at each other in surprise, but were too hungry to stop eating. Serval swallowed quickly. "How?"

"I caught the bus over to the Saunders' house to have a talk with Mrs. Saunders about Daddy gettin' fired. Serval, you know what? Mr. Saunders fired Daddy because he found two crates full of bootleg whiskey in the trunk of his touring car! Daddy could've gotten Mr. Saunders arrested! Well, anyway, Mrs. Saunders was goin' on about how they didn't know where they would find another chauffeur as efficient as Daddy, but that Mr. Saunders would never hire Daddy back after what he did—and I thought of Jack. I hope you don't mind, Serval. I know how you feel about the Saunders and all, but it might be just the thing for Jack."

"So, what did you do, baby? Tell Mrs. Saunders Jack would take the job?"

"Mm-hmm. I told her how he was a war veteran looking for work and all, and she said bring him over Wednesday to meet Mr. Saunders. I know her, too, Serval. Jack's as good as in. And the best part is, Jack, I know you've been worried about a place to stay, even though me and Serval don't mind if you stay forever with us. But if you work for the Saunders, you can live in the basement servants' quarters where me and Daddy used to live, and Aida'll cook you all the food you can eat and . . ." Opal stopped, suddenly aware that Serval and Jack were laughing at her. "What's so doggone funny, you two?"

Serval nodded at Jack. "You wanna tell her or should I?"

"You tell her. I don't have the heart."

"What?" Opal snapped. "One'a you better tell me!"

"Baby," Serval said, choking back a laugh. "Jack can't drive."

Opal glared first at Serval and then at Jack for a minute, before unfolding her napkin and placing it on her lap. Reaching for her fork, she said in a calm voice, "Is that all?"

Serval and Jack blinked at each other and Serval placed his fork on his plate. "Opal, didn't you hear me? How's Jack supposed to be the Saunders' chauffeur when he can't drive?"

Opal swallowed her food and took a leisurely drink of water. "Well, Jack, you've got three whole days to learn."

*   *   *

"Okay, Jack," Serval said, pointing at the floorboard. "This is the clutch and this is the brake. And this other one is the accelerator. Got it so far?"

"Uh-huh. Got it."

"Now. You remember the part about the gears, right?"

"Right."

Serval closed his eyes and shook his head. "Guess there's only one way to really get the feel of it. Take her for a spin."

"Who, *me*?"

"Who the hell else?"

"I thought you was gon' let me watch you do it first or sump'm, man."

"Jack, you've seen me drive every day since we got back from France. Haven't you been payin' attention?"

"Well . . ."

"Come on, now. Let's start her up."

Once the Pierce-Arrow's engine was rumbling, Serval said, "Okay, now what?"

"Uh, the accelerator? No, wait—the clutch, right?"

"But what gear is it supposed to be in, Jack?"

"Uh, damn. Ya better go over that gear stuff one mo' time, Serval."

Serval rolled his eyes and mimicked Opal in a high-pitched voice: "Don't know how to drive, Jack? Oh, is that all? Well, you've got three whole days to learn . . ."

"Come on, Serval," Jack groused. "Go over it again. I really want this job, man."

Serval looked hard at Jack for a moment. "You sure? I mean, the Saunders aren't exactly the nicest white folks in the world, Jack. You'll probably hate 'em."

"I needs me a job, Serval. Long as they gon' pay me a wage, I'll worry 'bout hatin' 'em later."

Serval shrugged. "Okay. Let's go over it again . . ."

\* \* \*

After taking intense driving lessons for three evenings, Jack and Serval burst into Opal's kitchen as she prepared supper, and abducted her.

"Lord, Serval! At least let me turn off the oven and take off my apron!"

After a bumpy start, Jack drove the Pierce-Arrow almost as smoothly as Serval did down 130th Street to Lenox Avenue, then turned left, and circled the block. His stops and starts were nearly perfect, and he turned a few extra corners to show off. As they pulled up to the front of the apartment, Opal squealed and applauded.

"See? I knew you could do it, Jack! Now, all you've gotta do is learn your way around New York!"

Jack put the car in park and rested his forehead on the steering wheel. "Aw, hell," he groaned. "How many hours I got left to learn that?"

\* \* \*

Aida Johnson stared up at Jack's face as he ducked under the kitchen doorjamb. "Mm-mm-mm!" she murmured, shaking her head. "It's gonna take me some time to get use'ta your height, boy! But sit on down here and I'll fix you a plate."

"Thank you, ma'am. Smells real good."

"It's pot roast, honey," Aida said, smiling. "My specialty. And I'm loadin' you down with mashed potatoes and gravy, 'cause a fella big as you just got to have an appetite to match. And you' gettin' some'a these greens too, whether you like it or not." She placed the steaming plate before Jack, and then pushed a basket covered with a tea towel in his direction. "Hot buttered biscuits," she said, lifting the tea towel. "And peach pie for desert."

Jack reached for his fork, then looked over at Aida. "Uh, ain'tchu eatin', ma'am?"

"Oh, I ate an hour ago. I been keepin' this hot for you. Now go on and eat, boy! Before you drool all over the table!"

The instant Jack began eating, Aida settled back in her chair. "Mm-hmm. I knew you were hungry. Go ahead! Wolf it down, boy! Ain't gotta put on airs for ol' Aida."

Jack nodded, and ate faster.

"You know Mr. Saunders really likes you, young man," Aida said.

Jack swallowed and looked up. "He do?"

"Mm-hmm. I heard him talkin' to the Missus at supper this evenin' and he said he had to spend a mint at his tailor's gettin' your uniform made special. You know, on account'a your height. He was talkin' 'bout, 'That Hawkins is certainly a quiet boy. Don't hear a peep out of him 'cept for yes, sir, Mr. Saunders and no, sir, Mr. Saunders.'" Aida laughed. "See, Leon was real talky. Ran his mouth constantly, but I sure do miss him. He was always in here tellin' us his silly stories, makin' us laugh 'til Miz Saunders had to come in here to shush us. Mr. Saunders likes a quiet house."

Jack shrugged. "Well, he seem patient enough, givin' me directions— tellin' me where to turn and where to wait. But I hate it when he be callin' me Hawkins."

Aida sighed. "I know. Sometimes a paycheck costs a lot'a pride." She patted his hand. Now, you ready for that pie?"

*　*　*

Two weeks later, Jack tapped on Serval's back door for their regular Sunday dinner. Opal opened the screen door and stretched up to hug him. "Well, you sure look happy this evenin', Jack!"

"I am," he said.

Serval was pulling out a chair from the table. "What's got you so happy, Jack? You meet a pretty girl or sump'm?"

Jack shook his head and sat down. "Nope. I quit on ol' man Saunders."

Opal gasped. "What are you talkin' about, Jack? You wanted a job so bad . . ."

Jack smiled cryptically. "Oh, I got me a job."

Serval passed Jack a plate and grinned with anticipation. "Doin' what?"

"I went down and got me a job with the Pullman Company. Ya know, as a porter. I'm fixin' to be a travelin' man! Now, what's cookin', Miz Opal?"

Opal laughed and stared at Serval, who grinned and shrugged his shoulders. "Well, Mrs. Rivard, you heard the man! Looks like we got another mouth to feed around here. Uh, you *will* be gracing us with your presence, won't you, Jack? When you're not off bein' a travelin' man, that is?"

"Sho' will. 'Til I can find a little place of my own."

# Chapter 20

William Mathis pushed the rolling chair away from his desk and yawned as he looked at his pocket watch. "Oh, my—eleven-twenty. Ruth will be angry." As he stood up to gather his papers, the front door to the UNIA office creaked open.

"Is that you, Cyril? Is the meeting just over?"

"Yes, Will. I've just left Mr. Garvey's residence. He has a new project in the works, and well, you know how excited he gets . . . But it looks like a late night for you, as well."

Will sighed. "Well . . . I was going over the books again, and the stock certificates. So much to do."

Cyril leaned his fists on the desk and leveled his eyes at him. "We need help. There are simply not enough of us to carry out the tasks already before us. And the plans he was talking about tonight . . . Will, it's happening. The global expansion he always speaks of is actually happening. The ships, the traveling . . ."

"Calm down, Cyril. We have a long list of men and women who are begging for assignments."

Cyril sighed and dropped into the chair across from Will. "So the time has come for delegation. And so another task." He laughed and rubbed his eyes.

"Wait a minute," Will said, shuffling through the papers on the desk. "There's a lad I've had my eye on since the first day he set foot in this very office. You met him yourself, Cyril. The soldier."

"Ah, yes, I remember. Very enthusiastic young man, as I recall," Cyril laughed.

Will produced the application and waved it in the air. "Not just enthusiastic, Cyril. This young man attended Morehouse. I wrote the school, and the Dean himself responded. Apparently, this Serval Rivard's grades were top drawer! He received high marks in every subject, but excelled in world history, creative writing, English grammar, and literature . . ." He looked up at Cyril and smiled broadly as he continued.

"And last but not least, it seems our Mr. Rivard was the captain of the debate team."

Cyril reached into his pocket and pulled out two cigars. Passing one to Will, he said, "A persuasive pitch man. Possibly a speech writer."

"An orator," Will added.

"If he's willing to travel, he could be a great asset to us in increasing membership."

Will lit Cyril's cigar, and then his own. "Not to mention selling Black Star stock."

"Do you think he's still available?"

A small laugh rumbled from Will's lips, then grew into loud laughter. "Oh, he's available. I'm afraid that for the last two months, our scholar has been slaving away at the UNIA's laundry facility—as a pants presser!"

Cyril sat forward in his chair. "He agreed to such menial labor? With his academic background?"

Will nodded. "Mrs. Abernathy told me that he hasn't missed a day. You said it yourself, Cyril. When it concerns Mr. Garvey and the UNIA, the young man is quite enthusiastic."

"It appears so! So when will you tell him that his enthusiasm has won him a ticket out of Mrs. Abernathy's steamy hell?"

"First thing tomorrow morning, Cyril. You may count on that."

Cyril exhaled a mist of cigar smoke. "And if he meets our expectations, then our only problem will be to find a hundred more like him."

\* \* \*

Serval wiped the steam from the face of his watch to check the time. "Two more hours," he muttered, reaching for a damp shirt. As he smoothed the sleeves, he felt Mrs. Abernathy's hard fingers jab his shoulder. He rolled his eyes, and turned around. "Yes, Mrs. . . ." Standing behind Lilah Abernathy was William Mathis. "Oh, good afternoon, Mr. Mathis," Serval shouted, extending his hand.

For the first time since he had been hired, Serval saw Mrs. Abernathy smile. "Good-bye, Mr. Rivard. You can be proud of your work here at the laundry. We'll miss you."

Serval blinked at her in confusion. "Uh, thank you, but . . ."

William Mathis reached for his arm. "Come with me, Mr. Rivard."

"Uh, but I don't get off until five . . ."

"It's all right, Mr. Rivard. You'll receive your full day's pay."

After Serval retrieved his personal items and signed out, he stepped outside with William Mathis and waited for an explanation. At last, Mr. Mathis smiled and patted Serval's back. "Mr. Rivard. I believe we've found a position for you in the UNIA more befitting your educational background."

"Oh, thank you, Mr. Mathis! What—well, sir, what sort of position?"

"Well, considering your skills, we're sure you'll start at a desk, handling correspondence, drafting slogans and short pieces for flyers—that sort of thing. We'd also like to let you try your hand at speech writing for Mr. Garvey."

Serval's mouth dropped open. "F-for Mr. Garvey?"

"Yes, son. He writes quite a bit himself, but he always enjoys speaking inspirational lines, no matter who has written them. And as long as we're on the subject, how are your oratorical skills?"

"Me?!"

"Of course. Mr. Garvey cannot be twenty places at once. We need intelligent people to be his voice in the places he cannot be. We must sell a lot of Black Star stock in order to realize the dream of the shipping line. And Mr. Garvey's message of pride and unity must be delivered. Do you understand?"

"Yes, sir!"

Mr. Mathis smiled. "And may I assume that you will tend to this assignment with as much zeal as you exhibited in our laundry?"

Serval nodded. "Zeal. Yes, sir, Mr. Mathis, you can count on my zeal. I'll be the first one there tomorrow morning."

"Well, that's not necessary since today is Friday. Your first day will be Monday. Report to the Liberty Hall office at 8:00 a.m. And one more thing . . ."

"What's that, sir?"

"I'm sure you'll enjoy the increase in your salary, Mr. Rivard."

"Thank you, Mr. Mathis! My wife will be happy to hear about that, sir."

Mr. Mathis laughed. "Wives usually are, Mr. Rivard. Perhaps you should go home now and tell her."

Serval shook his hand, then broke into a run. "I will! And thanks again!"

✳    ✳    ✳

Serval raced home and took the apartment steps two at a time, but his hand froze on the front door knob when he heard the muffled sound of classical music playing on the phonograph inside. *Chopin,* he thought, leaning his forehead against the door. *Les Sylphides — her favorite.* He listened to the small, muffled thumps made by the hardened ends of her pointe shoes as they met the creaking floorboards in time to the music. *All alone in that tiny living room with no audience, and she still dances.* He opened the door slowly, and watched her for a minute before she spun in his direction and caught sight of him.

"Oh, Lord, Serval!" she gasped, dropping to flat feet. "You scared the life out'a me! You should've said sump'm."

"I'm sorry, baby. I didn't want to disturb you." He smiled and wrapped his arms around her waist. "I'd almost forgotten how beautiful you are when you dance. It's been a long time."

Opal shrugged and pulled away from him. "You're home early," she said, leaning down to lift the needle from the phonograph record. "Everything okay?"

"I'll say it is! I've got news, Mrs. Rivard."

Opal sat down and smiled as she untied the ribbons on her ankles. "Good news?"

"Great news! Mr. Mathis promoted me. Mrs. Rivard, you are no longer the wife of a laundry man. My new duties will be performed behind a desk at the UNIA offices."

"Oh, Serval!" Opal cried, jumping into his arms. "That's what you wanted, huh? To write for Mr. Garvey's newspaper!"

"Well, it's actually better than that, Opal. One of the things I'll be doing is writing speeches for Mr. Garvey."

Opal's eyes widened, and she fell back onto the sofa. "No!"

"Yes. And you'll never believe the rest."

"Stop, Serval, I can't stand it. This is like your dream come true, huh?"

"Yeah. And it's still just sinking in. But you didn't let me finish."

"Oh, I'm sorry. Go on."

"I'll be traveling myself to make speeches and sell stock for the shipping line. Me! I'll be making speeches just like Mr. Garvey!"

Opal sat up straight and her smile faded. "Traveling?"

"Mm-hmm. But don't worry. It probably won't be that much traveling."

"I guess so. Oh, I'm being silly, Serval," she said, brightening. "I'm happy for you. You're a real Garvey man now, huh?"

"I'll be wearing a suit to work from now on, baby. Hey! Or maybe I'll wear a uniform like Mr. Mathis's. But I'll be writing speeches and selling Black Star stock. The shipping line! That's the biggest part of what Mr. Garvey's been talkin' about. Up to now, it's been like a dream but now . . . These are the ships that can get us the hell off this plantation. But baby, you realize the salary won't be anything too grand."

"Can't miss grand money if I never had it, Mr. Rivard. That smile on your face is a lot more important to me anyhow."

Serval laughed. "This smile is a wicked one, Mrs. Rivard. I was just thinkin' about the fight my Daddy and I are gonna have when he finds out I'm working for Mr. Garvey. Oooh! That'll be the granddaddy of 'em all!"

"Huh! Just think how he would've acted if you didn't get promoted, Serval. I'd love to see your Daddy's face if you'da told him you were workin' at a laundry for a career!"

Serval laughed. "Why do you think I've been layin' low the past two months? And now that I think of it, I haven't seen my parents but once since the first day I got back. Guess I ought'a go over there for a visit and act like a son before I drop this bomb on my Daddy."

"I think that's a good idea. You know how your Mama always makes a big fuss about her big breakfasts . . ."

"Brunch, remember? They always eat late, and they *always* call it brunch, my deah," Serval sniffed.

Opal rolled her eyes. "Oh, that's right—brunch. How could I forget? Anyway, why don't you surprise 'em tomorrow morning, Serval? Just show up for brunch."

"Okay. Go with me."

"I've got some errands to run with Miss Aida. Besides, I think after all this time, they'll probably want to talk to you by yourself. I'll go next time. And Serval?"

"Mm-hmm?"

"Maybe you ought'a wait to tell your Daddy about your new job 'til *after* breakfast . . . I mean brunch. You know, right before you leave to come home."

\* \* \*

Upon Serval's arrival the next morning, Kathryn Rivard smiled as she adjusted his collar. "I've missed you, Serval. Now I hope you'll try to get along with your father this morning. Since you've been back, I guess you've been too busy with Opal to visit. But Serval, your father really missed you while you were away, so perhaps you can find a bit of patience for him. Please? For me?"

"Okay, Mama. For you."

"Good. Now I have some letters to write upstairs, and the new cook's still trying to get that hollandaise sauce right, so it'll give you and your father a little time alone to have your coffee. I'll join you later. And please remember your promise, son."

"I'll try, Mama."

Serval stepped into the dining room and waited for his father to look up from his newspaper. A dark, willow-thin woman in an oversized maid's uniform gave Serval a startled look as she poured coffee into Charles Rivard's cup with a shaky hand.

"Thank you, Dora," Charles murmured. As he lifted the cup, he finally caught sight of Serval. "Oh! Good morning, son. This is a nice surprise. Sit down and have some coffee while I finish this article, and then we'll have a nice visit. Dora, this is my son, Serval."

Dora curtsied. "Good morning, sir," she said softly.

"Hello, Dora! Let me see if I can place that accent . . . You're Bahamian?"

Dora flashed a shy smile. "Yes, sir. Just arrived last month."

"Well, how's the old man treating you?"

Dora's eyes widened, then darted in Charles's direction. "Fine. Very fine, sir. I'll be in the kitchen if you need me, Mr. Rivard."

After Dora scurried out, Serval took a seat and stirred cream into his coffee while waiting for his father to finish reading. In the silence, he tried to think of a peaceful way to broach the subject of his work for the UNIA without starting an argument. But as he observed his father's disgusted reaction to the newspaper article, Serval sensed an explosion about to erupt.

"Hooligans!" Charles seethed, tossing the newspaper to the floor.

Serval sighed and stared into his coffee cup. "Who's a hooligan, Daddy?"

"All those fools rioting, Serval! Their actions reflect on all Negroes! Why, things have gotten so out of hand—so bloody—that these newspaper reporters have coined a new idiom for the headlines—'Red Summer.' That is not a label I want attached to people of my own race."

After taking a sip of his coffee, Serval mumbled, "Here we go."

"Did you say something, son?"

Charles's voice had that familiar irritated tone in it that always set Serval's teeth on edge. *I promised Mama,* he thought. "No, sir. I didn't say anything."

But Charles pushed. "There are ways of approaching a problem without resorting to hysteria."

Serval stirred his already well-mixed coffee once again, and dropped his spoon back onto the saucer with a loud clatter. When Charles looked up, Serval's angry eyes were waiting for him. "You don't believe those white-owned newspapers, do you, Daddy? Who do you think started those riots? You think the Negroes just went on a crazed rampage and started killing defenseless white folks in their beds?"

"Serval! For God's sake, will you never learn to listen? That is not what I said and you know it. All I'm saying is that perhaps it wouldn't have escalated to such violence if things had been handled differently."

"And that embarrasses you. The idea of just rolling up your sleeves and squaring off with those murderers is unthinkable to you. Better to smile and wait. And wait and wait, while they stockpile all the riches in this country, pass them on to their children, and keep us under their heel. But under no circumstances are we to stand up to them. Do you think *they'd* react with all this minstrel-show passivity if the situation were reversed, Daddy? Do you?"

Charles opened his mouth to protest, but Serval pounded the table with his fist and shot out of his chair. "Why the hell do you think they're rioting?" he shouted. "The reason's standing right in front of you. I was there, Daddy, remember? I was there and you weren't. I fought in your glorified Great World War, along with over 400,000 other Negro men, because you said to. You and Mr. god-almighty DuBois and the rest of your kind told us to go fight for the white folks, and then, maybe, after we proved ourselves to them, we'd get our piece of the pie. As far as I'm concerned, Daddy, I ain't got shit to prove to the white man. I never did. He's the one that needs to be provin' himself to me!"

Charles sighed. "You've learned a new trick, Serval. You use words like deadly weapons to wound me. And you don't even try to understand my . . ."

Serval cut him off. "I had *nothin'* to prove! But I went, Daddy. I went and I watched my friends get butchered, and wondered if I'd ever get back alive myself. And when I got back, what did I find? Jim Crow and the Klan . . . Stand in the back, nigger! White only! And more lynchings than ever before. Glory hallelujah! Three cheers for the god-damn red, white, and blue!"

Charles folded his newspaper and stared up at Serval. "It's a sad day when a father can no longer reach his son—when a son is too stubborn to accept the wisdom of his father's life experiences."

Serval picked up his napkin and wiped the perspiration from his forehead. "No, Daddy," he said softly. "It's a sad day when the son has lived through so much hell that his father's life experiences are as use-less as fairy tales." He sat back down. "Does it say there in your news-paper, Daddy, what the cause was for some of those riots? I'll tell you. Because some of the fellas being lynched were soldiers. War veterans who somehow made it through that . . . that bloodbath in Europe. Then they come back for their piece of pie and get hung—hung by the neck until dead. Isn't that the way they pronounce a death sentence, Daddy? To be hung by the neck until dead? They *executed* 'em, Daddy," he shouted, letting his tears fall. "*That* was their piece of the goddamn pie!"

Charles shook his head. "Son . . . must you use that gutter language?"

Serval blinked at his father, then laughed derisively as he wiped his eyes. "Yeah, Daddy, I guess I must. Keeps me in touch with reality. 'Cause, you know something? Out of all the fancy words your money bought me, I never found a better word for bullshit than *bullshit!*"

Now Charles pounded the table. "Stop it at once! Do you hear me, Serval? I understand your bitterness, son. I know about these lynch-ings, but that's just one side of the coin. We *have* won respect, Serval. Things are getting better. Just because the percentages might not be as high as . . ."

Serval slumped back in his chair and groaned. "Percentages. Damn, Daddy. Now you sound like Joseph Winfield. Him and his five percent theory. I'd like to tell him about his damn theory now."

"Joseph—Winfield?" Charles said haltingly.

Serval looked up. "Yes. Why do you say it like that?"

"Joseph . . . Oh, my God, Serval . . . Then you haven't heard . . ."

"Heard what? Daddy, what happened to . . ."

"Son, your friend Joseph . . . didn't make it home. He was killed in the war."

Serval shook his head. "No," he whispered. "No, he wasn't. That can't be true."

"I'm sorry, but I'm afraid it *is* true. Son, I attended the funeral in December. It was before you got back. I—I assumed you knew."

Serval stood up and stared at his father in silence for nearly a minute. Charles reached for his arm. "Son? Are you all right?"

Jerking his arm free, Serval hurried to the front door and ran out.

\* \* \*

When Serval returned to the apartment, Opal was gone. Sinking down onto the sofa, he dug the heels of his hands into his eyes, but couldn't stop the tears. The cold grip of death was back. *Not Joseph. Not Joseph too.*

Someone knocked on the front door and Serval jumped. He considered ignoring the caller, but at the second knock, he stood up, wiped his face with his handkerchief, and headed for the door. He opened it a crack and peered out at an overdressed dandy with a smooth caramel complexion and pomaded hair as shiny and black as the brocade vest he wore under his white suit. Certainly no costume for the morning.

"Yes?"

The stranger's thick black eyebrows creased together in perplexed annoyance. "Oh, sorry. Guess I got the wrong . . . Wait a minute. Your name Rivard?"

"Who wants to know?"

The man broke into a smile that Serval had seen before on a street grifter. "Well, sure! You must be Opal's husband! The war veteran, huh?"

"*Who* are you?"

"Oh! Sorry. Name's Chappie—Chappie James. From The Douglas Club? Aww, now I get it . . . You comin' home must be the reason Opal quit. You are one fortunate fella, Mr. Rivard! Opal is one sweet . . ."

Serval cut him off. "You mind telling me what the hell you're talkin' about? And before you answer, you'd best remember all those stories you've heard about us returning soldiers from the war. Some of us came back minus a few cards in our decks. So however you know my wife, you'd better give me the truth, and right now."

Chappie gave Serval a confused look, followed by a patronizing smile. "Oh, it's not what you're thinking, buddy. See, everybody loves Opal down at the club, and, well, she's always talkin' about you. It's good to finally meet you. Anyway, the reason I'm here is to see if Opal might consider coming back to work, even if it's just temporary. See, two of my best dancers quit on me today and . . ."

"Dancers?"

"Huh? Uh, yeah, dancers. Oh, wait a minute! Didn't she tell you about her job?"

"Dancers?" Serval repeated, eyeing Chappie's flashy suit. "What kind of *dancers?*"

"Aww, naw, buddy! You got the wrong idea. I mean, I'm sorry Opal didn't mention it to you but, well, see, she doesn't dance like—like what you're thinking. She's a *real* dancer. Best ballet training I ever saw. She does the artsy stuff, you know, not like Creola . . ."

"Creola?" Serval's voice dripped with contempt. "Swell. So that's how she met that little . . . Look, *buddy*, you can take it from me. Opal won't be back."

"But . . ." Chappie's protest froze on his lips when Serval slammed the door in his face.

\* \* \*

"Serval?" Opal called, upon arriving home that evening. "Where are you?"

No answer.

She headed into the kitchen. "How'd things go with your Daddy this . . . Where is he?" she murmured. "His car's here. . . . Serval?"

Silence.

Suddenly, she laughed. "Oh, I know! Somebody wants to play games, huh?" Walking into the bedroom, she was surprised to find the bed empty. Turning around, she noticed the bathroom door halfway shut and tapped on it gently. "Serval? You in here?" She flipped the light switch and saw him lying in a full tub of water, staring at the faucet.

"A bath in the dark? What's wrong?" she asked softly. "Did you . . . Oh. You and your Daddy got into another scuffle, huh?"

Still no answer.

"Serval?"

Without looking at her, he reached into the water and yanked the plug out of the drain, then stepped out of the tub. He seemed to be unaware of her presence as he reached past her for a towel and began to dry off his body.

Opal watched in confusion. When he headed for the bedroom, she followed him, unable to think of anything to say.

Throwing the towel onto the floor, he reached into the armoire for his trousers and slung them over his shoulder. He then yanked open a drawer and rummaged around for underwear and socks.

Opal sat quietly on the edge of the bed, trying to figure out what was wrong, while doing her best not to be distracted by his bare body.

It wasn't until he began to button his shirt that he looked into her eyes. Holding the stare for a moment, he finally spoke.

"Chappie came by," he said simply. "He was wonderin' when you'd be gettin' back to your job."

"Serval . . ." She reached out, but he jerked his arm free and headed for the door.

"Serval, wait," she pleaded. "Let me explain . . . Where are you going?"

"Out."

\* \* \*

Opal lifted her aching head and gazed out the bedroom window at a full moon. Reaching for the clock, she blinked her eyes. *Ten-twenty. I've been cryin' for two hours.* She hadn't experienced such distress since her nightmares about Serval being killed in the war. She longed for a shoulder to cry on, but Jack was away on a cross-country trip; it was too late to call Aida; and she hadn't heard from her father since he had left her home weeks earlier. But Opal knew that no one would have the power to comfort her tonight. The only person she wanted was Serval.

*Where is he?* She rose, shaking, and stumbled to the bathroom to splash water on her face. *What if I lost him? Oh, God, Serval. Come home, please.*

\* \* \*

Serval climbed out of his car, slammed the door, and crossed the street to The Douglas Club. Ever since his talk with Chappie James, he had felt a need to see the place. *A goddamn common cooch dancer!* Stepping into the dimly-lit entryway, he saw Chappie leaning over the bar, pointing at something and speaking sharply to the bartender. He looked up and, when their eyes met, nodded deferentially before approaching Serval. He led him to the front table and leaned over to smooth the tablecloth. "It's not as bad as you think, Mr. Rivard. And I don't know if it'll help, but most of our girls are good girls. But your wife—she's a real lady, and everybody knew it." Rising, he said louder, "Enjoy the show, sir. I'll send Mindy around to take your drink order."

Serval listened to the jazz band without hearing the music. His normal enthusiasm was numbed, even to the line of Chappie's Chorines, as they bumped and wiggled through their first number. *Opal was different. I was so sure she was different. How could she be happy doing this?* As hard as he tried, he simply couldn't picture Opal in one of the skimpy costumes, shaking her body for the entertainment of a roomful of leering drunks.

His thoughts were interrupted when Chappie sprang up onto the stage and clapped his hands sharply for attention.

"Ladies and gentlemen! Now that you're all warmed up, you just might be ready for the star attraction."

Wolf whistles pierced through Serval's alcohol-induced haze.

Chappie held up his hands for quiet and continued. "That's right! I'm talking about The Douglas Club's main event of the evening—the number one reason we all love being men! Give a nice hot welcome for the one and only Miss Creola Dorshay!"

Serval's eyes narrowed as he watched Creola flounce out onto the stage, her body sandwiched between two enormous fans made of flamingo-pink feathers. Batting her eyelashes seductively, she fluttered the front fan, exposing just enough thigh to elicit a wild cheer from the men in the audience. He watched as she whirled about the stage to the beat of slow jazz number, teasing the men with brazen flashes of skin followed by coy cover-ups with the fan.

She stopped suddenly, and Serval realized that she had spotted him. He regarded her with cold indifference, and she responded by moving in his direction. Her dancing took on a lewd quality, with pelvic thrusts accenting full exposure of her breasts. Her eyes were locked on his, as if daring him to fall victim to her seduction. Serval met the challenge by keeping his gaze trained only on her eyes.

The number was nearly over, and Serval was becoming amused at her obvious desperation to entice him. He maintained a cold, bored stare.

At last, Creola captured his attention. She stopped dancing. But just as the audience began to murmur their objection, she elicited a roaring cheer by dropping her fans on the floor and spinning slowly around to give them a view of her bare rear-end. She wore only a thin G-string, which all but disappeared when she took a wide-legged stance and bent over to point everything she had in Serval's direction.

Serval had to fight to keep from laughing when Chappie made a lunge for the stage and tackled Creola, covering her with his jacket. The audience erupted in wolf whistles, applause, and laughter.

With his head aching from too much alcohol, Serval reached into his wallet, threw a five dollar bill onto the table, and left.

Chappie shoved Creola into her dressing room and shut the door. "What the hell was that, huh? This has never been that kind'a club, Creola, and you know it!"

Creola's mind raced, trying to measure Chappie's anger. The answer came quickly. She was in trouble. For as long as she had known him, and as many times as she had tried his patience, she had never seen him this angry. Deciding that her partial nakedness was an advantage, she leaned against the dressing table and stretched, arching her back strategically, before reaching for a cigarette. "Got a light?" she purred.

Chappie squeezed his eyes shut and spoke to her through bared teeth. "Nice try, Creola, but I've had enough'a your illegal tits for one night. What you were doin' out there could shut us down, not to mention get your ass locked up. The legal term is 'lewd and lascivious behavior,' in case you're too stupid to know it. But I think you know it. You just didn't give a good goddamn. Put on some clothes or you're fired."

Something in his tone made Creola obey. Pouting, she pulled on a robe and lit her own cigarette.

Chappie paced the room angrily. "Goddamn, Creola. I'm not sure your popularity with the patrons is worth all the damn trouble you make."

"Okay, enough, Chappie!" she shouted. "I got a little carried away is all."

"It's called a fan dance, Creola. That means you're supposed to dance *with* the fans not—*around*'em. This is a class joint! What the hell were you thinkin'? I mean, your number is already as close as we get to bein' lowdown. You're just supposed to tease the men, Creola, not have 'em linin' up to take a damn number!"

Creola watched her unsmoked cigarette burn in the ashtray, as Chappie ranted, and was suddenly shocked at herself. *Why did I do that? I ain't never been that wild. Not when it came to my job.* Glancing up at her reflection in the mirror, she shivered and pulled the robe higher around her neck. Three names came to mind. Serval, Jack—and Opal. She couldn't figure out the connection, but for the first time in her life, Creola Dorshay was humbled.

*    *    *

After stopping at an all night cafe for coffee, Serval drove home as slowly and carefully as he could. He stumbled once on the front steps, but managed to let himself into the apartment with hardly a sound. Without turning on a light, he felt his way down the hallway to the bedroom. Still unable to make sense of his emotions, he stood at the foot of the bed and gazed at Opal's sleeping face. There was just enough moonlight beaming through the half-closed shade to remind him of their first night together after his return from the war. He blinked back the stinging sensation in his eyes and studied her body. Curled into a partial fetal position, there was a tenseness about her, most evident in her balled-up fists. Her nightgown was twisted and tangled around her thighs, like a child passing a fitful night of sleep. Watching her seemed to dissipate whatever anger was left, and before he could stop himself, Serval found himself sitting on the edge of the bed, reaching for her. "Opal."

Her eyes fluttered open and she moved into his arms. "I'm sorry I hurt you, Serval. I want you to trust me and I won't lie to you ever again, I promise . . ."

"Shh. We'll talk about it later. I love you, baby. And I'm sorry too."

"You didn't do anything, Serval. I feel like I lied to you."

"I'm sorry for thinking you could ever be like that tramp Creola."

\* \* \*

Serval woke to a case of nausea, brought on by his drinking the previous night, and was instantly plunged into depression. Reaching for Opal, he tried to force the haunting images of Red and Jimmy Coles out of his mind.

"Baby, you awake?" he whispered.

"Mm-hmm," she murmured, without opening her eyes.

"The next time I go stormin' out'a here, remind me I can't handle drinking. I feel like—well, I don't feel so good."

"Aww, poor baby. Le'me go see if we've got sump'm. Be right back."

When Opal returned with a glass of bromo, Serval regarded the fizzing concoction with revulsion and moaned loudly. "Aww, baby! I hate that stuff . . . Oh, okay. Give it to me."

As Opal watched Serval's facial expression contort while drinking the bromo, she laughed lightly. "That'll teach you, Mr. Rivard. You're sure not one for drinkin'."

"I'll say!"

"Where'd you go anyway?"

Lying back on the pillows, Serval avoided the question. "Opal, you know what's strange? We've only had two fights the whole time we've known each other, and both of 'em were about your dancing."

Opal lowered her head. "I quit, Serval. I—I don't dance anymore."

"You didn't let me finish."

"Huh?"

"Both fights were *about* your dancing, but they were *caused* by my stubbornness."

"What are you talkin' about, Serval? I should've told you I was dancing. I feel like I lied to you. Nobody likes to be lied to. I'd be mad if you lied to me, too."

Serval grinned. "If you're through beatin' yourself up, I'd like to finish."

"Okay."

"I trust you. I know you wouldn't do anything wrong. I mean, I know you weren't exactly dancing the ballet at that—place. But I'm sure that whatever you did was tasteful."

Opal smiled. "Matter of fact, it was so doggone tasteful, I almost got booed off the stage the first night."

"No!"

"Mm-hmm. Chappie put me on right before Creola. You know, it was kind'a late and the patrons were pretty liquored up by then, so they were just itchin' to see Creola. See, she does this kind'a burlesque peek-a-boo dance with a couple'a big fans. But she doesn't really show anything . . ."

Serval made a grunting sound, but gestured for her to continue.

"Anyway, my little dance was way too 'Mary Pickford' when everybody was waitin' to see Creola and her fan dance, and . . ."

"'Mary Pickford'?"

Opal rolled her eyes and sighed. "Yeah, Serval. You know who Mary Pickford is, don't you?"

"Mm-hmm. Little Miss Goody-Two-Shoes of the flickers. And I know how you meant it, too. You pickin' up street-slang on me, young lady?"

"*Anyway*, Serval, then Chappie changed my dance to the first number, you know, early in the evening before folks start actin' a fool. And the dinner crowd liked my act. Chappie started letting me pick out songs, and I guess I really started enjoying myself, Serval. I know I should've written you about it, but I was scared you'd be mad. So I just quit the day before you came back."

"I know."

"And Serval, you don't have to worry about my costumes. I was the most covered up girl in the place, believe me."

Serval pulled Opal against his chest and kissed her head. "You really love to dance, don't you? It might not be the ballet, but it's close enough, huh? God, I've been selfish."

Opal blinked at him. "You mean—you don't want me to quit? I can go back?"

"I mean I don't have the right to keep you from it. Damn! When I think of all those years you practiced . . ."

"Hours and hours, every day. With bleeding toes and aching legs all the time . . ."

"Okay, okay," he groaned. "Make me feel worse. Why is it that society frowns on a married woman who works anyway? Well, the hell with them. You dance, baby, if it makes you happy. That is—as long as you don't start doin' Creola's fan dance."

"Shoot! That's sump'm the world will never see!"

"Okay, Mrs. Rivard. Now that we've gotten all that straightened out, I've got a confession to make."

"What, Mr. Rivard?"

"Last night—you were wondering where I went. Well, I don't know why, but I just had to see the place—The Douglas Club. That's where I went."

Opal sat up and stared at him, but said nothing.

"I just had to see it, Opal. And it helped. I had all kinds of pictures in my head, but once I saw those other girls, I knew you couldn't be like that. I mean . . ."

Opal's expression changed into one Serval had never seen before. "A lot of those girls are real nice, Serval."

"Ooh, sorry. I just mean—well, I'm sure they are. I didn't mean anything by it. But that Creola . . ."

Opal crossed her arms. "Creola's not so bad once you get to know her."

"Wait a minute, Opal. I was about to leave when that tramp came on stage with her feathers and started doin'—whatever it is she does that passes for dancin'—and Opal . . ."

"Please don't call her a tramp, Serval."

"But baby, she was completely . . ."

"She was completely what?"

"Well, she—she was completely bare-breasted and . . ."

"What?!" Opal gasped. "Are you sure?"

Serval rolled his eyes. "Now, baby, I was a little drunk, but believe me, I wasn't so far gone that I couldn't spot a woman's breasts when she shook 'em at me."

Opal gasped. "*Shook* 'em at you? Creola shook—she shook her . . .? Oh, Serval!"

Serval reached for her, but she pulled away. "Opal! I didn't say I *liked* it."

"But you saw it—them! I can't believe she did that! Didn't Chappie . . ."

"Did he ever!" Serval laughed. "Let's just say that Creola won't be dancing that particular number at The Douglas Club any more. Hey, don't be mad at me! I left as soon as she . . ."

"You did? You left?"

"Of course I did. Don't you remember when I told you about those *ghostly* girls in France? Well, after Creola's peep show, I could tell that she's way too ghostly to do anything for me! Not when I got this pretty bronze goddess waitin' for me at home." His tone suddenly turned serious as he looked into her eyes. "Opal. Look at me. I love you. I wasn't there for some sort of thrill. I wanted to see where you worked. That's all."

Easing back into Serval's arms, Opal sighed, "Well . . ."

"I love you—and no *ghostly* cooch dancer is ever gonna steal me away!"

Opal giggled. "But Serval. Creola *is* colored, you know."

"Shee-it. Barely."

"Serval. Will you think I'm bad if I tell you some gossip?"

"Is it juicy?"

"Mm-hmm."

"Spill it, girl."

"Creola puts this stuff on her skin—to bleach it!"

"No!" he said, feigning amazement.

"Yes, she does!"

"Now, why doesn't that surprise me?"

"Okay. Now I feel bad. We've got to stop talkin' about Creola, Serval. She's not so bad deep down. And she's still my friend, you know."

Serval shook his head, but said nothing.

*      *      *

Opal returned to The Douglas Club with Serval at her side for support. Chappie James approached them when they walked in, and shook Serval's hand. "Got a seat for you, Mr. Rivard," he said. "And it's a little too early for a drink, but I can get you somethin' else if you want it."

"No, thanks. Coffee's fine. Listen, I hope me bein' here won't disrupt your rehearsal or anything . . ."

"Not at all," Chappie said, grinning. "I want you to see how classy your wife's number is. Opal, it's so good to have you back in the show."

"Thanks, Chappie," Opal said, waving at someone on the stage. "I'm so thrilled to be back!"

Serval leaned down to kiss her forehead, and Chappie shook his head. "Man! If I ever get caught and dragged to some altar, I hope I can have a marriage like you two have. This must be the way it's supposed to be."

"Just do me one favor, man," Serval said.

"What's that?"

"Let her do as much of that ballet stuff as you can. She loves it."

Chappie took Opal's hat and pulled out a chair for Serval. "White folks don't know what they're missin'. If she was white, she'd be the next Pavlova. I never even heard of Pavlova 'til your wife talked me into seein' her in a two-reeler at the Bijou. And you know sump'm? I think Opal dances circles around her."

"Oh, go on!" Opal laughed.

"No, he's right," Serval said. "That's what Anna Romanov always said."

Opal's smile faded.

"Who?" Chappie asked.

"Her teacher from Russia."

"Oh, yeah. Sorry, Opal. I know how upset you were when she passed away."

"I still miss her."

"I know. I wish I could'a been here," Serval whispered.

Chappie tugged at his collar and stood up. "Uh, well, guess I better get this rehearsal started. Good talking to you, Mr. Rivard." He clapped his hands as he headed for the stage. "Okay, girls, line up. Hey, Opal, while they're goin' over their routine, why don't you go over that list of songs and let me know what you want to start with."

"Okay, Chappie. See you later, Serval," Opal said, kissing him on the cheek. "Hope you enjoy the madness of rehearsal."

"Hey, I'm really curious," Serval said, grinning. "Go ahead and knock 'em dead, baby."

The stage began to buzz with activity. The piano player began the first number and Chappie ran through the new steps with the dancers. Halfway through the number, the tallest dancer stared out toward the entrance, crossed her arms, and let out a disgusted sigh. "Great. Guess we gotta start all over again for Mam'zelle White-folks."

Creola Dorshay had arrived.

Chappie hopped down from the stage to reprimand her. "Late again. Damn, Creola, just *once*, you think you could make it on time?"

Creola ascended the stairs onto the stage and walked directly toward Opal, who stared at her with a blank expression.

"So you're back," Creola said.

"Yes. I'm back." Opal's voice was uncharacteristically cool. She turned away from Creola and began stretching.

Creola glared at the other girls, who were watching the one-sided reunion and smirking. Creola leaned closer to Opal. "Come over here a minute, would you? I got sump'm I wanna ask you, but everybody's lookin' and . . . just come over here a minute."

Opal sighed. "Oh, all right." She followed Creola to the far left side of the stage and they stepped behind a large screen. "Well?"

Glancing over her shoulder, Creola whispered, "He told you, didn't he?"

Opal crossed her arms. "Who? Serval? Oh, you mean about your little burlesque number the other night? Yeah, he told me."

"And you're—you're mad?"

"No, not really mad, I guess. Just disappointed. But why should you care anyway?"

"I don't know," Creola said, looking at the floor. "I don't know why I care. Look, Opal, it was for somebody else—another fella. I got a little drunk, and I was jus' playin' around . . . it was stupid, I guess. But I want you to know I ain't after your man. Do you . . . forgive me?"

Opal shrugged. "Oh, all right."

"See . . ." Creola began, "I mean, I know we ain't been the best of friends or anything, but you' the only one around here who's nice to me. I know I act like I don't care, but sometimes it gets real lonely when you know everybody hates your guts." She took a swipe at a tear, and Opal touched her hand.

"Oh, girl! They don't hate you! They just—oh, you know how they are. They probably talk about me too when I'm not around."

"No, they don't," Creola said, sniffling. "Everybody likes you."

"Well . . ."

Creola rolled her eyes and reached into her pocketbook for her compact. "Oh, hell," she said, dabbing at her face with a powder puff. "I hate it when I get all weepy like this. That time of the month, ya know. Look, I really am glad you're back, that's all."

"Well, thanks, Creola. That's so sweet . . ."

"Yeah, well, don't go gettin' all syrupy on me, 'cause I got myself a sneaky reason. See, I was wonderin'—well, if that offer you made still stands. You remember when you told me you could teach me some of that ballet stuff?"

Opal laughed. "You just let me know when you're ready to start."

＊　＊　＊

Needing only two rehearsals to prepare, Opal was scheduled to appear in the Saturday night show to the regular packed house.

Serval stretched out on the bed and watched as Opal fussed around the room searching for something. "Why are you so nervous, baby?" he laughed. "You've danced to a full house before, haven't you?"

"Mm-hmm. Serval, have you seen my stockings? I just had 'em in my hand!"

"Come here and give me a kiss."

"Oh, Serval! I don't have time for any a'your smoochin' nonsense. You're gonna make me late!"

"One kiss."

Opal rolled her eyes and hurried over to him to deliver a quick peck. But before she could get away, Serval tugged at something around her neck, pulling her closer for another kiss. "What's this around your neck, Mrs. Rivard?"

"Oh, Lord! My stockings! I'ma mess up tonight, Serval, I just know it!"

"Calm down! You couldn't mess up if you tried. Mmm. Did I ever tell you how much I like to watch you get dressed? 'Specially when you get to the stockings part."

"Don't get any ideas, Mr. Rivard! I can't be late tonight. There's gonna be somebody real important in the audience and I want everything to be perfect! That's why I'm so nervous."

Serval was suddenly annoyed. "Who? Charlie Chaplin again? Or one'a those damn reporters who've suddenly discovered Harlem? Don't tell me—Winchell, right?"

Opal leaned down to kiss him again, and smiled. "No, crazy man. You."

*　*　*

As the small orchestra eased into Opal's intro, she emerged in a blue, gossamer costume that trailed around her legs as she danced. She danced on pointe only occasionally, in a unique blend of styles, closing her eyes and smiling serenely.

Serval watched her quietly from the front table with the same feeling he'd experienced the first time he had seen her dance at Madame's flat. Her beauty was enhanced by years of disciplined grace. Although the number seemed out of place for a nightclub, it charmed the audience. Opal became one with the music, blending into it with sweeping leg movements and ethereal spins.

At the last plaintive note of a lone violin, Opal slowly descended to the floor, and finished to a burst of applause from the audience. When she rose to take her bow, Serval smiled at her and applauded loudly.

Chappie's Chorines wiggled into the spotlight to the beat of "Ain't She Sweet" just as Opal disappeared backstage. Serval headed for the bar to join Chappie, who was waiting expectantly.

"Well?" Chappie asked.

"You were right, man. Very tasteful. My baby sure can dance, huh?"

"Best I've ever seen. Listen, Serval, I want you to meet somebody." Chappie gestured to a dark-skinned, muscular gentleman sitting to his right, whose most noticeable feature was his clean-shaven head. As Chappie began the introductions, Serval spotted the black derby resting beside the man's drink, and interrupted while reaching for his hand. "Why, sure! You're Jack Johnson! Heavyweight champion of the world! Good to meet'cha, Champ!"

Jack Johnson smiled, revealing the world-famous, gold-toothed grin that had inflamed Caucasian sportsmen into the frantic search for a "Great White Hope" to recover the championship belt for the white race. Johnson shrugged his shoulders as he shook Serval's hand. "Well, we all know I'm not champ any more. But thanks for rememberin'. Nice to meet you, Serval. Chappie told me that was your wife dancing. Class, man. Plenty of class! I'm likin' this place better every time I come."

Chappie leaned closer to Serval and whispered, "The Champ's thinkin' about buyin' the club."

_Up, you mighty race! You can accomplish what you will!_

—MARCUS GARVEY

# Chapter 21

Serval's first few days at work in the UNIA offices coincided with a flurry of activity surrounding the upcoming convention to be held at Madison Square Garden. At the end of his first week, Serval was invited to attend a planning meeting in the large conference room.

As the chief organizer of the Madison Square Garden event, William Mathis held the responsibility of delegating duties. "Mr. Rivard," he said, without looking up from his list, "Since you will soon be embarking on speaking tours across the states, I'd like you to stick close to me during the convention. It's important that you meet members from our visiting Southern branches, as well as the dignitaries from Africa and Cuba, and so forth. But I must confess I also have an ulterior motive. I'm afraid that your position as low man on the totem pole has won you the unenviable task of being my assistant, and, as any one of the fellows in this room will tell you, I'm not the easiest person to assist. For example—if I'm discussing global issues with someone from Haiti, and the man asks me a question about regional opinions, I'll expect you to provide to me—*quickly*—the UNIA's documented research and answers to that question. If I need an interpreter, you must be able to produce one for me immediately. It's grunt work, yes, but believe me, Mr. Rivard, it will be a stimulating learning experience at an intense level."

Before Serval had a chance to ask a question, Mr. Mathis turned his attention to the rest of the gathering, ostensibly ending his verbal engagement with "the low man on the totem pole."

"Mr. Garvey will be here in a few minutes," Mr. Mathis was saying. "He has a few points he'd like to go over with us, and, as you all know, his time is limited. So, if you have any questions, ask them now."

A few hands raised, but quickly lowered again when the door to the conference room opened. Marcus Garvey paused for a moment to scan the men in the room, as if calculating their worth down to the tiniest flaw. He strode to the head of the long mahogany conference table and laid out two stacks of papers, then pulled out his pocket watch to check the time. William Mathis offered him a chair, but Garvey shook his head and remained standing. Serval couldn't take his eyes off of him, and electric pinpricks danced on the back of his neck when he heard the familiar West Indian voice.

"Good afternoon, gentlemen!"

Serval listened intently as Mr. Garvey went down the planning list for the convention point by point. He spoke with efficiency, wasting neither time nor words, and seemed to answer every conceivable question before it could be asked. Marcus Garvey was often described as a visionary, and Serval now understood the reason. Possessing the ability to focus clearly on a goal, seeing beyond all obstacles, he was also a master at imprinting images in the minds of his listeners with the same clarity. He saw the convention in its successful completeness, and was determined to make it happen exactly as planned. As he wrapped up his talk, Serval was sure he detected a twinkle in Mr. Garvey's eyes as he asked, "Are there any questions?"

*Of course not.*

Garvey gathered his papers and stepped back from the head of the table. "Fine. Mr. Mathis, I'll turn the meeting back over to you, but before I leave, I'd like to meet this new young man I've been hearing so much about. A Mr. Rivard, I believe?"

Mr. Mathis gestured to Serval. "Mr. Rivard? Step up, please."

Serval stood up and prayed that no one would notice his shaking knees. Stepping close to Mr. Garvey, he extended his hand. "It's an honor to finally meet you, sir."

Marcus Garvey gripped Serval's hand tightly with both of his own. "I have heard nothing but good things about you, son. My expectations are high."

As he gazed deeply into the eyes of Marcus Garvey, the words echoed in his ears, and Serval could almost feel the mantle of responsibility settle about his shoulders. It felt intimidating, but strangely seductive.

＊　＊　＊

Serval began to hate Saturday nights. The Douglas Club opened early and stayed open late on Saturdays, and Opal never arrived home until after 4:00 a.m. On the Saturday before his scheduled departure on his first UNIA speaking tour, they had argued, leaving him in a worse mood than usual. He stood at the stove stirring a pot of leftover stew, and felt resentment creeping in to mingle with a vague loneliness.

Dumping the stew into a bowl, he grabbed a spoon and headed to the table. After dropping into a chair, he stared at the stew for a moment before pushing it away. "Maybe I ought to work on my speeches," he muttered, then stood up.

The creaking floorboards seemed to punctuate the emptiness of the apartment as he trudged into the living room. He settled into his desk chair and reached into his satchel for the clipped pages of the speech he'd been working on. Just as he was re-reading the opening for the fourth time, he was startled by a loud knock on the front door. As he reached for the doorknob, he heard Jack shouting.

"Open up, 'fo I call the law! I know what'chu two been drinkin' out them teacups, and it ain't tea!"

Serval laughed and yanked open the door. "Get in here, man, before you disturb my neighbors!"

"Aww, it's still early. 'Sides, they prob'ly in there stirrin' up sump'm in they own bathtub, man."

"When did you get in, Jack?" Serval asked, easing down onto the sofa.

"You see this bag in my hand, don'tcha? My train pulled in 'bout seven and I got me three days off. Now, I know Opal's workin' late tonight, and I know how evil you get on Saturdays, so get on in ya room and get dressed. I'll clean up and change in the bathroom."

Serval sprang to his feet and headed down the hallway toward the bedroom. "And I won't even ask where we're goin', Jack. Just get me out'a this apartment."

\* \* \*

Three hours later Serval and Jack were at the Bijou theater, sitting in the dark as the final credits rolled for a film entitled *Within Our Gates* by a Negro filmmaker named Oscar Micheaux. When the lights came on, the audience sat in stunned silence for awhile before slowly rising to leave.

The minute they stepped outside, Serval stared up at Jack and shook his head. "That Micheaux really set the record straight, didn't he? You ever see *Birth of a Nation*, Jack?"

"Naw, but I heard 'bout all them riots it kicked up."

"Well, I saw it. The most disgusting pack of lies I ever saw. I'm sure glad somebody had the guts to stand up to a big-shot director like Griffith and set the record straight. Makes me proud."

Jack nodded. "That was sump'm, man. I ain't never thought I'd see no colored folks in no flicker."

"But didn't you read the credits, Jack? That fella Micheaux—he wasn't just one of the actors. He wrote the film *and* directed it!"

Jack seemed suddenly distracted as he checked the time on his pocketwatch. "Huh? Oh, yeah. Guess I ain't noticed that. That sho' is progress. Hey, Serval, my stomach's growlin' like a junkyard dog. Sho' wish we'da brought the car 'stead'a walkin'. You got the stuff at home?"

"What stuff?"

Jack sighed and rolled his eyes. "Cawnmeal, man. Eggs, milk, bakin' powder—oh, and butter."

Serval laughed. "You and your cornbread. Yeah, we got the stuff. Might even have some catfish on ice."

Jack rubbed his stomach. "Now all we need's Opal to make the spaghetti, and we got ourselves a reg'lar feast."

Serval shoved his hands into his pockets and frowned. "Let's not talk about Opal right now."

"Uh-oh. What happened, man? Lovers' quarrel?"

"Come on," Serval said, sighing. "Let's walk." They crossed the street and covered nearly a block before he answered Jack's question. "I told Opal weeks ago about the UNIA sending me on this speaking tour, but now that it's actually happening, she's all upset."

"Aww, well, she jus' gon' miss you, that's all. That ain't nothin' to fight about."

"Well, it got worse, Jack. She exaggerated everything, talking about me being gone all the time as it is, and how these trips are gonna be increasing 'til I'm gone more than I'm home. She just panicked, Jack."

"Well . . . Is she wrong?"

"Hell, I don't know. Mr. Mathis said something about another trip in a month or two, but it's not definite."

"Well, Opal's actin' natural, ain't she, Serval? Most women want they men home wid 'em."

Serval stopped walking and stared at Jack. "You know what? It's strange you should say that. Because now that I think about it, once that part of the argument simmered down, the worst part was on account'a me . . ."

"On account'a you what?"

"All I said was . . . well, I *suggested* that she stay home with me tonight."

Jack leveled his eyes at Serval and grinned. "You *suggested?*"

Serval shrugged and began walking rapidly. "Hell, Jack. Here she was goin' on about me bein' gone all the damn time, and the whole argument's goin' on in the bathroom because she's busy puttin' on makeup to go to her cooch dancin' job 'til four in the goddamn morning. Hey. I got mad."

"Hold on, Serval. Opal ain't no cooch dancer. Don't call her that."

"Well, you know what I mean. She's the only married woman workin' in that place, and there's a reason for that. Not many husbands would tolerate their wives dancin' in a jazz club, even the kind'a dancin' Opal does. I mean, I'm not exactly a tyrant. And she does dance 'til four a.m., Jack. Sometimes later!"

"Only on Saturdays, Serval. Now who's exaggeratin'?"

"You're missin' my point, Jack. She's accusing me of being gone all the time, and she's gone as much as I am! I can't help it if my work is during the day and hers is at night."

"Hmm . . ."

"Hmm?! Is that all you can say?"

Jack cut his eyes at Serval. "Don't remember you axin' me—I mean, *asking* me for no answers."

"Okay, Jack. I'm asking."

"Well, Serval, way I see it is like this . . . Seem like y'all got a few bricks in y'all marriage. Folks and jobs and families and such—all steady tossin' bricks at'cha. Only thing I can say is—jus' don't start buildin' ya'self a wall wid 'em."

*　*　*

The UNIA International Convention of the Negro Peoples of the World was held on a sweltering night in August 1920, and drew thousands of delegates of African descent from twenty-five countries and four continents to Madison Square Garden. As local Negroes congregated by the hundreds in the surrounding streets to witness the historic event, the Caucasians of Manhattan were thrown into an uproar. For once, the white protests were ignored by city officials. No laws had been broken, every regulation had been observed, and the convention proceeded as planned.

After an orderly parade through the streets, representatives and visitors gathered on the convention floor to hear the opening address. Serval stood at his assigned table, straightening stacks of UNIA pamphlets, and carefully folding copies of the current issue of *The Negro World*. After answering a question and selling two books, he made his way through the crowd to find a good spot for watching Mr. Garvey, who was just stepping up to the podium. The buzzing crowd fell silent for a moment, and then Garvey's voice echoed throughout the expanse of Madison Square Garden.

"Good evening."

As Garvey delivered one of his most emotional speeches, Serval hung on every word, and was brought to tears by a segment that touched him in a deep, private place:

"*We Negroes are prepared to suffer no longer . . . For democracy the nations of the world wasted Europe in blood for four years. They called upon the Negroes of the world to fight. After the war we were deprived of all of the democracy we fought for. In many instances in the Southern States, colored soldiers in uniforms, returning from the battlefields of Europe, were beaten and a few lynched; before they were demobilized they were mobbed in this land of the brave. But we shall not give up. We shall raise the banner of democracy in Africa, or four hundred million of us will report to God the reason why . . . We pledge our blood to the battlefields of Africa, where we will fight for true liberty, democracy and the brotherhood of man.*"

Mr. Garvey ended his speech on a high note and soon everyone was buzzing about the unveiling of the Declaration of Rights of the Negro Peoples of the World. Serval's blood sizzled with excitement each time he engaged in a debate about the how's, why's, and what-if's. He encountered political views as diverse as the tongues being spoken around him by representatives from all regions of the world. Although the word "oppression" cropped up with expected frequency, the unity achieved brought the heady feeling of hope. Human eyes seemed somehow inadequate to take in all the colors and activity. With so many foreign dignitaries resplendent in their native dress, Madison Square Garden had never looked quite so regal.

Several times during the night, Serval caught himself drifting into complete distraction at the exotic sounds of different languages and dialects. Even English sounded melodic when spoken by someone from Liberia or the Islands. He was caught under the spell of two Jamaican women reminiscing about their childhood together when the harsh sound of his own name brought him back to the work at hand.

"Mr. Rivard! Are you quite deaf?"

"No, sir, Mr. Mathis. I'm sorry. I'm afraid I got distracted. What do you need?"

"Follow me. Your daydreaming has delayed Mr. Boley!"

Serval was careful to stay right at Mr. Mathis's heels as he threaded through the crowd. When they reached a group of men dressed in bright African robes, Serval was quick to apologize. "I'm so sorry to have kept you waiting. What can I do for you gentlemen?"

William Mathis made the introductions. "Mr. Boley, may I present Serval Rivard? Mr. Rivard will be one of our emissaries here in the States. You'll probably run into him from time to time on your travels here. Serval, I'd like you to meet Mr. Boley from Liberia. He is a very important link for the UNIA. We are working hand-in-hand with his organization to maintain ties with the Motherland. He will bring us news of Liberia and report the results of our efforts here in the United States."

As Mr. Boley shook Serval's hand, he murmured something to one of his associates in a language Serval didn't understand. Mr. Boley smiled. "Forgive me, Mr. Rivard. I was speaking Mande. My companion Mr. Buhari does not speak English, so I have been acting as his interpreter this evening. I was commenting to him that you are the least American-looking American I have met tonight. I thought you were from Western Africa. Do you have knowledge of your tribal ancestry?"

"No, Mr. Boley. I'm ashamed to admit that, like so many other Americans, that treasure has been stolen from me. But maybe you're right. Maybe my ancestors were from West Africa."

Mr. Boley studied Serval's face for a moment longer and murmured, "Yes, Krahn, perhaps. Well, who knows? Some Americans have been able to backtrack and find out about their heritage. At any rate, I am most happy to meet you, my brother from across the water, and I look forward to working with you on my travels in your country."

Mr. Mathis handed Serval a leather bag. "Mr. Rivard, will you see that our driver brings the car around to the front entrance for Mr. Boley? He has a train to catch."

"Yes, sir." Turning to Mr. Boley, Serval smiled. "It was an honor to be described as a native African. Thank you, Mr. Boley." Not wishing to make another mistake, Serval was careful to check with Mr. Mathis before leaving. "Do you need anything else, Brother?"

"Just get the driver quickly. And keep alert, please."

"Yes, sir."

After delivering the message to the driver and placing Mr. Boley's bag in the car, Serval returned to his table and smiled as he straightened his stacks of pamphlets and newspapers for the second time. *West Africa. Maybe my great, great grandfather was a warrior!* An image was forming in his mind of Africa in the times before greed had ravaged her people in the name of slavery. As the diversity of thousands of voices surrounded him with a backdrop of sound, the image became clearer. By the end of the evening, Serval was more certain than ever that Africa was his destiny.

*   *   *

*I wish Jack and Opal could'a been there tonight!* Serval thought, as he unlocked the front door of his apartment just before dawn. Yawning, he pulled off his shoes and padded down the hallway to the bedroom in his stocking feet. He smiled down at Opal as he undressed, wanting to wake her up to tell her about the convention, but stopped himself. Although he was sure he would be unable to close his eyes, the night's excitement had only masked his exhaustion, and the minute he settled down beside her, he was asleep.

*   *   *

*Green. Everything is so green! Where'd the cat go?*

A voice from far away called, "Serval?" It echoed again, "Serval?"

*Where'd the cat go? Did he get away? Why can't I talk louder?* He tried to shout. THE CAT!

"You mean Meow?" the echo said.

"No!" he shouted. "A *real* cat. It was—huh?" Suddenly aware of his own voice, Serval was instantly awake. Springing up in the bed, he blinked at Opal in confusion and tried to catch his breath.

"Serval? Was it—was it that dream again?"

"Was I—did I say something, Opal?"

"Mm-hmm. You were talkin' about a cat or sump'm. Was it the bad dream, Serval?"

Smiling ruefully, Serval eased back onto his pillow and stretched. "Naw. This was a good dream. Well, sort of. What did I say?"

Snuggling close to Serval, Opal giggled. "You kept saying 'where's the cat?' I thought you were worryin' about Meow."

"No. Now I remember. I was in Africa, Opal." Closing his eyes, Serval smiled serenely. "God! It was beautiful! And so real! I was an

African warrior on a hunt. I could feel the spear in my hand, baby! It was near a river, I think, because the ground was cool on my feet. I could see for miles—the horizon—everything! And baby, there was no wire, no rope, no Jimmy Coles—anywhere in sight. The sun was setting and . . . God! What a beautiful dream . . . Anyway, that's when I spotted the cat—I guess he was what I was after. Anyway, I stayed with him, step for step, until all of a sudden . . ."

"What?"

"That's when it turned a little weird. When the cat stopped, I realized that it wasn't a regular leopard like I thought; it was a black leopard. Then—don't ask me how I knew, but I realized that it wasn't a black leopard either—it was a serval cat. A black serval cat, the rarest kind, because they're usually spotted. And then, I knew I couldn't kill it—but I couldn't let it kill me either. Then it looked at me, right in the eyes, and this was the scary part—it—it was me. Myself. It was like I was killing my—I don't know, my own spirit, I guess. That's crazy, huh? Then he just disappeared. I guess I was asking for him because I wanted to explain to him that I didn't intend to kill him. That's crazy, huh?"

"Dreams are crazy, I guess."

Sighing, Serval pulled Opal closer and whispered, "Okay, beautiful, if you give me a *real* good kiss—one that lasts about thirty minutes—I'll tell you all about the convention and all the people I met last night."

"Oh! Tell me now, Serval! You and your crazy dream! I forgot to ask about the convention! I wish I didn't have to work last night. How was it?"

"Nuh-uh. My kiss first. *Then* I'll tell you about the convention."

Opal squirmed free and pulled on her robe. "You and your thirty-minute-long kisses! I'm hungry, Serval. Now come on in here and tell me about the convention while I fix us some breakfast."

"Aww, woman!" Serval complained loudly. "Please?"

But Opal was already halfway to the kitchen.

# Chapter 22

When Opal arrived at The Douglas Club for Saturday's extended show, she quietly headed to her corner of the dressing room and began unpacking her hair-dress articles and makeup. Dipping the tiny brush into the container of lip rouge, she carefully painted her lips the way Creola had taught her. With only her top lip painted, she stopped and stared at a stream of tears trickling down her cheeks.

Helen Fields, the resident blues singer, dropped her bag into a chair and draped one hefty arm around Opal's shoulders. "Opal? Baby? What'sa matter, sugah? You' the happiest, sweetest child I know! Now tell Helen what got'cha so upset."

"I'm not a sweet child, Helen," Opal sobbed, collapsing into the older woman's arms. "I'm horrible! I—I think . . . See, I'm—late."

"Late? Oh. Well, you' married, ain'tcha, child?"

Suddenly, Creola's voice piped in from the doorway. "Oh, Lord, Helen, just 'cause she's married don't mean she's ready to be droppin' babies every year. Damn!"

Without acknowledging Creola's presence, Helen settled into the chair next to Opal and began rummaging through her pocketbook. "Here, honey," she said, handing Opal a handkerchief. "Come on, now. Things couldn't be that bad. Don't you and your husband want babies?"

"He does. And right away," Opal said. "That's the problem, Helen." She searched Helen's eyes and lowered her voice. "See, I know I ought'a be happy but I—I don't wanna stop dancin'—just yet. I mean, we've got plenty of time for a family and . . ." She stopped for a moment, staring from Helen to Creola, and then began to cry again. "I'm a ballerina!" she sobbed. "I belong at the Metropolitan Opera House—dancing classical ballet! That's what I worked for ever since I was five years old, and I *want* it! What's so wrong with that?"

After a long silence, Helen said softly, "Aww, baby. Nothin's wrong wid'it. You ain't got to explain to me. I done seen you dance. We all got our dreams, and it ain't no reason you got to apologize for yours."

Creola flopped into a chair and stared at Opal in disbelief. "Wait a minute. Girl, you ain't tellin' us that you think them bluebloods down at the Met gonna let a colored girl dance wid' em! Opal, you done lost your mind!"

"Shut up, Creola," Helen snapped. "Bert Williams was a big Ziegfeld Follies star for years, wasn't he?"

"That's right, he was," Opal sniffled. "A headliner—right up there on Broadway with Fannie Brice and Will Rogers—all those white stars. And he's colored."

Creola rolled her eyes and crossed her arms. "Please. The Follies is a far cry from the Metropolitan Opera House! Look, I know you can dance and all that, Opal. All I'm sayin' is that, well, what'chu talkin' about just ain't ever gonna happen. Damn! You could prob'ly dance circles around all them white girls and they still wouldn't let you dance."

Helen shot Creola a warning look. "Leave her alone."

Opal jerked her chin up. "It could happen. Madame believed in me—and she was white. Somebody'll give me a chance."

"Well, baby," Helen said, turning her back on Creola, "I understand, even if some folks don't. But now, let's get back to your *late* problem. Opal, you must'a known what all that foolin' around in the bed was gonna get'cha, didn't you, child?"

"I—I guess I never thought about it—or sump'm," Opal mumbled.

"Oh, Lord!" Creola hooted. "That's it! Now I done heard everything. Ain'tcha ever heard of *timin'*, Opal?"

"Huh?"

"How's she supposed to know that, Creola?" Helen snapped. "Opal. Didn't you tell me your Daddy raised you?"

"Yes. See, Mama was . . . Well, she was gone by the time I was four."

"Mm-hmm. Well, ain'tcha ever been told—I mean, ain't a woman ever sat you down, child, and taught you . . ."

Opal shrugged. "Well, I only found out about the late stuff—you know, what missin' a period means—when I heard some'a the girls talkin' about it in the dressing room. Miss Aida told me about my period when I was twelve, but she never said a word about . . . gettin' pregnant."

"Shit!" Creola said. "That's 'cause *gettin'* pregnant is easy. Any man'll be more than happy to teach ya that! The hard part's *not* gettin' pregnant!"

Helen sighed. "Oh, Lawd . . . Listen to me, Opal. There's times of the month when you can get pregnant, and then there's times when you can fool around all you want to and—well, you jus' *can't* get pregnant."

Opal's eyebrows shot up. "When?"

Helen smiled and settled back in her chair. "Mm-hmm. That's what I thought. You been one lucky little lady so far, huh?"

"Guess so."

Creola threw back her head and laughed. "*Guess* so? I saw the way that man of yours kisses you—and child, I know he ain't one to waste a lot'a time usin' a bed for sleepin'!"

"Well, yeah," Opal laughed. "That's my Serval, all right."

"Awright, awright," Helen said, rolling her eyes. "Enough a'this lovey-dovey-rollin'-in-the-hay talk. That's how you got ya'self in this fix in the first place. Now. Jus' how late are you, baby?"

"A week."

"Only a week?" Creola chortled. "Shit, girl! If I started cryin' every time I was a week late . . ."

"Creola. Shut *up*," Helen commanded, then turned her attention back to Opal. "But she's right about that, Opal. Honey, you might not even *be* pregnant. But whether you are or you ain't, I got a book I want you to read . . ."

"I know that book," Creola interrupted. "I thought they got rid of 'em all! That's the one Emma Goldman and those other women's rights ladies use'ta pass out down at the clinic before she got arrested. It tells you all about ovulation and the safe days—you know, what days you gotta keep that man off you and what days you get to fool around."

"Uh, well . . . How many foolin' around days do I get?" Opal asked.

"Opal!" Helen laughed.

"Naw, Helen!" Creola said, shaking her head. "You ain't seen that man of hers. He's one hungry individual, I'll tell ya that!"

"And jus' how would you be knowin' that?" Helen asked.

"Hah! Please!" Creola sniffed. "The day Creola can't see sex in a man's eyes is the day I give up the ghost!" With that, she flounced out the door.

"And good riddance," Helen muttered with a wave of her hand. "Now, Opal. All you gotta do is talk to your husband and explain to him how much you wanna dance. He'll wait a couple'a years, won't he?"

Opal looked down at her hands.

"But baby . . . there's one mo' thing. Opal, look at me. If you' awready pregnant, then it's a little mo' complicated, baby. Then, you gotta go to Chappie. He knows a woman who . . . Well, never mind that now. You just wait a couple mo' weeks and let me know what happens. We'll talk about it then."

*   *   *

Five days after confiding in Helen, Opal tore into the Douglas Club like a hurricane, almost knocking Chappie over.

"Hey, hey!" he shouted. "What'chu so excited about? What'cha do? Hit the number?"

Opal flashed a smile. "Is Helen here yet, Chappie?"

Chappie grimaced. "In the dressing room tryin' on her new duds — some kind'a god-awful, raspberry-colored monstrosity with all kind'a damn spangles all over it. Lord, Opal. Try to talk her out'a wearin' that dress, would you? Please?"

Opal burst into the dressing room just as Helen was making the final adjustments to the enormous feathered headpiece that topped off her raspberry ensemble. For a split second, the sight sent Opal's news right out of her head.

"Lord, Helen! You look like Times Square and the Fourth of July all rolled up into one!"

Helen peered out from under the fringe of beads hanging from the headpiece and caught it just as it tipped dangerously to one side. "Hi, baby! The way you' smilin', you' prob'ly the only one in the joint that likes ma' new dress. Chappie hates it! But he jus' gon' have to *learn* to like it 'cause I'm sho' wearin' it tonight! I know it's loud and all, but I jus' *loves* me this color. Don'tcha jus' . . ." She stopped suddenly, and stared wide-eyed at Opal's smiling reflection in the mirror. "Oh! Child! Don't tell me — le'me guess. Ya monthly visitor came tappin' at the door this mornin'."

Throwing her arms around Helen's neck, Opal squealed, "Right! Now, where's that book you were tellin' me about?"

*   *   *

Serval's trip to Charleston provided Opal ample time to study the book. She read that the timing method worked best for women whose periods were regular, and prayed that her recent lateness would turn out to be an isolated incident. After figuring her "safe zone" on a calendar, she smiled. Serval's return fell on the first Monday of the days she had marked with the letters "F.A.O.K." which stood for "fooling around okay."

\* \* \*

Opal's timing strategy went haywire when Serval's trip was extended for two weeks. Instead of the romantic reunion she had planned, she spent the evening playing mouse to Serval's love-starved cat. She sighed with relief when he nodded off twice over supper, but a cup of coffee revived him. When he pushed away from the kitchen table and stretched, Opal saw a familiar grin on his face.

"Aww, baby! That was good! For a kid who was so spoiled by Aida's cookin', you're turnin' into a great chef!"

As Opal picked up his plate, it slipped from her fingers and crashed to the floor. "Oh, Serval! I'm sorry! I almost dropped it right on your head!"

Serval reached for her arm. "Well, you missed. And if you're tryin' to murder me for my money, forget it, 'cause I'm broke. Hey, what's the matter with you tonight, baby? You've been nervous ever since I got back."

Opal grabbed a dish towel and carefully squatted down to clean up the broken glass. "Nothin's wrong. I just dropped a plate is all. Go ahead and take your bath, Serval. I know how you like to take your little naps in the tub."

"You read my mind." Leaning over her, he kissed the back of her neck and whispered, "Why don't you come join me? If you wash my back, I'll be more than happy to wash your front."

Without looking up, she responded with a noncommittal "Mmmm."

"Opal? I said . . ."

"I heard you, Serval," she snapped. "I just—I—I already had a bath."

"You're in a strange mood, Mrs. Rivard!" Serval laughed. "Guess I better leave you alone for awhile. But wake me up if I'm in there too long. Don't let me drown!"

"I won't."

Opal fretted for the next half-hour, wondering what forms of trickery other women used at times like these. *Maybe he'll be too tired. Huh! Not likely. Maybe I'll tell him I've got a headache . . . No. Serval knows I never get headaches. I'll just say I'm not in the mood.* She shook her head, angry at her own displays of enthusiasm for sex since his return from the war. As she dawdled over the dishes, she muttered to herself. "Not in the mood? Huh! . . . Sorry, Dear, but me and Woodrow Wilson's got a date to smooch in Macy's window. He'll have an easier time believin' that!"

She was still puzzling about what to do when Serval's voice startled her. "Opal?"

She whirled around to face him, and his state of undress set her heart to thumping. He stood in the doorway wearing nothing but a towel, his bare chest still glistening with water from his bath. She swallowed hard. "Oh! Serval! I, uh . . ."

"What in the world is wrong with you, young lady?"

The faint smell of his shaving lotion hung in the air. Opal blinked and said nothing as he stepped nearer and enfolded her in his arms. She squirmed at the tickling sensation in her ear as Serval nuzzled it, humming a soft, lazy version of "Under the Bamboo Tree." She felt his thighs leaning against hers through the damp towel and a familiar hard pressure against her pelvis as he urged her toward the bedroom in a dance of wordless persuasion.

Opal clung tightly to him, afraid to open her eyes. "I—I missed you, Serval, but . . ." She stopped with a short gasp when she felt him lift her and ease her down onto the bed in one quick, fluid movement. Before she could protest, his lips were on hers, and she felt his thumb pulling gently down on her chin to ease her mouth open. An involuntary shiver ran down her spine when he murmured something unintelligible in her ear, then let out a long, deep sigh—the language of sex.

She realized that she was losing herself to his touch when she heard another sigh—her own. Pulling away from him quickly, Opal attempted to gather her wits. "Serval, I—I'm sorry. I . . ."

"What is it, baby? What's wrong with you tonight?"

"It's just—well . . . See, I pulled a muscle last night dancin' and— uh, well, I really think I hurt it bad, 'cause the pain is terrible."

"Oh, baby!" Serval's voice was filled with genuine concern. "Where? What muscle? I mean, do you need to go to a doctor or anything?"

Opal pointed to her left inner thigh area and winced. "Here, Serval. Chappie says it's not too bad, but it hurts all the way up and . . . Maybe I should see a doctor tomorrow if it doesn't feel better, huh?"

Serval gently touched her thigh with his fingertips, and Opal flinched. "Oh, baby, I'm sorry! It really hurts that bad, huh?"

"Well, yes. It—it hurts just to walk on it or move it at all."

"But you seemed okay fixin' supper."

"I—well, it really hurt . . . but—but I didn't want you to worry."

"Aw, baby. Don't keep things like that from me, okay?"

"Okay," she murmured.

"So, I guess this means you won't be dancing for a while, young lady."

"Huh? Oh, yeah. I guess not. But I prob'ly ought'a go to rehearsals—you know, just to watch and—uh—keep up with the new steps."

"Well, it's a good thing I'm home this week so I can drive you. I don't want you walking to the bus on that leg."

Opal's smile was joyless. "Thanks. That's real nice."

Serval adjusted the covers carefully, and Opal turned on her side, facing away from him. He settled against her back, spoon fashion, and she stiffened at the heat of his touch.

"This is okay, isn't it?" he whispered.

"Mm-hmm. Guess so. G'night."

Serval chuckled softly into the back of her neck.

"What are you laughin' about, Serval?"

"I just realized why you've been acting so strange all night. This is the first time you ever had to say no to me, huh? Is that it?"

*I wish it was the last,* she thought.

"Opal? Is that it?"

"Mm-hmm. Guess so."

He laughed wickedly. "Well, you were right to tell me, 'cause, believe me, baby, what I had in mind definitely involved stretchin' that particular muscle!"

"Serval!"

"Well, it did!" Kissing her cheek, he whispered, "I guess I'll survive another night or two without making love to you, although I barely made it through this last trip. I'm spoiled, I guess."

"Mm-hmm. You're spoiled, all right. But I'm sorry anyway, Serval. I really am. I miss you when you're gone, too. And I was really looking forward to . . ."

"What? Sex?" Serval laughed softly. "Why are you so shy about sayin' it? Just admit that you love sex, Mrs. Rivard. There's nothin' wrong with that. We *are* married, in case you forgot."

Turning to face him, Opal wrapped her arms tightly around Serval's neck. "I love *you.* Please don't ever forget that, okay?"

"Hey, hey, baby! Watch out for your leg! I love you, too. Now, let's get some sleep."

Opal nodded.

"Good-night, baby. . . . Uh, Opal?"

"Mm-hmm?"

"Did you ever pull a muscle before?"

"Oh, lots'a times. Why?"

"Well—how long does it take to heal?"

"Another week," Opal said quickly. "Uh, give or take a day."

Serval yawned. "Oh. Well, I've got another trip in ten days. Maybe if I'm real gentle and careful, we'll still have a little time to get to work on that first baby." His voice began to fade as he drifted toward sleep. "Mmmm. Pleasant work, though, Mrs. Rivard. Mighty pleasant work."

# Chapter 23

Opal was in no mood for a New Year's Eve celebration as she trudged through the corridor of Club Deluxe. Serval had sailed away to the Caribbean islands in mid-December, leaving her to spend Christmas alone, and his last letter made no mention of a return date. She pulled on her costume quickly, then joined the orchestra onstage for the first of three numbers.

She half-stepped through the orchestra's instrumental rendition of "I'm Just Wild About Harry," knowing that no one in the audience was paying attention anyway. At the end of the number, she bowed for the weak scatter of applause that could be heard above the drunken laughter and shouted conversation. The only person looking at her had also been her chief competition since she had stepped onstage: a waif-thin, caramel-colored man in shirtsleeves and dangling suspenders, who was perched atop one of the front tables, waving an empty champagne bottle and singing "Someday Sweetheart" for the third time. "When you gonna get Alberta Hunter in this joint, Champ?" the man shouted. "Hey! Where *is* the Champ anyhow? Ain't seen him in hours!" He finished his speech with a loud belch.

Hands on hips, Opal glared at him. "Go home, fool."

His response was a grimace followed by an off-key encore. Opal rolled her eyes at him and hurried offstage so fast, she nearly collided with Chappie, who was finally coming to her rescue with his megaphone.

"Don't let it bother you, Opal," he whispered. "You know this isn't our regular crowd. They're all bombed out of their minds."

Opal managed a nod, and headed in the direction of the dressing room.

"Opal!" Chappie shouted. "Please go out and mingle like the Champ asked you to. You know the patrons love it when the girls flirt a little. Come on, now."

Without looking at him, she turned around and slowly descended
the stage steps into the multicolored sea of balloons and paper stream-
ers at her feet. "I'll mingle," she muttered, "but flirtin' with these fools
is out." She folded her arms and stood still for a moment to survey the
madness surrounding her. Tiny party hats on the heads of grown men
and women gave the club its own army of drunken firemen, stumbling
Irish leprechauns, squealing fairy princesses, and enough red-horned
devils to crowd Satan out of hell. *I can't mingle with this mess. I gotta
get out'a here.*

As Opal made her way through the crush of revelers, she covered
her ears and avoided the eyes of anyone in her path. She slapped away
grabbing hands, and intently pressed toward the front door. But a sudden, deafening yell in her ear forced her to look up into the red eyes
of a balding Caucasian man wearing a pointed clown hat the size of
an ice cream cone and a tuxedo that had seen better days.

"Hey, sister!" he shouted. "Dansh wi'me!"

"No, thank you," she shouted back. "Please let me by. I need to get
outside."

"Nonshensh! There's no party out there!" He grabbed her wrist and
pressed a chipped teacup into her hand. "I got a flask in my hip pocket,
little cutie. My own recipe. Now, c'mon."

Opal narrowed her eyes. "Look, Mister, I'm sick. You don't want me
to throw up all over your fancy suit, do you?"

Releasing his grip on her wrist, he took a shaky step back, and Opal
was sure he would have fallen if not for the overcrowded condition of
the room. Turning her back on him, she craned her neck to plot her
course. The gilded framework of the front door beckoned to her like
the gates of heaven. Chappie's voice suddenly boomed above the din,
leading everyone in a countdown of the last seconds of 1921: "Four . . .
three . . . two . . . one . . . Happy New Year!" Just as the cheering
started, Opal slipped out the door.

Shivering in the cold midnight air, she wished she had grabbed her
coat on the way out. She folded her arms tightly and lowered her head
against the wind as she trotted across the street, taking care not to scuff
her new red dancing pumps. "The diner," she whispered to herself.
"I'll just run in here for some soup and warm up."

Just as she reached the door, it opened, and two Caucasian couples
stumbled out, nearly knocking Opal off her feet. The women appeared
to be twins, identical in every detail—from shiny black spitcurls on

foreheads to matching full-length ermine coats. They even giggled with the same high-pitched squeak. The men both wore expensive-looking tuxedos with evening capes, but looked nothing alike. One was silver-haired and portly; the other was lanky and college-aged. "Watch it, Dad," the younger man laughed. "You almost knocked this lovely lady down!" He reached for Opal's hand and kissed it while executing a wobbly bow. "A thousand pardons, my sepia princess. I say, would you care to join us? We're on the town with Delia here and uh . . . I'm sorry, my love. What was your name?"

The forgotten girl pouted. "Amelia."

"A thousand pardons. How could I forget? Delia and Amelia." He smiled at Opal. "And you are . . .?"

"Not interested," Opal said with a scowl.

The older man snorted a laugh, then applauded. "Leave her alone, son. Excuse us, my dear, but we're roaring drunk, as you can see. New Year's Eve, you know."

Opal forced a smile. "Mm-hmm. Well, Happy New Year to you then."

The son gasped and allowed his father to lead him away. "You don't mean we've missed it? Dad . . . it can't be midnight already?"

Opal watched the group stumble away, and noticed that a light snow had begun to fall. A glance through the diner window confirmed her fears; the group inside could easily be mistaken for the rowdy bunch she had just left. Apparently, Harlem was the place to be for ringing in 1922. Deciding that the middle of the street was her only possible oasis from the noise, Opal traded warmth for silence, and doggedly stood there shivering. *Wonder if he'll make it home by Easter? Guess I'll be lucky if he makes it for the fourth of July . . .* Her teeth began to chatter, so she hopped and shimmied for a moment, finally stopping to gaze up at the sign above the old Douglas Club. Blazing electric lights spelled out its new name: "Jack Johnson's Club Deluxe."

Opal stared at the sign until it blurred through her tears, and then reproached herself. *Mr. Garvey belongs to the people, and Serval belongs at his side. I've just gotta learn to share him, that's all. It's not like he planned this trip just so he could leave me all alone for the holidays on purpose.* She heaved a loud sigh. *Shoot, Serval! First you go off a whole year to that crazy war, and last year . . .* Her mental tirade was interrupted as the front door of Club Deluxe opened, spilling its light and noise out onto the new fallen snow. Without looking up, she saw

a long shadow sweep past her ankles, and then heard Chappie's familiar laugh.

"Opal! You look like some urchin who got lost makin' a break from
the orphanage. Come back in here before you freeze to death, girl!"

"I'm okay," she snapped.

"Okay. Guess I'll just have to tell the operator that I couldn't find
you then."

"What?" Opal shouted. "What operator?"

Chappie grinned. "Think she said she's got a call from a fella by the
name of, uh, what was it? Rivard or sump'm."

Opal broke into a teetering run and smacked Chappie's shoulder as
he held the door open for her. Flattening herself against the walls, she
made good time getting to the hallway outside the dressing room. She
snatched the receiver dangling from the wall-phone and shouted into
the mouthpiece, "Serval?"

"Opal? Well, there you are! Happy New Year, Mrs. Rivard!"

"Oh, Serval, it's good to hear your voice! Happy New Year! Where
are you?"

"Speak up, baby. I can hardly hear you."

"I said where *are* you, Mr. Rivard?"

"In Jamaica, Mrs. Rivard."

"Oh! So then you'll be back soon?"

"Oh, I don't know. We thought we might take a little vacation and
sail off to the Hawaiian Islands for a few months . . ."

"Serval, don't fool with me! I miss you! You've been gone a whole
month!"

Serval laughed. "I'm sorry, baby. I know I explained in my letters
about all the stops we had to make for repairs. Didn't you get my letters? Anyway we're on our way back. I should be home in a few days."

"I got your letters, Serval. So what day exactly? And what time? Me
and Jack'll pick you up at the pier."

"Well, barring any more delays . . . Wait, did you say Jack's in town?"

"Mm-hmm. He's gotta do a hop to Baltimore in the mornin' but
then he's got three days off."

"Good! Then have him bring you down to the pier on the evening
of the third at, oh, about six o'clock. Hey! How is Jack, anyway?"

"He's fine, Serval. Oh, shoot, they're callin' me! I gotta go do my
number now. I love you!"

"I love you, too. See you on the third. Oh, wait! Baby?"

"What, Serval? I really gotta go . . ."

"You know what I want."

"What, Serval? They're callin' me!"

"One kiss."

Opal giggled and reached up to give the mouthpiece a quick, audible smooch. "That's gonna have to do for now, Mr. Rivard. I'll give you a better one when you get back." As she hung up the receiver, Opal emitted a happy squeak. The timing couldn't have been more perfect. For the next seven days, her calendar was marked with nothing but "fooling around days."

*       *       *

The alliance of Jack's lanky body with the five-foot sofa in Serval's living room created an animated mountain range of shadows on the far wall. He shifted several times before settling into a passably comfortable position, then stared over at the silhouette of his left knee. *Mount Sinai. Moses an' the Lawd talkin' things over.* Yawning, he reached for the table lamp and pulled the chain. The darkness was reassuring, and he stretched his legs until they dangled over the end of his "bed." Despite the sofa's shortness, the headbumps he'd collected due to low doorways, and the cramped dimensions of the bathroom, the Rivard apartment was home to Jack Hawkins. He drifted easily to sleep.

The sound of the front door opening startled him awake, but he kept his eyes shut. He listened to Opal's quick, light steps over the usual creaky floorboards, and sensed her closeness. Jack's heartbeat quickened when he caught the scent of her hair, and he wondered why she was leaning over him. Pretending to turn over in his sleep, he saw her picking up the alarm clock he kept on the coffee table.

"Sorry, Jack," Opal whispered. "Didn't mean to wake you up. I was just checkin' to make sure you didn't forget to set the alarm on this thing. I didn't want you to be late like you were this mornin'. Now go on back to sleep."

Jack rubbed his eyes and gazed up at her. He paused for a moment, wishing he could think of something sweet to say, but settled on "Thanks."

"Oh, Jack! Guess what? Serval called the club tonight. You guessed it right. You said he'd prob'ly be gettin' in this week. Well, he's comin' home day after tomorrow!"

"Mmm-hmm. I thought that looked like a Serval smile."

"Guess it is. Anyway, go back to sleep now. You gotta get up in three hours. G'night, Jack!"

"G'night, Opal," he whispered.

Jack listened for the sound of the bedroom door closing, and peered down the hall to watch her shadow as it passed several times under the crack of the door. When the light went out, he heard her sigh, and he shut his eyes tightly at the sound. *My best friend's wife. But I can't help it.*

*     *     *

The S.S. Frederick Douglass was the crowning jewel of the Black Star Line Steamship Corporation. Originally christened the S.S. Yarmouth, the ship had been a costly but necessary factor in Garvey's plans, despite its need for repairs. He quietly paid the inflated asking price and acquired what would become his noisiest and most controversial weapon in the fight for racial advancement. After supervising its renovation to ensure the vessel's seaworthiness, Garvey renamed the steamer the S.S. Frederick Douglass, hired a captain and crew, and began the search for a second ship. While many UNIA stockholders held the romantic notion that the sole purpose of the shipping line was as transportation for the exodus back to Africa, members of Garvey's inner circle embraced it as a source of much needed capital. To Garvey, it was both. The Frederick Douglass was launched as a vessel of commerce and promotion on the high seas, engaging in Caribbean trade and travel, as well as transporting Serval and his associates to disseminate information and sell Black Star stock. In each port city visited by the flagship, UNIA membership soared.

On the night of Serval's return, Opal clung tightly to Jack's arm, squinting for signs of the ship. As six o'clock approached, the pier began to resemble a colorful backdrop for a lavish Broadway play. UNIA representatives in long coats and tall hats discussed future ventures of the shipping line, and family members of the returning crew gathered along the pier's edge to welcome their loved ones home. On the horizon, pink and orange clouds stole curtain calls from the sun as it melted into its own reflection in the water. But the show was lost on Jack, who patted Opal's hand as she fidgeted nervously. At last the long, mournful tone of a horn sounded the ship's approach. The Frederick

Douglass was by no means a grand ocean liner, but, gliding along in the flattering light of a hazy sunset, it was a stately apparition. On the deck stood a young man, his dark, muscled forearms in prominent contrast against the white rolled sleeves of his billowing shirt. He leaned against the rail and smiled.

"There he is!" Opal squealed. "Serval! Over here! Serval! Oh, Lord, Jack, why isn't that fool wearin' a jacket? He's gonna catch a cold for sure."

The minute the ship was secured, Serval ducked under a large net filled with fruit crates, and appeared not to hear the shouted warnings of crewmembers poised to guide the cargo to the deck for unloading. He ran down the gangplank and caught Opal as she flew into his arms. Jack hung back watching, and tried to smile. His eyes followed Serval's hands as they traveled from Opal's neck, down the length of her back, and up again, pulling her close for a kiss. Jack stared down at his own shoes and his smile faded. *I gotta git out that house tonight . . .* But when he heard the couple's hurried footsteps in his direction, then felt a strong arm around his neck, Jack looked up and found his misplaced smile in his best friend's eyes.

"Hey, buddy!" Serval said grinning. "I hear you're in for a few days, and you know what that means. Lively times must roll!"

"Yeah. I took a little time off. Been sleepin' on yo' couch the past two nights."

"That's not my couch. That's your bed, Jack. So how's everything goin', man?"

"Aww, things jus' the same—'cep we been missin' you. But now you' lookin' a little tired, man. You been sleepin'?"

Serval shrugged, then draped his left arm around Jack's shoulder and his right arm around Opal's waist as they walked. Opal stopped suddenly, and touched Serval's neck. "Oh, baby," she whispered. "Scratches. You had that dream again . . ."

Serval shot Jack a sharp look, then changed the subject. "So, what's for supper? I'm so hungry I could eat a whole pot of spaghetti and about ten or fifteen catfish."

"Shoot, man," Jack said, "Don't forget 'bout my cawnbread."

\* \* \*

Even before he had finished eating, Jack was planning his escape. Mumbling a barely audible excuse, he rose from his chair, and Serval protested loudly.

"Naw, Jack! You can't leave yet! We were gonna go catch a flicker, man!"

"Yeah, Jack," Opal said. "It's a new one called 'Four Horses in the Boxcars,' or sump'm like that." Serval leaned back in his chair laughing, and Opal cut her eyes at him. "Okay, I know that's wrong, huh? What is it then, Mr. Smart-aleck?"

"It's 'The Four Horsemen of the Apocalypse.' But hey, four horses in a boxcar sounds like more fun to me. What do you think, Jack?"

Jack shrugged his shoulders. "Aww, y'all jus' go. I got me some bidness to tend to."

Serval shot out of his chair in mock indignation and wrapped his arm around Opal's shoulders. "More important than *us?*"

"Cancel it, Jack," Opal chided. "When us three get together, there's nothin' more important, 'cause we—Hey! We ought'a call ourselves sump'm like . . ." Opal could barely contain her laughter. ". . . The Three Horsemen of the Boxcars—on account'a Jack's job."

Serval groaned. "What you need, young lady, is a long, quiet retreat at one of those *hospitals* . . ."

Only Jack didn't laugh, prompting Serval to nudge Opal while reprimanding him. "Jack's bein' a wet blanket. Come on, man! Cancel your plans . . ."

"I can't," Jack snapped. "I gotta go, hear? I—Look here, I be back tomorrow mawnin' for breakfas'. That okay?"

Opal crossed her arms and curled her top lip. "Shoot. At least he likes our food. Guess it's just our company he's got no use for."

Jack tried a half-hearted smile, then headed for the door. Serval's voice stopped him.

"Hey. Take care of yourself, brother."

"Yeah," Jack mumbled. "Y'all enjoy the flickers."

*   *   *

Seated in the dark theater, Opal nudged Serval with her elbow and pointed at the screen. "Serval! Look at this fella, would you?"

Serval's eyes fluttered open. "Huh?"

"I said look at him. That one—the one with the slanty eyes. And don't bother pretendin' like you're wide awake. I know you fell asleep."

"Huh-uh, baby. Not me. Wide awake. Great flicker."

"Liar. You've been snorin' for the last five minutes. The organ player just gave you a dirty look."

"Sorry. But it was probably his syrupy organ music that put me to sleep. Besides, I told you I like sword fights, not dancing boys wearin' lip rouge."

"Well, look at this one anyway, Serval."

"Which one?"

"That one . . . Oh, shoot! Another title. Wait . . . Waiting for sparks to fly . . ." Opal read in a whisper, "Marguerite wonders if her husband Laurier feels threatened by Julio, a man she has just met . . . There he is! Julio! The one with the slanty eyes! Who does he look like to you?"

Serval studied the face for a moment, then broke into a grin. "Jack! He looks like Jack Hawkins around the eyes. Hah! And the angles of his jaw . . . everything but his nose!"

"Shh! Not so loud, Serval!"

"Why? I'm not botherin' anybody, Opal. It's not like I've got a chance'a drownin' out the maestro and his corny organ." Sinking into his seat, he noticed several theater patrons directing icy stares his way.

"Look, Serval!" Opal gasped. "Julio's fixin' to go off to the war!"

Serval grunted. "Who, *him?* Swell. Nobody but the Krauts would'a signed him up. No wonder they lost."

"Shh! Oh, this is so sad. And he's wearin' an Allies uniform, smart-aleck. He could'a been fightin' in some trench with you."

"Opal. He's an actor. This isn't real. He never saw a trench in his life."

"Use your imagination, Serval. . . . Oh, Serval, look! He's at the war! They're shootin' at him!"

Serval rolled his eyes. "Use my imagination," he muttered. "Okay. I'll use my imagination and believe that his uniform could be that clean. And that the Army would'a signed up a fella wearin' lip rouge. But, Opal, my imagination fails me when . . ."

He was cut off by a loud female voice from a few rows back. "Hush, fool!"

Serval crossed his arms and shut his eyes. "Let me know when it's over."

Serval slept through the rest of the film, only waking when he heard Opal reading the list of credits. "So who was the white Jack Hawkins?" he asked through a yawn.

"Some new fella with a foreign name—Rodolfo Valentino. The ladies sure were sighin' over him, huh?"

Serval stood up to stretch, and cut his eyes at a group of giggling women dressed in the latest flapper attire—short, drop-waist dresses in loud colors, with skull-hugging cloche hats to match. "Crazy females. Acting so silly over a white boy wearin' lip rouge."

"Huh! You got a lot'a nerve, Serval. I bet you've seen every flicker Douglas Fairbanks ever made—twice. And he's white."

"That's different. I don't go around moonin' over Fairbanks. Look, I can't help it if I like a good sword-fight now and then, or pirates raisin' hell on the high seas. And yeah, Miss Smart-aleck. I *do* happen to get a kick out of Fairbanks when he does that backflip thing onto his horse. Anyway, I don't care how much the women go for this Val— Valentine . . . what's his name?"

"Valentino."

"Yeah, okay. But you mark my words. He'll never be as big as Fairbanks. Hell, he'd probably break his skinny little neck if he ever tried to do a backflip."

Opal laughed. "Serval, I hope it doesn't shock you, but I really don't think the ladies care if he ever does a doggone backflip."

✳    ✳    ✳

*Valentino*—Serval wrote in his journal that night—*some new actor who has the women sighing at the flickers—even Negro women! Just more nonsense that has newspaper columnists calling this decade "The Roaring Twenties." Can't help but get sore that some of our women have such short memories. It wasn't that long ago that masters and their sons visited slave row to add rape to their list of crimes against us. Some things never change. Are our people so determined to assimilate that they've gone blind? While these Caucasians who call themselves "jazz babies" swill their bathtub gin and invade Harlem to steal our music and dances, their southern cousins are lynching Negroes in record numbers. Slavery might be over, but the slave masters' descendants still inflict plantation standards on Negroes who dare to reach for progress. Who is Marcus Garvey but a modern-day slave trying to buy his freedom from the corporate masters in the form of ships? The only answer is to fight for our survival until we can build a new nation in Mother Africa. Damn! Carry me home, sweet Jesus—on a Black Star steamer!*

# Chapter 24

Leon burrowed deep into the warm softness of the big feather bed and dug his arms under the pillow as Manché's fingers worked warm mineral oil into the muscles of his back. "A little lower, baby," he murmured. "It's my low back always givin' me misery. Oh, yeah. Right there. That's the spot. Mmmmm."

Manché emitted a deep rumble of pleasure from her throat—the kind of laugh that comes from years of hard drinking. But it was an honest laugh. Manché Redriver enjoyed her time with Leon, and did her best to make him feel appreciated every minute. Now that they were spending more time together, she came to the realization that although Leon was certainly not the handsomest or smartest of men, his humor and sincerity had worked a miracle, gradually healing all her old wounds. Ever since he had moved into her little coldwater flat, she found that she was drinking with less frequency, and felt younger and more carefree than she had in years. She leaned down and kissed his back. "Ya had enough, Papa?"

"Manché, Manché. Woman, you sho' can give a backrub! I feels like a youngster again. Now, come on over here and lemme get my arms around all that sweet stuff you got workin' there, girl."

Manché snuggled close to Leon and let out a long, contented sigh. "You' a good man, Leon. I don't know what I done to deserve you."

Leon chuckled. "Well, honey. I ain't gonna argue wit'cha. I *am* good. But you know what I'm always tellin' you—only the best for my baby."

"Leon?"

"Mm-hmm?"

"I—uh . . ."

"What, baby?"

"I was supposed to talk to you about sump'm tonight—for Mr. Hightower."

"Mr. Hightower? What' he want wit' me?"

"Well . . . I—I think he heard about your little hustle and he asked me to see would you like to do a couple'a little ol' jobs for him."

"Aww now, baby. I don't know. See, I jus' been dealin' a little hooch for my buddies 'round the neighborhood and such. Hightower—shoot! He in with them big-shot Italians. Them's some dangerous fellas. I don't know, baby."

"Well, see, Sugah, I kind'a wanted to help him out on account'a all the pressure he been gettin'. See, I can't lose my job at The Brass Door. If Hightower don't keep up with the big boys, he'll get shut down and I'll be out'a my job, baby."

"Well . . . you really want me to do it?"

"Jus' go see what he wants, Sugah. If you don't feel right about it, then you jus' say no."

"Just say no? To Max Hightower?"

Manché squirmed away from him, and sighed. "Guess you shouldn't do it then."

"Aw, baby, don't be like that. Tell ya what. I'll think about it. How's that?"

"That' be jus' fine, Sugah. Now give Manché a kiss."

\* \* \*

The next afternoon Leon waited nervously outside Max Hightower's office to be announced, knowing that no matter what the request, he had already made the turn onto a one-way road. There was no turning back now.

"Mr. Jackson?" Peggy, Max Hightower's buxom red-headed secretary, smiled over at Leon. "You can go in now."

"Thank you, ma'am." Leon crossed the small reception area and opened the door to Hightower's dim inner office. The only light was provided by a green-shaded desk lamp, and a reading lamp at the end of an oxblood leather sofa. Leon cleared his throat and stepped inside. "Uh, Mr. Hightower?"

Max Hightower rose from behind an ornate mahogany desk, and walked over to greet Leon. He was an imposing figure of a man, about six feet, two inches in height, and good-looking in a swarthy Italian way, although only half Italian by birth. His only unattractive feature was his smile, which revealed teeth badly yellowed by years of chain-smoking. He flashed the yellow smile at Leon.

"Leon! Thanks for coming. Have a seat. You've met my associate Harry Bragg at the club, haven't you?" He gestured toward the sofa where a short, wiry white man with curly black hair was sprawled, perusing a racing form.

"Yes, sir. How you doin', Mr. Bragg?"

"Fine, Leon, just fine."

Max settled into the massive black leather chair behind the desk and studied Leon, the yellow smile still on display. "Now, let's get down to business. Leon, some'a my boys tell me you've got a nice, quiet little operation goin'. Is that true?"

Leon cleared his throat and tugged at his tie. "You mean the hooch? Aw, Mr. Hightower. Now that you lettin' me handle the numbers for you, I cut that back to jus' a little thing on the side. You know, hookin' up a friend or two, that's all. I mean, it sho' ain't no threat to what *you* doin' . . ." Leon stopped abruptly. *Gotdamn, Leon! How you gonna look a big-time gangster in the eye and tell him 'bout his illegal self?!* "Uh, Mr. Hightower, what I meant to say is . . ."

Max laughed easily, but Leon read a warning in his eyes. "It's okay, Leon. I've heard good things about you. You know your way around the block and you're discreet. You *are* discreet, aren'tcha, Leon? You know how to keep your mouth shut?"

"Oh, yes, sir. You can depend on that."

"Good. Because I want you to do a little job for me."

"Uh, well, sho', Mr. Hightower. What—what kind'a job?"

"We want you to pick up a shipment for us down in Florida. We need somebody who can get the job done fast and quiet, and who won't draw a lot of attention. Invisible, see?"

"Uh, well, Mr. Hightower, I don't know if I'm the best man for that job."

"Whadaya mean? You're perfect."

"Well, I'ma be drivin' alone, right?"

"Right. So?"

"Well, see, a colored man drivin' the highways by hisself . . . police sho' seem like they find a lot'a reasons to pull us over. See, now if I was to be chauffeurin' or sump'm . . ."

Max laughed. "You didn't let me finish, Leon. You got nothing to worry about. You'll be driving a supply truck and you'll be takin' side roads most of the way. You ever heard of Ace Construction? They're big. And half their drivers are colored, Leon. Don't worry. You won't get stopped. And if you do, then won't those cops be surprised when they open those back doors and find a supply of bricks! We're experts at camouflage, ya know, Leon. We know what we're doin'. What did you think? That we were gonna make you drive a truck with 'booze' written on the side of it in six-foot letters?"

Leon laughed nervously. "Well, uh . . . what if they get past them bricks and I get caught?"

Max leaned back and shot Harry a quick look before answering Leon's question. "Look, Leon. You just do what I tell you." As Harry handed Leon a piece of paper with written instructions, Max continued. "There's the warehouse address. You be there Monday at midnight and one of our boys'll show you how to load the shipment so the crates don't show. And don't be late. Then you follow this route down to Miami. When you get to the Racine address—it's a big, yellow boarding house—you go in and ask for Billy Greenleigh. Only talk to him, you hear me, Leon? You tell Billy you're one'a Joe Kennedy's new boys and you're pickin' up the shipment this week."

"Joe Kennedy?" Leon asked.

"You don't know Joe Kennedy?!" Max laughed. "Boy, where have you been? Kennedy and his boys practically supply the entire Eastern Seaboard!"

Harry rolled his eyes and leaned forward. "He's the guy you're working for, Leon."

Max rose and patted Leon on the back. "Now. I want you to make good time and when you get back, drive straight to the warehouse. And don't worry about getting stopped."

"Yes, sir, Mr. Hightower."

"Oh, and Leon . . ."

"Yes, sir?"

The yellow smile was abruptly replaced by another steely gaze. "You never heard of me."

Leon nodded. "Whatever you say, Mr.—uh, what'cha say yo' name was again?"

Max laughed. "See that, Harry? I told you Leon was a right guy!"

Leon backed out of the room and closed the door softly. When he turned to leave, he noticed that Peggy was nowhere in sight, and that the front door to the reception area was open. He headed for the door, but when he raised his hat to put it on, he noticed perspiration stains on the brim which was now badly twisted. "Gotdamn!" he muttered softly. "My best navy blue derby!" The sudden sound of loud laughter from inside Hightower's office startled him, and he overheard the name "Joe Kennedy." Keeping an eye out for Peggy, he edged closer to Hightower's office door and listened.

"Max, that's rich," Harry was saying. "Leon thinks he's workin' for that big-shot mick. That was genius!"

"Hey, Harry—whadaya think? That I don't have a sense of humor?"

"Yeah, but what happens if one'a the *real* boys finds out Leon's stealin' their shipment?"

"First, Kennedy's barely involved in that operation, if he is at all. I think he supplied a truck or somethin'. It's mostly his uncle's booze he fools with. And second, my man in Cuba can be trusted, believe me. Nobody but us knows this shipment's gettin' in a day early. By the time the boys get to Miami, Leon'll be back in Brooklyn. Besides, Harry, 'steal' is such an ugly word. Let's just call it—intercepting. And the real beauty of it is that if Leon does get stopped by the cops and talks, it'll be Kennedy's name he drops."

Harry laughed again. "Like I said—genius. Okay, but what if somebody other than the cops catches Leon *intercepting* . . .?"

Leon leaned closer to the door and held his breath as he waited to hear the answer. "Pal," Hightower said, "that's Leon's problem."

# Chapter 25

Opal fought her way out of a deep sleep in response to Serval's fingertips slowly gliding down the center of her back. Barely opening her eyes, she saw the golden paleness of early morning casting shadows on the wall. She smiled, lying completely still, curious to see how long his patience would last. As he eased closer to her, she felt a feather-light brush of his lips against the back of her neck, then on her earlobe, and she couldn't keep from trembling slightly.

"Wake up, Mrs. Rivard," he whispered. "Time to go to work."

"Huh? Work?"

"Not dancin' work. *Baby* work. You know, the *fun* kind," he chuckled. "Kiss me."

"Oh, Serval! What time is it?" Opal cried, scrambling out of bed. Without waiting for an answer, she grabbed her wrapper and hurried to the bathroom.

She stood in the bathroom for several minutes wondering what to do. Going back to bed was out of the question; if she ran a bath, he might try to join her; and if she started breakfast in such a rush, he would surely be suspicious. Finding no other alternative, she opted for the breakfast idea and headed for the kitchen.

*Maybe he'll fall back asleep.* As she turned to go to the cooler for eggs, she saw Serval standing in the kitchen doorway staring at her.

"Oh, Serval! I . . . How long have you been standing there?" She pretended to search the cupboard for something, then rearranged the pans on the stove.

After a long silence, he said, "Opal."

When she glanced over at him, he hadn't moved from the doorway, but his eyes were two inescapable magnets. "Just how stupid do you think I am, Opal?"

*Time for the showdown.* Opal lowered herself slowly into one of the kitchen chairs and covered her face with her hands. "I'm sorry," she murmured. "Serval, it's just that . . ."

"Don't. I don't want to hear how sorry you are. You don't have to be sorry if you want me to stop—touching you. Don't you think I saw through all your excuses, Opal? I didn't say anything because I just figured that, well, women aren't always in the mood, and I didn't want to force myself on you. But this morning was different. I know you, Opal, and I can tell when you want me. This morning, your body was more than ready, but the minute your brain woke up, you ran away from me like I was your worst nightmare. So . . . all I want to know is—why?"

A series of answers rushed through Opal's mind, but none made it as far as her lips.

Serval lowered his head. "Is it . . . another man? Did you meet somebody at the club?" His voice was almost a whisper.

Opal sprang from her chair and threw her arms around his waist. "No! Oh, Serval, no!"

Pushing her away, he stared into her eyes. "Then why? I thought you wanted a baby, and if . . ." He stopped and took a step back. "Aww, damn! That's it, isn't it? You *don't* want a baby!"

"Serval, I . . ."

He held up one hand and turned his back on her. "Don't."

"Serval . . ." Opal had to run to keep up with his angry stride as he headed down the hall to the bedroom. "Wait, Serval. Just listen— please?"

He pulled on one sock and sat poised to put on the other, but stopped suddenly to throw the sock across the room. "All this time, Opal. All this time I thought you loved me, but every time I was in this goddamn bed making love to you, all you were doing was just—submitting—and praying not to get pregnant! Goddamn!"

"No, Serval! It wasn't like that." Falling to her knees at his feet, she sobbed, "Listen, just listen to me, okay? I—I *do* want your baby. I want a family like we talked about—but . . ."

Serval shot her an evil look. "But what?"

"I—I just thought we could wait—a year or two. Maybe three . . ."

"A year or—did you say *three?* For what? We're young now! Why the hell should we wait?"

The answer came to her with such defiance that she scrambled to her feet. "What am I doin' on my knees?" she murmured.

"What?!" Serval shouted.

Opal straightened up and leveled her eyes at him. "I can't stop dancin' yet, Serval. I'm in my prime, and a dancer's only got but so many years. And even if I tried to get back in shape after havin' a baby,

I'd prob'ly never be able to make up that year. So . . . I'm only gonna say this one time. You can believe me or you don't have to believe me, but I'm tellin' you the truth. I love you—and I love makin' love with you. I want babies, but babies are gonna have to wait. I can't stop dancin' yet, Serval. Not now. I can't—and I *won't*."

\* \* \*

For the next four days, Serval worked later hours than usual, still hurt and confused by what he considered a betrayal of marriage vows. Torn between anger and a longing to patch things up, his pride outlasted his heart until his next out-of-town assignment. The day before his departure, Jack returned to Harlem from a two-week run. Serval smiled for the first time in days when he heard the familiar sound of Jack kicking the front door with the toe of his shoe.

"That's gotta be my buddy Jack with two armloads of groceries," he shouted as he opened the door. "Hey, man! It's really good to see you!"

"Mm-hmm, I know. What'cha mean is it's good to see these groceries, huh?"

Serval grabbed one of the bags. "You *and* the groceries! And right on time, too, 'cause I'm hungry as hell! You fix me some'a your prize-winnin' cornbread, Jack, and I'll fix the spaghetti."

"Got catfish too."

The joviality disappeared from Serval's voice. "Opal's at the club. We'll have to fry the catfish ourselves."

Jack set his bag on the table. "Uh, oh. Ain't like the sound'a that. What's wrong?"

"Nothin's wrong."

"Aw, man, don't gimme that! You and Opal get in a fight or sump'm?"

Straddling a kitchen chair, Serval laid his chin on the backrest. "Not just a fight, Jack," he sighed. "This is big. And I don't know what to do. I can't seem to—get rid of the anger."

"What' she do to get you so mad?"

After a long silence, Serval answered in a pained voice, "Remember how I told you we were tryin' to start a family? Well, I just found out— she doesn't want to. She doesn't want my child."

Jack shook his head. "What?! Aw, that don't even sound right. Opal? Naw, you read sump'm wrong, man . . ."

"No. She told me—she says she wants to wait—two or three years."

Jack began unloading the groceries. "Three years? For what?"

"That's what I asked her, Jack."

"Well?"

"She said she wants to dance. That ballet teacher she had put a lot'a notions into her head about dancin' the ballet. You know, Jack, *really* dancin' the ballet, like those Russians that come to the Metropolitan Opera House to dance. She's chasin' a dream that white folks won't ever let her catch."

"Yeah, but Serval, that's what some folks says about the UNIA too."

Serval felt something rising inside that at first felt like anger, but suddenly changed to confusion. "This is different. Ballet's not *ours*. It's not like jazz. That came from our people, all those rhythms and every innovation since ragtime—white folks can only copy what we play. That's why so many of 'em are hangin' out in our nightclubs. Bastards are probably takin' notes. And even . . ."

Jack rapped on the tabletop with his knuckles. "But then, if that's true . . ."

"Wait, Jack, I'm trying to make a point. We have our own poets, our own authors, great songwriters, and musicians, *and* our own dances. Why does she have this obsession with something from *their* culture? It's *theirs*, Jack. Why does she want that?"

"Shoot, she do it better'n them, ain't that what'cha told me?"

"Yes, but . . ."

"Then it' belong' to her, too. She love' to dance, Serval. Hell, you know that."

"No, Jack. You don't understand. She's just gonna get hurt. They'll never let her do it, and even if they did, why would she want to dance for an audience full'a white folks?"

Jack shrugged his shoulders. "I don't know. Maybe to show 'em she *can*."

Serval stared at Jack for a moment and opened his mouth to speak, but could find no serviceable response. After a silent standoff, he shook his head stubbornly. "No. It's theirs. It belongs to them and they can keep it, as far as I'm concerned."

"Okay, teacher," Jack chuckled, rising from his chair. "But I think it was you that told me they use'ta think slaves belonged to 'em, too. We ain't *never* belonged to 'em and neither does no doggone dance."

"Well, in theory, you're right, of course. But I'm talkin' about reality, Jack," Serval snapped.

Jack cracked an egg against the mixing bowl and gave Serval a long look. "Slavery was reality, too—once. Seem to me—reality be changin' all'a time. Ain't that right?"

Serval rolled his eyes and couldn't keep from laughing. "Damn, Jack, you'da been good on my college debate team."

Jack smiled and tossed a tomato at Serval. "Thought you was makin' spaghetti, man."

"Okay. But look, even if I agree with you that she's got the right to dance—and I guess I even admire her determination in a way—that won't solve our other marital problem. I still want a family and—damn! What if she decides she doesn't ever want to give up this dance idea?" He paused and stared at his hands. "I think I knew the first day I met her that I wanted her to be the mother of my children. Trouble is—I never stopped to think that she might not want me to be the father of hers . . ."

"Hey. Don't be thinkin' like that. She love' you, man. I know that. She jus' ain't ready yet. Give her a little time."

"Give her a little time? Jack, you don't know what that means. Do you have any idea what it's like to reach for your woman in bed and have her jerk away from you like you're some stranger? Goddamn! I guess I'm supposed to make an appointment for sex with my own wife!"

Jack shrugged in obvious discomfort. "Well, maybe you could use some'a them things they passed out when we was in the Army, man. You know—what they call 'em? Pro . . . pro-fa . . . "

"Prophylactics, Jack, and no thank you. Three years of rubbers? With my own wife? Goddamn! *Hell,* no!"

"Serval. I can't hardly give you no advice 'bout that. But I know one thing. Tellin' Opal not to dance—the way she' feelin' now . . ." He paused and shook his head. "Mm-mm-mm! That be like tellin' a bird not to fly."

\* \* \*

A full stomach and a long hot soak in the tub lulled Serval into a sleepy, almost contented state. For the first time in three days, a faint feeling of tenderness broke through his anger for Opal. When he finished packing for his early train, he decided to wait up for her, but the minute he stretched out in bed, he began to drift to sleep with one hazy thought buzzing around in his brain: *Telling Opal not to dance would be like telling a bird not to fly.*

Serval woke up hours later feeling his foot brush Opal's leg. Raising his head, he blinked at the clock: *3:20.* He wanted to touch her, but hesitated, unsure of the proper protocol for making up after a fight based, at least partially, on sex. After mentally debating the question for a few minutes, he decided to trust his instincts and eased one arm around her waist. Even asleep, her body responded to his touch, and he sighed.

"I love you," he whispered, holding her tighter.

Opal opened her eyes and returned the sentiment without speaking a word.

# Chapter 26

When Serval returned from a four-city speaking tour, the first order of business was a UNIA support rally on the corner of 125th Street and Lenox Avenue. With scores of new arrivals from the rural South, as well as from the Caribbean, the weekly rallies had become standard practice as a means to increase the membership of the UNIA. Mr. Garvey spoke to the crowd when he was in town, but, due to his heavy travel schedule, young Garveyites with oratorical skills took turns promoting the UNIA.

It was a bright afternoon, and Serval squinted as he stepped up onto the makeshift platform. He slowly scanned the murmuring crowd, and tried to shake the panic that always hit just as he was about to speak. It was always the same: parched throat, accelerated heartbeat, and, the most horrifying of all, his mind suddenly went completely blank. As a result of his many turns at the podium over the past year, he had discovered that the best solution was to focus on someone in the crowd — someone pleasant with a reassuring smile.

Today he found his nerve remedy in the eyes of a young boy — about fifteen years old, Serval figured. He smiled at the boy, recognizing a reflection of himself a few years before when he had stood almost on the same spot to listen to Marcus Garvey for the first time. He waited for the surge of confidence, and it came — right on schedule. "Good afternoon."

"Good afternoon!"

"I hope you are all enjoying another beautiful day as residents of Harlem."

The crowd smiled and murmured their approval.

Out of the corner of his eye, Serval saw a Greyhound bus shush to a stop across the street. "How many of you are permanent residents of Harlem?"

Nearly everyone in the crowd raised their hands. Serval nodded. "And how many of you are members of the Universal Negro Improvement Association?"

About half of the hands lowered.

"Well," Serval said, smiling, "It's a good thing we're having this little street-corner party today, then, isn't it?" Shading his eyes with one hand, he scanned the three people who had just stepped off the Greyhound bus across the street. Dressed in simple, threadbare coats, they appeared to be a family: a father, mother, and adolescent son. The father carried a battered straw suitcase secured by a thick leather belt, and the mother and son struggled with bulging carpetbags. Serval motioned in their direction. "Step right over, friends," he shouted.

The man and the woman exchanged a confused look, then slowly crossed the street.

"Let 'em through, please," Serval said. "Make way so they can come up front. There, now. That's better." He stooped down at the edge of the platform and extended his hand. "Where are you folks from?"

The man dropped his suitcase and shook hands with Serval. "We' from Tulsa, suh. Oklahoma."

A murmur went through the crowd, and Serval's smile faded as he straightened up. "Tulsa . . . We heard about all the trouble out there, Mr. . . ."

"Sutton, suh," the man said, removing his hat. "I be Harrison Sutton, and this' my family here—my wife Betsy, and my boy, Ned."

"Well, welcome to Harlem, folks. I'm Serval Rivard with the Harlem chapter of the UNIA. We sure hope you're here to stay."

Mr. Sutton lowered his head slightly, then looked around. "Well, thank you, Mr. Rivard. I ain't shamed to tell you we done lost everything back in Tulsa—got burnt out our house . . . and we wasn't the only ones. We all been hopin' the police, the gov'ment—somebody—come along to make things right for folks like us . . . but it ain't lookin' like that's gonna happen. So Betsy got some relations up here, and we figured we'd do better tryin' to start over from scratch . . ."

"Mr. Sutton," Serval said. "Would you mind if I borrowed your hat for a minute?"

Mr. Sutton blinked up at Serval in confusion, but handed him the hat. Serval reached into his pocket, pulled out his folding money, and peeled off three five-dollar bills. After dropping the money into the hat, he passed it down to a woman standing in the front. "Pass this around, would you please? Listen, folks," he said in a louder tone, "We all heard about the burning and lynching that went on in Tulsa last year.

The way I see it, the Suttons here were lucky to get away with their lives. Let's show 'em that Harlem has a heart. And when you reach down in your pockets, keep in mind that what happened to the Negroes of Tulsa could've happened to any of us. Mr. Sutton, if you'll stay close after my talk, I'd like to escort you and your family to the UNIA offices so that we can help you find your wife's relatives."

Mr. Sutton nodded at Serval. "We' grateful, suh. But I got one question."

"What's that, Mr. Sutton?"

"I believe I heard about you UNIA folks befo', but I can't for the life'a me remember what it means."

"Mr. Sutton, UNIA stands for—the Universal Negro *Improvement* Association," Serval said.

Mr. Sutton smiled. "Negro Improvement . . . Well, Mr. Rivard, I believe that be sump'm my family ought'a be part of, yes, suh."

"Then you may consider yourself a member. I'm sure that with a little help, you'll find employment in Harlem and make yourself a happy home here." Serval looked out at the crowd, which had now increased in size. "So, I hope that everybody learned a lesson from the Suttons. This is what the UNIA is all about. If we help each other, we all rise. Now, we have tables set up on the sidewalk to your left where UNIA representatives are ready to provide you with more information and sign you up. But before I close, I'd like to take a minute to speak to you about the Black Star Line stock certificates you've all been hearing about. For those of you who need more information about the benefit of investments, please pay close attention . . ."

As he went into his sales segment for Black Star certificates, he spotted a familiar face in the crowd, and froze for a moment. *Daddy.*

Although he regularly communicated with his mother by letter or telephone, Serval had neither seen nor spoken to his father in over two years. He managed to recover and close his speech, but found himself reaching for his handkerchief to dry off his perspiring palms. When his eyes met his father's, he nodded deferentially, and Charles nodded in return. For a second, Serval thought he saw pride in his father's face, but before he could be sure, it was gone—as quickly as it had appeared.

As the crowd dispersed, Serval stepped down to make arrangements for the Sutton family to be taken to Liberty Hall, and then to chat with a few remaining spectators. Keenly aware of Charles Rivard's location several yards away, Serval monitored his approach with a peripheral lock on the light-colored suit his father was wearing. As it gradually edged closer, Serval felt his heartbeat quicken.

He did his best to appear cool when his father was at last close enough to touch. *Daddy.* A surge of unexpected happiness blended with his nervousness as Serval extended his hand. "It's good to see you again, sir."

"Hello, Son."

"How are you . . . and Mama?"

"Fine. We're both fine. Are you—all right, Serval?"

"Yes, sir. Opal's doing just fine, too."

"Your health . . .?"

"Just fine."

After a pause, Charles asked, "Any children yet, Serval?"

Serval gritted his teeth. "Not yet, Daddy."

Another excruciating pause.

"Daddy—I . . ."

"Yes, Serval?"

"I know it's probably too late, but I'd like to—I'd like to apologize for all the childish things I've done over the years . . ."

Charles smiled. "Over the years, Serval. Those are the important words."

Serval shrugged. "Sir? I don't understand . . ."

"Son, think of the years you're talking about. You said childish things because you were still a child. Don't you think that every son feels the need to apologize to his father when he finally becomes a man? I certainly did."

Serval's eyes widened. "You?"

"Of course, Serval. Believe it or not, I was once a brash young dreamer like you. Maybe that's why I gave you the latitude I did. Some people even said I spoiled you, and perhaps that's true. But I kept my expectations high, and the courage it took for you to apologize is certainly a good sign. You'll understand when you have a son of your own. You'll want the best for him, and you'll expect the best from him."

Serval wondered how to respond, and suddenly heard himself babbling a graceless question: "So, Daddy—what did you think of my—uh—the speech?"

Charles took a deep breath, reached into his vest pocket for his watch, and gave the winding crown two deliberate twists. Serval had seen his father execute this exact movement countless times during arguments or discussions with respected colleagues, and he knew that Charles was taking great care in composing his response.

"Well, son . . . it appears that this back-to-Africa idea may have caught on—perhaps. With some of our people, at any rate. I—I suppose you're determined to do this thing—to—to relocate—move there yourself."

Fighting an ill-timed urge to embrace his father, Serval instead lifted his chin in preparation to defend the UNIA. He took care to keep his tone respectful. "Yes, sir. That's our long-term plan. For now, we're following Dr. DuBois's lead—there's a lot of work to do right here in the United States. But the return to Africa is . . . yes, I'll be going when and if I'm asked."

Charles smiled. "Well, well. We seem to have found a patch of that common ground you once spoke of. You seem to have discovered some of Dr. DuBois's logic."

"Yes, Daddy, but that doesn't mean . . ."

"Please don't misunderstand me, son. As impatient as I've been with your Mr. Garvey in the past, I can't help but see the pride he's instilled in so many of our folk. It's just that . . . well, when I think of you actually leaving your home and moving to Africa . . . please, forgive me, son, but the reason behind such a venture completely escapes me."

"Daddy . . ."

"Wait, son. I commend your dedication—I really do. But why not concentrate on conditions here at home instead of going to a strange land and trying to start everything from scratch? I know you must be aware of the difficulties you'll face—aren't you?"

Serval matched his father's tone in diplomacy, but persisted in making his point. "Daddy. White America just—they don't want us here . . . and they never will."

Silence.

"Daddy?"

"I know that, son."

"Then, why? Why can't you understand my wanting to find a better place?"

"There is terrible oppression in Africa, son."

"My God, Daddy, don't you think I know that? But at least there we're the majority. If we can just . . . No, wait. I won't stand here and lecture you about our philosophies. I don't want to argue with you, Daddy. Not any more. There are just certain questions you'll always have for me, and my answers will just never satisfy you. And vice versa, I'm sure."

"What is it you want to ask me, son?" Charles asked softly.

Serval opened his mouth to dodge the question, but remained quiet for a long moment. "Daddy, it feels like we're finally being completely honest here, so I will ask you one hard question—one that baffles me. Why . . . why are you so hellbent to stay in a place where you're not wanted? By a people who do everything in their power to make life hell for us?"

Charles raised his chin and stared at his son. "Because we built it."

Serval blinked.

"Serval?"

"Y-yes, sir?"

"That was my honest answer. Was it in some way satisfactory?"

Serval smiled and shook his head. "Let's just say you gave me something to think about."

"Good," Charles said. "That makes two of us. . . . Well, it was good to see you again, son. You take care of yourself—and Opal." He extended his hand.

Staring at the hand, Serval contemplated the formality for a moment, but came to the conclusion that it was the best his father could do. "Yes, sir. You do the same."

*   *   *

Serval felt a soft hand on his shoulder, and jumped, nearly falling back in his desk chair. Opal leaned over him to turn off the reading lamp. "Wake up, Serval," she whispered. "It's almost three in the mornin'. Come to bed."

"Huh? Opal? You just gettin' home?"

"Mm-hmm."

"Oh! Damn! I was supposed to pick you up! I'm sorry. I guess I fell asleep."

"Looks like it. Anyway, I got a ride. Serval, I don't know how you can sleep all twisted up like that. Doesn't your neck hurt?"

Leaning his head to one side, he winced. "Now that you mention it, yeah, it hurts like hell. I must'a fallen asleep right in the middle of my speech. Damn! I've still got so much more to do. Baby, go on to bed. I'll be in after a while."

"I thought you did that speech this afternoon."

"This is another one," he murmured grimly. "And I've gotta get it done, but I can't seem to concentrate. I keep gettin' distracted."

"With what?"

"I've got a lot on my mind, that's all."

Opal kicked off her shoes and stood behind his chair. "Here. Let me rub your neck while you tell me your troubles."

Serval sighed and shifted his body, leaning his head forward as Opal's hands worked to soothe his tense muscles. "I'll be leaving day after tomorrow."

He felt Opal's hands stop rubbing for a beat, then she continued. "Where to this time?"

"Atlanta. Charleston too, and a couple'a other towns, but Atlanta is—is the main stop."

"Why do you say it like that?"

"Like what?"

"Like—I don't know. Like you're dreadin' it or sump'm."

"Well . . . I guess I am. That's why I'm havin' so much trouble with this damn speech. I don't know what the hell to say."

"Why?"

"Opal, Mr. Garvey is going to Atlanta to . . ." He stopped and rubbed his eyes.

"What, Serval?"

"To meet with some—Grand Wizard or Dragon or—goddamn Grand Cockroach, or whatever silly name those fools call their chief clown . . . Mr. Garvey's meeting with the *Klan*, Opal! Isn't that the craziest thing you ever heard?"

"The Klan! Serval . . . you think Mr. Garvey's okay? I mean, he hasn't lost his senses, has he?"

"I keep hoping he's got some secret reason for it. You know, strategy."

"Serval! *You're* not meeting with 'em, are you?"

"Not if Mr. Garvey gave me a million dollars. I'm just going as part of the entourage. We'll be trying to broaden UNIA membership and keep everybody from panicking. But he's not telling us much. He just says to trust him."

"Well, do you? Trust him, I mean?"

Serval thought it over for a moment before answering. "I always have. I believe in Mr. Garvey, Opal. I guess I've just gotta trust that he's got his reasons for this trip. When the time's right, he'll explain it to us."

"Well, it sounds crazy to me. I sure would like to hear his reasons. But listen, you be sure and keep far away from those crackers, you hear?"

Serval laughed lightly. "*Crackers*, Mrs. Rivard?"

"*Far* away, Serval. I mean it. I worry about you enough as it is."

"Okay. I promise. Oh, Mrs. Rivard?"

"Mm-hmm?"

"This neck rub feels real good. And as long as you're back there, I've got a request."

"What?"

"One kiss."

Opal laughed. "Crazy man."

"On the back of the neck, please."

"Lord, Serval." Easing closer, she pressed her lips to his neck softly. "There. Now you feelin' better? Now that you got everything off your chest?"

Suddenly, his playful tone was gone. "Guess who I saw today."

"Who?"

"Daddy."

"Oh. . . . Did you talk to him?"

"Mm-hmm."

"Oh. Did . . . Serval, you didn't fight with him, did you?"

"No."

"Well, what did he say?"

Silence.

"Serval?"

"He asked me if we had any children yet."

Opal cleared her throat. "I—Serval, we'll have babies. We have lots'a time to have babies. Just not right . . ."

"You can stop now," he said, jerking free of her hands.

"Huh?"

"My neck—it feels much better."

"Oh. You sure?"

Serval reached for his papers and directed his attention to his speech. "Go on to bed now, Opal. I've really gotta finish this."

"Serval . . . Why don't you come to bed with me?"

*God*, he thought. *It must be one of her safe nights.* He leaned back in his chair and gazed up at her for a long moment. "No thanks. Good night."

Opal glared at him and scrambled to her feet. She turned to leave, but stopped suddenly. "Serval."

"What?"

"You can punish me all you like, but I will *not* stop dancing."

"I know," he said without looking up. "And you will *not* have a baby. Your position is clear. So good night."

# Chapter 27

Opal arrived at the Westfall rehearsal studio nearly an hour before the 9:00 a.m. call. Her decision to audition for the Denishawn Dance Company had been an impulsive one, and she began to have second thoughts the minute she approached the steps. But as she sipped her coffee and stared at the neat handwritten notice posted on the door, she could almost hear Madame's voice reading the words: *Denishawn Dance Company auditions—Thursday 9:00 a.m.—Openings: corps de ballet and two principal dancers for nationwide tour.* Opal closed her eyes. So many mornings of her life had been spent shivering near theater entrances in drafty alleys, listening to Madame's last-minute instructions as Miss Aida fussed with hairpins and lip rouge.

*This time, Shoo-Shoo! Show them who is greatest doncer!*

*That's right, Sista! Go on in there and take them heifahs to dancin' school!*

But the encouraging voices faded into the alley's silent stillness. This time Opal would face the skeptics alone. A solo.

She heard footsteps and turned around to see a middle-aged woman approaching with graceful, rapid strides. Stepping aside, Opal smiled as the woman unlocked the door.

"Is there something I can do for you, Miss?" the woman asked.

"I guess you don't remember me from last year, ma'am. I'm here to audition."

A familiar expression crossed the older woman's face—recognition that melted into pity. Opal smiled with well-practiced courtesy.

"What was your name again?"

"Opal Rivard, ma'am."

"Well, Opal, you're a lovely dancer as I recall, but our company is . . ."

"No, ma'am. You couldn't possibly recall, because I was never allowed to dance last year."

The woman stiffened, and her smile was gone. Opal pressed on. "I'd really like a chance to dance for Ruth St. Denis. Did she come on this trip?"

"Miss St. Denis does not have the time to accompany us on these talent searches, Miss—Miss . . ."

"Rivard. Opal Rivard."

"Miss Rivard. I assure you that you may regard me as an extension of Miss St. Denis herself. She and her husband trust me and my assistants to spot new talent for the company in Los Angeles. We are only following the guidelines set by Mr. Shawn and Miss St. Denis. I'm afraid that—well, we have a certain type in mind for our principals."

"You mean . . . Mr. Shawn and Miss St. Denis said not to hire colored dancers?"

"Of course not. It is certainly not the Denishawn Dance Company's policy to exclude . . . Listen. We have our patrons and sponsors to think of, Miss Rivard. To be blunt, I'm afraid they'd be shocked at seeing one of our male principals dancing an intimate pas de deux with a colored girl. Now that's not personal, it's just the way things are. You *must* know that."

Opal reached for the handrail and moved up to the next stair. "Then I'd be happy to audition for the corps de ballet, ma'am. Nobody even has to—to touch me—or anything."

"I'm sorry, Miss Rivard. It's just not possible." She pushed the door open and stepped halfway in before stopping. "Wait, Miss Rivard . . ."

"Yes, ma'am?"

"I'm curious about something, but please don't take this the wrong way."

"What is it?"

"Well . . . you seem like a smart girl, and I'm sure you've had enough doors shut in your face to know what to expect from professional ballet companies. Just what made you think you'd be allowed to audition?"

"I was trained by Madame Anna Romanov."

"Anna Romanov? I don't know the name," she said with a dismissive shrug. "I'm sorry."

"She was with the Bolshoi, Miss—uh, Miss . . . I'm sorry. What was your name?"

The woman raised her chin slowly, imperiously, without taking her eyes off Opal. "I am Helene DuQuesne."

"DuQuesne?" Opal murmured. "I'm sorry, I don't know the name."

She heard a sudden burst of giggles behind her, and saw moving shadows against the open door. She turned to see a group of four young women carrying shoe-bags. "Good morning, ladies," Opal said, and then turned back to face Helene DuQuesne. "Well, ma'am, it looks like we're all here to audition."

"Wait here, Miss Rivard."

Helene DuQuesne opened the door and gestured to the other dancers. As they swept past Opal, the last girl through the door whispered, "A colored girl trained by a Bolshoi alum? Ye Gods! Who does she think she's kidding?"

Opal pretended not to hear, and looked expectantly at Miss DuQuesne.

"Wait here for just a moment, would you, Miss Rivard?"

"Be happy to, ma'am."

The door closed and Opal exhaled. Within five minutes, Helene DuQuesne returned. "Come right in, Miss Rivard. You'll go first."

*    *    *

Opal was glad she hadn't cancelled Creola's lesson that day. Her entire audition, including travel time, had taken less than an hour and a half. After cleaning the apartment, she opened the front window and stood staring out at nothing, trying not to think about her morning and hoping that Creola would be early.

*I'm afraid you're not the type dancer we're looking for . . . Thank you for coming today, but I'm afraid the answer is no.*

"I'm afraid, I'm afraid," Opal muttered. "Why do they always say 'I'm afraid' when they say no? . . . I'm afraid you're not white enough, Miss Rivard. I'm afraid that if we let you dance, then everybody'll find out the big secret—that a colored dancer is just as good as a white dancer. Or maybe even better. So I'm afraid the answer is no, Miss Rivard. Because I'm afraid we need you to be our maid and our mammy, Miss Rivard . . ."

The sudden appearance of Creola standing on the sidewalk under her window interrupted Opal's conversation with herself, and she hurried to the front door to let her in.

Creola swept down the hallway and into the apartment, then tossed her bag onto the sofa. "Hey, girl! Who in the world were you just talkin' to out your window? You looked mad."

"Nobody," Opal said, waving her hand. "Just myself, I guess."

Creola laughed. "Mad at yourself, Miss Pickford? What'cha do?

Spill some milk on your clean kitchen floor? I know! You burned up some cookies, huh?"

"Hush, Creola. Look, I went for another audition this morning, that's all. And I guess I don't have to tell you how it went. You were right about everything. I'm wastin' my time."

"Uh-uh, wait a minute, girl. Don'tchu let them white folks give you the blues."

"But you said . . ."

Creola waved her hand in the air. "I know what I said, but since when do you listen to Creola?"

Opal shook her head and pointed toward the center of the floor. "Okay, Miss Pavlova, let's forget my morning and get to work. I hope you're ready, 'cause today we're gonna work on jetês. You've got to try a grand jetê sooner or later, you know."

"Oh, hell, Opal! You know I'm terrible at them pee-wee jetês, much less a damn grand one!"

"Lord, Creola!" Opal laughed. "If you were in Madame's class, you'da gotten smacked with her stick about a hundred times by now, girl."

"Oh, all right. I'll do the damn jetês. But sump'm tells me there ain't gonna be nothin' grand about 'em."

Opal sighed. "You're stalling, girl. Now stop all that groanin' and slouchin' and gimme twenty-five pliés. That'll loosen you right up for those grand jetês, and you *will* be doin' some today. And they *will* be grand, even if it kills both of us."

Creola lumbered into first position and rolled her eyes. "Ooh, you are *mean* when you ain't gettin' no sex, girl!"

"Creola!"

"What'chu need is a sweet daddy to keep you company when your Garvey-man is off savin' all the colored folks!"

"Okay, then," Opal said, folding her arms. "That'll be fifty pliés."

Creola groaned and executed a careful plié. "So, where is he this time, Opal?"

Opal hesitated before answering. "He's—uh—in Atlanta with Mr. Garvey. And keep your back straight. Anyway, he's just doin' all the regular kind'a business—sellin' Black Star stock and makin' speeches. But . . ."

"But what?"

"Oh, nothin'. Watch your turnout now!"

"Oh, damn! . . . Opal?"

"Huh?"

Creola stopped and placed her hands on her hips. "You think I'm gettin' this ballet business? I mean, I know you said it's better to start when you're little but—you think it's improvin' my dancin' at all?"

"Yeah, girl! All that cooch dancin' you been doin' all this time made you real flexible. You're doin' fine! When you really try, that is."

"Opal," Creola said, "I just thought of sump'm. Did you ever think about startin' your own dancin' school? You know—teachin' little kids—like you got taught?"

Opal felt the blood drain from her face. "I—I'm only twenty, Creola," she murmured.

"So? What the hell that got to do with it?"

"I'm still dancing, Creola! A dancer doesn't start teaching 'til she's *through*. And I don't care if you believe it or not, I am not ready to quit yet, so drop it."

After staring wide-eyed at Opal for a moment, Creola opened her mouth to speak, but was interrupted by a bumping noise at the door, followed by the sound of Jack's voice. "Anybody home?"

"In here, Jack! It's unlocked." Opal called, glad for the distraction.

"Could ya open the doe'? I got my arms full."

Creola froze, her hand clutching the back of the settee that doubled as a barre.

Opal opened the door and Jack squeezed in, smiling down at her. When he spotted Creola, the smile disappeared. "Oh. Uh—didn't know you had company. Hi, Creola."

Creola nodded, but said nothing.

Opal hopped up to give Jack a peck on the cheek before reaching for one of the bags. "Lord, Jack! What'cha do? Buy out the grocer? What is all this anyway?"

Jack looked puzzled. "Ain't Serval in town?"

"No. He left yesterday, Jack. Won't be back for a week or so."

"Damn! Oh, 'scuse me for cussin', ladies. I mean, thought he told me he'd be here this week."

"No, Jack. He's gone—again. Guess it was one of those *unexpected* trips." After peeking into the bag, Opal smiled at Jack and patted his shoulder. "Catfish and spaghetti, huh? Well, let's cook it up anyway. Creola's here. She'll help us eat it."

Jack smiled crookedly. "Well, uh, sho'. Creola can stay, I guess. I'll go start mixin' up the cawnbread. Oh, 'less y'all ain't finished wit'cha dancin' yet."

"Well . . ." Opal paused to wind the Victrola and brush off the needle. "We really just got started, Jack. Why don't you go take a shower and a little nap? You can use me and Serval's bed and close the door so the music doesn't bother you. And when we get done, we'll call you, okay? How's that sound?"

"Well, yeah. But I guess I better put the eggs and butter in the cooler first. Uh, Opal, could I talk to you a minute—in the kitchen?"

Following Jack into the kitchen, Opal called over her shoulder, "No sense in wastin' time, Miss Pavlova. Twenty-five more pliés, s'il vous plaît."

Once in the kitchen, Jack pulled Opal toward the back door and whispered, "Did you forget, Opal?"

"Huh? Forget about what?"

He sighed loudly.

"What, Jack?"

"'Member, Opal? What you promised last time I was in town— 'bout readin'?"

"Oh! Right! I'm sorry, Jack. Of course, I'll help you after supper."

"No! I mean—not wit' *her* here. I—I ain't want the whole world to know I can't read."

"But you can read some. You said you went to school when you were little."

"Opal. 'Bout all I 'member is my letters. Come on. You don't mind, do ya?"

Opal placed her hands on her hips and laughed. "'Course not, Jack. I'm happy to do it. I think I've still got my old primer from school and a couple'a story books, if you don't mind readin' about ducks and ponies and stuff."

"I'da axed Serval, but'cha know he ain't got no time," he mumbled, smiling with relief. "Wait. I mean *asked*. Mm. Still havin' trouble wit that one."

A puzzled look crossed Opal's face. "Wait a minute. Jack! I just thought of something . . ."

"What?"

"If you can't read, how'd you pass the test to get a chauffeur's license back when you were workin' for Mr. Saunders?"

Jack began unpacking the groceries and smiled cryptically. "Opal. I said I was uneducated. I ain't dumb."

Opal rolled her eyes. "Oh, Lord! Don't tell me . . . Serval helped you cheat, didn't he?"

Jack grinned. "Y'all go ahead on wit'cha dancin' now. Don't let me interrupt."

Opal left the kitchen and started the phonograph record from the beginning. "Okay, Miss Creola. Take your position."

Jack peeked out the door just as Creola began to dance, and cleared his throat loudly before re-entering the front room. Creola smiled at him, and nearly missed the high leg sweep in the segment. Trying to catch up, she kicked in a haphazard fashion, her toe just missing Jack's chin as he passed.

Without breaking stride, Jack deftly eluded the kick and grinned back at her while loosening his tie. "Too dangerous in here for me," he called over his shoulder as he headed down the hall.

*     *     *

When they sat down to supper, Creola stared at her plate in disbelief. "You were serious. Catfish and spaghetti? Opal, I thought you were pullin' my leg."

Opal and Jack exchanged a look and laughed. Then Jack shook his head, looking wounded. "Nobody ever mentions my cawnbread. Here, try this." Leaning over Creola, he buttered a square of cornbread and held it to her mouth.

Creola smiled up at him and took a bite. "Mmmm! Good!"

"See that, Miz Rivard?" Jack said. "This catfish better be up to snuff, hear?"

"Don't worry 'bout my part, Jack. You make sure Creola's not just being polite, 'cause you know I'll tell you the truth about your cooking. Oh! Jack, why don't you go the Bijou with us tonight?"

"Well . . ."

"Aww, come on, Jack. We need a gentleman escort," Creola said.

"Oh, awright. What's showin'?"

"The Sheik." Opal and Creola exchanged a look and giggled.

Jack rolled his eyes. "Oh, Lawd, Opal. That don't sound like my kind'a flicker. What is it? One'a them love stories?"

"Well, there's this new fella in it we want you to see, is all."

"Okay," he mumbled, shrugging his shoulders. "Guess I'm outnumbered. But ya wouldn't get away wit' seein' no Sheik if Serval was in town."

*      *      *

Jack did his best to scrunch down in his seat once the lights dimmed in the Bijou. He had just positioned his long legs comfortably under the seat in front of him when he caught Creola watching him.

He gave her a weak smile. "Uh, guess they ain't made this place for big fellas like me, huh?"

Creola leaned her face close to his ear and glanced over at Opal. "What happened to you, Jack? Why—why didn't you ever call me?"

*Oh, Lawd.* "I'm sorry. Let's watch the flicker, and uh, we'll talk about it later, okay?"

Creola nodded and remained quiet for the duration of the film.

Jack sat between Creola and Opal squirming. *Damn! When the hell this mess gon' be over?* He drifted into a pleasant nap, until a nudge from Opal's elbow startled him. "Huh? Time to go?" he asked.

"No, Jack!" she whispered. "That's the fella I was tellin' you about. Valentino. See? Don't you think he looks like you?"

Jack craned his neck, and his face contorted into a sour expression. "Him? Aw, Opal! Shoot! That boy wearin' a dress jus' like a woman! That what you think I look like?"

Opal giggled. "Oh, Jack. That's not a dress. That's one'a those robes those desert sheiks wear. What do you know anyway? He's handsome! He's what the girls at the club call a heartthrob!"

Creola leaned closer to him and whispered, "Yeah, Jack. If you don't believe us, jus' look around."

Jack rolled his eyes and impatiently scanned the row of theater patrons in front of them. He heard, more than saw, what Opal and Creola were talking about. Deep female sighs. From behind him, he heard a woman moan, as if physically aroused. Blinking his eyes in disbelief, he sank lower in his chair. At that moment, the action on the screen at last caught his attention. As his supposed look-alike was fighting off a whole gang of Arabs single-handedly, Jack became so absorbed that he didn't notice Creola reaching for his hand.

"The end" appeared on the screen as Valentino rode off into the sunset with his lady love in tow. A chorus of sighs rose from the women in the theater, and Jack stood up to stretch and make his escape. His stride was long and rapid, and Creola and Opal hurried after him. In the brightly lit lobby, he suddenly experienced a severe case of self-consciousness. He was accustomed to being stared at occasionally due to his towering height, but he had never drawn such ardent attention from so many females. His eyes pleaded with Opal for help, but she only laughed. "What' they all lookin' at?" he hissed.

Before she could answer, a chubby, light-skinned girl who looked to be about sixteen, squealed, "Ooh! The Sheik! You' the colored Sheik of Araby!"

As every pair of eyes turned in Jack's direction, Creola linked arms with him and glared at the women. Jack closed his eyes and groaned, "Oh, Lawd!"

*   *   *

Jack woke with a start and sat up quickly, trying to shake off the disoriented feeling. *Gold?* His eyes scanned his surroundings. Walls, door, windows—everything in this strange room was bathed in a dim, amber light. Blinking his eyes, he finally spotted the source—a lamp with a shade made of amber glass. *Creola's bedroom.* One tentative glance to his right confirmed his fear. Creola lay next to him, sound asleep. He grabbed his head with both hands. *Oh, Lawd, not again . . .*

Quietly slipping out of bed, Jack found his trousers and dug in the pocket for a cigarette and matches. He walked to the far window before lighting up and pulled the curtains aside. The sun was just coming up, tingeing the gray sky with streaks of gold, almost the same color as the room. *Why'd I let things get started up again?*

He heard Creola stir, and held his breath as he glanced over his shoulder. Her head fell back, and her breathing returned to a sleeping rhythm. Jack took a nervous pull on his cigarette and shook his head. *You know why, fool!*

Creola's body was smooth, lithe, and built for speed. And she was an expert at pleasing a man, at least physically. Jack pondered the empty feeling gnawing at him, and wondered how the body and the soul of one individual man could possibly have such opposite tastes. A few hours earlier, his body told him it couldn't get enough of Creola Dorshay. But now his heart thrilled at only one prospect: Opal's promise to teach him to read. After staring out the window for a few more minutes, he slipped into the bathroom for a quick shower before returning to wake Creola.

As a precaution, he paused to slip into his trousers before touching her shoulder. "Creola?"

"Mmmm," she moaned. "Huh? What time is it, baby?"

"Almost seven. I gotta go, and uh, I jus' wanted to say goodbye."

Reaching up to brush his chest with her fingertips, she smiled seductively. "Aww, Jack, don't go. Come back to bed. I promise you won't be sorry."

Jack smiled weakly. "Aww, uh, well, I'd like to—really. But I got lot'sa things to do today, Creola."

He buttoned his shirt quickly, trying to avoid the wicked gleam in Creola's eyes. Just as he was reaching for his tie, she emerged from under the sheet, threw back her head and stretched. The golden lamp-glow did beautiful things to her bare skin, and Jack froze, staring at her. As he sank back down onto the bed, his body did another quick battle with his soul, but it was no contest. Creola's fingers had just undone his last button when he closed his eyes and surrendered. *Damn! I was so close.*

\* \* \*

Jack felt considerably more comfortable that evening, sitting on the sofa that usually served as his bed, while he waited for Opal to find her books.

"Here they are, Jack," she said, dropping two books into his lap and sitting cross-legged on the floor. "This one here is the primer, and this one . . ." Covering her face with her hands, she giggled. "This one is my old fairy princess book."

"Look' like ya colored on it wit' some'a them wax colors."

"I was five. I got tired of the princess always bein' a white girl. So I decided there ought'a be a colored princess for a change."

Smiling down at her, Jack tugged at one of her short plaits. "Bet'chu was cute when you was little. An' I bet'cha wore ya hair jus' like this too, huh?"

Placing her hands on her hips, Opal shot him a stern look. "Page one, Jack. Give it a try."

"Wait a minute, girl! Jus' like that? I tol' you I barely 'member my letters!"

"If you remember your letters, Jack, then you can at least try to sound out that first word." Reaching across the coffee table, she pointed at the word and looked at him expectantly.

He cleared his throat twice. "Uh . . . let's see. This here's a T—I think. T-tuh-huh . . . oh, yeah! I 'member this word, awright. The. Right?"

"Right! That's good, Jack! Now try the next one."

"Tuh - tuh - ay - ul. Hmm. Tu - ay - ul. Oh! Tail?"

"Right again! See, Jack? This is gonna be easy for you. You'll see, it'll all come back to you, once you get started."

"Tail?" he repeated, tugging at her plait. "Who got a tail?"

Opal rolled her eyes and slapped his hand away. "Get serious, Jack."

"Awright. Tail. The—tail."

After Jack finished pronouncing all the words in the title, "The Tale of the Fairy Princess," he dabbed at his perspiring forehead with his handkerchief. He loosened his tie and grinned at Opal. "A princess wid' a tail?"

Opal let out a loud sigh. "You know it's not that kind of tail. A story kind'a tale, Jack. Like a fairy tale."

"I know it, girl. I was jus' messin' wit'cha. I'm nervous, I guess."

Her smile encouraged him. "Well don't be. You're doing so good, Jack. I'm real proud of you. Not too many men would swallow their pride and admit they couldn't read—much less sit here tryin' to read a silly book like this just so they could learn."

"Thanks, Opal. You' real sweet—to teach me."

"It's okay, Jack. It'll keep my mind busy so I don't worry about that big-head husband of mine so much. He called this mornin' from the train station in Charleston. They've still gotta go to Atlanta—and they're not comin' back for a whole week."

# Chapter 28

Cutter's Field was a small, unmapped patch of land hidden by a labyrinth of dirt roads far outside Atlanta's city limits. A carefully guarded secret among local Klansmen, the desolate field only came to life on special nights, such as this one.

Tonight a caravan of trucks, automobiles, and horsedrawn wagons crawled along the rutted roads, creating a crazy pattern of light in motion—long, shaky headlamp beams and bouncing lanterns—until Cutter's Field was illuminated by a large circular arrangement of vehicles. Ghostly white figures gathered quietly in the center to wait. Only the low murmuring and grunts of a few men struggling with a large object broke the air of solemnity. A shouted signal echoed, and all lights were abruptly extinguished. It was a moonless night, and the sudden darkness of Cutter's Field transformed the hooded visitors into a gathering of blind men.

L.T. Sullivan felt his little boy's hand go cold and stiffen, so he gripped it tighter. "Don't fret, boy," he whispered. "It's only fer a minute . . ." Suddenly, the black sky was lit with leaping flames in the shape of a cross, and the shouts of nearly a hundred men filled the air. L.T. managed a half-hearted yelp as he shook the bottom edge of his hood for ventilation, then felt his son tugging at his sleeve. The boy fidgeted with his small hood, tilting his head to one side, then the other, until at last a rapidly blinking eye appeared at one of the holes. L.T. suppressed a laugh, and bent down. "What is it, son?"

"Uh, well . . . What that fire for, Daddy? They gonna burn up some niggers or sump'm?"

"No, son. Now hush. I'll tell you again later after the Grand Wizard talks. You pay attention, hear? And stop pullin' on yer hood, boy. You can take it off in a minute."

Little Larry's shoulders rose and fell as he sighed loudly. "You sure 'bout that fire, Daddy?"

"I'm sure. Ain't nobody gettin' burned up in that fire, boy. It's jus' to look at. At least it ain't so dark. Now hush."

"Good," Little Larry whispered. "I was sceered."

L.T. smiled and patted his boy's head. "Well, don't be. Jus' stand still and—think about . . . about'cher frogs or sump'm."

L.T. turned his attention to Jim Mitchell, who was shouting a speech from the back of a pickup truck. L.T. didn't care much for Jim, but now that he was the Grand Wizard, the man's ego, as well as his ideas, had to be respected. L.T. felt a nudge to his ribs and groaned when he saw his brother Charlie standing behind him. "What the hell ya want now, Charlie?"

"L.T. Ya gotta do me a favor. I—I need . . ."

Impatiently yanking off his hood, L.T. nudged his brother away from the others and into the shadows. "I ain't loanin' you no more got-damn money, Charlie!" he hissed. "You ain't the only one out'a work, ya know. Besides, you ain't paid back the last five I loaned ya."

"I got me a prospect, L.T. Look, at least yer pickin' up day work. An' Ellen told me ya just got paid yesterday. Ya ain't spent it yet, L.T.?"

"Gotdamn her! Since when do you and my wife set around and talk about what money I got an' ain't got? I bet'cha I smack that scrawny bitch upside her empty head when . . ."

He stopped when he heard the sound of his own name. "L.T. Sullivan!" Jim Mitchell shouted from the truck. "If you and yer brother's through jabberin', maybe I can finish up here!"

"Sorry." L.T. shot his brother a withering look, and shivered at the resemblance he bore to their mother. After their abusive father's death, which no one in the family seemed to mind, L.T.'s mother had moved into L.T.'s cramped house. She was demanding, constantly whining about her aches and pains, and always took his wife's side in marital squabbles.

*An' the rotten apple don't fall far from the tree*, L.T. thought as he turned his back on his brother. *Charlie, Mama shore spit'cher sorry ass out.*

Only one good thing resulted from L.T. Sullivan's reluctant marriage to a visibly pregnant Ellen Reynolds—the surprising joy of fatherhood. L.T. liked the reflection he saw in Little Larry's eyes. He saw himself as a good father and a teacher, imparting the wisdom of Southern traditions to his son. Although L.T.'s deadly temper was known far and wide, it was never inflicted on his boy. The majority of his arguments with Ellen were over his spoiling of the child, and in some malicious corner of his mind, he actually preferred beating Ellen into submission rather than laying an angry hand on Little Larry. Occasionally, L.T. made an effort to get along with Ellen for Little Larry's benefit, but those phases never lasted long. He could stand neither the sight nor the sound of her: a spindly scarecrow of a woman, with stringy, mousy-brown hair, and a grating, whiny voice to top it off. He seriously considered running away with his son, leaving the rest of the Sullivans to rot, but, unable to stand Little Larry's tears when separated from Ellen for any length of time, L.T. grudgingly surrendered to the misery of his life.

Suddenly aware of an uneasy murmuring in the crowd around him, L.T. felt a light tap on his shoulder. He whirled around, expecting to see Charlie with his hand out. But to his surprise, it was his friend, Mac, who had arrived late.

"Ya hear *that*, L.T.?" Mac whispered, nodding in Jim Mitchell's direction.

"Uh, no. What' he say?"

"Shh. Listen."

Jim Mitchell extended his hands in a placating palms-down gesture. "Awright, now calm down. Jus' listen to me fer a minute. It ain't like we're sidin' with these niggers—it's jus' a meetin' and it's only with this one. Now, when ya think about it, which one would the Klan like to see leadin' all the niggers? That uppity DuBois fella—with all his talk about mixin' in with white folks and such? Or . . . would we like to see this Garvey fella lead all'a the niggers back to Africa? I don't know 'bout y'all, but if he can really get the niggers out'a the U.S.A., then I'll personally take up a collection to buy him some boats!"

As the crowd buzzed with mixed reactions, L.T. and Mac exchanged a look. "Gotdamn, L.T.! I seen pitchers a'that Garvey, all dressed up like a gotdamn go-rilla in a king uniform! If Jim really brings him down here, I'm quittin' the Klan!"

L.T. patted Mac on the shoulder. Mac was the only person he knew with a temper hotter than his own. "Calm down, Mac. Ol' Jim can't do nothin' unless we vote on it."

As if in answer to L.T.'s statement, Jim Mitchell concluded his announcement with a punch. "And in case some'a y'all don't like this strategy, yer jus' gonna have to learn to like it—'cause it comes directly from the top. It's all arranged, and like it or not, Garvey *is* comin' to Atlanta."

# Chapter 29

Serval scribbled furiously as his train approached the Atlanta station. He wanted to finish a list of points he knew he must cover as one of the reconnaissance men for Mr. Garvey, who was scheduled to arrive in two days. Serval's job was to divert public attention from Mr. Garvey's meeting with the Klan, while defusing any possible hysteria among the Negro population. Although Mr. Garvey had made it clear that he wanted the entire affair to be handled as quietly as possible, Serval received word during his stay in Charleston that Atlanta's UNIA membership was already buzzing with questions and demanding answers.

When the train pulled to a stop at the platform, Serval was confronted by the unwelcoming heat of Georgia. He loosened his collar and groaned. His neck was gritty and wet with perspiration, and his throat parched. *Lemonade. That's all I'd ask for if I met up with Aladdin's genie right now. No, wait. I get three wishes . . . Okay. Ice-cold lemonade, a long cool bath, and about twenty-four hours of sleep.* He laughed at the impossibility of his fantasy, considering the fact that he was scheduled to meet with officers of the Atlanta chapter of the UNIA in less than two hours. As he scanned the faces on the platform, he suddenly spotted his own name printed in large, neat letters on a placard. He headed in the direction of the placard and peeked over it at a bouquet of yellow spring flowers attached to a hat. He smiled and cleared his throat. "You're looking for Mr. Rivard?"

The placard fell as the hat leaned back to expose a tiny woman's nut-brown face. "Oh! Mr. Rivard!" Sticking out her hand, she continued before he could say another word. "Well, sho' you are! Good to meetcha, Mr. Rivard! Good to meetcha!" The take-charge enthusiasm in her voice contrasted sharply with her stature: about four feet, nine inches, Serval figured. He smiled down at her.

"And you must be Mrs. Thompson."

"That's right. I sho'ly am that. And me and Jasper's gonna see to it that'cho stay is a pleasant one, Mr. Rivard. Now, you jus' call me Lena, ya hear? Where is that Jasper anyhow? Oh! There he is! Jasper! Over here! I found him!"

Jasper hurried over and reached for one of Serval's bags. "Well, well, good to meetcha, Mr. Rivard! We done heard a lot'a great things about you and we' proud to have you stayin' in our home while you' visitin' Atlanta. Now, uh, I'm sorry 'bout rushin' you, but we expectin' a whole houseful of folks for this plannin' meetin' tonight and you' barely gonna have time for a quick supper 'fo everybody starts showin' up. Lena! Pour Mr. Rivard some'a that lemonade from the cooler. We thought you'd appreciate this on a hot day like today, Mr. Rivard. My Lena makes the best doggone lemonade in the county!"

"Well, thank you, Mr. Thompson," Serval said. "I was just wishing for some cold lemonade. You must've been reading my mind." . . . *Oh, well. One out'a three ain't too bad.*

\* \* \*

Serval had just enough time to clean up and change his shirt before sitting down to a supper of smothered chicken, mashed potatoes, and collard greens at the Thompsons'. As he ate, he found a pleasant diversion from his worries in Lena and Jasper's two children—David, who was two, and five-year-old Sistine. With a dark-chocolate complexion almost identical to Serval's own, Sistine was a charming, wide-eyed cherub who watched his every move. She rested her chin on the table, and her keen black eyes seemed to miss nothing.

"Look' like little Miss Somebody got a giant crush on big Mr. Somebody," Lena whispered to Serval as she refilled his glass.

Serval grinned across the table at his admirer and crooked his finger at her. "Come over here, Miss Sistine." Bashfully, she approached. Serval lifted her onto his lap and marveled at the heavenly paternal sensation of holding a small child. "Know what?"

"What?"

"I think you're the prettiest little girl I have ever seen. And your name! Sistine. Where'd you get such a pretty name?"

Staring at him in awe, Sistine pointed at her mother as a wordless answer. Then she whispered, "You smell good."

Serval smiled. "So do you. You smell like a sweet baby."

"I ain't no baby," she said, scowling. "I'm five now."

"Oh! Five. Well, I stand corrected. That's practically grown! I'll bet you can read already, huh?"

"A lidda bit. I know my ABC's. Wanna hear?"

"Your ABC's? You know *all* of 'em? Aww, now I don't know. You're gonna have to prove it to me. Go on. Say 'em."

As Sistine proudly recited her ABC's, Serval recalled his last argument with Opal about having a child. *If she could just see this baby, I know she'd change her mind.* But he knew there was truth in Opal's last stinging remark: *You're gone so much now, Serval. A child's supposed to have a Mama and a Daddy around, you know* . . . Sistine bounced and clapped her hands as she finished. ". . . X, Y, Z!"

"Bravo!" Serval shouted. "You must be the smartest little girl in the world, I'll bet. I sure wish I had a daughter like you."

Sistine patted Serval's shoulder sympathetically. "Ain'tcha got no chi'dren, Mr. uh—Mr. . . ."

"You can call me Serval."

Lena shot Sistine a warning look. "That's *Mister* Serval to you, Missy. She's got to mind her elders, Mr. Rivard."

Winking at Sistine, Serval said, "Miz Lena, if it wasn't impolite for a man to ask a woman her age, I'd get to the bottom of this 'Mr. Rivard' business. We'd see who's the elder around here. Now, *please* call me Serval."

Lena shook her head adamantly while drying off the last plate. "Naw, sir, Mr. Rivard. It ain't about age in the UNIA. You' one'a Mr. Garvey's soldiers, and 'round this house, you'll be addressed with a title of respect." Grinning slyly at him, she said, "After all, you still call Marcus Mosiah Garvey 'Mister'—now, don'tcha?"

Serval laughed. "Guilty." Lifting Sistine high in the air, he whirled her around until she screamed with laughter.

Jasper dipped his bread in a puddle of gravy, and grinned at Lena. "Lawd, you can tell he ain't got no children. Mr. Rivard, that child just ate a big supper. I'd put her down if I was you. That is, if you don't want to have to change ya shirt again 'fo everybody starts showin' up."

"Oh, right." Serval quickly put Sistine down and realized he had started something, when David reached up, shouting, "My turn!"

"Okay, okay! Now, me and your Mama and Daddy have got some business to take care of, so I'll make you a deal. Tomorrow, before anything else, I promise I'll throw you both around and wrestle and let'cha beat on me and whatever else you call fun. How's that?" Glancing up at Jasper for approval, he added, "Uh—*before* breakfast, that is."

Lena clapped her hands sharply. "Now you two go get ready for bed, hear?"

"Yes, ma'am," came the mournful unison response. Suddenly, Sistine darted back to Serval, and crooked her finger at him.

Suppressing a laugh, he leaned down.

"Can I still call you Mr. Ser—uh, Ser-val?" she whispered in his ear.

"I'll be heartbroken if you don't," he whispered back. "And Sistine?"

"Yes, sir?"

"You like secrets?"

"Yes, sir!"

"I'll tell you one, then. It's about my name. My name is the secret."

Wrinkling her nose, she giggled and whispered, "Nuh-uh."

"Uh-huh. It's not just a name. It means something."

"What?"

"A serval is . . . a wildcat! *RAAHRRR!*"

The shock of Serval's loud roar sent Sistine running out of the kitchen, squealing with laughter. But as the adults settled back down at the table for coffee, she stuck her head around the corner one last time. "Mr. Serval!"

"Yes?"

"*Raaahrr!*"

\* \* \*

Shortly after supper, a high-level UNIA organizer by the name of Ernest Davis arrived from New York. "Ernest!" Serval said, reaching for his hand. "I'm so glad you're here. I hope you remember me. I'm Serval Rivard. I met you at the convention."

"Yes, of course, Mr. Rivard. Mr. Mathis introduced us. He and Mr. Crichlow have had nothing but good things to say about you, and I've been looking forward to working with you."

Serval laughed. "Good things? I got the uneasy feeling that Mr. Mathis was about to fire me that night."

"Oh, he's tough on everyone, Mr. Rivard. But don't let him fool you. He's quite proud of his new young protege."

"Well, that's good to hear, Ernest, but please call me Serval, would you? Oh! I apologize for my rudeness. Ernest, say hello to the Thompsons. Jasper, Lena, this is Ernest Davis."

Jasper shook Ernest's hand, and Lena gave him a curious smile.

"Mr. Davis?" she said, "I hope you don't mind me askin', but where in the world are you from? That accent don't sound like Mr. Rivard's."

Serval's eyebrows shot up. "Accent? Why, I don't have an accent, Miz Lena. *You* have an accent."

Lena laughed. "Oh, no ya don't, Mr. Rivard. You' the foreigner around here. And you do too have an accent. A northern accent. But I ain't ever heard anybody talk like Mr. Davis here."

Ernest chuckled. "I don't mind you asking at all, Mrs. Thompson. I was born and educated in Jamaica. I continued my studies in England for awhile, but I now reside in Harlem, New York."

Lena's eyes widened, and she let out a long whistle. "Would'ja listen to him, Jasper? I ain't even heard white folks talk that proper! Shoot, Mr. Davis, I could listen to you talk all night! And call me Lena, please."

"I will, if you'll call me Ernest. And I'm sure you'll be tired of listening to my proper-sounding voice by the time we wrap up this meeting. The Atlanta branch of the UNIA is a large group. I'm afraid it may be a late night."

*   *   *

Ernest's prediction was accurate. Jasper had crammed fifteen wooden folding chairs into the small front room to provide additional seating, but by 8:30 even standing room was tight. The loud ticking of Lena's old wall clock seemed to amplify the tension as Serval stood up to open the meeting with a prepared statement. A polite silence prevailed as he spoke, but the minute he called for questions, the room erupted with strident voices. As the noise escalated, Serval dropped all formality and regained control by whistling sharply through his teeth. "Please! I understand you're all upset, but we can only listen to one person at a time." Pointing at the nearest woman, he sat down to listen. "All right, ma'am, you have the floor."

The woman's story was followed by hours of emotional testimonies from others about run-ins with the Klan, and ended with several members quitting the UNIA. It was nearly midnight when an elderly gentleman who hadn't spoken all night suddenly stepped to the center of the cramped room and faced Serval.

"Mr. Rivard . . ." he said in a choked voice, "come September, it' be ten years since I lost my wife Louise to them redneck butchers."

Serval swallowed hard. "They—they killed your wife, Mr. . . .? I'm sorry, sir, I didn't get your name."

"Cobb. Walter Cobb. Everybody 'round these parts knows what happened to my Louise." When Mr. Cobb paused, Serval snuck a look at Jasper, who silently mouthed one word: "Lynched."

Mr. Cobb continued. "Her daddy wasn't right in the head, ya see, creepin' up on ninety years and all, and he sassed some college boy, son'a Klan . . . I was workin' the day they come to get the ol' man. But my neighbor tol' me how my Louise fought them men like she was a man her own self, tryin' to save her daddy's life . . ."

Mr. Cobb stopped to wipe his eyes, then stared hard at Serval. "Mr. Rivard, you got any idea how a pitcha jus' kind'a burns into ya brain so ya can't never forget it? I had to cut 'em both down myself. My wife, with her dress half-to'e off her, and that pitiful ol' man who ain't never hurt a soul in all his life."

Serval's eyes remained locked on Mr. Cobb's, even as the old man tore up his Black Star stock certificates and threw the bits of paper into his face.

Mr. Cobb was crying freely now. "You come here an' you tell me Mr. Garvey fixin' to set down an' talk wit' them devils, Mr. Rivard, and I tell you this . . . The UNIA and Mr. Garvey was my last hope in this white man's world. So now it ain't nothin' lef' for me to do but die—a kicked down ol' nigga who jus' too tired to believe in any man—or any damn thing no mo'."

As Mr. Cobb turned to leave, the remnants of Atlanta's UNIA chapter stepped aside to clear a path for him. And a split-second after the slam of the screen door, they all filed out after him in a silent exodus.

Serval and Ernest blinked at each other, and Lena slumped into Jasper's arms with a sigh.

"Well," Serval said softly, "that ought'a show us what we're up against."

Ernest patted Serval's shoulder. "We can't be like Mr. Cobb. If we all decide to give up and die, then all is really lost. We all know the stories, but this is not a time for emotions. Agreed?"

Lena and Jasper nodded, and Serval stood up. "All right, then, Ernest. You up for some late night brainstorming?"

"I have no choice. Tomorrow we should see an even bigger crowd, and we need to work on a more convincing approach."

"We were reaching some of 'em . . ." Serval said, rubbing his eyes. "Until Mr. Cobb . . ."

"And tomorrow we'll reach the rest, my friend. I'm sure Atlanta has its share of optimistic folk."

Lena stood up. "Well, gentlemen, I'll make you a pot'a coffee, but then I gotta get to bed. Them little ones I got gonna be wakin' me up soon as the sun's up. Now, Jasper done set up them two rollaway beds for you in that back room. Hope you two won't be too cramped . . ."

"I'm sure it'll be fine, Miz Lena," Serval said. "I can sleep anywhere. Now go get yourself some sleep, please. Good night, Jasper. See you in the morning. And thanks for everything."

Jasper nodded his head and yawned as he stood up.

"Say, Jasper?" Serval said.

"Mm-hmm?"

"What do you think tomorrow's gonna *really* be like?"

"Lawd only knows, Mr. Rivard. You saw how those folks acted tonight. You fellas come from the nawth. Colored folks 'round these parts got no understandin' when it comes to consortin' with the Klan, no matter what Mr. Garvey say. I think you gonna get a mixed reaction, at best. But you'll find the right words. I know it. Good night, Mr. Rivard, Mr. Davis. Don't stay up too long, hear?"

"Good night, Jasper. And thanks again."

Serval sipped his coffee as he shuffled through his notes, scratching out words, rewriting, and scratching out again. "Ernest, you've known Mr. Garvey longer than I have. What in the world motivated him to meet with the *goddamn* Ku Klux Klan? Sorry for the profanity. Guess I'm tired—not to mention frustrated. 'Cause I've racked my brain and I still can't figure it out. Here I am in Atlanta to convince people of something I don't understand myself!"

Ernest smiled. "You're right, my friend. You're tired. In the morning, after you've had some sleep, things will be clear to you. Why, you spoke the answer only an hour or so before Mr. Cobb upset everyone. You were reaching them, I could tell."

"*I* spoke the answer? Me? How come I don't remember that? And exactly what did I say?"

"You said, as I recall, that Mr. Garvey couldn't possibly trust these devils. You said something to the effect that he must be using them. Because they are most definitely using him. Don't you see, Serval? You hit it on the head. Tomorrow—you just speak to the people about how

Mr. Garvey is using the Klan, the same way they are using him. The Klan and the UNIA are like opposite sides of the same coin. Separatists. They want us gone—to separate from them. Fine. We want the same thing—to form our own nation with Africa as the homebase. The only difference is that their methods are violent, bringing death to our people and disgrace to their own people. Our method is a device of *peaceful* separation—but separation, just the same. I have a feeling, Serval, that the Klan is willing to put up money to help Mr. Garvey with the shipping line, anything to get rid of the Negroes. And . . ."

"Wait, Ernest. You had my attention up until the money part. How can we allow ourselves to be financed, even partially, by those murdering, lowdown monsters? It's blood money, Ernest. No matter how I look at it . . ."

"No, my friend. It's *freedom* money. If they're stupid enough to buy us ships, then I say let's take the money and run. Serval, listen to me." Ernest leaned closer to Serval and smiled conspiratorially. "During slavery times, in the rare instance that a runaway slave killed an overseer during an escape, don't you think he had the good sense to go through the dead man's pockets?"

After a long silence, Serval rubbed his eyes and laughed hoarsely. "Thank you, Ernest. I think you just rewrote my speech for me."

\* \* \*

The controversy over the meeting of Marcus Garvey with the Ku Klux Klan brought Atlanta's Negroes out to Piedmont Park in record numbers the next day, a handful to show their support, some hungry for information from a source other than the local white-owned newspapers, but all demanding an explanation. A huge, ornate gazebo with thick ivy climbing over white latticework served as the park's band shell, as well as the speaker's platform for political gatherings. As Jasper led Serval and Ernest up the wide, curving steps to the podium, Serval gazed up at the high arch above his head and let out a long whistle. "I feel like President Harding, speaking from such a fancy stage, Jasper."

"The one you *should* be feelin' like is Booker T. Washington," Jasper said. "He gave a big speech here when I was a kid. It was the first time I saw white folks clappin' for a colored man. Made me proud, jus' like you' gon' make me proud today, Mr. Rivard."

Serval stared out at the growing throng. "Booker T. Washington, huh?"

"Mm-hmm. Standin' right 'bout nigh on where you standin' right now."

"Well, thanks, Jasper. Now I'm really nervous."

Jasper laughed. "No need to be nervous, Mr. Rivard. You' gon' do jus' fine."

*   *   *

Ernest's insight from the night before provided Serval with the words he needed to address the crowd's collective concern. Abandoning his notes, he launched into a parable about a slave achieving his freedom by hook, crook, and tricking his master out of ill-gotten money:

"... But the point is this: the master had all the resources, so communicating with the enemy was necessary if our runaway hero was to, uh, *relieve* him of some of that heavy gold he'd stockpiled off the sweat of his slaves. Now, none of us actually know what Mr. Garvey will discuss with the other participants of this meeting, but I think it's safe to say that he is not attending some sort of society tea party. Perhaps some of you folks are thinking of this meeting the wrong way. No one questioned President Wilson when he sat down with the Germans for armistice talks that ended the Great War. So perhaps we should view this meeting in a different light. A bloodless battle—fought over a table, using words as weapons, instead of guns. A debate, if you will. Or a strategy." He peered out at the gathering with a sly grin. "A *con* perhaps?"

A burst of laughter ended in applause, and at the conclusion of the speech, the crowd dispersed in a buzz of excited voices.

As Serval descended the gazebo steps, Ernest smiled broadly and grasped his hand. "I knew it! I knew you had the gift, my friend!"

Serval laughed lightly. "What gift?"

"Today, my friend, you reached into their hearts and then had them eating out of your hand! What a difference from last night! You actually made them laugh!"

"I couldn't have done it if we hadn't stayed up and had our little talk, Ernest. My speech would've flopped if you hadn't given me the key."

"Ah. That's where we're different. I think great thoughts all the time, but unfortunately, I don't have the gift to convey them very well."

"Well, then, looks like you and I make a good team, huh, Ernest?"

Suddenly, Serval's legs froze in mid-step. The unmistakable drawl of two approaching white men flooded his mind with thoughts of Spartanburg, Sergeant Fairgate, and Jimmy Coles.

The two men stopped, and the shorter one pointed at Serval. "Well, well. Here's that smartass big-talkin' nigger right here, L.T.!"

Serval saw Ernest's face register rage, and he placed a hand on his shoulder.

"Naw, Mac," the tall man said. "A nigger talkin' like that in the South ain't smart. He's stupid. Real stupid."

Ernest shook off Serval's grip and stepped closer to the white men. But before he could open his mouth to speak, Mac challenged him.

"Aw, look, L.T., this one looks mad! Ya better mind yer manners, nigger, if ya know what's good for ya!"

"Let me tell you something, *redneck* . . ."

Serval leaned close to Ernest's ear and hissed, "Calm down, please."

"Did'ja hear what that little black sumbitch called me, L.T.?" Mac sputtered. He raised a hand, but L.T. held him back. Mac strained and grunted, but couldn't break free. "Goddamn niggers! Ought'a line 'em up and lynch 'em all!" he screamed.

Despite the volume of Mac's voice, it was his quiet friend who held Serval's attention. He studied the white man while reaching for Ernest's arm.

Ernest pointed his finger dangerously close to Mac's face. "Why don't all of you Klan people do the world a great favor and go lynch *yourselves!*"

Mac lunged at Ernest, but L.T. again managed to restrain him, without taking his eyes off Serval.

"Don't talk crazy, Ernest," Serval said, meeting L.T.'s gaze. "Haven't you ever heard that old southern expression? Snakes don't *ever* commit suicide."

# Chapter 30

Leon sat up in bed and felt around on the bedside table for his cigarettes and matches. Fumbling with the matches in the darkness, he finally lit up and inhaled deeply. Manché shifted slightly beside him, but didn't wake up. Staring at the glow of the cigarette, Leon pondered his sleeplessness. Ever since his last brush with the police, he had found sleep an elusive prospect. While he enjoyed the fat roll of cash Hightower's operation provided, on nights like tonight, Leon longed for a less dangerous hustle, like the numbers game. But he knew that he was in too deep with Max Hightower to get out now.

The telephone outside jangled, snapping Leon out of his thoughts and startling him with the realization that the sun was up. Glancing over at the ashtray, he counted the butts—seven. Someone knocked on Manché's door, and before she could get up to answer it, an annoyed voice called, "Manché! Somebody's on this damn telephone askin' for your man! Shit! Folks gotta get some sleep 'round here, ya know!"

Leon pulled on his trousers and scurried to the door. "Sorry, Della," he whispered, taking the earpiece from the angry woman.

"Hello?"

"Daddy? I'm sorry to wake you up so early."

"Opal? Aw, baby, that's okay. I was awake anyhow. Anything wrong?"

"No, Daddy. Serval jus' called me to tell me he's comin' home tonight, and I guess I forgot how early it was—'til I heard your neighbor's voice. Ooh, she was mad, huh?"

Leon chuckled. "Aw, don't worry 'bout her. So you say Serval's comin' home, huh?"

"Uh-huh. That's why I called, Daddy. Serval's car is being repaired and, well . . . you think you could pick him up?" Her voice suddenly took on a surly tone. "I mean, if you're not too busy with that *woman,* that is."

Leon sighed and rolled his eyes. "Her name's Manché, Opal. And one'a these days, you gonna find out what a good woman she is."

"Hmmm. Maybe, Daddy."

"Anyway, baby, I'll be happy to pick him up. What train he comin' in on?"

"The nine-fifteen from Atlanta. And Daddy? Thank you."

*   *   *

As Serval squirmed into a more comfortable position in his seat on the train headed back to New York, he heard a familiar voice from above:

"Anything I can get fo' ya, suh?"

Serval grinned and opened his eyes. "Jack! Well, I figured sooner or later I'd end up on one of your runs! But hey, you're not supposed to be back here, are you? Aren't you supposed to be takin' care'a the rich white folks?" he said, grinning. "Better tips up there, I bet."

"I'm on a break from white folks. I saw you when you boarded in Atlanta, but I didn't get a chance to get back here 'til now. So, how'd it go? You' gettin' use'ta makin' speeches and all that?"

"Well, I guess I'm gettin' the hang of it. We managed to keep things under control while Mr. Garvey had his meeting and even signed up a few new members."

"Yeah? How many?"

"Oh, I don't know the exact number, but more and more folks are joinin' every trip, Jack. The UNIA is becoming a national phenomenon."

"Well, it's good to know all that hard work is payin' off, brotha, 'cause you sho' look tired. I—I wish I could get you sleepin' accommodations."

Serval patted Jack's arm. "It's okay. I can sleep anywhere."

Jack peered down at the two open books stacked on Serval's lap. "What'cha readin'?"

"Oh! Well, I was re-reading a little of 'Call of the Wild'—that was my favorite book when I was a kid, and it still stirs up my blood. Thought it might wake me up. But then I felt the need for a little soul-inspiration tonight, so I snuck in a couple'a poems. Langston Hughes. Did you ever pick up that book of poems I told you about, Jack? It has that one . . ."

"That one you read to me," Jack said. "The Negro speaks on rivers. My soul grows deep like rivers."

"So you *did* get the book, huh?"

"Naw. I just remembered that part 'cause I liked it. These ol' tracks reminds me a'rivers sometimes."

Serval sighed and closed his eyes. "Maybe one'a these days I'll get back to my poem."

Jack chuckled. "You still a poetry writin' man?"

"What's so funny about that? I wrote a lot'a poetry when I was at Morehouse. Well, at least I tried."

"Mm-hmm. Love poems to all them girls you was messin' wit', huh?"

Serval laughed. "Guilty. But this one's different. It's about the war. And Harlem. And me, I guess. Maybe that's why I can't finish it."

"Huh! You'll finish it. I ain't seen you quit at nothin' yet, brotha."

"Well, you're about to," Serval said, muffling a yawn. "'Cause I'm about to quit bein' awake."

"Yeah, I see that head noddin'. Go on, man. Get'cha some rest. I got a whole sleepin' car full'a shoes to shine anyhow."

Serval frowned. "Listen, Jack. Any more word on . . . you know, the union?"

"Yeah. Some talk. Lawd knows we need our own union. I done put in seventy-six hours this week, and if it ain't been for the tips . . . But some'a the fellas been sayin' unions jus' be mo trouble than anything. Another white man to answer to."

"Well, don't give up on the union, Jack. Union philosophy is sound—on its face. Just depends on who's runnin' the union. Now, see—Pullman's union is a joke 'cause it's run by the Pullman Company! If that's not the fox guardin' the chickenhouse, I don't know what is! And all the big unions ban Negroes from joinin' anyway. But you're on the right track. Just keep your ear to the ground and listen. When a fella with a *black* face comes along talkin' union for the Pullman Porters, then it's time to organize. But just make sure he's not hired by Mr. Pullman—you know, Jack, like those minstrel shows, a white man in blackface."

Jack looked over his shoulder and leaned down. "Well, now that you mention it, I did hear 'bout a colored fella name'a Randolph been talkin' 'bout organizin' the Pullman porters."

"Yeah. I seem to recall hearing sump'm about him, too. Asa Philip Randolph. He was against the war, too, Jack, just like Mr. Garvey." Serval laughed. "The White House called him 'the most dangerous Negro in America.' And you know me, Jack. I *like* those credentials. He just might be the guy who can do it. You let me know what else you hear."

"I will. I mean—damn! We work hard as any white man. And put up with a lot mo' mess. You know, jus' this mawnin' a little white girl—couldn't a'been but twelve, thirteen years old—looked me dead in my grown-man eyes and called me a boy! Talkin' 'bout 'Get that last bag, boy. And make it snappy!' Shoot, Serval! If I could find me a union wid a law against callin' men boys, I'd sho' join up fast. I hope this Mr. Randolph comes through. I mean, why should the unions all be jus' for the white folks?"

"They shouldn't. But equality takes a fight. Maybe even a war. But you just keep on workin', buddy. When it gets hard, just remember you're a man. That's sump'm they can't take away from you no matter how many times they call you out of your name."

Jack reached up and retrieved a pillow from the overhead storage shelf and plumped it. "Here, man. And thanks for the talk. Seem like . . ."

Serval interrupted him with a nudge and gestured toward the door connecting the cars. "White man at twelve o'clock," he hissed. "And by the looks of him, I'll bet he's your supervisor."

As Jack headed for the door, he whispered back over his shoulder, "'Least we gon' both be in the city at the same time. Wait for me when we get in."

Serval smiled and gave him a thumbs-up signal, but the smile faded as soon as Jack was gone. With a sigh, he crossed his arms over his chest and was instantly asleep.

*     *     *

Walking through Grand Central Station with Jack elevated Serval's spirits, almost letting him forget how exhausted he was. When he caught sight of Leon Jackson rushing in their direction with Manché Redriver on his arm, Serval grinned and extended his arms.

"Leon and his lady love! How' you folks doin'? Where' you headed?"

"Aww, we ain't goin' nowhere, son. We' here to pick you up. Opal called to tell me what train you'd be comin' in on and asked me to come get you."

"Oh, that's swell, Leon, 'cause my car's in the shop and I did *not* feel like hustlin' around for a ride." Giving Leon a once-over, Serval nudged Jack. "Look at Leon, would'ya, Jack! Man, where'd you get that suit? What's that thing the kids are sayin'? Ain't he jus' the *cat's meow*, Jack?"

"Mee-ooow!" Jack howled, grinning. "What is it, Leon? Purple?"

"Naw, man!" Leon laughed. "This here's what'cha call royal blue!"

"Oh, *royal* blue! Okay, your majesty, and I see your queen has on her royal garments too!" Serval hugged Manché and spun her around until she laughed.

"Aww, Lawd, Serval!" Leon said, "this woman got a whole closet full of fancy clothes! I'm lucky she' let a ol' fool like me hang around! Anyway, we headin' out to Crazy Eights and a couple'a other spots after we drop y'all off. Fletcher Henderson's playin' out there tonight."

Serval smiled. "Fletcher Henderson? Well, shoot, Leon. You don't have to be in such a hurry to get rid of us, ya know. Whadaya say, Jack? Wanna go hear some jazz?"

"Now, Serval," Leon began, and shook his head, "I ain't wantin' to get you in trouble with Miz Opal, now. I know my child, and I don't think she'd appreciate me keepin' you out all night yo' first night home and all . . ."

"Aww, Leon, you let me worry about Opal. We won't stay out late. But after spendin' the last two weeks in good ol' Confederate *Dixie*, I need you to get me to Harlem fast! I think I wanna get down on my knees and kiss Lenox Avenue."

"Thought you was tired, man," Jack said, grinning, as they followed Leon and Manché to Leon's new Chrysler.

"Gettin' home woke me up."

"Thought *Africa* was home."

"It is. But so is Harlem, brother. So is Harlem."

\*   \*   \*

Serval's mood quickly deflated upon their arrival at Crazy Eights. Just as they were seated, the floorshow began, eliciting wild wolf whistles from a party of intoxicated Caucasians occupying a large front table.

The waiter exchanged a look with Serval, and shrugged his shoulders. "That's the Ziegfeld crowd. Lately, they' been comin' here after the Follies instead of Roseland, and Lord, they' a noisy bunch."

"It's okay," Serval smiled. "Just bring us stingers all around. Oh, you still like stingers, Manché?"

"That's jus' fine, baby."

"Stingers," Serval confirmed with a nod to the waiter.

After the waiter left, Serval did his best to ignore the group at the front table, but found it impossible, as the slurred shouts interrupted his conversation with Leon:

"So, Leon, you been takin' good care of . . ."

"Aww, baby!" the drunk man roared. "See, Herb, I told'ya they' got beautiful asses! Shake it, baby!"

Leon smiled nervously at Serval. "Uh, what was that, son? What'cha say?"

"I said . . ."

Another interruption from the drunk, who was reaching for one of the dancers and waving money in the air: "What an ass! Here, baby. Here's a hundred—come sit on my lap for a while!"

Serval stared evilly at the drunk, then gazed at the dismayed expression of the girl. He closed his eyes and visualized Opal in her place. "I gotta go, Leon," he said, standing up. "You and Manché stay and enjoy yourself. You too, Jack. I'm sorry everybody, but I suddenly feel sick."

Jack stood up and tossed a five on the table. "Naw, man. I'll go wit'cha. I'm feelin' kind'a sick, ma'self."

*You must take responsibility upon your own shoulders to build something upon which you can depend—to get what you can take and keep what you can hold. You can't take anything without power and you can't keep anything without power. And you can't get power unless you're organized!*

—ASA PHILIP RANDOLPH

# Chapter 31

Each time Jack returned from one of his cross-country trips, he tried to convince himself that he was falling in love with Creola. Sexual deprivation for a two or three week stretch helped. Lusty first night reunions and the resultant fatigue allowed him to sleep soundly. But after two or three nights, he found himself standing at the window, smoking and staring blankly at nothing in particular. Not depression exactly—it was a nagging, hollow feeling in the center of his being, and it refused to leave him alone.

He missed spending time with Serval, but was haunted by their last exchange: a warning from Serval, which Jack absorbed with a judicious silence.

"Man, I'm tellin' you—that one's a she-wolf, Jack. You turn your back once and she'll chew your head off."

Jack closed his eyes and shrugged, glad that his friend couldn't read his thoughts. *Brotha, Creola Dorshay' the best friend you got. 'Cause she' the only thing keepin' me away from yo' wife.*

\* \* \*

But Jack's strength failed on the very day Serval left on another UNIA assignment. As he stood at the mirror straightening his tie, he tried to ignore the guilt and lied to his reflection. *Lunch, that's all. Lunch can't hurt. She' still my friend.*

Stepping off the bus at 125th Street, he hurried to catch the traffic light, and hoped that Opal hadn't already left to eat with some of her friends. When he opened the Club Deluxe entrance door, he was surprised to be met by an exceptionally tall white man dressed in an expensive-looking black suit.

"What the hell you want in here, boy?"

Jack was unaccustomed to conversing with anyone at eye-level, and was puzzled at the identity of this tall man. "Sorry, suh. I got a friend workin' here. Uh, Chappie know who I am."

"The choreographer?"

"Yes, suh. And the manager—I thought."

"New management, kid. New management and new owners. Chappie's still here—works with the dancers. Go around back and I'll send him out if I see him."

Unruffled, Jack continued in a polite tone. "Oh. Well, I was really lookin' for Miz Opal Rivard. She' my friend—one'a the dancers here. Leas' she use'ta be."

"Never heard of her. But the dancers are rehearsing. I'll ask when they get a break. But you gotta go around back to wait for her. The only colored allowed in here are the performers. See the sign?"

Jack gaped in disbelief at the sign hanging on the wall to his left: *White only.*

"But . . ."

"Look, kid. Don't argue with me. I'm under orders from Mr. Alphonse Capone. You've heard of Mr. Capone, ain'tcha, kid?"

Jack nodded and backed toward the door, but ventured one last question: "Ya mean the Champ sold Club Deluxe to—to *Al Capone?*"

"Nah. To Mr. Capone's associate, Mr. Madden. But don't make a mistake, kid. Mr. Capone's still the muscle behind the dough." He placed a beefy hand on Jack's chest. "Around back. *Now!* Get me?"

Jack slipped out the door and stepped out to the edge of the sidewalk. Shading his eyes with his hand, he squinted up at the new sign. "Mm-mm-mm. Ain't this sump'm?"

Pacing back and forth for a minute, Jack was about to leave when the door opened and Opal ran to him, throwing her arms around his neck.

"Jack! I went out back and didn't see you . . . I thought you left. When did you get back? Why didn't you call? We were mad at you for stayin' away so long without even callin'. We were worried."

"How'd you know it was me? I ain't gave that man my name."

"Big Frenchy came back to the dressin' room—he always comes in without knockin'—makes me so doggone mad. Anyway, he came back talkin' about some colored fella big as a house was lookin' for one'a the dancers. I knew it had to be you." Her smile faded. "So, did Frenchy tell you—'bout the Champ sellin' the club?"

After a long silence, Jack chuckled. "Ya know, I made a promise to ma'self a long time ago. I said I'd never set foot in no cotton field again, and look' like yo' Mr. Frenchy makin' sho' I keep my promise."

Stepping back, Jack shook his head and stared up at the club's new sign that now read "The Cotton Club."

*    *    *

The pattern of his relationship with the Rivards was beginning to trouble Jack more than ever. When Serval was in town, he was drawn to his best friend's side, and spent every free moment with him. But the minute Serval left on a trip for the UNIA, he found it impossible to resist Opal's company. He told himself he was breaking no rules, but the guilt was disturbing.

Serval's arrival later that week coincided with two of Jack's rare days off. After a supper of piecemeal leftovers, they talked until the coffee was cold, and stale cigarette smoke hung in the air like a thick London fog. At half-past-midnight Opal returned from work. She smiled at Jack and approached the table. Serval didn't look up.

"Got off early tonight," Opal said as she patted Jack's shoulder. "Creola got that crowd so stirred up, Chappie just let her encore her behind off. So they cut the finale." Staring at a stack of dirty dishes in the sink, she said, "So it looks like you fellas found sump'm to eat, huh?"

Serval said nothing, so Jack answered. "Mm-hmm. Shoot, y'all got all kind'a food to eat 'round here. We done fine, Opal. Sorry 'bout the dishes. We'll clean up in here, won't we, Serval?"

Serval took a silent pull on his cigarette, and stared into the smoke he exhaled.

Opal cut her eyes at him and sighed. "Well . . . good night."

Serval stood up and walked over to the counter. "More coffee, Jack?" he asked.

Jack glanced over at Opal, then at Serval's back. "Uh, yeah. Guess so."

Opal's lips pressed together in a tight frown. "None for me, Serval. Thanks anyway. Good night, Jack. I'd stay up and visit with you, but it's a little crowded in here for me." She whirled around, smacking Jack's chair with the beaded sash from her dress, then stomped down the hallway.

Jack's eyebrows shot up. "Guess I bed'not ask what that was all about."

Serval scraped his chair across the floor and positioned it with a bang before dropping into it. "That," he shouted, "was about the goddamn Cotton Club!"

* * *

Serval's mood appeared to be no better the next day when Jack joined him at the New York Public Library for a day of research. Jack recognized the distracted frown, and tried to concoct ways of erasing it.

"Hello, Mista Lion," Jack called, reaching up to touch one of the statue's stone paws. "Which one he be, Serval? Patience or Fortitude?"

"I'm never sure. They ought'a put up signs, huh? Anyway, come on, Jack. I want to show you this article I read last week about that Egyptian tomb they found. They say the king was just a boy when he died."

"Oh, yeah," Jack said, "King Toot. Little Rooty."

Serval shot him an impatient look. "Huh?"

Jack stuck his hands in his pockets and grinned. "Rooty-Toot."

Serval rolled his eyes. "It's Tutankhamen, but I know, I know. The slang-slingers are callin' him Tut. But Jack, it's still Tut, not *Toot*."

"I know. It was a joke. You ain't been in a joke-tellin' mood lately, so I thought I'd try one—to get you out that foul cloud you' been in, brotha."

"I'm not in a foul cloud, Jack. I just don't have the time for that Cotton Club type'a humor."

"What's Cotton Club about it?"

"Aw, you know. Burnt cork, banjos, and buck dancin'. Not in the mood."

Jack settled into one of the chairs at a long table in the reference room, and watched Serval as he searched the shelves for the items he wanted. When he returned to the reference table, Serval plunked down a copy of *The National Geographic* magazine, two books, and a backdated issue of the *New York Times*. He opened *The National Geographic* first, and read aloud: "At the tomb of Tutankhamen . . . an account of the opening of the royal Egyptian sepulchre which contained the most remarkable funeral treasures unearthed in historic times . . . Yeah," he said in a disgusted tone. "Treasures. That's enough reason for those Brits to violate the sacred burial ground of an African king . . ." He slid the magazine across the table to Jack. "Oh, by the way . . . Opal told me about your reading lessons—the last time we were speaking."

Jack shifted in his chair. "Oh, she did, huh?"

"Mm-hmm. I'm proud of you, man. I'm only sorry I never found the time to help you with it myself."

"It's okay. Opal's a real good teacher." He flipped through a few pages, then shook his head. "But I can't read none'a this here, Serval. I ain't that good yet."

"That's okay, Jack. You can pick through the words and look at the pictures while I do my research." Serval picked up one of the books and stood up.

"Awright," Jack said. "But wait a minute 'fo ya start . . ."

"What?"

"What's this trouble between you and Opal?"

"Who's talkin' about Opal?" Serval snapped. "I'm tryin' to teach you something, Jack, if you're still interested in learning, that is."

"Okay. If you don't wanna talk about it, okay, man."

Serval slammed the book back down on the table, then dropped heavily into a chair. Jack didn't move.

"I'm losin' her, Jack."

"Opal?" Jack laughed. "That woman love' yo' dirty draw's, man!"

"I'm losin' her to the white man."

"What?! Man, you' crazy. What white man?"

"*The* white man." He hesitated before continuing. "You know what she did, Jack? To keep her job at that goddamn white-only Cotton Club?"

Jack braced himself for a revelation of some unthinkable sin. "What?"

"That goddamn Frenchy told her she was too dark for the club, so she got Chappie to convince him that she could powder her face lighter— to look like the white man's ideal! You know, Jack, just dark enough to be exotic, but not African! Like that ridiculous sign they've got out front—'Tall, tan and terrific chorines.' I just can't stand it. My baby's up there dancin' for the white man while he drools all over himself, starin' at her body, and my black ass ain't even allowed in the joint!"

Jack held up his index finger. "You said ain't, Serval," he said softly. "You done tol' me not to say ain't a hundred times. Now what you should'a said was 'my black ass is *not* allowed in . . .'"

"I want her to *quit!*" Serval shouted, then lowered his voice. "Why can't she quit, Jack? Am—am I wrong?"

"Naw. You ain't wrong. I mean—you *aren't* wrong."

"They disrespect her husband—and she dances for 'em!"

Jack shook his head and sighed. "You *aren't* wrong, Serval. Opal's wrong. She' wrong as she can be."

# Chapter 32

The bathroom echoed with a piercing squeak as Opal gave a hard twist to the porcelain hot and cold faucet handles. She snatched a towel from the rack and ran into the hallway muttering and drying herself off as she went. "Oh, Lord! I'ma be late again!"

Her chemise skidded down her damp back and bunched up in a spot that she couldn't reach, but she ignored it and reached for one of her stockings. Just as she stuck in her toe, she heard the front door slam and leaned forward to peer down the hallway. "Serval?"

She heard his quick, heavy steps, and saw uncut rage in his face as he approached the bedroom. He stopped at the door and threw a piece of paper in her direction. "What the *hell* is this, Opal?"

Opal uncrossed her legs and the stocking dropped to the floor. "What, Serval? What are you talkin' about?"

"I said what the hell is this, goddammit?!"

"Hush, Serval! You want the neighbors to call the law? Now, let me see what you have there. You're stompin' around hollerin' at me and I don't even know what it is." Reaching for the rumpled paper, she laid it on the bed to smooth it, then caught her breath. It was a Cotton Club program featuring a lurid sketch of three muscular Negro men and two shapely Negro women, all naked. They were arranged in suggestive poses having nothing to do with dancing or the performing of music.

"Oh, God," Opal whispered.

Serval ripped off his necktie and threw it across the room. "You know who gave it to me? Huh? Cyril Crichlow! One of my superiors! He took it away from his little boy. Seems he didn't want him looking at dirty pictures. So he says to me, 'They tell me your wife works at this establishment, Mr. Rivard. Is this true?' What was I supposed to say, Opal? *What* was I supposed to say? Uh, yes, Mr. Crichlow, this is the little woman right here in the picture—the one spread out on the goddamn table with all her wild-eyed bucks crowded around! . . . *Answer* me, goddammit! What was I supposed to say, huh? . . . Are you gonna answer me or just sit there?"

Opal didn't bother trying to stop the tears she felt stinging her eyes, and only stared at the picture now lying on the floor at her feet.

"Goddamn!" Serval screamed. "Say something! You didn't have programs like this when a black man ran the club! Goddamn white man gets his hands on it and the next thing you know . . ."

"Serval!" she shouted. "You know nothing like this goes on at the club, and besides . . ."

"*What?* Now how the *hell* would I know what goes on at the club, Opal? You know a Negro man isn't allowed in the place! Not unless he's a performing *buck*, like in your program here."

"I mean—oh, Serval! You know what I mean—everybody wears clothes at the club! This picture's not right. It's just . . ."

"Just what? Just *what*, Opal? The way the white man sees you? I can't deal with this any more. I want you to quit. Tonight."

"But Serval . . ."

Snatching the program off the floor with one hand, Serval grabbed the back of Opal's head with the other and roughly forced her face close to it. "Look at it, Opal!" he screamed. "Is this what you want to be? The white man's *whore?*"

Opal jerked her head away so hard that a strand of her hair tangled in Serval's fingers and was ripped from her scalp. But she made no sound.

He let her go, but stood over her, his chest heaving. "Well, I guess maybe this *is* what you want to be. Guess this explains why you don't want a baby, huh? These women in this picture don't look much like young mothers either. No time to have babies when you have three wild-eyed, virile, black *bucks* lined up to satisfy! Is that what's next for the Cotton Club, Opal? They'll be expectin' you to strip down and have sex for the white folks' goddamn entertainment!"

"Shut-*up*, Serval! Stop saying that word!"

"What word?"

"Bucks! Just shut-*up*!" The sound of her own scream startled her and she scrambled to make her escape. Running down the hallway toward the bathroom, she sobbed, "I hate you, Serval Rivard!"

She slammed the door just as he reached it. "Of course you do!" he shouted. "Maybe you'd like me better if I were white! Huh, Opal?"

Opal watched the bathroom door shake on its hinges as he kicked it. A moment of silence was followed by the sounds of heavy footsteps and the slam of the front door.

After crying for several minutes, Opal finished dressing and headed for the corner to wait for her bus. But she was unable to dismiss the sound of Serval's voice: *Is this what you want to be? The white man's whore?*

"It's not like that picture," Opal murmured. "We just sing and dance—that's all. It's *not* like that horrible picture."

*       *       *

The Cotton Club's explosion of popularity soon made late nights for Opal a regular occurrence. Due to the audience response to the newest member of The Cotton Club's lineup of talent, a specialty dancer by the name of Earl "Snakehips" Tucker, Opal's late number was sometimes pushed back until almost 3:30 a.m. Serval picked her up from the club when he was in town, but late nights made it necessary for him to wait nearly two hours for her. Any patience he had was gone.

On the night of their argument over the program, Opal wondered whether Serval would show up to drive her home. Glancing at her watch, she gritted her teeth and peered out the rear door of the Cotton Club. Even if Serval had come to pick her up at 2:00, he would have left by now. It was well past 4:00 a.m. With a sigh, she went back inside and found Chappie pulling on his jacket in preparation to leave.

"Think you could drive me home, Chappie? I guess Serval got tired of waitin'."

Chappie yawned and stretched his arms. "Can't say I blame him for that. Tonight got completely out'a hand. Man! Guess Snakehips won't have to worry about employment for a while! Anyway, yeah, Opal. I'll take you home. One good thing about not bein' manager any more is I don't have to lock up. You know they still got about twenty people in there? Just sittin' around drinkin' with Mr. Madden."

"Oh, shoot, Chappie, let's get out'a here before Big Frenchy sees me and makes me dance another number."

Chappie laughed. "He won't. No musicians. They crawled out'a here a half-hour ago."

"Well, let's go anyway. They got a gramophone in there, ya know."

*       *       *

As they approached Opal's building, both Chappie and Opal were surprised to see the front windows ablaze with light.

"That's your apartment, isn't it, Opal?" Chappie asked.

Opal nodded slowly and opened the passenger door. "Yes, it is."

"You want me to wait 'til you get inside and make sure everything's all right?"

"No," she murmured, mentally rerunning her argument with Serval. "I'll be all right. He's probably just—waitin' up for me, is all. He's just worried 'cause it's so late. Thanks for the ride, Chappie. See you tomorrow."

"Good night, Opal."

Opal sprinted up the steps and into the foyer. When she reached her apartment door, she found it slightly ajar. Pushing it open, she heard the sound of male voices coming from the direction of the kitchen. She stole quietly toward the sound, listening. Picking up Ernest's unmistakable Jamaican accent, she quickly identified Jack's murmuring, but the tone of Serval's voice sent a shiver down her spine—a subdued, tired sound, like that of an old man.

"It can't be true. I—I just can't believe it's all over—in the blink of an eye," Serval croaked.

Opal stepped quietly into the kitchen, staring at Serval with wide eyes. He was clutching his head with both hands, as if the weight of it was too much to bear. "What—what's over, Serval?" Opal asked.

Serval looked up at her for a second or two, then stood up slowly, shaking his head. He walked to the sink and filled a glass with water, then remained there looking at it.

Ernest broke the tension by reaching for Opal's hand. "Sit down, Opal. Serval is quite upset, as we all are . . ."

"'Bout what?" she asked, blinking first at Ernest, then at Serval's back, then at Ernest again. "What happened?"

Ernest sighed deeply. "We're bankrupt. The Black Star Line has—has failed. And now somebody has got to face the stockholders to tell them . . ."

"What? That can't be! Serval . . .?"

Serval sank into a chair. "The money's gone, Opal. Everything is just—gone."

"But—but all the stocks and—oh, Serval! All that money you raised! I don't understand—I mean, it's gotta be *somewhere* . . . And what about all the ships . . .?" She stopped. It was apparent that each word was striking Serval like a physical blow.

"Opal," he began in a derisive tone, "it's not so hard to understand. It was the biggest rook of all time, that's all. And we were all the chumps—all the good, faithful people of Harlem who bought their shares because they believed in Mr. Garvey. And now, it's gone—the money, the ships—everything. Even the dream of Africa. It wasn't even a dream—it was just a lie." As the first tear splashed from his face onto the tabletop, Serval grabbed his glass and threw it across the room, sending shattered bits of it flying in all directions amidst a spray of water.

Jack stood up and gripped Serval's shoulder. "Enough."

Serval nodded, then lowered his head.

Silence was suddenly mandated, and no one broke it for several minutes. Opal grabbed the broom and dustpan, and began sweeping up the broken glass. Suddenly, she stopped. "Serval . . ."

Serval looked up at her, then reached over for her hand.

Opal's bottom lip quivered at his touch. The strong, confident hand she had held at her wedding was trembling. "S-serval, maybe it's not Mr. Garvey's fault," she said softly. "I mean, maybe it's grabbin' at straws . . . or like Daddy use'ta say—strikin' a match in a thunderstorm— but maybe Mr. Garvey didn't lie. Maybe *he* was the one who was swindled . . ." Her voice faded when she felt three pairs of eyes focusing on her.

Without taking his eyes off Opal, Serval said, "Ernest, where did you hear . . . Look, who told you the news?"

"It was—now that I think of it, it was Jules, and he got the story from his brother who works one of the printing presses for *The New York Times* . . ."

"Did he talk to Mr. Garvey?"

"I—I'm ashamed to say I didn't ask him. I was so shocked when he told me about the warrant for Mr. Garvey's arrest that I just rushed right over here to tell you . . ."

Opal sprang from her chair. "Come on, Jack. Drive me down to the newsstand. We'll wait for the truck to bring the early edition. Maybe somebody interviewed Mr. Garvey—we at least ought'a hear his side'a the story."

"Jack!" Serval said, "Do you mind? Pick up a copy of every fresh paper you can get your hands on—*The Amsterdam News* and *The Crisis*, too, if they're out yet. Let's see what Dr. DuBois is sayin' about all this. I'll make a pot of coffee, and . . . Opal?"

Opal was already at the door, and turned around to see Serval smiling at her. "Yes?"

"Thanks, baby," he said. "Thanks for striking that match."

＊　＊　＊

Jack and Opal returned in less than an hour's time. Just as they had all hoped, many of the newspapers displayed headlines about Mr. Garvey's impending arrest. As they tore apart each newspaper on the kitchen table, Serval's spirits were lifted. A number of denials appeared amidst the accusatory articles. Even *The Crisis* defended Garvey, demanding temperance in the absence of concrete evidence.

"There's still hope," Serval murmured. "But I'm not a hundred percent convinced yet . . . not until I hear the truth from Mr. Garvey, himself."

By the time Serval walked Ernest outside, the sun was coming up. "Get some sleep, buddy," Serval said, yawning. "And thanks for everything. I'm goin' to bed and sleep for about forty-eight hours."

"Serval!" Ernest laughed. "Have you forgotten all those telephone calls in the wee hours of the morning?"

"Oh, damn," Serval groaned. "Emergency meeting tonight. I'll have half of Harlem stuffed into my living room tonight."

"At seven o'clock, my friend, so set your alarm clock."

"I will, Ernest. See you at seven. And thanks again."

Serval trudged up the front steps, and Opal held the door open for him. As they stepped inside, Serval chuckled at the sight of Jack, who was sprawled halfway between the sofa and the floor, sound asleep. "Well, he's feelin' no pain."

Opal sighed. "I don't know how he sleeps on that tiny little sofa. And speakin' of sleep, let's go stretch out on our big, comfortable bed and get *us* some sleep."

"Good idea."

As they passed the telephone in the hallway, it rang, rattling Serval's nerves. He snatched the receiver from the cradle and summoned what was left of his voice. "Hello?" As he paused to listen, he looked at Opal with wide eyes.

"Who is it?" she whispered.

Shaking his head at her, Serval murmured into the mouthpiece, "It's gotta be a mistake. Are you sure it's her?"

Another long pause.

"Yes . . . All right . . . No. We—uh—we'll manage . . . Is he—is he all right? Yes . . . We're on our way." Serval hung up the receiver and grabbed Opal's shoulders firmly. "Okay, stay calm . . ."

"What happened, Serval? Who was it?"

"The police. They got Leon again . . ."

Opal closed her eyes. "Oh, Lord! What's Daddy gone and done now? They caught him with some more'a that bootleg mess again, huh, Serval?"

"No. It's worse this time, Opal, so brace yourself. It looks like your Daddy got himself into some real bad trouble. Seems that Manché Redriver got herself . . . Opal, somebody *killed* her last night."

"What?! Serval, how . . ."

"That's not the worst part, baby. For some reason, they think Leon's the one who did it."

Before Opal could react, the telephone rang again. Serval pulled Opal close to his chest and reached for the receiver with his free hand. "Hello? . . . Already? . . . All right, let me think a minute . . . No, Mr. Mathis is out of town. Call Ernest, if you would. He needs to be notified. No, wait. He's probably not home yet. Give him about fifteen minutes, then call him. In the meantime, I'll send Jack over there to keep things calm. Me? I've got a family emergency to tend to. I'll explain everything tonight. . . . Yes. And thanks, brother."

"What now," Opal whispered.

"Trouble at UNIA headquarters. Seems we weren't the only ones reading early newspapers this morning. Guess I'd better wake Jack up."

*   *   *

By the time Serval and Opal arrived at the Police station to see Leon, their entire world seemed to be collapsing around them. The Garvey scandal was the talk of Harlem, prompting crowds of stunned stockholders to line up outside the UNIA offices. As minutes stretched into hours, Opal's shock over her father's arrest gave way to tears. Serval tried to console her, but his words rang flat in the dank, gray waiting area of the station house.

It was nearly noon before Jack arrived to report on the situation at the UNIA offices. He appeared surprisingly calm when he finally joined Serval and Opal in the waiting area.

"Well," Serval said, "how bad was it?"

"Ernest and a few other fellas is stayin' 'round the office, tryin' to keep all the folks from jus' tearin' it up."

Serval covered his face with his hands. "Is it really *that* bad, Jack?"

"Well . . . if you ask me, I don't think them folks is in no mood to tear down no buildin'. That's jus' what Ernest and them other fellas is scared of."

Serval gazed at Jack quizzically. "What do you mean?"

"When folks is really hell-blazin' mad, it shows in they eyes. I talked to lots'a them folks today, Serval. Some put all they savin's in Black Star stock and a few even lost they houses behind this mess. When a man wakes up one mornin' and finds out he can't keep a roof over his kids' heads . . . well, the first thing he feels is scared. That's what I saw in them eyes today, Serval. They' jus' scared—and tired."

Serval's hands went limp at his sides. "I know they're tired. Tired of *losin'* all the damn time. What happened, Jack? This time—we were supposed to *win*."

A portly Caucasian officer with gray hair approached them, then glanced down at the clipboard he held in his hand. "You here for Leon Jackson?"

The trio scrambled to their feet. "Yes," Opal croaked. "He's my Daddy. Can we see him now?"

The officer scanned the three faces and sighed. "He's gonna need a lawyer, you know. Can you afford one or do you want . . ."

"Oh, God," Serval moaned. "I know I'm not thinking straight. That's the first thing I should've thought of. Look, Opal, you go on in and see Leon. I'm gonna make a few calls." Turning to the officer, Serval asked, "Has he been questioned yet?"

The officer answered with a nonchalant shrug.

Serval lifted his chin and adjusted the knot in his tie. "Well, it doesn't matter. We'll get things straightened out once and for all when the family lawyer gets here. He'll be here shortly. Now, I'd appreciate it if you'd take my wife in to see her father."

The officer's eyebrows shot up, and he hesitated before gesturing at Opal to follow him. Serval exchanged a nod with Jack, who trailed closely behind Opal and the officer.

Serval stood alone in the corridor for a moment, attempting to swallow enough pride to call his father for help. Taking a deep breath, he strode quickly to the sergeant's desk before he had a chance to change his mind.

＊　＊　＊

Opal's knees went weak at the sight of her father, sitting on a narrow bench in the dingy holding cell. Seemingly unaware of her presence,

Leon stared through her with dead eyes and appeared shrunken and old.

"Daddy?" she whispered.

No answer.

Sinking down beside him, she grabbed his hands, and was alarmed at their clammy coldness. "Daddy!" she sobbed, throwing her arms around his neck.

Leon didn't respond, and Opal pulled away to study his face.

"Daddy, you need a drink'a water. Your lips are all dry and cracked. Jack? Can we get him some . . .?"

Leon emitted a soft croak as his lips formed the word "baby." His eyes seemed to focus on her face, and he tried again: "Baby?"

"Daddy? What—what happened?"

He shifted his eyes away from her again, as if lost.

"It's okay, Daddy. You don't have to talk about it right now, okay?"

Jack finally intervened. "Yes he do. Least he gotta sort it all out in his head, Opal. If I know Serval, he done got some lawyer hot-footin' it over here right now. Sorry, Leon. But you the onliest one can tell yo' side'a the story."

Leon nodded slowly, and cleared his throat. "I'm sorry 'bout all this, baby. I know you ain't never liked . . . her."

"No, Daddy. I—I never really had anything against her," Opal lied. "I—I'm so sorry, Daddy . . ."

"She' gone now, Opal," he whispered. "My woman's gone. Second time a woman done broke my heart . . . First, ya Mama, and now my Manché. Aww, Opal, you know, she wasn't so bad. She—she liked her some hooch, but she was a real sweet woman, deep down. Treated ol' Leon real good . . ." His voice faded and his eyes glazed over again, any trace of light in them now extinguished.

"Daddy?"

Opal began to shake with sobs, and covered her face with her hands. She felt Jack's arms lifting her to her feet, and she pressed her face against his chest. "What am I gonna do, Jack?" she sobbed. "Help me . . . Help Daddy! Please!"

She felt Jack's arms tighten around her, and the steadiness of his voice warmed her like a blanket. "I will," he murmured. "You know ol' Jack ain't never let'cha down. I be right here."

\*   \*   \*

The same bored-looking officer approached Leon's cell, followed closely by Serval, who was speaking in hushed tones to a well-dressed Negro gentleman wearing round eyeglasses over studious black eyes, and carrying a brown leather satchel.

As he unlocked the door, the officer gestured at Jack and Opal. "You two will have to wait outside now. Only two at a time."

Serval nodded at Opal and kissed her cheek as she passed him. "It's okay, baby. You and Jack wait outside while I get Leon and Mr. Washington acquainted. I think he'll feel more comfortable if I'm here. I'll be out in a minute."

Opal choked back a sob. "No—no, Serval. You stay here with Daddy long as you want to—long as he needs you. I—I'm sorry. I know how tired you are."

"I'm all right. Jack? Why don't you take Opal and get some breakfast."

Jack nodded and led Opal away.

Mr. Washington was already situating himself on the bench near Leon with his pencil poised over a notepad. He peered up at Serval expectantly.

Serval made a quick introduction. "Leon, this is Nathaniel Washington. He's a lawyer my father recommended very highly. Leon?"

Leon's gaze drifted in Serval's direction, then shifted to Nathaniel Washington. A confused expression crossed his face, and he shook his head helplessly.

Serval knelt in front of Leon and shook his shoulders lightly. "No, Leon," he said, his voice firm. "I'm not lettin' you give up like this. I don't know what happened, but I know it's put you in a lot'a pain. I'm here, man. I'll help you all I can, Leon, but you have *got* to push past the pain for a few minutes and tell Mr. Washington what you remember. Opal and I love you, and we won't let you do this to yourself, you hear me? You've got to try, Leon. Now, here. I brought you some coffee. Drink it and tell Mr. Washington everything you can remember."

"Yes, Mr. Jackson," Nathaniel Washington said gently. "Let's just go back to yesterday morning. That's far enough for now." He smiled at Leon and patted his shoulder. "And by the way, you can just call me Nat."

Serval smiled gratefully at Nathaniel Washington, impressed with his style. *Thank you, Daddy,* he thought, closing his eyes. *You came through when it counted and I guess that makes up for everything.*

After a few sips of coffee, Leon nodded his head and murmured, "Okay, uh, Nat. Guess I'm ready to start."

"Take your time."

"Yeah. Okay, well, Manché . . . I been sort'a—I mean, we been kind'a—livin' together ever since . . ."

"Common law?"

Leon shrugged and stared at the floor. "I guess. I loved her like a real God-sanctified wife though. I really did. We was gonna get married . . ."

"Please continue—about what happened."

"Uh-huh. . . . Well, she' been worried 'bout her job at the Brass Door—that' the club she work' at."

"A speakeasy. She was worried about raids?"

"Well, yeah. But seem' like the pressure was comin' from all sides—the law *and* the lawbreakers. Some'a them cops on the take was threatenin' to close Hightower down on account'a he wouldn't pay 'em like the other club owners been doin'. Then some'a them big-time bootleggers started leanin' on him too, 'cause he, uh, well . . . Aw, hell, I don't care no more. Hightower wasn't usin' they' services."

"What do you mean?"

"Mr. Hightower had his own—well, he got his own hooch brought in his *own* self, if ya know what I mean. He was independent."

Serval broke in. "Leon. You have to tell Nat everything. The least of your problems now is runnin' a little liquor over state lines."

Nat scribbled a note and murmured, "So you were involved in Hightower's operation yourself, Leon?"

"Well, see, at first, Manché—she thought it might help if we kept it between us three, and like I said, she was worried about losin' her job and all . . ."

"So she persuaded you to help Hightower and you agreed."

"Yeah. I guess so."

Nat glanced at Serval, then peered at Leon awhile before asking his next question. "Leon, just how well did Manché know Mr. Hightower?"

Leon's eyes flashed. "What the hell you mean by that? He was her boss—that's *all*. Manché was *my* woman. She—she loved me."

"I didn't mean anything by that. Please understand—I must ask you these questions if I'm to find out what happened. Now, I usually like to just let a person tell his story at his own pace and in his own way, but I think in this case, that's the wrong approach. So, Leon, I'd like to get right to the point and see if backtracking will work a little better.

I'll start with the two obvious questions: One, did you kill Manché Redriver, and two . . . if *you* didn't, then who do you think . . .?

Leon held up his hand and his eyes filled with tears. "Ya ain't gotta ask that second question—'cause the answer to the first one is—yes."

\* \* \*

"He's lyin', Serval!" Opal cried, upon hearing the shocking news of her father's confession. "Daddy would never kill anybody! I know him better than anybody on earth and he couldn't do it!"

"I'm not arguing with you, baby. I don't think he could've killed her—especially as much in love as he was. I think he's lying too, but what we' gotta do is find out *why*."

"I'll go back and get the truth out'a Daddy. When can I visit him, Serval?"

"Tomorrow, I think. But tonight we both need some sleep. . . . Aww, damn!"

"What's wrong?"

"Nothin'. We're only supposed to have practically the entire UNIA membership at the house for a special meeting tonight. Ernest's been out all day spreadin' the word. What time is it?"

"Ten to three."

"Maybe I can sneak a little nap," he sighed.

"Serval, you haven't had a thing to eat since yesterday."

"I need sleep more. Come on, baby. You too. Call the club and tell 'em you've got to take the night off and get yourself some rest. I'll eat during the meeting—and let somebody else do the talkin' for a change."

\* \* \*

At seven that evening Serval woke confused and disoriented. Slowly, the swimming noise in his head took the form of human voices and his eyes began to focus. As he rose to a sitting position, every muscle in his body ached, and his voice was a barely perceptible croak when he called Opal's name. He pulled on his robe and stumbled down the hall to the bathroom.

The cold spray of the shower was brutal, but effective. He scrubbed his body quickly and reached for a towel, but found the towel rack bare. He stepped out of the tub wet and shivering.

"Damn! Son of a . . . ." He was stopped by the warmth of a fresh towel being wrapped around his midsection from behind.

Opal peeked around his shoulder and smiled. "What was that you was sayin', Mr. Rivard?"

"Thanks, baby. Who's here? I thought I heard voices."

"Ernest got here about an hour ago with a few fellas, and let's see— Eileen and her husband and a few other folks I know, but I can't remember their names. I've been tryin' to scuffle around and find sump'm for everybody to eat."

"Aww, baby. You don't have to cook." He grinned as his stomach rumbled loudly. "But if we've got any of Jack's cornbread left in the cooler, I could make quick work of that."

"I already made you a sandwich, Serval. You get dressed and I'll sneak it in to you. You can eat in the bedroom before the meeting starts."

"Thank you, baby."

As she turned to leave the bathroom, Serval caught Opal's wrist and leaned down to kiss her. "It's nice when we're not fightin', huh?" he whispered.

"Mm-hmm. Listen, Serval, about that picture—the one on the Cotton Club program . . . It's really not like that . . ."

"I know, Opal. I know you'd never take your clothes off like that. It's just that . . . I was mad because of the impression it gave and . . . Wait. I don't want to talk about that now. Right now we're getting along, and we've got so many more important things to think about."

"Mm-hmm," Opal agreed. "And we're both on the same side for a change, huh?"

"Sure seems like it."

Opal clung tightly to him for a moment. "I'll try harder, Serval. I really will."

"Me too."

\* \* \*

The UNIA meeting brought immediate results, both positive and negative. Emotions ran high, inciting arguments, but no one was ready to give up the ideology of the UNIA. After gathering bits of information from the membership, a picture began to take shape, of Garvey the visionary being betrayed by a handful of members who had handled finances.

"But that's not the way the papers are gonna paint it, you know," Serval said, raising his hands for quiet.

Ernest had to shout to be heard. "What we need . . . I said, *what we need . . .*"

"Shh. Please! Ernest is trying to say something," Serval pleaded. "Let's have some quiet."

"Thank you," Ernest said. "What we need is immediate repair to the damage already done by the newspapers. I think we need to strike from several different angles—our own newspaper, naturally, and we ought to arrange a meeting with Dr. DuBois. If we can get another positive article in *The Crisis*, that will have a healing effect. And from what I've heard, that's not as far-fetched as you might think. Dr. DuBois is quite upset at Mr. Garvey's arrest, believe it or not. And the other thing we need to do is send a contingent to each city—you know, the personal touch. The people need to see a real, live person—one who has the power to reassure them—to explain the situation to them so they won't lose faith in the UNIA." He gazed at Serval and smiled. "And of course, there's only one man for the job."

The group broke into applause.

"No, wait . . ." Serval began, looking helplessly at Opal. "I—please. I'm in the middle of a family crisis right now, and I really can't . . ."

"I know, my brother," Ernest said. "But we are all your family and the UNIA is in crisis. We will all pitch in and help your father-in-law in any way possible, but surely you can get away for, say, a ten day speaking trip?" Ernest turned to Opal. "Mrs. Rivard? He would be back before anything happens with your father's case anyway. I—we wouldn't ask if it were not an emergency. What do you think?"

Opal stared at the floor for a moment, then narrowed her eyes at Serval. "My husband will do what he thinks is best. I—I'll support his decision."

Serval glared at Ernest. "I will need at least a *little* time to think this over, Ernest. And I'd like to talk it over with my wife in private, if you don't mind." He looked at Opal, hoping to see some sign of approval. But he saw only a resolute flatness in her eyes.

# Chapter 33

Serval packed his bag quickly and mechanically, a familiar task he could now almost do in his sleep. But tonight he felt an urge to move a little faster, to finish before Opal got home from the club. In the three days since he had agreed to be the UNIA's good will ambassador on a ten-day speaking tour, Opal had barely spoken to him. Just as he finished packing, he heard the sound of the front door opening, followed by Jack's heavy footsteps.

"Were they still open?" Serval called.

"Yeah, man. Jus' caught 'em 'fo they closed. Come on and eat while it's hot."

Serval pulled up a chair and began opening the containers of steaming red beans and rice from Pop Duval's Diner. "You get cornbread?"

Jack scowled. "Yeah, I got some'a Pop's sorry cawnbread—for you, that is. As for me, I only eats my *own* cawnbread."

Serval grinned at him. "You and your damn cornbread. If it makes you feel any better, Jack, your cornbread is manna from heaven, but since nobody had time to cook, I'm just gonna have to choke down some'a Pop's. Sorry."

Jack cut his eyes at Serval as he passed the cornbread. "Traitor."

"Hey. You gonna be here when I get back from this trip, Jack?"

"Depends. When ya comin' back?"

"Well, it's only supposed to be ten days, but Ernest mentioned sump'm 'bout extending the trip if we get a positive response. You know, hit a few more cities while we're hot."

Jack shook his head. "Opal ain't gon' like that."

"I know."

After a long silence, Serval gazed up at Jack and studied him for a moment before speaking. "Jack?"

"Mm-hmm?"

"*You* understand, don't you? I mean, do you think I'm wrong for leavin' now?"

Jack put down his fork and pushed back from the table for a moment before answering. "Yes. My answer's yes on both questions. Yes, I understand—and yes, I think you' wrong for leavin' Opal right now. I know, I know, that don't make no sense, but it's my answer anyhow. See, you ain't got no choice . . ."

"I *don't* have *any* choice, Jack. Remember your double-negatives."

Jack sighed. "Awright, awright. You *don't* have *any* choice. 'Least far as I can see, Serval. You got a woman that needs you, but you also got the callin'—jus' like a preacher, only yours is a callin' for the people. So I know you gotta go, to try to keep folks together so they don't all drift off in different directions on account'a bein' all confused . . ." Jack stopped abruptly and shrugged his shoulders. "I ain't much on talkin'—like you, Serval, and I prob'ly ain't makin' much sense but . . ."

"You're makin' a world of sense," Serval said, rubbing his eyes. "Go on."

"Well, the way I see it, Opal' jus' gotta try to be strong and let you go do yo' work, even if the timin's bad. I know you love her, but you got a love for the people, too. And right now, what with folks gettin' lynched and kids losin' they daddies and all that—look like you gotta tend to the worst injuries first. I guess it be kind'a like—well, like a woman birthin' a child and prayin' for no pain. Can't have the child wit' no pain."

Serval closed his eyes and smiled. "Seems to me I recall this big, lanky fella savin' my ass during the war and then callin' himself dumb. And hell, he turned out to be the smartest person I ever met. There's more wisdom in your double-negatives than in the Talented Tenth's most articulate speechmaker. And that's not because you seem to be agreeing with me on this trip. Anyway, now I'ma have to ask you for another favor, Jack. Kind'a like pullin' me out'a the barbed wire again."

"You ain't gotta even ask. You ought'a know that, Serval. I'll trade some off-days wit' some'a the other fellas and I'll stick close to Opal while all this mess is goin' on wit' her Daddy—'til you get back."

"Now—how'd you know that was what I was gonna ask, Jack?"

Jack rolled his eyes and laughed. "Aw, Serval—come on now!"

*   *   *

Serval woke in the bathtub with a jerk, splashing himself with cold water. He reached for the hot water spigot, but the sound of Opal's light steps across the living room floor stopped him. Easing back into the tub, he closed his eyes. The footsteps stopped at the bathroom door, and he heard a soft tap. "Serval?"

He didn't answer.

The door opened a crack, and Opal stuck her head in. "Serval?"

"Huh? Oh . . . Come in."

"Uh-huh," Opal said smiling vaguely. "Fell asleep again, huh?"

Serval grinned and settled back in the tub. "Guilty. Would you mind washing my back?"

After a slight hesitation, Opal knelt down and dipped a washcloth into the water. "Ooh, Serval! This water's cold! Here. Let me run a little hot for a minute."

"Mmmmm."

"Lean forward," she said, kneeling down to turn the spigot. "You look so tired, Serval." As soon as she finished rubbing the warm washcloth on his chest and shoulders, he leaned back again and closed his eyes. When she moved close to his face, he smelled the Jasmine in her hair and knew that she was about to kiss him. It was a soft, sweet kiss— reminiscent of her honeymoon kisses. "I love you, Serval."

"Do you?" he whispered, slowly opening his eyes. As she eased away, he reached up with a wet hand to pull her face close again, and kissed her with a forceful intensity. "Do you?" he repeated, more demanding this time.

Opal squirmed free and stood up, dabbing at her hair and dress. "How can you ask me that, Serval? You jus' *tryin'* to hurt me? Of course I love you."

Serval sat forward and sighed. "Hand me a towel, would you, please?"

"Here."

Serval stepped out of the tub and began to dry himself. "You know I'm leavin' in the morning."

"I know. I'ma go change now, Serval. Then I'm goin' to bed."

"I was tryin' to wait up for you, Opal. I thought we could make love for a change."

"Oh, Serval," Opal fumed, "You sound like you're talkin' to some'a those high-tone businessmen up on Striver's Row. Tryin' to make some kind'a business deal. Maybe sell me some stock."

"I wanted to make love to you before I left," he said. "Oh, that is, if it's not the wrong time of the month."

Opal opened her mouth to speak, but said nothing. Shaking her head, she angrily left the bathroom, with Serval close at her heels.

She sat on the edge of the bed, and Serval stood over her. "Well?"

"I'm not your Daddy, Serval," she snapped.

"What?! What the hell's *that* supposed to mean?"

"Shh! Jack's asleep!"

"Fuck Jack! What the hell did you mean by that?"

Opal stood up, walked to the dresser and began to comb her hair. "I *mean* what I said, Serval. I am *not* your Daddy. Seem's like you've always gotta have somebody to argue with, and now you replaced him with me."

"That's the craziest goddamn thing you have *ever* said!"

Opal slammed her comb onto the dresser. "Why, Serval?!" she shouted. "Why couldn't you just put your arms around me and kiss me nicely if you wanted to make love? Like you used to? Why are you so . . ." Angrily swiping at the tears in her eyes, she softened her tone. "Oh, just forget it. You're leaving tomorrow anyway, and I'm tired. I'm tired of everything." She stepped out of her dress and slipped off her stockings, then eased into bed.

Serval didn't move. He stared first at Opal, then at his suitcase, which seemed to be beckoning to him. *I ought'a leave tonight. She doesn't understand anything. She won't even try.* But when Opal turned off the lamp, his anger was replaced by a heavy sadness—an emptiness that needed immediate attention if he were ever to get any sleep in the next few hours. Without a sound, he settled into his side of the bed. Turning his back to her, he lay on his side. As his eyes adjusted to the darkness, he found his gaze once again fixed on the suitcase. There was something frightful about it suddenly, and each time he shifted his eyes, it drew them back. Unable to stand the contest any more, he sighed and turned his back to the suitcase, tentatively placing his hand on Opal's waist. Leaning close to her ear, he whispered, "I'm sorry, baby. I don't want to leave like this."

Opal turned and was instantly in his arms. "I hate it when we fight! I was trying to make up with you. Please—Serval, please don't ever ask me if I love you again! I love you so much, I think . . . I'm gonna *die* from it sometimes!"

Unable to respond to Opal's words, Serval was only aware of his heart thumping in his chest. Whether it was the result of emotional need or physical need, he didn't know, but Opal suddenly blocked out all rational thought, just as she always did, and he held her a little too tightly, just as he always did, until he could speak. He gave her a soft, controlled kiss and whispered, "Take off your slip, baby. I need you— real bad tonight."

Pulling away slightly, Opal stared at him. "And I need you *tomorrow*, Serval."

He pulled her closer, and buried his face in her neck. "I know, baby. I'm sorry."

All was still for a moment. He felt her ease away slightly, and watched her as she lifted her slip over her head. Her body was warm with promise as she settled back into his arms. A sensual shiver danced down his spine when he felt her breath in his ear. "I'm sorry, too."

*    *    *

Serval shifted his body and felt Opal still lying on his chest. Her breathing was regular and calm and he knew that she was in a deep sleep. Carefully moving her over, he covered her with the sheet and squinted at the alarm clock. Without turning on a light, he padded down the hallway toward the kitchen for a drink of water. *Damn! Gotta get up in two hours.*

A nearly full moon provided enough light in the kitchen for him to find a glass. He quietly filled it with water, drank it all, then filled it again. As he cut through the living room on his way back to the bedroom, he was startled to see Jack's silhouette against the front window curtains. He was sitting up.

"Jack? You still awake?" Serval whispered, reaching for the lamp chain.

"Don't turn on the light." Jack's voice had a strange, congested sound—as if he had a cold.

"Jack? You all right? You sound . . ." Serval felt his heartbeat quicken. *He's crying!* he thought. Again, he reached for the lamp chain. "What the hell's wrong? Wait . . . Look, let me talk to you, brother."

"I *said*—don't turn on the light, Serval. Leave me alone."

"All right. Whatever you want, man."

Serval quietly returned to his room and climbed into bed next to Opal. Feeling the warmth of her body, he pulled her close and wrapped his arms tightly around her, but couldn't forget the choked sound of Jack's voice. He felt Opal stir slightly. "I love you, baby," he whispered.

"Mmmm? Oh. Mm-hmm. I love you, too."

Usually, sleep came easily for Serval after sex, but not this time. Long after Opal drifted back off, he lay awake, vacillating between thoughts of Opal and their marital conflicts, Leon's disturbing confession to murder, and the fate of Marcus Garvey. But for some reason, the thought of Jack sitting alone in the dark crying troubled him more deeply than anything else on his list of problems. What did it mean? His eyes burned with the need for sleep but he couldn't force them to close as he tried to piece things together in his mind—disjointed, crazy thoughts—interspersed with UNIA slogans. The last thing he saw before drifting to a short respite of sleep was his suitcase, standing at the door like an usher waiting patiently to guide him to his destiny.

# Chapter 34

In the days that followed, Jack worked a light schedule on the local lines, which kept him in Harlem more than usual. Creola was pleased when he accepted a key to her apartment and began spending all his nights with her, until she noticed the development of a disturbing pattern. After spending all of his free daylight hours with Opal Rivard, he never seemed to find the time for dinner with Creola, and was usually asleep when she returned from the Cotton Club. Creola held her anger in check, wondering when she would reach her breaking point.

It happened on a Saturday morning when she was startled awake by the jangling of her alarm clock. She slapped at it twice, knocking it off the nightstand, then sat up to shake Jack awake. "Jack! Why the hell's this alarm set for seven on a goddamn Saturday?"

Jack rubbed his head and stretched, then sat up on the edge of the bed. "Opal needs me today, Creola. I gotta take her to see that lawyer fella and then her Daddy after that."

Creola sat up and punched her pillow before leaning against it. "But I took today off from rehearsal," she fumed. "You said today was mine. You were gonna take me shopping, remember?"

"Can't be helped. It's important, and Opal needs me."

"You know sump'm, Jack? That Opal Rivard' been a thorn in my side long enough. You run out'a here talkin' 'bout, 'Opal's kind'a lonesome, so I thought I'd run her over to see Miz Aida.' Or if it ain't that, she got you runnin' around pickin' up papers from that lawyer. Shit! Let her husband send one'a them Garvey men over to cart that heifah around. I am a Cotton Club star, Jack, and I don't need these triflin' little chorus girls laughin' and whisperin' behind my back, talkin' 'bout 'Guess Creola ain't woman enough for Jack Hawkins. He got to have him *two* women.'"

"She needs me, Creola," he said again, reaching for his robe. "I promised Serval."

Creola's tone softened. "Wait a minute. Come back to bed jus' a minute, baby."

Jack sighed and stood up. "I ain't got time, Creola."

"Just for a minute, Jack *baby*. Please?"

Jack peered at her over his shoulder, then sighed as he eased back into bed. "I gotta leave by eight."

Creola wrapped a leg around his waist and rubbed the back of his thigh with her foot. "Well, now," she purred, "that's a whole hour. And you *know* it don't take me no whole hour to make you feel good."

She began a trail of wet kisses down his chest and stomach, and Jack responded instantly. She noticed a change in the way he handled her body. For such a large man, he was usually graceful in bed—passionate but gentle. But this time, his movements were urgent, his rhythm hasty, and within minutes, Creola was nearing an explosive climax. She felt his body convulse as his head jerked back, and he moaned a name as he sank back into her arms: "Opal."

The physical bliss Creola had been experiencing abruptly died. Unable to think coherently, she waited to hear an excuse or an apology— something. As his breathing returned to normal, he eased his body over and kissed her gently. "You awright?" he whispered.

Creola stared at him, amazed. *Damn! He don't even know he said her name!* After a momentary struggle with her anger, she said, "Jus' fine, baby. Was it good?"

"Mmm-hmm."

She cut her eyes at him, but managed to keep her voice velvety. "Well, guess you better get up, Jack. Opal's waitin'."

Jack leaned over and kissed her without taking his eyes off the clock. He missed her mouth completely, landing the kiss on the side of her nose. "Yeah. I'ma get me a bath."

As he walked out of the room, Creola stared at the ceiling. *Okay, Miss Opal. Now it's war, honey.*

# Chapter 35

Opal tightened her grip on Jack's arm as they climbed the foyer steps to Nathaniel Washington's law office on Lenox Avenue. After only one tap on the frosted glass door, Nathaniel opened it and motioned them inside. "Good morning, Mrs. Rivard, Mr. Hawkins," he said. "My secretary doesn't come in on weekends, so it's a good thing I know how to make coffee. Make yourself comfortable in my private office and I'll be right with you."

By the time Opal and Jack were settled into the armchairs that faced Nathaniel's large mahogany desk, he was back with a steaming mug of coffee in each hand. "Here you are, Mr. Hawkins. Light on the cream and heavy on the sugar, as I recall. And Mrs. Rivard, you like yours black, is that right?"

"Yes, but not now, thanks." Opal leaned forward and placed one hand on the desk. "Mr. Washington, did you talk to him?"

Sliding into his chair, Nathaniel opened a thick, tan file folder, and sighed as he peered at Opal over his eyeglasses. "Yes, I did, Mrs. Rivard. He wants his confession to stand. Your father specifically told me to plead guilty."

Opal's mouth dropped open, but she said nothing.

"Mrs. Rivard? Did you hear me?"

As she nodded her head, a flood of tears spilled down her face. Jack reached over and gently pressed his handkerchief into her hand.

"I'm okay, Jack," she said, lifting her head. "Look, Mr. Washington. Daddy's lying. At first, I thought it was just 'cause he was sad about losin' his lady friend, but now he's just not makin' any kind'a sense. I don't know why he'd want to do such a fool thing, but I *know* he's lying. And that's the God's truth."

Nathaniel Washington made a quick notation on his ever-present notepad, and nodded his head. "I'm inclined to agree with you, Mrs. Rivard. However, my hands are tied. I've talked and cajoled and begged, but if he still insists on pleading guilty, there's nothing more I can do.

But you, on the other hand . . . perhaps you can persuade him to change his plea."

Opal rose from her chair quickly and headed for the door. "Thank you for your time, Mr. Washington. Don't you worry. I'ma go see Daddy right now, and the next time you talk to him, he *will* change his plea."

*   *   *

Jack sat quietly next to Opal as they waited to see Leon that afternoon, and wondered what methods of persuasion were going through her mind. Her jaw was set in a tight square, and her steely stare never moved from a spot on the far wall. She was a determined, immovable rock.

Jack shook his head and let out a low whistle. *Leon' fixin' to catch hell.*

A guard appeared suddenly and glanced from Opal to Jack. "You're here to see Leon Jackson, right?"

"Yes," Jack said, rising.

"Sorry. Only one visit per day."

Jack nodded in Opal's direction. "Well, that's awright. I'll wait out here. This' Mr. Jackson's daughter and she' the one . . ."

"You don't understand. He already had visitors today."

"My Daddy? Who visited my Daddy?" Opal demanded.

Before the guard could answer, Jack spotted two familiar figures passing, several feet away. He recognized one as Max Hightower, but it was the other man, one of a small circle of Hightower's trusted associates, that ran a cold chill down Jack's spine. This particular man, whose real name remained a mystery, had attained a reputation for being one of Hightower's deadliest cronies. The thick shock of silver hair, out of place on a man with such a youthful face, earned him the moniker "Silver Boy" among Harlemites, and rumor had it that his role was that of a bloody executioner.

Vaguely aware of Opal arguing with the guard, Jack studied Hightower and Silver Boy carefully but discreetly. In one silent exchange between the two men, he found the missing piece of Leon Jackson's puzzle. As Hightower shifted his eyes in Opal's direction, he gave an almost imperceptible nod of his head, which Silver Boy acknowledged in split-second rhythm. Jack stopped breathing for a moment, and quickly looked at the floor.

After what seemed like an eternity, Jack ventured another look and caught a glimpse of Hightower's jacket through the crack of the door just before it closed. Reaching for Opal, who was still engaged in a heated debate with the guard, Jack leaned close to her ear and hissed, "Enough. I'll bring you to see him tomorrow, Opal. I'm takin' you home now."

"But Jack . . ."

"I said *now*, Opal."

*　*　*

Early the next morning, Jack broke his promise to Opal, arriving at the holding facility without her. A perplexed look crossed Leon's face as he took his seat. "Where's my baby?"

"Home. Listen, Leon. It's sump'm I gotta ask you—and I got a feelin' you ain't gonna be able to answer me. So I'm jus' gonna talk, and you shake yo' head if I go off on the wrong track."

With a nervous shift of his eyes, Leon mumbled, "I don't know what the hell you talkin' 'bout, big fella."

"You ain't gotta say nothin', Leon. You just answer me yes or no if you can. Is Opal in any danger right now?"

Leon's eyes suddenly filled with dread, but he didn't move.

Jack nodded. "Okay, then . . . Is she awright—long as you plead guilty? You can trust me, Leon. This' between me and you."

Leon's eyes held a fear Jack had never seen before, but finally he nodded.

Staring down at his hands, Jack shook his head. "I knew it." After a long, silent exchange, Jack finally rose. "Don'tchu worry, Leon."

"Jack?"

"Yes?"

"Think you could bring my baby to see me now and again? I mean, Serval's out'a town so much, and I don't want her comin' here . . . or whatever place I get sent to . . . I don't want her comin' alone."

"I will."

"And Jack—one more thing. I know how close you are wit' Serval, but that boy can be a hothead sometimes, and if he was to find out . . ."

"Naw, sir. You ain't got to worry. You' a man and you done made yo' decision. It ain't my secret to tell."

"Thank you, Jack. Bring her to see me soon, hear? She' all I got now."

\* \* \*

Serval's ten-day speaking tour for the UNIA turned into weeks, and visits home became an infrequent occurrence. By the week of her father's hearing, Opal was barely speaking to Serval. She no longer accompanied Jack to pick him up at the train station or the pier, and made a point of being asleep by the time Jack dropped him off. But on the morning Serval discovered that Opal had taken time off from The Cotton Club to prepare with Nathaniel Washington for Leon's hearing, weeks of chilly silence culminated in a heated screaming match.

"You couldn't take time off to have a baby, but you can take all this time off to prepare for Leon's hearing. How goddamned interesting!"

"Ooh! Don't you dare bring my Daddy into this! And you know this is different anyway, Serval. A baby means I gotta quit dancin' for good. Who's supposed to watch the baby while I go to work? His Daddy? No! He's off sailin' to Jamaica or someplace. Probably wouldn't even know what Daddy looks like anyway, 'cause the day after he's born, *Daddy's* gone again!"

"What do you want from me, Opal? Huh? There's nothing for me to do here. I already swallowed my pride to get Leon the best lawyer my Daddy's money could buy—and I'll probably be payin' him back for the rest'a my goddamn life! What the hell else you want me to do? Sit around here 'til the hearing and hold your hand while the UNIA goes to hell?"

"Hold my hand? *Hold my hand?!* You don't even touch me any more, Serval! Of course, I don't expect you to hold my hand. I wouldn't dream of asking."

Serval suddenly sobered and redirected the conversation. "Opal," he said softly.

"What?"

"You never really planned to go to Africa with me did you?"

"*What?*"

"That's why you kept putting off starting a family." He paused and confronted her eyes. "Isn't it?"

Opal glared at him. "That's what you think? Is *that* what you think of me, Serval Rivard?"

"Don't answer a question with a question, Opal. That's your reason for not having a baby, isn't it?"

Opal stood up and grabbed her handbag. "I'm leaving."

"Where the hell are you goin'?"

"To see my Daddy."

"Wait. I'll go with you."

"No. It's okay. Jack's takin' me. He'll be here any minute."

*   *   *

Despite the widening chasm between them, Serval sat at Opal's side for the duration of Leon's trial. On Leon's behalf, Nathaniel Washington pleaded guilty to involuntary manslaughter, claiming that Manché Redriver's death was accidental. The prosecution lawyer countered with crowd-pleasing sarcasm, charging that Manché Redriver being "accidentally shot through the head" was as far-fetched a notion as the man in the moon. Nathaniel Washington deftly steered the focus to the lack of solid evidence to support premeditation, and pushed for leniency.

But when the proceedings ended, Leon remained the sole suspect, and managed to confess himself into a life sentence at the Ossining facility, better known as Sing Sing.

As the sentence was pronounced, Opal fell into Serval's arms, sobbing. "Why? Oh, God, Serval, why'd he lie?"

Jack stood at her other side, gazing at Leon as he was led away. Their eyes met, and Leon lifted his head. Jack raised his right hand and tapped his temple in a private salute.

# Chapter 36

Leon's transfer to Sing Sing blurred into a series of terrifying images and sounds. He was unprepared for the psychological jolt when the leg-irons were clamped around his ankles for transport. His natural free stride was gone, replaced by the lowly shuffle inflicted on him by a standardized measure of chain. With each step it rattled, reminding him that his life was no longer his own, but the property of the federal prison system.

Leon counted the men before him. He was twelfth in line. They filed outside into a foggy drizzle, and boarded a gray bus marked "New York State Department of Criminal Justice—Ossining." Leon sank into his seat, damp from the rain, and stared out the window. It was raining hard now. After the initial grinding of gears, the bus lurched forward, and Leon surrendered—somewhere inside the comforting rhythm of windshield wipers taking futile slaps at a relentless rain.

* * *

When the bus rumbled through the gates of Sing Sing, Leon stared up at the high gray walls, and suddenly realized that he was trembling. Four armed guards in dark uniforms approached the bus as it rolled to a stop, then began shouting at the new inmates, pushing and prodding them with short black sticks. By the time Leon stumbled down the steps, the trembling had taken such a powerful hold that he could hardly walk. He felt the blunt pain of the guard's stick in his ribs, and doubled over.

"Move, old man!"

Leon could only nod. The guard pushed him and he stumbled forward, staring down at raindrops making high splashes in a puddle. He stopped again.

"Goddammit, old man! Get your ass in gear!"

In response to repeated shoves and bumps, Leon forced his legs to move until he found himself standing on a splintered wooden floor inside the prison. He raised his head slightly to take in his surroundings—

three wooden benches lining one drab wall of a long corridor. At the end of the corridor were bars.

"Sit down, old man."

Leon sat, nearly missing the bench, and felt someone jerking him up by his left arm. He felt the leg-irons slip off his ankles, and heard a swirl of voices over his head. A sharp, cracking pain in his temple startled him, and one of the voices broke through the haze: "I said stand your ass up, old man! Or do you want the stick against your skull again?"

Leon scrambled to his feet.

"Undress."

*Please . . . I ain't killed nobody,* Leon pleaded, but the words travelled no farther than his brain. *I was jus' tryin' to do what's right. Please . . . I don't belong in here . . .*

He felt himself being assaulted by a pair of rough hands, and realized that every stitch of his clothing had been removed.

"Open your mouth! Come on, I ain't got all day! . . . Bend over. . . . No, goddammit! Put your hands up on the wall! Somebody help me with this sorry old bastard!"

He felt fingers inside his mouth, then hands probing and groping every part of his body. Ignoring the shaking in his knees, Leon willed himself to remain standing. *Stop it, fool! Stop shakin' . . . Don't let 'em see how bad scared you are . . . Be a man.* He finally raised his head and saw on the guard's face a sadistic open-mouthed grin that reminded him of a snake about to strike. Leon stared at him with the words that were in his mind: *I'm a man too—jus' like you.*

The guard stared back at him with an amused expression, then let out a loud laugh. "Look at the old man! He's bawlin' like a goddamn baby!"

Leon was still crying when they threw him into his cell.

*   *   *

Jack kept his distance from Opal and Serval once the hearing was over. He stayed with Creola for two days, then abruptly left one night while she was at work. After notifying the Pullman Company of his availability for any and all overtime, he escaped on the rails. He busied himself through the first week, but found himself sneaking out to the observation car after the passengers were tucked away in compartments or berths. Time to face his demons.

In the dark of night, he watched the world whiz by as he did battle with himself. *How the hell can I be lovin' Serval's wife? 'Cause I ain't nothin' but a lowdown dog. I gotta forget it. Come on, Jack, it can't never be, so jus' let it die. . . . But it won't die. I done waited, but it jus' won't die. . . . Then ain't nothin' else to do but find some way—to kill it.*

The next stop was Baltimore.

*       *       *

Jack straightened his tie, then tapped on the compartment door marked 3-B. It was opened by a portly, red-faced man dressed in trousers and an undershirt. "Delay?" the man asked.

"Naw, suh, Mista Barlow," Jack said. "We' right on schedule. I was jus' stoppin' by to see 'bout some'a them hand-carries you always be havin'."

"Well," Mr. Barlow said, smiling. "That's certainly nice of you. I'll be racing to get back to the office, so yes. Come on in, uh . . ."

"Jack, Mista Barlow. Jack Hawkins."

"That's right. I won't forget again. And thanks, Jack. Let me throw a few things together and you can take this one . . ."

"Uh, Mista Barlow?"

"Yes?"

"You been livin' in Baltimo' a long time, huh?"

"All my life. Why?"

"Well, uh, suh . . . Would you maybe know 'bout some kind'a place a fella like me could . . . See, I need to buy me a—a engagement ring. Ain't got a whole lot to spend, but . . ."

Mr. Barlow smiled and nudged Jack's shoulder. "Got yourself a little girlfriend, eh, Jack?"

"Yes, suh. But like I said, I ain't got a whole lot to spend, and . . ."

"I know just the place. Wait, I'll write down the address."

"Mista Barlow?"

"Mm-hmm?"

"This place, uh . . . you sho' they gon' let me in?"

"Tell you what, Jack. The owner's name is Jed Steinberg and he happens to be a good friend of mine. Now, I'm writing the address on the back of my business card, along with a little note about your budget concerns. You give this to Jed and tell him I said you were okay. And if any of his employees gives you any trouble, you just tell 'em to get Mr. Steinberg. He'll take care of you."

Jack took the card and tipped his hat. "Thank you, Mista Barlow. That's mighty nice'a you."

* * *

Upon his return to Harlem early on a Friday evening, Jack stopped to buy Creola flowers, and then headed for her apartment. Knowing that she would be at the Cotton Club, he fished his key out of his pocket and let himself in. As usual, Creola had left the place in a shambles — stockings on the floor, dresser drawers half-opened with the contents spilling out, and, in the middle of the unmade bed was a plate containing remnants of dried-out scrambled eggs. Turning slowly in a circle to survey the room, Jack shook his head. "Lawd."

With a sigh, he rolled up his sleeves and headed into the kitchen to wash the dishes while rehearsing his proposal. "I'ma jus' say it — Creola, will you marry me — jus' like that. And then she' say yeah or oh, Lawd, Jack, I thought you was never gonna ax me, or sump'm like that. And then cry a little. And then I say . . ." He looked up from the dishwater and his hand stopped scrubbing. "Sho' would be a laugh on me if she was to say no." He chuckled and rinsed the plate in his hand. "Naw. She been hintin' at it too much. So then I say, I know you gon' be a better housekeeper, Creola. Aww, wait a minute now. Nuh-uh. She ain't gon' like that. But it ain't her fault," he muttered. "She ain't never had nobody to take care of befo'." As he dried his hands, another potential problem arose. "Wonder if she gon' be ready to quit that cooch dancin'? 'Cause ain't no sense'a gettin' married if ya ain't ready to start a family." He thought about his conversation with Serval on the subject of children. *But Opal don't want babies neither.* He grabbed the broom and began sweeping the kitchen floor. *Forget her.*

By the time he dusted the bedside table, he was surprised to read the time on the clock: 1:15. "Man! I just got time to clean my own self up!"

* * *

By 4:00 a.m., the only thing moving on Lenox Avenue was a large black Mercedes touring car. It crawled along like a lost foreigner until making the turn onto 132nd Street, and then slowed to a stop.

"Here it is, Daddy. This is where I live," Creola said, batting her eyelashes at her escort.

"Shtop the car, Jarvish," he bellowed to his Negro chauffeur. "This little danshin' lady and me're goin' upstairs to bed for awhile! You shtay right here and wait."

Creola laughed. "Aw, now, wait a minute, Daddy! I ain't said nothin' about takin' you up to my bed, now." Shooting a glance at Jarvis's disapproving eyes peering at her from the rear view mirror, Creola felt a quick pang of embarrassment, then slapped away one of "Daddy's" hands as it feebly squeezed her left breast. "Now, none'a that, hear me?" she scolded playfully, pinching his cheek. Creola knew all too well that middle-aged, balding Caucasian patrons of the Cotton Club were the most generous with baubles of the twenty-four carat variety, and, if a girl played her cards right, she might not even have to sleep with him. So she was not about to alienate Daddy just yet—Jarvis or no Jarvis.

As Daddy began to breath heavily and kiss her neck, Creola felt a wet trail of spittle rolling slowly down to her shoulder, and decided that now would be a good time to play hard to get. Pulling away from him, she fixed an artificial smile on her face and cooed, "Creola's gotta get up early in the mornin', Daddy. Rehearsal, ya know."

"Oh, baby. Lemme come with you. I'll let'cha go to sleep—in a couple of hours!" he roared.

*Good Lord! Why are these drunk-ass men so damn loud?* "Aww, Daddy," she pouted, "you want Creola to be good when she does her fan dance, now don'tcha? You want me to practice my wigglin' that you like so much, now don'tcha?"

Wobbling his head in a drunken nod, Daddy was as defenseless as a newborn kitten.

"Well, then, Daddy, Creola's gotta get her sleep or she won't get up in the mornin', and that mean ol' Chappie jus' gonna go fire Creola. You wouldn't want that, now would'ya? Huh?"

"Nooo," he crooned, gazing into her eyes.

Creola smiled. Instinct told her that he was ripe for the picking, and she moved in for the kill. With a breathless sigh, she gazed seductively at him and leaned close to his face. Ignoring the smell of stale liquor and cigars, she eased her tongue over the corner of his mouth in a slow, licking motion. He was hers.

"G'night, Daddy," she said as Jarvis opened the limousine door for her.

She managed to avoid Jarvis's eyes, concentrating only on reeling in Daddy. She climbed the steps carefully, shifting her hips in a slow, practiced sway.

"Creola?" Daddy called.

Turning halfway around to face him, she lifted her skirt a few inches and pretended to check the seams in her stockings. "Yes, Daddy?"

"Tomorrow I'm bringin' you a surprise, you hear me? I'm going to Tiffany's tomorrow and pick it out myself."

"Oh, Daddy," she gushed, taking another step back, "how sweet!"

"Creola?"

"Mm-hmm?"

Daddy looked like a six-year old with a bad case of puppy-love when he hung his head out the window and mumbled, "I love you."

Creola smiled and blew him a kiss. *'Course ya do, sucka,* she thought contemptuously. *You never had a chance.*

She stepped inside the foyer, yanked off her shoes, and began trudging up the three flights of stairs to her apartment. *This ain't even fun any more,* she thought. *But well . . . I sure can't count on Jack—the way he jus' up and disappears all the damn time. Come on, girl, don't break your own rule. Creola does the gettin', not the givin'.* But a sudden heaviness in her chest warned of imminent tears. *Uh-uh, no. I ain't lettin' Jack break my heart. Not when Daddy's talkin' 'bout pickin' me out sump'm from Tiffany's.* She smiled for a moment, wondering what expensive trinket she might receive, but by the time she reached her apartment door, the tingle had already worn off.

She rummaged for her key, then opened the door and dropped her bag on the floor. Without turning on a light, she headed straight for the bathroom to wash the last two hours with Daddy off her body. As she passed the bed, a hand grabbed her leg and she opened her mouth to scream, but a familiar voice stopped her.

"I been waitin' for you, girl."

"Jack?"

"Come to bed. I wanna talk to you 'bout sump'm, and uh, I got sump'm for you, too."

She stopped herself from throwing her arms around his neck. "I'm so glad you're back. Uh, wait a minute, okay, baby? I been dancin' and sweatin' all night. Let Creola take a quick bath before I climb in bed wit'chu, you big, beautiful man."

"Okay. But hurry up, hear? I can't wait much longer."

"Five minutes, baby. Be right back." Once inside the bathroom, she pressed the door shut and breathed a sigh of relief. *Damn! That was close!*

✻   ✻   ✻

Creola and Jack made up for lost time and remained in bed for most of the next day. Finally, at 6:15 that evening, she got up to get ready for work. After her bath, Jack watched her reflection in the mirror as she put the finishing touches on her makeup.

"What'cha gonna do with yourself tonight, Jack?" she asked.

"Aw, I don't know. Is Serval in town this week?"

"No. He left three days ago and Opal's face been draggin' the floor ever since."

"Well, I'll find sump'm to do."

"Jack?"

"Hmm?"

"Last night you said you wanted to talk about sump'm. And I seem to recall you sayin' you had sump'm for me, too. You holdin' out on me, baby? You got a little present for Creola?"

Jack gazed at Creola's expectant face and gulped. *Now. Right now. Jus' ax her, man.* He smiled and opened his mouth, but no sound came out.

"Jack? What's wrong, baby? You got the oddest look on your face."

"Shoot, woman. I'm jus' hurt, that's all. 'Cause I done *gave* you yo' present—all last night, and today too. Ain't you liked it?"

"Mmm-mmm-mmm," Creola laughed. "I loved it. So I hope you don't find anything *too* interestin' to do tonight, 'cause I'm comin' straight home tonight for some more, hear?"

He smiled. "Guess I'll be here, then."

"Well, if I don't leave right now, I'ma be late, baby."

"Awright then." When she leaned close to kiss him, Jack saw something unfamiliar in her eyes—something that looked vaguely sad.

"You know what, Jack?" she whispered, "I thought you wasn't comin' back this time. I missed you sump'm awful. I—I guess I really love you."

With a gentle touch to her face, Jack said, "Well then—I love you, too."

Creola let out a soft gasp. "You—you never said that before!"

*Not a proposal, but 'least it was a start,* he thought. *Maybe later tonight.* "Now, don't go gettin' all weepy on me, girl," he said firmly, smacking her backside. "You gon' be late to work!"

\*   \*   \*

Creola arrived at the Cotton Club in an uncharacteristically buoyant mood. "Evenin', ladies!" she chirped as she passed the chorines' dressing room.

"What the hell's wrong wit' Miss Uppity? Damned if that wasn't a smile on her face!"

"Naw, girl, that wasn't no smile. 'Cause if the bitch smiled, her C.J. Walker-bleach-wearin' face would'a cracked off!"

Opal sighed and rolled her eyes. "Y'all leave Creola alone, hear? Shoot, the girl's happy about sump'm, that's all. Ooh! I know, Jack must be in town!"

Dashing down to Creola's dressing table, Opal leaned against it, crossed her arms, and grinned. "He's back, huh? Ooh, look at these roses! From Jack?"

Creola sat reading a notecard, and barely looked up. "Huh? Oh, no. He brought me daisies last night. These are from . . . Uh, yeah. Jack got back last night, and girl, the man wore me out!" Her smile faded as she looked back down at the card.

Opal threw her arms around Creola's neck. "I'm glad, girl. 'Least one of us has got a man actin' right. But who sent you these gorgeous roses?"

But Creola didn't hear the question. "Opal," she said in a serious tone. "You gotta do sump'm for me."

"Okay. What?"

Placing the card back in the envelope, Creola reached around the vase of roses and retrieved a long, black velvet box. Around the box was a silver ribbon bearing the "Tiffany & Co." logo. "Take this card and this gift and give 'em back to that man that always sits up front."

"Ooh, girl, you mean that ol' bald-headed fool that's always screamin' for you when you're dancin'?"

"That's the fool."

Opal smiled. "Creola Dorshay givin' back a present—a present from Tiffany's?! Shoot, girl, Jack must'a put a spell on you! You better marry that man."

# Chapter 37

Serval had just opened his eyes when a loud knocking startled him completely awake. He sat up straight in his chair and looked around the room. Before he was able to distinguish his surroundings, another knock sounded. "One minute, please," he croaked. "Uh, who is it?"

"It's Ernest."

Serval stared at the pencil still clenched in his right hand, and then dropped it. He stood up stiffly and stretched as he tried to recall what city he was in. *Chattanooga. That's right—Delbert Martin's home.* Crossing the room, he opened the door and let Ernest in. "Sorry, Brother. I guess I fell asleep writing that outline."

"Before you finished?" Ernest asked with a smile.

"You're a hard taskmaster, Ernest. And to tell you the truth, I don't have any idea how far I got. I'm sure it'll be just as much of a surprise to me as to you."

"Well, sorry to wake you, Serval, but I have two pieces of good news that just couldn't wait."

Sinking back down in the desk chair, Serval rubbed his eyes and held out his palms expectantly. "Number one is . . .?"

"Number one is that luscious down-home breakfast that even your sleep-deprived nose cannot help but detect."

Serval's stomach rumbled with hunger as he picked up the unmistakable smell of bacon frying. "Good news to my stomach. Number two?"

"We have the honor of entertaining very special guests tonight at our meeting. The Liberian representatives have arrived."

Serval shot out of his chair. "When? Aww, Ernest, we weren't expecting them for another week. Damn! Do we have accommodations ready? How many of 'em came?"

"Calm down, my Brother," Ernest laughed. "They arrived late last night and were very patient with us. We had to wake a few people up, but, as usual, the UNIA membership came through. Mr. Boley is staying in this very house. In fact, he'll be joining us for breakfast."

"Aww, Ernest. I wanted to make a good impression on 'em and I slept right through their arrival. Oh, all right . . . Let me wash up and I'll come out to welcome Mr. Boley properly."

"Not so fast, my Brother. Don't you want to be prepared for what awaits you?"

"Huh? Please, Ernest, I haven't had my coffee yet. Talk straight."

"I'm afraid I'm guilty of the crime of eavesdropping. Serval, I overheard Mr. Boley talking to Delbert while I helped Anna prepare a place for him to sleep."

"And?"

Ernest suddenly threw up his hands and smiled as he danced a clumsy jig.

Serval stepped back and laughed. "You know, you're scaring me, Ernest. You definitely should'a brought coffee. I've never seen you like this."

Ernest stopped, and his smile disappeared. "Like what?"

Serval raised his hands in the air and mimicked Ernest's footwork. "You're uh, oh, let's see . . . I know! You're giddy, Ernest, that's what you are."

Ernest laughed and grabbed Serval's shoulders. "I am. I admit to being a giddy man. And I'll tell you why. Serval, I think — no, I'm sure — that Mr. Boley is going to ask you to head up the UNIA contingent in Liberia. He wants you to organize a group to go, and of course, I will be expecting a lofty assignment. Think of it, Serval! Africa! It may not be on the grand scale that Mr. Garvey dreamed of, but perhaps you and I can still make it!"

Serval's response to the unexpected news was a forced smile. The dream for which he had worked the past five years beckoned to him from the very next room. And now, to his surprise, he felt nothing but uncertainty.

# 1925

*Malcolm X is born.*

# Chapter 38

Opal slung her shoe-bag over her shoulder, and pulled the collar of her coat tightly around her neck before stepping out the back door of the Cotton Club. Bowing her head against the icy 3:00 a.m. wind, she almost didn't see the Pierce-Arrow parked across the street. Serval stood leaning against the driver's side door, coatless.

"Serval!" she called. "When—when did you get back?"

"A few hours ago."

She approached him slowly. "Serval. Are you crazy, runnin' around on a night like this without a coat?"

"We need to talk."

She looked down for a moment, then nodded. "I know."

Opening the passenger door for her, he said, "Is Jack at the apartment?"

"You mean you haven't gone home yet, Serval?"

"Is he *there*?"

"No."

"Good. That's where we'll go then."

*   *   *

After a silent ride home, Opal unlocked the front door. "Would you mind lightin' a fire, Serval? It's awful cold in here."

Without answering, he dug through the bin for a likely piece of wood and began building a fire. By the time Opal returned from changing, the room was beginning to warm up.

"Sit down, Opal."

Opal sat down and brushed away a tear. "You're leaving me."

Serval sat down next to her and reached for her hand, but stopped short of touching it. "I know you think it's because of the club, but it's not. I was wrong for making you feel . . . I was just wrong."

"Then why, Serval? *Why*? Do you . . . Don't you love me anymore?"

He looked into her eyes, and was surprised at the ragged sound of his own voice. "I love you. From the minute you made me drink cream and lemon in my tea at the Saunders house that day—even through all the fighting. I'll always love you, Opal."

A sob escaped her throat. "Then *why?*"

Grabbing her suddenly, he pulled her face against his neck and whispered, "God! I can't stand to hold you—and I can't stand *not* to hold you."

After a moment, he eased away from her and stared at the fire. "Opal. How much time do you think we've spent together this year?"

"I don't know, Serval. I guess 'bout six or eight months."

"No. I looked back at my logbook and I was gone over eight months this year, if you count all the little three and four-day trips."

"But Serval . . ."

"And when I *am* home, all we do is fight."

"But that's 'cause of me, Serval. I'll stop dancin' at that damn Cotton Club. I was just bein' evil 'cause I thought you were tryin' to rule me—and Serval, you know how stubborn I can be . . ."

Serval's lips twitched into a half-smile. "That *damn* Cotton Club?"

"Don't leave me."

Leaning his head back, Serval closed his eyes and Jack's words filled his head: *Tellin' Opal to stop dancin' would be like tellin' a bird not to fly.* He took a deep breath. "God, Opal, don't you see? We've already left each other."

"No! I'd never leave you, Serval! You—you're just tryin' to make excuses to leave me!" she shouted angrily. "Did you meet some other woman? One'a those UNIA nurses from Liberty Hall?"

Serval opened his eyes but didn't move. "Opal, have I ever lied to you?"

No answer.

"I've got my shortcomings, but Opal, you *know* lying isn't one of 'em."

"I know."

"Look at me. Since the day I met you, I haven't been with, or even thought about bein' with anybody but you."

"Stop it, Serval!" Opal wailed. "Why are you doing this? I believe you but—why are you telling me this—how much you love me and you don't want anybody else—but then you tell me you're leaving me. Why are you doing this to me?"

"Because I want you to know it's not you. And it's not me, either. It's the circumstances. I—Opal, I'm leaving for Africa in three months. And this time . . ." he stopped.

"This time—you're not coming back. That's it. That's what you've been tryin' to tell me, huh?"

"Opal, ever since they arrested Mr. Garvey, our membership has been falling off by the hundreds. Don't you see? It's up to us—he's counting on us—to keep the dream from dying."

"But Serval, even Jack says . . ."

Serval frowned. "What does Jack say?"

"Well, you know how he sets store by what Mr. Randolph says—and well, Serval, I think I kind'a agree with 'em. Goin' back to Africa just isn't gonna work. I don't think your dream is gonna come true, Serval. White folks rule over there, too, you know. We need to stay here and try to—to make things better *here*. That's what Dr. DuBois says too."

Shaking his head, Serval stood up and began to pace. "Mr. Garvey always said we could move mountains if we could just maintain unity. Maybe it's the *unity* that's just a dream. 'Cause Opal, I am *going* to Africa. I couldn't live with myself if I didn't at least try. I've spent over five years working my fingers to the bone, depriving myself of the pleasure of my wife, and living on three hours of sleep every night—for what? To just throw in the towel when things get tough? This is the age of the Pan-African. If we keep thinking small, we'll never move forward. I'm not saying that DuBois and Randolph—and Jack—don't have a point. We need leadership here. But we also need the international connection. They can play their roles—the roles they believe in—but I've got to do what I believe in. After all the groundwork we've laid, we've got to keep the international connection. This is what I do. It's who I *am*." He stopped suddenly and shrugged his shoulders. "I know, I know. You've heard it all before . . ."

A long silence hung in the room before Opal finally spoke. "I was deprived too, Serval."

"I know," he groaned. "I was never there for you when I should have been. You're right. I keep telling myself it's nobody's fault, but . . . Look. The blame falls directly on my shoulders, Opal. I . . . I'm sorry. I should've never married you. Maybe you'd be happier."

"Oh, just stop it, Serval! There must be some way we can work things out."

Serval sat back down next to her and took her hand. "I thought about that all the way back this trip. I think there is a way. But I don't think I could ask it of you . . ."

"What? I'll try anything if it means . . . You want me to quit dancin'?"

"It's not about your dancing, Opal. Well, not entirely."

"Then what?"

"Come with me."

"To—you mean to—*Africa?* But—but Serval, what about Daddy?"

Seeing the horrified expression on her face, Serval pulled her close and stroked her hair. "Yes. There's Leon to consider. I'd be tearin' you away from your Daddy, and you're all he's got." He sighed. "Now maybe you can understand what I meant when I said that it's the circumstances. We love each other, but we constantly fight each other. And we fight because deep down inside, we need different things. You need to stay here and find a way to make that dancing dream come true. Come on, tell the truth. Even if it weren't for Leon, you wouldn't really want to move to Africa, would you?"

Opal shrugged. "No, Serval. Harlem's home to me."

"That's honest. As for me, I keep feeling this pull—to make this global dream of mine come true. And Africa just keeps calling me. I love Harlem too, Opal. There's no other place in this country I'd rather live, but I just can't pass up this chance to go to Africa, to see if it's the true home I think it is."

"But Serval, are you sure it's not . . ."

"What?"

"Well, are you sure it's not just your sense of adventure? I see your face when you come back on those ships. Don't get mad, but to me it seems like some part of you is playin' Douglas Fairbanks—bein' a pirate and all that."

Serval sat forward and shook his head. "Douglas Fairbanks? Damn! If that's what you think, Opal, then you don't know me at all, and I can add that to my list of why things won't work out between us. You see how hard I work. I never accused you of pretending to be Pavlova or some Russian ballet star, did I? You're dream is legitimate, and so is mine."

"But you wanted me to stop dancing, didn't you?"

"I've got no reason to lie now. Yes. I wanted you to stop dancing, have a baby, and come with me to Africa. That's my idea of happily ever after. But now I realize that my happily ever after would've made you miserable. And I understand your concerns for Leon . . . You loved your Daddy long before you loved me. You could no more leave him than I could leave my . . . my mission. See, it's not a dream, Opal. I know it sounds crazy, but I feel like this was what I was born to do. Somebody's gotta change all this—this nightmare."

"But Serval, why does it have to be *you?*"

Serval laughed lightly. "Well, thanks for makin' me sound so noble, but it's not just me. I'm only a small part. But if you get a million fellas like me together—united—then, maybe . . ." His voice trailed off.

"Then . . . I guess you're right, Serval," Opal whispered. "I—I just don't wanna fight anymore."

"Neither do I." He saw the surrender in her face, and knew that the discussion was over. "What time is it, Opal?"

"Almost six."

With a quick squeeze of her hand, he whispered, "Guess it's time for me to go."

"You don't have to go, Serval. This is still your home."

Serval smiled. "We didn't even get a chance to talk about—arrangements—like the rent. I'll make sure you're taken care of, Opal. I'll come and see you when I get back from Boston and we'll work everything out."

"But—where—where' you gonna stay while you're here in town, Serval? Really, you can stay here . . ."

Serval shook his head and stood up. "Opal, you know if I stay here, I'll want to make love to you, and I can't do that to you. Not when we both know . . . I mean, make love to you and then just—leave? I couldn't do that to you—and to tell the truth, I don't think I could stand it myself. It'd just make it that much harder to go. No. I'll go stay with Ernest." He headed for the door.

"Well . . ."

Serval reached for the front doorknob, but Opal's shout stopped him from touching it. "Wait!"

"What is it?"

"Let me—let me get one of your old coats from the back closet, Serval," she said, wiping the tears from her face. "You'll make yourself sick runnin' around in this cold with no coat. Don't leave. I'll be right back."

He watched her as she ran down the hall to the bedroom, and as soon as he heard her open the closet door, he quietly slipped out. He hurried outside to his car, and started the engine. Just as he pulled away, he saw Opal running down the steps in her stocking feet, with his heavy blue coat clutched in her hand. She was shaking with sobs. He shifted gears just as she jumped onto the running board.

"Serval! Wait!"

He stopped the automobile with a jerk, and rested his forehead against the steering wheel. "Please, Opal. Please just say goodbye. I'm not as strong as you think I am."

"Look at me, Serval," she said softly.

After a slight hesitation, he turned his head and gazed at her tear-stained face. "What, Opal?"

"One—one kiss."

He pressed his eyes shut as tightly as he could, but couldn't stop the flood of tears. Shutting off the engine, he stepped out of the car and quietly followed Opal back up the steps to the apartment.

Once inside, she closed the door and turned to him. "You got to give me this, Serval. This—this last time with you. Then I promise . . . I promise I'll let you go and . . ."

"Opal . . ."

"You said yourself you never gave me enough of your time. You're here now, and we're not fighting. Please. An hour. One hour, Serval. You owe me that."

She stretched out her hand, and he allowed her to lead him down the hallway to the bedroom. He sank down onto the edge of the bed and shook his head sadly as she slipped off her dress. "Don't, Opal. This isn't right, not like this."

Flinging her dress across the room, she fell to her knees in the center of the floor, sobbing. "Don't you even want me for—for sex anymore?"

He pulled her to her feet and wrapped his arms around her. "Don't make me weak. *Please* don't make me weak. You know how easy it would be for me to just stay here with you—and give up on everything else? But it's my work, Opal, and I've gotta go where it leads me. Please. I'm hangin' on by my fingernails. I've gotta stay strong."

Opal pulled away and gave him a long, steady look. "You're askin' me to be strong enough to give you up, Serval. To let you just walk out that door and out'a my life! So you better figure out a way to be a little stronger for me, 'cause I'm holdin' on by my fingernails too. You're gonna have to be strong enough to say goodbye to your wife properly, Serval. And not just for me, for *both* of us." She stepped out of her slip, and streams of tears made their way down her face. "One last beautiful memory, Serval—that's all I ask. So we can forget all—all the fighting we did. I promise I'll make it last the rest of my life."

Stunned into silence, he allowed Opal to unbutton his shirt and then ease his arms out of the sleeves. "You know how much I love you, Opal," he whispered. "It wouldn't be this painful if I didn't."

"I love you, too. Now don't think anymore, Serval. Just lay beside me and hold me like you used to. Just stay with me—a little longer."

Easing down onto the bed next to her, Serval buried his face in her neck and surrendered to Opal's soothing touch one last time.

*     *     *

Opal lay staring at the ceiling for several hours after Serval left that afternoon. Having no conception of how much time had gone by, her first coherent thought came when she heard the front door opening, followed by the sound of Jack's voice.

"Damn, it sho' is cold in here! Opal! You home?"

*Jack.* Her mind told her body to get up, if only to break the news to Jack, but she remained still. She heard his footsteps in the bathroom, then sensed his presence at the bedroom door.

"Opal?"

*Answer him.*

Now he was standing at the foot of the bed. "Opal? You sick or sump'm, girl? Creola called and said Frenchy was mad you ain't showed up at the club, so I came to see if . . ." His voice was tinged with alarm. He sat beside her on the bed and grabbed her shoulders. "Opal! What's wrong wit'chu?"

With great effort, she tore her gaze from the ceiling and blinked at Jack. "I'm—I'm awright, Jack. I'm not sick."

He continued to stare at her. "Opal, yo' lips is all cracked. Lemme' get you some water."

"It's okay, Jack. I'll get it myself." Easing to a sitting position, she suddenly realized her state of undress and pulled the sheet up higher around her neck. "Oh, you'd better wait outside."

Backing out, Jack started to close the door, but stopped. "Opal, it feels like about thirty degrees in this place, and you layin' there wit' nothin' but a sheet on? What's . . . ? Oh. Serval must be in town, huh? Where'd he go?"

A sob caught in her throat as she answered. "He—he's gone, Jack! I—guess he's with Ernest. He left me, Jack. He just . . . Oh, God! Just— get out my room! Get out my room and leave me alone!"

After Jack shut the door, Opal heard his heavy, rapid steps heading to the front room. The sound of the linen door opening and slamming shut was followed by a pounding on the bedroom door. "Opal!" Jack yelled. "You put sump'm on and get ya'sef out here so you can wrap up in these here blankets. I turned on the radiator, and I'm leavin'."

Opal pulled on her wrapper, and ran to open the bedroom door. Jack's face registered a rage she had never seen before. "I—I'm sorry, Jack. I was just upset. You don't have to leave."

He headed toward the front door, still barking orders. "And eat sump'm. I know you ain't had nothin' to eat."

"Jack—where are you goin'?"

He looked back at her as he opened the front door. "To find Serval."

\* \* \*

Serval sat in Ernest's small, cluttered kitchen and watched his friend eat his second plate of beef stew. "I don't pretend to be a fancy cook," Ernest said, "but it's really not so terrible. Serval, you haven't taken a bite."

"Huh? Oh, I'm sorry, Ernest. I'm sure it's good. Maybe I'll eat a little later."

"I understand. You have a lot on your mind."

For the next few minutes, the only sound came from outside where the wind was rattling a dry tree branch against the kitchen window. A sudden insistent pounding on the front door nearly startled Ernest out of his chair. Serval didn't so much as blink, and calmly patted Ernest's arm as he stood up. "Let me get it, Ernest. It's for me." *Jack*, he thought, as he headed for the door. *Right on schedule.*

He opened the door slowly, and stood returning Jack's icy stare for a moment before stepping outside.

Jerking up his chin, Jack growled, "Get a coat. I'll wait."

Answering him with a contemptuous look, Serval circled Jack slowly. "I'm not cold and what the hell do you want here?"

"I came to take you home."

Leaning against the front door, Serval crossed his arms. "Home? Haven't you heard? I'm in transit, Jack. Get to the *real* point—you came to beat my ass for leavin' Opal."

Jack's eyes narrowed to two slits, and his nostrils flared. "Maybe. If that's what it takes. How you gon' hurt her like this, man?"

Serval's upper lip quivered with anger, and he knew he was close to losing control. He moved to within an inch of Jack's chin. "Why the hell should you care so much?" he hissed.

"Step back, Serval."

"Or what?"

"I *said*—step back."

Serval read the fury in Jack's eyes, and nodded. "You know me well enough to practically read my mind right now, don't you, Jack? So you must know I'm teetering on the edge of a razor right now, I wanna spill your blood so bad . . ."

Jack blinked. "What?"

"The way I see it I've got two choices. I could grit my teeth and be a disciplined UNIA soldier—be rational. I could do what you said—step back, and just ask you the question. And then I could pretend I believed you while you stood there lyin' your ass off. Or, on the other hand, I could . . ."

"What the hell you talkin' about?"

" . . . on the other hand, I *could* refuse to step back, and . . . See, Jack, sometimes a man's just gotta pay—in blood . . . even if he is the closest thing to a brother . . ." Serval stopped, and after a tense moment, he stepped back. "So I guess this is the moment of truth, huh?" he said quietly.

"I still ain't knowin' what the hell you' talkin' 'bout, Serval," Jack said. "But yeah, truth would be a nice start."

"I faced the truth already, and so did Opal. It doesn't work—*we* just don't work. That's our truth, anyway. You're the only one who won't face your own truth, Jack."

"My . . . ? What the hell I got to do wid'it?"

Serval stared at him as if for the first time. *The closest thing to a brother* . . . "I know you love her, Jack," he whispered. "You love my wife."

Jack blinked. "*What?!*"

"You love her."

"Well, yeah . . . I—I love you, too."

"I don't mean how you love me. You're my brother. I know how you feel about me. But I also know how you feel about Opal. You're in love with her. You can't deny it 'cause it's true. Don't you see, Jack? I've known for a while. I could'a never left Opal all alone. I guess without understanding why at the time, I was always throwing the two of you together. Because I knew she'd be happy with you. I don't know why I got so angry just then. None'a this is anybody's fault. You take care of her, Jack. Take care of her for me."

"No," Jack said, shaking his head. "You ain't got no kind'a right to even say that, man. You can't jus' hand her over to me, talkin' 'bout 'take care of her.' B'sides, she love' *you*, not me. So how you gon' . . . Don't you love her anymore?"

"Very much. I love her so much I can't ask her to wait when . . ."

"When what?"

". . . When I might not come back."

"Naw, man. She be waitin' no matter how long it take."

"You don't understand, Jack. I'm fightin' a war. This is a war just like the Great War, Jack. Remember that feeling we used to have all the time? Wonderin' if we'd ever get back home again? That feeling is all over me—every minute. And even if I do survive, man, this is no kind'a life for Opal. She wants to dance . . . I'm always gone. I'm going all the way to Africa, for God's sake. And a woman wants a man who's gonna be there for her when she needs him. A steady kind'a fella—like you. And even with all that—do you have any idea how many death threats I get—day in and day out? I might—I might not be *able* to come back—even if things were different."

"But Serval . . . Why you? Why you gotta be the one who . . ."

Serval laughed softly. "You and Opal are so much alike. That's the same thing she asked me. Look, Jack . . ." He stopped and stared out at the darkening sky. "Remember that fella I told you about—Jimmy Coles?"

"Mm-hmm. He the one got lynched."

"Yeah, Jack, standing up to a whole room full'a hateful, ignorant white men. Now there's a lot'a folks who'd say he was a damn fool. I thought it myself for awhile. But I've been thinkin' about Jimmy a lot lately, Jack. Do you believe in fate? Destiny—a person having a purpose in his life and that kind'a thing?"

Jack shrugged.

"Well, maybe . . ." Serval felt tears stinging his eyes, but blinked them back. "What if Jimmy Coles had a purpose in his life? What if his whole purpose was—to be one of my teachers? To teach me how to stand up to the white man? How to make others follow my example, so things could change?"

Jack sighed and shook his head. "I don't know, Serval . . ."

"No, Jack, listen. It's kind'a like a relay race. One fella runs as fast as he can, knowing he'll never see the finish line. He'll never get any farther than handing the baton to the next runner, and watching him take off. But he knows that the last man on the team is *going* to cross that finish line, Jack. See?"

"Kind'a makes sense, when you tell it like that," Jack said.

"Right. See, it's no different from what your Mr. Randolph is doing with his union talk. If he can get all of you to stand together, then maybe things'll really change at the Pullman Company. It all starts with one. I'm not stupid, Jack. I know that a lot'a what Mr. Garvey dreamed about probably won't happen, but I'm gonna take the best of what I learned and . . ." He stopped.

"And what?"

"Fight!" he shouted, ". . . scream . . . run as fast as I can . . . whatever it takes to make all this madness stop. All the lynchings . . . all the . . . It's gotta stop. That's why I need to know you'll take care of Opal for me. Does—does she know? Does she know how you feel about her?"

"Naw," Jack said softly. "She don't know."

Serval closed his eyes. "It means a lot to me that you never acted on it."

"Aw, man. I'da never did that to you. B'sides, I told you. She don't love me. She love' you, and she ain't never gon' stop."

"Look, Jack. I know you're right when you say I don't have the right to just hand her over to you. I'm not tryin' to *arrange* anything here. All I'm tellin' you is that if the two of you naturally drift together after I'm gone, you shouldn't feel guilty about it, that's all. I'm sorry I got sore a few minutes ago. I'd rather see her with you than anybody else on earth. I trust you."

He stared up at Jack, and saw tears standing in his eyes. "You know, I always wanted a brother, and I guess you turned out to be him." Serval smiled. "But I could'a never beat your ass anyway. You're too goddamn big."

A nervous laugh escaped Jack's lips. "I—Serval . . ."

Serval reached for the doorknob. "You know, Jack, it *is* cold out here. Guess I better go on in and warm up."

"Wait! When you leavin'?"

"Well, we're not scheduled to go to Liberia for about three months, but I've gotta go out for one last U.S. sweep day after tomorrow. One of the last stops is Boston so I'll stop back here then—to tie up a few loose ends before . . ."

"I wanna be here, Serval—so I can . . . so I can say goodbye."

Serval nodded. "I'll call Opal when I know the date. She'll let you know."

Jack gazed at him, but said nothing.

"Oh, Jack! I nearly forgot . . ." Serval reached into his trouser pocket and retrieved a folded piece of notepaper. He unfolded it and smoothed the creases before handing it to Jack. "Remember that poem I was working on? Well, I . . . I finally finished it. I, uh, wrote it out in printed letters instead of longhand. You know, so you could read it easier."

Jack stared at the paper and nodded. "I—I might have trouble wit' some'a these words, Serval, but I'll try."

"You'll read every word someday. Opal's a real good teacher."

"Serval, I . . ."

Serval smiled. "I know."

*   *   *

Jack found Opal sitting on the sofa when he returned that night, still wrapped in the blankets he had given her. He sat next to her, trying to think of a way to tell her that he had failed. He cleared his throat and opened his mouth, but she spoke first.

"He's not comin' back, I know. I'm okay, Jack. You don't have to fuss over me."

"You—you want me to stay here and keep you company?"

"No. Go home."

Jack stared at the streaks of tears on Opal's face and tried to figure out exactly where "home" was. "You call me if you need me, Opal. I'll check on you tomorrow."

"No, Jack," she said firmly. "You need to spend some time with Creola, and I need to spend some time by myself."

*   *   *

Creola woke up abruptly. She had been dreaming, she was sure, but couldn't remember the dream. Without turning over, she knew that Jack was not beside her. The smell of cigarette smoke hung in the room, and she heard him sigh.

"Why, Jack?" she said softly.

"What? Oh, sorry. Didn't mean to wake you."

"Jack . . . why?"

"Why what?" There was a note of annoyance in his voice.

"Why do you stand there every morning starin' out the window?"

The silence stretched for too long, and Creola felt her eyes fill with tears. Finally he answered. "It settles me."

*   *   *

For the next few weeks Jack worried about Opal, but honored her wish to be left alone. His plan to marry Creola was a distant memory, and he was sullen and distant with her. Even sleeping with her became unbearable. Finally, he could stand no more and headed to Opal's apartment for a showdown.

Knocking loudly on the front door, he was not surprised when she ignored it. Using his key, he let himself in. "Opal?"

No answer.

"Opal, you come out here and talk to me or I'm comin' to find you. Opal?" He strode down the hallway toward the open bedroom door and peered in. Opal was curled up in the center of the bed asleep. "Hey!" he shouted. "Wake up, girl!"

Opal's eyes fluttered open, and then she scowled at him. "Huh? Jack? What're you doin' bustin' in my room like that?" Reaching up, she ran her hands through her badly matted hair. "Go home."

"You broke yo' promise."

She shot him an evil look, then settled back against the pillow. "I don't know what you're talkin' about, Jack. I don't have time for you and your damn games."

"You ain't got time? Oh, right. I see how busy you been these last few weeks—bein' evil and layin' around lettin' ya'self go to hell. You way too busy to keep a promise, huh?"

"I *said*—go *home*, Jack."

"I *am* home."

Spotting her robe lying on the floor, Jack picked it up and threw it at her. "You promised to teach me to read and now it' been so long, I'm forgettin' everything you done taught me. Now. I'ma be waitin' in the front room for my lesson." He turned around and strode back down the hall.

As he waited on the sofa, Jack picked up Opal's old fairy princess book, still lying on the coffee table from his last lesson. It was dusty. As he turned the pages and tried to make out the words, he heard a sound that made him smile. Opal was running water for a bath.

Several minutes later, she walked in and took her usual place on the floor, sitting cross-legged with her knees under the coffee table. Without looking up, she said, "I'm sorry. Now, go ahead on and read, Jack. I'm listenin'."

"Well awright then. Now ya sound like my teacher I use'ta know. Okay . . . The . . . tay-ul . . . of the . . . fairy princess. Long, long ay-go . . . in an . . . en-chan-ted . . . land . . ."

"Jack?"

He looked up. "Huh?"

"I got fired."

"You got . . . Oh. Who fired you?"

"Oh, it's my own fault. I was skippin' rehearsals and, well, Chappie came by the other day and told me that Frenchy hit the roof when I missed that second show. He felt real bad, but I told him not to."

"I'm sorry, Opal. But you' so good, you'll find another dancin' job. They' openin' new clubs every day."

"Mmm. Well, anyway, we better get back to your reading."

"Awright. Le'see, where was I?"

"Jack?"

"Yes?"

Opal hesitated.

"What'chu wanna say, girl?"

"Well . . . You know how much Serval wanted a baby?"

"Uh-huh."

Her voice caught, and Opal finished in a whisper. "I should've given him a baby, huh? I was wrong. He wanted a family so bad. I should've gotten pregnant and—maybe he'd still be here."

"Hey. Ain't no sense thinkin' 'bout that now, Opal. He done a lot'a things wrong too, ya know."

"But Jack, I should've gotten pregnant a long time ago—not *now*—now, when it's too late . . ."

Jack dropped the book in his lap. "What? Opal, you . . ."

"Serval's finally gonna be a daddy and he'll never even see his own baby! Oh, Jack, I'm so sick of crying."

Jack lowered himself on one knee and gathered Opal into his arms. "Shh. Hush, now. Opal, you' so crazy. You really think Serval could still go off to Africa if he got a baby on the way? This' jus' the thing to bring him to his senses. He'll come back, you'll see."

Opal pulled away from him suddenly and wiped her face with the back of her hand. "No, Jack. You didn't see him—how much fight he had in him. If he doesn't go to Africa, I think the man—I think he'd just die. I can't stop him. Besides, I don't want him back just on account of a baby. If we couldn't work things out between ourselves when it was just me and him, then what's a baby gonna fix?" She jerked her chin up. "No. I can do this by myself, Jack. Women have babies every day. I'll learn—and take care of my baby by myself. Just face it, he's gone and it's too late."

"Opal. Please let me tell him. He ain't *really* gone yet. He' still down south somewhere. I can go down to the UNIA office and find out where we can send him a wire or sump'm . . ."

"No. I'ma do this by myself, and let Serval do what he's gotta do."

Seeing the determined set of her jaw, he sighed. "Well. You won't be alone anyway. I'll be here—anytime you need me."

"Thank you, Jack. Now. Gimme a handkerchief so I can blow my nose, and we can get back to your reading."

\* \* \*

As soon as Jack got back from a two-day trip, he showered at the YMCA and headed straight for Opal's apartment. It was a bright morning, and he was ready to read, but when Opal opened the front door, Jack grew alarmed.

"Opal! You ain't lookin' too good . . ."

Opal's eyes widened, and she crumpled into a heap on the floor, retching.

"Aww, Lawd!" Jack said. "I'll get sump'm, Opal."

When he returned with towels, Opal was resting her head on the arm of the sofa. "I'm sorry, Jack. I usually make it to the bathroom . . ."

"Don'tchu worry 'bout it," Jack said as he helped her to her feet. "I'll clean it up. Le'me help you to the bathroom, and then you jus' go lay down for a minute. I'll bring you some soda crackers when I'm done in here."

"Thanks, Jack. The mop's in the utility closet, and the Bon Ami . . ."

"I know where everything is, Opal."

After he finished cleaning up the floor, he sat on the bed next to Opal and pressed a damp washcloth to her forehead. "Hey," he said, grinning at her. "How long this mornin' sickness stuff gonna last?"

"Shoot, Jack. How am I supposed to know? This is my first time goin' through this mess, too, ya know."

"Ya feel like eatin' some'a these crackers?"

"In a minute." Opal touched his arm. "Jack?"

"Huh?"

"Lean down here so I can give you a kiss on the jaw."

Gazing at her soft expression, Jack hesitated.

"Okay, then, stubborn." Opal raised up on her elbow and kissed him quickly. "You and Miss Aida take such good care'a me. I didn't count on all this sickness."

"Oh, you told Miz Aida 'bout the baby?"

"I didn't have to. She came over last Sunday morning so we could go to church together, and I was in the same shape I was a few minutes ago. She just stood there smilin' at me, and then asked me when I was due."

"Did you tell her 'bout Serval?"

Opal shrugged. "No. I didn't want her to worry. Guess you're the only one I can really talk to 'bout all this. Jack—I don't know what I'da done without you these past few weeks. I—I'da been awfully lonely."

"I miss him too, Opal."

Opal smiled. "Well . . . I'm feelin' better now, Jack. Go get your book. You got lots'a readin' to catch up on."

# Chapter 39

Spring's arrival that year coincided with the second phase of Opal's pregnancy, and the combined effect lifted her spirits. As she rode with Jack along the isolated road on the way to the Ossining facility, she leaned her head back on the soft leather seat of Leon's Chrysler and began to hum softly.

"What'chu so happy 'bout, woman?" Jack laughed.

"Well, Jack, for the first time in days I'm not sick. And I'm goin' to see my Daddy. And this breeze feels so good. Look's like spring's finally here, huh? It's a mighty pretty day."

"Mm-hmm. And that's a mighty pretty smile, too. Listen, I'm sorry I couldn't take you last Sunday. The fella I switched days wit' got sick and . . ."

"It's okay, Jack. I'm sure Daddy understands."

"Well, I still felt bad. I worry 'bout ol' Leon."

Opal's smile faded. "I do too. I can't even sleep nights worryin' about Daddy, and then Serval, and then Daddy again . . ."

Jack turned to look at her, and saw her dabbing at her eyes. "He' be awright, Opal. And ya know that Mista Washington still talkin' 'bout maybe . . ."

"He's always so quiet when we visit him."

Jack made the turn into the prison entrance. "Hey, now. We here, so you bed'not let Leon catch you frownin' like that. That smile a'yours prob'ly like sunshine to him."

Opal nodded. "You're right, Jack. I'll try."

*  *  *

Opal sat fidgeting at the visitor's table, and staring at the door until Leon finally came in behind a guard. "Daddy!" she called.

He raised his head and gave her a bland smile.

"Oh, Jack!" Opal whispered. "Daddy looks terrible!"

"Aw, he don't look so bad, Opal. He' jus' gotta settle in."

Opal stood up and embraced her father, as Jack looked on. When they sat down, Jack saw tears standing in Leon's eyes and noticed a severe trembling in his hands.

"Leon . . .?"

"Oh, Daddy!" Opal cried. "What's wrong?"

Leon stared down at the table and spoke in a hoarse voice. "Where was you at last week, baby? I waited and waited for the guard to call my name last week and . . . y'all never came. I ain't never spent such a long day in my whole life."

"It's my fault, Leon," Jack said. "See, the fella I switched wit' . . ."

"But Opal," Leon said, "you could'a got somebody else to drive you up, couldn't you, baby? You got my Chrysler—I done gave you that. I—I jus' . . ."

"Oh, Daddy, I'm sorry. Miss Aida can't drive and . . ."

"But what about Serval?"

Opal blinked and took a deep breath. "He—he's still out'a town, Daddy. I'm sorry, but I'm here now. Let's just have a nice visit."

Leon shook his head. "You don't know how it is in here. You should'a came, girl. I need you. I done took care'a you all by myself all these years. You should'a came!"

Jack saw Opal looking at him, but couldn't take his eyes off Leon, who was crying freely now.

"Daddy?" Opal said. "Calm down, now. There's no reason for you to get so upset just because I missed one Sunday."

"You don't know," he said. "You jus' don't know. Sinjin told me . . . Sinjin—he' this real o'nery fella in the next cell from me—he' been tellin' me since the first day, 'You might as well be dead, ol' man. Sho', they remember you at first—comes to see you and all that—but in a while, it' jus' be a letter now and then—and after a year or two, you be lucky to get that.' That's what he said, Opal—and when you ain't showed last Sunday . . . You don't know how bad it is . . ."

"Daddy!" she sobbed. "You know I can't forget about you. You think I come here just to do you a favor? I miss you! I come and see you because—I miss you. And that's never gonna change. Now, promise me that if I ever miss a Sunday, you won't think all that nonsense." She grabbed his hands. "Please!"

The guard stepped up and tapped Leon's shoulder. "No touching. Come on, Leon, you know the rules. Only at the beginning and end of the visit—and over by the door where I can see you."

"Yes, sir."

Opal shot the guard an evil look, and Jack touched her arm. "Don't get us kicked out, now," he whispered.

Opal took an angry swipe at her tears, then crossed her arms. "I wanna tell him, Jack."

"Tell me what?" Leon asked.

"You think it be a good idea?" Jack asked.

"What, baby?" Leon pleaded. "What'chu wanna tell me?"

"I just don't want you to worry if I miss a Sunday or two in about six months, Daddy. 'Cause I'm liable to be feelin' kind'a weak when—when the baby comes."

A bright smile suddenly appeared on Leon's face. "A baby? You mean . . ."

"That's right, Daddy. You're fixin' to be a grampaw. How do you feel about that?"

Leon smacked the tabletop with both palms. "How do I feel? How you think I feel? This' the first happy thing since . . . Well, will you bring the baby to see me?"

"Yes, sir," Opal laughed. "If they let me. Every Sunday, without missin'—just like church."

"Well, maybe after *real* church. I wouldn't want the little fella growin' up thinkin' that Sing Sing was *church*. Mm-mm-mm. My little sweetheart gonna be a Mama. And I guess that means I'll be seein' mo' of that travelin' husband a'yours, too, huh? 'Cause I know Serval' gon' be stayin' closer to home now that he finally got his family started."

*　*　*

The drive back to Harlem was painfully quiet. Jack decided not to disturb Opal's thoughts until they rolled to a stop in front of her building.

"Okay, le'me walk you upstairs, and then I guess you need to get some rest, so I'ma be headin' off."

"Aren'tcha gonna take the car, Jack?"

"I'll take the bus. Shoot, this automobile ain't mine. It's Leon's."

Opal smiled. "Daddy gave it to me. But you know I can't drive. Tell you what, Jack. I'll make you a present of it."

Jack shook his head. "Uh-uh. No."

"No, really, Jack. You can have it as long as you take me to the places I need to go when you're in town. And when you're gone, you can just leave it here. Otherwise, it'll just sit out here and rust."

"Well, then you gotta let me pay you for it."

"No arguments. Take it, Jack, and we'll talk about that later. I wanna get inside. I've got a lot of thinking to do."

Jack squeezed her hand. "I'll call you later."

✳   ✳   ✳

As Jack climbed the stairs to Creola's apartment, he realized that he had put off the inevitable for long enough. Ever since he had returned her engagement ring to Mr. Steinberg's jewelry store on his last stop in Baltimore, he had been plagued by guilt. It was time to set things straight.

He paced the floor of her apartment waiting for her to return from the Cotton Club. She was late. By three a.m., Jack was too tired for conversation, and decided to delay the discussion until morning. He stretched out on the bed and was just dozing off when he heard the click of the doorknob.

"Jack?" Creola whispered. "You awake, honey?"

Jack played possum until he heard her running a bath, then relaxed into a natural sleep.

Opal's face came to him in a dream. She was smiling at him—not with the sweet smile she always gave him—this was a smile that radiated love—the smile she reserved for Serval. Her eyes gazed at him, and he could feel her breath on his face, her breasts against his chest. He spoke to her, but knew that she couldn't hear him. *I love you.* A sudden, urgent fear gripped him, and she swirled away from him. *Stay wit' me, Opal!* He could feel her fingertips as they slipped from his grasp.

He sat bolt upright and stared at the face next to him in bed. "Creola? What'chu doin' here?"

"What am I doin' here?" she whispered. "What's wrong with you, Jack? What is it? A nightmare?"

Easing away from her, Jack sat up on the edge of the bed and held his head in his hands. "I'm sorry," he murmured.

"What? Sorry for what, Jack?"

Without answering, he turned on the lamp and began to take his Pullman uniforms out of the closet. He opened his suitcase and quietly began to pack.

"Don't, Jack," Creola murmured, crawling quickly across the bed to him. "You're leaving me, aren't you? Don't go. Can't we talk about it?"

Silence.

Her voice caught as she began to cry. "Jack—please. You can't be still carryin' a torch for Opal? That's your best friend's wife. You—you ought'a stay with me. I'll be good to you, Jack."

He opened a small leather shaving case, and pulled out a stack of twenty dollar bills. Counting out five of them, he laid the money on the nightstand. Creola slapped her hand over it, then crumpled up the bills and threw them at him. "You're always givin' me money! I don't want your damn money, Jack! You jus' keep it! And keep the guilt that goes with it!"

Jack shut his eyes as tightly as he could, and repeated the only words he could call to mind. "I'm sorry."

Creola slumped back onto her pillow in tearful surrender. Aside from the occasional muffled catch in her throat, the room was quiet.

Jack dressed mechanically. After stacking his things by the door, he leaned over to switch off the lamp, then sank heavily on the edge of the bed near her. "I'm sorry," he whispered. "You take care'a ya'self, Creola."

There was no response, not even a sniffle. "Creola? You awright?" She moved away from him without answering.

Jack sighed and headed for the door to gather his bags. Just as he stepped out into the hallway, he heard Creola's voice in an unintelligible tumble of words. He paused and peered back in. "Did—did you say sump'm?"

"I said . . . my name ain't Creola. It's Addie."

*     *     *

As Jack drove through the dark streets, the stillness of predawn haunted him with a familiar uneasy feeling. He searched his mind for a memory, and gazed at the headlight beams stretching before him on the lonely road. A train whistle sounded in the distance, triggering the answer. *On the train from Alabama,* he thought. *After the war.* He pulled over to the side of the road and turned off the headlights, then stepped out. It wasn't a particularly cold night, but he pulled up his collar against some inexplicable chill. As his eyes began to adjust, he saw the train's silhouette off to his left, small and black against the deep blue of night's final hour. *I can see all the little farm houses and trees y'all passin'. Pullman fella rushin' to finish up them shoes befo' folks starts wakin' up. Next stop—Penn Station.* The tiny train sounded one last, faint whistle before disappearing from Jack's sight and into his memory.

*     *     *

Opal's eyes fluttered open at the sound of someone knocking on her front door. She shifted her legs to the side of the bed, but began to drift back to sleep before her feet touched the floor. The second knock was more persistent, and she jumped to a sitting position. Pulling on her wrapper, she stumbled down the hallway and reached for the chain on the living room lamp. Another knock. "Okay!" she muttered.

She slid the cover away from the peep-hole and tried to focus, but saw only a dark blur. "Who is it?" she asked.

"It's me, Opal. Jack."

Opal unlocked the door and stepped back as Jack walked in. "Jack! Why didn't you just use your key? You know the sofa's yours anytime you want to use it."

"I—I ain't came to visit the sofa, Opal. I gotta talk to you."

"Well, Lord, Jack! Couldn't it wait 'til morning? What time is it anyway?"

"'Bout five thirty, I reckon."

She sighed and shook her head. "Well, come on in the kitchen, Jack, and I'll fix us some coffee."

As Opal stepped into the pantry to fetch the coffee grinder, she smiled at Jack over her shoulder. "Hey, tall man. I can't reach that doggone percolator without climbin' on a chair. Get it for me, would you?"

"Okay. Where?"

"That highest shelf, Jack."

Jack retrieved the percolator and set it on the counter. "What' it doin' way up there where you can't reach it?"

Opal shrugged. "I don't really drink it when I'm—by myself. I used to fix coffee for Serval—when he was here." Turning the crank on the coffee grinder, she studied Jack. "So, what do you want to talk about?"

After a long silence, Jack settled into a chair and said, "Sit down, Opal."

"Okay—almost finished. There. It'll be done in a while. Oh, Jack! I don't think I have any cream," she said, heading for the cooler.

He sighed. "Opal, please sit down. I'll drink it black."

Opal took a seat across the table from Jack, but found it difficult to look at him. "Is sump'm wrong?"

"Guess that be dependin' on how you look at it."

"Huh?"

He took a deep breath. "How—uh, I mean . . . Awright. Look, what would you say if I told you . . . I love you?"

Opal swallowed and stared at him for a moment before answering.
"I—Jack, I guess I know it. I mean, I didn't know—not 'til right now, but
as soon as you said it . . . it felt like I always knew." Shaking her head,
she laughed softly. "That doesn't make sense, huh?"

"Yes it do. Sometimes our head don't keep up wid our hearts, I guess."

"But Jack . . ."

"I know. You ain't gotta say it. I know you still love Serval, but . . ."

Opal gazed at her hands. "But Serval's gone. That's what you were
gonna say, huh? And he's not comin' back."

Jack covered her hands with one of his. "I—I want you to know,
Opal, this would'a never happened if he ain't lef' like he done."

"Oh, I know that, Jack. I know it's not in you to hurt Serval." She
shrugged her shoulders and blinked back tears. "It's me that hurt him.
I guess we hurt each other. But you never hurt anybody, Jack. So don't
worry about that."

Jack shook his head. "I done my share'a hurtin'. I think I hurt
Creola real bad."

"Oh, Jack! You didn't tell Creola how—how you feel about me?"

"Naw. But seem' like she knew somehow. I lef' her tonight, Opal.
And she was cryin'. I ain't never seen Creola Dorshay cry. I tried to love
her. I really did. But I jus' couldn't stop thinkin' 'bout you. Opal . . ."

"Mm-hmm?"

"I know you ain't ready for all'a this—but how' you feel? 'Bout me,
I mean?"

"I don't know," she said softly.

"It's awright," Jack said quickly, releasing her hands. "I understand."

"No, you don't. I love you, Jack. It's just not the same way I love—
my husband." She laughed softly. "My husband—guess I can't really
call him that any more, huh?"

"Did—did Serval say anything about . . . a divorce?"

"No. He said sump'm 'bout tyin' up loose ends, though. You know,
before he leaves for Africa. Guess that's what I am, Jack. One'a those
loose ends. But I guess with him in Africa and me here, and things the
way they are . . ."

"Opal, I ain't meant to come over here to make you feel sad. I jus' . . ."

"It's not your fault, Jack. Do you . . . think you could give me a little
time? I haven't sorted out my feelings yet, but I know I—I need you.
Please don't—don't leave me too, Jack."

"I ain't goin' noplace, Opal. You take all the time you need to figure things out."

Opal smiled at him and stood up. "Coffee's done, Jack. I'll get you a cup. But I don't think I better have any," she said, placing her hand on her abdomen. "I don't feel so good, all of a sudden."

Jack sprang to his feet and placed one arm around Opal's waist. "Forget about that damn coffee, Opal. I'll help you to ya room."

"Aww, Jack," she whispered. "You better make that the bathroom. And hurry! Oh, God, I thought this was over . . ."

Arriving in the bathroom in the nick of time, Jack ran cold water on a towel as Opal fell to her knees and succumbed to a severe bout of morning sickness.

"Opal," he said, kneeling beside her, "if you feel awright about it, maybe I ought'a move back in here. 'Course I'll sleep on the sofa like I always done. But you need somebody to take care'a you, girl—leas' 'til you get to feelin' better."

Unable to speak, Opal nodded her head and leaned against Jack as he pressed the cool towel against her forehead.

*   *   *

After Jack moved in with her, Opal noticed a distinct coolness in her neighbors. Mrs. Emerson who lived across the hall answered good-mornings and smiles with a silent, judgmental stare. Two women from down the block became Mrs. Emerson's constant companions, and the trio instantly pressed their heads together in whispered conferences whenever Jack and Opal stepped outside. Opal began to wonder how long it would take before Creola found out where Jack was staying.

It took six days.

On the morning that Opal saw Creola coming up her sidewalk, she was stricken with a combination of anxiety and nausea. It had been months since Creola had stopped taking ballet lessons, and there could be only one reason for this unannounced visit. As she opened the door, Opal said a silent prayer of thanks that Jack was out of town.

"Mornin', Creola! It sure is good to see you, girl!"

Creola scowled, then walked across the living room floor to peer into the kitchen. "He's stayin' here, isn't he?" she snapped.

"Uh, who?"

"You know who, Opal," she said. "Jack. Bet he came straight here that night when he . . ." She stopped suddenly, and sank down onto the sofa in tears.

"Oh, Creola! Please don't cry, girl. I—I'm sorry things didn't work out for you and Jack, really I am. But I never did anything to . . . Don't blame me, please. It's not like you think, ya know. He sleeps right on that sofa you're sittin' on. We didn't—I mean, he hasn't touched me, Creola."

Creola gave her a hard look, and yanked a handkerchief from her pocketbook. "You think that's supposed to make me feel better, Opal? You think I'm some kind'a damn fool or sump'm? I gave that man enough sex to kill a horse, and you know what it got me? Huh?"

Opal shook her head and clutched her mid-section.

"I hope it happens to you, Miss Pickford," Creola hissed. "I don't know what's goin' on with you and that missin' person husband a'yours, but I hope you find out how it feels to have him—or Jack—or whoever your man is—to be layin' up on top'a you—and then call out another woman's name."

Opal's mouth fell open. "Not—not *my* name! Jack called *my* name?"

Creola rose and gave Opal a contemptuous look. "So Serval's gone, and Jack ain't touched you, huh? And that's supposed to make me feel relieved 'cause everything's so damn nice and pure and friendly. You' so stupid, Opal—if you don't think he's layin' awake on this sofa every night tossin' and turnin'—and jus' *sweatin'* to sneak into your bed! He's a man, Opal! The only reason he ain't touched you is that . . ." The volume of her voice dropped suddenly. ". . . he's willin' to wait— 'cause—'cause you're the one he really loves."

"Creola, wait . . ."

Creola took a rough swipe at her tears, then lifted her chin and stared coldly at Opal. "Aw, sit down. I'll see my damn self out. Oh, and Opal? Thanks for makin' me feel *so* much better."

*      *      *

For the rest of the day Opal tried and failed to shake off the dismal feeling Creola had left hanging in her home. Late that afternoon, the telephone rang and Jack's gentle voice reassured her.

"Hey, Opal. It's me, ya wanderin' Pullman friend."

"I'm so glad you called, Jack," she said.

"Hey, now, wait a minute. Sump'n don't sound right in yo' voice. Ya sound kind'a shaky, girl."

"Well, it's just that . . . Creola came over today."

"Aw, Lawd," he moaned. "What' she say?"

"Well . . . things I didn't want to hear."

"Mm-mm-mm. Like what?"

"Well . . . I'm a little embarrassed to say it, Jack."

"Please, Opal. You can talk to me."

"She—well, she told me . . . She was real upset, Jack."

"I know. I'm sorry 'bout all that, but we gotta get on past it. Sometimes folks jus' be in love alone, that's all. I tried to love her, Opal, but . . . well, you know how I feel . . ."

"No, but Jack . . . See, I understand all that, but what upset me was the part about . . . Jack, she told me that you called out my name . . . one night when—well, when you should've been callin' out hers."

Silence.

"Jack?"

"Opal, I . . . I don't remember that, but . . . look. You been on my mind, and I guess . . . But Opal, that ain't the way . . . I mean, that ain't the only way I . . . Oh, Lawd . . ."

"It's okay, Jack. You don't have to explain. I'm not mad at you."

"You ain't?"

"No. And I'm not so upset about it any more, I guess. Will you be comin' home soon?"

"Well, I got Ignatius to fill in for me on that long California trip, so I'll be back day after tomorrow. But listen. Far as all that stuff Creola got'chu worryin' 'bout? Opal, it jus' seem' like we all been steady hurtin' each other for a long time. Ya know what I think? I think it's time for all'a us to start fresh."

"Thanks, Jack. I think that's a real good idea."

✻ ✻ ✻

Jack returned the following Wednesday. Opal had just drifted to sleep when the squeak of the front door woke her. Still too sleepy to get up, she lay listening to the sound of his heavy footsteps in the hallway, followed by the coat closet opening. She closed her eyes and smiled. *Now he's hanging up his Pullman jacket—real careful—and buttoning all the buttons.* Two shoes plopped onto the floor, and the springs of the sofa creaked in protest as Jack settled down. Opal was barely awake a few minutes later, when she vaguely heard the footsteps again; then the sound of Jack running a bath. *It's good to have him home.*

The room was silent and dark when Opal woke up an hour later. She sprang to a sitting position and her heart was racing. . . . *If you don't think he's layin' awake on this sofa every night tossin' and turnin'—and jus' sweatin' to sneak into your bed* . . . She stared at the bedroom door. *What would I do if he did come in here one night?* "Oh, Serval," she moaned. "How could you do this to us?"

She heard the sofa springs squeak from the living room . . . then quiet . . . then footsteps fading into the kitchen. The sound of water running . . . footsteps . . . the settling of Jack's weight on the sofa again. *He can't sleep either.* Opal squirmed uncomfortably, hating herself for the physical arousal creeping up on her. The tears that followed were almost a welcome attack.

*   *   *

When Jack returned from work the next night, Opal was in the kitchen preparing supper. "What'chu doin', girl?" he asked. "You sure you feel like cookin'?"

"Mm-hmm. I've been feelin' pretty steady today. So how does mashed potatoes sound?"

"Well . . ." He paused to yawn. "That sounds good fo' a start. But hungry as I am, ya gonna have to throw in a chicken or two, and maybe some biscuits."

"You are hungry!" Opal laughed. "Sure you don't want me throw in a side'a beef, too, Jack?"

"Hey," he said, grinning. "I'm a big fella. Takes a lot to fill me up." Impulsively, he leaned down and kissed her cheek gently.

Opal stopped peeling the potatoes and gazed up into his eyes. "Jack?"

*Uh-oh. Shouldn'ta done that.* He took a step back. "What's wrong, Opal?"

"Jack . . .?"

"Oh," he said, placing his arm around her waist. "You ain't feelin' good, huh?"

Opal shook her head. "I feel fine," she whispered. "Kiss me—again." "Huh?"

She moved closer to him. "Kiss me again."

He studied her face for a moment and whispered, "You sure?"

"No. But kiss me, Jack. I have to know—I mean . . ."

"Shh." Leaning down, he grazed her lips lightly with his, before gently settling there—for a soft kiss that bordered somewhere between friendship and desire. Opening his eyes, he stared at her and touched her face with his fingertips. "Opal."

"Hmm?"

"You sure now?"

"No. But kiss me again, Jack."

Finding courage in her eyes, Jack pulled her close to his body and kissed her again, more intimately this time. When he felt her lips part and her body press against him, all the passion he had harbored for so long rushed out in a low moan.

Opal pulled away from him and picked up a potato. "I still don't know if—if I'm sure, Jack. And I don't even know if it's right or wrong—with me bein' pregnant and all—but I know one thing . . ."

"What, Opal?"

"I know—I liked that kiss. I probably shouldn't—but I did . . ."

Jack smiled and kissed the back of her neck. "And I probably shouldn't want you much as I do, but girl, I think I was born wantin' you."

"But we have to move slow, Jack. I'm still tryin' to sort out the other part. You know—my feelings for Serval. But maybe I shouldn't talk about him—I'm sorry."

"No. I don't mind talkin' 'bout Serval. I know all this ain't makin' no sense, but I miss him. I miss him jus' like you. Maybe we *should* talk about him. Maybe that' be how we move on."

"You know what I miss the most, Jack? How we used to hold hands when we were first together. When we started fightin' all the time, he never held my hand any more. That's a funny thing to miss, huh?"

"Naw. It ain't funny. I think I miss the way he use'ta cuss and get mad when he couldn't get his way. Now that's sump'm funny to miss."

"I used to get so mad at him, Jack. But now I guess it's easier for me to understand him. Like how he stopped holdin' my hand. He was stubborn like that. I'd say, 'Serval, why don't you hold my hand any more?' And he'd jus' look at me that way he had, and say, 'I'll hold your hand when I feel like it, girl. If you want to hold my hand, don't tell me to hold yours, just reach out and grab mine!' Seemed like everything was a contest with him."

"Maybe he was jus' tryin' to get'chu to show ya own feelin's," Jack said, smiling.

"You two," Opal laughed, rolling her eyes. "You're still defendin' him and he' not even here."

"Naw, I ain't. But I gotta admit I miss him."

Opal smiled. "And I guess that's all right."

"Hey, you know what? Since we' talkin' 'bout Serval, I been meanin' to read you this poem I been holdin' onto. I been practicin' and . . ."

"That's good, Jack! I'd love to hear you read sump'm new. Where is it?"

"I got it right here in my pocket."

Jack pulled out the poem and unfolded it. He studied it for a moment, then handed it to Opal. "I can't."

"Aw, Jack. Yes, you can. Come on, now. Try."

"Naw, Opal. It ain't like I *can't* read it. I just think . . . see, Serval wrote it. He said he started it on the way back from the war. I was gonna give it to you . . ."

Opal stared at the paper, but said nothing.

"Look," Jack said, "you ain't got to read it right now. Read it later when you' by ya'self."

"Okay. I will."

"Good."

All was quiet for a moment until Opal snapped her fingers and hurried to the living room, with Jack close behind. "Hey," he said, "Thought you was fixin' supper?"

"I will, Jack, in a minute. But right now I feel like dancin'." She headed for the coat closet, and reached for the hatbox on the top shelf. "Hey, Jack! You ever seen a pregnant lady dance *Swan Lake?*"

"Huh? Swan . . .?"

"*Swan Lake.* It's a ballet. I don't feel like bein' sad thinkin' about Serval and the war. I feel like dancin', Jack. 'Course I'm so out'a practice, I'll prob'ly stomp around here like a buffalo, but I'ma try anyhow. And you better not laugh at me! Now help me move the coffee table."

Once the coffee table was moved and the rug rolled up, Opal began rummaging through the hatbox. "Jack, crank up the Victrola and dust off the phonograph record, would'ya?"

"Which one?"

Opal rolled her eyes at him. "Well, I don't think I'm fast enough to ballet-dance to *Sweet Georgia Brown!* Which one do you think, Jack? The one that says *Swan Lake*, of course!"

Jack chuckled as he dusted off the record. "Jus' for that, I ain't gon' give ya no applause. . . . Okay. Ya orchestra's all ready to play, Miss Ballet Dancer. And yo' audience is gettin' impatient—so come on."

"Okay, Jack. You just sit down and let me get my shoes on and we'll

see if I can make you applaud or not. 'Course, remember I *am* pregnant, so I won't be the most graceful thing you've ever seen."

"Aw, woman! Yo' belly ain't even big yet! So quit makin' excuses."

Jack watched Opal carefully lift the toe shoes out of the pink tissue
paper and tie the ribbons around her ankles. After a bit of abbreviated
stretching, she stood up on pointe for a moment, then stepped over to
the Victrola to start the music.

Jack immediately recognized the haunting strains of *Swan Lake* as
one of the pieces Opal played repeatedly when she practiced. The
emotion of the music floated through the room and seemed to lift
Opal until she became one with the air. Jack's eyes travelled from her
head to the tip of her weight-bearing foot as she executed a series of
quick pirouettes.

"Mm-mm-mm . . . I still can't figure out how you balance ya'self on
ya toetips like that . . ."

"Shhh!"

"Sorry."

With great difficulty, he forced his eyes away from her feet and studied her face, which was lit with some inner peace. Her eyes were closed
and she swayed and spun slowly to the melancholy theme until, toward
the finale, the rise in volume and accompanying cymbal crashes dictated more vigorous movements, topped off by a leap so impossible
that Jack reached out to catch her. But she didn't fall. As the sound of
violins faded, Opal descended in a slow bow, folding one leg beneath
her and stretching her arms out over the extended leg. Her head came
to rest on her knee, as peaceful and still as a child's head on a pillow.
When the silence was broken by the scratchy skipping of the phonograph needle, Jack stood up and clapped his hands.

"Lawd, Opal! Shoot, girl, I ain't never seen you get that carried away
practicin' in here! How' you' do that jump thing? I thought you was
gon' fly through the ceilin' for a minute!"

She smiled at Jack, then began untying the ribbons on her shoes.
With a sigh, she placed the shoes back in the hatbox and returned it
to the closet. "Guess it was jus' a dream, huh, Jack? Me dancin' the ballet, I mean."

Jack shrugged. "I don't know 'bout that, but Opal, you sho' can
dance, girl. It was like—well, at the beginnin' it was kind'a like a flower
blowin' in the breeze. But that second part—shoot, I don't even know
how to tell you 'bout that."

Opal sat down next to him. "That was real pretty, Jack—what you said about the flower in the breeze—kind'a like poetry."

Jack shrugged.

"No, Jack, really. You oughta talk more. I—I wanna hear what you're thinkin' about. And you don't have to worry about talkin' good. I don't talk as proper as Serval either. So talk to me, Jack. You talk and I'll dance." Leaning close to his face, Opal kissed him lightly once, then again, lingering close for a moment. "Well," she whispered. "I guess I'll go finish makin' supper now. And thanks for the applause."

*      *      *

After supper that night, Opal relaxed in the bathtub with a long, meditative soak, then went to bed early. After turning down the sheets and settling in, she remembered the poem and turned on the lamp. She took the paper out of the drawer, unfolded it, and began to read:

> *Dawn—prismatic morning colors*
> *refracting lies called "white" and*
> *a war called "Great" leaving*
> *Dark Paradise eclipsed by light*
> *Uncle Sam wants you too!*
> *Fight for the country your father built and*
> *your mother suckled and nurtured and*
> *tried to make clean*
> *A renaissance dream laid bare*
> *as New Negroes line up for "nigger" weapons*
> *at the armory of shovels, mops, and*
> *shoe-shine rags*
> *To serve at dream-stealers' feet*
> *"over there, over there . . ."*
>
> *High noon—blinding eyes to truths of*
> *a lynching en masse—over there*
> *Shovels gladly traded for colored pride*
> *Hut, two, three, four—move out!*
> *Sharecroppers, chauffeurs and*
> *ragtime-side-men*
> *French heroes overnight*

*over there*
*in burning blasts of light and*
*rocket's red glare*
*blind and lost to white man's truths*
*Talented tenths—*
*percentages caught*
*in a barbed-wire noose*

*Sunset, shadows—enigma of twists*
*Mama's tears and sweetheart's kiss and*
*Jim Crow's mocking grin*
*Sing it loud!*
*Here Comes My Daddy Now!*
*A sho'nuff natural man—at last . . .*
*Respect at five percent*
*'til uniforms are torn and burned by*
*white-sheets on a midnight ride*
*Uncle Sam wants you to*
*line up for mops and*
*shoe-shine rags*
*to serve at dream-stealers' feet*
*outside doors to "cotton" clubs as*
*nights grow late with*
*twisted dreams on flop house beds*
*of twisted wire and burning flesh*
*lynched and*
*dead and*
*caught in*
*red, white, and blue barbed-ropes of*
*Armistice. Victory. Dishonor.*
*And Harlem weeps.*

Opal read the poem several times before placing it back in the drawer and turning off the light. Within seconds the darkness stirred up memories of "the nightmare"—being jarred from a deep sleep by the sound of labored breathing and a jerking agitation in the bed beside her. Anguished, disjointed murmuring: *Cut him down! Help—help me . . . Red? Where is it? Where—where's your goddamn dogtags? . . . I'm good . . . I'm good, Daddy. I'm a good killer . . .*

Choking back tears, Opal stretched out her hand to the empty space beside her and twisted the sheet tightly in her fist. *Let me go . . .*

*   *   *

A few hours later a violent crash of thunder shook Jack awake. Scrambling up to turn on the lamp, he clicked it twice before realizing that the storm had knocked out the electricity. A sudden streak of lightning illuminated the room, followed immediately by an intense rumbling, ending in an earsplitting crack. Jack ran into the kitchen and wrestled with Opal's curtains, which were whipping in a frenzied wind, until he finally managed to shut the window. By the time he finished with all the windows in the front room, his shirt was drenched and he had counted five thunderclaps. It was the worst storm he could ever remember, and it was close.

"Opal!" he shouted.

No answer.

He hurried down the hall to her bedroom and opened the door just as Opal slammed her window shut. Another loud clap of thunder startled her and she jumped.

"Opal! You awright?" Jack shouted.

Opal gasped and spun around. "Oh, Jack! You scared the life out'a me!"

The room was dimly lit by a large, flickering candle on the bedside table. Eying the candle, Jack smiled. "You scared'a the storm, Opal?"

"No," she said, cutting her eyes at him.

"How'd you find a candle so quick?"

"I got candles all over the house, Jack. You know that. In case of emergency, like now."

"What emergency, Opal?" he smiled. "We' safe."

"Okay, Jack," she snapped. "Thunderstorms rattle me a little. I admit it. You' satisfied now?"

He laughed. "I gotta go dry off, Opal. I got wet closin' all them windows. Wait a minute."

Jack felt his way to the bathroom and peeled off his wet shirt. Just as his hands found a dry towel, he heard Opal calling him. "Jack? Come on in here and keep me company. But you bed'not make fun of me for bein scared."

Jack walked back in, drying off his chest with a towel, and smiled. Opal was in the center of her bed, hugging her knees. "Aww, I ain't gon' make fun'a you," he said softly. "My Mama used to get real scared'a thunderstorms, and if I wasn't tryin' to act like a he-man, I might haf'ta admit they make me jumpy too."

"Really, Jack?"

"Mm-hmm. Really. . . . Hey! Opal, I jus' thought'a sump'm."

"What?"

"'Member when you was dancin' earlier and I said I didn't know how to tell you how—you know, what it was like? Well, now it jus' come to me." He grinned broadly. "You must'a been dancin' up a storm."

Opal groaned. "Awww, Jack! Guess you ready for the Vaudeville now, huh?"

"Nope. I'ma go straight to the Follies. See can I give Bert Williams a run fo' his money," Jack said, bowing.

"Mm-hmm. Well, one thing's for sure, Jack. You'll be the biggest thing on Broadway."

Jack grimaced, then sat quietly at the end of the bed for a moment. "So—did you read it?"

Opal's smile faded. "Yes. I read it."

"Good."

"But let's not talk about it now, Jack."

"Awright." At the next crack of thunder, Opal jumped again, and Jack covered a smile. "I ain't laughin'."

"That's 'cause you jumped too, Jack!" Opal said, laughing. "I saw you."

"Okay, okay."

"Jack—you can stay in here with me if you want to. I mean, jus' to sleep."

"You sure?"

"Mm-hmm." She reached over to plump a pillow for him.

All conversation ceased as Jack leaned against the pillow and stretched out his long legs on the bed. Opal rested her head on his shoulder, and he felt her relax. After awhile, the storm weakened into a steady rain, and Opal's breathing grew regular. Careful not to wake her, Jack eased her into a prone position and covered her with the sheet. As he settled down next to her, he closed his eyes and wrapped his fingers around her hand.

# Chapter 40

Serval's train pulled into Grand Central at 8:20 on a bright Monday morning. After picking up his car at the parking garage on 42nd Street, he headed uptown, running an itinerary of the day's business through his mind.

But the instant he crossed 110th Street, all thoughts of business dissolved. It was May in Harlem—when morning sparkled like a string of polished pearls around a young girl's neck. Serval blinked at the unique colors of the neighborhood as if he'd never seen them, and its sounds danced in his ears like jazz. The bright awning of Lovely Lady House of Beauty rolled its green and white stripes out toward the street, and right next door was the ornate front entrance of the Verbena Perfumery Company. Each woman who reached this stretch of sidewalk stopped in her tracks to peer at photographs of the latest hairstyles, and sigh over the elegant display of draping blue velvet and cut-crystal perfume bottles glittering in the early sun.

Serval sat at a stop sign watching the ladies until his attention was diverted by the shrill chatter of birds perched along the flowering branches of five saplings standing in a neat row in the center of Lenox Avenue. On the far corner, a newsboy wearing patched green plaid knickers waved a newspaper and shouted the headlines to men and women who scurried past in fresh-pressed business attire and stylish hats. Even the street sweeper looked dapper in his crisp white uniform and cap. From an open window across the street, the tentative do-re-mi of musical scales rang out; a piano lesson was underway. Directly under the window was a high-backed shoe-shine stand—a three-seater made of solid oak—with three jackets on hangers dangling from brass hooks on one side.

Serval smiled. *Dan the Shoe-Shine Man . . . And he's got himself a full house.* Dan moved like a young dancer from one shoe to the next, and his brushes and rags were a blur of motion. The only thing that gave away his age was a row of wiry white curls peeking out from under his black leather cap, which he always wore backwards when he worked. Suddenly, Dan's rapid movements came to a stop, and his three customers leaned forward. He brandished his brushes high in the air, and Serval held back the laugh he felt rising. *Here comes the punchline . . .* The raucous laughter exploded in the air like confetti at a parade, and the high-backed shoe-shine stand rocked precariously with the concerted glee of three full-grown, well-dressed gentlemen. Serval laughed as if he had heard the joke himself, and pulled up to the curb. "It was a dirty one, wasn't it, Dan?" he shouted.

Dan leaned down to peer into the car window, then stepped back, straightened his cap, and bowed from the waist. Serval chuckled as he drove away with the snorting laughs and shouts of "Tell another one, Dan!" fading behind him.

Two blocks up, Serval was forced to slow to a crawl, stuck between an ice wagon and a Model-T, but he didn't mind. He soaked up the sweet sound of the horses' hooves clip-clopping along, with the old wagon wheels squeaking in rhythm behind them, until a series of wheezing horn blasts from the Model-T broke in. As the ice wagon pulled over to let the Model-T pass, a familiar noise rumbled in Serval's ears. . . . *Like a giant rolltop desk opening,* he thought. He pressed the accelerator until he reached the end of the block and saw old Mr. Sampson hoisting up the heavy door of his corner market. His three sons were close behind, opening crates containing oranges, bananas, and apples and arranging them at the edge of the sidewalk to tempt passersby.

Serval leaned out the window and waved. "Good morning, Mr. Sampson!"

Mr. Sampson squinted over his eyeglasses at Serval, and broke into a smile. "Aww, hey now, that's that Rivard boy, ain't it?" he shouted. "How' you doin', boy? You jus' gettin' back into town?"

"Yes, sir," Serval answered.

"Well, you come by and see us 'fo ya leave out again, ya hear? And say hello to the folks."

Serval opened his mouth to explain his circumstances, but the words died in his throat. Besides, Mr. Sampson was occupied with a delivery of fresh fish. Serval smiled. "Goodbye, Mr. Sampson," he whispered.

By the time he reached 135th Street, Serval made up his mind to postpone his business for awhile, and take a walk. After a few minutes on foot, he realized his need to memorize Harlem—to mentally photograph and record the sights and sounds exclusively found within its narrow parameters. He stopped at a newsstand to peruse its offerings—the distinctive banner of *The Amsterdam News; The Opportunity*, the voice of the Urban League. Serval smiled when he saw the familiar decorative lettering of Dr. DuBois's paper, *The Crisis*. He couldn't picture his father without a neatly folded copy in his hand. He scanned the cover story of A. Phillip Randolph's *Messenger* and its subtitle: "The Only Radical Magazine Published by Negroes." *Give 'em hell, Mr. Randolph.* He checked to make sure that the UNIA newspaper *The Negro World* was prominently displayed, then moved down to the book section.

"Langston Hughes is selling like hotcakes," the merchant said as he straightened a row of magazines.

"I've practically got that memorized," Serval said, reaching for a book in the back row. "But what do you hear about this new one—*Harlem Shadows*?

"Oh, that's Claude McKay's collection. I highly recommend it."

Serval extended his hand. "Sold. Thanks, uh . . ."

"Oh. I'm Cal. Cal Harris."

"And I'm Serval Rivard. Thanks for the tip, Cal. I'm going on a long trip, and I'll need something inspiring to read. But listen, you don't by any chance carry anything by a poet by the name of Edna St. Vincent Millay, do you?"

Cal reached behind a stack of thin books and retrieved a small journal. "Well, I mostly carry the works of Negro poets, but I happen to be an admirer of Miss Millay. So . . . is this what you had in mind?"

Serval reached for the book and began flipping through the pages. "Yes! But there was one poem in particular . . . Here it is. I'll take this one too, Cal."

"That'll be one twenty five."

Serval paid for the books, and smiled at Cal. "Thanks a lot, man."

"Hey, come by again sometime, Serval. I'm always getting new titles in."

Serval's smile faded. "Well . . . maybe. You take care, Cal."

"You too. Have a good trip."

Serval strolled along slowly, flipping through pages and reading random passages from the books. By the time he looked up, he was standing in front of James Van Der Zee's photographic studio. He lingered near the front window gazing at the images of formal wedding parties, pulsing street scenes, and portraits with eyes that spoke to him. The spell was broken by two little ebony-skinned girls dressed in identical white pinafores, who ran past him in a swirl of lace, hair ribbons, and giggles.

"Rachel!" a woman's voice called. "Rose! You two stop running this instant!"

Serval took off his hat when the woman hurried past him to the entrance of Van Der Zee's studio. "Good afternoon," he said.

"Oh, my! I'm sorry if my girls bumped into you, sir," the woman said, nodding at him as she pulled off her beige gloves.

"Not at all."

She sighed and shook her head. "They're here to have their picture made, and if I don't hurry, I'm afraid they'll be a couple of nappy ragamuffins. Rose! Rachel! Get over here right now!"

The two girls ran over, breathless and losing hair ribbons. Serval smiled as he watched their mother fuss with their hair and smooth eyebrows with a tongue-moistened thumb. Braids were straightened and sashes were retied into perky bows, and at last, the girls stood at the studio door looking like twin dolls. Serval let out a long whistle. "That's gonna be a beautiful picture, ma'am."

The mother smiled back at him as she opened the door. "Thank you, sir. It's going to be a gift for their Dad this Father's Day."

"I'm sure he'll love it. Bye, Rachel. Bye, Rose."

"Bye!" the girls called.

Serval put on his hat and headed up the street, feeling a sudden urge to visit every shop and speak to every Harlem resident. *There's so much I'll miss . . .*

Serval quickened his pace and scoured Harlem like an explorer— up 135th Street, down 137th; across Fifth Avenue; cutting through alleys, between buildings, and back again. Memories played on every sidewalk, floated above his head, and jumped out at him from corners. The YMCA—his second home during high school. The manicured grounds of Harlem Hospital. The "White Only" signs outside Connie's Inn and the Cotton Club were answered by the "All Welcome" elegance of the Renaissance Ballroom and Casino. But Leroy's up the street thumbed its nose at all the nonsense with a prominently displayed "Negroes Only" sign.

Another sign posted in front of the 135th Street Branch of the New York Library announced "The Literary Event of the Year!—The Records of a Race in Literature, History, Art and Science—Grand Opening of the Department of Negro History Literature and Art."

Serval stopped at the foot of the wide entry steps to the hulking National Guard Armory for the 369th Regiment and stared up at the carved lettering above the ornate archway. He thought of Joseph Winfield, Red, and Jimmy Coles, and all the Harlem men who had never seen the grand new armory dedicated in their honor.

When he reached the UNIA offices he considered going inside, but hung back when the front door opened, and two men he had never met walked down the steps, engaged in excited dialogue. Serval took a few steps back, then turned and walked away slowly, already feeling like a foreigner in Harlem.

*  *  *

The afternoon was nearly over by the time he arrived at Nathaniel Washington's office. He rushed through the door, nearly bumping into him.

"I'm sorry I'm so late, Nat. You weren't leaving, were you?"

"Actually, I was stepping out to see if you were lurking around anywhere."

"Aww, I'm sorry I kept you waiting. I was—I guess I was saying goodbye to Harlem."

Nat smiled. "Must've been hard. Have a seat."

"Thanks. Yes, it was harder than I ever imagined. But I know your time's precious, so let's get to business. Listen, I really appreciate you handling this for me."

"Well, it's not my area of expertise, but my fiance is studying tax and estate law, and between the two of us, I think we can manage. So you said on the telephone that you have a trust fund . . .?"

"Yes. I'd like to have the rent on the apartment paid out of that. And there's a life insurance policy too . . . I've spoken to my father, and he's arranged to have all the paperwork sent to you. If you can just draw something up that'll take care of Opal—you know, provide some kind of monthly stipend or whatever you want to call it. Look, it's important to me that she's taken care of."

Nat sighed and leaned back in his chair. "I'm so sorry to hear about you and Opal. You two seemed so . . . Oh, look, I apologize. That's none of my business, so let's get back your arrangements. Do you have a central office or residence where I can contact you in Liberia?"

"Yes. I have everything right here . . ." Serval reached inside his brown satchel and retrieved a clipped stack of papers. "I drafted a breakdown of anticipated expenses, and here's the address I'd like things sent to."

Nat reached across the desk for the papers, then nodded as he scanned the first page. "Well, you've made my job easier. I'll need you to sign a power of attorney."

"Of course."

"Will you be shipping the Pierce-Arrow?"

"No, actually I'll be giving that to Opal. She has her father's car, but I figure she can sell the Pierce-Arrow for a good price. Maybe you could help her with that."

"I'd be happy to. Will you be in town for awhile in case I have any questions?"

"Only today. My train leaves for Atlanta tomorrow at noon."

Nat shook his head slowly. "That's right, I read where Mr. Garvey's being incarcerated in Atlanta. So you're going to visit him?"

"Yes. But I'm also scheduled to speak at a big support rally the local UNIA chapter is planning down there, so I'll be in Atlanta for a couple of days."

"And then you'll be back here to catch your boat?"

"No, actually this is my last visit to Harlem. I'm sailing out of Charleston, so that'll be my last stop after Atlanta." Serval rubbed his eyes and sighed. "My first time on a commercial ocean liner. Guess I don't have to tell you I won't be travelling first class."

"Oh, that's right. I read in the newspaper about the ships . . . Losing the shipping line must've been quite a blow to Mr. Garvey. Those ships were his pride and joy."

Serval nodded and stared at the space above Nat's head. "I read a very unflattering article the last time I was in Charleston. No, it was beyond unflattering—it was insulting. Called the Frederick Douglass 'Garvey's Folly.' Oh, well. I guess they were just old steamer ships, but they meant a lot more to us—a concrete symbol of everything, I guess. 'Cause when I stood on the deck of that ship, it wasn't just a dream. Everything was possible."

"I guess it'll be sort of bittersweet," Nat said softly.

"What?"

"Well, you'll be living the dream. I mean, there's only a small group of you going, but as you said, it's symbolic. When you sail away to Africa, you become the embodiment of the exodus of the entire Negro race. But the irony is that instead of arriving on a Black Star ship, you've got to make the passage on a white-owned commercial liner."

"Yeah. I get the irony. But you're wrong about it being bittersweet. It's just bitter. Damn bitter."

Nat smiled. "I know how dedicated you are, Serval. The results of your hard work—that'll be the sweet part."

"Thanks, Nat. Thanks for everything. Oh, there's just one last thing . . ."

"Name it."

"Actually, it's two. If it wouldn't be too much trouble . . . could you check on Opal from time to time—without being too obvious about it? Just a friendly visit. You see, I think she may be wanting to file for divorce once I'm gone awhile, and maybe you can help her find somebody who's good."

"You mean you haven't . . ."

Serval shrugged. "I couldn't file for divorce. I'll let her do it—when she's ready."

"And the other?"

"Huh?"

"You said there were two things."

"Oh, yes. If you wouldn't mind, could you write me now and then to let me know how she is? Even after the divorce? It's very important to me that she's all right."

"I understand, Serval. You can count on me."

*    *    *

When Serval stepped outside, his shadow was long on the sidewalk. *It's late. I can't put off sayin' goodbye to Mama any longer.* He hurried back to Lenox Avenue, but stopped to take one more look around before climbing into his car. *Next stop—Striver's Row.*

*    *    *

Serval was puzzled when Kathryn took a seat to his left that night at the long dining table. For as long as he could remember, Serval had sat in the center chair between his mother at one end, and his father at the other.

"I'll say grace tonight, Charles," Kathryn announced.

Charles nodded. "Of course, my dear."

Serval stared at them both, but said nothing.

Kathryn gripped his left hand with her right, and lowered her head. "Dear Lord," she said, "You have seen fit in your infinite wisdom to bless me with only one son. And you have made him a hardheaded son, Lord—a son who has gone out into the world—too often and too long for my tastes. You have given me a son who has butted his head against his father's hard head at every turn, and you know that these two fools have been the reason for many a headache for me, your humble daughter. And now, Lord, my son has decided to live his life in a land as far away as Africa. Now, you know I have questioned you on all this in the past, and it's not until today that I have found my understanding. The son that was born of my body is not my possession, but my greatest blessing. He has the courage of ten men, and the kindness of my own sweet mother and my grandmother, God rest their souls. He has the intelligence of a whole classroom of A-students, and my God, he has such vision! My husband knows this, Lord, although only you know why he won't admit it—not out loud anyway. You have given my son a job to do, and maybe only you and he know the dangers involved and the glorious victory he will achieve through this work. So I guess what I've learned, Lord, is that it's not the quantity of children one receives, or the easy rearing of a child that counts . . . it's the child himself. He was worth all the headaches, Lord, so I have to thank you for giving me this time with such a son . . . even if I never see him again."

She leaned forward and gazed at Charles with clear, dry eyes, and he smiled back at her. "Well said, my dear," he murmured. "Oh, I mean—amen."

"Oh, and Lord," Kathryn added, "Thank you for the food too."

Serval couldn't raise his head, and blinked as a teardrop fell onto his thigh. Kathryn squeezed his left hand with her right, and then picked up her fork with her left. Serval smiled broadly and squeezed back. "You plan to hold my hand all through dinner, Mama?"

"I'm left-handed and you're right-handed, Serval, so it works no hardship on you. I may be willing to let you go off into the world, but I'm not letting go until absolutely necessary. Now eat your vegetables."

\* \* \*

The next morning Serval was up before the sun. He had two difficult goodbyes to deal with before his noon train departed—Leon and Opal.

The street was dark and deserted when he stepped outside. Fishing out the key Ernest had given him, Serval locked the front door. As he walked down the steps, he smiled at the silhouette of his Pierce-Arrow. *One last spin around New York, huh, car? Just you and me.*

*   *   *

Serval stood at the front door of what had formerly been his home, and poised his fist to knock. *It's too early. I knew it was too early. She's still asleep.* After quietly pacing in front of the stoop for several minutes, Serval strode out to his car, climbed inside and turned on the small interior lamp. Reaching into his satchel, he pulled out a pen and paper and began writing:

> *Dear Opal,*
>
> *I don't know where to begin. I stood outside intending to knock, but it's still dark and I know you're asleep. Besides, the last time we were together was too painful for a repeat performance.*
>
> *I've made arrangements for the rent to be paid, and you will be receiving monthly checks starting on the first of June. Call Nathaniel Washington if you have any questions. He's handling everything. Please say goodbye to Jack for me. I was going to leave him a note with one of the Pullman supervisors at Grand Central, but, as I said, I don't know where to begin. For a man who usually has so much to say, I seem to be at a loss these days.*
>
> *There's just one last piece of business I must address. I want you to sell the Pierce-Arrow. I have one more stop to make before my train leaves, and then I'll leave the car at the parking garage on 42nd Street. (Jack knows where it is.) I'll leave the key with the attendant, and pay the ticket in advance. All Jack has to do is pick it up when he has time. Nat will help you with the sale arrangements.*
>
> *I know it must seem the height of audacity, but I must ask you to do me a favor, Opal. Please try to forgive me, and try to be happy. Love, Serval.*

Without re-reading what he had written, Serval sprinted up the steps. Folding the paper lengthwise, he slipped it into the mailbox so that the top third was plainly visible, then hurried back toward the street. He climbed into his car and rested his head against the steering wheel. *You're a goddamn coward, Serval Rivard.* Looking back at the building, he prayed to see a front light go on, but the windows remained dark. "Oh, well . . ." he whispered. "Next stop—Sing Sing."

*   *   *

Serval waited for nearly an hour before Leon was brought to the visitor's table. He stood up and stepped into Leon's arms for a long, emotional embrace. "God, Leon," he whispered. "I can't tell you how good it is to see you."

"Aww, son, it's mighty good to see you too! Been a long time! Set ya'self down here and tell me what's been goin' on in the world."

"I will, I will. But first let's talk about you. You're lookin' a lot better than the last time I saw you, Leon. Are you doin' all right in here?"

Leon shrugged. "Good as I can, son. Good as I can."

"Well, you're a tough man, Leon, I'll tell you that. Listen . . . I came to see you because, uh . . . see, I'm leavin' tonight on another trip and . . ."

Leon shook his head and smiled. "Guess you' gonna be cuttin' down on them trips pretty soon, huh? Ya know, with Opal's time comin' and all."

Serval blinked at him in confusion. "Uh, Opal's—what?"

"Her time, boy. The baby!"

Serval leaned back in his chair, sure that he had misunderstood. "Baby?" he said. ". . . Did you say—*baby?*"

Leon's eyes widened. "You mean you ain't heard . . . Good Lawd, boy! What the hell kind'a nonsense you two got goin' on in that marriage a'yours? Now, why wouldn't Opal tell you that you' gonna be a Daddy? Shoot! You should'a been the one tellin' me, 'stead'a the other way 'round! Now ain't that right?"

Serval nodded dumbly. "Things have been—well, things haven't been so good between us lately, Leon. . . . Uh, look, Leon?" he murmured.

Holding up one hand, Leon smiled and stood up. "I understand, son. Don'tchu worry 'bout me. You got mo' important things to do. Like straightenin' out that child a'mine 'bout how you really feel. And you put all that man-pride on the back shelf, you hear me, son? You two got to patch things up 'fo my grandbaby gets here."

*   *   *

As Serval raced back to Harlem, his mind was a jumble of ecstasy and painful insecurity. *Why didn't she tell me? . . . Maybe she tried but she couldn't locate me. But she could've gotten word to me through the office. They would've tracked me down . . . Oh, damn! What if she doesn't want*

*me back? After the way I left her . . . and she didn't want a baby yet. God,*
*please don't let her be too disappointed . . .*

Pulling his car up in front of Ernest's apartment, he ran up the steps
and unlocked the door. He unbuttoned his shirt on the way to the bathroom, and nervously began to rehearse what he would say. "Opal . . .
Uh, Opal, I visited your father this morning and . . . No, stupid! If you
say that, then she'll think that you're only comin' back because of the
baby." He sighed and filled the tub for a relaxing, mind-clearing soak.

*       *       *

The last streaks of sunset had just disappeared from the sky when Serval
climbed the foyer steps to Opal's apartment for the second time that day.
Glancing at the mailbox, he noticed that his note was gone and suddenly
heard two distant but familiar voices in low conversation: Jack and
Opal. As Serval debated about whether or not to knock, the voices suddenly fell silent. Curious, he leaned down to peer into the front window,
and discovered the reason for the abrupt break in the conversation. His
best friend and his wife were locked in an intimate kiss. Serval couldn't
move, and listened in stunned silence when they resumed their talk.

"Don't worry 'bout anything," Jack was saying. "I'm here. I'ma always be here."

"But Jack, I—I just can't believe he could leave without seein' me,
with nothin' but a note—a note about his car!"

"I know him, Opal. He jus' couldn't face sayin' goodbye, that's all.
You know he ain't never meant to hurt you."

Opal gazed up at Jack with a look of adoration that stung Serval
more deeply than the kiss he had just witnessed.

"I don't know what I'da done without you, Jack," she whispered,
stretching up on tiptoes for another kiss. As Jack gathered Opal tightly
in his arms again, Serval gritted his teeth, suddenly unable to take any
more. Opening the foyer door, he strode down the hallway to the apartment. He knocked sharply on the door, then opened it.

Opal gasped when she saw Serval. Jack lowered his head and closed
his eyes. Serval stepped closer, staring and waiting to see who would be
the first to speak.

To his surprise, Serval heard his own voice break the silence. "Don't
feel guilty—either one of you." He paused and shrugged his shoulders.
"Just like Jack said, Opal, I never meant to hurt you, but—I know that
neither one of you meant to hurt me, either." He managed a smile.

"But Serval . . ." Opal began.

Serval held up his hand and shook his head. "Let me finish—please? I—I'm sorry we couldn't make it work, Opal. And I don't blame you for turning to Jack. I did everything to push you away, and if I'm alone, it's nobody's fault but my own." His eyes drifted to Opal's midsection, which she quickly covered with her hand. "Just—hold on to Jack, Opal. He's a good man and he deserves a good woman. I know all this sounds strange but—I guess we're livin' in strange times. I guess people have just got to hold onto whatever happiness they can get while they try to survive. Just remember that I love you forever in my heart. And about the baby . . ."

Opal gasped, and Jack's eyes met Serval's. "It's yours, Serval. The baby is *your* child."

Serval nodded. "I believe you, Jack."

"How—how'd you know about . . .?" Opal whispered.

"It doesn't matter, Opal," he whispered. "It's too late now anyway. Just do one thing for me. Tell—tell my boy that the work I'm doin'—is for him . . ." He smiled. ". . . or her, if it's a daughter."

He glanced once more at Jack before aiming his gaze back at Opal. "One kiss?"

Opal looked up at Jack, and her voice caught as she whispered, "I—I need a minute."

Jack nodded, turned his back, and lit a cigarette as he headed for the kitchen.

Serval opened his arms and felt Opal pressing herself tightly against him. He stroked her hair and rested his chin on the top of her head. "Don't forget me, baby. Don't forget the best parts—the good days we had." He held her for a moment longer, then eased away from her and nudged her toward the kitchen. "Hey, Jack."

Jack walked back in and stood next to Opal, his eyes fixed on Serval's. Serval nodded and smiled at them, then quietly slipped out the door. He took the stairs quickly, and didn't look back until he reached his car, which was parked across the street. When he turned, he saw Opal's face at the window. He froze for a moment, straining to hear her voice calling him back, but the only sound breaking the silence was the faint whistle of a train somewhere in the distant night. He watched her as she inclined her head to the left and then to the right. *She can't see me.* An involuntary shiver ran through Serval's body. It was as if the night had suddenly swallowed him.

# Chapter 41

After a long day of traveling, followed by a planning meeting with Atlanta's last remaining UNIA loyalists in the Thompsons' living room, Serval retired to his regular room in the back of the house. Hearing a tap on the door, he sighed. "Come in."

Lena Thompson opened the door and peeked in. "Just checkin' on you, Mr. Rivard. Anything I can get for you?"

Serval smiled. "Miz Lena, I'd really appreciate it if you'd just call me Serval. And to answer your question—no. As usual, you've anticipated my every need—pitcher of water by the bed, clean sheets and plenty of towels for my bath in the morning."

"Well, then. You get yourself some sleep. You got a lot'a folks to educate tomorrow. We're all lookin' forward to your speech. Oh, and Mr. Garvey told Jasper during his visit yesterday that he'll be wantin' a full report on what you got to say. He's got a lot'a faith in you, Mr. Rivard."

"Well, then. I guess I'd better finish up with my work and get to bed."

"All right. I'll wake you up about seven-thirty. You just holler if you need anything, Mr. Rivard. Good night."

"Good night."

Sitting down at the small corner desk, Serval rubbed his eyes and opened his journal to make a brief entry:

*May 17, 1925. Arrived in Atlanta to small gathering at the home of Lena and Jasper Thompson. General unrest and anger over Garvey's incarceration, but at least no one quit this time. Tired but hopeful about tomorrow's speech. Ernest predicts a good turnout, but he's a die-hard optimist. Looking forward to visit with Mr. Garvey, and anticipating his usual inspirational talk. With luck, should make Charleston in plenty of time for departure to Africa.*

He closed the journal, then sat thinking for a moment. Reopening the journal, he made another entry:

*In five days, I am scheduled to sail thousands of miles away from my beloved Harlem, in all likelihood, never to return. My best friend is in love with my wife, and apparently, she feels the same way about him. And now, as I stand in the wreckage of my failed marriage, fatherhood looms.*

Serval stared at the pen resting on the paper and waited for more words to flow from it. When the pen began to move, he felt a great quaking inside, as if his whole being would shatter.

*I think of Jimmy Coles more than ever now . . .*

Serval continued writing in a rapid scrawl, his normally neat handwriting spoiled by his shaking hand. When he finished, he dropped the pen and read his entry twice. The shaking in his hand had stopped, but he was suddenly overcome by exhaustion. He took off his shirt and walked across the room toward the bed, but was stopped in his tracks by the sight of his reflection in the dresser mirror. Leaning closer, he stared at himself and was reminded of a similar moment of self-scrutiny several years before. *It's my eyes that are different.* As he peered into the blackness of his own eyes, a rush of memories flew by in no logical order. He was sitting with Opal in front of Anna Romanov's kitchen stove, bathed in warmth and innocence. *I'm not a child, Serval. I know about what goes on between men and women. It's just that—I guess I never felt it before. Now I understand. Nature just makes you crave each other, huh?* The warm faded to cool, then cold, and he was kneeling in a scatter of dry Autumn leaves holding Jimmy Coles in his arms—smothering in the silent stillness. *So this is death.* He thought of Joseph Winfield, and his smiling face appeared, but quickly faded into a vision of charred trees. Suddenly Serval's view became aerial—he was suspended without form in the fetid air over a battlefield in France to witness Joseph Winfield's last choking breath—a percentage point on a casualty list.

Serval shook the image from his mind, and hurried to a happier place and time: He was seventeen again, standing on the corner of 135th Street and Lenox Avenue, and tingling at a voice that rang with the urgency of a firehouse bell—Marcus Mosiah Garvey calling him to his destiny: *Up, you mighty race!*

The memories began to spin and race, hurrying him. Back to Opal's arms. Back to his parents' dinner table, his mother's hand, warm and reassuring. Back to happy days with Jack—the joy of seeing him at the parade. . . . The parade . . . The lions guarding the New York Public Library. Back to the battlefield—to Red. To the wire. Back to Jimmy Coles' eyes. Opal's eyes . . .

Serval squeezed out the visions and leaned forward until he felt his forehead bump against the mirror. *What's my baby gonna look like? I'll never see my child . . .* His eyes fluttered open, and his breath caught at the sight of his own reflection. Beads of perspiration stood out on his face, and his chest heaved with labored breathing. And he was staring into the familiar eyes of Jimmy Coles.

✻   ✻   ✻

Serval attempted to sleep late on the morning of the rally. He stirred at the sound of Lena shushing the children, and then heard her talking to Ernest as they prepared to leave. When the house was quiet again, Serval drifted back to sleep.

It was 10:00. a.m. when Jasper tapped on the door. "Mr. Rivard? Time to be gettin' up now."

Serval sat up. "Come in, Jasper."

Jasper came in carrying a cup of steaming coffee. "Here ya go. Thought this might help. Lena and Ernest done lef' hours ago to set things up with the committee. You and me can be a little late. I figured you could use a little extra sleep."

"Thanks, Jasper. I'll be ready in no time."

✻   ✻   ✻

Serval worked on his speech as Jasper's old Ford bumped along the road leading to town. "Hey, Jasper," he said, tapping his pencil against the paper. "I'm stuck on sump'm here."

"What'cha say, Mr. Rivard?" Jasper shouted. "I can't hear over Lizzie's chuggin'. You' gonna haf'ta holler."

Serval nodded. "Remember last night when Lena was talking about her grandmother being a slave? I was tryin' to make this very specific connection to . . ."

Suddenly, the engine sputtered and fell silent.

"Aww, hell!" Jasper groaned as he climbed out of the car.

"What happened?" Serval asked.

Jasper slid up the engine cover, and a swirl of black smoke rose into the air. "Overheated. Lawd, Mr. Rivard," Jasper said, "I sho' am sorry 'bout this. But listen, we got time before the rally starts. We'll just stop awhile and get some water into this ol' heap, and we'll still get there in plenty of time."

"Well, I was hopin' to spend some time with Mr. Garvey before the rally to check a few points with him. Look, Jasper—maybe I could just walk the rest of the way and meet you there. 'Cause you're right about lettin' that engine cool off, and I know you don't want to leave your car sittin' on the road."

Jasper squinted back at Serval and shrugged. "In that nice white suit you got on? Shoot, Mr. Rivard—now you know that ain't a good idea. It's still a long stretch into town, and ain't nothin' looks worse than a wilted use'ta-be-white suit jacket wit' sweat stains under the arms. You' the main speaker. You wanna look fresh."

"Well, I could take off my jacket . . ."

Jasper held up one hand and stepped around to the passenger side. "Look," he said, his voice suddenly grave. "Lemme tell it straight. See this road? This road runs through a section where some'a them Klan fellas live. Now, drivin' through is one thing, but if they see a colored man walkin' 'round in they' neighborhood . . . Well, let's not give 'em no excuses for some'a that Klan nonsense."

"Oh. Understood. Well, then I guess we ought'a find some water. Unless the car runs on lemonade, that is."

Jasper laughed. "My ol' Lizzie's barely hangin' on, Mr. Rivard. Good as my Lena's lemonade is, I think it might jus' kill this heap dead. But ya know—there's a little ol' creek that runs through here somewhere. Lemme empty out that lemonade container and take a look."

"Good idea. Tell you what, Jasper. You look on that side, and I'll check my side over here. If I see anything, I'll give you a shout."

"Awright."

Serval slipped off his jacket and headed in the direction of a patch of green brush, hoping that the vegetation might be evidence of a water source. As he pushed through the branches, he felt a tug and noticed a small hole in the knee of his trousers. "Damn," he muttered. "How the hell . . .?" His complaint was stopped by a sound in the distance— a child's voice singing "Jimmy Cracked Corn."

After taking a few more steps, Serval spotted the singer and smiled— it was a small white boy dragging a jagged stick along the rocky bank of a narrow creek. *Water.* Serval was just about to shout Jasper's name when the boy suddenly stopped singing and squatted at the water's edge, reaching for something.

"Okay, frog," the boy shouted, "Yer mine now!"

But as the fat bullfrog escaped in a long arcing leap, the little boy lunged face-first into the water and began to wail.

Serval hurried toward the edge of the water and did his best not to soil his shoes as he reached for the boy's flailing arms. "Hey, hey! I'll get you out, but don't splash me, okay?"

"Not me! Get my frog, Mister!" the boy shouted.

"Well, you can get him next time."

For the first time the boy glanced back at Serval. His mouth opened in a gasp of shock. "Yer a . . ." He stopped abruptly and took a fearful step backward.

Serval reached for the boy's hand just in time to keep him from falling back into the water. "Careful, now. Now what were you saying? I'm a—what?"

The boy looked at his muddy feet. "Nothin'. Umm—sorry."

Serval hesitated a moment, then extended his hand. *He's only about Sistine's age.* He spoke to the top of the boy's straw-colored head. "Well, since you won't tell me what you think I am, I'll tell you. I'm Serval Rivard and I'm visiting some friends down here. What's your name, Frogman?"

The boy giggled, but didn't look up. "Larry. I like frogs."

"Nice to meet'cha, Larry. I like frogs too. They sure are fun to catch, huh? Tell me—do you let yours go after you catch 'em? Or are you a collecting-type Frogman?"

Larry leaned his head back and squinted up at Serval. "I got me five at home—in a big tub wif' a rock island and everything."

"A rock island? Well, you *are* a collector, huh?"

"Yeah. But I ain't got none big as him," he said, pointing upstream.

"Oh, the one that got away, huh? Well, maybe you'll catch him tomorrow. But be careful, or he might catch you—like he nearly did today."

Larry sighed and tugged at his muddy shirt. "Mama's gonna make me take a bath now, huh?"

"Well, the way you look right now, I think you can count on it, Larry. Sorry. Hey, listen. Speaking of your Mama, does she know you're out here all by yourself?"

"Umm, well, see—I was out here wif Bruce. He's my friend, but he got lost or sump'm."

"Oh, *he* got lost, huh? Well, maybe . . ."

The sound of an angry high-pitched voice startled Serval and he spun around. A heavy-set white woman with dark hair hurried down the rise of high grass toward them.

"What'chu doin' to that child?" she shrieked. Before Serval could react, she reached for Larry and yanked his arm roughly. "Larry! What's your Mama gonna say when I tell her yer out here talkin' to niggers? I been lookin' for you ever since Bruce come home by hisself. Now you git on back to the house right now, boy!"

After sending Larry away with a swat to his rear-end, the woman glared at Serval. "You better git on back to your side'a town, you hear me?"

Serval decided to say nothing as he watched her lumber away. As he trudged back through the tall grass and bushes toward the road, he couldn't stop thinking about the little boy. *In ten years he'll be just like her.*

✻ ✻ ✻

When Jasper and Serval arrived at the old boat house near the 12th Street entrance, Piedmont Park was already overflowing with Atlanta's Negro residents. Ernest smiled and waved at Serval from the gazebo, then hurried down the steps. "I was beginning to worry," he called. "I expected you earlier."

"We ran into a little trouble, Ernest," Serval said.

Alarm registered on Ernest's face. "What kind of trouble?"

Serval patted his shoulder and scanned the crowd gathering around the gazebo. "Only car trouble, so don't worry. Hey, Ernest! Seems your prediction of a good turnout was wrong, wasn't it?"

"What do you mean?"

"This isn't a good turnout. It's great! It looks like the convention again! How in the world did you do it?"

"I thank you for the kind exaggeration, my friend, but I think we're a few hundred short of the convention. But I must say I'm surprised at the turnout myself. From the people I've spoken with, it seems that the tide of sympathy has shifted in Mr. Garvey's favor."

Serval sighed. "At least for the moment."

"Then let's capitalize on the moment while we have it in our grasp. Here. I have the program schedule all typed up for you. Let's go over it."

Serval leaned near Ernest to study the notes on his clipboard, but a vague distraction made him look up. Something was amiss, but his eyes couldn't find it. He nodded at something Ernest was saying, and then felt himself being nudged toward the platform steps. It wasn't until he had arranged his notes on the podium and looked out at the crowd that he spotted the trouble—two white faces standing slightly apart from the dark crowd. The second they caught his eye, he saw the short one cup his hands around his mouth. "Well, well," the man shouted. "If it ain't our old nigger friends from up North."

The people standing in the front turned around, and a buzz of murmuring ran through the crowd.

Ernest groaned. "Oh, God. Not them again."

"Yep," Serval said. "Mac the loudmouth and his friend Silent Sam."

"Who?" Ernest asked.

"Oh, I don't remember his name, Ernest, but he's challenging me to another one of his tiresome staring contests." Serval rolled his eyes, and turned his attention to his notes. "Ignore 'em," he muttered softly. "We've got business to attend to."

But Mac pushed his way through the crowd and raised his voice a few decibels. "They ain't never gonna let'cher big hot-shot Garvey out'a jail—but if they do, we know how to make quick work of his kind."

Ernest started down the steps, and Serval followed him, grabbing for his arm.

"You low-lifes touch one hair on Mr. Garvey's head and you—are—*dead*," Ernest shouted. The crowd fell quiet.

After a slight pause, Mac countered with volume. "Y'all niggers might get away with this shit up North, but things is different here! This is the South, goddammit!"

Ernest opened his mouth, but it was Serval who answered. "I've been to the South before. Now, if you'll excuse us, we have work to do." Giving the two angry white men a full view of his back, Serval calmly climbed up the stairs and approached the podium. He did a quick visual sweep of the crowd, and tried to reassure them with his smile. "Good morning."

"Good morning!" they answered.

He detected a note of hope in their voices and felt a surge of his old confidence. Shooting a look over at L.T. and Mac, who were retreating to the outer fringe of the crowd, Serval rubbed his palms together in anticipation.

"A little more than sixty years ago, some of you were slaves. Many of your parents were slaves, and the majority of your grandparents were slaves. Some of you have relatives who now live up North, having run away from the conditions in the South. I come from such a family. Although my father was the son of a free black man, his grandfather came from these parts. He was one of the few who possessed the courage to escape and the good fortune to make it to his destination. I, myself, have never called anywhere home but Harlem, but I know the South. You might even say I grew up here—and I still carry the sour taste in my mouth."

He paused, as the expected murmurs rumbled through the crowd.

"Wait, wait, now . . . Don't get me wrong. The South is a beautiful part of the country. You and I know this because we grew it, nurtured it, and built it—your ancestors and mine—at the end of whip. But just like an ugly blemish on an otherwise beautiful face, you have the misfortune of living in a region that's the breeding ground for a misguided group of white folks known as the Ku Klux Klan. Now, I know you folks don't need some fella from Harlem standin' up here tellin' you about the Klan, so I won't. I've spoken that unsavory name the one and only time I intend to. And the only reason for it is to point out the foundation for all your confusion these many years. When slavery was outlawed, white folks said, 'There. Now you're free and everything's equal.' But things were never equal. One new law does not pay for hundreds of years of oppression. They never intended things to be equal, any more than they intended to give you forty acres and a mule. They opened up the gates of their plantations and looked at you standing there—with no money, no education, no language or religion of your own, no dignity, no roots, and most significantly, no *land*."

He paused to let the word "land" sink in, then continued. "And they said, 'Now. You're free. Go make something of yourself.' But they didn't send you away empty-handed. Oh, no. They gave you words to live by: spoken and unspoken—like 'Jim Crow'—and words painted on signs, like 'white only.' But the most damaging thing they did was to make you hate yourself. And you do, you know."

Rumbles of protest rose from the crowd.

"No? How many of you would like to be a shade or two lighter than you are? How many of you refer to tight, nappy hair as 'bad hair' and soft, wavy hair as 'good hair'?" He smiled. "Don't lie, now. How many of you young ladies are thinking, 'Hmm. The speaker might be a handsome fella if he just wasn't so doggone *dark!*'"

At last, a laugh.

"All right. I know that many of you are Garveyites—still Garveyites, despite the difficulties of the past year. And to those folks, I apologize. I know you've been loyal to Mr. Garvey's philosophy. That's what I really want to talk to you about today. For those of you who don't understand the nobility of your heritage, Mr. Garvey's words are necessary. His vision will help you to see things clearer. It's true that the Black Star Line failed—and many of you lost your investments. The white-owned newspapers would have you believe that Mr. Garvey is the sole responsible party, but we all know the way they slant their opinions. I'm here today to tell you about the man I know—the man they've locked up, not for the charges they claim—white men get away with more grievous offenses and never see the inside of a jail. Think about it. When has the misfortune of the black man been of any interest to the white man? None of the investors in the Black Star Line were white. The injured parties in this business failure were Negro investors. No, Mr. Garvey's crime was his philosophy. They consider him a dangerous man—not for how much money Black Star investors lost, but for instilling pride and dignity in the hearts of Negro people. And that's why we cannot abandon him now."

The emotion of the crowd was palpable, and Serval answered it with the most effective words he knew: "Up! You mighty race!" he shouted. "You can accomplish what you will!"

A roaring cheer went up from the crowd, and Serval stepped back to smile at Ernest, who was giving him a thumbs-up signal from the left side of the platform. When the crowd quieted, Serval continued in a somber tone. "Of course, I don't achieve the same effect as Mr. Garvey does when he says it. Those are *his* words. He believes in you. Believe in him. A man doesn't give his whole life to his people just so he can swindle them. And just how has he swindled anyone? The man is penniless! The worst that can be said about Mr. Garvey is that he is not the world's greatest businessman—at least not in the shipping industry, which is one of the most competitive industries around. Many people warned Mr. Garvey not to engage in the shipping business, but he forged ahead because it was a necessary part of his dream—the dream you've heard so much about—the dream of returning to Mother Africa." Serval paused when his voice broke with emotion. "The—the dream might not be possible—just now. But while we wait, the global unification of people of African descent goes on. It can't be stopped just because one man is behind bars. We will continue to make alliances with our oppressed brothers and sisters in Jamaica, Cuba, Panama, and, of course, Africa. That's what Mr. Garvey meant when he said, 'Africa for the Africans—at home and abroad.' We don't have to actually live in Africa to work hand-in-hand with her people. We can send representatives of our own and welcome African delegates here. Communication is the key. We must begin to think of ourselves as a large part of the world, not a small part of the South or of Harlem. I am a perfect example, on a smaller scale. I have worked in your community as a Harlem emissary, to bring you the news from the North and bring back your views and ideas. But this trip is different. Instead of my being the courier of your voices back to Harlem, this time I'll be carrying them much farther— all the way to Africa."

He smiled and waited for the excited buzz to die down. "We may not all be able to go back to Africa, but I have been chosen to be a—kind of ambassador for our people. And your own Lena and Jasper Thompson will welcome our African guests to America. Through correspondence and growth of the UNIA, the free exchange of ideas, cultural and political, we will forge a solid connection with the Motherland. I must admit I'll miss Harlem, the only home I've ever known, just as you would miss the South if you left it. But we've got to get it into our heads that America has never been our true home. Africa is home. And even though there are battles to be waged there, just like here, we of the UNIA believe that our place is with the Africans, fighting shoulder to shoulder with them for a unified Africa. If all the stolen children return, then black Africa will prevail!"

The deafening cheer rolled into a rhythmic pulse that had a name: *Gar-vey, Gar-vey, Gar-vey, Gar-vey* . . . Serval's eyes were drawn to something above, and he smiled; the thunder of voices seemed to ride on the wings of the birds scattering in all directions from the surrounding trees. *Gar-vey, Gar-vey, Gar-vey, Gar-vey* . . . It went on for nearly five minutes, until Serval raised his hands for quiet, then continued.

"Because of recent setbacks, our progress has been impeded— impeded but not stopped. The dream of Africa remains the cornerstone of the UNIA, and no matter how long it takes, we must hold on and never lose sight of it. But in the meantime, life in America goes on. Life in Harlem goes on, and life in the South goes on. So I must speak for a minute about making things better for our people while we work toward Africa. The solution is to apply the same global efforts I've been speaking about to the local front. It would be an easy thing for folks in Harlem to sit back and enjoy our community without giving the troubles of our folks in the South a second thought. Many of you have visited Harlem and know that it's a wonderful place to live. Our culture, our music, or, as some of our 'New Negro' writers and poets would say, our 'Negritude' is thriving in Harlem. But that would be isolating ourselves from our own brothers and sisters. Not that the practice of lynching is unheard of in the North—it happens there, too. Unfortunately, when it comes to Jim Crow ideas, we're quite similar to the South, only we call our Mason-Dixon Line '110th Street.' But back to the barbaric practice of lynching—in the South, it seems to have become an epidemic. I don't have to tell you the statistics—already over sixty lynchings this year alone, and those are only the *reported* incidents. We all know that the majority of these murders go unreported because of the threatening presence of the local do-nothing law enforcement officials, who are usually card-carrying members of that gang of bedsheet-wearing cowards, themselves. There are many lynchings that are never reported. Many dead men and women whose stories have never been told . . . They lump them together as a number—a statistic."

Serval stopped and closed his eyes. He heard the murmurs of the crowd, but remained silent until he felt Ernest's hand on his shoulder. "Serval?" he whispered.

Serval nodded and looked up. Turning his head completely to his right, he drilled a defiant stare into L.T. Sullivan's eyes. "Join the UNIA and this *will* stop. Unity is the only possible solution—a strong network, South and North, East and West, working within the boundaries of this plantation called America, and growing stronger all over the world. Remember, we are only a minority in America. From a global viewpoint, the dark races are the *majority*."

Serval pounded the podium with his fist, and shouted to be heard above the cheering: "They've been trying to annihilate us for hundreds of years! But here we are! Standing tall, unbent, and proud. We are truly, as Mr. Garvey says, a *mighty* race of people!"

As the crowd applauded, Serval again met the angry gaze of the two white men. He smiled, then turned back to the crowd and raised his arms in a conductor's gesture to lead the chant: *Gar-vey, Gar-vey, Gar-vey, Gar-vey . . .*

\* \* \*

For nearly an hour after the rally ended, Mac ranted about Serval's speech. "Did'ya see them uppity goddamn niggers, L.T.?" he sputtered. "Lookin' down their noses at us like they was better than us! And all that sumbitch done was stir 'em up more! Back to Africa! Shit, I'll send his black ass back to Africa—in a *box!*"

"Calm down, Mac," L.T. growled. "And slow this gotdamn truck down! Yer bouncin' my brains out on this bumpy road. Look, all them troublemakers'll be gone in a couple'a days. And you know how these niggers 'round these parts are—lazy and shiftless. They'll forget all this nonsense in a week or two."

"But what if they don't? Gotdamn, L.T.! I can't stand no nigger lookin' at me like he's my better!"

L.T. shrugged. "They'll settle down, Mac. And if they don't, then we'll settle 'em down—our way. Hey, where' you goin'? Here's yer house."

"Thought you wanted to go on home? I was gonna drop ya, L.T."

"Now, ain't you said you got some beer in the cooler at home? I need to numb up some 'fore I go home to that hag I done married."

Mac stopped the truck and hopped out. "Well, come on in then."

After drinking three glasses of beer, L.T. was too annoyed to listen to any more of Mac's commentary about the rally. "I'm tired, Mac. Come on. Take me home."

"Aw, L.T., relax awhile."

L.T. stood up and glared impatiently at Mac. "Look, I'm awready in a bad mood and it's almost Little Larry's bedtime. Now, I done told you I ain't seen him since yesterday, so you gonna take me or do I haf'ta walk?"

"Awright, awright, L.T. Jus' lemme pour ma'self another glass for the road."

\* \* \*

When the truck rounded the corner to his house, L.T. saw a crowd of people overflowing from his front porch onto the dirt yard. He jumped out of the truck before it had come to a complete stop and called over his shoulder, "Don't leave, Mac. Sump'm must be wrong."

"Right behind ya, L.T."

L.T. strode across the yard and pushed open the front screen door. As he stepped inside, he comprehended something dreadful in the blur of faces in the room. "What happened?" he shouted.

Ellen sobbed incoherently, and the others stared without answering.

L.T. suddenly felt the hairs on the back of his neck stand on end. Grabbing Ellen roughly, he hissed, "Where's my boy?"

He was answered by another sob—louder this time.

Shoving her aside, L.T. strode down the hallway and into Little Larry's room.

"Boy?" But his voice only echoed the emptiness.

Returning to the front room, he screamed at the frozen faces, "Got-dammit! Where's my boy?!"

Ellen sank to her knees and screamed, "He's dead!"

L.T.'s left eye twitched, then he shook his head.

"He's dead, L.T.!" Ellen screamed again. "Awww, God, ain'tchu hearin' me? They—they took him away! They took my baby away . . ."

Before she could finish, L.T. slapped her with the back of his hand. "You gotdamn lyin' *bitch!* Where's my *boy?!*"

For the first time he identified one of the faces as his brother Charlie. He was saying something in a low, indulgent tone as he sheltered Ellen with his arms. L.T. stared at him until the sounds became words. "Don't hit her no more, L.T.," Charlie said. "She ain't lyin'. We found the boy down by that ol' creek. You know where he was always goin' frog catchin' with his little friend?"

Adele McVey took a timid step forward. "My Bruce," she said. "He was playin' with my Bruce today, but every time I turned around he was sneakin' off to that doggone creek, L.T. After I dragged him back that last time—caught him down there talkin' to that fancy nigger, and I told that boy . . ."

"What fancy nigger?" L.T. growled.

Adele stepped back. "I—I ain't sure, L.T., but I think it was that Garvey nigger that's been stayin' out there with Lena and Jasper Thompson—the one always handin' out them flyers and things to the niggers in town. But I ran him off, L.T. Little Larry was okay then . . . but he wandered back down there, and that's when he got bit . . ."

L.T. made a lunge for the front door, but Charlie stopped him. "A snake, L.T.! It was a snake bit him—a water moccasin or sump'm. There wasn't nothin' nobody could do. We didn't find him in time."

L.T. stared at him. "A—a *snake?*"

"I'm sorry, L.T. You know how many of them damn snakes there are down by that creek."

Adele dabbed at her nose with a handkerchief. "Can't watch them kids every minute, L.T. It could'a been Bruce. I'm so sorry."

L.T. shot a confused look at Adele and then at Charlie before pushing through the front screen door and striding in the direction of Mac's truck. Yanking the passenger door open, he climbed in and stared at the windshield.

Mac climbed in on the other side and grabbed the steering wheel. "L.T.?"

"Drive," L.T. said.

Mac blinked at him. "Drive?"

"Gotdammit! Just drive me the hell away from here!"

"Okay, L.T. Whatever you say."

As Mac put the truck into gear, Charlie approached the truck, shouting. "L.T.! Why don'tcha come on back inside . . ."

L.T. grabbed at Mac's throat and screamed again, "I said *drive*, gotdammit! I gotta find my boy!"

Just as the truck began to move, Charlie crossed in front of the truck and pounded the hood with his fist. Mac hit the brake pedal. "You gotta listen to me, L.T.!" Charlie shouted, leaning into the passenger window. "You ain't gonna find the boy! Now come on in the house. You ain't—you ain't in yer right mind. I done told you a snake got'cher boy—a *water moccasin*, L.T.! He's—he's just gone. Now come on back in the house."

Perspiration ran down L.T.'s face, and his breathing was labored. "Please, Mac . . ."

Mac patted L.T.'s shoulder and pressed the accelerator.

✳   ✳   ✳

An hour later, Mac stopped at Old Man Watson's filling station just as his son Tommy was closing up for the evening. "Fill'er up, Tommy," Mac shouted out the window. Then he turned to look at L.T. "You don't look so good, buddy . . . Hey, Tommy!" he yelled. "Ya got some hooch in the back?"

"Aw, hell, Mac, I told ya I'm closin'."

"Come on, Tommy. My buddy's in a bad way."

"Oh, awright. I'll bring ya out a few bottles."

Within minutes, the truck tank was full and L.T. was gulping Tommy's homemade corn liquor.

"That's right, buddy," Mac said. "Drink up. You'll feel better."

L.T. glanced out the window to his right. "Where the hell we goin', Mac?"

"You said to drive, L.T. So we goin' for a drive."

L.T. shook his head. "This is nigger town. What the hell we doin' in nigger town?"

Mac chuckled. "Thought maybe you might feel like lettin' off a little steam."

"Well, I don't," L.T. growled. "Turn around."

"Wait a minute, L.T.," Mac said. "Ain't that Jasper Thompson's ol' jalopy up ahead?"

L.T. didn't answer.

"Shore is," Mac murmured. "They're turnin' up ahead . . . This must be where that damn troublemaker lives."

"I ain't in the mood for this, Mac. Now turn around and let's go back to your house."

"Now wait a minute," Mac said as he pulled the car over. Rolling into a patch of tall grass across the street, he watched as the car doors opened and the Thompson family piled out—Jasper, Lena, Sistine, and David. When their guest stepped out, Mac let out a soft whistle. "L.T.! Look at that! There's that Garvey sumbitch from the park!"

L.T. took a drink and blinked as he craned his neck. "Yup. It's him, awright."

"L.T., what was it he said about snakes?"

A pained expression crossed L.T.'s face. "Snakes?"

"He said sump'm 'bout snakes killin' theirselves or sump'm, remember? You don't think . . ."

"What?"

"Aww, nothin'."

"What, gotdammit?"

"Well, didn't that lady say sump'm about Little Larry talkin' to that fancy Garvey nigger down by the creek? What if he lured him down there, L.T.? What if it was some kind'a message or sump'm. Shore is strange—him talkin' about snakes and killin', and then yer boy walks right into a snake's fangs."

L.T. leaned his head against the passenger door and stared across the street as the front screen door slammed shut at the Thompson residence. "Shut-up, Mac," he muttered.

# Chapter 42

Tapping lightly on the guestroom door, Lena poked her head in and smiled at Serval. "We're leavin' now, Mr. Rivard. Goin' to the evenin' prayer meetin' to see how many folks we can pull onto the bandwagon. You need anything 'fore we go?"

"No, thank you. You think Ernest got to the train station on time?"

"Oh, I'm sure he did. And remember, your own tickets are in on the kitchen table if you want to put 'em in your suit pocket or sump'm. How was your visit with Mr. Garvey?"

Serval closed his eyes and sighed. "It was like—I can't explain it, Miz Lena. He sits there so calmly and reminds me not to fall into the same traps he has. And when he talks about Africa . . . He tried not to show it, but I know he'd give anything to be in my shoes. You know they're talking about sending him back to Jamaica."

"Yes, I heard about that," Lena said softly.

"He tried to be upbeat, but I could see the sadness in his eyes."

"Well, Mr. Rivard," Lena said, "Mr. Garvey's a fighter. Don'tchu worry 'bout him. No matter where they send him, that man's gonna be fightin' for the people 'til he draws his last breath. Well, I really gotta get goin'. Now the kids are in bed, so you shouldn't have no trouble with 'em. Well, 'cept they might try to test you a little," she laughed. "You know, like askin' for eighteen glasses of water or givin' you a whole passel of excuses to stay up. You just keep tellin' 'em no enough times, they'll wear theyselves out and fall asleep."

Serval smiled. "I think I can handle it, Miz Lena."

"You *sure* you don't mind? 'Cause I can call my sister . . ."

"Stop worryin'! It's the least I can do. Now, you go on to your meeting and give 'em hell!"

Lena giggled. "Can't give 'em hell, Mr. Rivard! Not at a prayer meetin'! See you in a few hours."

Lena only made it halfway to the door when she heard the sound of Sistine's dramatic whine. "Oh, Lord, Sistine . . ."

"Go, Miz Lena," Serval laughed. "I'll tend to that little play-actor."

"You sure?"

Heading toward the children's bedroom, Serval called over his shoulder, "You better make your escape while you can!"

"Well, all right. Good-night, Mr. Rivard."

"Good-night."

Serval fought to maintain his stern expression when he peered into the room and caught Sistine burrowing hastily back under her covers. "What are you still doin' up, young lady? Your Mama said it was bedtime."

"But it ain't even dark yet, Mr. Serval," she pouted.

"That's because it's summer. But it's still bedtime for little folks."

After an exaggerated yawn, Sistine's voice became suspiciously frail. "Ooh, Mr. Serval . . . I—don't—*feel* very good."

Rolling his eyes, Serval covered his laughter with a cough and sat down on the edge of her bed. "Okay. What seems to be the trouble, Miss Sistine?"

"My headache hurts," she said, sighing dramatically.

"Your headache hurts? Hmm. Well, what does your Mama usually do when your headache hurts?"

"Uh, mmm, she—she reads me a story—'til I feel better."

"You know what, Miss Sistine?"

"What?" she murmured weakly.

Serval leaned his face close to hers and frowned. "You are a little fraud."

"Am *not* a frog," she snapped.

"Not a frog—a fraud!" Surrendering to his laughter, Serval reached down and tickled Sistine. "You don't have a headache, girl! Know what you are?"

Sistine's shrieks and giggles woke David, who scrambled out of his bed and into Sistine's.

"Aww, Lord!" Serval laughed as he scooped David into his arms. "I lost control here, huh? Now, what do you want, David? Hey! You know what your sister is? Huh? She's a—a frog-fraud!"

"Sistine's a frog-frog!" David shrieked.

"Nuh-uh! David's a frog-frog!" Sistine shouted.

Serval collapsed on the end of the bed laughing. "What's a frog-frog?"

Sistine gasped for air, choking back giggles. "You are! Mr. Serval's a frog-frog, too! Cribbit! Cribbit!"

Serval dabbed at his watering eyes. "Cribbit? What's a cribbit?"

"It's a frog word, Mr. Serval. Ain'tcha ever heard the frogs talkin' in the creek?" She squatted in the center of the bed, and sprang up and down. "Cribbit," she croaked.

Serval rolled his eyes and carried David to the other bed. "Okay, enough tickling. Enough giggling. And enough cribbits. It's way past your bedtime. Now get under the covers and I'll bring you each a drink of water. A short one."

Serval fetched the water and watched the children drink it. Sistine opened her mouth to speak, but Serval placed his index finger to his lips. "Shhh . . . Not another word or cribbit out'a you, Miss Frog-Frog. Now you two go to sleep. I got work to do before I leave in the mornin'."

He made it as far as the door before Sistine whispered, "Mr. Serval?"

"Yes, Sistine?"

"Are you comin' back to visit us again?"

He paused to steal a look at David who was already falling asleep, then crossed back over to Sistine's bed and sat beside her. "Don't you remember?" he whispered. "I've gotta go far away—to Africa, Sistine. You heard your Daddy and Mama and me talkin' about that, didn't you?"

"Yes, sir. But can'tcha come back?"

He swallowed back a sugar-coated lie; Sistine was too intelligent for such things. "Sistine, I might not see you for a long time—maybe 'til you're all grown up."

Sistine stared at him sadly, then whispered, "Daddy was gonna take us to Africa too, but then he said no. They' got tigers in Africa, ya know. Better be careful."

"I'll be okay. I'm an African wildcat myself, remember? Tigers won't eat me."

Sistine smiled. "I forgot."

"Mm-hmm." Lifting her into his arms, Serval closed his eyes and held her tightly for a minute. "You know what, Sistine? I got another secret to tell you."

She raised her head from his shoulder, and grinned. "What?"

"I'm a Daddy. Well, I'll be a Daddy soon. I mean, my wife has a baby, but I won't see it. See, she can't go with me to Africa—she has to stay here, and well . . ."

"Is it a lidda girl or a lidda boy?"

Serval blinked back the stinging in his eyes, caught off-guard by the question. "Well . . . I don't know yet. It's, uh, not born yet."

"Oh," she said, nodding. "It didn't get sent from heaven yet—like Miz Coolidge' baby."

"Miz Coolidge?"

"Mm-hmm. She's fat."

Serval shook his head. "Uh . . . ?"

"Daddy said when a lady gets fat, then God sends her a baby from heaven. Then she gets skinny again. But it didn't work wif Miz Coolidge."

Serval smiled.

"Mr. Serval, why you gotta go to Africa all by yourself? Won't your baby miss you? He won't have a Daddy, huh?"

Serval stared at her, unable to respond.

"Why, Mr. Serval?" she pressed. "Why you gotta go to Africa all by yourself? Do you gotta work or sump'm?"

"Well, yes, Sistine. I have an important job to do."

With a worried expression, she reached up and gently patted the side of his face. "Why? Why ya gotta work so *hard* all the time?"

Serval took her shoulders in his hands. "To make things better for you, Sistine. That's what your Daddy and Mama are doin' too. They work just as hard as I do so that by the time you grow up, things will be better for Negroes here. And if we work real, real hard, then maybe your own little children will be born in Africa. That's why we work so hard, baby. It's all for you and David—and my baby too."

". . . when it comes from heaven?" she whispered.

"Yes. When it comes from heaven."

A look of panic suddenly crossed Sistine's face. "My Daddy ain't goin' to Africa, is he?"

Serval gathered her in his arms. "Oh, no, honey. Your Daddy's gonna stay right here with you and work in Atlanta. Don't you worry about that."

Sistine pulled away and crossed her arms. "But Mr. Serval, why can't you work here too? Then the lidda baby can still have a Daddy."

Gazing into Sistine's questioning eyes, Serval could find no logical answer to give her. *Because my wife is in love with my best friend?* As soon as the thought formed in his mind, he was struck with the absurdity of it. Closing his eyes, he forced his mind back to the last time he held Opal in his arms; the softness in her eyes. *She still loves me. Whatever she feels for Jack couldn't be the same as what we had.*

"Sistine?" he whispered.

"Yes, sir?"

"You are a very wise little girl and—you know what? I'm gonna think about what you said."

Sistine yawned. "Good. Think real hard, Mr. Serval, so the lidda baby can have a Daddy like me."

Serval kissed her forehead and tucked the covers around her shoulders. "You go to sleep now, Sistine. And thank you for helpin' me with my problem."

As he reached the door he heard a sleepy mumble from the bed: "Mr. Serval?"

He peered back at her suspiciously. "Yes?"

"Can we come visit you and your baby at your house sometime? And his Mama too?"

"I'll be heartbroken if you don't."

"G'night, Mr. Serval."

"Good-night, Sistine."

Serval returned to the desk and sat in stunned silence for several minutes before pulling out a sheet of paper and beginning a very difficult letter.

*May 18, 1925*

*Dear Mr. Boley,*

*It is with a mixture of apprehension and joy that I write this letter to you, and I pray that you will find it in your heart to understand.*

*For the last five years of my life, the UNIA has been my primary focus and I hope I have been able to give as much to our people as I have gained from them. They have inspired me to work harder than I ever thought possible and to reach beyond boundaries for goals previously denied to Negro people. Only one thing could tear me away from my mission in Liberia—the mission you have so graciously entrusted to my hands . . .*

After the first few tentative lines, the letter began to flow naturally and Serval was filled with hope. Suddenly, because of the words of a small child, everything seemed possible.

Just as he started the last paragraph of the letter, his train of thought was interrupted by the sound of the front door being kicked open, followed by the sounds of heavy footsteps and Sistine's frightened cry. He bolted out of his chair and ran down the hall toward the children's room, but stopped at the sight of a white man standing frozen in their doorway. The man turned his head and stared at Serval with a deranged expression.

*It's him . . .* Serval thought. *From the rally . . .* He took two rapid steps, then lunged at him, but was caught from behind by a second man, who held him with a crushing choke-hold.

Serval couldn't see his face, but his voice was all too familiar. "Well, well. Looks like we found our troublemaker all by his lonesome, L.T. What happened? All yer big strong nigger buddies sail fer Africa without ya?"

Serval felt an opening, but just as he drew his elbow forward in preparation for a shot to the man's belly, he saw the glint of gunmetal in L.T.'s hand. His hesitation resulted in his being thrown against the wall, then shoved toward the front door. Out of the corner of his right eye, he saw Sistine creep out from the hallway. In his left ear was the hissing voice of his captor: "Come on, nigger. Me and L.T.'s gonna show you some Southern hospitality. Yer goin' for a little ride in the country."

"No!" Sistine screamed, and lunged at Serval.

"It's—it's okay, honey," Serval said, keeping his voice calm. "Now, listen to me. You go back to bed and stay there 'til your Mama comes home, you hear me?"

David stared at him with wide eyes as he clung tightly to his sister's arm. Sistine nodded and emitted a sound that was half-wail and half-answer: "Mmm-huhmmm."

As Mac shoved him out the door, Serval jerked his head around to look back toward the house where Sistine and David stood staring at him through the screen door. He gazed at the fear in Sistine's eyes, and flashed a reassuring smile.

*      *      *

A drop of perspiration rolled down Serval's face as he bumped along in the truck between Mac, who was driving, and L.T., who sat to his right. Feeling the pressure of the handgun against his ribs, Serval studied them by turn with his peripheral vision. Mac was a maniacal blend of contempt and merriment, laughing, gesturing with his fist, and repeatedly snapping his head to the right to punctuate something he was saying.

After a while, his nonstop insults and threats became a vague curtain of sound, but L.T.'s silence was as jarring as a scream. His face was as pale as death, with eyes devoid of expression. Despite the coolness of the evening, wet strands of his hair stuck like plaster to the perspiration on his forehead, and his breathing was shallow and rapid. Serval went cold. *He's insane. They both are.*

After traveling through a seemingly endless maze of dusty backroads, Mac abruptly stopped the truck and jumped out. At last, L.T. spoke. "Out."

Serval hesitated for a moment, then slid across the seat and stepped out. Pulling himself up to his full height, he stepped close enough to L.T. to bump against the barrel of the gun. Their eyes met, and Serval spoke to him in their own silent language. *I'm not scared'a you or your gun.*

He felt Mac's grip on his arms before being shoved against the rough bark of a tree. Mac pushed him harder against the tree, and cackled in his ear. "Hope ya like pea-cawns, nigger, 'cause yer gonna be hangin' up there with some of 'em."

Serval jerked away from the tree and felt his heart begin to thump in his chest. The fear washed over him so quickly that his plans for escape lost all sense of order. His worst nightmare ran rampant through his mind, and words he had written in his own journal screamed down at him from the claw-like branches of the tree. *To hang on display . . . as an object of the white man's derision.* His eyes darted from left to right, but froze on L.T. when he spoke.

"You come out here stirrin' up trouble. And you left my boy with them snakes," L.T. said, his voice flat. "So you gotta die, nigger."

"You *are* crazy," Serval murmured, shaking his head. A thumping sound caught his attention, and he spun around to see Mac pulling a rope from the bed of the truck. Words ran through his mind, but were too jumbled to use as tools of reason. He stared first at the gun in L.T.'s hand, then at the rope, and made a split-second choice. He lunged away from the two white men in the direction of a thick stand of trees, but felt his foot catch when L.T. tripped him. He stumbled and clawed at the ground to regain his footing, but a kick sent him sprawling in the dirt. He heard a sound—wild, like the cry of a wounded animal—and realized that it had come from his own mouth. When he scrambled up on all-fours, another kick rolled him over. Letting his head drop back, he looked up into two inhuman masks, contorted by hatred and rage.

The butt of the handgun crashed into his temple, and Serval felt himself falling into a deep blue foxhole, spiraling into gray, then black, with blasts of pain jolting intermittent flashes of red . . . red . . . Red.

*Red! Where are you? No! Fight, Red! Run!* His fingers scratched at trench-mud, but it dissolved into thin air. His eyelids fluttered open, and he blinked to regain control of his vision. Standing over him were two hazy forms shouting a language he couldn't understand. *Krauts!* he thought. *I'm captured!* Serval stretched out his hand for his rifle, but before he could find it, the rain began. Harder and harder it poured, until the driving raindrops were like the blows of fists and the kicks of sharp-toed boots. The blur of motion above his head was dizzying, so he closed his eyes while fending off the rain with his arms. But a sticky wetness made him look up at his hands. "Blood!" he screamed. "It's raining somebody's blood!"

The rain stopped. Serval gazed up at one of the Krauts, wondering about the object he held in his hands—a coil of the wire. *No. I'll crawl under it . . . Where's my gun?* He scratched frantically at his neck. *Where's my dogtags?*

The rain started up again, harder this time. Thunder and lightning— and hail. Serval tried to raise his head just as the biggest hailstone hit, and he felt something break loose in his face. Then a strange calmness covered him like a warm blanket, and the pain grew dimmer. He exhaled and settled into the mud as he regarded his enemies. He saw one of them kick him, and knew that his ribs were broken by the loose rattle he felt. The crashing confusion in his mind quieted, and, one by one, clear thoughts began to flow like a placid stream. Serval smiled. *Not Krauts . . .*

A voice broke through: "Gotdamn nigger's laughin', L.T.!"

*They're mad.* Serval tasted blood in his mouth, and smiled broadly to show them. He heard the angry voices rise once more, then fade to a low hum as he stared up at the darkening sky. A scattering of faint evening stars showed themselves against a canopy of blue shadows. *So this is death . . .*

*It's finally here, Jimmy. It wasn't rain at all. . . . Opal? I'm dying tonight, Opal. But don't cry. It's not so bad. All I can do is smile, but it makes 'em mad. So I'll just lie here and keep smiling at 'em . . . I'll make 'em kill me before they get a chance to put that rope around my neck. And—and then it won't matter what they do to my body, Opal . . . 'cause I won't—I won't be in it any more. I'll be . . . gone—somewhere else. I wish I knew where* . . . He experienced a heaviness in his chest, but the pain was remote and muted. *Jimmy?* . . . *They can beat me and kick me—and kill me. And they can keep on killing me—over and over and over again.* As he exhaled, his own breath seemed to spin above his head, leaving him in a vacuum. He finally managed a gulp of air and saw the men staring down at him. The laugh that was in his throat emerged as a feeble cough. *They're so stupid. Don't they know I'll just come back? I'll be back* . . . *and I'll be—stronger—and blacker—I'll come back and I'll give 'em so much hell* . . .

. . . *God?*

✻ ✻ ✻

The body at his feet was limp, but L.T. delivered another vicious kick to the ribs, which caved in loosely to the pressure of his boot. Breathing heavily from over-exertion, he gazed down at the black man and felt a sudden wave of nausea. "Gotdamn nigger's still—still laughin' at me!" He pulled himself up tall, waiting for the soothing sensation of vengeance, but felt only a rattling terror when the bloody smile forced him to turn his back. "Mac, see if he's . . . see if his heart's still beatin'."

Mac leaned down and pressed his palm against Serval's chest for a long moment, then chortled, "He's the best kind'a nigger, L.T.—dead. Now let's string him up. You know—an example fer his uppity Garvey buddies."

L.T. forced his eyes back to his victim, and was again struck by the dead man's enigmatic, other-worldly smile. "No."

"Huh? Come on, L.T."

"Gotdammit!" L.T. shouted. "He's dead as he's gonna get, ain't he? Just—just put the rope back in the truck. It's too damn much work anyhow."

# Chapter 43

On the morning of Little Larry's funeral, L.T. sat at the kitchen table, his gaze fixed on a drop of water stretching longer and longer from the rim of the spigot in the sink. He held his breath, waiting. *Why don't it fall?* he wondered.

Ellen wandered in, pathetic in her best Sunday dress, her face red and puffy from crying. "Please, L.T.," she whimpered. "It's the boy's funeral. What'll folks say if—if his own Daddy don't come?"

But L.T. didn't hear her. He was too caught up in the suspense unfolding in the kitchen sink.

*DRIP.*

Ellen touched his shoulder, then gasped when he mechanically slapped her hand away. When Charlie appeared at her side, L.T. took a swipe at him, but missed.

Charlie led Ellen quickly to the back door, then paused and said softly, "L.T.? We're goin' now. You come on later—if ya want to."

L.T. didn't answer. His only concern was the new drip forming at the bottom of the spigot. He heard the back screen door slam shut, followed by the sound of the truck as it drove away. *Wonder if I can make it back in time?* he mused. Walking swiftly down the hallway to his bedroom, he fished a small key out of his pocket. He opened the closet door, reached down for the metal box in the corner, and unlocked it. Lying in the center of the box was the pearl-handled pistol his father had given him at his first Klan meeting. He snatched the pistol from the box and hurried back to the kitchen—just in time to witness the event that consumed his thoughts.

*DRIP.*

He settled back in his chair and calmly loaded the gun, checking every few seconds on the newest drop. Wiping the perspiration off his forehead, he was ready. *When the next one falls . . .*

He placed the gun barrel in his mouth with a steady hand as he watched the drop engorge with water—heavier and fatter—and he fleetingly marvelled at his lack of nervousness.

*DRIP.*

Silence.

Expecting to hear the report of the gun, at least for a split second before the longed-for nothingness, L.T. sat in momentary confusion. Although his brain had sent the message to shoot, his paralyzed hand had not responded. The gun slipped through his limp fingers to the floor, and his eyes filled with tears as the voice of a dead man displaced his obsession with the faucet:

*Snakes don't ever commit suicide.*

*   *   *

The morning after the discovery of Serval's body, Ernest Davis arranged to transport him home to Harlem. He had considered calling Opal and Serval's parents to tell them, but concluded that such news should be delivered in person. He spoke to no one for the entire two-day trip as he tried to compose the appropriate words.

As the train neared New York, Ernest sat alone in the afternoon heat at the back of the Jim Crow car. The rhythmic clacking of the metal wheels over miles of rail lulled him away from theorizing the violent details of Serval's death. *Cli-clack, cli-clack* . . . He settled into the endlessness of the sound, ignoring the inevitability of the final stop. But the irony kept creeping in, of his friend traveling home in the connecting baggage car while lying in the eternal stillness of a coffin.

Ernest had packed all of Serval's personal belongings in a trunk, with one exception. The satchel that had become an extension of Serval's hand in the last two years of his life now rested on Ernest's lap. He stared down at it, and impulsively reached inside to examine the contents: the Atlanta trip itinerary, which was clipped to the annotated pages of his last speech, a ticket for the voyage to Liberia, a thick manilla envelope from Nathaniel Washington's office, and Serval's personal journal. *How many times have I seen him scribbling down his thoughts in this book?*

Ernest turned the pages slowly, reading random passages until he reached the last entry. He shivered as he read the date: May 17, 1925.

*Sleep is elusive tonight. Thoughts of death demand to be written down, so I take pen in hand, and see what appears on the page.*

*Death is the final personal act of a human being. It is the cessation of a life, all the memories, happy and sad, every failure and*

*triumph. How much information can a human brain hold? All
the things we learn, the skills and artistry we work so hard to de-
velop—the details that make each human unique—it all ends
with that most private moment. The masterpiece is destroyed,
never to be replicated. If there is ever a truly reverent moment in a
person's life, it is the moment the body takes leave of the soul. The
mighty heart that pumped vitality into every vein falls weak, and
finally surrenders. The muscles go slack, no longer able to carry the
vessel to distant places at the command of the inquisitive brain.
Curious fingertips lose the sensation of touch. Nothing more to
discover. Nothing more to learn or feel. And the eyes—the recep-
tors of millions of colors and breathtaking images—sunsets, dew
on spring grass, a child's smiling face—even these shining mirrors
of the soul go flat and refuse to see. It must be a moment of si-
multaneous mourning and great joy. To lose your best friend, your
body, while being lifted into the unknown bliss and freedom of
spirituality. It is a human being's most private moment with self.
Your last awareness of your birthright—the majesty and honor of
your humanity.*

*The men who killed Jimmy Coles stripped him of his birthright.
Like two thieving hands working in concert, the left hand robbed
him of his life, while the right hand stole from him the reverence of
his own death. A man named Jimmy Coles was made to spend his
final precious moment—as an object. He was made to hang on
display at the end of a rope as an object of the white man's derision. An object—of derision."*

*   *   *

The sun was setting when Opal opened her front door and saw death in
Ernest Davis's eyes. Before he said a word, her legs went weak and she
grabbed the door jamb for support. "Tell me!" she said in a shrill voice.
"Something happened. Just say it! It's Serval, isn't it? My Serval . . ."

"Opal," Ernest said weakly, "May I come inside? I—I've really got
to sit down. Please."

When she stepped back to let him in, Ernest reached for her hand,
but Opal recoiled. Shrinking against the wall, she pointed at the sofa.
"Sit down."

Ernest sank down on the edge of the sofa and stared at the floor a long
time before he spoke. His voice was a whisper. "It's exactly what you're

thinking, Opal. They—they killed him. I don't know how else to say it. Serval Rivard is dead."

Opal glared at him, hating him. *Breathe. Breathe so you can ask it.* "Did they—how did they—kill him?"

"They—oh, God, I'm so sorry . . ."

"Just tell me!" she shouted. "How?"

"They—they beat him. They just—beat him to death, Opal."

"But . . ." She paused. "Did you—did you see him? How did they *find* him?"

Covering his face with his hands, Ernest moaned, "I saw him. I went back from Charleston as soon as I received the news that he was missing."

Opal clawed at one of his hands, with a desperate need to see his eyes. "But—how *was* he when they found him? Did you see—did you notice any marks—on his neck?"

Ernest dropped his hands and stared at her, then shook his head slowly. "No. There was no rope. Jasper Thompson and six other men had just given up the search for the night when I arrived. An old Negro gentleman who lived near the creek showed up at the Thompsons' the next morning just as we were gathering for another search. He told us he had found a dead Negro man lying in a clearing. He was afraid to go to the police, but he trusted the UNIA. So he led us to—to the spot."

Opal closed her eyes. "And it was Serval."

"Yes."

"And—and there was no rope."

"No rope. In fact, Jasper Thompson said it was a miracle. You see, we found him lying on the ground directly under a tree. Jasper said it was a miracle that we didn't find him hanging from it. . . . I'm sorry, Opal. I know you two had something special—even if you weren't—together any more. He always told me that if anything ever happened to him, to tell you and Jack—and to make sure you were taken care of."

But Opal was no longer listening. Closing her eyes, she wrapped her arms around herself to keep from shaking. *They didn't hang him. Thank you, God.*

\* \* \*

The bedroom was dark when Opal heard the front door opening. *Jack. How do I tell Jack?* She heard his heavy footsteps in the kitchen, then his voice: "Opal?"

She tried to answer, but couldn't. *How do I tell him?* Jack's footsteps grew louder as he came down the hallway, then stopped at the door.

"Opal? Girl, what'chu doin' sittin' on the flo' like that?"

Opal continued to stare blankly at the wall as Jack crossed the room. "What is it?" he whispered. "What happened?"

Opal remained silent. *I can't say it yet, Jack. I need more time.*

Jack sat heavily on the edge of the bed. "Opal. Please say sump'm."

She tried to remember how she had been told. It seemed years since she had asked Ernest to leave. What words had he used? She struggled with her malfunctioning memory, then opened her mouth to speak, but hesitated, unsure of what she would force out—speech, or the bile she felt rising in her throat. At last the impossible words came: "Serval— Serval's dead."

Speaking seemed to release her from her trance, and she twisted around to look up at Jack. His face resembled some inanimate object— more statue-like than human—but reflected no trace of shock. He seemed to be expecting the news.

"Do his Daddy and Mama know?"

"I told Ernest I'd tell 'em. I just haven't been able to . . ."

"I'll do it, Opal. I'll drive over—I'll jus' . . ." He leaned forward, as if preparing to stand, but slumped back down and lowered his head. "Opal?"

"Yes, Jack?"

"Did they—did they hang him—like how he used to dream?"

Opal shook her head, then whispered, "No."

"How—how'd they kill him?"

"I—I didn't say anybody killed him. It could've been . . ."

"But it wasn't." Tears began to pool in Jack's eyes, but his expression remained unchanged. "They killed him. I lived around them rednecks, Opal. They couldn't stand no black man like Serval comin' down there all proud . . . How'd they do it?"

"They—beat him. They just beat him to death, Jack. But he wasn't hung."

Jack nodded. "I knew he'd never let 'em put a rope 'round his neck."

Opal felt her heart drop, as if from a great height. Still seated on the floor, she clamped her arms around his leg and pressed her forehead into his knee as the horror began—the unbearable drowning-on-air sounds of Jack fighting back the grief—holding in all the pain, all the rage. She squeezed her eyes shut and held her breath as he choked back a scream that she knew would dissolve somewhere deep in his soul, never to be heard by the outside world.

Opal tightened her grip on his leg until she felt the silent scream enter her. She held it for a moment, touching Serval's pain and tasting Jack's tears. But unable to contain it, she opened her mouth and gave it voice.

# Chapter 44

It was nearly eleven p.m. when Jack climbed the steps to the home of Mr. and Mrs. Charles Rivard and rang the bell. He stared at a moon shadow on the door—criss-crossing tree branches swaying with the breeze. When the door opened, the shadow fell across the angry face of Charles Rivard.

"Sir! Have you any idea what time it is?"

"I'm sorry, Mistah Rivard. I know it's late an' all. I wouldn't be botherin' y'all if it wasn't—important." Jack snatched off his hat and tried not to twist it in his hand. "You never met me, but I'm Serval's friend. We was in the war together."

Charles leaned out and peered down the steps. "He isn't with you?"

Jack felt his heart thump harder. "Naw, suh. I'm—by myself . . . Mistah Rivard, you think I could come inside for jus' a minute?"

Charles hesitated for a moment, and Jack saw the fear flash in his eyes.

"Is something wrong? . . . I'm sorry. Please come in. What's your name, son?"

"Hawkins, suh. Jack Hawkins." Jack stopped in the entryway and faced Charles Rivard squarely. "Mistah Rivard . . . I don't rightly know how to tell you this . . ."

Charles Rivard's anxious expression suddenly changed to dread. "What's happened?" he murmured.

Jack took a deep breath. "I'm sorry to tell you this, Mistah Rivard, but . . . Serval was—was killed."

After a slight sway, Charles Rivard didn't move. A clock began to chime somewhere in the house, and Jack heard the squeak of a door opening. Then a woman's voice: "Charles?"

Without taking his eyes off Jack, Charles answered, "Yes, my dear. I'll be right up."

"But who is it at this hour, Charles? . . . Charles?"

"I—I'll be right there, Kathryn."

Jack nodded and reached for the doorknob. "I ought'a . . . Guess I ought'a go now so you can tend to ya wife, suh."

Charles touched Jack's arm. "Where—where is he?"

"I don't rightly know jus' now. The UNIA been handlin' everything so far. But . . ."

"*Garvey's* people?"

"Yes, suh. But I was fixin' to say that Ernest told Opal . . ."

"Who is Ernest?"

"Ernest was Serval's assistant—an' his friend. He the one brought him back on the train. He'll prob'ly be the one callin' on you tomorrow, Mistah Rivard. To see about the church and all."

Charles closed his eyes.

"They ain't bad people, Mistah Rivard," Jack said softly. "They loved Serval . . . jus' like us."

After a long silence, Charles extended his hand to Jack. "Thank you," he whispered.

✳ ✳ ✳

The next two days were a blur to Opal as Jack and Ernest went about the grim business of breaking the news to Serval's friends. After the wake, visits from devoted UNIA associates went on into the late night hours, but Opal relied only on Jack, who seemed to sense her teetering on the edge.

Since Serval had always loved the early morning hours, the funeral had been set for 8:30 a.m. After a sleepless night, Opal watched the sunrise from her kitchen window and wished for the day to be over. Jack suddenly appeared beside her and took several oranges out of the fruit basket on the counter.

"Here," he said, as he began cutting the oranges, "I'ma make you some juice and I want you to drink it."

Opal shook her head.

"Come on, now, Opal," he said. "You gon' need ya strength today."

Opal clutched her midsection and hurried out of the kitchen.

Jack dropped the knife and hurried after her. "Aww, you sick again, huh? Is it sump'm I can do to help?"

"No, Jack," she moaned as she stumbled into the bathroom. "Nobody can help me today."

✳ ✳ ✳

Mother Zion AME Church was not a grand building in the structural sense, but nevertheless asserted a towering presence among the dwellings in Harlem. With dramatic processions that stretched out along Seventh Avenue before making the turn onto 137th Street, Mother Zion AME was known far and wide as the venue for Harlem's most illustrious funerals. The mourners gathering in front of the church on the morning of Serval's memorial service were a colorful, international mix of people, and local residents leaned out their windows, whispering among themselves the stories that would spin into Harlem mythology.

By the time Opal arrived, a crowd was already overflowing into the street. Many of the faces were unfamiliar to her, and those that she did recognize quickly became a blur of mouths spilling the same condolences. She began to shake, so she tried to lose herself in the colors and spectacle of a hero's memorial service. Banners of red, green, and black were held high by Harlem's remaining contingent of UNIA loyals, who wore black armbands on their full dress uniforms. A group of about fifteen UNIA nurses lined the sidewalk, their crisp, white uniforms dazzling in the early morning sun. Standing on the church steps was a small group of men dressed in colorful African robes of gold and green. And their voices all rang in Opal's ears with the sound of her husband's name. Leaning against Jack, she found it difficult to focus until she passed a petite grief-stricken young woman sobbing into her handkerchief. Opal stopped and watched for a moment as a tall man in a black suit consoled the woman. Stepping away from Jack, Opal extended her hand. "I—I'm Opal Rivard."

The woman's eyes widened. "Oh! Oh, Miz Rivard! I'm so sorry! Your husband was such a dear friend to us. He was a great man."

"I'm sorry I never got a chance to meet you . . ."

The man in the black suit offered the woman his own handkerchief and stepped closer. "Oh, we ain't from these parts, Miz Rivard. We're the Thompsons—I'm Jasper and this here's my wife Lena. Your husband stayed with us whenever he was in Atlanta. He was like a second daddy to our kids. We—we're so upset that all this happened while he was stayin' wid us. If I'da stayed home that night . . ."

"Oh, no, Mr. Thompson. Please don't blame yourself. It was nobody's fault," Opal said. "Well—not yours, anyway. I—I'm glad to meet such good friends of my husband's. And he did tell me about you. He told me all about your children."

"Oh, yes, Miz Rivard," Lena sniffled. "He loved my babies, awright. And they loved him too. And—and so did we!" She broke down again, and leaned against Jasper for a moment, then waved her hand as she composed herself.

"He spoke very highly 'bout you," Jasper said. "He loved you so much—you was the world to that man."

Opal stared at Lena as Jasper began introducing the African representatives to her. She felt as if she were under water, and couldn't seem to hear their voices as she shook their hands. *He still loved me. I was his world.*

As Jack led her away, Opal felt a tug at her sleeve, and Lena thrust two envelopes into her hands—one large manilla envelope and a small pink envelope. "I almost forgot, Miz Rivard," Lena said softly. "This is— I think it's a letter your husband wrote somebody while he was stayin' with us. I didn't read it, I just saw that symbol at the top, and it looks jus' like Jasper's UNIA letter paper. Anyway, Ernest must'a missed it when he collected all—all Mr. Rivard's things from the house. I thought you ought'a have it. And this—well, this is a letter from my little girl, Sistine. Mr. Rivard was sorta partial to her. We—we had to explain to her the best we could, and she asked me if—if folks could get letters in heaven, so I helped her write it. She wanted to come today, but we thought it might upset her too much." Her voice dropped to a whisper. "You ain't got to look at 'em now, Miz Rivard. Jus' read 'em whenever you feel like it."

Opal continued to stare at Lena blankly until she felt Jack leading her toward the door of the church.

When she stepped inside, she saw an even larger crowd than the one congregated outside. There were people standing wherever there was space, and Opal felt hundreds of eyes staring at her. As she walked up the aisle, she clung tightly to Jack's arm and tried to acknowledge all the whispered greetings.

"So many folks are crying, Jack," she said softly.

Jack leaned down and pressed his handkerchief to Opal's cheek. "Yeah. This is a day for cryin', awright."

When they finally reached the front row, Opal could hardly control her trembling. She took her seat next to Jack and leaned close to him. "Where is he?" she whispered.

"They' gon' bring him in directly, Opal."

Opal shot a worried glance at Jack. "But—but Serval would want you to be carryin' him, Jack. How come you're not . . . ?"

"Naw, Opal," he said firmly. "Serval would want me right where I am."

She nodded. "That's right, I guess."

Out of the corner of her eye, Opal spotted Charles and Kathryn Rivard seated in the same row on the other side of the aisle. Kathryn's eyes were puffy and rimmed with dark circles as she cried softly into a handkerchief. Charles appeared stiff and mechanical as he sat beside her patting her hand.

"Jack, look!" Opal whispered. "They came!"

Jack continued to stare staight ahead. "I saw 'em."

"I wasn't sure he'd come."

Jack squeezed her hand. "Oh, I knew he'd come."

"But they never got along, Jack."

"They got along—in they own way," Jack said.

Opal questioned Jack with her eyes, and he answered her with a smile.

Suddenly, Opal remembered the envelopes she clutched in her hands, and thought about the little girl who had sent the letter. Slowly she opened the pink envelope and began to read the rickety-looking scrawl.

*Dear Mr. Serval,*

*Mama said not to cry so I'm trying to not. I'm sorry you didn't get to go home to be a daddy or to Africa, but maybe Heaven is just as good too. I think so. They might even have tigers there too. I know they got a Serval now. Roar! Me and David miss you, and we play frog-frog all the time now. Don't be sad, Mr. Serval. You can be a daddy a little while in Heaven before the baby gets sent. Tell him Sistine say hello and be a good boy or girl. Okay? I love you very much. Good-bye. Here a picture for you. —Love, Sistine*

Underneath the writing was a picture of what Opal guessed must be a black cat, and beside that, the word "Roar!" Surprised to feel the corners of her mouth turn up, Opal thought she might actually laugh. *It's a serval cat*, she thought. Folding the letter, she turned her attention to the manilla envelope. Sliding out the crisp linen stationery, she ran her fingers across the embossed UNIA insignia in the upper left-hand corner, and stared at Serval's handwriting. It was a letter dated May 18, 1925—the date of his death.

*Dear Mr. Boley,*

*It is with a mixture of apprehension and joy that I write this letter to you, and I pray that you will find it in your heart to understand.*

*For the last five years of my life, the UNIA has been my primary focus, and I hope I have been able to give as much to our people as I have gained from them. They have inspired me to work harder than I ever thought possible and to reach beyond boundaries for goals previously denied Negro people. Only one thing could tear me away from my mission in Liberia—the mission you have so graciously entrusted to my hands. Although I am sure I don't deserve it, I recently received a great blessing. I am going to be a father. You have never questioned me about my decision to make the trip to Liberia alone, leaving my wife behind, but I would like to explain myself now, if I may.*

*Any problems in my marriage were my fault. My stubbornness and failure to understand my wife's ambition—her right to have a dream of her own—drove a wedge between us that we were both either too angry or childish to remove. But with the news of the baby, I find that it is undoubtedly the time for us both to grow up and work together, instead of against each other. I haven't discussed any of these things with my wife, and I pray that she will forgive me and take me back . . .*

Opal gasped, and Jack patted her hand gently. Several teardrops fell, smudging the ink, and Opal quickly dabbed at them, afraid that she might miss a word. Keeping her handkerchief poised, she read on.

*As for my appointment in Liberia, please know that I am fully aware of the importance of the mission—of the struggle for global unity for our people and the idea of nation-building, but I have just made the discovery that the raising of a child is an integral part of nation-building, as well. Therefore, after much soul searching, I find that I must beg your forgiveness, but I simply cannot accept the appointment. I belong with my family. I humbly leave you with one recommendation for a replacement. Without the assistance of Ernest Da . . .*

The letter ended in mid-sentence, and Opal shuddered. *He was trying to come home . . .*

"You awright, Opal?" Jack whispered.

"Mm-hmm."

"What's that you readin'?"

Opal slipped the letter back into the envelope. "It was just some of Serval's business."

"What it say?"

Opal slipped her hand into Jack's, and gazed into his eyes for a long moment. "Nothin'," she said finally. "Just some talk about—Africa."

The congregation stirred and began turning to look in the direction of the front entrance of the church. Six uniformed pall-bearers, walking in a slow march-step, carried a flag-draped coffin on their shoulders. Opal read the words emblazoned on the side of the flag: *One God; One Aim; One Destiny.* Her hands went cold, and her trembling became severe. *One destiny? He's dead. My Serval's dead in that box.*

After a few minutes, the trembling began to subside, but a new shock settled over her—a tense, rigid feeling, as if she had turned to stone. Unable to hear the words of the preacher, she found it took considerable effort to listen, until Jack got up to speak at Reverend Webster's request.

The pulpit was dwarfed by Jack's towering height when he stepped behind it. He gazed out at the congregation and cleared his throat. "I ain't got much to say. My name's Jack Hawkins and—Serval was my best friend. He use'ta say I was his brother—only brother he had. And I guess if blood make men brothers, then we' brothers awright, 'cause we was in a bloody war together. But wit' Serval and me, it was different. Seem like we was always brothers . . ." He paused and appeared to be struggling with his emotions as a sudden stream of tears made its way down his face. "Guess all I—I really wanted to say was . . . The first thing . . . and the last thing Serval Rivard taught me was one word . . . truth." Shoving his hands into his pockets, he stepped down and joined Opal in their pew.

Reverend Webster's face registered surprise as he returned to the pulpit. "Thank you, Brother Hawkins. That was short but heartfelt, I'm sure. Now, if everyone will please turn to page . . ." He was interrupted by a sudden stir in the front row.

Opal turned and saw Charles Rivard stepping into the aisle. He held up his hand, and Opal could see that it was shaking. "Reverend Webster?" he said in a choked voice. "Is it too late for me . . . May I please say something . . . to my son?"

Reverend Webster extended his arms. "Certainly, my brother. We're all glad you came today, and it's never too late for a father to speak to his son." He stepped aside as Charles took his place behind the pulpit.

Opal studied her father-in-law's face. Charles Rivard appeared to have aged at least a decade since the last time she had seen him.

He met her gaze and smiled, then stared out at the congregation. "So many people loved my son. My boy. I'm sorry. Let me begin again. Good morning. My—my name is Charles Rivard. I'm so grateful that so many people came to pay their respects to my son. I—call him my son although I'm not sure I have the right any more . . ."

He was interrupted by reassuring murmurs from the crowd.

Charles nodded appreciatively. "My son and I spoke very little during the past few years. It seems to me we spent most of his young life arguing, but now, I—I can't for the life of me remember what was so monumental that it could—divide us this way. I hope he can hear me now. I—I want him to know."

He lowered his head, and Opal could see the tears falling from his eyes.

When he lifted his head, he was staring directly at her. "If he can hear me now, I know he'd want me to correct a great wrong . . . Opal, my dear, please forgive me for . . . for so much—for everything."

Opal smiled though her tears and nodded.

Charles finally managed to compose himself, and continued. "Is it possible . . . is it possible to fight bitterly with a man, in total conflict—and still be filled with admiration for him? Because that's how I always felt about my son. It seems we disagreed on everything, but I was never more proud of anyone in my life. When he was a boy, Serval was always reaching—always asking 'why, Daddy?' By the time he got to school, it seemed he was always trying to do ten things at once, and rather than being proud of the nine things he did well, he'd be miserable over one failure. I told him time and again, 'Slow down, son. Don't burn the candle at both ends. You're always in such a hurry. You can't burn the candle at both ends or else . . .'"

His words faded into a long silence, and Kathryn Rivard's voice echoed in the cavernous church. "Go on, Charles," she said, "Finish what you came to do."

Opal stared at Serval's mother as if seeing her for the first time.

Charles continued haltingly. "I—saw my son last year, speaking on Lenox Avenue, with all the b-beautiful courage of his convictions. We spoke but . . . I wanted to tell him how proud I was . . . I wanted to—but I—I just didn't know—how. Well, I guess he sensed it, because two days later, a book arrived. My son sent me a book of poetry by Edna St. Vincent Millay, with a note marking a page where he had underlined a short passage. I guess it was his way of explaining himself—of making peace with me—and I must admit, it made me smile. I'd like to read it for you now, if I may." With shaking hands, Charles opened the book and put on his reading glasses.

> *My candle burns at both ends*
> *It will not last the night*
> *But ah, my foes, and, oh, my friends*
> *. . . It gives a lovely light!*

# 1940

President Franklin D. Roosevelt remains undecided
about U.S. involvement in the Second World War.

The NAACP continues its nationwide protest of the film
"Gone With The Wind" for its negative depiction of
Negroes and for its blatant romanticization of slavery.

Marcus Garvey dies in England.

# Chapter 45

The wake-up bell at the Ossining prison facility jangled loudly, and within minutes all inmates lined up for the orderly trek to the mess hall.

All but one.

Seymour Webber had worked as a guard at Sing Sing for twelve years, and, aside from an occasional violent outburst, most days followed their usual routine course. So when his fellow guard, Ed Paxton, who also worked the morning shift, reported one missing inmate, Seymour was annoyed.

"You sure, Ed?"

"Yeah."

Seymour scratched his head uncertainly. "Well, before we panic, let's give the cells a quick look. Then I guess we'd better call downstairs."

As the two guards scanned each cell, Seymour found his own step quickening, and he repeatedly glanced in the direction of the stairs. If an escape attempt was in the works and he delayed in reporting it, it could mean his job.

"Seymour?" Ed called over his shoulder.

"What is it?"

"Over here."

Seymour breathed a sigh of relief. "What? Somebody sick?"

"Look."

Seymour approached the cell and peered in at an elderly Negro inmate lying in a fetal position on his bunk. "Hey!" Ed yelled, banging his nightstick against the bars. But the inmate didn't move. His face was a dark ashy gray, and he appeared to have stopped breathing. Unlocking the cell door, Ed stepped in and reached for the man's wrist, but quickly pulled his hand away.

"Ice cold. Ain't gotta check this guy's pulse. He's been dead for hours. Check your list for his name."

Seymour shook his head and murmured, "I don't have to check. His name's Leon Jackson. He's been in here for years—since before I started workin' here."

"Any family to notify?"

"Yeah. A daughter, I think."

* * *

Creola Dorshay opened her apartment door and smiled at her guest as she motioned him in with a sweep of her arm. Aware that his eyes were riveted to her body, she sucked in her belly and crossed the room to her dressing table, then perched on the edge of the chair to give her hair a quick, last minute brush. "How 'bout a little drink, sugar?" she said, applying a bit of face powder to the dark circles under her eyes.

"Naw," he said, running the back of his hand across his lips. "I wants to be sober for you, baby. Mmm! My, my! You is one fine baby, though."

Peering at the man's reflection in her vanity mirror, Creola lit a cigarette. *Damn! He's old enough to be one of Mama's old gentleman callers* . . . Her head was suddenly filled with derisive laughter. . . . *but this one's one'a mine.*

Her mind drifted back to the business at hand when she realized that the man had been saying something to her. "Huh? What'cha say, Daddy?"

He pulled off his coat and hat, revealing a balding head and an enormous paunch. Dropping into the bed, he leered at her as he began to unbutton his rumpled shirt. Creola clenched her teeth before taking another pull off her cigarette.

"I was sayin' come on over here, you pretty red thang," he said, patting the bed. "Lemme get my hands on that pretty, bright skin 'a yours. Mmm, mmm! You sho' is sump'm, gal!"

Creola crushed the end of her half-smoked cigarette into the ashtray and struggled to conjure up a smile. "Yeah," she murmured, gazing at the flat deadness of her own eyes in the mirror. "Ain't I sump'm, though."

# 1972

# Chapter 46

Opal never closed the door to her office and knew that it would cause a stir on such a special day, but decided she needed a bit of privacy after discovering an unusual item in the afternoon mail. She stared at the envelope with the California postdate and smiled; its thickness intrigued her. As busy as her son was, she was lucky to get a hastily scrawled postcard whenever his work took him out of town. "Wonder what's got the child so talky all of a sudden? Well . . . guess there's only one way to find out!" She groaned and muttered as she slowly settled into her chair, then reached for her reading glasses and tore open the envelope.

*Dear Mama:*

*It's late, I'm tired, and way behind in so many things, but Mama, "My Heart"—I know I've been neglecting you lately, so I thought I'd sit myself down to write.*

*As I've griped on so many occasions, I must've been out of my mind when I decided it was possible to preserve the integrity of union organizing. It seems management wants us banished from the face of the earth so that they can reinstitute slavery, and the workers think we're either communists or some gun-happy Mafioso characters from "On The Waterfront." But every once in a blue moon, I have a day that makes it all worthwhile. At today's talks, I got a strong feeling that all our hard work is beginning to pay off. Management conceded on two major points, which leads me to believe that they're finally beginning to take us seriously—but only after bringing out the worst in everyone. Mama, just when I think I've seen everything, and that nothing else can shock me, the cruelty of this world escalates to a new, impossible level. But I guess we've got to focus on those few steps forward and not the many steps back.*

*Oh! I almost forget to tell you—I met Cesar Chavez! I had a chance to compare notes with him about our respective struggles, and the man is simply inspiring, Mama. God! There's so much go-*

*ing on in California! Politics has an entirely different momentum out here—there's a youthful energy that just sizzles, whether it's the Black Power Movement, or the Vietnam protesters, or even us, I suppose. I think it's these young people who are pumping the life blood back into the union, Mama. And Mr. Chavez—he's just a young spirit with plenty of energy. And whenever I meet someone like him, I'm reminded of my father. In fact, lately, I've been thinking a lot about him. Funny, isn't it, Mama? This man who died so many years ago—a man I never even met—yet he looms so real in my mind (thanks to you and Daddy). I never told you this before (maybe exhaustion breeds confession), but I sometimes have long talks with Serval Rivard, and yet I've never felt his presence so intensely as this past week. Maybe he's sticking close to give me pointers. I don't know. I only know that I'm feeling him with me every step of the way.*

Opal's gaze drifted up to the arrangement of framed family pictures standing on the shelf above her desk. Removing her glasses, she stared at the faded sepia image of herself at age eighteen clinging tightly to Serval's arm on their wedding day. His eyes smiled down at her, and she smiled back, then continued reading.

*By the way, thanks for the birthday cookies. You were right—cookies mail better than cake—and even the cookies were a bit damaged, so I can imagine how a cake would have looked after the long postal journey to California. But never fear, Mama—crumbs and all, your cookies lived up to their lofty reputation and we all enjoyed them. Can you believe I'm forty-six? It's a strange feeling—but not so bad, I guess. I'm sure some people would say I don't have much to show for my forty-six years on this earth, but somehow, I feel like a very rich man. When I was in college, I remember how some of my buddies were pressured by their parents into "brass ring" professions—"get that money, son!"—and that sort of thing. How blessed I was to have parents who never made material demands on me. You and Daddy always taught me that a man's work shouldn't be measured by how much money he pulls down, but the purpose behind the work. Perhaps that's why I'm so well-adjusted—even when I don't have two nickels to rub together (and this situation occurs a little more often than I'd care to admit),*

*I can still find something to smile about, and some way to make
ends meet. Hmm . . . I guess I'm rambling now.*

*Anyway, the only good thing about aging is the natural acqui-
sition of wisdom that comes along with it. Things I never understood before are now clear to me. Recently, I solved a puzzle that
had me stumped since I was a little boy. You and Daddy used to
tell me that even though my real Daddy was killed by white men,
it was a blessing that they didn't hang him. Mama, that used to
make me so angry, I wanted to go out and kill all the white folks I
saw. Well, I finally grew up enough to understand that going
around killing folks wouldn't solve anything, but I never could rec-
oncile myself to thinking it was somehow a "victory" that he wasn't
hanged. Man! What a consolation prize! Even when you explained
about his nightmares, I still didn't get it. Well, Mama, like I told
you, Daddy's been hovering close to me lately, and I guess I'm finally
able to understand. I can't put it into words, but I understand now.*

*I hope it doesn't pain you when I go on and on about my real
Daddy, and not Jack. Jack was a wonderful father and I miss him
every day. How are you holding up? I know the last two years have
been lonely ones for you since he passed away. And you know,
Mama, better than anyone, how hard it was for me to think of him
as a stepfather. He treated all of us kids exactly the same, but that
was his way, wasn't it? Fair and equal. So he might not like the
way I always felt about my family, because I always felt a little
more blessed. I was the only one with two fathers and one lovely
mother. I feel like Jack was my "earth father" and Serval was my
"spiritual father." When I think about the story you told me about
how my Daddy gave you and Jack his blessing, I know that somewhere deep inside, that was his intention all along. He probably
knew he would die a warrior's death — young.*

Opal reached into her pocket for a handkerchief and lifted her glasses
to dab at her eyes. Again she found herself studying the pictures on the
shelf, and she smiled up at her favorite picture of Jack. It was a photo
she had taken of him at their surprise thirtieth wedding anniversary
party. He was seated in his big green lounge chair in the living room,
with his three children standing behind him. In a heap on his lap was
a tangle of unruly arms and gangly legs belonging to his grandchildren,
always referred to by Jack as "the seven dwarves." With the exception

of his thinning gray hair, Jack looked almost the same as the day of their wedding. Every face was smiling and irresistible, and Opal kissed the picture three times. After placing it back in its spot, she reached for the picture next to it: of her eldest son in cap and gown, waving his Columbia University diploma high in the air. His smile was Serval's smile, but the dimples were inherited from Opal. And the bright, wide-set eyes were one hundred percent Leon Jackson. She kept the graduation picture in her hand, and went on with her reading.

*So Mama, as I think about all these things, all the pieces fall into place. Now I know why you and Daddy didn't name me after Serval. He was one of a kind. Besides, a name like "Serval" just doesn't sound right with a "Junior" attached to it. I guess you could have named me after Jack—but I already know the answer to that one. Daddy was never one to let his ego rule him. If that had been the case, he wouldn't have been so insistent that I keep the name "Rivard" instead of taking "Hawkins." That was important to him, huh? It was his way of honoring Serval. How you two got so wise at such young ages is beyond me. It took me forty-six years to figure out what was second nature to you and Daddy in your twenties. Thanks for never making me feel slow.*

*It's funny how life seems to run in cycles, isn't it? Remember when Sheila and I first got married (you raised hell about us being too young), and we moved in with you and Daddy? Even with us struggling with jobs and college, and you and Daddy juggling finances to get your dancing school started, those were some of the best days—the Four Musketeers gorging on catfish, spaghetti, and Daddy's world-famous cornbread. Great times. And now that we've managed to get all three of our own kids through college, Sheila and I seem to gravitate to your house a lot more. I miss you both so much, and God, I miss Daddy. But I'll be home soon—a few more days. That reminds me—tomorrow's project is to write to Sheila. I don't want her divorcing me now! Not after two months of sleeping alone!*

*Please forgive the scribble, Mama, but your son is tired. Think I'll catch a little sleep now.*

*With all my love, as the struggle continues,*

*Your son, Marcus*

Opal folded her reading glasses and placed them in their case, then settled back into her chair for a long visit with her family pictures. But the sound of a frantic tapping on her office door startled her back to the present. "Come in."

The door opened and a dark-skinned teenage girl dressed in a black-feathered "Odile" tutu peeked in. "Mrs. Hawkins? Uh, 'scuse me . . ."

"Oh, my, Terry! Don't tell me our guest is here already?"

Terry bounced excitedly, setting her formal black tutu rustling with a rhythm more reminiscent of ragtime than *Swan Lake*. "Yes, ma'am. And he's so beautiful! I—I hope it's all right—I got him a chair and some tea and—well, he's waitin' for you."

Opal kissed the letter from her son, folded it quickly, and tucked it into her skirt pocket as she stood up. "Relax, Terry," she laughed. "The man's been on your side of the street, himself, you know. You've worked hard, child, and this is where it all pays off. The training is what carries you through these audition jitters, you see? Now get on out there and take your position. I'll be right out."

Opal checked her appearance in the mirror hanging next to her office door. As she adjusted a hairpin and smoothed her skirt, she remembered Miss Aida's good-luck wink and the feel of Madame's hand on the small of her back, gently pushing her out to center stage. *This time, Shoo-Shoo! Show them who is greatest doncer!*

When she stepped out of her office, Opal's eyes were instantly drawn to the dark gentleman seated in a folding chair near the recital stage at the end of the long, mirrored room. She lifted her chin and smiled as she took a step in his direction, but then stopped suddenly, distracted by the mirror's reflection of the large center window facing the street. "Who left those damn shades up?" she muttered. But as the man rose from his chair, Opal forgot the shades and crossed the room, studying him with each step. He was everything she had expected, and more. His skin glowed with the rich color and sparkle of fresh black coffee, and he filled the room with a quiet dignity. He wore a crisp, pale gray suit with a charcoal shirt and wine-colored tie, and gold cuff links gleamed from the edges of his sleeves when he extended his hands. His smile was dazzling, and intelligence burned in his dark eyes. Opal felt her heart begin to pound as she reached for his hands. "Mr. Mitchell?"

"Ah, Mrs. Hawkins. After all our telephone conversations, it's a pleasure to finally meet you."

She turned and smiled at her students. "Class, I'd like you to meet

Mr. Arthur Mitchell, Director of the Dance Theater of Harlem. Mr. Mitchell—my dancers."

Arthur Mitchell bowed slightly from the waist, and years of dance experience were evident in the movement.

After the excited buzz died down, Opal cued the pianist and took a seat in the chair next to Arthur Mitchell. She snuck a peek at him from the corner of her eye and sighed. *It sure is a new day, Madame.*

From the beginning of the first number, she held her breath and mentally danced each abbreviated piece with her students. From *Swan Lake* to *The Firebird*, she willed them to execute each movement, each lift, to perfection. At the conclusion of a short piece dedicated to Katherine Dunham, the lights came up and Terry appeared at the center of the floor. She was now costumed as an exotic bird, complete with red and black feathers trailing from her headpiece.

Her voice faltered slightly when she made her announcement. "And now, Mr. Mitchell—our finale. I guess it's weird for a finale, but we call it *The Beginning.*"

Opal stiffened in her chair and reminded herself to breathe. She had given the class a free hand in the creation of the full-length finale, which featured the entire corps de ballet in their own homemade mix of African regalia—kente and kuba cloth draped over cocoa-colored leotards, with feathers and cowrie shells decorating necks, wrists, and ankles. Exchange students from West Africa who attended Terry's college had offered their talents along with four traditional drums called *djembes* to accompany the dancers. And the students had recruited two baby brothers and three little sisters from their own families to portray "the offspring."

The piece began with the first drummer playing a slow, rhythmic pattern reminiscent of rain. One by one, the dancers emerged to play out their roles in the story of Africa's bounty. And one by one, the other drummers fell in with the rhythms of life. Opal twisted the fabic of her skirt as she counted the beats to Terry's entrance—a grand Kitri leap followed by a solo packed with complicated pointe work and rapid aerial combinations. The drums rose to a fevered crescendo, and Terry suddenly appeared like a bolt of lightning high above center stage, the trailing red feathers of her headpiece streaking behind her like a fiery comet. The sight brought an instant flood of tears to Opal's eyes, and she pressed her palm to her heart. *Oh, Madame . . . I think this one's gonna make it.* She exhaled slowly and finally settled back in her chair.

As she watched the story and listened to the ancient sounds of the *djembes*, Opal experienced an odd blend of feelings—at once sexual and spiritual. She closed her eyes, and Serval's image was waiting for her—still youthful, frozen in time. The rhythm lulled her hypnotically until it carried another tone—Serval's voice, speaking clearly to her through the drums, relaying a fifty-year-old dream.

. . . *I was in Africa, Opal. God! It was beautiful! And so real! I was an African warrior on a hunt. I could feel the spear in my hand, baby! It was near a river, I think, because the ground was cool on my feet. I could see for miles—the horizon—everything! And baby, there was no wire, no rope, no Jimmy Coles—anywhere in sight. The sun was setting and . . . God! What a beautiful dream . . .*

The final drumbeat signaled a collective shout from the dancers as they fell to the floor in a dramatic cascade of bright colors and rattling shells. Then all was still, and Opal's eyes slowly opened.

After a long silence, Arthur Mitchell rose slowly and began to applaud. "Bravo!" Leaning closer to Opal, he whispered, "I can't think of any words . . . except that you've taught them well, Mrs. Hawkins. I think we might have a few stars in this bunch. Call me tomorrow. I'm particularly interested in the pair that danced that second pas de deux, and my God! That soloist in the finale! Breathtaking."

"Thank you so much, Mr. Mitchell. We were hoping you'd like it."

"I loved it. And I'd love to stay and watch your class—to study your teaching technique," he said, smiling at her. "But I've got a rehearsal of my own to get to. We're performing at the Met next month. I'll send you a special invitation."

Opal's fingers wrapped tightly around the letter in her pocket. "The—the Metropolitan Opera House! How wonderful!"

"And the company is a nervous wreck," he laughed. "So, Mrs. Hawkins, I really must go, but I'll leave you with one thought. From what I saw here today, some of your students will be dancing at the Met in a season or two."

"The Met," she whispered.

Arthur Mitchell smiled warmly at the class as he turned to leave. "Magnificent."

The minute he left, the class gathered around Opal and erupted with questions.

Opal clapped her hands. "Wait a minute! A visit shouldn't disrupt our work. Now. We've got ourselves a recital to get ready for, and it's time to get to work. But I promise I'll tell you everything he said—*after* class." She broke into a smile, then nodded at the pianist. "Lily, let's start with the corps de ballet piece from *Giselle*, shall we? Ladies and gentlemen . . . you can dance in those leotards, but lose the shells and sashes," she said, pointing to a large box near her office door. "In the storage box. And all the headpieces go back on the racks—in order, please."

As she waited for the students to put away their costumes, Opal again caught sight of the window with the open shades, and strode over to lower them. As she tugged the pull-cord, she sighed impatiently. "I don't know how many times I have to say it—I want this shade pulled down! Now I've . . ." She stopped in mid-sentence as her eyes were drawn to the crumbling, graffiti-ridden walls of the abandoned building across the street. The sight of it had always disturbed her, so keeping the shades down had become a strictly enforced rule. She tugged harder on the pull-cord, but it wouldn't budge, and once again she was filled with an eerie mix of anger and fear as she stared out the window. It was more than annoyance over a neighborhood eyesore; she was sure that something dreadful was hiding there—in plain sight.

Someone coughed, and Opal heard the low murmuring of her students. She knew that they were curious—perhaps impatient—but she could not tear her eyes from one of the ruins of her grand old Harlem. Before its abandonment, it had been a bookstore, and before that, a small drugstore. But to Opal it would always be a ghost of the old millinery shop, with its sparkling front window filled with colorful hats—hats that she was not allowed to try on.

The image of the bright shop window quickly faded, but her eyes were still held captive by some phantom she couldn't quite find. She tried to ignore the sudden, familiar scream of a police siren from a nearby street, and focused harder. It appeared that the decaying structure was being swallowed, brick by brick, into the very ground on which it rested. The high weeds nearly reached the top of a wood fence dividing it from the adjacent property. Her eyes trailed up the fence, and suddenly, the answer was there—even though she knew it had been there all along. Sprawled across the top of the fence was a large, ominous twist of barbed wire. To the left of the fence was a storage facility with its own barricade of spikey wire. For the second time that day, Serval's voice filled her memory.

*The wire, Opal. The barbed wire. It was like this—this demon butcher all over the landscape. It snatched human life like it was nothing—men with souls—and swallowed 'em. It was the devil, sitting right there in the open, making us kill each other when we didn't even know why. We were like—like an army of goddamn puppets, and he just laid out there and waited for a fella to make one false step so he could swallow him down right into hell.*

Opal stared at the wire as if confronting a lifelong enemy, then turned to look back at her students. The thrill of Arthur Mitchell's visit still danced on their faces, and their eyes sparkled with hope. A gradual calm settled over her, and she took a deep breath. Once again, the window commanded her attention, but this time her eyes were drawn away from the barbed wire to a closer image—her own business sign in twelve-inch black script letters against a stark white background. It hung just outside the window, near enough to reach out and touch. "The Black Star Dance Academy."

Leaving the shades open, Opal sent the pull-cord sailing in a high arc, then turned to smile at her students. "And now . . . we begin."

*It is always darkest before the dawn—*
*Thank God for the darkness!*
*Because without it*
*the moon and the stars would remain hidden*
*in the light*
*and we would miss the birth*
*of the new morning . . .*